THE RETRIBUTION SERIES

BOOK 1:
THE RISING

BY SHANNON FIGALLO

Retribution, Book 1: The Rising
Author: Shannon Figallo
Published by: Shannon Catherine Figallo
ABN: 27861275760
Facebook: Shannon Figallo
Instagram: shannon_figallo
LinkedIn: Shannon Figallo
Tumbler: shannon-figallo
TikTok: @shannon_figallo
You Tube: Shannon Figallo
Twitter: @FigalloShannon

ISBN: 978-0-6487812-9-5

With thanks to:

My sister, Aria Triggell.
Without your love, support and sarcasm to match mine, I never would have
done this. I would also still be stuck on page 50.

My husband, Paul, for putting up with me: I love you lots.

My children, for driving me nuts and keeping me there: I love you.
The rest of my family and friends: I love you all.

CONTENTS

Retribution

NOUN: Punishment inflicted on someone as vengeance for a wrong or criminal act (www.lexico.com)

TRIGGER WARNING

This novel depicts events containing sexual assault, violence, violence against women, bullying, and gruesome acts. I did not write this story to upset anyone, and in no way does it relate to people I know, whether living or dead.

To all those who have been through the violence and have escaped: you are stronger than you will ever know. To those who are trapped: you are not alone and help is out there, don't ever doubt your strength to leave. You have a chance at freedom

TAKE IT.

When you see this symbol, ▣, the story will continue from a different character. I hope you enjoy reading my novel as much as I have enjoyed writing it.

CHAPTER 1

The Meeting

January 2010

The sound and the smell of the ocean…
It's so peaceful, relaxing, and beautiful.
I grew up camping on the beach with my family and friends.
Every chance we got, we rode dirt bikes, went four-wheel driving, played beach football and cricket, and went surfing.
My grandparents had property, so it was all about riding dirt bikes or horses and shooting.
I remember feeling free, safe, and loved.
I remember being myself…
Laughing, joking, and having fun with my family and friends.

I was happy… Once.

Now, I stand alone in my kitchen, looking out the window.
With no family, and a wish that maybe, just maybe, I can let myself love someone and receive love in return, and somehow have a family of my own — one day.
My past is filled with pain and loss.
I can see the scars whenever I look in the mirror.

The vast ocean gives me a tiny glitter of chance.
A chance to feel free: free to be safe, free to breathe and—possibly—free to fall in love and be myself again…
Well, kind of.
I don't know if I will ever get back to being who I was.
All I know for certain is that there are some things I'll never go back to.
I am hiding from someone, an evil that could consume me.
It's the past I'm fighting against.

I was once young and carefree, at nineteen-years-old, but then everything changed.
Seven and a half years of my life were stolen from me, as well as the family I can never go back to.
It's the past I'm fighting against.

I know I have a lot of healing to do, and having the visible scars to prove it makes it hard to escape the past, sometimes.
Right now, all I can do is take it one day at a time, and do the small things that make me happy.
It's a start, at least.

I still have five months till I'm due to go back to work.
I'm lucky enough to do what I've always wanted to do ever since I was a child: being a paramedic.
So for the next five months I have a to-do list as long as my arm, which includes joining a gym and getting back on a surfboard and dirt bike.
I'm also going back to studying, as so much has changed since I first graduated, and I want to expand my skill set within my chosen career.

I can't wait to start making my little house a home filled with laughter, music, food, and special people to share it all with.
When they hid me for over 18 months, moving me from motel to motel and from safe house to safe house, I was unsettled, depressed, and on edge.
I found it hard to be happy, or positive, with no place to call my own, and no safe place to breathe.
So, as soon as I could, I looked for my own place.

I fell in love with the house the first time I saw it.
It was a lovely, old, partially-renovated double storey home in a small town called Moore Park Beach, in Queensland.
It had an amazing view of the beach and was situated on an acre.

I moved into my new home in September 2009.

I have a folder full of ideas and zero talent or knowledge with which to actually achieve any of it.
However, it's a new year and a new start.
I finally feel like I might be able to move forward and keep my most important promise to myself.

I spent the first couple of months redrawing plans and finalizing approvals for the house.
The previous owners had started to renovate, but never got to finish it.
The front of the home had been enclosed to make two extra bedrooms.
The bathroom had been ripped out and moved to make the lounge bigger, and to allow for a study.
The main bathroom is now between my bedroom and the spare room.

The kitchen has been partly demolished and has a hole in the floor for internal stairs.

My bedroom is a brand new extension to one side of the home, a big open space with plenty of windows, a walk-in closet and an absolutely beautiful en-suite.

It has a rain shower head and a claw-foot bathtub with a window overlooking the backyard and the ocean.

It's the perfect spot for some self-indulgence; you just need a glass (or a bottle) of wine, chocolate (or a big jar of Nutella and a spoon), music, and a good book.

The hole in the kitchen floor, that will eventually have stairs, leads to the laundry room and the third bathroom.

There will also be a spare room, along with a bar, a kitchenette, and an entertainment area.

I plan to make the kitchen an open-plan space filled with light.

The dining room itself will open out onto a deck.

But right now, all I have is an old electric stove, four DIY cupboards, and some kind of bench with half a table screwed to it.

The other half of the table has been screwed to the wall, under a window.

I know it's not much, but it's mine and I love it.

While listening to a music mix of The Travelling Wilburys, Fleetwood Mac, The Big O and Creedence, I smile as I watch kangaroos hop through my backyard.

I make myself breakfast and a cup of tea as I dance and hum to myself.

I'm in my own little world and completely oblivious to the fact that I have an appointment at eight-thirty, and that it's already eight-twenty-five.

I look out my window and see the trees rustle from the gentle breeze.

Setting down my cup of tea on the bench, I get on tippy-toes and lean over to open the window, inhaling the fresh ocean air that rushes in.

It's cool and sensuous on my bare skin.

I stay there for a minute with my eyes closed, enjoying the moment.

I really need to get a few surfboards this week.

The sooner I can get into the ocean the better.

Maybe I'll even get a dirt bike at the same time.

I smile to myself.

Moore Park has a beach that goes on for ages, and very few people.

A quiet beach with a few waves and beautiful weather is the perfect place to rebuild myself.

I open my eyes.

I get the feeling that I'm not alone, and I giggle to myself because it's obviously all in my head.

This isn't the first time I have felt like this, but the outcome is always the same: I am alone.

I mean, I changed hospitals, states, cities, and even changed my name. I'm constantly hiding and looking over my shoulder every time I leave the house.

I freeze, realising that I'm not alone right now, and that someone is indeed watching me.

Then I hear someone behind me, and I smell something different but pleasant— this smell does not belong here.

My body starts to tremble slightly and my heart rate increases.

Have I been found?

As I tremble, I quickly realise that my body is not reacting to fear, this is something else.

It feels like waking up on Christmas morning with the anticipation of opening your presents.

It feels like excitement.

I close my eyes and focus on my breathing, taking in a deep breath and releasing it.

Whatever this smell is, I don't want to lose it.

I take another deep breath and let the smell engulf my senses.

I have no idea why I feel like this; it's something I have never experienced.

How can I even begin to understand my body's reaction?

This strange feeling makes me feel almost safe; it's something that I don't want to lose.

It makes me feel warm, despite the cool breeze.

I get down off my tippy-toes and breathe deeply, in and out. I slowly turn around, and I see him standing there, at my glass sliding door.

I'm glued to the spot and I can't drag my eyes away.

I almost forget that I need to breathe.

Well!

Oh, my holy moly, good god!

Hello, builder.

He is a tall, tanned, muscled tradesman, in a khaki-coloured, button-up shirt tucked into his shorts, steel-cap boots, and what looks like a New Zealand Warriors NRL cap, slightly covered by his sunglasses. Warriors?

Oh well, no one's perfect, I guess.
It could be worse, I mean, could have been the Broncos!

On his left arm, I can see the start of what looks like an intricate tattoo, beginning at the wrist and wrapping up and around his arm.
He also has a light brown leather band on his left wrist.

My body starts to calm down, my breathing slowing and deepening.
I feel warm desire moving through me, and coming to rest between my thighs.
I clench my thighs together, trying to suppress the sudden onset of want and need.

My right hand fidgets along my neck and collarbone, while the other rests on the bench.
There is a man standing at my glass door and my body is reacting to his presence in a way I have never experienced.
I want him, and not just his body, but all of him and I don't even know him.
Why?
What is happening?
What is wrong with me?
My eyes travel up and down the length of him.
How can my body react this way to someone I don't even know?
I stand there looking at him, inhaling his scent.
I watch as he adjusts his hat and the sunglasses on his head.
He cocks his head to one side and I realise he's talking, but I can't hear anything he is saying.

I snap out of my trance when my plate hits the floor and shatters, spilling my Vegemite toast on the floor.
I look down at the broken plate and the remains of my breakfast, then back at him.
'Are you alright?' he asks.
'What?' I reply, thinking, oh god, my voice sounds weird.

'Are you alright?' He repeats the question as he looks at me with such intensity that I could hand him my panties and tell him to take me right here, right now.
My body shivers and I feel the quiver between my thighs.
My god, I'm wet and most likely blushing crimson red!

'I'm fine, why?' I reply as I wave dismissively, trying to stem the complete dissipation of what remains of my dignity.

He smiles.
Yup, my dignity is going in three, two…

'You've knocked your breakfast off the bench, and you kind of look like a kangaroo caught in headlights,' he says with that stupid, sexy accent, and that stupid, sexy smile.
'Umm yes, yes I'm… I'm yes, no, I'm good,' I stammer, scolding myself mentally for being so stupid.
Oh my god, he looks, um, so um… Flustered, much? I scoff at myself.

'Um, who are you, and what are you doing here?' I ask, trying to clean up my mess.
'I'm Dominic Taumata, we have an appointment for eight-thirty. I'm the builder,' he says as he leans against the door frame.
He smiles at me again and my mind turns to mush.

'Oh shit! I mean, right! Crap, what time is it? I'm so sorry.' Focus, Lizzy, jeez, I admonish myself.
If a sinkhole could appear right now and swallow me whole, I would really appreciate it.
Come on, Elizabeth, at least say something intelligent.
I look at him and he smiles again.
Yeah, nah, let's just go with kangaroo-caught-in-headlights.

'Don't worry, it only just got to eight-thirty now,' he says, still smiling at me.
Oh, for the love of god, stop smiling at me, please.
'Are you sure you are alright? I can help you clean up,' he asks.
'No, sorry, I mean, I'm all good, I've got it,' I say, trying not to look at him.

He's still smiling at me.
Oh, my good golly gosh, that smile…
It's making me weak at the knees.
I stand up, turn, and put the broken plate and my ruined breakfast in the bin.
Then I turn back to face him and dry my hands nervously on my shirt.
Shit!! That's all I'm wearing!
An oversized white shirt that exposes my shoulder and, of course, my bra strap, and only just covers my arse…
Which, of course, would have been the first thing he saw: my arse in red lace underwear.
Oh well, on the bright side, at least I was wearing some.

He is still smiling.

Please stop smiling.

'Right, well, the kettle has just boiled, here is a cup. The tea, coffee, and sugar are next to the kettle, and milk is in the fridge. Feel free to make yourself a cuppa while I get cleaned up,' I say, trying to move without giving him more of a show. 'I'll be back in a minute.'

Don't look at his lips, his beautiful lips.

Focus, Lizzy! I scold myself again.

He's not saying anything, why is he not saying anything?

Why does he just stand there with a smile that makes my knees weak?

👀 DOMINIC 👀

She is beautiful. She doesn't realise just how beautiful she is, or the effect she is having on me.

Her auburn hair, with wavy, loose curls, falls just below her shoulders, and her eyes—wow, piercing green.

Her lips look soft; they were lips I could happily claim.

I drop my A4 notebook on the counter to cover the growing need to take her; right here, right now.

I notice her breathing has quickened slightly and see her draw some deep breaths.

I watch as she blushes and licks her lips, then she bites her bottom lip as her eyes meet mine and she smiles before looking at the floor.

I watch as her hand moves to her neck; she seems nervous.

Her hands look small, delicate, and soft.

I wonder what they would feel like on my body with her lips on mine.

She looks completely and utterly beautiful and pure.

I have never wanted anyone that I have just met like I want her.

She has me completely mesmerised and speechless; I can't look away.

She's not helping my predicament, with her shirt exposing a red bra strap, and that arse!

Well, it looks really fucking good in red lace.

I'm fighting the urge to walk up to her, to claim her lips with mine, teasing her with my tongue and tangling my hands in her hair.

I need to hold her, not caring about anything or anyone except us.

How the hell am I supposed to concentrate with her around?

All I can see is her; her subtle moves, the way her breathing changes when I smile at her.
The way she touches her neck when she is trying to calm her nerves.
The way her green eyes sparkle when she smiles and blushes.
I can't focus on anything else but her.
But why is she nervous?

The breeze through the kitchen window gently blows past her and her alluring smell hits my nose.
I walk further inside.
What is it about her?
Why do I need her?
I crave not just her body, but all of her.
Even though I don't know her, I know I need her with me.
What the fuck dude! I scold myself.
Say something, don't just stare at her perfectly beautiful lips—she'll think you're an idiot.
You're a builder here to provide her with a quote.
Now focus on your job!
I mean, she's probably not even single.
I bet she has some model-looking boyfriend or husband.
She might even be gay!
But I can't deny that she looks even better when she blushes and nervously bites her bottom lip.
Yep, she has no idea just how beautiful she is.
I take a deep breath.

👀 ELIZABETH 👀

'Thank you, I would love a cuppa,' he says, removing his hat and running his hand through his dark brown hair.
His fringe lands perfectly on the side of his face, as he sizes me up.
My face is so red I can feel it glowing like sunburn.
Great first impression, Liz, he probably thinks you're a complete idiot.

I start talking while walking backwards towards my room.
'Right, well, I'll be just a minute!' I say as I hit the door frame. 'Whoopsie daisy!'
Then I just stand there, looking at him, at a complete loss.

…One! Yep, my dignity has left the building.
It exited stage left, yelling, 'Peace out, bitch!'

I'm such an idiot!
Focus, Liz!
'Are you sure you are alright?' he asks again.
All I can do is look at him and nod.

He moves towards me.
I quickly back into my room before he can come any closer.
'Yeah, no, I'm all good, I just need a minute,' I reply.
Just hurry up and close the goddamn door, woman!
You really need to get a hold of yourself, I whisper to myself as I lean back on
the closed door, rolling my eyes.
Why does he have to smell so good?
Why does he have to be so goddamn good-looking?
And I'm so, well, plain and so, totally, not good enough for him.
At this point, I realise that I still have no idea how to behave around another
man without permission, and not be fearful of punishment.
But I need to try; I can't keep hiding forever.
I just need to try and be who I was before, right?
Too easy, right?

Shaking my head, I go into my walk-in closet and put on a pair of black denim
shorts with the white button-up shirt.
I mean, he's probably not even single.
I bet he has some model-looking girlfriend or wife or, even better, he might
be gay!

I walk into my en suite and look at myself in the mirror.
Really, Liz? You made yourself look like a complete loser, I tell my reflection.
Hello! There's a hot guy in your kitchen, and you're hiding here in your en-suite,
arguing with yourself! I shake my head and roll my eyes at myself.
Dumb arse! I chuckle.
I close my eyes and take a deep breath before appraising myself in the mirror
again.
'Right, let's do this.'

Step 1. Get dressed. Already done, next.
Step 2. Brush hair and teeth.
Step 3. Deodorant.
Step 4. Remember where all the bats are hidden. (Yes, I have cricket and baseball
bats hidden throughout the house.)
Step 5. Don't freak out, just breathe and walk out there like a boss.

Step 6. Check to make sure I'm actually fully clothed first, and did I put deodorant on?

I look down and sniff myself at the same time; check and check.
Right, let's walk out there, one foot in front of the other, and don't trip!
I grab my house folder; I'm okay and I can do this, I'm ready.

I'm standing at my bedroom door, with my hand on the doorknob.
'Open the door, Elizabeth,' I whisper to myself.
'You can do this, take a deep breath and just open the door.' I nod.
'I'm confident and strong. I can be anything and do anything I want,' I mutter to myself, nodding my head.

I close my eyes, take a nervous, deep breath and open my eyes again.
'Ready,' I murmur.
I open my bedroom door.
'Hello Dominic, I'm so sorry about earlier, I was in my own little world and forgot about the time,' I say as I walk towards him.
He's sitting at my kitchen bench, holding a cup in both hands as he turns to face me with a smile.
Damnit, that smile! It seems like a permanent fixture on his face.
I blush, bite my bottom lip, and look at the floor.
Crap! No hole to fall through!

I place my folder near him on the bench.
Taking a deep breath, I look back up to see him watching me.
Damn, he has beautiful, dark brown eyes.
Oh dear lord!
The path to temptation has never looked so… So perfectly delectable!
My body shivers, despite feeling hot enough to melt on the spot.

He chuckles as he places his cup on the counter.
'Don't worry about it, I have been greeted a lot… Umm, worse,' he says as he tilts his head to the side and runs his hand through his hair.
I want to run my fingers through his hair as he claims my body.
I smile and blush as I turn around to make myself a fresh cup of tea.
How the hell am I supposed to focus on this when all I can think of is him?
I take a deep breath; mmm, he smells so good.
The way he moves.
The way he looks at me.
The way he smells.

I want him to walk up to me and claim my lips with his, teasing them with his tongue, with his hands in my hair. Oh god, am I even going to be able to sit without sliding off the chair?

I am in so much trouble.
I have no idea what to do when it comes to being around the opposite sex.
I wasn't allowed to talk or even look at another man, and they too weren't allowed to talk to or touch me without permission.
I was to be seen and not heard.
But that's behind me, isn't it? I mean, I should be able to talk to other people, even men, without fear of retribution.
I want to be intimate with someone.
I want to be intimate with Dominic, a man I don't even know.

Maybe I should Google it?
I mean, surely. Stop, Liz.
Make yourself a cup of tea and when he leaves, have a shower.
A very cold shower. I have to laugh at myself.

👀 DOMINIC 👀

Wow, she is absolutely beautiful.
She has put her hair up with a clip, which makes her eyes and lips stand out even more.
Man, her lips are so perfect, and she just has to bite the bottom one and make it so much harder to maintain some sort of dignity.
I shift in my seat; damn work pants!
They are not good for growing… enthusiasm.
I look at her and smile and she smiles back, thank god I'm sitting down.
I glance at her hand: no ring.
Man, I hope she is single.

She turns around to make herself a cup of tea.
She is wearing shorts, not short-shorts, but still—her butt looks good; although it looked better in red lace. I take a deep breath, trying to focus on anything but her, but it's not working.

Her body looks tiny.
I look her up and down and I notice scars.
I feel my chest constrict at the thought of her being hurt in an accident.
I watch her run her foot up the back of her opposite leg.

I imagine what they would feel like wrapped around me as I lift her up onto the bench, my hands holding her hips and squeezing as I pull her onto me.
 My hands in her hair, kissing her hard, full of lust and desire.
I hold the cup in both hands and bring it to my lips, wishing it was her.
I can just make out the red bra through her shirt.
Oh, sweet Jesus, please, for the love of fucking god, be single!
And can I please grow the balls to ask her out?

🔖 ELIZABETH 🔖

I have managed to compose myself enough to make a fresh cup of tea.
I smile to myself before turning back to him.
'Right, well, I'm Elizabeth, but you can call me Liz or Lizzy,' I say as I bring the cup to my lips and blow before taking a sip.
He shifts in his chair and looks down at his cup before picking it up.
He looks up at me and smiles again.
Wowzers! I like his smile, I have to admit. It certainly has a magical effect on me,
Breathe Elizabeth, just breathe, I remind myself.

'Hi Liz, I'm Dominic. We have an appointment regarding the building work you would like completed,' I smile.
'Thank you for coming to see me, Dominic. I have heaps of things I would like to show you and get your thoughts on,' I say as my phone rings.
'Sorry, I have to take this, just a minute,' I pick up my phone.
'Hello, Amber, sorry, I can't chat. I'm in the middle of an appointment with the builder.'
'No worries, can I call you back later? Or I'll text you when I'm on my way.' Amber replies.
I nod automatically as she talks, 'Excellent, we'll chat when you get here around noon. Thank you, Amber, bye for now.'
I hang up and turn back to Dominic.

Amber is my handler while I'm in hiding.
Now she is also helping me reintegrate back into society, something I'm still struggling with.
We have a code during calls that lets her know whether I'm OK, or I need her to intervene.
She is from Western Australian, like me, and works for the Australian Federal Police.

She is proud of her part-indigenous heritage—her dad is Aboriginal and her mum is Scottish.

They met while her mum was here on a holiday, and it was love at first sight.

Amber is funny, loyal, tough, and a force to be reckoned with.

I classify her as a very close friend even though it's her job to protect me, as she treats me like a friend, not a witness.

She works with Bundaberg Police and no-one there, except for those who need to, know who she really is.

We both decided that I can't have Amber with me twenty-four seven if I'm going back to work.

So when she's at work, I try to go grocery shopping on my own.

Baby steps, right?

'Sorry about that, Dominic. Right, as I was saying, lots of ideas,' I say, getting my notebook out of my folder and sitting next to him.

Oh, my good golly gosh, he smells good!

He has his A4 notebook in his hand as well, and as he starts writing, I notice that he is left-handed.

His tattoo looks amazingly intricate, and from what I can see of his wristband, it has his family's name on it.

I watch his hands and begin to wonder what they would feel like on my body.

Are they rough, or soft?

They look big and soft.

I imagine him lifting me onto the bench as his hands grab and squeeze my hips, before snarling in my hair.

I imagine his kiss, hard and filled with desire.

I start to imagine him slowly undressing me, his lips and hands on my body…

I grip my cup tighter, almost spilling my tea.

Focus, Liz! I mentally yell at myself.

Focus on the house, woman! You are a grown woman and you are engaging his services as a builder. Let's get on with the appointment and focus on the fireplace.

A cold night, a warm fire, a nice rug with me on it, under him…

Oh crap! Just breathe, Lizzy, just breathe.

It's okay!

He's just a guy,… okay?

A really, really hot guy, sitting in my kitchen next to me.

Drink your tea, Elizabeth.

Meanwhile, if I grip this cup any tighter it will break.

I feel like a schoolgirl, sitting next to her high school crush in the back of the classroom.

Stop checking him out! I scold myself.

I take another sip of my tea.

'Right, so there are a few things that need to be repaired or replaced entirely,' I say, turning a page in my notebook. 'I would like the deck extended and part of it covered.'

I look at him.

He looks up at me and smiles.

'Right, let's start at number one on your list and go from there, how does that sound?' he asks.

I can't help but get distracted by his beautiful eyes and lips again.

'Elizabeth?'

'Sorry, what?' I blink myself back to reality.

'Umm, yes, sorry. Yes, let's start with item number one,' I stammer, looking back down at my notebook. Just breathe.

'Okay, item number one: The windows. I want the old timber ones removed and louvers installed, and stainless steel security screens added to all my windows and doors,'

I watch him write.

We sit for over an hour, going through more of my ideas and the plans I had drawn up.

Every now and then he would lean in a little closer, and my breath would catch in my throat.

I watch as he takes notes and moves his hand over the plans.

'Would you mind emailing these to me?' he asks, looking at the plans.

'You can have those, if you like. I can print more.'

'Thank you,' he smiles at me.

My body shivers involuntarily, and I try to hide my hands when they start to shake.

I have a feeling he notices nonetheless, but he just smiles as his eyes move over me.

I try to hide the scars on my arms.

He must find them, me, disgusting.

I show him the rooms at the front that have already been completed, along with my room and the en suite.

Then I show him the main bathroom and lounge, which I want to change.

'I want to have a fireplace installed in that corner. Would it be possible?' I ask.

'Should be okay, I'll just need to take some measurements. It will need new sheeting as it needs to be fire rated, unless you go with a wood heater,' he replies, looking at me.
'Wood heater?' I enquire, lifting my eyes to meet his.
'Personally, I would go with the wood heater. Less maintenance, and cleaner,' he smiles at me.
I smile back and look away, embarrassed by my reaction to him, hoping that he doesn't see my face flushed with colour, and sense my desire for him to reach out and touch me.
The fact that I really want him to take me to bed isn't helping.

'Okay, can you add that to your quote, please?' I ask as my phone rings.
'Excuse me, I'll leave you to measure or whatever it is you need to do.'
He nods and begins to measure and look around.
I sigh, would I ever be good enough for him?
Even if we did share a night together, would I disappoint him?
With everything I have gone through I'm not sure of myself. I'm constantly second guessing myself.
Am I destined to be alone, unloved and untouched, till the day I die?
I walk into the kitchen to take the call.

🦉 DOMINIC 🦉

'Hello, Elizabeth speaking,' she says into the phone.
'Hello Marshall, I'm good thank you, and yourself?' She rolls her eyes.
'Yes, I can talk, is everything okay? I did speak to David at QAS, and to my lawyer, they told me that everything has been submitted. I signed and submitted all my documents on Friday. Is there something wrong?'
She leans on the bench.
'Lawyer? Is there something I missed?'

I watch from the corner of my eye.
She looks nervous, almost afraid.
What could have her looking that way?
Is it something to do with a family member?
Could it be an accident, and if so what kind of accident had she been in?
I watch her discreetly.
She is pale, hugging her body.
I suppress the urge to go to her, to pull her against me and hold her tight.
I wish I could remove all her worries and fears and let her shine.

'That's not fair, it was never a part of the agreement.' Liz walks to her bedroom.
'No, I'm sorry, I can't meet with you. I'm sorry if I sound rude, but I really need to go. I have a visitor and I really need to get back to him,' Liz pauses briefly.
'I would appreciate it if you could contact my lawyer regarding any further issues.' She pauses again.
'No, thank you. Goodbye, Marshall.'

I hear her sit down on her bed, sigh and put the phone on her bedside table.
I know I shouldn't be thinking what I'm thinking, but she is so beautiful, and so freaking hot.
The way she talks, moves, and smells—up until this stage I have resisted every urge to ask her out.
She is going through a break-up by the sounds of it, and judging by the scars, it's not a good one.
I also get the feeling she has rejected Marshall's invite for a 'meeting' more than once, and judging by the eye-roll, he won't take no for an answer.
Could he be the one responsible for her scars?
Could he be the ex, trying to get her back?

I spend the next two hours with her going through the plans she had drawn up for the work to be done underneath her house, the deck extension and the kitchen.
It's getting harder not to touch her, or just walk up and kiss her.
'Well, I think we have covered pretty much everything,' she smiles at me.
She looks me over and blushes when I catch her.
I need to stall the end of our appointment.
I can see in her eyes that she wants me, but there is also something stopping her.
I notice how her hands shake when I get too close.
I move to give her space, and let her come towards me.
I want her to trust me.

'Why did you buy this house?' I ask.
'Umm, I loved it the first time I saw it. I was just sitting in a hotel room, and bought it on impulse.'
She smiles, but it seems forced, never reaching her eyes.
'Well, you're not from the area, so where have you moved from?' I look at her enquiringly.
'My last post was in Western Australia, but I needed a fresh start, so I packed up and here I am,' Liz responds, her eyes on the floor.
'Post? Are you in the Defence Force or Police?'
She chuckles.

'No, I'm a paramedic. I'm on leave for the next five months, then I'm going back to work and study.'
'What are you studying?'
'I want to increase my skill set and advance my career, so I'm studying paramedic critical care.'
'Is that something you've always wanted to do?'
'Yep, ever since I was a kid,' she replies, smiling at me.
Her eyes shine as she talks about her job. Yep, she's definitely making it hard to leave.

👓 ELIZABETH 👓

'Elizabeth.' Oh god, my name sounds good coming from his lips.
'Yes?' I reply.
'Can I ask why you want all the glass changed to safety glass? Some of the windows are brand new and have nothing wrong with them.' He looks at me.
'Personally, I don't think you need to, and it would save you a lot of money.'
The curiosity in his eyes tells me he is being honest, and wants to help, but my fight-or-flight anxiety makes me a little cautious about his question.
Step four, remember where all the bats are.
Just breathe, Liz, I tell myself.
I close my eyes, take a deep breath, and open them again.
He is watching me closely.

'I was burgled and it was, umm…' I trail off.
Please, for the love of god, DON'T CRY!
'Say no more.' The concern in his voice matches his eyes.
I nod and look down at the deck.
It needs a clean.
'I'll work through all the notes, get some prices, and then I'll have a quote for you in the next few days or so.' I look at my watch and realise it's noon already.
Ask him now. It's now or never, I say to myself.
I decide to lower my defences and muster the courage to ask.

'Um, Dominic, would you like something to eat? I seem to have kept you awhile,' I ask him as we walk back into the kitchen.
Please say yes, please say you will stay. I want you to stay.
He smiles as he grabs his hat and sunglasses off the bench.
'Thank you for the offer, but I should probably get going,' he replies.
Rejection; it feels like a kick to the gut and I retreat behind my walls again.
My hands start to shake.

How could I be so stupid?

Why would he stay with me?

'I'm so sorry, you're right,' I say, looking down at the floor, my hand rubbing my neck.

'You probably have someone waiting for you. I'm so sorry, I shouldn't have asked,' I stammer, too embarrassed to look up.

My hand rubs the scar on my right wrist.

'Hey, Elizabeth,' Dominic takes a step towards me.

'Yes?' I ask, moving backwards, away from him.

I can't even look at him, I'm too busy trying to hide my anxiety.

'What have you got planned for this Saturday?' he asks.

'Just catching up with a friend,' I reply.

'A group of us are going up the beach for the day. BBQ, drinks, cricket and a few laughs. You and your friend should join us.' He smiles, taking another step towards me.

'Umm, I don't know. I'm not good…' is all I manage before a sudden stab of anxiety prevents me from saying anything else.

I stumble backwards, grab the door frame of my room and manage to look up at him.

He can tell I'm broken.

I can see it in his eyes.

His face is creased in a frown.

My panic escalates.

I tell myself to breathe, but I can't, my chest hurts and I can't focus.

Darks spots appear in my vision.

My body suddenly feels heavy, and I look back down and take a deep, shaky breath.

Amber, I need to call Amber.

I look up, my vision blurry. I can just make him out, taking a step towards me.

'Help' I whisper, as I try to reach for him.

'Dominic' I stumble towards him.

The last thing I hear is him calling my name, then everything goes black.

ᗜ DOMINIC ᗜ

Liz stumbles and calls out to me to help her.

I run over, and just manage to catch her before she hits the floor.

Shit! I shake my head.

What just happened?

We were talking and she asked if I was hungry, which I am but I didn't want to push my luck.
Why would my refusal to stay cause her to panic?
It's obvious that something has happened to her.
I have so many questions, who, what, when, where, and why, but I take a moment to still my mind and focus.
I'm starting to realise that it must have taken a lot of courage for her to ask if I wanted to stay for lunch.
Liz looks pale, but is breathing softly.
I sit with her for about ten minutes, just holding her.

I look at the scar on her collarbone and neck; I've noticed how she rubs at them when she is nervous. The scar on her right wrist: she rubs that when she starts to say something, but then stops.
The scars look bad, like they were from a really bad accident.
It's not like someone could have done that to her on purpose, could they?
How could anyone do that to someone?
I find myself angry at the thought that someone could have hurt her on purpose.
Angry, because I wasn't there to stop them and to protect her.
Could I ask her what happened?
Would she tell me?
I close my eyes, I feel bad for not accepting her offer.
But if I stayed, I wouldn't have wanted to leave without trying to kiss her.

I remember seeing her watching me and feeling the tension between us.
Watching the way she moves, the way her fingers touched her lips.
The way her eyes shone even more when she really smiled.
I could happily have lost myself in them.

I take a deep breath and feel warmth spread through my body.
I have never felt anything like it before, and I want her to feel the same.

It's crazy, I know.
We have only just met.

She smells amazing, like coconut, vanilla, and a soft hint of something floral, maybe jasmine.
Please, for the love of god, be single!
I don't want to let her go, and this realisation scares the shit out of me.
I can't explain it, but the pull is huge.

I move carefully, lifting her up and carrying her to her room, where I lay her down gently on the bed and carefully remove her hair clip.
I stand there for a moment, watching her, before I go and get a glass of water for when she wakes up.
I get a washer in her bathroom, dampen it, and dab her forehead, face, and neck.
Then I just watch her for a while.
She is so beautiful.
I sit down next to her, and when she starts to stir, I quietly say her name and brush the hair from her face.

👀 ELIZABETH 👀

What is that smell? Sawdust, why can I smell sawdust?
Sawdust mixed with deodorant, aftershave, and…
'Elizabeth,' a voice says. Who the hell is that?
'Elizabeth,' the strange voice says again.
I feel someone touch me as I come to.
I sit up quickly.
'NO!' I scream, 'No! Please, don't hurt me anymore!'
I shrink away, trying to shield myself from the incoming beating.
I'm breathing heavily, I can hear my heart pounding in my chest like it's about to burst.
I look out from under my arms.
Where am I?

'You're okay, Elizabeth, you're okay. Just take nice, easy breaths.' The voice continues.
No, I'm not okay! Where am I?
I scan my surroundings.
I'm in my room, on my bed.
My clothes, my clothes!
I look down and touch my clothes, as I realise I'm not naked.
I look over my arms and legs, there are no new marks or cuts.
No blood.

I need to ring Amber.
The bat, I need to get to my...

'Elizabeth, look at me,' the voice pleads.
My body trembles.
'Please look at me.'

I feel someone touch me, and I flinch.
I look up to see his eyes.
My whole body is shaking violently, and I feel ice-cold.
I realise it's Dominic, the builder, touching me, that his is the voice talking to me.
He holds his hands up in front of me.
'You are safe. You are okay, just look at me and breathe nice and easy.'
I nod as he slowly brings his hands down, resting one on my shoulder.
Wow, he's even better up close, and I'm probably a mess.
Why does this have to happen to me?
There is a totally gorgeous man, sitting on my bed, in my room, and I make a complete fool of myself.
I'm sorry,' I stutter, as the tears start to fall.
I feel so stupid and embarrassed.
I try to turn away, but he won't let me.
'Just keep looking at me,' he says softly.
'Breathe in and out, nice and easy.' He smiles at me.
Why won't the floor open up and swallow me whole?

'Don't apologise, you have nothing to be sorry for,' he murmurs.
He is still holding my hands, and his eyes never leave mine.
Right now, all I want is for him to kiss me, I'm completely mesmerised by him.
'How long was I out for?' I ask.
'About 30 minutes.'
'Did you carry me to my bed? I don't really remember much.'
'Yes I did. I hope that's okay.'
'Thank you,' I nod.
'You're welcome,' he responds, his hands still holding mine.

I smile and he smiles back before handing me a glass of water.
We sit together for a long while, not saying a word.
My hands start to shake, and he takes the glass from me and holds them gently.
His thumb moves along my fingers as he reaches over and touches my cheek with his other hand.
I close my eyes as his fingers move along my cheek, tucking lose strands of hair behind my ear.
I can feel myself starting to calm down and breathe normally.
He doesn't even know me, yet it feels like he knows exactly what I need.
His touch feels warm and safe.

It's not until my phone vibrates on the bedside table that I notice the time.
I don't even remember putting it on silent.

'Oh my god, I'm so sorry!' I groan.
'What, why?' he asks, incredulous, as he lets go of my hands.
'The time, oh my god! I have kept you here. You need to be elsewhere and instead you're here, babysitting me!'
The tears start to fall again.
'Hey, look at me', he says, gently.
'I'm so stupid.'
'No you're not,' he shakes his head.
I look at him and he smiles.
'I don't need to or want to be anywhere other than right where I am now,' he smiles as he takes my hands again.
'I'm so sorry...'
'Elizabeth, stop, it's okay,' Dominic cuts me off before I can finish.
'I'm not going anywhere. I'll stay here with you as long as you need me to.'
He moves closer to me and takes my face in both hands, tilting it up so I can see his eyes.
With his thumbs he gently wipes away my tears, smiling.
'Elizabeth, it seems to me that you have been through something that still has a huge hold on you. I think you should give yourself time to heal. Now, I understand that it's not easy letting go of things that still hurt you but...'
Dominic pauses, looking at me intently, and I can feel his gaze reaching right to the very depths of my soul.
I try to look away, but he makes me hold his gaze.
'It doesn't mean you won't heal, in time.' He smiles again.

I sigh as I look into his eyes.
I feel warmth spread through me, my nipples harden, and I feel an ache between my thighs.
Please kiss me.
I need to feel your lips on mine.
I need you to hold me.
I smile as I close my eyes, his hands are moving down to my neck.
His touch is relaxing my whole body, making me feel warm and safe.
Why can't I take the lead and kiss him first?
Why don't I have the courage to feel him against me?

I made a promise to myself to let someone in.
I plead with myself to let him in.
Opening my eyes, I see him still watching me, like he is silently asking for permission.

I moisten my lips with my tongue as he watches me.

His eyes find mine again and he starts to move in, my body filling with anticipation.

He's going to kiss me, and I'm going to let him.

I part my lips.

My breathing quickens.

Is this what your first time is supposed to feel like?

He runs his thumb along my cheek.

'ELIZABETH! Elizabeth, where are you?' a woman's voice calls.

'Oh crap!' Not now, please don't come in.

'ELIZABETH!? Fuck!' Amber calls out again.

I hear her bag drop to the floor.

She is going to freak out when she comes through my bedroom door.

Dominic's hands drop as he stands and turns, putting himself between the bedroom door and me.

I stand up behind him and move to his side.

'Who is it, Elizabeth?' he asks, his voice protective as he moves in front of me.

'It's okay, Dominic, it's my…' I manage before Amber barges through my door, almost running straight into Dominic.

'Who the fuck are you?' Amber demands, her hand moving automatically to her hip.

'Who are you?' he retorts, his voice hard as he pushes me further behind him.

Dominic stands his ground, his fists clenched, his posture tense.

'Don't push it,' Amber's voice is threatening.

'Amber, it's okay.' I say, moving out from behind Dominic.

He instantly pushes me back behind him.

'My, my, my. Now I know why you haven't been answering your phone, or returning my messages.

Too busy with your builder, huh?' She winks. 'Go Lizzy!'

She laughs, all tension gone from her voice.

The whole time, Dominic has been standing in front of me, his arm preventing me from moving and Amber from getting to me. He stands there, listening, somewhat stunned by Amber's abrupt arrival.

I am still standing behind him.

He reaches behind, pulling me closer to him and I find myself leaning against his back, holding onto his shirt. Usually I would be fearful of impending punishment but I feel safe right now. I just wish Amber would leave, right now!

My reassurances do not make Dominic back down, however, his demeanour is still tense and protective. He is still blocking my way, until I place my hand on his arm.
He turns to look at me.
I nod that it's okay and he turns back to look at Amber.

He drops his arm but takes my hand and I don't pull away.
He keeps himself between Amber and I.
I look over at Amber; far from stopping him, she is allowing him to stay between us.
'Hi, I'm Amber, Lizzy's best friend. I'm sorry for barging in and interrupting,' she winks.
Oh my god, Amber, you're not helping!
Dominic releases my hand to shake Amber's, before taking mine again.
Oh, dear lord! I could really get used to his touch.

'Amber, stop it, nothing is going on,' I say, blushing beside Dominic.
Why am I blushing? I feel so stupid and my body starts to tremble.
Dominic picks up on my unease, grips my hand tighter and runs his thumb soothingly along my fingers.
I allow his soothing touch to calm me.
I take another deep breath and start to relax again.
Meanwhile, Amber is standing there, smiling at me.
'This is Dominic. He is my builder and he was helping me,' I falter, looking down, and then looking back at Amber.
Dominic squeezes my hand.
'I kinda had a moment,' I stammer.
His thumb caresses the scars on my hand.
I let his warmth spread through my body, restoring my calm a little more.
His touch feels so good.
Please, let me find it in myself to open up to him.

Amber's smile fades and is replaced by a concerned frown.
'Oh, hon, are you okay?'
She looks from me to Dominic as she moves closer.
His body stiffens as he tightens his grip on my hand.
I hang onto his, not wanting to let go.

Dominic looks at Amber and nods.
She brings her hands up in front of her, palms up, signifying that she isn't trying to interfere.

I watch what is going on between them.
Then Amber looks at him and smiles.

'Thank you for looking after her,' she moves to hug me.
She looks down at our hands, then back up at Dominic, still smiling.
I look up at Dominic, too, and blush as he smiles at me.

'You're welcome, I'm just glad I was able to catch her,' he responds, his eyes on mine.
'I let my imagination run away with me there for a bit, didn't I?' Amber grins.
'No worries, I'll leave you both to it.'
He releases my hand and turns to me.
'The offer still stands for this Saturday, for you both, if you're up for it?'
I look at him, and he watches as I lick my lips and nervously bite my bottom lip.
I can feel myself blushing again.
Why the hell did Amber have to interrupt us?
'Thank you, I will talk with Amber,' I reply.
I see Amber out of the corner of my eye, moving backwards toward my bedroom door.
The smile on her face is huge.

'There is nothing better than a day on the beach, sun, surf, and food,' he flashes me a huge grin.
There's that damn smile again!
Oh, dear lord!
I've gone weak at the knees.
Amber is standing , behind him, with two thumbs up and a pleading smile.
'We'll be there!' She chimes in, with no idea about what the invite is for.
'Okay, nine AM, Saturday, south entrance to the beach. Bring your own drinks and whatever you want to put on the barbie.'
We look at each other like there is no one else with us.

Dominic, on a beach, with no shirt on…
Oh, dear lord, it got hot all of a sudden!
I blush and sway slightly, and Dominic reaches out a hand to steady me.
I'm all class, I know, but what the hell, I already lost my dignity.
'I don't have a car that can drive on the beach,' I blurt out suddenly, feeling somewhat flustered.
'I'll pick up both of you, about eight-forty-five,' he replies.
'Lizzy and I will be ready,' Amber seems very chipper and winks at me. 'Thank you for the invite.'
'Excellent!' He smiles at me.

'I'll even give her a list of food to prepare,' Amber beams.
Go away, Amber.
'Sounds great!' Dominic beams in return.

His eyes have barely left mine; we smile at each other again.
I suddenly realise his hand is still on my waist, and I'm really starting to feel hot and bothered.
What the hell is going on with me?
I feel my chest rise and fall with heavy breaths.
All I can think of is Dominic, on a beach, no shirt, the water beading off him and that amazing, makes-my-knees-weak, perfectly sexy smile.

Oh, dear lord, I'm so, so out of my depth, I have no idea what to do.
I'm not asking Amber, either, she will be absolutely no help at all.
Her mind has already hit the gutter and I'm not far off.
I think the two years of being around Amber has rubbed off her dirty mind on me.
I close my eyes, trying to focus.
Cold shower, music, washing clothes, cooking food in a hot oven.
Beach, water, hot sun, no shirt. I need a cold shower—a very cold one.
I open my eyes, giving up trying to focus. It's never going to happen while he is touching me.

'Well, I should get going, I have to get this quote done,' he says, still smiling.
'Yeah' is all I manage as I take a small step backwards.
Amber is absolutely loving whatever is going on between Dominic and I.
'Well, I'll be in the kitchen making food. Bye, Dominic,' she grins.
'Bye, Amber,' Dominic says, but he's still looking at me.
Amber leaves the room and I move to follow her.
'I'll walk you to your car, I blush.
Shit! That's not what I wanted to say.
My body is screaming at me to let him in, but I still can't find the courage to kiss him.
'I'd like that,' he smiles, as he brushes a lock of hair off his forehead.

We walk past Amber in the kitchen, where she is starting to make a mess, trying to cook.
Dominic grabs his book, hat, sunnies and keys off the bench and says goodbye to Amber again.
Amber smiles broadly and waves.
'Take your time, I'm all good here!' She winks.

I roll my eyes at Dominic and he smiles at me as he turns and walks out the door.
I shoot Amber a what the fuck look, but she just shrugs her shoulders and smiles.
Then she comes around the bench and practically pushes me out the door.
'Go, Liz, I'll manage not to burn the water, I promise,' she chuckles and turns back to the kitchen.
Amber can't cook to save her life, but she likes to pretend, occasionally.
I think she messes up on purpose so that I will take over.

Shaking my head at her, I turn and walk towards Dominic, who is waiting at the top of the stairs.
I follow him downstairs, replaying the events of the morning in my head.
I miss the bottom step, stumble forward and he catches me.
'Are you sure you're alright?' he asks, his eyes searching.
I focus on his lips, it would be so easy to…
Please, just once let me kiss someone I actually want to kiss.
I nod, feeling utterly embarrassed.
I'm a smart person, but socially awkward and completely out of my depth with the opposite sex.

I look down and close my eyes, his hands are on me again.
I shiver, breaking out in goosebumps despite the warm weather.
I open my eyes to see his book lying on the ground.
I bend down and pick it up, taking a step back to hand it to him.
'Thank you' he murmurs, taking the book from me.
I can see my hands shaking, so I stuff them in the tiny pockets of my shorts, hoping he didn't see.
I walk past him down the short pathway to where his car is parked.
Reaching his car, I turn back to him.
'I'm sorry that you had to witness my moment earlier…'
'You don't have to apologise, Elizabeth,' he interrupts gently.
'Well, I should at least thank you.'
'You don't have to thank me, either.'
'Well, thank you anyway, you did way more than you needed to.' I blush and look down.
I need to sweep the path.
His hand lifts my chin so my eyes meet his.
His touch sends shockwaves through my body like nothing I have ever felt.
My breathing deepens; he smells amazing.
My hand runs over the scar on my right wrist.
Just this once, please, I beg myself.

🔖 DOMINIC 🔖

Touching her feels great.
She runs her hand over the scar on her right wrist.
I feel like she wants to say something, but doesn't know how.
I feel as if I instinctively understand her, even though I don't know how.
She doesn't need to say anything, her body is doing all that for her.
She just can't bring herself to say what's on her mind.
All I can hope for is that, given time, she will.
I run my fingers along her cheek and tuck her hair behind her ear.

Stepping in, I close the gap between us.
I can feel the tension between us building, the calm before the storm, and I want so badly to kiss her.
I feel her body's reaction to my touch, and savour it.
She has absolutely no idea of the effect she has on me when she licks and bites her lip nervously.
I run my thumb gently over her lips.
My god, they feel amazing.
Elizabeth closes her eyes, her breathing deepens.
My thumb traces her jawline as she opens her big beautiful green eyes.

I put my book down on the hood of my car and hold her waist, pulling her towards me.
Her body shudders under my touch.
I'm about to kiss her when my phone rings, ruining the moment.
I can't stop looking at her.
She steps back from me and lowers her gaze.

No, no, no! I breathe, exasperated, as my left hand drops to my pocket, the right staying on her waist.
I can hear her breathing heavily and I know she wants me, but she is holding back.
Liz looks back up at me, her beautiful eyes making it hard to look away.
Looking at her, I imagine what it would feel like to kiss her, to taste her.

Please, ask me again to stay.
I want to stay, but I don't want to push her.
The break-in must have really been serious for her to hide from everything.
But something doesn't seem to add up.
Is there more to the story than she has let on?
Were they looking for someone else?

Someone she was protecting?
Is that why she has those scars?
As much as I want to stay with her, I need to win her trust first.
I pick my book without taking my eyes off her.
I imagine what she would feel like in my arms.
As I make love to her.
My phone rings again.

'Don't you need to answer that?' I ask.
'No, no, I don't,' he replies without looking at his phone.
'Thank you for coming today, and for your invite.' I look down and back up at him.
'I'm looking forward to Saturday.'
I wave at him, turn, and walk back towards the house.
'Elizabeth?' He calls after me.
'Yes?' I turn back to look at him.
'I, um,…' He fiddles with his keys, 'I'm really looking forward to Saturday as well.'
He opens the door to his black Landcruiser Ute. 'I'll call you later.'
'I'd like that,' I smile, wishing I had the courage to walk up to him and tell him exactly what I want him to do to me.
'Can I ask you a question?' He asks suddenly, walking back towards me.
'Yes,' I nod   slowly, praying he doesn't ask about my panic attack. I feel embarrassed enough as it is.
'Um…' He lets out an uncomfortable laugh and looks away.
'I, um, overheard…' He looks up at me, 'Something about a lawyer.'
'The lawyer is dealing with the purchase of this house and an investment home I'm looking to buy.'

'Elizabeth, I would really like to see you again.'
I smile at him and he smiles back.
I'm sure he is only saying that to be polite, but it is still nice to hear.
'Okay, well, I'm not going anywhere.'
He walks backwards to his car.
'Good,' he says, a boyish grin on his face.
'Dominic…' I start, but I can't bring myself to finish the question.
'Yeah?'
'Oh, umm. I was wondering...'
Come on, Liz, just ask him.
'Are you...' I stall again as I shove my shaking hands back into my pockets.
'Single? Yes, if that's what you were going to ask.'
I nod, not lifting my gaze. I'm too embarrassed to look at him.

'Elizabeth,'
I force myself to look up into his eyes and smile.
I wish I could bring myself to kiss him.
My hands are still in my pockets, shaking.
I clench them into fists, digging my nails into my palms.

I lick my lips at the thought of his lips on mine.
His phone rings again.
'I should, um, get going,' he mutters, getting into his Ute.
He starts his car, and the V8 engine in his twin turbo diesel Landcruiser roars
to life.
We wave at each other as he drives away, then I turn and walk back to the house
to face Amber.
I walk upstairs and take a deep breath.
Amber is not going to shut up, so I will have to bake a big chocolate cake as a
bribe, that should slow her down… For a while.
I chuckle to myself as I walk in the door.
'Well, did he kiss you?' Amber asks me as soon as I'm in the door.
I shake my head as I walk towards the window.
'I'm making a chocolate cake. Is there anything else you would like me to cook?'
I sigh, trying to change the subject.

I stare out the window and touch my lips.
I close my eyes, remembering his touch.
I can't help but smile, thinking about how he almost kissed me, twice, and I was
going to let him.
His touch was so warm, so calming, my body just responded to him.
I want Dominic on so many levels, and it isn't just about sex, regardless of how
it sounds.
There was something there I couldn't explain.
I only hope that he feels the same, and that we can explore whatever this is,
together.
I hope we get the chance.

'Earth to Lizzy.'
'Sorry, what was that?' I ask, my fingers still touching my lips.
'Where did your mind just wander off to then?' Amber comes to stand beside
me.
'Um, maybe you should go on your own on Saturday.'
'Oh heeeeellll no! After what I just saw, you are going!' Amber scoffs, a huge
smile on her face.
'What did you see?'

'You like him, he likes you. The tension between you two was, how should I put this? It was undeniable, there is definitely something there. He was holding you and you were letting him. You should allow yourself to enjoy whatever comes from it. You did promise yourself, remember?' Amber touches my shoulder and smiles.

'But what if I don't satisfy him? And…'

Amber laughs, 'Liz, you have satisfied yourself for long enough!'

I look at her, totally confused.

'Um, Liz, come on, surely you have pleasured yourself?'

'Um, no, never.' I blush, my eyes on the ground.

When I look up, Amber has shock written all over her face.

'Wow! I mean… um, ok. Well, I guess it's your lover's job to satisfy you…'

'But my body is so scarred!' I cut her off.

I feel tears coming.

'Oh, hon, I know you're scared. But I know Dominic will see past that.' Amber says, hugging me.

'How? How do you know that?' I wail.

'Well, he stayed with you when you blacked out. He still wanted you to join him on Saturday. And he wouldn't let me near you when I barged into your room. Even when you told him it was okay, he was still protective of you. Dominic feels what you feel, I know it—it's meant to be.'

'I couldn't even bring myself to ask him to kiss me. I really want him, and it's not just about sex. His touch felt warm and safe. I just don't feel good enough to have him.' I sob, miserable.

'Liz, hon, you deserve more than most to find someone who makes you happy. You are good enough for him, please remember that.'

I smile at her through my tears.

'Besides, I thought you were hot when I first saw you at the hospital. I was bummed when I found out you weren't interested in women.' She winks at me.

'Amber. Why couldn't I? Why did I pull away?'

I was in his arms, I saw him looking at my mouth.

I watched his tongue run over his lips.

Amber takes a moment to gaze out the window before looking back at me.

'Hon, Michael groomed you into thinking you could only do things when he gave you permission.'

'But he is not here! Why can't I do what I want?'

'Elizabeth, you need to give yourself permission.' Amber puts her hand on my shoulder. 'You need to stop thinking about the what-ifs and just let yourself go. Let Dominic in and you will find yourself, trust me.' She squeezes my shoulder.

'Now you have some chocolate cake to bake,' she smiles.
'Yes ma'am!' I return her smile.

The week drags on, and I restock the freezer with all of Amber's favourites; in triplicate.
I make enough chocolate cake, vanilla slices, lamingtons, and pavlova to feed the entire Australian Defence Force.
I still can't believe how Amber manages to eat nearly all of it.
We laugh a lot as she revels in reminding me of my lusting after Dominic.
She even wants me to go shopping for some new outfits, but I manage to get out of it.
Every time she mentions him, I swear I blush and my body feels hot and feverish.
I do get to speak to him a few times on the phone, and I manage to bang on for ages about all sorts of things, so that I don't have to hang up.

'Hi, Elizabeth, it's Dominic. Are you free to talk for a minute?'
'Yes, of course.' I feel my cheeks warm as I smile.
'I just need to ask you about the wood heater. Do you have a preference?' He asks, 'I'm here at the hardware store now and there are a few styles to choose from.'
'No I don't. I just want one that looks good, but no fancy designs.'
I hear someone talking to him.
'The tile heath that it needs to sit on, do you want it in a glossy tile, or a timber finish?' They ask.
'I would suggest tile, because the timber look won't match what she already has,', he replies before turning the conversation back to me. 'Are you okay with that, Elizabeth?'
'Yes, of course, that sounds great. Thank you.'
'Elizabeth, would you mind just holding on a sec while I finalise this?'
'Mmm hmm,' I nod as I walk out onto the deck.

I listen to Dominic talk to the sales staff. His phone must be on the counter, because I can hear a pen scratching on paper.
'All done.' The salesperson says. 'Your wife will be very happy with the selection. Just let us know when you are ready to collect.'
Wife? Dominic didn't even try to correct them. I stare dumbfounded at the ocean view, before Dominic's voice snaps me out of my trance.
'Elizabeth? Are you still there?'
'Yes, sorry, I'm here.'
We talk for another half an hour before we hang up, and the only job related thing we spoke about was the wood heater.

There is something about his voice that makes me feel safe, like I could trust him.

I just need to trust myself to let go.

As much as I want to go on Saturday, the whole idea freaks me out.

Out of a group of people I would only know two: Amber and Dominic.

I don't want to hang off either of them.

I want Amber to enjoy herself and I don't want Dominic to feel he has to babysit me the entire time.

I agonise over whether or not to cancel, but I just can't bring myself to.

I'm positively counting down the minutes to seeing him again.

Amber is also looking forward to getting out of this house and mixing with people other than me —not that she ever complains.

The closer to Saturday it gets, the more nervous I become.

It's Thursday morning and Dominic calls me.

'Hello, this is Elizabeth.'

'Hi, Elizabeth. It's Dominic, are you free to speak?'

'Of course.' I smile as I place a cake tin in the oven and close the door.

'I have just put a cake in the oven, so I'm all good.'

He has rung a few times with some questions about the renovations, and I feel like a teenager every time.

'I'll try not to keep you too long.' He pauses when someone in the background calls his name.

'Sorry, just a second. Yeah, Luke?' He calls back.

The voices are muffled, but I can hear him laughing.

'Sorry about that, Elizabeth.'

'No worries, Dominic, you're working, after all.' I sit down in the lounge and pull a cushion onto my lap.

'Um, well, I have completed your quotes. I'll email them to you shortly.'

'That's great, thank you. Where are you working today?'

I give myself a mental facepalm.

Why on earth did I ask him that?

'I'm heading to Burnett Heads soon. I have to deliver something for a new deck we are finishing today. The owners have added a spa bath, so I have to go back and make some changes so that it meets the building codes.'

'Sounds very interesting.' Ugh, I'm so awkward.

'Yeah, the weather has held off for us, so that helps.'

'Yes, the weather has been beautiful this week. I hope it stays for the weekend, I would hate for your beach day to be cancelled.' Okay, now tell him you can't go.

'Yeah, so do I. I'm really looking forward to taking you there, it's always a great day out.' I can hear the sincerity in his voice.

My heart beats harder and faster, and I just can't say no to him.

Again, I manage to talk for ages about all sorts of things, just so I don't have to hang up.

He has his phone on hands-free while driving to his job. It almost sounds like he doesn't want to hang up either.

After we get off the phone, I find the quotes he emailed through, sign them, and send it right back.

It is Thursday night, and Amber and I decide to have dinner at the pub.

We're just finishing our desserts when I look up to see Amber smiling.

'What?' I ask her.

She is looking past me, and I start to turn around.

'What are you wearing on Saturday?' She asks suddenly.

I stop and look back at her and start to say something, but I notice her expression has changed.

'She can wear me,' a familiar, sleazy voice answers from behind me.

I look at Amber.

Why can't this guy get the hint and leave me alone!

I never even look at him, let alone talk to him.

Yet, he tries to talk to me every time we come here.

And I tell him the same thing every time—I'm not interested.

His presence makes my skin crawl.

I can't move or speak, my whole being is screaming at me to run.

I realise that I'm trembling.

His demeanour and even his smell remind me of Michael.

'Sorry, not interested. Do you mind?' Amber retorts.

'Come on, there is enough of me for the both of you, if you want,' he continues.

I can hear him behind me as he moves closer to my chair.

I keep my eyes on Amber and move slightly to try and see his reflection in the window.

I grip my glass tighter.

'You can't say no to this forever,' he motions to himself.

'Oh god, I think I just threw up in my mouth. I tell you what, how about I make a phone call and have my friends in blue take you for a drive. Then I'll make your life a living hell.' Amber glares at him.

I don't turn around, I'm frozen in my seat.

I can just make out his reflection in the glass, but I can't see his face.

He starts to lift his hand towards me.

'You touch her, and I'll take great pleasure in breaking all ten of your fingers,' Amber says with a huge, menacing smile on her face.

'I guess I'll have to try another day, when you're not hogging the goods.' His voice sounds vile.

Oh god, now I think I've actually thrown up in my mouth.

'No, you won't, she is spoken for and I don't like to share. I have a badge, a gun, and a get-out-of-jail-free card, so please feel free to try your luck. It's been a while since I last got my hands dirty,' Amber challenges him.

'Well, I guess I'll have to watch and wait.'

'I'll tell you what, you can have her when, oh wait, never. Now if you would kindly fuck off and let us finish our dinner and drinks, the exit is behind you,' Amber sneers, pointing at the door.

I watch his reflection as he turns and retreats toward the bar.

Amber watches him leave, then gets out her notepad.

'What are you doing?' I ask.

'Writing down this idiot's description. Then I'll keep an eye out for him, get his car registration number and put him on my watch and wait, he will do something stupid-list.' She looks up and smiles sweetly at me.

'Right, now as I was asking before we were so rudely interrupted. What are you planning on wearing for Dominic on Saturday?'

I blush. 'Amber, sshhh!'

'Okay, buzzkill, what are you wearing on Saturday?' Amber asks more quietly.

'I don't know. I haven't thought about it. Probably just my swimmers, with a shirt and sarong,' I muse.

'I don't have enough clothes to worry about what to wear, I finish, playing with the straw in my drink.

'Well, I'll help you. One or two-piece swimsuit?'

'One-piece, Amber,' I answer quickly.

I look up to see that she is glancing at something behind me, smiling a kooky kind of smile, before looking back at me.

'Fine,' Amber sighs dramatically. 'I'll have a look through mine. I probably have swimmers I haven't even worn.'

'Elizabeth!' A familiar voice calls behind me.

I turn around to see Dominic walking towards us.

He looks amazing in black denim jeans that fit snugly in all the right places and a light grey button-up shirt. His hair is freshly washed and brushed, falling over his forehead. I feel like a schoolgirl seeing her crush.

'Crap!' I hiss as I turn back to Amber.

She has a huge grin on her face; she is no help at all.

'Hey!' Dominic says.

'Hey!' I smile back nervously.

'Hello, Dominic,' Amber grins.
'Hello, Amber,' Dominic replies.
'Would you like to join us? We have finished eating, though,' she asks.
'Thank you,' Dominic says as he sits next to me. 'I won't bother you for too long,
I ordered a take away.'

Oh my god, he smells so good!
I can feel his warmth and my body responds immediately.
'You can stay with our Liz as long as you like, I don't mind at all,' Amber replies
mischievously, snapping me out of my little fantasy.
I glare at Amber and she smiles innocently at me.
I am mortified, I've let my imagination run wild and Amber was no help.
'We were just talking about Saturday, and what Liz will be wearing,' Amber
remarks, winking at me with a wicked smirk on her face.
I look down at my lap, blushing.
Once again my body is hopeless when he is around.
Why won't a sinkhole appear and swallow me?

'Just as long as you join me on Saturday and have a good time, that's all I care
about,' I hear Dominic say.
I look up to see him looking at me.
His smile is big and infectious.

'I'm looking forward to it,' I reply, smiling and playing with the straw in my
drink.
'I'm going to the ladies room,' Amber says, beating a hasty retreat, leaving
Dominic and I alone.

We sit at the table and smile at each other.
'So,...' I start.
'So,' he says.
We smile at each other.
'So, a day at the beach. I hope that means cricket and football,' I say, nervously,
trying to hide at least some of my excitement about seeing him.
'Of course. Not to mention jet-skiing and surfing,' he adds, as someone calls his
name.
'Sounds like it's going to be fun,' I respond, hoping my voice sounds convincing
as I stir my drink.
'You will have to come out on my jet-ski with me,' he grins, with a cheeky glint
in his eye.
His comment almost makes me knock over my drink.
My hands start to shake.

What's wrong with me?
I automatically start to decline his offer when I look up to see him looking at me.
My mind goes poof! and I can't say a word.
I feel like red jelly—my face bright red and my body trembling.

His eyes, however, don't leave mine.
He smiles at me and I feel like I'm the only person in the room.
He reaches for my hand.
I take a shaky, tentative breath and let him in, a little.
I turn my hand over and let his fingers run over my palm.
They are soft, and my mind wanders to his hands exploring my body.
I look at our hands and let him hold mine in both of his.
I feel anxious, but I can't bring myself to pull my hand away.
It feels so good to be touched like this and I don't want him to let go.
I'm sure he can feel my hand quivering under his, but he doesn't say anything.

I slowly reach out with my shaking fingers and stroke his.
I have no idea what is happening between us; I have never felt anything like this before.
I look at Dominic, he is keenly watching my reaction.
He smiles and, feeling myself blush, I duck my head and look back down at our hands.
He lifts my hands up in his, and I can feel his breath on my fingers.
My lips part and my breathing accelerates at the anticipation of his lips touching my fingers.
I can't remember the last time someone touched me like this.
I had no idea that a person could render me so completely at their mercy without fear of pain or punishment.

🔲 DOMINIC 🔲

I watch her close her eyes and drop her head slightly.
I hate it when she hides herself. I smile as I wait for her to lift her head and open her eyes again.
I would give anything to make this beautiful woman in front of me happy, just to see that amazing smile every day.
I can feel her hand trembling in mine.
It is soft, even though there are scars all over it.
I know she is holding back.
Her body is giving the game away, but she can't bring herself to let go.

I will wait, and I don't care how long.

Elizabeth is, without a doubt, worth waiting for. I want so much for her to trust me.

I long for her to let go of whatever is holding her back. I want her to want me as much as I want her.

I watch as she licks her lips and bites her bottom lip nervously, it makes my body respond and I shift in my seat.

She makes it hard to maintain my dignity, I chuckle at myself.

I can't explain this feeling I have for her.

The need to be with her, to hold her and protect her with everything I am, is overwhelming.

I'm drawn to her on so many levels, and I can only hope she feels the same.

I watch her face closely and see her blush.

She really is beautiful and I wish she could see what I see: a beautiful, strong, and intelligent woman.

She runs her fingers along her neck before slowly bringing her hand down to touch mine.

Her green eyes shine and I get lost in them.

All I want to do is hold her and never let go.

I long to feel her on my lips.

To feel her under me as I make love to her.

I lift both of her hands up and gently blow against her fingers, watching her whole body react.

She blushes and smiles.

I watch as she parts her lips and her breathing quickens, anticipating me kissing her fingers.

🔍 ELIZABETH 🔍

'Hey, Dominic, here's your order,' a waitress announces loudly as she comes up to the table.

She comes to stand between Dominic and I.

I watch as she puts her hand on his shoulder seductively.

She smells of cigarettes, beer, and men's cologne, it stings my nose.

Dominic releases my hands and the loss of his warmth instantly causes me to panic.

'Thank you,' he says, clearing his throat.

'So, I haven't seen you for a while,' she purrs, ignoring me.

'I have to get going, goodbye Dominic.' I get up to leave.

'Elizabeth, please wait.' He stands.

I stop and look back at him.

'It's okay. I'll see you Saturday morning at eight-forty-five.' I turn to leave as Amber comes back.

She looks from the waitress to Dominic.

'What's…'

'Can we go, please?' I snap, cutting her off.

'Sure,' she replies, still looking uncertainly at the two of them.

I practically run to the car.

'I can't. I can't do this. I'm not good for him, I'm not safe to be with. He's too good for me,' I stammer to myself, pacing at the front of Amber's car, my arms wrapped tightly around myself.

Amber grabs me, turning me to look at her.

'Hon, what happened? You are trembling, are you okay? What did he do to you?' Amber asks me, concerned.

'I can't. I can't do this.' I shake my head, repeating myself.

'Liz! Look at me, what happened?' Amber shoves me lightly.

'I don't know,' I sigh, and take a deep breath. 'I let him touch me, he held my hand. It felt good. It felt warm and safe. I started to panic when the waitress came over and stood between us, and he let go of my hand. I'm an idiot, I panicked and did what I do best, I ran.'

'No, you are not Elizabeth!' Amber squeezes my shoulders tightly, trying to get me to focus.

'Maybe I should cancel.'

'No! No, you won't,' Amber cut me off.

'I can't do this. I'm not good for him, I'm not safe to be with,' I repeat, looking miserably at Amber.

'Liz, that's not true,' Amber says, shaking her head.

'But…'

'No!' Amber says loudly, cutting me off. 'Remember the promise you made to yourself?'

Then she hugs me tight, trying to calm my nerves.

'I'm so scared, Amber. I'm scared to let him in and then have him leave me. He will find out the real me and all my baggage, and then find someone easier to be with.

Someone who doesn't…' I take a deep breath and try not to cry.

'I mean, how stupid does that sound? We aren't even together and I'm acting like a, a jealous girlfriend!' Then I really start to cry.

'Liz, hon, look at me,' Amber asks, gently, as she pulls back from me.

I lift my eyes to meet Amber's.

'After everything you have been through, you have every right to feel the way you do now.' She pulls me into a tight embrace, letting me cry on her shoulder.
'I want this, Amber. But I don't know if I can let myself get it.'
'Liz look at me, you're okay,' she says, taking a step back to smile at me.
'Come on, let's get into the car and go home.' She opens my door.
'We have a whole tub of Hokey Pokey ice cream and chocolate topping to eat.'
She shoots me a grin.
I giggle and nod as I comply.

🦉 DOMINIC 🦉

I run out of the pub to see if I can catch her and apologize for what happened with the waitress.
I see her with Amber and it looks like Amber is trying to calm her down.
Liz's hand is on the scar on her neck..
She isn't rubbing the scar on her right wrist yet, and I want to go over to her.
I want to hold her, but I can't bring myself to do so, I just stand and watch.

I'm starting to understand why Elizabeth is the way she is.
I suspect she is hiding, but why?
Who is she hiding from?
Did she see something she wasn't supposed to?
Was she caught up in something before she realised it, and got hurt because of it?
I have so many questions, and judging by Amber's protectiveness, and the way her hand had quickly moved to her hip when she burst into Elizabeth's room, there is a whole lot more to her than just being Elizabeth's best friend.

Who is she? Clearly she doesn't trust just anyone around Elizabeth.
Then I realise I'm not the only person watching them.
Standing in the shadows, I can just make out the shape of a man.
Is he the one who hurt her?
My hands squeeze the pizza box tight as I watch him.
Liz is hiding. Is she hiding something other than herself?
The question grinding me the most is, why?
Has she been found?
And the hardest question of all, will she let me protect her?
I watch the man in the shadows as he brings his phone to his ear and walks away.
Shit, I think to myself, he has found her!

I wake up Friday morning feeling stupid about how I reacted the previous night.
He's not mine, we aren't together.
I had no reason to act jealous and panic.
Maybe I should cancel, after all.
I don't know if I can face him after last night.
I go to the kitchen and find a note from Amber, a request for food and a P.S.:

The way to a man's .... heart is through food
Xo Amber

I look at the list and laugh; it's all her favourites.
Amber knows cooking is my safe place, my distraction from the world.
I make a shopping list and go to get all the ingredients.

I make everything on her list, it's not like I have anything better to do, or anywhere else to be.
Considering Amber is my handler, she never treats me like anything other than a friend.
In fact, she has gone above and beyond to help me.
I asked her to train me in basic self-defence a few months ago.
I had to wait to get the all-clear from my doctors; the body doesn't heal quickly after enduring horrific trauma.
She is a hard taskmaster, but in the end I loved it.
I have started to feel empowered, less weak and helpless.
I still have a long way to go, but it's a start.
Due to the injuries I suffered, my fingers and shoulders dislocate easily, so she taught me a few extra things that may come in handy.
The first was: 'Always have nice long thumb nails; eyeballs and thumbs are not best friends.'
The second thing she is teaching me is how to use the attackers' own weight against them.
Not to mention, the sweet spots to hit.

The anxiety is hard to overcome, but I'm trying to get past it.
All the doctors have been saying the same thing, 'With the amount of trauma you have endured, you must take it day by day.'
Yeah, well, day by day might sound great to them, but in reality it sucks.
I just want me back, I want to go to work, I want a normal life.
Amber is helping me the best way she can, and I love her for it.

She never hides things from me and always gives me an honest answer, even if I don't want to hear it. The Australian Federal Police set Amber's cover up as a consultant with Bundaberg Police.

She travels to schools and talks to the students about the pros and cons of donning the uniform, trying to get them to stay on the right side of the law.

This way, Amber's roster makes it possible for her to protect me, but also gives me some space.

I can integrate myself back into society slowly, preparing for the day that I won't need her anymore.

I still only use check-outs with female staff, and I choose queues where I won't have to stand near men. There are times when I have to have some form of contact, but I can't bring myself to make eye contact with them, and I do everything possible to keep them from touching me.

My doctors and legal team are all female, except for one medical specialist.

Our Friday night routine goes like this.

Amber comes home and does her weekly report.

She does a full circuit around the house and gets updates on my case.

She spends about an hour on the phone while eating throughout.

I don't even think she chews.

It's more of a straight inhale, and the food's gone.

It's a good thing that I make double, sometimes triple of everything.

I smile, she is my only friend, and she treats me like one, and nothing else.

We may be complete opposites of each other, but we have a great time together.

'Earth to Liz.'

'Sorry, what did you say?' I look at Amber.

'We are out of wine,' Amber smirks, 'What are you thinking?'

'Um, just about stuff,' I sigh. 'I'm trying, Amber, I really am.'

'Don't push yourself, you'll get there.' She smiles at me.

I nod and smile. Amber knows all too well how bad I take being unable to talk to men.

I was not allowed to talk to anyone, especially men, without express permission.

She takes me to places where I will have interactions with other people.

As soon as a man comes near me, I panic.

My body shuts down when they are within touching distance.

Dominic is the only man that hasn't scared me.

It's been different with him.

No other man that I have come into contact with has made me feel at ease, even with a shop counter or a desk between us.

He got close to me.
We talked.
He touched me and I let him.
He was going to kiss me, and I was going to let him.

There is something about him that makes me feel that I can trust him.
That I can trust myself to let him in.
Nonetheless, the question remains; if he finds out the truth, will he accept my dark past and still want to be with me?

CHAPTER 2

The Beginning of?

On Saturday morning, my alarm goes off just as Amber barges in.
'Wakey, wakey, hands off your…'
'AMBER!' I yell.
'What?' She shrugs.
I sigh and pull the covers over my head.
'It's too early for your crude personality,' I grumble.
She rips the covers off me. I don't know if I can do this. I mean, I want to.
I've been waiting all week for this day.
'Elizabeth?' Amber interrupts my thoughts. 'Get up, it's seven-thirty.'
'So?' I groan.
'He will be here soon,' she grins.
'As previously stated, so?' I whine, secretly excited and terrified at the same time.
There is no way I'm telling Amber that, it's already hard enough to shut her up.
I snicker quietly to myself, then I get up and make my way to the bathroom.
'Well, he has it bad for you, and wants to…'
'Amber, no!' I say shooting daggers at her as I close the door.
'Ahh, yes you will!' I hear her call from my bedroom.
'You know, you're not really helping!' I shout back.

'Now, I have personally selected your outfit for today and put it in the bathroom
for you. I want you to put it on, come out and show me before you say anything.'
'And Elizabeth,' she adds, before I can say anything.
'No arguing with me.'
'Dominic will not be able to take his eyes, or his hands, off you.'

I walk out fifteen minutes later and there she sits, on the foot of my bed with a
naughty grin on her face.
'What the hell, Amber! Where's the rest of the outfit?' I gape at her.
'Wow! You look fucking wow! Why couldn't you be gay, or even bi? I can share.'
Amber sighs.
I raise my eyebrow at her, giving her the that's-a-load-of-bullshit look.
I know for a fact she is terrible at sharing.

'Kind of,' she shrugs and smiles.
I shake my head and laugh.
'What?' she asks in a mockingly innocent tone.
'I swear, these shorts will cut me in half if I sit down. I'm not wearing them,' I glare at her.
'That hurts, Lizzy. I spent ages looking for the purrrfect outfit for you.' She holds her hand over her heart like I have broken it.
'I mean, your arse looks a whole lot yummy in those shorts. I reckon Dominic is an arse-man. I really think you should wear them.'
'No thank you, Amber. I appreciate your fashion guidance, but I think your taste is a little more, um, revealing than I feel I can pull off.'
'Oh, you pull it off, trust me. Dominic will want to pull it off you.'
She flashes me a cheeky grin.
Then she winks, blows me a kiss and starts fanning herself.

I roll my eyes, change out of the shorts and put on my favourite shirt.
I keep the swimmers.
Thankfully, it's a one-piece, even though it shows more cleavage than I would usually allow myself.
It is beautiful, though; deep purple with black crisscross stripes over my breasts and cleavage, and it really doesn't cover much of my butt.
I swap the shorts for my favourite white sarong with purple Singapore Irises around the edges.
My white cheese-cloth shirt has a low V-neck that hangs off one shoulder.
I walk back out into my bedroom and Amber shakes her head.
'I prefer the first outfit. You looked hot.'
'What's wrong with what I'm wearing?' I ask.
She shrugs, stands up and smiles.
'You're still gorgeous.'

Amber, on the other hand, is wearing a barely-there white bikini, with even smaller shorts.
Paired with highly reflective sunglasses that she calls her perving glasses.
She is absolutely stunning, and the white bikini accentuates her flawless dark skin.
I stare at her, wondering again where she puts all that food.
I wish I could have a body like hers.
She is gorgeous and strong.
My body is scarred and broken.

We are having a breakfast of avocado and egg on toast when Amber breaks the silence.
'Come on, Liz, we can't keep your hot-for-you builder waiting.'
'I still don't know if I should go,' I start.
'Oh, you are going,' Amber says, looking at me. 'What else would you do?'
'Um, I have stuff…'
'No you don't. You are coming, so don't bother arguing with me.'
'I'll call him now, he will understand. You can still go and have fun.'
I pick up my phone, which Amber snatches out of my hands.
'You, Miss Miller, are going, and I don't want to hear another word about it!'
'Please, Amber, look at me! I don't have anything to offer anyone, especially someone like Dominic.' I sigh.
'I am looking at you. Give yourself a chance.'
'I'll only make a mistake…' I start to say.
'How would you know? You haven't even given him, or yourself, a chance. Besides, he is the first man you have allowed close to you. You made yourself a promise to find him and let him in. Trust me when I tell you, Dominic is that guy.'
'I'm sure Dominic thinks I'm a freak, and I don't blame him,' I sniff, trying to hold it together.

🔱 DOMINIC 🔱

I pull up to Elizabeth's house, terribly nervous.
I really wish it was just the two of us going to the beach.
Just speaking on the phone with her this week has been special.
She is so easy to talk to, and maybe having the phone between us gave her the confidence to come today and not cancel.
Luke, my work mate and best friend, hasn't let me get away with anything all week, he knows something is happening.
As I walk up to the door I hear Amber and Elizabeth talking.
Elizabeth sounds nervous, too.
I stand there listening to everything they are saying.

I watch as Amber takes Elizabeth's phone away and I smile.
Thank you, Amber. Elizabeth's hands tremble as she looks down at the floor.
'Please, Amber, look at me. I don't have anything to offer anyone, especially someone like Dominic.' Elizabeth sighs. I am mesmerised by her, blind to everything else.
Please give me the chance to show you what I see, I plead with her silently.
She could never be a mistake, the only mistake would be letting her go.

I look down at my hands.
Once I hold her, once I kiss her, I will make sure to be everything she needs.
'I'm sure Dominic thinks I'm a freak, and I don't blame him,' Elizabeth sniffs.
Her voice falters and I watch as her hand covers the scar on her wrist.

👀 ELIZABETH 👀

'Who's a freak?'
I freeze at the sound of his voice, turn around and there he is, standing in my doorway.
Oh my god!
He looks so … Wait, what?
Did he overhear our entire conversation?
I'm red, scarlet red. I cover my mouth with my hand involuntarily before I speak.
'Umm, well… I … Crap!'
He smiles at my discomfort.
'You're early, Dominic,' Amber pipes up.
'Well, I can't keep you waiting, I am the hot builder after all.'
He leans against the door frame with a smirk, never once breaking eye contact with me.
Crap! He heard all of it!

Great start to the day, I think to myself, feeling the panic start to stir.
I'm doomed to be single, unloved and untouched until I die.
'Well, I hope for your safety's sake that there are some single ladies, 'cause I'm on the prowl.' Amber says as she licks her lips lasciviously.
'Amber! Really?' I glare at her, then glance at Dominic with an apologetic look on my face.
She shrugs her shoulders and smiles as Dominic bursts out laughing.

'Um, okay,' Dominic stifles his laughter. 'I'm sure there will be someone you could meet.'
He walks inside and leans against the glass.
My hand automatically goes to my wrist.
I need to tell him I can't go.
It's a mistake.
I'm no good.

But I want him, all of him.
His smile, the warmth of his touch, his lips on mine, and his hands holding me close.

I can feel myself yearning to let go with him, but I'm so scared that I will disgust him or make him angry. I'm so afraid that I'll never be good enough for him.

'Are you ready to go?' He asks.
His phone rings before I can answer.
He looks at it and lets it ring off before looking back at me.
'Yes, we are ready,' Amber looks at me.
'The cooler is next to you,' she adds, walking towards him.
He turns, looks at the cooler and back at us.
'I gave her a list of food to make, you can thank me later,' Amber says as she walks past and pats him on the shoulder.
'I'll be in the car, take all the time you want, no need to rush!' She calls over her shoulder.
I swear, I would kill her if I wasn't glued to the spot, dying of embarrassment.

Dominic smiles and scratches the back of his head.
'She is very, um…'
'You have no idea,' I chip in before he can finish.
I stare at the floor again.
It could use a wash.
Um, hello! Hot guy in your kitchen and you're thinking of washing your floor.
Just walk over to him, please, just do it.
My breath catches in my throat as I look up to see him smiling at me.

👀 DOMINIC 👀

She looks absolutely stunning, her eyes luminous.
I watch as her hand reaches for her neck.
'I really am glad you are coming, Liz,' I say, watching her.
She looks up at me and smiles.
'I, um, never mind,' she blushes, looking back down at the floor as she rubs her wrist.

I know what she wants to say; her body is giving it away again.
As much as I want to walk up to her and kiss her right now, I know I need to give her time.
I want her to let me in, to let me touch her, let me kiss her.
Most of all, I want her to allow herself to relax with me.
'As much as I would love to stay here, alone with you, we probably should get going,' I say, watching her move.
Oh my god, I love it when she blushes.

'Okay,' she smiles at me, her hand still covering the scar on her left wrist.
I swear, every time she smiles at me, I fall harder for her.
The moment I get to hold her I will never let go.
She is becoming my weakness.

Liz grabs the drinks cooler as I pick up the one with the food.
'Jeez, how many people are you planning on feeding?' I tease.
I love it when she smiles.
Yep, I'm never letting her go.

👀 ELIZABETH 👀

'Blame Amber and her huge appetite. I swear she eats enough for three people at once.'
He chuckles as he walks out the door carrying the cooler.
I grab my bag off the bench and follow him nervously out the door.
We get to his car when my phone beeps with a message from Amber.

I said not to rush.
Xoxo

I look over at her in the backseat and shake my head.
She shrugs her shoulders, grinning.
Dominic takes the drinks cooler from me and opens the front passenger door.

The drive to the beach is interesting, spiced up with Amber's comments and suggestions.
Dominic looks over at me and smiles.
I blush, again. I can't help it, he makes me feel like a schoolgirl.
My cheeks go from warm to hot.
Pink to red.
Damn woman, get your shit together! Your head looks like a giant beetroot!

The beach is beautiful, and the weather is perfect.
I fiddle with the hem of my sarong, trying to hide my nerves.
I notice my shaking hands and hope he doesn't see it.
I take a deep breath and close my eyes.
I want to enjoy this day and not let my anxiety get the better of me.

I look at all the cars, and feel myself beginning to freak out. 'I can't do this,' I whisper under my breath.

I start shifting nervously in my seat, my chest tight.

Then I feel a warm hand on mine.

'You will be fine, Elizabeth. I will be right next to you,' Dominic says, calming me.

I open my eyes and look at him.

'Okay,' I whisper and nod.

I get out of the car as he comes around and takes my hand.

My heart skips a beat and I feel flushed.

I look over at the group to see Amber already introducing herself.

Why can't I have her confidence?

I used to be confident, I think.

I used to be a lot of things.

I look up at Dominic.

He brings his hand up and runs the back of his fingers along my cheek and down to my neck.

His eyes never leave mine, and I feel myself relax.

His other arm wraps around my waist, I move closer to him and slowly bring my hands to rest on his chest.

He doesn't pull me in, but just stands there with me, allowing me to move closer to him.

I close my eyes and take a moment to let Dominic's presence calm me.

When I open them again and look up at him, he smiles warmly, and I smile back at him.

'Shall we?' He asks, giving me a squeeze.

I look up at him and nod.

'If at any time you need to leave, just tell me and I will take you home.'

'Thank you, Dominic.'

He releases me, taking my hand while his other hand plays with a lock of my hair.

We walk over to the group, hand in hand, and Dominic introduces me to his friends.

'Okay, around the circle we have David and Amanda, Gavin, Cassie, Luke, Simon, Louise, and at the back is Shane and Chantelle. Everyone, this is Elizabeth.'

I tremble and squeeze his hand at the name Chantelle, but I manage to wave at everyone and say hello.

Amber looks at me, and Dominic notices the change in her demeanour and mine.

He looks down at me.

'Are you okay?' he asks quietly.

'I, um, used to know a girl named Chantelle, but she passed away. I'll be fine.' I look up at him, smiling wanly.

I have a feeling he doesn't quite believe me, but he doesn't push it.

He just smiles and holds my hand a little tighter.

David and Amanda are both P.E. teachers at different schools and very competitive, funny, and easy to talk to.

Gavin works as a mechanic, but is training to be a fireman.

He clearly has no interest in talking to me, which kind of suits me, so I don't spend much time trying to get to know him.

Cassie is lovely; she works at a salon doing waxing, hair and makeup.

Amber and Cassie make eyes at each other and I give Amber an I like her nod and thumbs-up, to which she smiles and licks her lips.

I smile, shaking my head; she will probably never change and I really hope she never does.

Next up is Shane and Chantelle.

He is a plumber, and Chantelle is not working at the moment, she is studying nursing.

I don't get the chance to really talk to them, as they are too busy with each other.

Louise works in retail and I get a feeling that she may fancy Dominic.

She spends all her time talking to everyone else and pretty much ignores me.

Which leaves Simon and Luke, two completely single guys, and they are hilarious.

Simon is a nurse at the Bundaberg Base Hospital in the Department of Emergency Medicine, and is very happy to learn that I'm a paramedic.

Luke works with Dominic sometimes, he is a bit of a jack-of-all trades, but mainly works as a carpenter.

Dominic hardly leaves my side, and I sense his body language change when Luke and Simon come over to talk to me.

'Okay, so you're a paramedic from Western Australia, and you moved here, of all places. Why?' Luke asks.

'A fresh start,' I respond.

'Ah, relationship break-up. Am I right?' Simon inquires.

'I guess you could say that.'

👓 DOMINIC 👓

Luke and Simon are talking to Liz as I stand next to her.
I watch her from the corner of my eye, she shuffles closer to me and won't make eye contact with them.

Her hands shake slightly as she fidgets with the hem of her sarong.
She seems to get nervous around people she doesn't know, and I can see men definitely scare her.

I'm surprised by how protective and almost possessive I feel, and I look down at my hands trying to get my head around my feelings for her.
My need to be with her is unlike anything I have ever experienced, and my protective instinct is through the roof.

'So, are you seeing anyone?' Luke blurts out.
I glare at him, and both he and Simon take a step back.
I glance back at Liz; her hand is on the scar on her wrist and she has suddenly gone very quiet.
'Sorry, Liz, I didn't mean to pry,' Luke apologises.
She nods mutely. Luke and Simon nod at me awkwardly and walk away.
I look back at her just in time to see a tear fall, her hands are shaking.
Taking both her hands in mine, I give her a reassuring squeeze.
'I'm sorry,' she whispers.
'Don't be,' I say, bringing my hands to her neck and covering the scar.
She takes a deep breath, looks up at me and smiles bravely.
I pull her down to sit on a log with me.

👓 ELIZABETH 👓

'Are you okay?' Dominic asks.
'I'm…'
'Liz, I can tell there is something going on, do you want to talk about it?'
'I want to, but…'
'You're scared,' he finishes, quietly.
He runs the backs of his fingers along my cheek.
I close my eyes as he cradles my face in his hand.
My body's need for him screams from the top of my head all the way down to the tips of my toes.
I look in his eyes. Dark brown, framed by long lashes, watching me intently.
I feel totally safe with him.

'You're scared, but I'm not going anywhere. I'll help you.' His voice is earnest and I believe him, I trust him; it's me that I'm worried about.

I close my eyes and take a deep breath before looking at him again.

'The break-in was, … It was very bad.' I suck in a deep breath and look away.

'He hurt me; I almost died. I spent a long time in hospital, and when I got out I was so scared I ran.'

Amber comes over and shuffles in between Dominic and I, laying her head on my lap and her legs on his. I shoot him an apologetic look.

'Well, dearest Dominic, I'm happy to say you're safe. Cassie is yummy.'

'Well, I'm glad you have found someone to your liking,' Dominic smiles at me.

'So, what are your intentions, Dominic?' Amber suddenly asks him.

'Intentions?' he asks.

'With my best friend,' she quips.

My body stiffens.

'Um, sorry, I need to, um, get a drink.' I stammer, jumping up and walking away.

🦉 DOMINIC 🦉

I watch Liz get up and walk away. Amber sits up, looks at me and sighs.

'Please be patient with her, she has suffered…' Amber starts to say.

'I know,' I cut her off before she can say any more.

'She told you?' Amber asks, astonished.

'No, not in so many words. But I'm not blind or stupid. She was just telling me about the break-in.'

'She wants to let you in.'

'When she is ready.'

Then she smiles and puts her hand on my shoulder.

'The thing that scares her is that the person who hurt her was supposed to care for her.'

'Amber,' I stop her. 'If anyone is going to tell me, I would rather it be Liz. I want her to trust me enough to open up and let me in. But only when she is ready.'

Amber smiles and her whole face lights up, then she leans in.

'So, do I have to give you the if-you-hurt-her-I'll-hurt-you speech?' She looks menacingly at me and I can tell she means it.

'Nope,' I shake my head.

'Well, I shall leave you to go to your Liz while I go back to my Cassie,' she winks and bumps my shoulder with hers.

Amber walks back to Cassie and I see Louise talking to Liz.

I can tell by Liz's body language that it's not a friendly chat.

She nods as she looks down, her hand is on her neck.

Louise looks up and sees me watching.

She starts walking towards me as I stand up, but I'm still watching Liz.

She hasn't moved and her hand is now on her wrist.

Fuck! This is not good.

I need to let Liz know I'm not with anyone, and that I don't play with people's emotions.

'So, Dominic, how about we go for a walk?' Louise suggests as she comes up to me.

She tries to wrap her arms around me, but I step back.

'What were you and Liz talking about?'

'Group stuff, who is with who,' she replies glibly.

'Louise, what exactly did you say?'

'Nothing much, just something about you and I,' she smiles smugly.

'You and I are friends, we are not together. We have had this discussion, Louise,' I look at her, annoyed.

She just shrugs and walks off.

I make a move to go to Liz as Simon walks up to me.

He watches Louise skulk off and shakes his head before turning back to me.

We start towards the cars to get the cricket gear.

'Jeez, someone needs to take her happy pills. What's wrong with her?'

I look down, not sure what to say.

'Oh, you didn't!' Simon exclaims.

'It was a once-off. We discussed it and agreed we should stay friends.'

'And now she is letting Elizabeth know that you are off-limits,' Simon remarks as he glances over at Liz before looking back at me.

'I told Liz I'm single.'

'Hey, do you think her and Amber… You know?' Simon asks, looking at Liz.

'No, I don't. They are best friends, that's all.'

'Oi, you two! Are we playing cricket?' David yells.

Amanda is with Liz, they are walking over to David.

Amanda has her arm slung around Liz, and I wonder what she is saying to make Liz laugh.

'We are coming, Mr, Bradnam,' Simon yells back, making me laugh.

Amanda comes up and wraps her arm around my shoulders.

'Please tell me you like cricket?'

'I love cricket. I'm a big fan of Sir Donald Bradnam, Rod Marsh, Dean Jones, and Glenn Magrath.'

'Oi, you two. Are we playing cricket?' David yells to Simon and Dominic.

'David, sorry, Mr. Bradnam, Liz here is going to play,' Amanda announces.

'Mr. Bradnam?' I gape.

'It's because of his batting average, except in this case it's him batting above his stature, with me.' Amanda says sweetly, smiling at David.

I laugh.

'We are coming, Mr. Bradnam,' Simon yells back and I can hear Dominic laugh.

'Hey, you're only just taller than me,' David replies Amanda.

We spend the morning playing cricket, which at some point in time, becomes a contact sport when a catch is required.

Cricket is followed by football. Amber, Cassie, Louise, and Chantelle sit out for this, but Amanda is adamant that I need to be a part of the game.

I watch Chantelle closely.

I suspect she is pregnant, but hasn't told anyone, by the way Shane dotes on her.

I make sure I hardly get the ball so no-one will touch me.

Every now and then, when I try to sneak over to Amber, Amanda catches me.

I look over and see Dominic watching me.

He winks, making me blush.

'You two are so cute together,' Amanda remarks when she sees me blushing.

'We aren't together,' I reply automatically.

She laughs.

'Yeah you are,' she smiles. 'You might not know it yet, but we all do.'

She winks at me as we walk back to the game.

'Oi, you two, get your butts back here, we have a game to win!' David calls out.

Amanda grabs my hand, pulling me back towards the game and away from Amber and the group watching us.

'Shall we?' She asks.

'Well, he is right, we do have a game to win. We are tied, so I suppose we should do the right thing and help them win easy,' I reply.

'Oh, we are going to get on just great,' Amanda beams.

The teams are tied at five tries each, and it's down to whoever scores next.

We have the ball and David passes to Amanda, who then passes it to me.

I manage to get past Luke and Simon, but am tackled by Dominic just as I pass the ball back to David. We land on the sand with a thump, and he smiles down at me.

'Hmmm, tackled without the ball, isn't that a penalty?' I ask, looking up at him.
'Well, to be fair, you did have the ball when I went for the tackle,' he smiles back at me, his arms still around me and his body pressed hard up against mine.
Sparks surge through me and I'm sure he feels it too, judging by how his pupils dilate.
He leans down and takes a deep breath.
Oh sweet Jesus, I feel his leg between my thighs.
The sensation sets off my longing throb of desire.
I fight the urge to drop my gaze.
Dominic brings his hand to my face and brushes sand off my cheek, causing me to shiver.
His other hand moves to my waist and squeezes gently.

I bring my hands to his sides and feel his body react to my touch.
'Oi!' David yells, 'Opposition won't release the player once the tackle is complete.'
Everyone has a laugh.
I try to move, but Dominic won't let up just yet.
Oh my god, he feels good on me.
I look into his eyes, willing myself to kiss him, but I can't bring myself to pull his face down to mine.
His thumb brushes over my lips and he moves closer.
I feel my body respond and my hands hold him tighter.
My lips part with anticipation, I can almost feel his lips on mine.

'Dominic!' Louise calls sharply, 'You need to get the BBQ ready.'
He groans and looks up, annoyed.
Then he looks back down at me and smiles.
I can see the frustration at our moment being interrupted in his eyes.
I smile as I lightly run my hands up his sides and feel his muscles tense.
His heated stare excites me.

'We have a kind of rule when it comes to football.'
'What rule?' I ask innocently.
'Whoever concedes a penalty has to buy dinner or drinks for the person awarded the penalty,' he winks and gets up, then pulls me to my feet.
His arms wrap around me.
Oh, for the love of god, he smells so good.
I bring my hands to his chest; I can feel his heart beating.

It almost feels like time stands still and we are completely alone.
I can hear my heart pounding and I so badly want to taste his lips.
A nervous tremor spreads through my body and I lick my lips at the thought of his lips on mine.
I look up at him.
'So, that means you have to buy me dinner and drinks,' I cock an eyebrow at him, trying to sound confident.

He smiles, his hand playing with loose locks of my hair before he tucks it behind my ear.
He leans in and brushes his lips against my ear, his breath warm against my skin.
Holy crap!
My mind goes on a fast descent, straight into the gutter.
Breathe, Elizabeth, I admonish myself, it's no good if you collapse from lack of oxygen.
But hey, mouth-to-mouth could be worth it.
I blush and break into a big smile.
'I think I could live with that,' Dominic pushes his body against mine and I feel my nipples harden.
'Sooner rather than later,' he murmurs against my cheek before he releases me, and walks to his Ute to get the BBQ ready.

I stand there, gazing over the ocean and catching my breath.
What the fuck is going on with me?
Oh man, I have never felt this way before.
I want so badly to fuck him, I can't think straight.
My brain is screaming at me, giddy up! Get on that man, woman! Ride him! I chuckle just listening to myself.

I realise my body yearns for his warmth, just from being so close to him.
I shiver at the thought of him touching me, and I can't help but smile as I bring my fingers to my lips.
I want him to hold me, talk to me, make love to me.
I wonder if he wants me like that too?
Would I satisfy him?
Was Michael right?
He always told me no-one would ever really want me.
My self-doubt kicks in and my anxiety flaps its wings.
I am already back to thinking what I've been conditioned to: that I have nothing to offer anyone.

Amanda walks up and wraps her arms around me, resting her head on my shoulder and breaking through my thoughts.

'Wow, you and Dominic have it bad,' she says with a smile.

'I'm sure he was just being polite, I'm not that special.'

'He's a good guy, and I can tell he likes you a lot, trust me. He's not the kind of guy that goes around with different girls. He is also very protective of you, I've never seen him act like that before,' she moves around to face me.

'At first I thought he was just saying that you're off limits. But I see the way you are around the guys and I can tell there is more to it. He is like a lion around you, and I can tell you like him too. What are you holding back for? Go for it!' She brings her hands to my shoulders.

'Let him in, he really likes you,' she chides, gently.

'I like him too,' I reply, blushing.

'Good, because David and I would really like you and Dominic to be a couple. You guys are super cute together,' Amanda's smile widens.

'What about…'

'Louise?' Amanda cuts me off, shaking her head.

All I can do is nod.

'They are close, but not in the way Louise would like, she wants more. You and Dominic though,' she glances toward the group before looking back at me, smiling. 'You and Dominic, no one will step in between you, not a chance. We can all see that already.'

Amanda hooks her arm in mine and we make our way back to the others.

I really hope Amanda is right about us.

'Excuse me, Elizabeth, but I'm stealing my girl,' David says as he grabs Amanda and kisses her.

They walk to their car hand in hand.

Luke and Simon remove my cooler from the back of Dominic's Ute as he sets up the Weber BBQ with Gavin. I make my way towards them.

'Jeez, Liz, what did you pack in this?' Simon groans as he lifts it.

'Blame Amber, she gave me a list of food to make,' I reply, not looking directly at him.

'You do know you only have to feed yourself, not everyone,' Simon smiles.

'You don't know Amber. Like I said, she gave me a list and I made it,' I reply.

'What have you got in here?' Luke asks, opening the cooler.

'Get fucked! Is that vanilla slice?' Luke gapes at me.

'Um, yes, that's vanilla slice,' I answer uncertainly.

'Homemade?' He smiles in disbelief.

'Yes.'

'May I?' Luke's eyes are huge.
'Of course,' I nod.
'Share, Luke!' Simon grabs the container off him.

'What else have you got?' Luke asks as he grabs another piece of vanilla slice.
'Um, that one is mini lemon meringues, those are mini custard tarts, this is marinated lamb rib,' I say as I kneel down, pulling out a few containers and handing them to Luke and Simon.
'And over here is cheesecake.'
I smile as I watch them dig into the mini lemon meringues.
'That one is, um, marinated chicken,' I continue, pointing. 'Here are turkey burger patties, and this one has homemade pork and veal sausage. There're also other nibbles and things in there, as well,' I finish.

'Do you have bread?' Simon asks hopefully.
'Yep, it's in the bag in the front of Dominic's car, along with buns. I made them yesterday so I hope they will still be good,' I reply, smiling.
'Onion?' Luke asks, chewing.
'Yes, it's in this container here,' I pass it to him.
'Yo, Dom?' Luke calls out, his mouth still full of food, peering into the cooler.
'Yeah?' He replies, walking up.
'Can we keep her?' Luke looks imploringly at Dominic, 'Please?'

Dominic laughs as he gets to us.
'Dude, she has vanilla slice, homemade vanilla slice,' Simon says, looking meaningfully at him and offering him one. Dominic winks and smiles as he takes a bite. I look back down at my cooler, trying to hide the fact that I'm blushing… Again…
I'm so screwed.
'Dom, try these lemon thingies,' Luke says through a mouthful.
'I also made some lamingtons, a chocolate cake and a pavlova, but I couldn't fit them in the cooler,' I say apologetically, glancing back up.

The three of them look at me, mouths agape.
'What?' I ask.
'Dom, get the woman a bigger cooler,' Luke says, punching him in the shoulder.
'Marry her or I will,' Simon adds, shoving Dominic playfully.
'Oi, David! Looks like you're not the prettiest cook in the group anymore!' Simon yells.
'Haha! Fuck off, Simon!' David yells back, Amanda doubles over in laughter.
"David can't cook. We don't even let him near a barbie." Simon shakes his head.
"But he is pretty."

"Don't worry, Liz, I'll help keep your cooking safe." Luke says with a mouthful of food and a huge grin on his face.

Dominic comes around to my side of the cooler and helps me up.

'So, what were you and Amanda talking about?' He asks softly.

I smile and blush as my hand rubs my wrist.

His warmth reaches deep into my body, arousing me.

He smiles, the fingers of his left hand brushing my cheek as his right rests lightly on my neck.

I find myself looking into his eyes, unable to look away.

I feel like it's just the two of us standing there, as my body cries out for more of him.

He snakes a hand around my waist and I move closer to him without even thinking about it.

I find my head tilting back, my lips parting while I rest my hands on his waist.

His body tenses as I slowly move my hands up.

He leans in, his eyes never leaving mine.

'Dominic!' He sighs and looks up. 'Can you help me over here, please?'

'Louise,' his voice is low and angry. 'Why don't you ask Gavin to help you with your cooler.'

He looks back at me and leans in.

My chest tightens as his lips brush my ear.

'I'll be back to finish our chat as soon as I am done with the BBQ,' he says, inhaling deeply, 'Mmmm.' His murmur vibrates all the way to my thighs.

'Don't go too far,' he smiles as the back of his fingers trace my cheek.

'Okay,' is all I manage.

'I still want to know what you and Amanda were talking about. She was making you blush redder than usual.'

I smile and nod. Oh dear lord, I'm so horny, and he hasn't even done anything to me yet.

Dominic winks at me before he walks over to Louise.

Once his warmth leaves, a cold shiver runs down my spine and I realise I'm holding my breath.

I watch everyone interact, but I stay away from the guys except when Dominic is with me.

I look over and lock eyes with him, his lips curve up and I feel like he is stripping me naked with his eyes. As I watch, he brings his thumb to his mouth, slowly sucking the juice off it while holding my gaze.

I'm so aroused that I look away before he sees me blushing and drooling over him like Homer Simpson over a donut.

Bib and mop in aisle 4, please!

Lunch is great. It's nice to meet other people and actually enjoy myself.

They get the jet-ski out and tow tubes behind them.

Dominic comes up to me and takes my hand, pulling me up and leading me down to the water's edge.

'Dominic!' I giggle in protest.

'You're coming out with me,' he says, still holding my hand.

'I don't know,' I falter.

He brings his hand up to cradle a side of my face and I can't find it in me to say no.

He smiles and pulls me into him, his hands resting on my sides as mine rests on his chest.

'I'll make sure you're safe,' he says.

'I'm not scared of the water,' I whisper.

My body enjoys the warmth of his touch, and I'm willing myself to give in and enjoy whatever comes.

I mean, come on, Elizabeth, you've already been thinking it. You want it, so jump on and have a ride—you never know, you might want more. I scold myself; it's like having Amber in my head.

He smiles and winks at me encouragingly as he gets on.

I rest my hands on his sides and he pulls them around so I'm hugging him.

He rests his left hand on mine as I hold onto him.

'You ready?' He asks, turning his head to me.

'Mmm-hmm,' is all I can muster.

'Hold on,' he smiles.

Dominic turns to the front and takes off, heading straight for an incoming wave.

I find myself laughing, enjoying the speed.

He turns, fast, and it reminds me of when I raced motocross and went on dirt-bike trips with my brothers.

Due to the settlement given to me by the Australian Government and some smart financial moves, I have already ordered my new car.

I guess I can get myself a four-wheel drive and a jet-ski too..

I find myself remembering the times my brothers and I would repeat the line from Top Gun: I feel the need. The need for speed!

Then we'd high-five each other, laughing before taking off into the forest.

I'm enjoying myself immensely, but at the same time missing the most important people in my life. My family was everything to me, I miss them terribly and a day like today just cements the fact that I'm never going to see them again.

Whatever life I had before Michael has been lost and is now just a memory.

Lost in my own thoughts, Dominic's laughter pulls me back to the present.
These are the new memories I need to cherish.
Smiling as I tighten my hold on Dominic, I wonder: dare I wish for a happy-ever-after with him?
I close my eyes and hold on as Dominic guns the jet-ski again.
He is towing Simon and turns sharply, plunging him under the water.
'Asshole!' Simon yells, sputtering and laughing as he surfaces.

I'm laughing too as Dominic brings the jet-ski back to shore; I don't really want to let go. He holds my hands to him and turns his head, smiling at me.
Maybe he doesn't want me to let go either.
I decline a ride on the tube, and go to sit with Amanda on the beach.
We watch as the others are pulled along behind the jet-ski on the surfboard.

'Having fun?' She asks as she rests her head on my shoulder.
I can tell we would be great friends. She is funny and caring and doesn't make me feel judged.
In fact, she has welcomed me like an old friend she hasn't seen in years.

'Very much so. This day has been perfect,' I reply.
'Well, you're coming to the next one, David and I will make sure of it.' She gets a naughty grin on her face,
'That's if you and Dominic can bear to leave the bedroom.'
'You are as bad as Amber!' I laugh.
'I knew there was a reason I really like her,' she laughs.
'Looks like Amber and Cassie are getting on really well, too.'
'That they are. Amber told Dominic he better have some single ladies here today, because she was on the prowl.'
'No, she didn't!?' Amanda sits up, chuckling.
'She did!' I laugh, 'I was so embarrassed, and all Dominic could do was say 'I'll see what I can do for you.' I shake my head.
'She is definitely not backward in being forward,' Amanda laughs as she looks out to the horizon, then back at me.
'Amber has no filter. She is all about eating, inappropriate conversations and having a laugh. I don't ever want her to change.'
I bring my knees up to my chest and hug them tightly.
'She is my best friend, and has helped me more than she knows,' I smile.

'I thought my ears were burning,' Ambers smirks as she sits down beside me.
'So, please do enlighten me on what I have missed.'
'Dominic and Elizabeth!' Amanda exclaims ecstatically, 'He likes her, she likes him.'

'See, hon?' Amber thumps my shoulder, laughing. 'I'm not the only one who thinks you should go for it!'

'Shhh, Amber,' I hush her, quite flushed.
'What?' She grins, 'Hey, if I was straight I would be on my knees blowing him like a champion!' She shrugs, watching Dominic.
Amanda completely loses it as I sit there, mouth wide open, as Amber just grins innocently.
'Fuck me! That was hilarious!' Amanda hoots, trying to catch her breath.
Amber grins and leans over to hug me before jumping up and heading back to Cassie.
'She really doesn't have a filter,' Amanda states, still holding her stomach with one arm, and wiping the tears from her eyes with the other.
I still haven't recovered enough to say anything, I'm just glad no-one else heard her.

'Amanda!' David calls from the water. She lifts her head, then looks at me. 'Looks like someone wants a little attention, I'll be back,' she smiles as she stands up.
'No rush,' I smile back at her.
I watch as Amanda saunters up to David.
He wraps his arms around her, lifting her as he plants a kiss firmly on her lips.
I smile as I watch them, hoping that I might be lucky enough to sample a taste of what they have.
I watch as Dominic comes out of the water carrying his board.
His tattoo runs the entire length of his left arm, around to his back and up the left side of his neck.
It has intricate detailing and is all in black, and I wonder what it means and how long it took to get it done. I also can't help but notice how the water beads off his perfect body.
He is walking towards me, smiling, when Louise sidles up to him with a towel.
I quickly look away, embarrassed by how much I want him.

I get up and go for a walk along the water's edge.
I want the rest of my days to feel exactly like this; no more fear, no more pain.
I want to spend these days in Dominic's arms, laughing and enjoying each other.
I was told for years that I was nothing, and meant nothing to the world, that I was disposable.
Now I'm finally edging closer to thinking that maybe, just maybe, that might not be true.

👀 DOMINIC 👀

I watch Liz get up and walk away, her arms wrapped around herself.
I want to wrap my arms around her, and have her wrap hers around me so that she can never walk away from me.
Forever in my arms; the thought hits me like lightning.
'So, Dominic, I was thinking we should have dinner together tomorrow night,' Louise purrs, handing me a towel, interrupting my thoughts of Elizabeth.
I glance at Louise as I hang the towel on my board.

'Sorry, Louise, I can't,' I reply, turning my head back to look at Liz's retreating figure.
Louise touches my arm, running her fingers up to my shoulder.
'But I thought…'
'Louise,' I turn and look at her. 'We talked about this.
Our friendship is important to me, it's not something I want to lose,' I sigh.
'We tried having sex and it didn't work. Please, Louise, just… Stop.' I look out over the ocean, trying to figure out how to get through to her.
'Louise,' I let out an exasperated breath.
'You told me how you felt, and I told you that I don't feel the same. I never lied to you or led you into thinking we could have more.'

'But that's just it, Dominic,' her hand lingers on my shoulder. 'The more I think about it, the more I want it.'
'No!' I cut her off, shaking her hand from my shoulder.
'Look,' I sigh, looking up at the sky and back at her.
'I won't lie to you. At the time it felt good, but risking the loss of your friendship wasn't worth it.'
'Fine, whatever,' Louise glares at me angrily, 'I won't wait for you to realise the mistake you're making with her.' She flicks a glance behind her before looking back at me.
'Louise!' I gape at her, shocked.
'Go to hell, Dominic!' Louise spits and walks off.

She is pissed at me because I can't give her what she has decided she wants from me.
Do I regret taking that step with her and trying?
We can't blame alcohol or a spur of the moment decision.
Having sex was a conscious decision that we made.
However, the next day was awkward.
We barely spoke for an hour, and were both relieved after finally discussing our feelings.

I look back up and can't see Liz anymore, she must have walked around the bend.

I head up to my car to wash off and put my board away.

I want to go and find her.

I want to ask her if she would consider dating me.

Fuck, I'm so nervous.

I am just finishing my shower as Luke and Simon walk up.

'So, you and Liz, hey?' Luke teases.

I look up and see Liz strolling back towards the group.

'Man, you have it bad,' Simon laughs.

'What about Sarah and Sally?' I ask them, 'Any dates yet?'

'Hey, don't change the subject. Everyone can see the chemistry between you two. Besides, I saw you the day after you met her. I only wish I had it on video.'

'Fuck off, Luke,' I laugh.

'Please do tell, I feel left out,' Simon smirks, but I just shake my head.

'What is stopping you?' Luke asks, leaning on my car, his eyes on Elizabeth.

'If you don't, someone else will,' Simon warns, watching her.

'Yeah, Amber described some guy at the pub, and it sounded a lot like fucking Daniel. He has been trying to get into Elizabeth's...' Luke stops and looks at me apologetically.

My fists are clenched. I fucking hate Daniel, they both know how much I loathe him.

'Don't worry,' Simon pats my shoulder, 'Elizabeth won't even acknowledge him, and Amber threatened to break all ten of his fingers if he touched Elizabeth.'

'How do you know that?' I ask Simon sharply.

'Amber told us. Apparently, he tried his luck last Thursday while they were at the pub having dinner. Amber reminds me of The Terminator when he is sent back as a protector. I do not want to get on her bad side,' Luke shivers. 'She looks all cute and cuddly, but I'm too scared to even try and hug her,' he laughs.

I look up to see Liz sitting down, hugging her knees to her chest.

I want her so much it hurts.

'Dominic, go to her,' Luke practically pushes me in her direction.

I shoot a look back at them and they both give me two thumbs up, grinning from ear to ear.

Taking a deep breath, I jog over to her, putting my shirt back on.

⌗ ELIZABETH ⌗

I sit down, knees to my chest, close my eyes and exhale.

The late afternoon sun feels fantastic on my skin, and the salty breeze strips away my anxiety. For a brief moment I am lost in my own little world.

'Can I join you?'

I didn't even hear him walk up, but I don't need to open my eyes to know that it's Dominic.

'I would like that,' I reply.

He sits down next to me, our shoulders touching.

A warm spark runs through my body.

I breathe deeply, letting his presence envelop me like a cocoon.

My head and heart are starting to come together, giving me a little bit of confidence in taking the next step with him.

I'm going to let myself enjoy being with him, in the moment.

I am, aren't I? I ask myself, like I'm still trying to make sure I'm thinking with my head and not the horny throb between my thighs.

I inhale deeply, revelling in his scent, and my mind dives head-first into the gutter, faster than a submarine evading the enemy.

I need to come back up to periscope depth, my lungs are burning.

I didn't even realise I was holding my breath.

I wonder if his kisses are as good as his smell.

I shiver, my hands tingling at the thought of running them over his body and through his hair.

I open my eyes and turn to face him, only to find him looking at me.

'Thank you for the invite,' I say softly, 'I can't remember the last time I did any of this.'

Making conversation to hide my deep desire for him.

He smiles.

Thank god I'm already sitting down, because my knees are jelly right now.

'Well, judging by your empty cooler and the requests for buying you a bigger one, I might get in trouble if I don't invite you again next time.'

His smile lights up his face and the delicious, dark brown pools of his eyes are making me hot.

'Give me a list of food, like Amber does,' I smile.

'Simon and Luke said they would start their lists and give them to me in time for the next beach day.'

We both laugh, and I find myself stealing a quick look at his lips.

'I enjoy cooking,' I nod. 'It's my safe place, where no one can hurt me.'

I blurt out before I realise what I'm saying.

I quickly look back out over the ocean. Oh shit, Panic sets in and dark spots appear in front of my eyes. No, no, no! Not now, please, for the love of god!
Okay, oky, just breathe, in and out. I start trembling.
Suddenly, I feel Dominic move.
He sits down behind me, his legs on either side of me.
He wraps me in his arms and pulls me back against him.
I let him pull me in closer, I let him hold me.
My god, he smells so good.

He leans in, his lips against my ear, and whispers, 'I've got you, just breathe. Close your eyes and listen to the ocean. I'm not going anywhere, I'll keep you safe.'
He tightens his arms around me. 'Just breathe, Elizabeth.'
His face is buried in my neck and I feel his lips on my skin as he talks to me.
'Breathe with me, I'm right here with you, and I am not letting go.'
I do as he says and feel my body relax against him.

🔭 DOMINIC 🔭

I feel her body start to relax as she lets me pull her tighter against me.
She smells amazing and feels so warm and good to touch.
I notice more scars on her arms and bare shoulder; they don't look like they were ever tended to properly. I feel a surge of anger at the person who hurt her so badly.
It makes me furious knowing she suffered so much and was scared and alone. I need to hold her, I need to protect her.
Now that I have her in my arms I'm never going to let her go.

Her breathing has returned to normal and her body has relaxed.
I realise that she isn't trying to get up and move away from me, if anything she is letting me hold her. Elizabeth is finally starting to trust me, I smile to myself.
Her head is resting against me and I rest my head against the side of her head.
We sit there together not saying anything just listening to the sounds of the ocean.
After a while I rest my chin on her shoulder.
I run my hands along her bare skin and watch the effect my touch has on her.
I move slowly, watching and listening for any sign that she needs me to stop.
But she doesn't, her breathing quickens, and she pushes back into me.
A faint sigh escapes her lips as I take her hands in mine.

I relish her body against mine as I let go of her hands and snake my arms around her.
We softly rock side to side and she is still relaxed.
Fuck me, I let out a silent groan to myself, her body fits against me perfectly.
Thankfully my self-control is holding….just. Down boy, I tell myself, otherwise I'm going for a swim to relieve my body of its failing self-control.
'Hey Dom!' Luke calls out, like a bucket of cold water that has just been thrown over me.
I sigh and lift my head.

👀 ELIZABETH 👀

He doesn't let go of me; we just sit together, listening to the sound of the ocean.
I feel his hands run along my arms and when he takes my hands in his, it sets my body alight.
His chin is resting on my shoulder and I can feel his breath on my neck.
My breathing quickens.
I want him so much it almost hurts.
My mind is going into overdrive with thoughts that would make even Amber blush, and trust me that is no easy task.
'Hey, Dom!'
Our moment is interrupted.
I feel him sigh before lifting his head to answer.

'Yeah, Luke?' He says, sounding a little annoyed.
'Mate, we are on the beach, please tell me you remembered the guitar?'
'Yes, it's in the back of my Ute.' Dominic replies, before resting his chin back on my shoulder
'Sweet, move your arse, we have a tradition to continue!' Luke calls back.

'Sorry, our moment has been cut short,' he says, kissing my shoulder.
Oh my god, his lips feel good on my skin.
I move forward a little and turn to face him.
I find him smiling at me and I smile back.
My body is screaming at me to kiss him.
He brings his hands to touch either side of my face, and my breathing quickens.
His fingers brush along my cheeks.
'Elizabeth' His voice is deep and husky.
His eyes search mine. 'I want to kiss you.'
'Yes.' I smile and nod slightly.

He moves in slowly as he watches me and brings his lips to mine.
Dominic's hand is in my hair.
I hear the group cheer behind us, I can feel him smile.
I sigh softly as I melt into him.
His lips are soft, his tongue begs for entrance to which I happily grant him.
I melt even more as his tongue touches mine, I don't ever want this kiss to stop.
He gently nips at my bottom lip causing my body to surge with heat.
I crave more.
More kisses, more touches, more of Dominic.

I place my hands on his chest before sliding them up to his neck holding him to me.
I feel his hands move down to my back pulling me in closer to him.
Please don't let go of me.
I don't want this sweet moment to end.
Sparks are flying through my body, the kiss was… It felt like my heart was about to burst out of my chest.

👀 DOMINIC 👀

Her body trembles slightly as I bring my hands to her face.
I want to kiss her so badly and I can tell she wants to kiss me too.
This time she is not putting up her walls.
Elizabeth is allowing me to get close, giving me permission to kiss her.
I lean in, bringing my lips to hers. She sighs softly and parts her lips.
I can hear them cheer behind us, and I smile as our kiss deepens.
Her lips are every bit as soft and luscious as I imagined.
I feel her slide her hands up my chest before bringing them to my neck, holding me to her.
Liz's soft sigh drives me wild.

I need her, I need all of her.
My need is not possessive or obsessive, seeking to bend her to my wants and desires.
It's more of a need to protect her.
I want to shield her from harm, make sure that no one ever scares or hurts her ever again.
That the only tears she should ever shed are tears of happiness.
Liz deserves the world, and I want to be the one to show her.
I want to put her happiness first—it's the most important thing I can think of.
Please, for the love of god, want me as much as I want you.

We look at each other, he smiles as I bite my bottom lip in an attempt to steady my breathing.

One kiss and I'm hooked, I could tell he wanted more, heck I wanted more than a kiss; but would he accept my body once he saw all of it and just how ugly it is? It was still on my mind, haunting me.

Please, for the love of god, want me as much as I want you.

Dominic brings his lips back to mine, his kiss is hungrier this time.

He pulls me closer to him.

He slides his hands up under my shirt, squeezing my sides.

There are scars where his hands come to rest, but he doesn't acknowledge them.

My senses go off like fireworks, my body tingling from the touch of his hands and lips.

He groans as he breaks our kiss and looks at me.

The space between us is heated by my desire, to have him holding me hard against him.

I want him to dominate my lips, heck he can dominate all of me with his lips and his body.

I would let him take me and become completely lost to all else.

His lips come back to mine and my mind goes completely scrambled, a small moan escapes me, causing him to pull me in tighter.

I dig my fingers into his sides and his whole body vibrates as he growls lightly, it excites me.

'Unfortunately, I'm wanted elsewhere,' he says, getting up and offering me his hand.

'I would rather stay with you.'

He helps me up and takes a moment to kiss me again as he slides his hands to my waist.

I stand on my tiptoes and grab his shirt at his chest, pulling myself in closer.

'Don't go anywhere, I would like to share another kiss.'

He smiles and runs his thumb over my lips, his eyes never leaving mine.

'Well, I came in your car, so I'm kinda stuck here,' I joke, rolling my eyes.

He chuckles as his hand lightly traces my face.

I close my eyes as my body reacts to his touch, I'm sure he can feel it.

His lips brush mine, my tongue teasing him.

Dominic pulls me in tighter and his hand snakes through my hair.

His kiss fills me with excitement.

He can feel that I want more.
My hands move up his body, I can feel his body's reaction to my touch, he wants more.
'I would like to share more than a kiss with you,' he whispers, his fingers brushing my cheeks.
'Yes, I want it too,' I answer, looking shyly into his eyes.

I want it more than I thought, even though it scares the absolute crap out of me.
I smile as his thumb brushes along my lips.
I part them and touch his thumb with the tip of my tongue.
He smiles as he watches me kiss his thumb, then he pulls me in and kisses me again.
My arms wrap around his neck as his hands slide down and grab my butt.

He releases me and we walk back to the group hand in hand, they have got the fire going.
I realise then that it's almost 6:30pm.
I watch the group talking and laughing.

David and Amanda are high school sweethearts, and recently got engaged, they look great together. Gavin has tried hopelessly to get with Amber, but she only has eyes for Cassie.
He is still kind of ignoring me, but I'm fine with that.
Shane and Chantelle have been together for seven years, they have been off and on for the last two, and judging by their body language they are definitely on—and pregnant.

I have a feeling that Simon likes Sarah, and I think she feels the same about him.
Luke, in turn, has been making puppy dog eyes at Sally from the moment she turned up with Sarah. Louise, on the other hand, let me know in our brief exchange that I'm an outsider and not welcome, well at least not by her.
She took extra delight in telling me that Dominic is thinking of going back to New Zealand to be with his family.
I know she likes Dominic, but the feeling is not mutual, it seems.

Dominic pulls me in and kisses me softly before he lets go of my hand and walks to the back of his Ute with Luke.
I can't hear what Luke says, but he gets a punch to the arm for it.
Luke laughs and Dominic shakes his head and punches him again.
He looks up to see me watching, winks and smiles at me.
I smile back.

Then I turn and walk over to the fire.
Amanda comes over to me and hugs me.

'See, I told you he likes you a lot, I can tell he won't let you go now.'
'I'm nervous,'
'Why?' Amanda asks, confused.
'That was my first real…'
'Oh my, you're…' Amanda smiles and hugs me tight.

'What about Louise? I mean, she really likes him. I…'
Amanda stops me, 'Louise is, um, complicated.'
I wonder if Louise might be bipolar, I think to myself.
Whatever the reason for her behaviour is, she seems unable to balance her emotions, so I vow to do my best to stay away from her.
I know mental illness isn't the fault of the person who suffers from it.

'She's hot and cold with everyone. She doesn't even like me and hates Chantelle,' Amanda continues.
'Why?'
'Shaun turned her down and got back with Chantelle. They have a long history together and there is no room in his life for anyone other than Chantelle. I guess losing a child at birth makes your own issues seem less important.'
'Shaun and Chantelle lost a child?'
'Yeah, just over a year and a half ago. But judging by how protective Shaun is right now, Chantelle could be pregnant again.'
Amanda looks at me.
'You and Dominic will have beautiful babies.'

David comes up behind her and grabs her around the waist.
'My lap is cold, and I need attention,' he says against her neck.
Amanda smiles as she turns in his arms.
David holds her as he kisses her neck.
'Sorry, Elizabeth, but I'm stealing my girl from you again,' he smiles sheepishly.
'Well, I would hate to be the reason your lap is cold.' I reply.
I turn my attention back to the fire and sit down.

I really want to have something with Dominic, but my past is something I'm never going to escape from.
I look up and Amber gives me a huge grin with two thumbs up.
She doesn't have to say a thing, I know where her mind is, but I beat her to it.
I nod and smile back at her as Dominic sits down on my left with a beautiful, black acoustic guitar.

I look at his guitar and notice the red pinstripe artwork entwined with an intricate silver fern.
The light from the fire dances over the surface of the guitar, making the artwork come alive.

'Hey, you,' I smile at him.
'Miss me?' He smiles back.
I shrug my shoulders nonchalantly. He leans over, bringing his lips to mine.
Oh, my good golly gosh! I really like his kisses!
We spend the next couple of hours laughing and singing.
I'm having a great time, but just as I'm starting to feel tired, Dominic leans in.

'You ready to go?' He asks.
'How can you tell?' I yawn.
'I'm just that good,' he jokes, his fingers trailing down my arm.
'Besides,' he kisses my bare shoulder, sending shivers all over my body, 'I would like to continue…'
'I would like that too,' I reply quickly, before he can finish.
I turn to face him, bringing my hand to his face and running my fingers across his cheek, up into his hair. Leaning in, I bring my lips to his, teasing.
I close my eyes and let him hold my lips to his.
When he pulls away to look at me, I can feel myself blush.
He smiles and kisses my forehead.

Dominic looks at his phone.
'All right, tide's down, let's go!' He calls.
Everyone groans in protest, no one wants to leave.
Amber comes up to the back of Dominic's Ute where we have just finished putting everything away.
'Hey, I'm going back with Cassie, will you be okay without me?'
'I'm sure Dominic will get me home safely,' I answer her.

She looks from me to Dominic and smiles.
'Hey, Dom, do you like pancakes? Because our Lizzy here makes yummy pancakes.' She smiles suggestively.
'Well, how can I say no to pancakes?' He winks at her.
'Good. I won't be home till very late tomorrow afternoon or night, if you get what I mean,' Amber winks at us, turns and walks back to Cassie.

Dominic looks at me and smiles. I'm so red you could think the sun was still up.
I look down at my feet.
I want to know what sex feels like when both people want it.

I have allowed myself to touch him, kiss him, and hold him.
I fought my nerves and let myself feel.
But a kiss is just a kiss, sex is intensely intimate, and I want it, with him.
However, I'm also scared that after one night with me he will regret it.

I start getting nervous. Dominic senses it, walks up behind me and wraps me in his arms.
I relax against his chest.
He places delicate kisses along my neck, and my breathing quickens.
His hands move slowly down to my waist and he turns me around to face him.
His lips brush against mine, sending my body into overdrive.
'I really like you Liz and I want you. I really…'
'I like you a lot too,' my breathing hitches as he presses his lips against mine again.
'And I want you to be my first…' I start, but Dominic kisses me deeply before I can finish.

🔲 DOMINIC 🔲

I kiss her softly, my hands on her waist, pulling her against me.
I feel her hands move up my body.
She is returning my kiss and it's setting my body alight.
Elizabeth wants me to be her first, did I hear that correctly?
Her hands move up, her arms wrapping around my neck.
I kiss her harder as my hands slide down to cradle her butt.
She makes no move to stop me.
She moans softly and presses against me, her fingers running through my hair.
I push her up against the tailgate of my car.
She gives no indication that she needs me to stop. I push a little harder and deepen our kiss.
She makes a small sound in her throat, driving my body to the edge of desire.
Our tongues meld together as my hands move up her back.
I can feel the heat emanating from her as her body melts again into mine.
My hands are in her hair, gently pulling her head back as I nip at her bottom lip, causing her to whimper softly and pull me in closer.
I don't want to stop, and I don't want to let her go.

I groan as I pull away. I look at her; she is perfect.
Her eyes are wide and dazed, looking directly into mine. Her cheeks are flushed, her lips showing how hard I kissed her: red and swollen, in a good way.
Elizabeth smiles and her whole face lights up.

She is trying hard not to let her fear take over, fighting the urge to turn away
and hide her face.

'We should get going,' I murmur against her lips before kissing her again, softly.
I untangle my hands from her hair as she steadies herself.
My hands cover the scars on her neck as I watch her close her eyes.
She takes a breath before opening them again.
The whole world falls away and it's just Liz and I, alone on a beach.
'Yes, we should,' she says, smiling up at me.

👀 ELIZABETH 👀

'Bye, Liz!' Amanda calls out, waving as she leaves.
I wave back as Dominic takes my other hand.
'Don't do anything I wouldn't. Love you! See you tomorrow night!' Amber calls
through the window of Cassie's car.
Coming from Amber that doesn't rule out much. I smile and wave.
'Bye, Liz!' Simon and Luke call out in unison as they walk to their cars.
'I will definitely get in trouble if I don't invite you to our next gathering,' Dominic
observes, wrapping his arm around my waist.
'That's what Amanda said,' I smile, leaning against his chest.
'What else did Amanda say?'
'Um, well…' I can't quite bring myself to finish and blush.
I rub my neck. His fingers replace mine and I feel his warmth run through me.
'That good, huh?'
I look up and smile, I'm blushing again and his smile isn't helping.
Dominic kisses me softly.

On the drive home, when he isn't changing gears, he is holding my hand.
I find myself really wanting this, even if I don't satisfy him, even if it's only for
one night.
We get back to my place and Dominic carries the cooler inside.
I barely make it to the kitchen bench when he gently pushes me up against it,
pinning me from behind.
He leaves a trail of soft bites and kisses along my shoulder.
I tilt my head to the side, giving him full access to my neck.
Wildfire runs through my body.
I have never felt anything like it.
I hang onto the bench, my breathing fast and heavy.
My body is giving all the answers I can't bring myself to say.

I moan softly, which seems to excite him; his hands explore my body, intensifying the sensations.

I turn my head and kiss him on the lips.

His hands slide up under my shirt and up to my breasts. I shiver.

In one movement Dominic spins me round and his lips find mine, his tongue beg for entry to my mouth.

I tilt my head back and grant him access.

He grabs my behind and lifts me onto the bench.

I wrap my legs around his waist, my hands on either side of his neck.

His left hand comes down to cup the side of my face after releasing the clip holding my hair, while his other hand holds me to him.

His left hand moves from my face, tracing his fingers along my arm, up and down.

I shiver under his touch.

I can feel him smile as I moan with desire.

He never once breaks our kiss.

Dominic's hands move up to my neck before gently pulling my hair, exposing my neck to his mouth.

His lips tickle my skin as he slowly moves down towards my breasts.

I inhale sharply as his hands move down my back to my hips and grips them, firmly.

My hands run through his hair and he moves his hand back up to my neck.

I exhale shakily, his hands moving back down to my waist and squeezing.

'Elizabeth,' he murmurs my name softly.

'Mmm Dominic,' I breathe.

His lips brush against mine.

I move my hands down his chest, I can feel his muscles ripple under my fingers.

My hands rest on his waist as my tongue teases his lips.

I run my hands up under his shirt, up from his waist, along his abs.

His body tenses under my touch.

He breaks our kiss to remove his shirt.

I can't help but stare; my goodness, he is absolutely gorgeous.

I hesitate, feeling self-conscious about the scars from my past all over my body.

'Liz, what's wrong?' He asks, stepping back a little.

His concern makes me blush.

'I'm just a little nervous.' I take a deep breath.

'I want this, I really do,' I take another deep, shaky breath.

'I have never… I mean, I have… I've just never had it feel this good.'

The words pour out in a rush.

'And you are so beautiful, and I'm so … not. I have scars, lots of scars and I'm worried that you will find me ugly and unsatisfying' I stare at the floor, fidgeting with the hem of my sarong, my hands shaking.

His hands cover mine.
'Liz,' he says, moving back against me.
'I have never consented before and …'
Dominic looks at me as he gently tucks my hair behind my ear. I look away.
'I want you to be the first.' I finish as his hands cup my face, making me look at him.
I can see the concern in his eyes.
'You are beautiful, Liz. Your scars won't change my opinion of you. If you want to stop and wait, I understand.'
'No,' I cut him off, 'I want this, tonight, with you. That is, if you still do?' I ask, looking up at him nervously.
'As long as this is what you want, I want you.'
'I want you, Dominic.'

And with that he claims my lips again.
His hands slide down my sides, sending shockwaves through my body.
I wrap my arms around his neck and my legs around his waist, pulling his muscular body against my small frame.
I can feel him smile as I moan and he gently bites my bottom lip.
He slides his hands under me and lifts me up, carrying me towards my room, never breaking our kiss.
We collide with the door frame of my bedroom and he pushes hard against me.

His hands grasp my butt harder. He groans.
He wants this; his kiss is urgent and hungry.
He sits down on my bed, with me on his lap.
I can feel his erection pressing against my crotch.
He removes my shirt and his kisses follow my swimsuit straps as he slides them from my shoulders and down my arms.
I lift my hands through the straps as he cups my breasts, my body shuddering as his thumbs rub over my nipples.

Oh my god, his hands are warm and feel incredible on my body.
He starts to kiss my breasts as I grab his hair, throw my head back, and gasp in ecstasy.
His fingers find scars and he senses the apprehension in me.
He brings his hand up to the side of my neck and his thumb traces the line of my jaw.

Delicately, he trails kisses up my neck and finds my lips.
He is breathing fast and exhales, forcing himself to slow down.
His other arm runs up my back and holds me tightly against him.

'Liz,' he whispers as his tongue teases my neck, 'You feel so fucking good.'
'I want…' I breathe. I can't finish, my body is on fire with the anticipation of sex with Dominic.
His hands feel every bit as good as I imagined.
His lips feel unbelievable against mine, against my body.
'I want you, Elizabeth.'
I can feel his erection harden against me as his mouth finds my breasts, gently teasing them in turn, nipping and sucking my nipples.
'Dominic!' I exclaim softly.
I push my fears and doubts aside.
I want this, I need this, I deserve this.
After everything, I want just one night where I have consented.
I want to be with him.
I want him to be mine.

👀 DOMINIC 👀

I can feel her body's reaction to my touch.
I savour her taste, her touch, and her smell.
Her nails slowly trace down my neck as my lips find hers, her hands run through my hair.
Man, she feels good.
She breaks off our kiss and slides to her knees on the floor, her hands running over my chest and down over my abs.
My body shudders under her touch.
I have never wanted someone as much as I want her.
I really want to be with Liz.
I want to be hers and I want her to be mine.
I watch as she begins to undo the drawstring of my boardshorts.
I stand to remove them.

She cups my balls in her hand, taking my cock in her mouth.
I was not expecting this, but damn, I'm going to enjoy it.
I moan, spread my feet a little wider and grab a handful of her hair as she takes me in all the way.
She teases me with her tongue before taking my cock in deeply again.
'Don't stop,' I gasp as my head snaps back.

Her hands tease me as she takes me, deep.
'Fuuuck!' I moan.
Her hands are like magic as they run along my shaft; mine are tangled in her hair and I'm thinking of all the ways I want to make love to her.
My hips match her rhythm, my head rolls back as she takes me deep again.
'Liz…' I groan.
She seems to be enjoying this as much as I am.
'Fuck, Liz,' I moan again, under my breath, 'Mmmm, my god, Liz.'
Every time I utter her name she takes me deep in her mouth.
'Fuck, fuck, fuck, Liz!' I groan, louder.

She is driving me crazy.
I look down as I grab more of her hair and push against her.
Her hand moves up my leg.
I take it and our fingers intertwine while her other hand tickles the underside of my balls.
'Fuck me,' I sigh, 'My god, Liz, you are…' I moan out loud again, '…Amazing.'
She is a drug that I could enjoy being addicted to.

Liz lets go of my hand and lightly traces her fingers around my waist to my lower back.
Her hands feel incredible on my body.
I can feel her lightly digging her nails in, pulling me in as she takes me deep in her mouth again.

Both of my hands are tangled in her hair now and she's clearly enjoying hearing me moan in ecstasy.
'Fuck, Liz, what are you doing to me?' I rasp, breathing heavily.
I groan as she teases the tip of my cock with her tongue, running her right hand up and down my shaft while the left fondles my balls. I tip my head back.
'Oh my god, Liz!'
She takes me all the way in her mouth as I gasp and run my fingers through her hair.
A 'FUCK, LIZ!' tears out from deep within me.

I look down at her and our eyes lock, mirroring pure, raw, mutual desire.
My balls contract.
If I don't stop her I'm going to blow.
There is no way I'm going to go off like a teenager without making her scream first.
I pull her up and claim her lips, I need to be inside her, I need her under me.
I need her to know how much I want her, I need her to know she is mine.

'Liz…' I breathe against her lips.
'Yes, Dominic,' she responds as I kiss her neck.
'I want you,' I whisper as I look into her eyes, making sure she is still okay.

I want her to know just how much I want to be hers; I need to show her that I am hers.
Liz looks up at me and smiles, her whole face lighting up and her eyes shining brighter.
I bury my hands back into her hair, pulling her lips to mine.
I kiss her, passionately. I feel her body shudder as she moans.
Grabbing her buttocks with both hands, in one swift movement I turn and lift her onto the bed.
She feels fantastic under me.
I begin to trail kisses to her ear and down her neck as I hold both her wrists above her head.
They are delicate enough to fit in one of my hands.
My free hand travels down over her breasts as I kiss and gently nip at her neck.
She arches her back and wraps her legs around me, pulling me against her.

I release her wrists as I kiss her collarbone.
I stop and look into her eyes.
My god, she is breathtaking.
I kiss her again; will I ever be able to get enough of this woman?
I bury my face in her cleavage as I cup her breasts with my hands; her nipples erect.
I trail kisses around them and I feel the goosebumps break out on her skin.
She moans as she runs her hands through my hair, grabbing a handful.

I trail kisses down as I start to remove her swimwear.
Her breathing hitches as she becomes nervous.
I move back up to her lips, I need her to know that I see past her scars.
Moving more slowly back down her neck, I follow the scar to her collarbone and down, over her breast to her stomach.
'Liz,' I say against her skin,
'You are so beautiful.' I kiss her stomach softly.

I run my tongue back up to her left breast, taking it gently in my mouth before sucking her nipple, hard, making her gasp.
My hands grip her waist as I move my mouth back down.
'Scars and all,' I murmur, kissing the scars on her stomach.
Her fingers move along my shoulders to my head, and she runs her fingers through my hair as she softly whispers my name.

I untie the sarong, she lifts her hips so I can remove it, and I toss it on the floor.
I run my hands up her thighs and, feeling the scars, I begin to kiss them, gently.
She gasps and moans as her body shudders under my touch.

🐾 ELIZABETH 🐾

His hands move over my body and I am loving every moment.
I love every touch of his lips, his tongue moving along my scars.
The touch of his hands and lips set my senses on fire.
I feel like I could orgasm without penetration and be completely satisfied.
The way Dominic kisses me is so new to me; I feel wanted, desired, almost beautiful.

I trace my fingers up his back, over his shoulders and up to his head, running my fingers through his hair. My god, his lips feel unbelievable on my body.
His hands move with delicate purpose, and squeeze my waist.
He tells me I'm beautiful, scars and all.
I want to believe him, and in this moment, I do.

'Elizabeth,'
His voice vibrates over my skin, intensified by the sensation of his warm breath.
The heat rises through my body as I drag my fingernails along his back.
I gasp and moan under his touch and I don't ever want this feeling to stop.
I have wanted this since I met him, and I don't want to give it up.
I want to please him, I need to please him.
'Mmm, Dominic,' I moan.

I feel his grip tighten slightly around my middle as he moves his mouth further down.
His fingers move to my swimsuit, slowly inching it down.
His lips follow, kissing my scars.
A moan escapes my lips. Please don't stop, I think to myself.
'I need you, Elizabeth,' Dominic breathes against my skin.
'I need you, Dominic.' I reply as I arch my back.
His fingers and lips move along my scars.
The feeling of his touch is so intense.
My body shudders and begs him to give me what I desire most from him: all of him and nothing else.
'Oh, hmmm, Dominic,' I exclaim and run my fingers through his hair as he continues to move down my body.

👓 DOMINIC 👓

I start to pull her swimwear down and I see even more scars.
I kiss them gently, hoping to show her that I accept them, that I accept her as she is and never want her to change.
I slowly remove her swimsuit as I trail kisses along her thighs.
I discard it on the floor with her sarong.
My hands move up her thighs and I begin to gently nibble and kiss her inner thigh.
I tease her scars with my tongue while rubbing her clitoris with my thumb.
Her body erupts and she gasps and moans, loudly.
I bring my tongue to her clitoris.
I massage it with my tongue and suck, my thumb entering her.
Her whole body shudders as she gasps.

'I've never had…' She breathes heavily, '…this before.'
The more she grabs my hair, and the louder she moans, the harder I suck her clitoris.
Her hips buck and grind.
Smiling, I pull back and blow softly against her nub and moist lips, causing her to shudder with pleasure.
Fuck, she is so wet and tight.
I slide my finger into her and she responds by calling out my name and begging for more.
I bring my mouth back down and gently nip and suck.
I feel her getting close to climaxing.
She moans my name, bucking her hips.
'Dominic, oh my,… I … you are…' The words get lost in her throat.

👓 ELIZABETH 👓

I have never received oral before.
It feels amazing, the way his tongue moves, his mouth sucking my clitoris. I moan, loudly.
'Oh my…' I gasp as my back arches.
'Dom…' I breathe heavily, I don't think I can hold back much longer.
He can feel I'm close and increases the force of his finger moving in and out of me.
With his other hand he starts rubbing the rim of my anus, and it feels incredible.
My body convulses and I gasp and moan loudly.
The ecstasy envelops my body and I can't hold back anymore.

'Dominic!' I cry out his name.
Dominic goes harder and my body erupts with pleasure as I grip fistfuls of his hair. I have been taken to the edge of oblivion and pushed beyond.

👀 DOMINIC 👀

I use my thumb to keep teasing her, while using my free hand to get a condom from my shorts and put it on. I continue to tease and suck her clitoris, penetrating her with my fingers.
I use my other hand to rub her rim.
'Oh my!' Liz cries out, 'Dominic!'
Her whole body begins to shudder as she climaxes.
'Dominic,' She calls out my name in the throes of pure ecstasy.
I run kisses over her stomach.
'Dominic,' She gasps.
Her body is reacting to my kisses as I reach for her breasts. I cup them as her legs wrap around me again.
I flick my tongue over her nipples, then I bury my face in her neck as I enter her, and our bodies begin to move as one.
Her hands run up and down my back, igniting a trail of fire.

👀 ELIZABETH 👀

Dominic moves back up my body, kissing and nipping as he reaches my breasts.
Oh my god, we are about to…
He enters me as he buries his face in my neck.
Our bodies move together and I run my fingers up his back, moaning deep in my throat.
My legs wrap around him, holding him to me.
'Elizabeth,' he says as he pushes deeper into me.
'Yes, Dominic,' I breathe against his neck.

I'm giving him all the access I can give.
I want it harder.
He pins my wrists above my head with one hand as the other moves down to my breast.
His movements become more insistent as he rolls his hips and my body responds.
I call his name and moan in ecstasy.

He pinches my nipple and it sends a sharp stab of pleasure rippling through my body.
'Dominic!' I gasp hoarsely as he brings his lips to mine.

His tongue teases mine, and he sucks it before gently biting my bottom lip as I begin to orgasm and call out his name again.
But he doesn't stop.
His body moves on top of mine with increasing urgency.
I can feel him push harder, deeper, and faster.
Dominic growls, and it vibrates through his body as he releases my hands.
I wrap my arms around him, digging my nails into his shoulders, dragging them down his back.
I feel his tongue move along my neck, up to my ear, taking my earlobe into his mouth before making his way to my lips.
'Yes, Dominic,'
I want him with every fibre of my being.

🔳 DOMINIC 🔳

'Elizabeth,' I say as I push deeper inside of her.
I pin her wrists above her head again with one hand, while the other moves down to her breast.
I hold it and gently pinch her nipple.
Liz calls out my name in between gasps.
I push harder and deeper, rolling my hips, bringing her to climax again.
'Dominic!' She cries out my name.
I start to fuck her harder, and as I release her hands I feel her nails dig into my back.
I kiss her hard as she moans, and I can feel my body tense.
I suck her bottom lip into to my mouth, gently biting it, revelling in the immediate reaction of her nails dragging up my back.
She pushes her lips harder onto mine.

I want to hold back and make her climax again.
I pull her wrists up above her head again as I intertwine my fingers with hers and move harder against her.
Elizabeth said yes to me, the first time she has ever consented.
I want her to fully enjoy every part of our night together.
She feels fantastic against me and I vow never to give up on her.
I bring my lips to hers again, kissing her harder.
She returns the kiss.

I release her wrists and run my arm along her back, lifting her slightly.
I tangle my fingers in her hair as I thrust harder.
Her legs tighten around me as she orgasms again.
I can't hold back much longer.
She feels too good, smells too good, tastes too good, and sounds too good.

The way she calls my name as she orgasms drives me wild and my body aches for her.
'Fuck, Liz,' I roll my head back. I'm so close.
Elizabeth is hot, wet, and so fucking tight, when she cums it's like my cock is being strangled.
Fuck me, it's so good.
I look back down at her, Elizabeth is fucking perfect.

🔞 ELIZABETH 🔞

His breathing is getting heavier, his kisses harder.
I tighten my legs around him, the pleasure I'm feeling right now is mixed with pain.
The pain of my whole body aching with deep desire as he makes me cum again and again.
I have never felt anything so amazing in my life.

'Dominic!' I call out his name. 'Don't stop, I want you to…' I moan loudly, 'Cum with me.'
He kisses me again, his hand grabs my thigh and he pushes deep within me.
With every thrust and roll of his hips I can feel him getting closer.
He starts to moan.
'Liz.'
'Dominic.'
His body shudders with mine and we climax together.
He breathes into my neck, whispering my name.
He trails kisses along my neck to my lips.
His kiss is full of passion and wanting.
He props himself up on his elbow and looks at me, his breathing still hard and deep.
I rest my hand over his heart, it's beating just as hard and fast as mine.
Please want me like I want you, Dominic. I look into his eyes, trying to get a sense of what he is feeling and thinking.
'Dominic,' I blush as I begin to ask him, 'What…?'

'You are amazing, Liz, and…,' he pauses as he runs his eyes over my body, trailing his hand up over my breasts to my face, running his thumb over my lips.

'…Absolutely fucking stunning.'

I smile back at him, not sure what to say.

He leans in and kisses me softly.

Then he lays down beside me and pulls me in to him.

I rest my head on his chest as he runs his hand through my hair.

His other hand holds me, protecting me from harm.

I feel him kiss the top of my head as I drift off to sleep.

👀 DOMINIC 👀

I look down at her as she smiles up at me, blushing.

It's no lie, she is absolutely fucking stunning.

Her body is perfect, she is perfect.

I lie down beside her and pull her into me, holding her tight.

Liz lays her head on my chest, she is still breathing heavily.

She rests her hand on my abs and her warmth spreads through me.

I run my fingers through her hair as she drifts off to sleep.

I bring my hand to hers and hold it.

Her hands are small, soft, and delicate.

I can't fathom the amount of scars she has.

I will never let anyone hurt her ever again.

Elizabeth is my girl.

I drift off to sleep holding my girl.

CHAPTER 3

A New Dawn

I wake up early in a state of euphoria, and roll over to see him still asleep.
He really is so handsome.
I lie there for a minute remembering last night.
Am I able to walk? I snicker to myself.
My legs do feel a little weak as I get up and steady myself.
I can't help but smile.
I love this feeling.
I make my way to the bathroom, I need a shower and I'm guessing my hair is
a mess.
I stand in the shower remembering every touch, kiss, and sensation.
I run my hands over my body.
I can feel the scars, but he didn't care about them.
Dominic's touches made them fade away; forgotten if not gone.

I get out of the shower and as I dry myself, I see a condom in the bin.
I smile to myself.
As I brush my teeth, I look in the mirror and see the reflection of a person
glowing and happy.
Wow, this feels fantastic.
I never thought I would ever get the chance to experience sex I actually wanted.
It was just like Amber described it.
I'm so thankful that she made me believe that I could have that with someone.
I made myself a promise to find him and let him in.
I so badly want that person to be Dominic.
I want to be his and only his.
I want him to want me, I want him to be mine.

After years at the hands of a monster, I believed that I would die alone and
unloved; a nobody.
I want to prove that wrong.
I'm strong, independent, and I am someone who can be loved.

I finish brushing my teeth, put my hair up in a clip, and don a black bra and undies.

I wear a black cotton sarong on top.

Dominic is still asleep, so I leave a towel and new toothbrush on the bed for him.

I pick up his clothes and throw them in the washing machine for a quick wash as I get the ingredients ready for the promised pancakes.

I put some music on after I hang out his clothes, not too loud, but just enough to revel in my happy place. Right now, on my playlist, James Blunt and Michael Buble are belting it out.

I take a deep breath, close my eyes and smile.

I open my eyes again and lose myself in the music.

Singing to myself and moving to the music while I make breakfast.

🔲 DOMINIC 🔲

I get out of the shower and I can hear the music playing softly.

I can also smell pancakes.

I smile as I wrap the towel around my waist and walk out.

I stop and watch her from the bedroom doorway.

She is humming and moving to the music.

Lost in her safe place.

I want to be her safe place.

I lean against the door frame, watching her body moving to the music and starting to resent that black sarong for blocking the view.

I need to feel her in my arms again.

I need to feel her lips on mine.

I need to feel her under me as she moans my name.

I need to be the one she wants.

I need to be good enough for her.

I don't want her to feel alone, scared, and unloved ever again.

I want to give her the world.

🔲 ELIZABETH 🔲

I didn't realise that Dominic was standing in my bedroom doorway, watching me.

It's not until he comes up behind me, wrapping his arms around me, that I realise he has been watching me for a while.

'Morning,' he says as he kisses my shoulder and pulls me hard against him.
'Morning to you,' I reply as I remove the last pancake from the pan and turn the stove off.
I turn in his arms to face him.

'Would you…' is all I get out before his lips crash into mine.
He pulls me in against himself, thank god he is holding me up, because my legs aren't.
I feel his fingers dig into my sides as he tightens his hold on me.
My hands run through his hair, still damp from his shower.
Oh my, I want to shower with him.
My body shivers.
My god, this man is … I moan softly, which fuels his desire.

Dominic breaks the kiss and rests his forehead on mine.
He is wearing nothing but a towel, and is clearly aroused.
I really want to feel him again.
'Do you have any more condoms?' He asks.
'No, I don't,' I respond, looking at the floor.
'I'm clean and I, I can't have children.' I finish in a whisper as I play with the hem of my sarong.
I take a deep breath and try to keep my emotions in check.
Not being able to have children devastates me beyond words.
I will never be able to give a man a biological child.
I will never be able to be a biological mother.
It's another reason why I'm not good to be with.

'Liz,' Dominic's voice breaks through my thoughts of self-doubt and worthlessness.
'I'm so sorry, Liz.' He pulls me in and kisses the top of my head.
'It's okay, you don't have to apologise, you didn't know.
I was in a bad accident.
I came to terms with it a long time ago.
Does it change your opinion of me?' I ask him.
He releases me, sighs, and takes a step back.
Oh no! It has! Just breathe, Lizzy, you knew it was only a fling.
I start to tremble and my hands tighten on the hem of my sarong.
I stare at the floor.

🦉 DOMINIC 🦉

Accident?
I don't believe her.
I think some fucker did something to her, he fucking took it, he fucking stole it from her.
I want to destroy him, erase him from her life so she never has to fear him ever again.
I look at her and I can tell she hasn't come to terms with losing something that is so special.
I want to be the one she turns to.

I watch as her body starts to tremble; her hands move along her scars and she looks down.
I lift her face gently, holding it so she can look at me.
'Elizabeth,' I say, looking into her green eyes.
I move in close, bringing my lips down to brush against hers.
Her breathing hitches and her body stills.
'No,' I answer. She is still perfect.
I kiss her softly as I move my hands along her body.
I can feel her relax and she smiles, returning my kiss.

🦉 ELIZABETH 🦉

'Elizabeth,' he says, holding my face and making me look at him.
He leans in, his lips close to mine.
His eyes never leaving mine.
I close my eyes and almost forget how to breathe.
My body freezes.
'No,' he answers my question as he pulls me in and kisses me.
His kiss is soft, his touch purposeful.
Dominic's kiss makes me smile and gives me a feeling of safety and acceptance.

'You are wearing too many clothes.'
I giggle at his comment and take a deep breath.
'Down, boy. Eat first, then you can play.'
I finish as I bite my bottom lip nervously.
I hate feeling nervous.
'You really shouldn't do that,' he grumbles, looking at my lips.

His look is almost primal, and it excites me right down to my swollen sex.
It takes a lot of resolve not to strip down and let him throw me over his shoulder,
caveman style, and carry me to bed.
'Go, sit and I'll bring you some pancakes,' I instruct as I turn around in his arms.
'Tease!' He replies as he plants kisses along my collarbone and up my neck.

I close my eyes and shiver as his hands move along my body up to my neck.
He blows softly where he kissed my neck, and my lips part as I take a sharp
breath.
With a groan, he lets me go and I feel my sarong drop.
'Like I said, you were wearing too much,' he whispers in my ear, then kisses my
temple.
I can't help but smile as his hands move along my bare skin.
His lips brush my shoulder and travel up to my neck.
'You don't have to hide anything about yourself from me,' he murmurs against
my ear.
His fingers squeeze my hips before grabbing my butt as he goes to sit down.
I take the pancakes over to the table.
Dominic is smiling at me and I can feel myself blush as I return his smile.

Can I tell him? Will he accept the truth?
Would he still want me?
He tells me he will listen and be there for me, that he accepts me as I am and
doesn't want me to change. He makes me feel safe, he makes me feel that I'm
valued as a person, not a possession.
 We haven't known each other very long, yet I feel like he is the one I was
waiting for, even when I was with Michael.
At the start, before… Before he took my self-worth away from me.
It's easy to say that you accept someone, regardless, before hearing their story.
My hands aren't clean, they are stained red.
Amber tells me that it's not my fault, that it's all Michael's doing.
Easy for her to say, but not so easy for me to believe.
Will Dominic accept my stained hands?
I turn and take the coffee to the table and sit.
I see Dominic staring at me, and it makes me feel self-conscious. I put my
sarong back on.

🔖 DOMINIC 🔖

I watch as she brings over the plate of pancakes, then as she moves around the kitchen getting the coffee ready.
She has no idea just how beautiful she really is.
The scars cover her body, I lost count of them.
It still astounds me, the amount she has.
I know that whatever happened, it wasn't a home invasion or an accident.
That's just a cover story for a very ugly truth.
These scars are from the hands of another man, a man she is hiding from, a man I need to protect her from.
I just know it.
I clench my fists, the anger I have towards the man responsible is hard to process.
I just hope she finds it in herself to trust me enough to tell me what happened.

There is one jagged scar that runs almost the entire length of her back.
There is one running across her left collarbone, down over her breast and to her bellybutton.
When I imagine her alone and scared, screaming in pain, I feel my fists clench again.

Elizabeth picks up her sarong with her toes and grabs it.
When she comes back to the table and notices me watching her, her body language changes.
She becomes self-conscious and reaches to put her sarong back on.
'Please don't,' I say softly, grabbing her hand.
'My scars,' her voice trembles. 'They are disgusting.'
'I still think your body is beautiful, please trust me?' I ask, looking at her.
'I… I do, Dominic, it's just that I'm not ready. My past is…'
She won't even look at me.
'Liz, it's okay. When you are ready, I'll be here.' I smile up at her.
'Thank you, Dominic.'
She looks relieved.

She smiles as she tucks loose strands of hair behind her ear.
I clear my throat.
'Right, well, we better eat before it ends up on the floor and you end up on the table.'
I look at her with raised eyebrows.
She blushes and giggles.
She has no idea how much I want to fuck her right now.

I have no idea how I manage to eat, but I do.
All I can think of is her; how she feels, how she tastes, how she smells.

I walk up behind her and run my hands up her thighs, kissing the scars on her right shoulder.
I can feel her body's reaction and her breathing quickens.
My hand slides into her panties and I slide a finger into her.
'You did say I could play after breakfast,' I whisper in her ear as I hold her to me.
'I want you, right here, right now.'
'Okay,' She sighs as she leans back into me.

I turn her to face me.
I kiss her passionately, stroking her breast and teasing her nipple.
Her hand moves up to mine and she wraps her arm around my neck.
I bring her to orgasm, her body shaking as I hold her against me.
I remove her bra and panties, then my towel.
'I want you,' I state as I kiss her, hard.
She is giving me all the access I need to please her.

Liz sighs as my kisses move down her neck to her breasts.
My hands squeeze her sides as she runs her fingers through my hair.
My lips trail further down and her breathing gets faster.
'Dominic,' she moans my name softly.
My hands move up her legs, squeezing gently, making her moan my name again.
My tongue teases her left thigh before moving to her clit; the response is instant.
Liz rolls her head back as her hands hold my face there.
My hand grabs her arse, pushing her against me.

ᗜ ELIZABETH ᗜ

Dominic's lips trail kisses down my neck to my breasts.
His lips feel incredible against my body.
He continues down and my breathing gets quicker, my body shivering as his hands move with smooth purpose.
The sensation causes me to moan his name out loud.
I run my fingers through his hair, my body responding to him.
I can't believe that I got to have him last night, and now I get to experience it all over again with him.
He gently squeezes my legs as his hands move up.
I moan his name again.
His tongue teases my left thigh, then he begins to suck me again.

I grab his hair as I roll my head back.
'Dominic.'
His hand grabs my arse and pulls me into him.
I can feel his need to go harder, and I let him.
I don't want him to stop.
Dominic lifts me up onto the bench, pushes me back and continues to give me oral.
His hands move up to my breasts, his fingers teasing my nipples.
I feel his thumb enter me as his fingers tease my rim.
I run my hands through his hair, back to his shoulders and I dig my nails in.
I feel his reaction.
My whole body erupts and shudders, my back arches as I orgasm, calling his name.
The more I call his name, the harder he sucks my clitoris.
'Dominic, I want you inside me,' I say breathlessly.

👀 DOMINIC 👀

Liz calls for me, she needs me. I need her.
I move back up her body, lifting her as my lips tease.
I reach her lips and Liz pulls me against her, kissing me hard.
Her hands move down my chest to my back, her fingers igniting my body.
I enter her as she buries her head against my neck.
She feels even better than last night.
Her fingernails dig into my back, causing me to shudder.
My lips tease her neck and move down to her breasts as I push her down gently.
I hold her breast as I start to go harder, still making sure I don't hurt her.
Her body responds to me.
I pull her to me, and I look into her beautiful, green eyes.
She smiles and nods.
I didn't even have to say a word, she knows what I want.
She moans softly as I pull out and kiss her passionately.
My hands slide down and grab her firmly.
Lifting her off the bench, I turn her back and bend her over.
I enter her again, pushing hard and deep into her.
She moans loudly, calling out my name.
She grabs my hand at her waist and pulls me closer.
'Fuck, Liz, I want you,' I say as my lips follow the scar along her back.
I want her so bad it hurts.
Liz smiles and nods as I push her hard against the bench.

🔖 ELIZABETH 🔖

Oh my god, it feels better than last night.

His hands hold my waist as he pushes me against the bench and pushes deep into me.

I grab his hand and pull him closer into me.

He kisses my shoulder as I moan and push back against him.

His hands move to my breasts and hold them as he starts getting harder, pushing deeper.

I gasp at the pleasure, it's so intense and hot.

I feel his balls hit against my clitoris when he thrusts hard.

'Dominic, oh my, don't stop!' I gasp as my body drips with the high I'm on.

'Mmm, Dominic.'

I can feel him getting close, he starts to growl deeply, and his hold tightens.

He pulls out suddenly and turns me around, kissing me fiercely.

His fingers dig into my sides, exciting me further as he directs me towards my bedroom door, pinning me against the door frame as he pulls back and looks at me.

He is breathing hard and fast, and so am I.

I lick my lips, tasting him, as I slide my hands down his chest slowly before bringing them around his hips and fanning my fingers wide over his arse, pulling him back to me.

Dominic smiles as he lifts me, bringing my lips back to his; we manage to find our way to my bed.

🔖 DOMINIC 🔖

I pull out and turn her to face me. I kiss her hard, she drives me wild but we manage to get to her bed. Once inside her, she wraps her legs around me, pulling me hard against her.

Liz arches her back, her breathing quickens, her body shudders, she turns me on so much I can't hold back.

She is moaning my name, her fingers running through my hair to my back.

They dig in and the feeling drives me; my woman drives me to give her more.

I thrust deeper, harder, faster holding her tight against me.

Kissing her as we orgasm together.

Everything about her has drawn me to her.

I'm addicted… Addicted to her.

👓 ELIZABETH 👓

We make our way out to the deck and sit, soaking in the summer sun and gentle breeze.
The light smell of the ocean is mixed with the jasmine growing in the garden.
I take a deep breath, close my eyes, and stretch my arms high above my head.
I can hear the ocean, right now everything is absolutely perfect.
'I need to get a daybed for my deck, I think,' I say, more to myself than to Dominic, as I open my eyes.
'Daybed?' He asks.
'Yep, right here, with a fire pit. Lazy summer weekends with drinks and good food.
Winter nights with a blanket, a glass or two of wine and a good book.'
'I could think of a few other things you could do with your daybed,' Dominic says, grinning.
'I think you're trying to corrupt me.' I look over at him and he winks at me.
'I suppose I could get a good soft rug with a couple of throw pillows for in front of the fireplace inside.'
'It does get cold in winter.' Dominic points out suggestively.

I close my eyes and put my feet up on the railing, enjoying the warm sea breeze.
I feel him run his fingers up my leg.
I smile as my body reacts to his touch.

He brings his Ute and jet-ski around to the beach side of my house, where there is grass, so we can wash the sand and salt water off it.
Somehow washing his car turns into a water fight.
He has an unfair advantage, having the hose.
I end up getting completely soaked, but at least his Ute, trailer, and jet-ski are clean.
He takes his Ute back around the other side of the house while I pack up the car wash products and sponges.
I grab a towel off the line and take my wet clothes off in the laundry.
I am just wrapping myself in a towel when he finds me in the laundry.

👓 DOMINIC 👓

I come around the corner to find her wrapping a towel around herself.
Her body drives me wild and I hate seeing her dressed.
I walk up behind her, running my hands up her arms.
She shivers and I can feel the goosebumps.

Her breathing is fast and her lips part as I gently squeeze and kiss her shoulders.
She moves her head to the side, giving me access to her neck.

Liz moans softly, enjoying my touch.
I turn her around and bring my hands to her neck, running my thumbs along
her jawline.
Her eyes shine brighter today and she is even more beautiful than yesterday.
I lift her up onto the bench and bring my hands back to her neck, covering her
scars with my hands and kissing her with as much passion as I can give her.

I feel her hands untuck her towel and move to my boardshorts.
Her hands push them down as she grabs my arse, pulling me into her.
She rolls her head back and moans as I enter her.
My god, she feels even better than yesterday as I begin to make love to her.
Her hands slide under my shirt and up my chest.
I remove my shirt and she digs her nails into my back.

👀 ELIZABETH 👀

I remove my towel and his boardshorts and grab his arse, pulling him into me.
I need to feel him inside me again.
I slide my hands under his shirt and I feel his body react instantly.
Pushing his shirt up, he removes it as my lips move up his chest to his neck.
His body responds to me as much as mine responds to him.
I dig my nails into his back and he buries his face into my neck, groaning deeply.
I let him go as hard as he wants and I enjoy every bit of it.

He has one hand pushing against the wall behind me, and the other on the
small of my back as he pushes deeper into me.
I lean back against the wall and his hand grabs my waist before moving up to
my breast.
He brings his lips to mine before moving them along my neck down to my
breast, sucking hard.
I moan loudly, he hungrily claims my lips again before pulling me back into
him.
Things fall from the shelves onto the bench, and roll to the floor.

His hands grab my hips as he pulls me in, and he thrusts harder and deeper.
His grip tightens as we make eye contact.
I drag my nails down his back to his butt, holding him to me as he gets more
vigorous.

My body responds, the harder he goes, the more I want it and I moan loudly, letting him know.
My hands move to his waist and I squeeze before running them up, holding him to me.
Dominic's hand grabs my hair, pulling my head back gently so my lips meet his as I trail my nails softly down his back.
His hands move to the sides of my face as I tease his lips with my tongue.
'Dominic,' I say against his lips.

He moans deeply as he kisses me hard.
I sigh in pleasure and that only seems to feed his hunger.
He groans and pushes me back against the wall, going harder.
He pulls me back to him hard, claiming my lips, his kiss causes my body to surrender to him more. Dominic's lips move down my neck as his hands push against the wall.
I lean back and gasp as he takes my breast in his mouth.
'Dominic,' I murmur his name.
I can feel he is close.
I am as well, and I want him to climax with me.
'Cum with me, Dominic.' I say against his neck.

His lips find mine as he starts going harder.
I orgasm as he kisses me hard.
He orgasms as well, I feel his cock pulsing.
I have never felt it before.
We stay there holding each other, breathing heavily.
His lips find mine and he kisses me tenderly.
'Are you okay? I kind of got a little…'
'Don't be sorry, I wanted it as much as you did. I trust you.' I say, not letting him finish.
I bring my hands to his face and smile.
He smiles back and kisses me.

I found someone to let in, I'm trusting him with my body.
He holds me tight.
I feel like there is no one else in the world, just us in our moment.
I hope with everything that this moment continues.
I can't remember the last time I wasn't scared to be near a man, let alone having him touch me.
Dominic is resting his head on my shoulder as he holds me, oh boy it feels good.

We spend the rest of the day laughing, talking, kissing and I lose track of how many times we make love. I even manage to make a cheesecake.
Good thing my neighbours aren't too close and can't see in, I smile to myself.
I'm feeling so good, I can't believe what's happened this weekend.
I'm so thankful to Amber for making me go to the beach yesterday.
Dominic makes me feel like I am important, like what I say, think and feel matter.
I really want him to be with me.
I swear I'm walking bow-legged.

It's getting dark and Dominic goes to have a shower.
I put some music on and begin prepping dinner.
He comes up behind me, holding me tight.
I move my head to the side and he buries his face against my neck, inhaling deeply.
'I could really get used to this with you, Liz,' he says, running kisses along my collarbone.
He unbuttons the top of my shirt and slides his hand in to cup my breast.
My breathing increases and I lean back into him as his other arm stays wrapped around me.
I run my fingers along his arm and intertwine them with his as I wrap my other arm around his neck.
'Mmmm, no bra,' he growls approvingly, rubbing his thumb over my nipple.
My body responds to him in more ways than I have ever experienced.
I turn my head and pull his lips to mine, teasing his lips with my tongue.

'I wouldn't mind it either.' I say against his lips.
'Elizabeth,' he turns me around.
'Yes, Dominic.'
'Be mine?' His eyes look directly into mine.
'Yes.' I didn't even have to think about it.

I promised myself not to let my past rule my future.
No sooner have I answered him that his hands cup my face and his lips find mine.
This kiss is different from his other kisses.
This one is the feeling of passion, of deep desire.
Dominic's hunger for me makes me weak at the knees and leaves me wanting more.
His tongue explores my mouth and he gently bites my bottom lip, his hands sliding down and grabbing my butt, lifting me up onto the bench.
His arousal is very evident as he starts to unbutton my shirt.

I lean back and wrap my legs around him, and he takes my breast in his mouth.
'Dominic,' I moan and run my hand through his hair.
I feel his tongue following my scar and he makes his way back up to my lips.
'HELLO BITCHES, MISS ME?!' Amber yells as she walks through the door.

Dominic groans and rests his head on my shoulder.
My hands move to his face as I smile and kiss the side of his head.
I try to do the buttons on my shirt quickly as she walks towards us.
'Hello, Amber,' I stammer.
Dominic stands and looks at me; his hard-on is still evident.
He looks very flustered, his hands moving to the back of my head as he smiles
and kisses my forehead.
I close my eyes, take a deep breath and smile.
I am his and he is mine.

Amber moves next to us and leans on the bench with a very smug look on her
face.
'Oops, sorry, I didn't realise you two were still...'
'How was your day?' I ask, cutting her off, still trying to do up my buttons.
Dominic has kind of composed himself enough to turn around to greet Amber.
'Tiger needs a shower.' Amber looks down and smiles before looking back up at
Dominic and raising her eyebrow. 'A cold shower.' She winks at him.
Dominic nods and I don't know what to say or do.
'Right, well, I'll leave you two ladies to catch up.' He turns to face me.
'I'll go and shower.'
He kisses my neck and then my lips, pulling me in tight against him.
My hands run up his chest as his grip tightens.
He pulls away, looking deeply into my eyes as his hand moves along my cheek,
down to my neck.
He doesn't say anything, but I get the hint as he winks and heads to my room.

Amber watches him walk away, then turns back and looks at me with wide eyes
and a huge grin on her face.
'Spill, now! And you may want to fix a few of your buttons.' She points and
smiles at me.
I look down and then back up with a smile, blushing.
I hop off the bench, fix my buttons and go back to getting dinner ready while
she makes drinks.
'I don't kiss and tell, but today, today has been perfect.' I say as she hands me a
drink.
'Oh come on!' Amber slaps her hands on the sides of her legs and stomps her
foot.

'I need more than that, I made your favourite drink!' She pleads.
Handing me a glass of Bundaberg Rum and Bundaberg Brewed Ginger Beer.
She even does the whole sad puppy thing.
I roll my eyes and laugh.

'Fine, but you're making the salad and spilling the goss on your day first.' I answer her as I smile.
'Deal!' She replies.
'Now I'll have to give you the MA15 version, because any more detail and your blushing will give you heart failure.'
I laugh, I know exactly what she is talking about.
Amber has never hidden that side of herself from me.
She has always been open and honest and never tried anything on with me, and I'm thankful for that.
I look up at her as she makes the salad and talks about her day.
'Man, that girl is flexible, and I made her scream, I have to say she taught me a thing or two.'
She rambles before adding, 'And then she returned the favour and made me scream.'
She winks. 'Oh, and by the way, we sat in your driveway and did the whole Titanic in the car.'
'Okay!' I cut her short. 'Can you please start the BBQ?'
'Okay.' She throws her hands up and walks out to the BBQ.
'Your turn!' She calls back.
I roll my eyes and follow her with the meat.
'I'm waiting.' She looks at me. 'Well, well, well, judging by the flushed cheeks, yours was just as naughty as mine.' She laughs.
'So?' Amber prods with a huge grin on her face. 'I'm waiting.'

I turn back to the house and check to see if Dominic is there before turning back to face Amber.
I put the tray down and look back at her.
'It was, umm, hot and umm, multiple times, places…' I trail off.
'Yay! So happy for you!' She exclaims, hugging me.

'You deserve all the happiness in the world.'
'Thank you, Amber,' I smile and hug her back.

'Am I interrupting or is it safe to come out?' Dominic asks.
Amber looks at me, winks and nods.
She has done a full background check on him and all his friends.
I smile at her.

'You're safe,' I giggle as I turn to him.
'Can I help with anything?' Dominic asks, walking up to us.
'You can cook the meat.' Amber chips in.
'Lizzy is on music and drinks duty.'
'No worries, I can do that.' He walks up and kisses me.

Oh dear god, his kisses and my weak knees, thank god he is holding me.
I head inside for drinks and music, tonight it's Dark 'n' Stormy, good old Aussie
Rock playing in the background.
As I make the drinks in a jug, I look up to see Dominic at the BBQ, cooking the
meat while being interrogated by Amber.
I have to laugh as he looks over at me with a help-me look on his face.
Picking up the tray, I head back out to the deck.
As I place the drinks tray on the table, I hear the end of Amber's don't-hurt-her
speech.

'Did I miss anything?' I ask.
'Nope, just idle chit-chat,' Amber answers glibly.
'Drink?' I ask.
Amber pours me a glass, then herself.
'Not for me tonight, thanks, I'm driving.' Dominic says, shaking his head.
'I think I have some light beer in the fridge. Would you like one?' I ask.
'Yes please.'
He smiles.
I turn to go back to the house when Dominic grabs my hand and pulls me back
to him.
'Don't be too long.' He kisses me softly.
'Come find me if I'm gone too long.'

We chat, laugh, and eat dinner.
Amber refills her glass, then mine.
Dominic declines.
'Well, I'm just going to confiscate your keys, cause you are staying with our
Lizzy here.'
'Sorry, there's work early tomorrow.' Dominic replies.
'But aren't you working here?' Amber asks.
'Yes, but not till about nine, I have a small job to do at my neighbour's first,' he
replies.

'It's okay, Amber, he has to work,' I say, shaking my head at her.
'I promise that I will come back,' Dominic says.
'Well, I'm not happy. Lizzy deserves to be…'

'Dessert, who wants dessert?' I ask, cutting her off and getting up.
'But I'm not finished eating, and don't change the subject!' Amber reprimands, emptying her glass then refilling it.

She reaches over to top up mine, finishing off the last of the jug.
'It's cheesecake,' I announce.
Amber looks directly at me, then at Dominic.
'Your cheesecake?'
'Yes,' I reply, looking at her.
'You better not be joking.' She threatens, looking directly at me.
'Would I do that to you?' I ask, holding my hand over my heart, pretending that I'm hurt.
'Wow, I'm impressed!' She grins.
'Why?' I ask, looking innocently at her.
'Well, judging by what I walked in on when I got home, cooking was the last thing you would have done.'
She looks at Dominic and I, crossing her arms.

Dominic grabs my thigh under the table and squeezes, looking directly at Amber.
'Well, we did go through our fair share of chocolate and cream,' he says.
Amber sits there, I don't think I have ever seen her lost for words till now.
'I even had to do a shop run for more,' he finishes.
I can feel myself blushing, Amber still hasn't said a word.
Dominic's hand moves up my thigh, causing goosebumps even though the warmth of his touch spreads through my body.
I look at him, his gaze holds Amber's and then he continues to explain a few finer points.
Amber's face is red, her eyes moving from Dominic to me.

'Well, I have to say,' Amber clears her throat and has a drink. 'Yay for Lizzy and thank you, Dominic.'
'Thank you? Why, what for?' Dominic asks her.
'Our girl here hasn't had any in, like, forever.'
'I'm sure it hasn't been that long,' I protest.
'How long have we known each other?' Amber asks me.
I don't answer her.
Dominic holds my hand and gives it a reassuring squeeze, he can tell I feel a little embarrassed.
'Two years, give or take, a month or two and you haven't done anything.
She may as well be a vir...'
'So, do you want dessert?' I ask quickly, cutting her off.

We spend the next couple of hours chatting and laughing.
This really has been the best weekend I have had in such a long time.
Dominic's hand never leaves mine and every now and then I feel his thumb rub along my hand.
His touch feels so warm and safe.

I sit there listening but not really paying attention, thinking back to when I was kid.
I miss my family so much.
Sundays, when we were home, was always a big family gathering filled with food, drinks, laughter, and love.
I wish that I could get to have that again.

'Liz?' Amber calls out.
'Earth to Liz,' Dominic says, rubbing his hand along my arm.
'Sorry, what?' I blink.
Dominic squeezes my hand.
'Are you alright?' He asks me.
'Um, yep,' I say getting up.
'I'm, I'm just going to the bathroom, can I get anyone anything?' I ask.
'One of your coffees, please. Dom, you should have one, they are yummy.'
'Sure, why not,' he responds.
'Okay, coffee coming up,' I say, turning to go.

Dominic grabs my hand and pulls me down to him.
'Are you sure you are okay?' He asks.
'Yep.' I smile and kiss him.
'Liz?'
'I'm okay, Dominic, I'll be back shortly.' I smile and walk inside.
I have a feeling he doesn't believe me, but he doesn't push it and I'm thankful for that.

👓 DOMINIC 👓

I watch Liz walk inside, something is wrong.
Her body language has changed and her smile was forced.
Her eyes don't shine when she forces her smile.
I so badly want her to open up to me and let me in.
I need to wait and be patient, hold her when she needs me and listen when she needs to tell me what happened.
I want her to trust me.

She is such a beautiful person.
I hate that some fucking asshole broke and hurt her.
I turn back to Amber to ask if she can see the change in Liz, and what she thinks could have upset her. Only to find Amber staring at me.

'What?' I ask her.
'Good, she is gone.' Amber says looking directly at me.
'Why, what's wrong?' I ask.
Amber leans forward and folds her arms on top of the table.
'You stayed last night, yeah?'
'Yes, why?' I reply, not sure where she is going with this.

'How was she? She has a lot of trouble sleeping.'
'Liz slept fine. Why?' I ask.
'I assume you saw her scars.'
'Yes, Amber I did. Where are you going with this?' I ask, sitting forward and leaning on the table.
'Due to um...really bad things that were done to her by her ex, Liz has horrible nightmares. Like waking up screaming, covered in sweat.'
Her fucking ex!
Her fucking ex did this to her!
Fucking mongrel, I bloody knew it was a guy.

The fact that she was hurt by the hands of someone she loved, someone she trusted, makes me rage.
I clench my fists, he will never get close to her again.
I can feel the anger building in me, but manage to control myself.
I know from how Amber is talking about Liz, there is a whole lot more to the story, and judging by her scars it's bad, really bad.

'Well last night she didn't, I mean she woke before me' I reply.
'Did she take her sleeping pills?' Amber asks me.
'Sleeping pills?' I question.
'Please, Dominic, this is important,' Amber pleads with me.

'Well, once we got back and made it to bed, we never left it and she fell asleep before me. I did get up during the night, but as far as I know, Liz didn't. Why do you want to know?' I ask.
Before I can say any more, Amber changes the subject.
'So, what's happening tomorrow?' She asks.
'I have a delivery truck arriving tomorrow morning with the first lot of materials between nine and nine-thirty AM.' I reply.

'Okay, three of Amber's favourite coffees.' I place the tray down and hand him a cup.
'Yours is half strength because you have to drive, hope it tastes okay.'
He takes a sip.
'Mmm, not bad. What's in it?'
'Bundaberg Rum Salted Caramel Royal Liqueur,' I answer.

'Liz is always playing with flavours and I unfortunately have to be the guinea pig,' Amber sighs.
'A selfless and thankless job,' Dominic jokes.
'Oh, it is.' Amber grins.

We sit for a while longer enjoying the coffee and the whole time Dominic is holding my hand, every now and then he gives it a reassuring squeeze.
'As much as I would like to stay, I really have to go,' Dominic says, giving me a wink.
'Okay, I'll walk you out,' I offer, I can feel myself blushing.

'Bye, Amber.' Dominic gives her a quick hug.
'Bye, Dominic.' Amber says with a wink over his shoulder.
They release each other and Amber looks hard at him and nods, before turning to me and smiling. Dominic takes my hand and we walk towards the steps.

'What was that about?' I ask.
'Probably something to do with her don't-hurt-my-bestie speech, or the chocolate and cream.' He replies as we walk down the steps.

We walk hand in hand to his Ute in silence, a perfect weekend coming to an end.
We get to his car and I lean against the driver's side.
Dominic runs his fingers through my hair, bringing his hands to rest on my neck.

'Thank you, I have had a great weekend.' I say.
His thumbs run along my jawline.

'So have I,' he answers.
Before I can say anything else, he pins me up against his car and his lips find mine.

I wrap my arms around his waist pulling him into me and his hands start to unbutton my shirt.
My hands move around and I begin to untie his board shorts.
His hands move slowly down to my waist and slide down to my arse, grabbing it hard and lifting me up. He pushes me harder up against his car as I wrap my legs and arms around him.
He finishes unbuttoning my shirt and his mouth finds my breasts; I grab fistfuls of his hair as I moan.

He stops, we are both breathing heavily.
Before I realise it, he has unlocked his car, pulling me into the back seat.
We remove our clothes hastily and Dominic pulls me onto him as he buries his face in my cleavage.
He is hard and ready, and I moan as he slides into me.

Dominic's hands run up and down my back.
My hands are in his hair, pulling him in closer to me.
His lips leave a trail of fire as he kisses and bites along my neck, ears and down to my breasts.
One of his hands pulls my hair making my head tilt back further as the other hand grabs my arse, hard, pushing me as he goes deeper in me.

His lips find mine again and he moans and kisses me harder.
I tease him as my tongue runs along his neck and I gently grab his earlobe with my teeth.
'Liz,' his voice is deep and husky. 'Liz, my god woman, you drive me wild.'
Dominic's hands hold me to him as I move along his cock, I can feel him deep inside.

His hands move along my body. He takes mine, pulling them behind me.
Holding my hands behind me, his free hand grabs my hip and squeezes before moving up to my breast.
He moves his hand and grabs my hair, pushing my lips to his.
The heat is rising, and I can feel myself start to shudder as I climax.
'Oh my, Dominic!'

He releases my hands, holds me tighter and pushes in deeper as he climaxes as well.
We are breathing heavily and holding each other.
I kissed him and the way he kissed me back…It felt like it could move mountains.
'I really have to go,' he says, breathing heavily as he kisses my neck.
'I know.' I answer him in a breathless whisper.

He rests his head over my heart and holds me tight.
I hold him to me and kiss the top of his head, breathing in his scent.
He takes a deep breath.
'Mmm, you feel so good. You're making it very difficult to leave,' he sighs.
I giggle coyly.
'Well, you're not making it easy to let you leave,' I say, trying to sound confident.
He sits back, running his hands over my body.

'I'll make you a deal,' I offer.
'A deal? I'm listening,' he says, raising an eyebrow.
'The days when you're working here, I'll make you lunch, and cook dinner and…'
'…you'll be my dessert,' he finishes, before adding, 'And I get to stay the night.'
'You want to stay the night?' I ask. 'With me, again?'
'Yes, I would very much like to.' He smiles as he runs his fingers along my face,
brushing away my hair.

'So is breakfast on you or me?' I ask him.
'Well, you could be breakfast.' He kisses my neck.
'But, I guess I could make breakfast. You like Vegemite on toast, don't you?'
'Deal, who doesn't like Vegemite on toast?' I laugh as his lips find mine again.

We finally get dressed and say our goodbyes, and I turn to walk back inside,
thinking to myself,
Oh my god, best weekend ever! I'm sure I'm walking bow-legged!
Amber is waiting as I walk in the door.
'Well, well, you naughty little minx. I had to clean up all by myself.' She pouts
and crosses her arms.

'I'm sorry Amber, I was distracted.'
'I can just imagine what you mean by that.'
'Titanic.' I say, blushing.
We both laugh.

'So, my little Lizzy, are you two together?'
'Yes, we are.' I smile and nod.
Amber pretends to cry.
'My baby is growing up,' she says as she walks around the bench and hugs me.
I giggle at her performance.

'Anyway,' I say, 'I'm heading for a shower and then straight to bed.'
'No worries, I have a couple of reports to do and I'll check around the house and
then I'm crashing, too.'

After a long relaxing shower, I sit on my bed with my sleeping pills.
I take the lid off and think about taking them.
Setting them on my bedside table, I crawl into bed.

Mmm, my bed still smells like him.
I snuggle in remembering our night and day together, I still can't believe what happened.
Dominic wants me. I smile and snuggle in more as I fall asleep.

CHAPTER 4

Dreamcatcher

'Lizzy!' A voice calls out.
'Lizzy, wake up.' The same voice.
Who the hell is yelling? Am I dreaming?
'Come on, Lizzy, wake up!'
What the hell? I feel someone shake my shoulders.
I cop a slap that wakes me up.
'No, don't hurt me!' I call out as I sit up fast, coming face to face with Amber and Dominic sitting on my bed.
Fear starts to set in. I have to run again.
I reach back to the bedhead sliding my hand down, looking for my pouch.
'Lizzy, no.' Amber looks at me.

She knew instantly what I was thinking.
I pull the covers up looking at Amber and Dominic as I move, curling up and away from them both.
'What? What's going on? What's wrong?' I stammer, starting to shake.
'How many did you take?' Amber asks urgently.
'Huh? What are you talking about?' My voice breaks.
'Sleeping pills! How many did you take?' Amber asks, holding the bottle up.
I look at Dominic. I'm so confused.
'I didn't take any. Why?'

'Are you sure? Do I need to call an ambulance?' Amber grabs my arm.
'Ambulance? Amber, what the hell are you talking about?' I look at her, my whole body is shaking with cold fear.
'Liz, babe. Look at me.' Dominic's voice cracks.
His face looks concerned as he moves along the bed towards me.
I start to shake more and pull the covers up, cowering away from him.
'I didn't take anything! I thought about taking them but fell asleep before I did.'
I feel the tears start to fall.
'Please, Amber, I didn't,' I take heavy breaths. 'I promise you.'

My whole body shakes violently.
Amber and Dominic look at each other then back to me.

'Liz, do you have any idea what time it is?' Amber asks.
'No!' I shake my head, tears stinging my eyes.
'It's nine-fucking-am! You never sleep this late. You scared the hell out of me!'
'I'm sorry, Amber.'
'Oh hun, I'm sorry, don't apologise, you didn't do anything wrong.' Amber hugs
me hard.
She releases me and I rub my cheek.
'Right. Sorry about the slap. I'll ah, leave you with Dominic and he can kiss it
better.' Amber gets up and leaves the room quickly, closing the door behind her.
Dominic moves closer and he touches my hand.
I panic and pull further away from him.

'Sorry I, I, I need to use the bathroom,' I stammer, getting up.
'I'm not going anywhere,' he answers.
I don't even look at him as I practically run to the bathroom and close the door.
Oh crap, great, now he will think I'm some sort of can't-sleep-without-her-pills
type of person.
I grab the vanity with my hands, close my eyes, and try to focus on my breathing.
It's over before it even began, isn't it?
I mean it could be, I just, I mean, I, shit…I pulled away from him.
Will he be angry with me?
This isn't fair. I really like him…a lot.
I start pacing in the bathroom trying not to freak out.
Just breathe, I tell myself, in and out, in and out.
I manage to brush my teeth and my hair.

👀 DOMINIC 👀

I watch Liz pull away from me and panic.
I want to hold her and tell her it's ok.
Why would Amber think Liz would have taken an overdose?
Has she threatened to, or actually overdosed before?
I can't imagine her being pushed to the brink where she thought death was her
only option.
I feel like shit. My girl needs me to be better.
I sit on her bed waiting for her to come out.
Liz is amazing and I don't want to lose her.
I watch her as she emerges from her en-suite, looking pale and fragile.

I can't stand the way she looks right now, it breaks my heart.
I resist the urge to pull her into me, but instead wait for her to come to me.
I sit and wait for her to be ready to talk to me.

👀 ELIZABETH 👀

I emerge a few minutes later and sit down next to Dominic as I finish putting my hair up.
I look at the floor and fidget with the pillow I'd pulled onto my lap.
He's leaning forward with his elbows on his knees, resting his head on his hands.
'I'm sorry, Dominic, I didn't mean to pull away from you earlier. Please don't be angry with me. I honestly didn't take any sleeping pills.'
'Liz, you don't have to apologise, and I'm definitely not angry with you.'
He sits up and turns to me, his hand brings my face around to make me look at him.
'You're not angry with me? I don't understand,'
'Why would I be angry with you?' Dominic asks as he gently touches my hand.
'Because I pulled away from you. I'm so sorry. I promise I won't…'
'I should be apologising to you,' he says before I could finish.
'Why?' I ask, shocked.

By now Michael would have lost it.
If I wasn't up at five in the morning getting his breakfast and coffee ready for him by six, and his day bag packed for him to leave at seven, I would have been beaten.
Depending on his mood that would determine what I was beaten with.
But Dominic isn't even a little bit angry. I don't even know how to behave right now.
'I should have given you more credit.' He says softly and smiles at me.
'Do you still want me?' I ask him quietly, too scared to even look at him.
'Why would you ask me that?'
'Because I'm broken and I take pills to sleep, usually,' I whisper.

He leans in and I take a deep breath. He smells amazing.
He gently takes my chin in his hand and turns my face to look at him.
'You are not broken. I'm glad you didn't need them to sleep on Saturday night or last night,' he smiles at me.
I blush and smile back tentatively.
'And yes, I still want to be with you… Never a doubt about that,' he adds as he kisses me softly.

He then pulls me in and holds me, and we sit for a few minutes not saying a word.
I snuggle into his embrace more and I feel him kiss the top of my head.
He holds me tighter—I'm in my safe place… In his arms.
'Dominic.' I whisper.
'Yeah, babe?'
'Thank you.' I snuggle in more.
'You don't have to thank me, babe. I just want to help you, make sure you're safe, and be with you.'
He kisses the top of my head.

👀 DOMINIC 👀

I pull her in and hold her, I can feel her body rigid and trembling.
I don't care that she takes sleeping pills to help her sleep.
I know even though she hasn't told me herself that someone has hurt her.
I want to know more, but at the same time I don't.
Even imagining someone hurting her stabs me in the heart.
We sit, not saying anything, and I can slowly feel her body relax.
As I hold her I feel a huge pull to protect her, no matter the cost.
I feel this overwhelming need to help her heal, look forward, and live.

Her smile is infectious and there is nothing sexier.
Her beautiful green eyes shine even brighter.
Liz snuggles in more, and I tighten my hold and kiss the top of her head.
I need her with me, I need to show her what she means to me.
I need Liz to know that I will never betray or hurt her.

'Liz, I don't ever want you to think that suicide is your only option.
I'm here with you, I want to be with you.
If you need the sleeping pills take them,
I won't think any less of you. I promise I will do what I can to help you.' I hold her face up so I can see her eyes.
'If you get scared, or have a bad dream and I'm not with you, I want you to ring me. I don't care what time it is, or where I am. Promise me that you will call me.'
She nods slowly.
'Elizabeth?'
'I promise I will call you,' she says quietly.

I can tell she is still trying to process what I have told her.
Whatever this fucker did to her has her believing that care and affection is not something she is allowed to have.
The thing that hurts the most is that she will likely never fully escape it.
I kiss her softly and hold her tight.
It's hard to understand how I feel so much for her in such little time.

👀 ELIZABETH 👀

We emerge from my room to see Amber waiting in the kitchen.
'Are we all good?' She asks sheepishly.
'What kind of a silly question is that? You are my best friend, of course we are good,' I say as I walk up to her and hug her tightly.
'Good. I kind of went a little overboard; sorry about that.'
We laugh and break our embrace.
'Right, well I'm late for work so I really have to get going. Oh, before I forget, Dominic, there's a truck driver out the front waiting for you.'
'Will you be home tonight?' I ask her.
'I don't know.' She smiles and throws a wink at me.

Amber grabs her stuff and heads out, waving and blowing kisses.
Dominic walks up behind me wrapping his arms around me.
I feel him kiss my neck, I run my hands along his arms and turn my head.
His lips find mine and I sigh softly.
Dominic turns me around and pushes me against the bench.
He lifts me up onto it, his kiss more urgent.
I wrap my legs around him, holding him closer.

He reluctantly pulls away and looks at me, running his fingers along my cheek and down my neck.
My eyes drop as I smile, and I can feel myself blush.
'Please don't look away.'
I take a deep breath and lift my eyes back up to see him smiling.
'There's my girl.' He kisses me softly.
'I had better get to that truck.'
'Do you want a cuppa? I'll put the kettle on while you do your thing.'
'Sounds good. Mine has gone cold and I blame Amber for that,' he says as he walks out the door.
I slide off the bench and put the kettle on and ponder over my music choice; I select Cold Chisel. Humming to myself while making a late breakfast, I get lost in my own little world.

👀 DOMINIC 👀

Coming back upstairs after the truck left, I hear the music.
I stand at the door watching her singing to herself.
I find myself completely mesmerised by her.
I watch as she moves to the music.
I look down at the floor and smile as I look back up at her.
I realise it's going to be hard to get work done with her around.
I walk up behind her, put my hands on her waist, and slide them down to her hips.

I take a deep breath, my god she smells good, and she feels fantastic in my hands. I pull her into me, wrap my arms around her, hold her tight, and kiss her shoulder.
I hate how her clothes ruin the view. Unless it's that red set she was wearing the day I met her, I smile to myself.
'I made you a fresh coffee. Would you like something to eat?' She asks.
'No, just coffee for now.'
She turns around in my arms, looks up at me and smiles, her eyes shine.
'So, what are your plans for today?' Liz asks me.

I kiss her and pull her in hard against me; her hands are on my waist sending shockwaves through me. Her lips are soft, and she fits perfectly in my hands, I can't let her go.
She moans softly as I reluctantly break off our kiss. I step back and look at her.
'Well I can tick that off my to-do list, for a start.' I say as my phone rings.
I kiss her forehead, grab my coffee, and head outside to answer my phone.

👀 ELIZABETH 👀

The next couple weeks go by in a flurry of deliveries and studying.
January turns to February and I'm feeling good.
Valentine's Day; I have never had a Valentine so I make him all of his favourites and put on his surprise under my red silk robe.
I look at the time.
He is running late. Dominic's never late.
I better send him a message, but I don't want to sound like I'm nagging or being a controlling girlfriend.

Hey, just checking that everything is okay.

So sorry, got held up with a few problems. I'll call you as soon as I'm done.

No worries.

I sigh and put everything away, but I don't get changed.
Grabbing the laptop and sitting on the couch, I transfer more money over to Dominic's account, then I continue studying.
My phone beeps with a message from Amber.

Hope you're having fun, I am! Wink Wink. xoxoxo

I smile at her message.
Amber and Cassie seem to be going well and she spends a fair amount of time with her.
I'm so happy for her, every now and then I get a message from her pleading for one of her favourites, and I'm happy to oblige.
I drift off to sleep reading about cardiothoracic surgery procedures.

👀 DOMINIC 👀

I pull up to Liz's house and quietly walk up to the glass sliding door.
I can hear soft music playing.
I feel bad for not buying her something, I completely forgot.
I walk in and find her asleep on the couch with one of her textbooks on her chest.
She is absolutely stunning.
I stand there and watch her sleep.
She moves, knocking the book off her chest and it lands on the rug.
I kneel down beside her and gently run my fingers along her cheek.
'Liz,'
'Mmmm.' She moans softly as she stretches.

'Liz,'
'Hey you,' she says softly as she opens her beautiful green eyes and smiles.
'There's my girl.'
She pulls me in and kisses me softly.
I wrap my arms around her pulling her up into me and holding her tight.
'Sorry I missed spending the day with you.'
'You're here now.' She says softly.

'I had to help a friend, and it went longer than I wanted.'
'Dominic, it's okay, you were needed by a friend. It's just a day.'
'Yes, but I wanted to spend it with you.'
Liz reaches up, touches my face, and smiles.
I bring my lips back to hers, I can feel her smile.

'What?'
'Are you hungry?' She asks me.
'Define hungry.'
'I made your favourites.'
'Mmm, sounds tempting, but I don't think I want food unless it's dessert.' I slide my hand up her thigh.
I watch her body react to my touch as I slowly move my hand further up.
She moans softly and pulls me to her, she feels amazing.
I stop when my hand touches what feels like lace, I look at her in surprise and smile.
Liz starts to untie her robe. I can see her hands shaking.
I take her hands and lean in and kiss her, my fingers moving along her neck and pulling down the material.
Her breathing quickens.
I look over her body, Liz is wearing a red lace strapless corset and g-string.
Fuck me, she looks incredible.
'Definitely dessert in bed,' I say, picking her up and taking her to bed.

I wake and see day breaking, Liz is still asleep.
Laying there watching her sleep, I feel bad about yesterday.
I want to tell her the truth.
Will she understand and accept it?
I run my fingers along her back following the scar.
Liz stirs and I lean in and start kissing her shoulder.
'Morning,' Liz says, smiling.
'Morning.'

I pull her into me and kiss her softly, I feel her hands pull me in close.
The warmth of her touch spreads through me and my body tenses.
I run my hand along her bare skin up to her neck and along her cheek.
'How about you and I spend the day at the beach?' I ask her.
'Sounds perfect.' She smiles.
'Good, 'cause I don't want to share you with anyone today,' I grin.
Liz giggles and turns in my arms and starts getting out of bed.
'Yeah, no you don't.' I say, grabbing her and pulling her back.
'Dominic!' Liz laughs.

We eventually made our way to the beach. Dominic is happy and we have the beach to ourselves.

'Dominic, your phone is ringing again.'

'Ignore it.'

'Shouldn't you at least check it? It might be an emergency.'

'No, I know who it is, besides, I'm busy with you.'

Dominic pulls me into him and kisses me as his phone starts ringing again.

'Fuck me!' Dominic exclaims angrily.

He gets up and answers his phone.

'What?'

He sounds angry at whoever is calling.

'No!'

I can hear him talking even though he has moved away.

'Stop calling, Louise, I'm with Liz,' he says, pacing.

'No, Louise, we have had this discussion and after yesterday it's definitely not happening again. I'm with Elizabeth and that's final. I'm right where I want to be. Goodbye, Louise.'

Yesterday is not happening again? What does he mean by that?

I get up and wrap myself in my towel, not sure what to make of it.

'Liz, what's wrong?'

He reaches for me, but I step back not looking at him.

'Can I ask you something?'

'Liz, babe, talk to me, you're shaking.' He sounds concerned, moving towards me.

I move backwards away from him again with my hand out in front, trying to stop him from moving closer.

I feel his Ute behind me and I can't go any further.

'I need you to be honest with me.' I can't even bring myself to look at him.

'Of course,' he answers without hesitation.

'The phone calls today. Are you and Louise sleeping with each other? Is that where you were yesterday? If you want to be with her I won't interfere,' I say, my whole body trembling.

'Liz, babe, no, I'm not sleeping with Louise and I don't want to be with her. I was helping her move yesterday and my ex turned up. It wasn't pretty.'

'I'm so sorry, I shouldn't have questioned you.' I still can't bring myself to look at him.

I feel so ashamed. The tears start to fall.

'Are… Are you angry with me?'

Dominic pulls me in and holds me tight.
'No babe, I'm not angry with you. I understand why you asked.'
His hands bring my face up so our eyes meet.
His thumbs wipe my tears away and he smiles at me.
'I could never be angry with you.'
He leans in and kisses me softly.
I feel my body relax.
'Now we need to do something about this towel.'
I blush and look away.
I take a deep breath and let my towel fall away.

Dominic's hands move around to the small of my back.
'You are absolutely gorgeous.'
I look up and smile. His hands move up to my face and his lips claim mine.
His kiss is hungry.
I bring my hands up to his sides and I feel his reaction instantly.
His hands move to my sides, pulling me in to him.
I moan softly and dig my fingers into his sides; this only fuels his urge.
He moves me and pins me against his car.

He slides his hands over my body and down to my butt.
He squeezes and groans as he breaks off our kiss.
'These next few weeks away from you are going to be torture!' He groans.
'But I need to get this other job complete now that everything has finally arrived.'
'Well, I'm not going anywhere, if you're hungry for dessert…' I giggle coyly.
We spend the rest of the day enjoying the sun and being completely alone with each other.
Dominic goes for a swim and I drift off to sleep as I watch him.

👀 DOMINIC 👀

I walk back up to where Liz is sitting and notice she is asleep.
I sit next to her and watch her sleep.
Her hands are clenched, she is dreaming of something bad.
I wrap my hands over hers and I feel her relax.
I need to tell her what happened between Louise and I.
'Hey you, what are you in deep thought about?' Liz asks sleepily.
'I need to talk to you about yesterday.'
'Okay.' Liz sits up and grabs her towel.
She is building her walls again, her hands trembling.
I take her hands in mine.

'Please trust me?' I ask her.
Liz nods her head but won't look at me and I can still feel small trembles.

'I was helping Louise move and didn't even think of what the day was. It wasn't till Louise gave me a gift that it dawned on me what day it was. My first thought was that I need to get to you. She then proceeded to undress. I declined her advances, as well as her gift, and wrapped her in a blanket. I told her I'm with you and I couldn't be with her, but she didn't take it well. I felt bad, but I was honest with her. We have known each other for a long time, and I won't lie—we are close, but I want to be with you, Elizabeth.'
I touch her cheeks and my fingers tilt her face up so I can see her eyes.
Liz is trying so hard to hold it together.

'Louise started yelling and crying and I waited for her to calm down. I was worried about her and at some stage she must have sent a message. My ex, Stephanie, who is her best friend, turns up and starts accusing me of leading her on, and playing the field. I can take whatever she calls me, but I drew the line when she mentioned you.'
I take a deep breath.

'I don't want anyone else except for you. I just want to be with you.'
I look at her trying to read her expression.
I couldn't bring myself to tell her that I slept with Louise the weekend before I met her.
Even though I told Louise after that I couldn't be with her, and she agreed that it wouldn't work, I still feel like I have done something wrong.
'Thank you for telling me, Dominic.'
Liz brings her hands to my face and smiles.
I can feel her body start to relax.
'I am sorry for doubting you, it's just...'
'Liz, it's okay.' I say as I run my fingers through her hair.

'Dominic, I wasn't broken into. My ex... My ex... He hurt me very badly and I struggle with it.'
'I promise you, Elizabeth, I will never do anything to make you feel scared or unsafe. I also promise you that he will never hurt you again.'
'Dominic,' Liz's hand runs along the scars on her arm. 'He is a bad man, a monster.' Her hand covers the scar on her wrist and her whole body trembles.
She is not ready.
'Liz, I know you're not ready to talk about it. But when you are, I'll be here for you.' I pull her in and hold her.
'Thank you, Dominic.' She snuggles in closer.

I can tell she feels relieved, as I sit there holding her.
Liz wants to talk, but her hand covers her wrist every time.
I figure she either doesn't know how to tell me or feels ashamed.
Maybe she is scared that I will turn away from her.

🔯 ELIZABETH 🔯

The weeks drag on.
I don't get to see Dominic much, but when I do see him, I feel like a kid at Christmas.
It's finally Friday and Dominic is working here, and as promised I make him lunch.
Late afternoon, I duck into the shops to grab some stuff for dinner.
On the way back home I stop at the Moore Park Beach Tavern's bottle shop for drinks, and I run into Luke and Simon stocking up for the weekend.
'I need some help,' I say.
'Well, we are here to offer assistance,' Luke says gallantly.
'Dominic's favourites: beer, spirits and or wine?' I ask them.
'He likes Millers Chill, Corona with lemon, and he drinks Canadian Club with Dry.' Simon replies.
'Awesome!' I nod.
l grab a cold six-pack of each.
Luke and Simon get the cartons and I grab the rest and they help me take the alcohol to the car.

'So, we are having another beach gathering in a few weeks. Do you need a bigger cooler? Wink, wink.' Simon pleads with a smile.
'You get me the bigger cooler and I will happily fill it,' I smile at them.
'Sweet! I'll send Dominic a message and let him know the day,' Luke says as he closes the boot of my car.

'I don't suppose we could hire your cooking services to help us with a surprise party for Louise?' Simon asks me. 'It's still a while away but she has family interstate and overseas.'
'Sure, I would love to, would you like me to cater the food and cake?'
'Hell, yeah!' Luke smiles at me.
'I tell you what, I will look after the food if you handle the drinks, venue, and decorations etc' I say.
'Really?' Simon asks.
'Yep, I enjoy cooking.'
'Perfect!' Luke smiles.

'Just give me plenty of time to organise food and cake.'
'We should catch up at yours to plan,' Simon suggests.
'Okay, I'll give you my number.' I hand Simon my phone and he rings both their phones.

'My shifts are crazy over the next few months. I will call or message you.'
'Well, I'm studying from home, so I'm pretty much free most of the time.'
'What are you studying?' Luke asks me.
'Critical care paramedics.'
We say our goodbyes and I head home.
I smile to myself.
This is the first time I have been so close to two men and not felt uneasy.
I only hope that Dominic will be okay with it.

It is almost 6pm by the time I get home.
I put the cold drinks in the fridge.
I hear the shower turn on and I head down to get the last of the groceries out of the car.
I turn the BBQ on to heat up, light the citronella lanterns and head back inside.
I go old-school with my music: The Chords, Sh-Boom.
I head back into the kitchen and get the meat ready.
I turn around to head back out to the BBQ and see him standing there and my mind goes blank.
Oh jeez, only a towel… Don't drop the plate.
Oh my god, he looks so incredibly handsome.
Don't drop the plate.
Remember to breathe, and don't drop the plate.

'Fri…beer?' I stutter, biting my lip.
'Say again?' He looks at me with a smile.
'Fridge is in the beer. I mean towel wants a beer.' Oh crap. I'm so red.
He starts laughing.

'Would you like a beer? They are in the fridge.' Phew, finally got a sentence together.
'Flustered?' He says, raising an eyebrow.
'Yes, I mean, no.' I bite my bottom lip.
Breathe and don't drop the plate, I remind myself.
'Hmm, cold beer and what looks like a T-bone?' He says approvingly, moving towards me.
'What are you planning?' He looks at me with a predatory look in his eyes.
I back into the bench.

I'm trapped and I'm still holding the plate and looking him up and down.
Just a towel, I keep telling myself.
He closes the gap until all that is between us is the plate.
He leans in and my breathing quickens.
My god, he smells good.
I close my eyes as his lips brush my ear, I shudder at the feeling.
I grip the plate tighter.

'I'll take this,' he says softly, grabbing the plate as he backs away and heads out to the BBQ, laughing.
'Well, that's just mean!' I scoff, standing there trying to compose myself.
'Hey, I told you not to bite your bottom lip and look at me like that,' he calls back.
'I hate you right now!' I say, more flustered than annoyed.
He laughs.
'No, you don't!'

He's right, I hate that stupid towel!
He puts the meat on the BBQ and heads back inside to get dressed.
While he cooks the meat, I finish the salad and gravy.
I put on some music Russell Morris and Johnny Diesel strong Australian blues rock mix.I walk out with the tray of plates, cutlery, and food. I'm setting the table when Dominic walks up behind me, wrapping his arms around me.
He holds me tight and rests his head on my shoulder, his lips brushing my neck.
'Mmm, hey you.'
'There's my girl.'
I turn in his arms and wrap mine around his neck.
We move together to the music, lost in our own perfect little piece of paradise.
He brings his hands up to my face and kisses me softly.
His hands move to my waist and gently squeeze.
Thank god he is holding me against him, because my knees go completely jelly.

'So, I'm thinking, Easter is coming up and there's a long weekend. How about you and I go camping?'
'Yes, please. I loved camping when I was a kid,' I respond eagerly before he finishes.
'Where would you like to go?' He asks, smiling.
'I have always wanted to go to Fraser Island.'
'Done. Fraser Island it is,' he smiles.

We sit down to eat, and I tell him about my chat with Luke and Simon about Louise's surprise birthday party, and how I'm supplying the food and cake.

'Engaging my girlfriend to cater for Louise's birthday?' Dominic smirks.
'What?' I ask him.
'Luke and Simon have been trying to get with her for a while.'
'I thought they liked Sarah and Sally,' I say.
'Yeah they do, I guess they have given up on Louise.'
'I don't think she likes me very much.'
'How did you come to that conclusion?' He looks at me.
'She pretty much ignored me that day at the beach when you said that I came with you. The only time she did speak to me was to tell me…' I look down. 'To tell me that you, um…' I'm too embarrassed to look at him.

'Hey, look at me, I don't want anyone but you.' He kneels down at my side.
'I trust you, Dominic.' I say, looking at him.
'I don't think for a second you would do anything to hurt the person you are with.'
'And I'm with you,' he says as his fingers lightly brush my cheek.
I lean in and kiss him.
I do trust him, it's Louise I don't trust.
My circle of trust is small, Amber and Dominic are the only two people that are close to me.
I want to be able to trust more, but it's hard when I don't really trust myself.
I do not want to disappoint Amber and Dominic.
We clean up after dinner and his phone beeps.

'Simon is organising another beach day. Apparently, I'm only allowed to come if you come with me and bring a full cooler,' Dominic announces as he walks up to me and pulls me in.
'Well, give me a list and a cooler and I will happily fill it,' I respond as he kisses me softly.

 I go and have a shower while he is on the phone.
He is still on the phone when I get out, so I leave him to it and hop into bed and read until he joins me.
'What are you reading?' He asks as he snuggles in.
'A book,' I reply with a smirk.
'Smart arse.'
I giggle and take a deep breath as his hand moves over my body.
'What's it called?' He kisses my neck.
'Scarecrow, by Matthew Reilly.' I close my eyes and my book, enjoying his touch.

He starts kissing along my shoulder and up to my collarbone, then he pulls me against him, his erection clearly visible. I put my book down and enjoy his kisses.

They travel up my neck to my ear as he slides his hand under my shirt and cups my breast.

'I do not like this shirt.'

I shudder under his touch.

'What's wrong with my shirt?' I ask, breathlessly.

'You're still wearing it,' he growls as he gently bites my earlobe.

I roll over to face him. He slides his hand down and removes my underwear, and runs his hand back up as my breathing gets quicker.

His hand reaches my waist and he pulls me on top of him.

I moan as he enters me.

He sits up as I take my shirt off and takes my breast in his mouth.

My body reacts to his touch and I moan in ecstasy.

His hands glide down to my arse and grab it, pulling me in harder against him.

I wrap my arms around his neck and run my hands through his hair as he kisses me hard, full of hunger and passion.

🦉 DOMINIC 🦉

I have her all to myself and she feels so fucking good.

Sliding my hand slowly from her arse up her back, I hold her to me.

I remove the hair tie and let her hair fall down her back.

Grabbing a handful, I pull her head back, breaking off our kiss and exposing her neck to my mouth. Her body reacts to my touch and I can feel the goosebumps on her skin.

She moans my name.

I trail kisses and bites down her neck, her arms around mine and her fingers in my hair.

Her breathing quickens as she moves against me, my hand is on her butt, pushing her harder against me as I push deeper inside her.

She runs her fingers along my back and shoulders.

I can feel her getting close to climax as she tightens around my cock and calls out my name.

My hand slides back down to her waist.

I trail kisses back up from her breast to her neck before claiming her lips again as our bodies move as one.

I gently take her arms and hold them behind her with one hand as I hold her breast with the other, teasing her nipple.

'Dominic!' She calls out as she climaxes.

I hold her tight against me, pulling her harder against me as I place little bites along her neck.

In one movement I have her under me.

Pushing deep inside of her as she arches her back, I trail bites along the side of her breast and kisses over her nipple.

Her whole body reacts, and she moans my name.

I have one hand beside her and the other on the bedhead.

I start to go harder as her legs wrap around me pushing me deeper.

Her hands move down my chest to my waist where I feel her nails dig in lightly, driving me wild.

I feel myself letting go, I want to, but can I with her?

I don't want to hurt her.

'Please, Dominic, don't stop.'

'Liz, babe,' as I say her name, she begins to orgasm again.

But I'm not done making her scream yet.

I pull out and pull her up hard against me, looking into her eyes.

I need her to let me, I need her permission.

Liz brings her hands to my face, we are both breathing hard.

'Liz, I want to so badly, but I don't want to hurt you.'

Liz smiles and nods, she trusts me.

I feel her hands move over my body, I tilt my head back, enjoying her touch.

'Dominic,'

I bring my eyes back to hers.

'I want you, I want all of you, Dominic.'

'You are amazing, Liz.'

I pull her in and kiss her fiercely, holding her against me.

I dig my fingers into her sides and she moans softly, her body shuddering.

Her hands move to my sides and around to my lower back, and my body responds to her immediately.

I hold her tighter and kiss her harder, she does nothing to stop me.

Turning her around, with her body still against mine, my hands travel from her breasts down to her waist, where I bend her over to grab the bedhead.

I trail kisses over her butt cheeks and begin to finger her.

She moans and throws her head back.

My thumb teases her rim and my other fingers rub her clit.

I can feel her body start to shudder.

'Dominiiic!' She calls as she climaxes.

Fuck, I love hearing her call my name during sex.

As much as I want to try anal sex with her, I don't think she is ready for it.

Kneeling behind her, I slide my cock into her.

Fuck, she is so wet.
With one hand on her waist, the other takes a handful of her hair.
'Liz…' I moan.

I start to fuck her as hard as I dare and she calls out my name, urging me to go harder.
With both hands on her waist, I push in as deep I can and she moans louder and louder.
Fuck she feels good, smells good, tastes good, and sounds good.
I throw my head back and groan.
I know I'm not far from coming, I won't be able to hold back much more and she knows it.
I grip her waist tighter, groan loudly, and start going faster and harder.

'Dominic, don't stop!' She cries.
'Dominic!' She screams as she begins to climax.
Hearing her scream my name, I feel myself start to orgasm.
I push hard against her.
'Fuck, Liz!' I call out as I orgasm.
I keep both hands on her waist as I move in and out of her.
I lean in as I finish and kiss her back, running my hands along her sides, bringing a gasp from her lips.
She lets a little moan escape her when I pull out.

I stay behind her, running my hands from the top of her back down to her butt.
I feel the goosebumps on her skin.
I notice more scars, and I feel a white-hot surge of anger at the person who caused her so much pain and suffering.
The one that runs almost the entire length of her back is so hard to look at without getting angry.
I struggle to think what they were made with, a whip?
I pull her up to me and hold her against me.
'Liz, I…'
'I wanted you to, Dominic, I wanted it with you.'
'I didn't…'
'No, you didn't,' she answers before I can finish.

She is breathing hard.
She wraps one of her arms around my neck and moves her head to the side, exposing her neck.

I run my hands down her sides, to her hips, and back up to cup her breasts, pinching her nipples sharply. The sensation makes her gasp again, and I feel my arousal pressing against her.

I move one hand up to her chin, turning her face to mine.
I lick her lips as she parts them and her tongue meets mine.
I hold her face as I kiss her while my other hand slides down to her clitoris.
She moans and moves seductively against me.
She feels my erection, moves and bends back down, giving my cock access.
I slide back into her and start fucking her again, hard and fast.
She calls out for more, begging me to go harder.
I grab her hips and push deep.
'Liz,' I moan, rolling my head back.
This woman is my drug and I'm addicted.

🔱 ELIZABETH 🔱

He's behind me. I feel him deep inside me, his fingers digging into my waist.
I tell him I want it hard. I want it fast. I want him.
I throw my head back and grab the bedhead.
'Dominic.'
I grab his hand, pulling him down to me.
He takes my hands, pulling my arms behind me, and pushes my head into the pillow as he moans and goes harder and deeper.
My body is responding to him and I'm left wanting more, wanting it harder.
I feel myself getting close to coming, and Dominic can feel it too.
'Dominic!' I call out his name.
My body shudders as I orgasm.

He pulls out and spins me around, grabbing the back of my head, pulling me up as his lips devour mine. He moves against me, pushing me back up against the headboard.
He grabs my leg, wrapping it around his waist as he starts to fuck me.
He looks into my eyes, watching me, watching as I bite my bottom lip.
I gasp as he pushes against me and his tongue plunges into my mouth, his kiss as primal as the sex we are having.
'Fuck me, Dominic,' I say, breathing hard.
I'm giving him permission, I want it, I want him.
He kisses me passionately again.
I moan into the kiss as he lays me down.
He enters me as his tongue explores my mouth.

Dominic grabs my arse hard, but I can feel him holding back.
'Dominic, yes, Dominic.'
His body tenses as my fingers run up and down his back.
'Fuck, Liz,'
'Yes, Dominic!'
'I… You are… Fuck, Liz!' Dominic rasps, breathlessly.
I pull him in and kiss him as hard I can, his arms wrapping around me.
He pulls me up as he continues to thrust deep.
Then he lets me go as he grabs the bedhead with both hands.
I wrap my legs around him tighter.
Dominic thrusts hard and deep, his body tense.
He groans as I run my hands over his body, down to my own and grab my breasts.
He watches hungrily as I play with my breasts and pinch my nipples.
He continues to fuck me and watch my hands moving over my body.
I lick my lips and bite my bottom lip. I feel the effect it has on him, feel myself shudder.

Dominic stays on his knees and he runs his hands from my knees along my thighs, up to my breasts, and holds them.
'Mmm, Dominic.'
I feel one of his hands slide down and he begins to thumb my clitoris as he fucks me.
Arching my back I call out his name, which makes him go harder, pushing deeper into me.
I can feel myself getting close to climaxing.
'Dominic!' I call out his name as I start to orgasm.
He throws his head back as he orgasms loudly, his whole body convulsing with mine.
His hands grip my sides, hard.
'Liz!' He calls my name, breathlessly.
He moves beside me, breathing heavily, and pulls me into him, leaning down and kissing me hard.
His kiss leaves me breathless.
He looks down at me and smiles.

'Are you okay?' He asks after a while.
'I'm more than okay, that was amazing.'
His hand runs down from my shoulder, following the scar over my breast and down my stomach.
I break out in goosebumps as his fingers trace the scars.
It almost feels like he is trying to erase them.

I look up at him. I think I'm falling in love with him.
Whatever it is, I'm going to enjoy the here-and-now, I think to myself as my hand runs up his chest to his face. I look into his eyes. Is he caught up in the moment too?

'What are you thinking about?' He asks.
'I'm happy, and I haven't been this happy for so long, it kind of scares me,' I answer.
'Scares you?' He asks, concerned.
'I have never had this before.'
'Had what?' His fingers brush my cheek and go down to my neck.
'A relationship that wasn't…'
'Liz, I promise that I will never hurt you.'
'I just don't want my past to scare you away, because I really want to see where our relationship will go.'
He smiles and runs his hand along the side of my face.
'I can't say if we will be together forever, but right now I want you and only you. I don't want to be where you're not. I want to see where this goes as well,' he says, kissing me gently.

'Dominic,'
'Yes,' he murmurs.
'When I tell you everything, and I will tell you, I just need you to listen. After that I will accept your decision if you want to leave me.' I look at him, trying to gauge his reaction.
'I promise that when you are ready to tell me, I will listen and support you as best I can,' he says, gently, as his hand rests on my neck and his thumb traces my jawline.
'I will be by your side.' He kisses my lips, then my forehead.
I close my eyes and breathe in his scent.
He pulls me in and holds me tight as his free hand runs through my hair.
I take a deep breath as I sink further into his embrace and fall asleep.

I wake up cold and alone, something is wrong.
Something is very wrong.
I hear a voice that doesn't belong here.
I don't even think, I just run!
I'm running, my chest hurts. I'm running out of breath, but I can't stop.
It doesn't matter, all I know is that I can't stop.
I have to keep running.
I burst out of the tree line and I fall hard onto the sand.
I feel someone grab me by the hair and pull me up.

I scream in pain as I try to get free, calling for help.

I get spun around and I'm face to face with HIM.

Michael has found me! I stop fighting, there is no use.

He is bigger, stronger, and faster.

Whatever I do to him he will just do to me ten-fold.

His black eyes are filled with disgust and anger; he stands over me and I notice his hair is dishevelled and that he hasn't shaven for a while.

This is totally unlike Michael, he always looks immaculately clean and well-dressed, even when he has a five o'clock shadow.

He growls as he yanks me in closer, he is not in control of himself right now.

This is bad, very bad.

He half-drags me by the hair and half-pulls me all the way back to my house, and pushes me up the stairs by my head.

I get to the top and see Amber's lifeless body on the deck.

She has been shot multiple times, judging by the two big guys standing on the deck behind her, she went out fighting.

I want to cry but that will only enrage him more and he hasn't given me permission to cry.

We get to the door and he throws me across the floor.

I skid along it into the bench, splitting my eyebrow.

I start to get up and he kicks me hard in the stomach.

I roll into the cupboards as he comes up and kicks me again.

'Get up you bitch!' He yells.

'Yes, master,' I cower.

I stand up, only to be backhanded and knocked down again, busting my lip.

I crawl across the floor as he walks up beside me and kicks me, hard, into the bench, then kicks me again and again.

Struggling for a breath, I hold my hand out and look up at him as his fists rain down on my face.

I taste the blood in my mouth, and spit it out onto the floor.

Michael kicks me again and my hands slide in the blood on the floor.

I can hear him removing his belt.

'My, my, that arse, Chantelle.'

I cringe at his words.

'The things I'm going to do to you.. I have missed my plaything, my beast-tamer.'

His words are full of venom and malicious purpose.

'I'm going to make you bleed, make you scream. I'm going to break you all over again.' His tone is demonic.

He hits me with his leather belt across my shoulders.
I get up and turn around as he walks up to me, grabbing my hair.
He punches me so hard that I vomit, for which I get hit again and shoved back down to the ground.
'Clean that up, you stupid fucking bitch!' He yells at me.
'Yes, Michael.'
'Yes, what?' He hisses, grabbing my hair and ripping my head back with so much force that I feel the hair tearing from my scalp.
'Yes, master.' I stammer.
'That's better. Do not forget who you are fucking talking to.'

Michael pushes me back down.
I hear footsteps entering the kitchen.
'Hey, Michael,' I recognise the familiar voice of one of Michael's right-hand men, Brian.
Brian enjoys the hunt just as much as the kill.
A monster, but nowhere near the calibre of Michael.
'Did you find him?' Michael asks.
'Yes, we are bringing him in now, he put up a fight.' The equally familiar voice of Sam, Michael's other right-hand man.
His forte is the business of human trafficking, and whatever else Michael asks for, Sam finds it.
I hear something being dragged along the floor.
I look up and see Dominic, out cold. No, please, no! I think to myself.
I need to do something, I need to save Dominic.
I begin to crawl further across the floor, trying to get away and get to one of my bats.

'Take him to the bedroom and tie him to the chair. And wake him up, I want him to watch.'
'No worries, Michael.' Brian nods and drags Dominic to the bedroom with the help of Sam.
I move away from Michael, trying to get to my kit and my bat.
'Where do you think you are going? We have a movie to make.'
I don't answer him, I keep moving.
Michael comes up beside me and kneels down, he grabs a handful of my hair, forcing me to my knees and making me look at him.
'I asked you a question. Where are you going?'
'I thought you wanted to play harder, master.'
'Play harder?'
'We have been apart for so long. I thought you would like me to be harder to get.'

'Harder?' He questions.
I close my eyes and take a deep breath, before opening them and looking at him.
My fingers touch his face and I smile, licking my lips.
He watches my mouth.
'Fuck you!' I shout, slapping him.

Michael rips me up by my throat, pulling me up to his height and slamming me
against the wall.
Leaning in, he runs his tongue along my cheek.
He groans deeply before bringing his eyes back to mine and releasing me, resting
his hands on the wall on either side of me.
'What are you doing, Chantelle?' He asks me, looking over me with a demonic
look in his eyes.
'What took you so long finding me? I have been waiting for you.' I yell, pushing
him away.
'I was behind fucking bars,'
'But you're Michael Webster. You're un-fucking-touchable.' I spit, cutting him
off and hitting his chest with my fists.
He looks at me, stunned.
I have never spoken to him like this, or fought back before.

'They took me away and told me horrible things, and I waited for you. I told
them that you love me and that you will save me. But you didn't, you left me, you
fucking left me! You left me alone at the whim of those…' I cry as he watches
me, curiously, 'They waterboarded me to get to you. It's all your fault!' I push
him again.
Michael's hand moves to my throat as his other hand grips my side, squeezing
hard.
'I was…' He starts to say.
I slap him as hard as I can.
'Stop!' I yell, 'Don't lie to me. You're Michael fucking Webster.'
'Mmm, say my name again.' He purrs as he leans in and tightens his grip on my
throat.
'Michael Webster.'
I grab his collar and pull him in, kissing him hard and trying not to throw up.
I run my hands over his body looking for his knife.

'I want you to take me, Michael. I love you, I need you. I can't live without you.'
I say as I rip open his button-down business shirt.
He looks at me and smiles before crushing his lips back onto mine.
I push his shirt off his shoulders, and he grabs my arse, hard.
I dig my nails in and drag them down his back.

I need him off guard, that's the only way to save Dominic.

He doesn't have a knife, shit, he always has a knife! I move my hands to his waist.
I start to undo his pants when his hands grab mine.
'Stop.' He groans.
'No! I want what is mine,' I hiss against his ear as I bite down on his earlobe.
'Chantelle,' he moans, 'Wait.' He pulls away.
'Why? You need me as much as I need you. I want it now!'
'I have a surprise for you.'
'Keep it, I don't want it.'
Michael steps back and backhands me again.
He wraps his belt around my neck like a dog collar, pulling it tight.
Then he drags me by the belt to my room, lifts me and throws me on to the bed.
He's ready to play, but I'm going to play harder.
He pushes my head down as he tears away my shirt.

Michael rolls me onto my back, raking his nails over my breasts, and becomes enraged.
He slaps me across the face and grabs me by my throat, lifting me off the bed.
My feet just barely touch the ground and I try to grab at him.
'Is that the best you've got? You're slipping, Michael.' I gasp, smiling through my blood as his grip tightens.

I can hear mumbles and movement behind me.
I think they punched Dominic.
'What the fuck have you done, you ungrateful slut!' Michael yells in my face.
'Did he make you do it?' He yells, pointing at Dominic.
I can hear mumbling behind me.
'No, master, they removed them in the hospital.' I answer him.
'Why?' His grip tightens.
'The implants ruptured,' I reply, feeling light-headed.
'Fuck!' He screams as he throws me to the ground and kicks me forcefully.
I take in deep breaths as I spit blood on the floor.

'Chantelle,'
'Yes, master,' I say in between breaths.
Michael stands in front of me.
'Stand up and look at me.'
'Yes, master,' I say as I stand and look up to him.
'Are you crying?'
'No, master,' I reply.

'Good girl.'
'Thank you, master.'
'Face the door.'
'Yes, master,' I comply, meekly.

He walks up behind me, lifting my hands above my head.
I instantly know what's coming, and brace myself.
He runs his hands over my breasts and buries his face in the back of my neck, taking a deep breath.
He groans and steps back.

'It's been a long time and I have had trouble containing my rage without you, Chantelle, to tame the beast in me.' He sneers, his voice laced with venom.
I hear his bag open. I need to get to the bag.
His knife must be in the bag.
I can smell leather, he has bought his whips.

They are forcing Dominic to watch.
I tell myself not to cry, not to scream.
I know this game.
'Did you let this man touch you?'
'Yes.'
He hits me with the leather flogger.
'Did he fuck you?'
'No, I fucked him.'
He hits me again.
'Did you tell him who you belong to?'
'No, I lied to him.'
He hits me again.
'Why did you fuck him?'
'I needed it, but only you do me right. I love you, Michael.'

He hits me again and I feel my back start to bleed, but I never drop my arms.
I can hear mumbling and movement behind me again.
Michael stands in front of me, smiling.
'You are lying, Chantelle,' he hisses, grabbing my face.
'No, no, I'm not. The police— they made me do it. I wanted to go back, I did.'
The words tumble out as I look him in the eyes.
He rams the handle of the leather flogger into my stomach, making me fall to the ground.
He walks up beside me and kicks me hard into the bedside table.
I'm gasping for air.

He smiles and touches my face.
Ripping me up by my hair, he makes me stand.
I'm unsteady on my feet.

'You are out of practice, Michael. Are you tired already?' I challenge him.
'No, are you?' He asks, moving closer, only to have me backhand him, busting his lip.
Not yet, I smile to myself.
'What are you smiling for?' He asks.
'After all the time apart I'm finally standing in front of you, and it appears you haven't missed me at all. Who were you fucking? You know who I was fucking.'
'Chantelle,'
I push him out of my room, back into the kitchen.
'You disappoint me, Michael.'

He looks at me and I see the snap.
He loses control and doesn't focus, that's why he needs me.
He looks down, trying to regain his focus, his breathing hard and fast.
I see his fists clench.
I wipe my face with my hands and walk up to him, wiping my blood on his chest.
'I'm bleeding for you, what are you doing for me?'
I bring his face to mine.
'Master,' I spit, spitefully.
I kiss him hard, grabbing fistfuls of his hair, pulling hard.
He responds by pulling me in tight before abruptly pulling away and smiling.

His smile is pure villainy.
I have seen this smile once before.
I had to watch him kill a man for touching me without his permission.
Michael was covered in the man's blood as he claimed me on the floor next to the dead body.
Michael grabs my throat and shoves me back to my room.
 I feel the sting of a needle.
'You fucking coward!' I look at him, shocked.
He has never used drugs on me, this was unexpected.
My plan is failing.
'You fucking coward.' My voice sounds groggy.

Michael turns away before swinging back and punching me in the face, making me spin around and land on my bed.
I start to feel dizzy, like I'm about to black out, but I need to focus.

Dominic's life depends on me.
My whole body is screaming in pain.
Michael grabs my hair, forcing my head up.
I see Dominic bound to the chair with tape across his mouth.
He has a cut above his eye and dried blood on his knuckles and in his hair.
Dominic looks directly at me, his eyes wide with fear and anger.
I mouth the words: I love you, I'm so sorry.

I now know what's coming, the reason for the drugs.
He is planning on taking his time and this will go on for days.
But I won't let Michael hurt Dominic.
I will stop him, and I'll do whatever it takes.
'Your boyfriend here is going to learn not to touch what is not his.
He is going to watch me torture you for weeks.
I'm going to fuck you so hard that you will scream, and you will be just out of his reach.
I will break you all over again before I kill him.'
I see the knife above Dominic's fingers.
'We are going to cut off a finger every time I make you scream,' Michael continues, his voice low and menacing.
'But I want a finger now. I have a hungry friend,' he whispers in my ear.
Pure fear courses through my body.

'NO!!!' I scream as I sit up, trying to get to him.
Two hands grab me, and I hit out wildly at the person holding me.
'Dominic!' I shout in panic, 'No, Michael, please don't hurt him!'
I'm grabbed again.
'Liz, stop it's okay, it's me, Dominic. You're safe, just breathe.'
I sit there, stunned, staring dazedly at the chair in my room, at the bed covers.
'Liz, look at me.'
There's no blood, there is no blood.

I touch my face and look at my hands: no blood, no pain.
'Liz, please look at me.'
I look up to see Dominic, his eyes. I'm home, I'm okay.
'Liz, speak to me, please,' he pleads with me.
I look at him and notice his lip is bleeding.
My fingers tremble as I touch his cheek.
'I... I... I'm so sorry,' I stammer as the tears come.
He pulls me in.
'Shhh, it's okay.' He runs his hand up and down my back.
I listen to his heart beating.

'I'll be fine, I've got you.' He kisses the top of my head.
I let myself sink into his embrace and listen to his heartbeat.
'I didn't mean to hurt you, I'm so sorry, Dominic.'
My breathing returns to normal, but I'm still trembling.
'You have a mean backhand, remind me never to sneak up on you and try to scare you,' he smirks.
I manage a stifled laugh at his statement.
'Dominic.'
'Yeah, babe?'
'Thank you.'
'Don't thank me, I just want to help you, I just want to be with you,' he says as he pulls me in tighter and kisses my hair.
I can see daybreak through the curtains.

'Can we go for a walk on the beach?' I ask him.
'Sounds perfect,' he says.
His hand tilts my face up to his, he kisses me tenderly.
I bring my arm up and wrap it around his neck, pulling him into the kiss.
I feel him wince. I pull away.
'I'm sorry,' I start to say as he pulls me back in and continues our kiss.
'Don't be,' he replies, resting his forehead on mine.
We get up, get dressed, and walk to the beach hand in hand.

DOMINIC

She is different this morning. That dream has really rattled her.
I want to ask her, but I don't want to push her.
I look down at her as we walk hand in hand, she looks pale and fragile.
It kills me to see her this way.
I can feel her trembling as she tries to hold it together.
I have so much anger towards the person responsible.
Do I love her? I don't know, but I'm right where I want to be.
That I do know for certain.

'Dominic,' her voice breaks through the silence.
'Yeah, babe?' I look at her.
She stops and looks over the ocean.
'Please talk to me, Liz, don't shut me out.'
She looks at me and nods.
'My dreams are my deepest fears.'

I don't say anything, I just stand beside her.
She looks back over the ocean and takes a deep breath.
'I have had this dream before, but,' she pauses.
'But this time it was worse.'
She stops again and her breathing becomes faster.
'Who is Michael?' I ask her.
She rubs her neck, running her fingers over the scars.
'He is the one who gave me the scars.' Her voice breaks.
I can feel the anger inside me begin to boil as my fists clench.
'He would do horrible things to me if I didn't do what I was told, or if he was angry with something or someone.'
She starts to tremble more violently.
I stand behind her and pull her to me. Her whole body is shaking.

'He would tell me that each scar was a reminder that I had to be better, do better, lose more weight.
That I shouldn't want or ask for anything, that I should do what he wants when he wants it.' She starts to cry.
'This dream, though, was the worst I have ever had, it started off the same as my other dreams. But this time it was different.' She sobs.
'Why?' I ask her.
She wipes her face and turns to face me, the look in her eyes absolutely floor me. It's pure unadulterated fear.
'Because now I have someone to lose,' she says, never once looking away.
'For the first time in a long time I have a safe place and now I have someone.'
She is looking at me and trying not to cry.

I bring my hands up to her face, I can feel her trying not to crumble.
I lean in and kiss her tenderly.
We sit down on the beach and she tells me what happened in her dream.
What Michael did, what he used, and the threat he made against me.
We sit there watching the waves rolling in.

'Are you okay?' Liz asks.
'I'm fine, why?' I ask her.
'Because of everything I just told you, and I really hurt you.'
'Liz,' I say, wrapping my arms around her. 'Like I said earlier, I'm right where I want to be—with you. I don't want to be anywhere you're not.'
I lean in and kiss her as I pull her onto my lap.
She has become my whole world and I'm not giving her up without a fight.
I need her to know, I need her to feel what I feel.
I need her and only her.

Our kiss deepens and I feel her arms tighten around me.
I hold her tight, not wanting to let her go.
I look into her eyes, she hasn't recovered from her dream, but she is stronger than she gives herself credit for.
Her strength amazes me.
After everything she has been through, she is still a warm, helpful and beautiful person, and she is all mine to fall in love with.
I smile at her and she smiles back, I hold her tight and kiss the top of her head.
We walk back hand in hand. I have to go into town today, but I really don't want to leave her alone.
I want her with me.
We can see Amber on the deck, waving to us as we walk back up to the house.

'Hey there, lovebirds,' she smiles.
'Morning, Amber, just got here?' I ask her.
'Yep,' she winks.
'Hi, Amber, I'm going in for a shower', Liz says quietly, 'I won't be long.'
Liz heads inside, I look at Amber and she knows instantly something is wrong, and notices my lip.
We head into the kitchen, I turn the kettle on and start making coffee.
I walk to the bedroom door and hear the shower. Amber finishes making coffee and we head back out onto the deck.
I tell her everything, from Liz's dream to our talk on the beach.
The look on Amber's face right now confirms everything Liz told me. It was bad, really bad.

'Dom,'
'Yeah?' I reply.
Amber doesn't say anything, her look is enough.
She is thinking the same thing I am, Liz has been gone too long and this worries us both.
'I'll go and check on her,' I say as I get up.
I turn and start to walk inside, I'm almost to the door when I see her standing there.
Her hair is still wet and her eyes are red from crying.
It's just at that moment when I see her body give up.
'LIZ!' I shout as I start to run to her.

I get to her just as she collapses.
I hold her as Amber rushes to my side.
'Shit! Shit! Shit!' Amber shouts.
'What?'

'Her breathing is shallow and I'm having trouble getting a pulse,' Amber replies. I can see that Amber is just as concerned as I am. She gets up and makes a phone call, cites a badge number.

I look down at Liz and back up to Amber, she is pacing in the kitchen on the phone.

What the hell is Area Seven?

What the fuck is going on?

I look at Liz again, she is really pale.

I look up as Amber comes back over to us.

'What was all that about?' I ask as I hold Liz tighter.

Amber looks at me.

'Dominic, please trust me, Elizabeth will be in good hands and you will be able to be with her. I…' She stops as her phone rings.

She takes the call as she walks into Liz's room, talking to someone about Fox Gant.

She comes back with Liz's handbag.

'Ambulance is 20-25 minutes away,' She announces as she puts her hand on my shoulder.

'Dominic?'

'What's going on, Amber?' I ask, looking at her.

She looks at me, then at Liz.

'AMBER! What the fuck is going on?' I can feel the tears building.

'What I'm about to tell you cannot go any further, and you can't tell Liz I told you. She needs to tell you…'

'Amber, please, for the love of god just fucking tell me!' I hear my voice break.

'Um, look, Michael is … Um, well, for lack of a better word, a psychopath.' She checks her phone.

'In short, when she tells you, you have to promise me that you will listen and not judge. And most importantly, take care how you react and what you say.' Amber looks at me.

'Okay, I promise I will. But can you please tell me what this is all about? What is Area Seven, and who is Fox Gant?' I ask, looking down at Liz.

'Dominic, I'm Elizabeth's handler,' she sighs, answering me.

'Handler?'

'I work for the Australian Federal Police. Area Seven is code for this house and Fox Gant is Elizabeth's codename.' She looks at her phone again.

'Liz chose the code names we use; they are from one of her favourite authors.'

I'm lost for words, I really don't know what to say.

Amber sighs and looks at me.
'Look, when we got to her, she was in a very bad way.'
'Surgery was touch and go, she died on the table a few times.' Amber checks her phone again and continues.
'They put her into a medically induced coma.'
I find myself subconsciously pulling her in closer to protect her.

'He broke her, physically, mentally and emotionally,' Amber says, tearing up, 'We changed her name and hid her.'
'Amber, who is he?'
Her phone rings and I grab her arm.
'Amber! Who the fuck is he?' My voice breaks.
Amber sighs.
'Michael Webster. He is organised crime, she didn't know until it was too late to leave.'

I sit there holding her.
I don't know what to do.
I look down at her until I hear the ambulance.
Amber puts her hand on my shoulder and goes to meet the ambulance,
'I'm here, Liz, come back to me. I'm not going anywhere,' I whisper as I gently kiss her forehead.
'Come back to me babe, I can't be without you'.
A tear drops.

👀 ELIZABETH 👀

I can hear muffled voices as I open my eyes, my mouth feels dry and my hand feels heavy.
I look around and get my bearings; hospital, I'm in a hospital.
I remember being at home, Dominic calling out to me and then nothing.
Amber is in the hallway on the phone and has her back to me.
I look down and see Dominic holding my hand, he is asleep.
I tried to move without waking him, but my movement woke him anyway.
There is a look of intense relief in his face when his eyes meet mine.
'Liz, babe, my god, you scared the crap out of me!' He moves closer.
'I'm so sorry.' My voice is scratchy.

Dominic brings his hand to my face, he feels so warm.
He runs his thumb across my lips as I turn my head in his hand.
I close my eyes and breathe in his scent.

I open my eyes and smile at him as I kiss his thumb that is still on my lips.
I melt when he smiles back at me.
He lays next to me on the bed and I hold his hand to my face.
'Stop apologising,' he leans in.
His lips feel great on mine, his kiss is firm and wonderful, albeit interrupted by Amber coughing.

'Stop hogging my bestie.'
Dominic sits up as Amber, who is sitting on the other side of my bed holding my hand, comes over and hugs me, .
'The doctor will be in shortly.' She smiles at me.
I notice the look she gives Dominic.
'Amber, how much did you tell him?' I ask.
'The doctor is aware.'
'No, how much did you tell Dominic?' I ask, cutting her off.
'Enough for him to understand the gravity of your um, situation,' she replies.
I look at Dominic.
'You stayed?'
'I told you, I'm right where I want to be, next to you,' he replies.
He smiles at me and caresses my face. I can feel myself blush.

'So, what happened? I mean, I know I fainted, but I mean what happened?' I ask them.
'Amber and I were on the deck. I had just finished telling her about your dream when we realised you have been gone a while. I was almost to the door when I saw you, your hair was still wet and I could tell you had been crying. You just collapsed. I caught you and now you are here,' Dominic explains.
'How long have I been out for, and why?'
'You have been out for a few hours. It's best to leave the rest up to the doctor. Way too many big words that I'm not even going to try to pronounce, spell or understand,' Amber replies as she eats the hospital food. Judging by the look on her face, it's not great.

Amber and Dominic help me sit up straighter, and Dominic hands me some water.
'Mrs. Elizabeth Miller?'
I look towards the door to see a doctor. I'm guessing early forties and, judging by his accent, Scottish.
'Yes, that is me,' I reply.
'Who else do we have in the room?' He enquires.
'I'm Amber, her over-protective best friend.' She shakes his hand.
'I'm Dominic,' He shakes the doctor's hand as well.

'You're the husband? I'm Dr. Marcus MacDougall.'
Yep, definitely Scottish.
Wait!
What?
Back up, did he just refer to Dominic as my husband?
I bring my hand to my mouth.

'Elizabeth?'
'Sorry, what?' I look up to see the doctor watching me.
Dominic's hand squeezes mine.
I look at him, he sits back down and smiles, his fingers running along my cheek as he kisses my left hand and winks.
'May I discuss your medical details in front of your guests?' The doctor asks politely.
'Of course,' I reply without hesitation.
'Okay, I have been looking through your file from your previous admission in Brisbane. The fact that you are here right now amazes me. I have never seen anything like it. I looked up your accident, your car basically disintegrated into nothing.' He looks at me.
Okay, he doesn't know as much as I thought.
'You suffered a perforated liver and kidney. Both are working at a reduced rate, but are still healthy.'
Dominic's hand squeezes mine.
'You also sustained a ruptured spleen and bleeding on the brain.'
The doctor continues to list broken bones, my dislocated shoulders, hips and shattered pelvis.
I can feel Dominic stiffen beside me.
'Your appendix needed to be removed, and due to the horrific internal injuries to your lower abdomen, you had an emergency hysterectomy to prevent you from haemorrhaging further and bleeding to death.'
I look up to see Dominic staring at me, and I can't read his expression.
His face is white and his body rigid; it doesn't even look like he is breathing.
I start to pull my hand away, but his grip tightens and he shakes his head.
Now he knows just how damaged and broken I am, but his hand never lets go of mine.

'Now, we have done a full blood screen, MRI, CT, x-ray, and ECG; everything has come back clean and clear.' He closes my file and holds it against his chest with his left hand.
'There is nothing to suggest your body is not healing, but with what you endured, and a month in an induced coma, your body still needs time.' He looks at me.
'So, what does that say about my collapse?' I ask him.

'Amber and Dominic told the paramedics and the staff here about your bad dream and how it rattled you. With what I have read about your accident and your body's fight to survive,' he clears his throat,
'I believe that it was some sort of stress-induced panic attack. Your body shut itself down to protect itself,' he finished.

'So, like a reboot?' Amber asks as she continues eating.
The doctor looks at her.
'Yes, I guess you could say a reboot.' Dr. MacDougall shrugs his shoulders and nods.
'So, when can I take my girl home?' Dominic asks.

I smile to myself. My girl. He still wants me, for now.
'The nurse will be in shortly to do more ops, but I don't see why Elizabeth should stay, so possibly this afternoon,' the doctor replies.
'I'll be back later to check on you.' He smiles and leaves the room.

'Thank god you're going home, hospital food sucks, home cooked is so much better,' Amber remarks.
Dominic and I look at her.
'What?' She shrugs her shoulders, 'It's true.'
'Sorry, Amber, Liz will be coming home with me.' Dominic smiles at me.
'You will have to fend for yourself a little longer.'
'I have some of your favourites in the freezer, and there's some Apricot Chicken in the fridge. Oh, and cheesecake.' I say, blushing.
'I have to go, but I love you, bestie.' Amber hugs me.
'Where are you going?' I ask her
'I have some paperwork to complete, call me later, okay?' She winks at me, 'I'll leave you two lovebirds to it.'
She blows us a kiss as she leaves.

I know she doesn't have to work.
She is just giving us time alone together without actually saying as much.
After Amber leaves, I begin to feel nervous; I have never seen Dominic's home.
Dominic picks up on my mood change and lays down on my bed, pulling me to him. "What's wrong Liz?"
"I've never seen your home."
"I have wanted to take you there for a while but I wasn't sure. I want you to be comfortable there."
"I want to see your home." I smile up t him.
He smiles and kisses my forehead lie there for a while, his hand running through my hair.

'Dominic?' I ask as I curl up closer against him.

'Yeah, babe?'

'Please be honest with me.'

'Of course, I'll always be honest with you,' he replies, holding me tight.

'Do you still want me? I know I'm broken and…'

'Liz,' he stops me. 'I am right where I want to be.'

He kisses my hair.

'Wherever you are, I want to be beside you.'

'I'm sorry if I keep asking, it's just…' I sit up to look at him. 'I feel insecure and I hate that about myself.'

'Whenever you feel unsure or insecure about anything, ask me, I won't judge you,' he brings his hand to my face, sitting up.

'Thank you,' I say, smiling at him.

'I booked Fraser Island. We leave on the thirteenth of April for two whole weeks of just you and me on a beach with the dingoes.' He kisses me softly.

'Can't wait,' I smile.

A few hours later, after a few more tests, we're done and my doctor returns.

'Okay, Elizabeth, Dominic, I'm satisfied with your test results. Everything has come back good, so you are free to go home. But please rest for a few days, and no strenuous exercise.'

'Thank you,' I say.

Dominic stands up and walks to the end of the bed.

'Thanks, Doc,' he says as he shakes his hand, 'I'll make sure she gets some rest.'

He turns to me and smiles, 'Come on, let's go home.'

'Sounds good to me,' I say, getting up.

On the drive home he holds my hand every chance he gets.

'What are you thinking?' He asks.

'Fireplaces. I want to add two fireplaces; another one inside, and one downstairs.'

'Fireplaces,' he smiles, 'I think I can do that.' He places his hand on my leg.

Yep, I am absolutely and irrevocably in love with Dominic. I sing out in my head.

I sit there looking out the car window, and make a startled noise at the revelation of my feelings for him.

'Liz, what's the matter? Do you need me to pull over?' He looks over at me.

I can hear the concern in his voice.

'I, um, I'm…'

Dominic pulls the car over and reaches over to me.

'Liz?' His hand touches my face.

'Ah, yeah, I'm okay. I am okay, really, Dominic.' I smile at him.

'Can we stop at the shops and the tavern, please?' I ask.
'Sure, anything in particular you want?' He asks, looking a bit puzzled.
'Apart from chocolate and alcohol,' I pause and think to myself, you, naked, making love to me.
'I feel like cooking something,' I finish after a moment.
'Well, I'm all for you cooking, I love your cooking, but if you like we could have dinner at the tavern, you know, like a dinner date.' He looks at me, his hand still touching my face.

'Liz, you are the last thing I think of when I go to sleep, and the first thing I think of when I wake up. You are everything I want and everything I need.'
I can feel myself blush as I bring my hand up, holding his to my face.
He looks into my eyes, trying to read my expression, but it's not hard.
I kiss his thumb as he runs it over my lips.
'Dominic, I want you, and only you. I…'
I don't get to finish as his lips find mine and I melt into him. He is an amazing kisser.
'Change of plans,' he announces, his lips still against mine. 'Take-aways and a movie.'
'Sounds per…' I don't get to finish my answer.
I'm pretty sure I don't need to, though.

👀 DOMINIC 👀

We pull into the tavern and Liz heads into the bottle shop.
We ordered on the drive back into Moore Park Beach: her favourite Surf and Turf pizza with cheesy garlic bread, and I added a BBQ Meatlovers.
After raiding the vending machines for chocolate, I go and wait for the pizza.
I grab a beer while I wait, and take out my phone.
As I scroll through pictures and footage, I can't help but smile.
How did I get her?
She is absolutely stunning.
I'm looking at a picture of us, taken by Amber, when I'm interrupted by someone calling my name.
'Dom, is that you?'
Crap! I think to myself, I really don't want to deal with this now. I just want to get the food and take my girl home and hold her.
'Hello Stephanie, going to have another go at me, are you?' I reply as I turn around.
'I haven't seen you in ages,' she says as she hugs me, ignoring my comment.
She reeks of beer and cigarettes.

'I have missed you,' she slides her hands down to my waist.
'I have a girlfriend.' I push her hands away and try to change the subject.

'Order for Dominic.'
I turn, finishing my beer, and grab the food.
'Thanks,' I nod at the waitress.
I turn around and start to walk back through the bar.
Stephanie grabs my arm.
'Come on, Dom, we should catch up, just like old times.'
'Stephanie, no. I have a girlfriend.'
She takes a step back, clearly not impressed.
'Don't play hard to get, I know how much you enjoyed fucking me,' she sneers,
running her fingers over her cleavage.
'Yeah well, not everyone wants another spin on the town bicycle,' Liz says from
behind me.
I didn't even see her come in, or hear her walk up beside me, but her timing was
perfect.
I look at her and smile, pulling her against me and kissing her.

Stephanie is taken back by Liz's comment, and looks back and forth between
Liz and I.
Then she regains her composure, but before I can say anything, Liz motions for
me to go.
We turn to leave when Stephanie decides to have one last dig at Liz.
'Just remember, little whatever-your-name-is,'
We stop and turn around.
'Elizabeth, my name is Elizabeth,'
I can see Liz's hands shake, and I reach down and take one of her hands in mine,
gently squeezing it as I run my thumb over her hand.
'Whatever, just remember, I had him first.' Stephanie struts towards us.
Everybody in the bar has stopped to watch the show.

'And I never left him unsatisfied.' She finishes with a raised eyebrow.
I go to say something, but Liz stops me.
'Look, I don't care what you think of me, but my boyfriend clearly declined your
advances. I'm sure that you should be able to find yourself another buyer quite
easily.' Liz turns and grabs my hand and we walk away.
'Fucking slut!' Stephanie calls out, 'He will be back!'
I stand at the door, holding it open, when Liz turns back to Stephanie.
'You see, the thing with smart people is, when they take out the trash, they don't
usually take it back in.' Liz turns back around and winks at me.
'Wow, she is a bitch.'

I look around the bar quickly, people don't seem to know whether to laugh, clap or just have another drink.

We walk out, leaving Stephanie standing there with her mouth gaping open in shock.
'You have no idea,' I reply as I walk out the door after Liz.
We walk back to my car.
'We were…'
'Dominic, it was before you were with me, you don't have to explain,' Liz looks at me.
'I need to.'
She stops and looks at me.
'Okay,' she says apprehensively.

'We were together for two years; I thought she was the one. We broke up, I got very drunk one night and ended up at her house, and in bed with her. Big mistake.'
'When?' She asks.
'We have been over for about 18 months now, and hooked up about eight months ago. But she has never been inside my home.'
'What do you mean? You were together?'
'It wasn't finished,' I look away, feeling embarrassed about my moment of weakness.
'Hey, look at me,' Liz touches my face, 'Thank you, I don't think any less of you. But I am glad I heard it from you and not from someone else.'
We get back to my car. Liz had left the alcohol on the back of the Ute tray.
I put the takeout on the back seat with the alcohol and open Liz's door.
'You know you're pretty amazing, right?' I ask her.
I can see her hands still shaking, confrontation in any form is not something she is comfortable with.
'I know,' she laughs.
I pull her in and kiss her, thinking, I will never get enough of kissing this woman.
'Come on, let's go home,' I say.
'Yes please,' she replies, looking up at me.

👀 ELIZABETH 👀

We drive to his home.
I didn't know he was only about five hundred meters down the road from me.
His driveway winds through the trees and opens up to what looks like a three storey home with a big shed to the left.

It is a dark render with timber accents.
We park in front of the shed and get out.
'I lived in the shed while I built the house,' he says.
'Wow, you built this?'
'Sure did.'
'Well, I got the right builder then,' I smile at him.
'Ha ha, smart arse. Come on, let's get inside before the food goes cold.'
We walk up the steps and through the front door to be greeted by two very excited dogs.
A Staffie and a Labrador.
'Liz, I would like you to meet Bonnie and Clyde. I'm looking after them for my neighbours.'
I get down and pet them.
They are absolutely adorable.
'Bonnie is the Labrador, and this hurricane is Clyde, two of the biggest sooks going around, who will do anything for food and pets.'
'Kind of like the person looking after them, perfect match!' I joke as I get Clyde's tongue across my cheek.
'Well, it looks like we have more than food and pets in common,' Dominic says, smiling, as he helps me up.
We put the food on the bench and Dominic shows me the main bathroom so I can wash my face.
His home is open, with big glass windows looking over his back yard, pool and down to the beach.
There is a huge back deck which wraps around the sides.
It's surprisingly clean for a bachelor pad.

He gets dinner for Bonnie and Clyde and puts them downstairs.
We have our pizza and drinks in the living room and watch Walking Tall, followed by The Dukes of Hazzard. Dominic pulls me in against him and I snuggle in.
He is playing with some of my loose curls, resting his hand on my bare skin under my shirt. We clean up after dinner and Dominic takes me upstairs.
I am exhausted, all I want is a shower and bed.
He shows me the en-suite, and gives me a towel and toothbrush.
One wall of the shower is a huge pane of glass, where I can see the moonlight over the ocean.
The hot water feels so good on my tired skin.
I manage to stay awake long enough to brush my teeth, and realise that I have no spare clothes.
Oh well, I'm too tired to care, I'll just grab one of Dominic's shirts, I think to myself.

I climb into his bed.
I fall asleep before my head hits the pillow.

🔱 DOMINIC 🔱

I come back inside from the deck off my bedroom after making a phone call.
She is asleep, my god, she is beautiful.
Her hair is still damp from the shower, and it cascades down her face.
I gently tuck it behind her ear, run my hand softly over her cheek and kiss her forehead.
I notice that she has grabbed one of my New Zealand Warrior NRL jerseys; it looks better on her than on me anyway.
I send Amber a message asking if she can drop some clothes over in the morning for Liz, along with my address.

I head in for a shower, and stand there letting the water run over me, daydreaming about spending the rest of my life with Liz.
I want to be with her, laugh with, cry with, and grow old with her.
To be honest, the thought excites and scares the crap out of me in equal parts.
Fuck, I want her to want me as much as I want her.
We have only been together for a short time, but I have never had anything like this.
I'm sure I'm in love already, but it surprises me because it's so early in the relationship.

I return to the bedroom, she has moved.
The covers have slipped off her, exposing her perfect butt.
I groan, she has no underwear on.
As I climb into bed behind her, I see even more scars.
These are faint, running up the backs of both her legs, from the bottom to the very top.
I follow them over her butt cheeks to her lower back.
I have seen scars similar to these before, some remind me of electric shock burns, and the others look like the burn marks you get when you grab a hot handle.
I battle with the feelings I'm having, thinking about someone harming her.

I pull her to me. spooning her, when she turns and snuggles into me.
I pull the covers over us and hold her tight, not wanting to let her go.
I fall asleep, holding my girl as I play with her hair.

CHAPTER 5

Chocolate Cake

I wake the next morning with a jolt; her side of the bed is empty.
I sit up and see her outside on the phone.
Judging by her body language and the fact she is pacing, it's not good.
My phone buzzes, it's from Amber, she is downstairs and has a bag for Liz.
I quickly chuck on some board shorts, run downstairs and let Amber in.
I point to the kitchen before I race back upstairs.

I find Liz on the bed looking somewhat deflated.
I cup her face with my hands so she will look at me.
'Liz, babe, what's wrong?'
She remains quiet.
'Liz, who were you taking to? What's happened? Is it Michael?' I ask her.
Liz looks at me, shakes her head and offers me a small smile.
'I just got off the phone with David, he is from Queensland Ambulance in Bundaberg.
They have delayed my return to work for another four months,' she replies.
She sighs and puts her phone on the bed, and I take her hands in mine.

'I'm sorry babe, I know how much you were looking forward to going back to work,' I say as I kiss her hands. 'Did they say why?'
'My panic attack,' she answers, and draws in a deep breath. 'I'm not angry with their decision. I understand why and I accept it; it's about patient safety, and mine.' She brings her hands to my face. 'They feel I need more time.'
'Well,' I say, 'I can see one positive out of this extra time.' I smile.
She looks at me, unsure what to say.
'More free time with me,' I finish as I kiss her.
I can feel her smile and her arms fold around my neck.
We hold each other for a minute.
'Thank you, Dominic.'

'Anything for my girl.' I say kissing her again.
'As much as I want to stay right here,' I get up to leave. 'Amber is downstairs with your bag. I'll go grab it for you.'
'Wait,' Liz says, getting up.

'What's…'
I don't get to finish, she pulls me in and kisses my lips.
Her lips are soft against mine, and our tongues move as one as her hands slide around my waist and come to rest on my lower back.
My whole body reacts to her touch.
I move my hands down to her waist and pull her in against me, but she breaks away, leaving me breathless and wanting more.

'I think this free time is exactly what I need,' she looks at me with a raised eyebrow.
She can feel exactly how aroused I am.
She winks at me, bites her bottom lip and walks off to the bathroom.
'That is just mean, Elizabeth,' I call out to her, 'Cruel and unusual punishment!'
I can hear her laughing from the en suite.
'Just remember, Elizabeth, karma's a bitch, and she bites!'
'I look forward to it!'

I have managed to compose myself by the time I get back downstairs and come face to face with Amber. She rolls her eyes.
'What?' I shrug.
'I was starting to think I had to go up there and hose you both down.'
'Haha! I'll be back in a minute. I need to take her bag up.'

I come back downstairs.
Amber is leaning against the bench with a smirk and her arms folded, looking at me.
The glint in her eyes tells me her thoughts are not clean.
'Amber, I wish that was the reason, but trust me, it's not.' I shake my head giving her a stifled laugh.
'WHAT?' Her voice reminds me of when I was busted for swearing at school by the teacher.
Her arms are still folded as she turns around, watching me, waiting for my explanation.
She is not going to be happy when I tell her about the phone call Liz just had.
I put on the kettle and walk to the bottom of the stairs.
I can just make out the noise of the shower.
Putting my hands behind my head I look at Amber and walk back to the kitchen.
I lean against the bench.

'They have delayed her return to work by another four months'
'Those assholes!' She slams her fist on the bench.
I swear you can see the steam coming off her. She is pissed.

'She needs this, Dominic.

A return to work will give her purpose, routine, a fucking distraction from this fucking case...' Amber trails off.

'Actually, she is surprisingly okay with it. Yes, she is upset, but she understands and accepts their decision.'

'It's not the same, Dominic. Everything she has been through, and done since moving here, has taken a lot of effort from her. I was all she knew; me, that house, and her fucking dream of going back to work.'

I hand Amber her coffee.

'I admire her, Dominic, she is stronger than she gives herself credit for.'

I nod in agreement.

'Being with people again is such a huge step. I remember when I first became her handler, I would take her out for dinner hoping she'd get used to being around others. The moment anyone spoke to her, she'd go into her shell. You may not get this, but her being with you is a massive milestone in her journey to finding and being herself again.'

I watch Amber for a minute and smile.

'What's that smile for?' She asks me.

'I need a favour.'

'What do you need?' She asks, leaning in.

I place my hands on the bench and lean in, looking Amber in the eye.

'How soon can you get Liz a passport?' I ask her quietly.

'If I can pull some strings and call in a favour, maybe two weeks... Three, tops. Where are you taking our girl?'

'New Zealand.' I stop as I hear Liz coming downstairs.

👀 ELIZABETH 👀

'Hey, Amber,' I say, getting to the bottom of the steps.

Amber walks up and gives me a hug.

'How are you feeling, did you get any sleep? Or did Dominic keep you up?'

'Hey, I was the perfect boyfriend, thank you,' he says, acting hurt.

'I'm fine thank you, and Dominic was a good boy.'

'Woof!' Dominic barks as he leans against the bench, and Bonnie and Clyde respond.

We laugh.

'Anyway, I better go. I have to work, so please don't enjoy my suffering too much.' Amber pouts.

Dominic sees Amber out as I sip my coffee, looking out the kitchen window, watching as the rain starts to fall.

Dominic walks up behind me and wraps his arms around me.

'Hey, you.'

'Mmm, there's my girl.'

I lean back into him and run my hand along his arm.

I so love him, I smile to myself.

'What would you like to do today?' I ask him.

'You and me on the couch, with a movie.' He smiles.

'Sounds perfect,' I say as I turn in his arms.

He holds me tight and kisses the top of my head, and I take in a deep breath and enjoy his warmth.

'I'll go feed the dogs while you pick a movie,' Dominic says as his fingers brush my cheek.

I look up and nod as he kisses me softly.

Dominic walks back towards the stairs before he turns back and smiles at me.

I smile back and watch him go downstairs.

I sit on the floor in the lounge, looking through Dominic's movies.

There are so many that I haven't seen.

I look through them and find Misery, I hold it in my hands as they start to shake.

Michael used to tell me how much he enjoyed hobbling people, and if I ever tried to escape he would do it to me. He made me watch the movie then watch as he did it to people.

What is a great movie and book by a brilliant author now scares the hell out of me.

'Liz, what's wrong?' Dominic comes to my side. 'Babe, you're shaking.'

'It's, umm…'

Dominic takes the movie from me.

'Michael?' He asks.

'Yes, one of his favourite punishments for people who disobeyed him came from that movie.'

I see a mixture of concern for me and a simmering anger in Dominic's eyes.

'Are you okay?' he asks.

'He used to threaten me. He would say that if I ever ran, he would hobble me that way. I would still be useful, but unable to escape.'

Dominic puts the movie down and pulls me against him, holding me tight.

In his arms I'm in my safe place.

I close my eyes and hold him.

'Thank you, Dominic.'
'No need to thank me'.
Casting Misery off to the side, he focuses on the rest of the selection and asks,
'Did you see any movies you like, or should we go to the cinema?'
'I have never seen Lord of the Rings.'
'Perfect! They were all filmed in New Zealand.'
'Really?' I ask, looking up at him. 'I've always wanted to go to New Zealand.'
Dominic smiles as he runs his fingers along my cheek and brings his lips to mine.
I make popcorn while he gets the movie ready.
We spend the morning snuggled together on the couch with a blanket.
I made it through the first movie, but not the second.

🦉 DOMINIC 🦉

I look at Liz, she has fallen asleep curled up in my arms.
I turn the movie off and snuggle up to her more, drifting off to sleep, playing with her hair.
I'm woken by the sound of my doorbell and phone ringing.
Liz is still asleep.
Carefully getting up, I make my way to the front door and open it.
'Hey, Simon, what's going on?'
I greet him while I stretch.
'We have been ringing, but you didn't answer.'
'Sorry, mate. Watching a movie with Liz and fell asleep.'
'Sweet, bring her as well. Pub in twenty minutes, Sunday sesh.'
'I'll ask Liz and see if she feels up to it. She wasn't well yesterday.'
'I know,'
'You know?' I ask, looking at him.
'I was at work yesterday when she was brought in. I saw you and Amber, but I was called to a critical and couldn't get back to see you,' Simon answers.
'How is she?'
'Better.'
'Good, I'll see you both in twenty.' He smiles and heads downstairs to his car.
I wave and close the door.
Liz is awake when I get back to the lounge.

She smiles as I sit down next to her.
'Sunday sesh? I probably should get ready then,' she says as I kiss her hand.
'Only if you are feeling up to it.'
Liz nods and gets up.

'Sorry I fell asleep on you.'
'I turned the movie off, snuggled into you and slept as well.'

We get ready and head to the pub, we are the last to arrive.
'Hey Liz,' Simon says as he comes up to us.
He hugs Liz and I feel her hand tighten around mine.
'I'll get drinks, would you like anything, babe?'
'Bundaberg Rum with Ginger Beer, please.'
I watch Liz from the bar.
She still keeps her distance from Luke, Simon, and the other guys.
I look around to see if Daniel is here, but I can't see him.
I do see Louise with Stephanie and a couple of other people
I can't make out, sitting right at the back.
I hope they stay out there, Liz doesn't need the drama.

👀 ELIZABETH 👀

I watch Dominic laugh with his mates and play pool, while I sit with Amanda
and Chantelle.
I notice Chantelle getting pale, and I know she needs to go.
'Amanda, go and get Shaun and Simon. Chantelle doesn't look well, I'll stay
with her.'
Amanda nods and I move next to Chantelle.
'How far along are you?' I ask her.
'Almost eight months,' she answers softly.
Her pulse is fast, and she is clammy to the touch.
'When did you last eat?'
'A couple of hours ago,' Chantelle mumbles.
'Okay. Can you have a sip of soft drink, please?'
Chantelle nods and I help her have a drink.
Shaun and Simon rush to us.
'Shaun, you need to take her to the hospital, now,' I say as I put my hand on his
shoulder.
'Chantelle, hey, look at me,' Simon asks as he kneels in front of her, searching
her face for signs of what is happening.
'I'll ring work and let them know you're coming.' Simon gets up and makes
a call.

Dominic and David help Shaun with Chantelle.
Shaun comes up and hugs me.
'Thank you,' he says before getting in his car.

I stand there and watch as he drives away.
Dominic comes up to me.

'Babe, you're shaking.'
'I…' I look at the ground.
'Is it because Shaun hugged you?'
'Yes,' I whisper. 'I'm sorry,'
'Don't apologise, it's OK.' He brings my face up to his.
He smiles and softly kisses me, before giving me a hug.
'Are you all good?' He asks, kissing the top of my head.
'I'm fine, but even better now,' I reply as I snuggle in.
'Do you want to go home?'
'No, you haven't beaten David at pool yet!' I snicker.

His hands slide down and grab my butt.
'Well, I'm going to need a kiss for good luck.'
His lips feel wonderful on mine, and he tightens his hold on me.
'Just a kiss?' I ask.
'For now,' he whispers as his lips brush mine.
'Oi, Dom! Waiting on you!' David calls out.
I feel Dominic smile.
We spend the next few hours playing pool and laughing.
Shaun rings to let us know everything is okay.
Chantelle's blood sugar had dropped to 2.9, and they are keeping her overnight
for observation.
We head home and let the dogs out for their dinner.
They manage to trip me again.
I head upstairs for a shower and only just make it to bed before I fall asleep.

I wake up early the next morning and find myself in his arms.
I managed to get up without waking him.
I get out of the shower, dry off and wrap myself up in a towel as he walks in.
'Morning,' he says as he kisses me softly.
'Morning, shall I make breakfast?'
'What are you offering?' He asks as his hands slide down to my butt.
'Pancakes.'
'Mmm, yum, do you come as breakfast, as well?'
I shrug and walk out of the bathroom to get dressed and make pancakes.
Dominic comes up behind me putting his hands on my hips.
'Hey, you.'
He holds me as I make pancakes.

'Are you okay?' I ask him.
'Yep. I have you right where I want you, in my arms.'

Dominic makes coffee as I set the table and bring over the pancakes.
He walks up behind me, pulling me onto his lap as he sits at the table.
'Are you sure you are okay?' I ask him again.
'Yep, I'm okay. I have just been thinking about what you told me yesterday.'
'I told you too much didn't I?' I ask, looking away.

He turns me around to face him.
'No. But I want you to know that I don't ever want you to feel like that again. I
want you to talk to me about anything. I don't care if you think it's stupid or silly,
I want to be the one you feel you can turn to.'
'I want to tell you I really do…I just need time.'
'I'm not going anywhere. I don't want to be anywhere you're not.'
I nod and smile as I run my fingers through his hair.

We eat the pancakes, and he tells me how he came to be a builder and live in
Moore Park Beach.
About his mum being an only child and her parents living in Moore Park Beach
till they passed away.
His family moved back to New Zealand to live and be near his dad's family.
The grandparents left the three grandchildren money, and Dominic used his
share to buy land and build his home.
His phone rings as we are cleaning up.
I look out over the backyard down to the beach; the day is beautiful and clear.
'It's a nice day, how about we pack a cooler and head to the beach? There is a
small swell I could teach you to surf,' he suggests as he hugs me from behind.

I smile. He has no idea that I grew up surfing.
'Don't you have to work today?' I ask as I turn around in his arms.
'That's the great thing about being my own boss and sleeping with the client'
His hands slide down and grab my arse as he leans in.
'I think I can wrangle a day off,' he says, kissing my cheek.
He kisses the corner of my mouth.
My body's reaction to him is instant.
My lips part in anticipation as I sigh softly.
'Thank you.'
'Anything for my girl,' he whispers against my lips.

Our kiss starts gently.

My hands are on his hips and I slide them under his shirt and up to his shoulders as I push up onto my tippy-toes. I slide his shirt up over his head.

'Liz, are you sure?'

I don't say anything, I just remove my shirt.

I run my tongue over my lips as I reach for him again.

I need him, I need him to make love to me, I need to feel him.

🔍 DOMINIC 🔍

We don't even bother going upstairs.

I grab her butt and lift her up carrying her to the lounge as her legs wrap around me.

Our kiss never falters.

My god I need her, I want her so bad.

The corner couch has an ottoman, which makes for a perfect makeshift bed.

I lay her down, her auburn hair fanning out above her head.

I look down at her and I'm lost in her piercing green eyes and for a moment, I can see our whole future together.

I run my hands up her thighs.

I feel her flinch under my touch.

I know she is still self-conscious about her scars, even though she tries to hide it.

I slowly undo her shorts and remove them, then her underwear, kissing and nipping as I do.

My hands run back up her thighs to her waist.

I run my tongue along her stomach and trail kisses down to her clitoris.

My tongue starts to tease her, and my hand slides up her thigh and squeezes.

I reach up and touch her breast, I feel her hand slide on top mine.

She calls out my name as her hands run through my hair.

I love that sound, my name on her lips, nothing is sexier.

I untie my board shorts, I want her under me so bad, but I'll be patient and make her come first.

I start to suck her, and her body's reaction is instant.

I feel her arch her back, gasp and moan as she pulls at my hair.

I can feel her getting wetter.

She is so close.

I go harder, my mouth more urgent.

'Dominic!' She calls out as she climaxes.

Grabbing the cushions, I place them under my knees while I remove my shorts, taking her by the waist I pull her onto my cock.

I watch her, her movements, the way her hands move up my arms, the way she bites her lip, the way she enjoys me.

My hands hold her breasts and I tease her nipples.

Liz arches her back and I slide my arm under her, lifting her up to me.

Her lips find mine and her arms envelop me.

Her legs wrap around my waist, pulling my cock into her.

'Dominic,' she whispers my name against my lips.

'Dominic, I want you, I need you.'

My hand is in her hair, holding her lips to mine.

She feels so fucking good.

We move to the couch.

I need her under me, I need to feel her body under me as I bring her to orgasm.

Our fingers lace together above her head.

I start fucking her harder, her body starts to shudder.

'Don't stop, Dominic, I want you to…'

She orgasms and screams my name. I
 can't stop, hearing her drives me wild.

'Dom,'

I kiss her hard, my body craves her, I crave her.

I orgasm as I bury my face against her neck.

I love her taste, her smell, her touches, her smile, and her laugh.

👀 ELIZABETH 👀

He lies beside me, still holding me against him.

'Are you okay?' He asks as he comes up onto his elbow.

'Of course, why do you ask?'

'Doc said no strenuous exercise.'

I laugh as his fingers trace my side, down my leg, and back up.

His eyes follow them.

'Well, in my professional opinion, as a qualified paramedic with heaps of free time, that was more of a stress release.' I smile up at him.

'Stress release,' his hand grabs my arse as he looks at me and smiles.

'Yep,' my hand traces down his chest and over his stomach.

I feel him react to my touch.

'Yes, stress release, and I'm very stressed.' I sit up, looking at him.

'Very stressed, with lots of free time.' I lean in.

With my tongue against his neck, up to his earlobe, I gently bite and tease him.
I feel his fingers grip my waist as I bring my leg to his side, and he sits up.
'Well, I suppose I should be the dutiful boyfriend then and…' his head rolls back as I kiss his neck.
He groans as he enters me.
'…Help reduce your stress,' he finishes.
His body feels amazing against mine, his arms hold me to him as I move against him.
I place kisses along his jawline before his lips find mine.
I kiss him with everything I have to give.
The way he makes me feel, the way he makes love to me.
All the things I thought I was never going to have.
In our short time together, he has given it all to me.

His hands explore my body, igniting it.
He kisses my neck as I roll my head back and moan.
He buries his face in my cleavage as both hands brush over my breasts.
He calls out my name.
I can feel myself getting close, but I need him to want it as much as I do.
'Dominic,' I pull his head back and kiss him deeply.
His hands slide down and grab my arse firmly.
'Liz,' he groans as he kisses me.
'Fuck, Elizabeth.' He pulls my hair to give himself access to my neck.
His tongue moves along my scar.
I feel the goosebumps all over my body.
I shiver with anticipation.
I arch my back as he continues down to my breast, his tongue teasing my nipples.
My fingers intertwine in his hair.
He can feel me shiver.
He knows I'm getting close.
'I want you to cum, Liz, cum for me.'

👀 DOMINIC 👀

I can feel the light sweat beads on her skin as I trail kisses along her neck.
She moves against me and she starts to orgasm.
I hold her tightly as I orgasm, too.
The things she does to me and the way she makes me feel, I can't explain it, but I don't ever want to give it up.
I don't want to give her up.
I don't want to give her a reason to leave me.

I press my ear to her chest and listen to her heartbeat.
She rests her head on top of mine, we are both breathing heavily.
I still have one hand on her butt, the other entwined in her hair.
I don't want her to move, I want her right where she is.
I move my hand up along her spine as she leans back.
I look into her eyes.
Elizabeth's smile lights up the room, and all I can see is her.

👀 ELIZABETH 👀

I giggle.
'Dominic,' he silences me with a kiss, pulls me in tighter and holds me tight.
I moan lightly into the kiss, my god he feels good against me.
'Dominic,' I say in the kiss, before his lips move to my neck.
'Mmmm, yes, babe?' He replies, still kissing my neck.
'You promised to take me surfing.'
'Mmm ,you in a bikini is very tempting, I'm not sure how much teaching I will get done.' He kisses me lightly on my shoulder.
'Well,' I pause, enjoying my body's reaction to his kisses, 'It's a good thing… Mmm…' I sigh, 'I already know how to surf, then.'
He stops and looks up at me.
He has a huge smile on his face.
'What?' I ask.
'Can you get any hotter?'
I get up, put my shorts back on and pass him his.
I look for my shirt and I find it on the kitchen floor along with his.
He comes up behind me and spins me around, pulling me against him.

'What else can my Lizzy do?' He asks with a smile.
I place my hands on his chest and kiss him before pulling away and walking towards the stairs, putting my shirt back on.
'Let's see,' I say, turning around to face him.
'I can throw a ball, love cricket and football. Um, I can change a spark-plug and a tyre. Bathurst should be a national long weekend. You have had the computer in your car remapped with a straight-through two-point-five-inch exhaust system, which, by the way, is only slightly illegal. Oh, and I can ride a dirt bike.'
I wink and turn to walk up the stairs.
'I'm going for another shower, while you feed the dogs!' I call back to him.

I only make it halfway up when he catches me and pins me against the wall with his body, which is still naked.

His lips brush over mine.
'You forgot to mention you make a mean chocolate cake,' he says as his lips brush against mine.
His hands slide up under my shirt as he kisses me.
I moan as he brushes over my breasts and lifts my shirt over my head, pinning my arms above me.
His lips move down my neck to my breasts, and I feel his tongue lick my nipple before he takes my breast in his mouth.
I moan as he finds my mouth with his.
His arm wraps around me and pulls me in, holding me against him.
I can feel his erection pressing against me.
'Dominic,'
'Liz,'
I moan, I still have my hands pinned against the wall above my head.
He pulls back and looks at me.

'I'm going to have a cold shower, you can feed the dogs,' he says.
'Really?' I look at him and say, 'You would tease me like that?'
'Karma, my dear Elizabeth, karma.' He laughs.
He looks over my body. I'm still breathing hard.
'A very cold shower,' he sighs.

He releases my hands and turns to walk up the stairs.
I grab his arm and stop him from going any further, pulling him back to me.
I wrap my arms around him.
I can feel him smile in the kiss as his arms pull me against him.
This kiss isn't about sex, or him being naked.
It's about us, here and now, together.
Just us and no one else.
We break off our kiss and look at each other, his hands touching my face and mine resting on his chest.
He pulls me in and holds me tight for what feels like hours, and I don't want him to let me go.

'I guess I better feed the dogs, then,' I say eventually.
'Yeah, but in a minute. I'm not ready to let you go yet.'
'Okay,' I giggle coyly.
He rests his forehead on mine, his eyes closed.
I bring my hands to the side of his face.
'Dominic, what are you thinking?'
'I just realised something,' he says, his eyes are still closed.
'Really, and what's that?'

He stands in front of me with the biggest smile on his face.
'We just christened my house.'
'Really?' I raise my eyebrow.
He smacks my arse and heads upstairs for a shower.

I go downstairs and let the dogs up for their breakfast.
Clyde manages to trip me, and I'm almost licked to death by both of them.
I swear they do it on purpose.
From down in the kitchen I can hear him on the phone.
I have just finished packing the cooler for the beach when he comes downstairs,
dressed for work.

'A quick change of plans,' he announces, walking up to me.
'That's okay, work has to come first.,' I sigh, turning to him.
'Oh, we are still going to the beach,' he says, looking me up and down.
He grabs me and lifts me onto the bench.
'I just have to help Luke for a couple of hours.'
He kisses me hard and I wrap my arms and legs around him, returning his kiss.
He pulls back and looks at me.
'Right now, I hate Luke,' he says.
I giggle.

'No, you don't,' I laugh.
'Yeah, I do,' he chuckles as he kisses me again.
I laugh again, putting my hands on his chest, pushing back.
'Come on. The sooner you help Luke, the sooner we can go to the beach.' I slide
off the bench.
'Grab the cooler,' I say, sashaying towards the door.
'And stop looking at my arse!' I call back as I walk out the door.
I hear him groan, 'Yep, I hate him.'

He drops me home with the cooler and the surfboards.
Before he leaves, he grabs my hand and pulls me in, bringing his other hand up
to my face.
He looks me in the eyes, not saying anything, just smiling.
'What?' I ask him.
'Just admiring the view,' he sighs. 'I really need to go, if anything happens, call
me.'
'Of course,' is all I get to say before he kisses me.
It starts off soft, but only gets hungrier as his hand leaves my wrist and snakes
around my lower back.
I moan softly which makes him pull me closer.

'Dominic,' I say, 'Go, I'm not going anywhere.'
Dominic groans as he releases me.
'Fine, but I'm not happy. I'll be back as soon as I can.'
'And I'll be here, pining. Waiting for your return,' I say with sad puppy eyes.
'Smart arse.'
'Yeah, but I'm cute, so, you know.' I shrug, smiling at him.
He kisses me again.
'Go,' I giggle.
He slaps my arse and gives it a good squeeze before getting back in his car and heading off.
I look at the time, it's a little after nine AM.

I head inside with Dominic's bag with his clothes in it, and the cooler.
It will be a few hours before he gets back so, there is plenty of time to make a mean chocolate cake, I think to myself.
I preheat the oven and put the Beach Boys on, loudly, not caring about the neighbours, and chuck in some washing.
I quickly check to see if Amber needs any of her uniforms washed and ironed; she does.
I laugh to myself.
I get the cake ingredients out and then decide to make it a layered mud cake.
I unpack the cooler and then begin to sing and dance around the kitchen.
I get the cake tins in the oven and head down to hang out the washing.
I'm washing Amber's uniforms when my phone beeps in my pocket.
It's a message from Dominic.

I hate Luke!!

Poor baby, I reply, chuckling to myself.

MEANWHILE:
Casuarina Prison Maximum Security Prison, Western Australia.

Sitting alone in an interview room, a lawyer awaits the arrival of a prisoner.
The door opens, and the guards bring in a prisoner in heavy chains and shackles.
The guards remove his restraints and he watches them leave.
Even in prison clothes and chains, he cuts a striking figure.
Tall, tanned, and well built.
Dark hair, medium, side-swept, and a well-groomed, short beard.
He is incredibly handsome and knows it, but his eyes are black and devoid of even a hint of anything—it's like staring into the abyss.

'Mister Webster. Please take a seat.' The attorney stands to greet him and motions for him to sit.

'I trust you have come here with good news, for your sake, Donald.' His voice is venomous.

'Well, yes,' he stammers, 'And, no.' The attorney is nervous.

'Get to the point, I am not a patient man!' Michael snaps and slams his fists on the table, making the attorney flinch.

He fusses with his glasses and then puts them on.

He opens the file on the table in front of him.

'Right,' he begins, 'Well, with all the evidence against you, the prosecution is campaigning to have you held till trial.' He swallows. 'Now, if, sorry, when you make bail, it will be high and very strict. You will be confined to the state of Western Australia.'

'Wow, just fucking wow! I pay you to tell me what I already fucking know?' Michael yells.

'I believe I may, sorry, I will get you out on a technicality. The warrant you were arrested on appears not to be completely accurate.' Donald shifts in his seat and clears his throat. 'I also have some matters that require your urgent attention.'

He pulls out a document folder from his briefcase.

'Is that all you have to tell me, Donald?' Michael asks.

'No,' the attorney pauses, 'We found her.'

Michael sits back, folds his arms, and smiles.

👀 ELIZABETH 👀

I have just finished icing the cake when I hear his car.

I can't mistake the sound of his Diesel V8 twin turbo Landcruiser Ute.

I quickly finish cleaning up and turn around to see him reach the top of the stairs and walk onto the deck. He gets to the door, puts his sunglasses on the back of his hat, and bends down to remove his boots and socks.

Oh my, he is all hot, dirty and sweaty….in a good way.

I stay right where I am, holding onto the bench with weak knees.

He looks up and smiles.

Oh, good golly gosh, that damn smile.

I take a deep breath, hold onto the bench even tighter, and smile back.

Even covered in dirt and sawdust, smelling of deodorant, aftershave, and sweat, he is still as gorgeous as ever.

He walks toward me, removing his hat and putting it on the bench, and running his hand through his hair. I can't even string a sentence together.

He grabs me by the waist and his eyes haven't left mine, the anticipation causes me to stumble slightly into him.
His hands hold either side of my face, his eyes searching mine, as he leans in and finds my lips.
I melt into him and moan, my arms tightening around his waist.
He has never kissed me like this.
He breathes deeply into the kiss, like I'm the oxygen his body requires.
A surge of heat shoots through my body, setting off every nerve like fireworks.
Holy moly, this man knows how to kiss.
My toes curl, and I may have even done a little princess leg lift.

He stops and steps back, looking at me.
A sense of fear creeps in, is this a goodbye kiss?
What's happening?
I start to panic when his lips claim mine again.
This time with more urgency; his tongue explores my mouth and dances with mine.
He pulls me in hard against him, my hands on his chest, holding onto his shirt.
He pulls away again and rests his forehead on mine.
'Is everything okay?' I ask, 'Are you okay?'
'I am, now,' he replies, 'I missed you.'
He brings his hands back up to my face, and smiles.
He kisses me gently.
'Now, what do we have here behind you?'
'I may or may not have made a chocolate layered mud cake,' I reply tartly.
'Cake and barely-there shorts, if you have cold beer I'm never letting you go.' He smiles and raises his eyebrow.
'Beer is in the fridge,' I say, biting my lip.
He groans as he kisses me again.

'If we don't go to the beach now, we will never get there,' he says, letting me go.
He walks into my room for a quick shower while I repack the cooler and add a few beers for him.
We grab the boards, cooler, blanket and towels, and head up the path to the beach.
We spend the rest of the afternoon enjoying the water.
The waves are small, so I get to show off my goofy-foot talent on the longboard.
We have good weather and each other.
The waves die off even more, so I lie back on the board, looking up at the sky, with my fingers in the water, listening to the ocean.
I missed this.

I hear him paddle up to me.
'Come on, my little goofy-foot, it's about time we head in.'
'Can we stay a little while longer?' I ask him.
'Come on, I have a lighter in the lid of the cooler, I'll make a fire.'
'Yay!' I say as I roll over and sit up on the board.
He leans in, his kiss is soft and tender.
'Last one in cooks dinner!' I say as I push him off his board and paddle in.
'Elizabeth!' He calls out.
I laugh and look back as he gets back on his board.
Shit he is quick, but I still make it to shore before him, just.
I get the board up on the beach as he catches me.
'I hope you're not a sore loser,' I say, looking up at him.
'You cheated!'
'No, I played the advantage, it's not my fault you were distracted.' I raise my eyebrow.

I shiver as his hands run up my sides and his lips brush mine.
Before I realise it, his arms wrap around me and he takes my legs from under me, pinning me on the blanket under him.
'Now who is distracted?' He asks.
'Guilty, sir,' I giggle.
He helps me up and wraps me in a towel.
'Shall I get a fire going?'
'Yes, please,' I reply, 'Only if you want to, as well.'
'Hell, yeah.' He kisses me.
He goes to find some timber. I watch him build the fire, smiling to myself.
'What?' He asks.
'Oh, nothing, just admiring the view,' I shrug.

He sits behind me, pulling me in.
We sit for ages, not saying a thing.
'Where is your mind right now?' He asks.
'Um, back to the day at the beach. I was so nervous, I thought that you only invited me because you felt sorry for me.'
He kisses the top of my head and chuckles.
'What?' I ask him nervously.
'I was nervous.'
'You were nervous, really?' I'm shocked by his statement.
'Yep, the first time I saw you, you kinda hit me for a six. I stood in your doorway completely lost for words.'
'Me?'

'I so badly wanted to kiss you when I was sitting on your bed, and when I was leaving. Every time you called, or I called you, I would pray that you weren't going to say you couldn't come. I would delay the end of the call, just so I could listen to your voice.' He clears his throat.

'It sounds childish, but when we played football, I made sure I was on the opposite team just so I could get the chance to hold you. When I saw you sitting by yourself, I thought—it's now or never. When I kissed you, I was hooked. When you kissed me back, I was so elated.'
He pauses, kisses me on the head, and pulls me in tighter.
'I could tell someone hurt you. I didn't know the extent at the time. But you took a chance to let me in. I have never once thought you were a freak.'
I turn to look at him.
I knew he cared, but hearing all this was another thing.
Hearing that he was nervous around me completely shocked me.

'Dominic, I, um… Wow! I made you nervous? Me? You make me feel special,' I can feel myself blushing.
'Liz, you are special to me. The more I get to know you, see how you treat people and do life, it makes me only want you more. After everything, you are still a loving, thoughtful, beautiful person, and incredibly sexy.'
'Thank you,' I smile.
'What for?'
'Taking a chance on me.'
I kiss him and I feel his arms tighten around me.

It is dark when we get back and wash the boards.
Dominic has a shower while I unpack the cooler.
I'm replaying everything Dominic said to me on the beach.
He comes out wrapped in a towel as I come up from hanging out the washing.
I head in for a shower, and I'm still smiling to myself when I get out.
I dry myself off, put my hair up in a clip and wrap myself in a towel.
I head into the kitchen to find Dominic stuffing his face with cake; he looks at me as if to say, What?
'Well, I guess the cake tastes okay, then' I smile.
He shrugs and nods as he continues eating.
I smile at him.
I'll give him his surprise tonight.

I notice I have a message.

Hey Elizabeth, It's Simon, Dominic's friend. Luke and I have nailed down a date for Louise's birthday. Can I drop by tomorrow with a food list and ideas?

I reply with my address and let him know early morning is best.
He responds, I'll see you at 8:30 before I start work.

I turn back to Dominic, who is still eating cake.
I walk over to him and a devilish thought crosses my mind.
I can't help but smile.
He looks up with a mouth full of cake and realises he is cornered.
I get to him and all that's between us is two towels and a plate.
I look at the cake and then back at him.
He still has a mouthful of cake and is looking somewhat concerned.

I raise my eyebrow and bite my bottom lip.
I walk backwards as I pull his towel off.
'Mmm, much better,' I giggle as I turn and walk away.
I turn around, releasing my hairclip as I remove my towel.
Turning my head to look over my shoulder, I see his heated stare as he watches me drop the towel.
I hear him growl, and the plate gets dropped into the sink.
I shiver with anticipation.
I only just make it to my bedroom door before he catches me.
He grabs my hips and spins me around.
His lips devour mine as he uses his foot to close the door and moves with me to the bed.

I manage to turn him around and get him on the bed as he pulls me down onto himself.
He leaves a trail of kisses and bites along my neck as his hands grab my arse.
I reach over and grab a black box off my bedside table.
He looks at me as I hand him the box.
There is a part of me that is really, really nervous.
He looks at the box and then back at me.
He opens the box to reveal condoms and lubricant; he knows exactly what this is for.
He looks up at me, and I nervously smile and nod.
He twists his fingers through my hair, and pulls my face to his as I move along his cock.

'You are amazing, Elizabeth.'
'I want you, Dominic.' I moan softly.
I feel him deep inside me, I know how much he wants this.
I kiss him hard and he returns it.
His hand is still tangled in my hair, and the other hand slides down to my butt as I move on him.
His fingers start caressing my rim.
Our movements become harder and faster.
I can feel the heat rising in me.
He slides his finger in as I climax, calling his name.

He turns and pins me under him, never once stopping.
He pushes deeper and harder, and moans as his lips find mine and I run my fingernails along his back.
I can feel his body's reaction to my touch.
He pins my hands above my head with one hand, using his free hand to sit up enough to look at me as I wrap my legs around him holding him to me.
'Dominic,' I whisper his name.
His movements become harder and more dominant; he never breaks eye contact with me.
I reach for him, pulling him down to me as I arch my back and start to orgasm.
He grabs my breast and pinches my nipple, kissing me as I cry out in ecstasy.

We are both breathing heavily when he looks at me.
'Liz,'
'Yes?'
'Are you…?'
'Yes,' I confirm.
I'm feeling confident right now, and some of my worst scars are on my back.
I want this, I want it while I still feel confident enough to initiate it, not in the heat of the moment when we are both lost in the intensity of it.
He kisses me softly.
'Let me know if you need me to stop.'
'Okay,' I nod.

I pull him in and kiss him, his hunger matching mine.
As I turn my body to the bed, he pulls me against him.
I feel his chest against my back.
He is hard and is breathing heavily.
With one of his hands planted firmly on the bed, keeping his weight from crushing me, the other reaches around me, finding my breast.
My body responds to him.

I feel his lips brush against my shoulder.
His fingers search my core, moving down to find and rub my clit.
The feeling causes me to moan and gasp.
My arm reaches up behind his head as I turn to look up at him. He smiles as he kisses me.
His kiss gets harder as his fingers slide into me, causing an explosion through my body.
I moan his name loudly as he continues.
He pushes me against the bedhead.

My breathing gets quicker as his hands move along my back, and his kisses trail softly with his tongue.
I hear the foil packet being opened.
The lubricate is cold and quickly melts against my heat, sending shivers over my body.
He enters me, slowly, carefully, whispering to me and making sure that I'm okay.
His hands run along the scars down to my waist.
His fingers dig softly into my hip, and his movements are gentle.
I can tell he is holding back, he doesn't want to hurt me.
It's not long before he is all the way inside me, and I hear him moan.

The feeling is unbelievable, and the pleasure spreading through my entire body is insane.
I turn my head to see him, he looks like he is lost in the pleasure as well.
He leans forward, pushing in deeper, and I moan loudly.
'Liz?' He asks me, sounding concerned.
'Don't stop. Dominic, please don't stop,' I pant; it's intense and I want to explore it.
He kisses me, his tongue moving with mine, as we both moan with pleasure.
With each movement I can feel myself getting closer to climax.
I start to feel how much he is enjoying this.
His grip on my waist tightens.
His movements become harder, faster.

I try to hold back and he senses it.
His hand moves under me and his fingers start to tease my clitoris, and this tips me immediately over the edge.
My whole body erupts, my hands grabbing the bedhead, nearly breaking it, as I cum.
I look back at him, pleading with him not to stop and go harder.
I have never had or felt anything like this before.
I've never even orgasmed this intensely in my life.

He stops briefly to apply more lubricate, not to moisten me, but to cool me down.
I can feel the heat burning between my legs.
He enters me again.
I gasp, the pleasure overcoming me again.
'Liz,' he moans my name.
His voice is raspy, his breathing is rapid and heavy.
He pulls me up to my knees and holds my breasts in his hands.
I turn my head and pull his head to mine, hungry for his lips.

'Liz,' he whispers.
'Yes, Dominic, I need you,' I moan against his lips.
His kiss starts soft and becomes more vigorous.
He pushes me against the headboard and leans in.
His fingers intertwined with mine, neither of us can hold back any longer.
We both tremble as we let go and orgasm together.
It's the most intimate experience I have ever had, sharing it with him feels so much more sweeter.
His hands find mine and hold them as his kisses trail up my back, to my neck, finding my lips again.

'Liz?'
'Mmm.'
'How are you feeling?' He whispers in my ear.
He slowly pulls out and I turn to face him.
'Amazing,' I answer, 'And were you satis-'
He silences me with a kiss. A kiss full of passion and desire.
'Do you even have to ask?' He looks at me.

We somehow made it to the shower and he proceeded to wash me, his hands lingering over my breasts.
I look up at him and smile.
Water droplets fall from his hair down to his chest.
I run my hands up his arms and lace my fingers together behind his neck.
He holds me closer.
'Am I ever going to get enough of you, Miss Miller?'
'I certainly hope not, Mister Taumata, but I do suppose I could find you additional jobs. I would like to continue our mutually beneficial arrangement.' I answer as I lick my lips.
'Like what? I have already added an additional fireplace and a fire pit.' He smiles.

'Well, maybe I could buy some land and get you to build me an entire home. I could make the deck bigger, get a pool… Oh, maybe even a spa on the deck.'
'A spa?' He smirks.

'Mmm, just think about it: After a long day of watching you work, I could sit in my spa with a drink or two, and have you join me. Unless, of course, you have received a better offer,' I say as my hand traces down his chest to his abs and back up.
I look at him with a raised eyebrow, biting my bottom lip.
He grins and leans in.
'Nope, definitely no better offer.' He says as his hands slide down to my arse.
I giggle.

'You better get that spa.'
I giggle again.
His lips feel good against mine.
'Really? I can have the spa?'
'On one condition,'
'Which is?' I ask him.
'Clothing is optional.'
I giggle some more as his lips find my neck.

He holds me tight as our wet bodies feel alight.
Our kiss leaves no room for imagination.
I can feel him harden against me.
He lifts me up and pushes me against the shower wall.
I wrap my legs around him as he presses against me and enters me.
The way he makes me feel is incredible.
His movements are hard, and I moan louder as he pushes deep into me.
I can feel his breath against my neck.

He leans down, moving his lips from my mouth to my breasts, his teeth teasing my nipples.
His movements become urgent as he brings me to orgasm, sucking my breast.
I dig my nails in, continuing to climax, trembling.
'Do you trust me?' He asks, breathing heavily, asking permission.
'Always,' I answer breathlessly.

He lets me down and turns me, pinning me against the wall.
I know exactly what he wants, and I let him.
I bend slightly, pushing against him, letting him know I want it as much as he does.

He enters slowly and it feels even better and more intense than before.
'Dominic,' I moan.
His response is immediate.
I feel his hand slide up my stomach and I hold it to me, his fingers intertwined with mine.
His other hand holds my waist and he grips me tighter.
I push harder against him and he starts to moan.
'Liz,' he moans, 'Can I pl...,'
'Yes, Dominic,' I answer.
I know he wants to fill me up, and I want him to.
'Tell me if I,' he moans, 'If you...' He moans again.

I don't have to answer because my body does it for me.
With both hands grabbing my waist, he thrusts harder and deeper.
I feel an explosion of heat and ecstasy, building up.
The pleasure is intense.
I turn my head and place my hand on his as I watch him.
I can feel myself start to shake.
I try to hold back, but I can't, the sensation is so overpowering.
He throws his head back and cries out.
His thrusts become faster, his hold tighter.

He calls my name when he starts to feel me tighten around him as I climax.
'Yes, Dominic!' I call out.
He leans forward as he starts to orgasm.
He is breathing hard and he wraps his arms around me, waiting for his body and mine to steady before gently pulling out.

He kisses my shoulder and I turn to face him, and lean on the wall.
He puts his hands on either side of me, looking at me.
'You feel so amazing, Liz,' he whispers.
I turn to him and meet his lips.

Eventually we get out of the shower and make our way to bed.
Dominic, however, decides he needs more cake and heads to the kitchen.
Spent, I don't even bother to get dressed, but climb into bed and snuggle in.
I fall asleep so quickly that I don't even feel him climb into bed and cuddle me.

CHAPTER 6

Michael

MEANWHILE:

Casuarina Maximum Security Prison, Western Australia.

'Hello Donald, to what do I owe the pleasure of your company this late on a Monday?' Michael smirks.
'I was able to get a meeting with Judge Harper. I got him to sign off and your hearing date is set.' Donald replies.
'Well, what are you waiting for?'
'Right. Um. The earliest I was able to secure was Friday, the fourteenth of May.'
'Not good enough, Donald!' Michael slams his fists on the table.

'I have been in here for too long, I have a business to run, and clients that I need to see.' Michael stands and paces the room.
'I need to arrange a meeting. I need to see Brian and Sam.'
'Of course. I will get to it as soon as possible. Is there anything else I can do for you?' Donald asks.
'Get a bitch here to see to my… Needs,' he sneers with a villainous smile.
'The female guards are getting a little too clingy.'
'That will take some time, and payment.' Donald looks at him nervously.
'Who am I?'
'Michael Webster,' Donald answers.
Michael nods and sits back down.
He folds his arms and leans back, putting his feet on the table.

'So, when I get out, how soon before she joins me?' Michael asks
'Two of your most trusted men are watching her,' Donald replies.
'Good, I want what belongs to me, no one takes my belongings without retribution from me. Mark my words, Donald, my vengeance will be a masterpiece.' Michael leans back in his seat further.

'We do have a development, though.' Donald says nervously.
'Well, please do enlighten me as to this development.'
'It appears she has found a boyfriend.' Donald clears his throat.

'Well, well, well, now that is an interesting development. This is going to be fun.'
His voice drips with venom.
'Donald, I have changed my mind, I'm going to them, so I want everything set up.'
'Of course, I will see it done.'

'Don't forget my toys,' Michael sits up and looks at Donald.
Even Donald gets deathly cold chills at the word toys.
'I'm sure that everything will be arranged as per your requirements,' Donald shifts in his seat.
'Excellent, is there anything else you need to discuss? Time is getting on.'
'Just, ah, um, a few issues,' Donald says, fidgeting with the papers in front of him.
'I don't like issues, Donald. I like jobs being done correctly!' Michael raises his voice. 'If there is a problem, I expect you to fix it and come to me with solutions,' Michael demands.

Donald passes him a letter, which Michael reads, his eyes showing nothing but evil.
'Pen please, Donald, and make sure it is red, my favourite colour.'
'Why is red your favourite colour?' Donald asks as he passes Michael a red pen.
'Because my Chantelle bleeds it so beautifully,' Michael smiles as he begins writing.

'Now, Donald, please make sure the men know this is to be followed precisely. I will not accept any fuck-ups this time, the last one had my Chantelle stolen from me.'
Michael looks up, 'Tell Sam and Brian I want to see them tomorrow. The sooner they get things moving, the better. Make sure they get this.'

Michael leans forward on the table and slides the letter over to Donald.
Donald opens it and reads.
He instantly goes pale, and looks up at Michael.
'I told you it will be a masterpiece,' Michael says, standing up.
Donald stands and nods.
'Oh, and, Donald, please contact Joe, he is our closest asset. Tell him to prepare a hole.' Michael bangs on the prison door. 'Time for my ladies to sponge bath me.'

I wake early the next morning to see sunlight peeking through the curtains.
Dominic is still sleeping.
Careful not to wake him, I slide out of bed and tiptoe to the bathroom.
I feel a little tender, but I smile, remembering the passion and intensity Dominic and I experienced last night.
I emerge from the bathroom and get dressed.
He is still asleep.
I make us both a cup of tea in travel mugs, leave a note for Dominic and head down to the beach.

The beach is beautiful and calm this morning.
It's just me, some kangaroos and people in the distance.
The sun is hiding behind the clouds, the water is glossy and reflects the beautiful orange, yellow, and purple tones.
The water is cool on my feet and I close my eyes, letting the cool breeze wash over me as I listen to the small shore waves.
The tide is up, almost to where Dominic and I were sitting with the fire.

I remember pushing him off the board, and him telling me how nervous I made him.
I still can't believe I'm with him, how happy I am. How happy he has made me, and knowing I have made him happy as well makes everything just perfect.
I sit on the beach, watching the waves. I look up the beach and see people on horseback.
The horses are galloping through the water towards me.
They slow as they get closer and pass me before they set off again.
I hear footsteps behind me, and I turn to see Dominic.

'Hey, you!'
'There's my girl.'
Dominic sits behind me and I lean back into him, closing my eyes.
'How are you feeling?' He asks, as he kisses the top of my head.
'A little tender. But I love the feeling. It's never felt so intimate and sensual.'
I turn and look at him.
'What about you? How do you feel?'

He smiles and leans in, his hands moving up my arms to my neck as he brings his lips to mine.
His kiss makes me feel like I'm floating in the clouds.
It's hard but it's also passionate, dominating but also caring.

He responds to my hands under his shirt, resting on his bare skin.
His tongue explores my mouth and teases my lips.
I moan as he softly bites my bottom lip.
'You have me completely amazed, Elizabeth. What I feel for you is hard to explain; how you make me feel… I don't have the right words to say how much you mean to me. Don't ask me if, just trust me when I tell you that you always satisfy me.'
I blush and he pulls me in, holding me tight.

'Shall we start heading back?' He asks.
'Do we have to?' I sulk.
He laughs and says, 'Yes, I have a few things I want done before we leave next week.'
He stands and helps me up.

We walk back hand in hand.
I can't wait to go on our little getaway.
Just Dominic and I with no distractions, and most importantly—a chance to let him in a little more.
He knows Michael is a bad person, but not to the full extent.
I need to be sure I can protect him.
'Liz?' His voice breaks through my thoughts.
'Sorry, what?' I look up at him.
'I was asking you if you are okay. You went really quiet and looked like you were a million miles away.'
I nod as I bring my hand to my wrist.

He sees me rubbing my wrist and understands immediately.
'Babe, don't rush yourself. You can tell me when you're ready, and I'll help. I'm not pushing you.'
'I do want to tell you. I will, I just need some more time. He made me think….'
'What, what did he make you think?'
'He, umm, made me think I'm expendable, a nothing and a nobody. I was only his possession… To use as he saw fit. I was good for cooking, cleaning, fucking, and beating.' I say, looking at the floor of my kitchen.
'I'm so sorry that he made you feel that way. Please trust me when I tell you, you are nothing of what he made you feel. You are someone special, my someone special.' Dominic kisses the top of my head and runs his hands over mine.

I look up to meet his eyes.
He brings his hands to my face and his kiss starts off soft, becoming harder, more forceful, but still passionate.

I place my hands on his hips and melt into him.
I replay every kiss in my head and apart from our first kiss, this one is my favourite.
It's by far the most meaningful.
His tongue explores my mouth, licking my lips and his teeth gently biting my bottom lip.
He rests his forehead against mine, my eyes are closed, savouring his touch, his smell, his lips.

'Why did you stop?' I ask him.
'If I didn't now, I wouldn't be able to, and I really need to get ready for work.'
I take a deep breath and open my eyes to find him watching me with a smile.
I move my hands up his shirt, grab the collar and bring his lips back to mine.
He groans as he holds me tight and lifts me up onto the bench, we only stop to catch our breath.

'Okay, now you can go get ready,' I say.
Even though my legs still hold him to me, and his hands haven't left my sides, he looks at his watch and then back at me.
'One more,' he brings his lips back to mine.
His hand slides along my thigh, sending shock waves through my body.
'Okay, now I really need to…' He says, still kissing me.
I moan as his hands slide up under my shirt.
He breaks away.
'…to stop, I have a truck arriving at seven-thirty-ish,' Dominic looks at his watch.

I release my legs from around him and pout.
He chuckles and runs his hand through his hair.
'Not fair, Liz,'
'Fine, go then, get ready for work. I suppose I should get ready myself, anyway.'
'Ready for?' He asks.
'Oh, just this hot builder I've got working on my deck extension,' I say, fanning myself.
'Oh, right, the hot-for-you builder, I might have to hang around then.' He winks as he turns to go get ready.

My phone beeps with a message from Simon.

Can I come now? I have to go to work early.

Kettle is on, I send back.

I start getting ingredients out for something savoury and perfect for lunch and put the kettle on.
Dominic's phone beeps so I pick it up and take it to him.
I walk into the bathroom.
He's wrapped in a towel and water still beads on his body.
I look him over and hold up his phone.
'Trade?' I suggest as I raise my eyebrow.
'No,' he says, trying to grab his phone.

I duck away out of reach and give him my best pout face.
He groans and gives in, pinning me against the door frame.
His kiss starts off soft as he pulls his phone from my hand, and becomes more forceful.
'Knock, knock, Elizabeth?'
'Shit,' I say
'Don't go anywhere, this isn't over.'
'It is, for now,' he replies as he starts to get dressed.
'Agreed,' I smile and leave to greet Simon.

'Hi, Simon, come in, the kettle has just boiled. Are you hungry?'
'Coffee would be great, thanks, but I can't stay.'
'I'll make it in a travel mug for you. How do you take it?
'Black, two sugars, please.'
'Hey, thanks for this, I really want to give you a heads-up for the food,' he adds.
I turn and start making coffee.
'If you want, I can give you some vanilla slice and lamingtons to take and share at work.'
'Are they yours?' He asks.
'Yep, I made them for Dominic, but I can make more.'
'Well, I won't say no, and neither will the nurses in the staffroom. You sure Dominic won't mind?'
I grab the containers from the fridge, put them on the bench in front of him, and smile.
I turn back to finish the coffee when Dominic walks out into the kitchen.

'Hey mate,' Dominic says as they shake hands.
'Hey, didn't expect to see you here. Early start or sleep over?' Simon enquires.
Dominic doesn't answer, he just walks up behind me and puts his hands on my hips, leaning in.
'Do I get one?' He asks, as his hands slide up my legs.
I lean back into him, enjoying his touch.
'Yes,' I whisper.

He kisses my neck and slaps my butt, then walks over to Simon and they head out onto the deck.

I stand there for a minute, smiling to myself, then I finish making coffee.

I walk out with the tray of coffee as Dominic's phone rings.

He winks at me and walks down to the grass to take the call.

I grab the containers off the bench and sit opposite Simon.

'So, what do you have for me?' I ask.

'Be completely honest with me, you don't have to do this if it's too much.'

'I'm happy to do it,' I reply

'Okay, well, I had a chat with Luke and we are thinking of finger foods, platters, BBQ meats and salads, etc. Nothing too formal,' he says, looking at me while having a mouthful of coffee.

'That sounds great. I have a whole folder of that, I can go get it.' I start to get up.

'No, not today, but if you could email a list of what you want, Luke and I will buy it. I, sorry, we do have another two favours to ask you, though.' He says with fingers crossed.

'Okay, what would you like?' I ask him.

'Can you make a white chocolate mud cake?'

'Yes, not a problem,' I reply. 'So, what's favour number two?'

'Would it be possible to have the party here?' He asks with a pleading look.

'Sure.'

He looks at me, kind of shocked. I'm guessing he was expecting me to say no.

'Really? Are you sure? I mean you didn't even take time to think about it'.

'Yes, I'm serious, I would be happy for you and Luke to host the party here. I mean, she has never been here, and it is a surprise party, so it makes perfect sense,' I answer.

'Oh my god, thank you, thank you, thank you!' He flashes a huge smile.

'So, when would you be free to settle the menu?' I ask him.

'Um, today is Thursday…' He looks at his phone, 'Next Tuesday morning?'

'Perfect, I look forward to it.'

'Look forward to what?' Dominic asks.

I hand him coffee as he sits down between Simon and I and takes my hand.

'Menu planning for Louise's birthday,' I reply.

Dominic lifts my hand to his lips and smiles at me.

'Our dear Elizabeth here has agreed to let us have the party here,' Simon adds.

'Is that a good idea, Simon?' Dominic asks.

'Why? I don't have a problem with it,' I interject.

'Louise and Stephanie are best friends, so that means she will be here.' Dominic looks at Simon.

'So, we can rub it in her face that you have traded up,' Simon jokes.

'Let her come, I don't care, besides I can always take out the trash or let Amber loose,' I smile at him.

Dominic leans forward and grabs a lamington from the container.

'Hey, those are mine!' Simon complains as he snatches the container from Dominic.

Dominic turns to look at me.

'What, you're giving him my goodies?'

'I will make you some more, besides—you still have some in the fridge and chocolate cake.'

'Can I have those mini lemon things you made last week? And I'm not sharing,' he says, looking over at Simon.

'Why do you get to have all the food?' Simon asks.

'Cause I'm her boyfriend, not you,' he replies.

'Now, boys. Simon, bring those containers back and I will restock them for you. Dominic, I promise you will get more than him,' I say, laughing at their childish exchange.

'Can I do what Amber does?' Simon asks.

'Give me a list and I will make it for you,' I nod, smiling.

'Would you like me to refill the travel mug before you go?' I ask Simon.

'Yes, please,' he replies.

I head inside to refill the mug for Simon and they continue to chat.

I come back with his mug.

'I really have to go, thank you so much, Elizabeth!' He stands.

I hand him the mug as he pulls me in for a hug and kisses my cheek, and I completely freeze.

Dominic notices straight away.

'Oi, hands off my girl and take your food!' He jokes.

Simon laughs and releases me and grabs the containers, before walking off with Dominic.

I stand there regaining my composure. Dominic returns and finds me pacing in the kitchen.

'I'm so sorry, I didn't mean to panic. I just...'

'Liz, babe, it's okay.' He walks over to me.

'Breathe, Liz, don't worry—he didn't even notice. He was more concerned about me taking my goodies back.'

Dominic pulls me against him.
'I still feel stupid, it's just that…' I pause.
'What?'
'It doesn't matter, it's stupid, really,' I say, feeling embarrassed.
'No, it's not Liz. It has upset you, please tell me.' He looks at me.
'Promise you won't… You won't laugh?' I ask, looking at the floor.
I start fidgeting with the tea towel. Dominic reaches for my hands.
He can feel me trembling.
'Yo, Dominic!' A voice calls out.
'Shit, sorry, Liz. I'll be right back.' Dominic says.
'No, it's okay, you go do your thing.' I give a forced smile and walk away.

👀 DOMINIC 👀

I watch her pull away.
I remember what Amber told me: the doctors and the account of the injuries
she sustained at the hands of another man, a man she trusted.
A man she loved.
I feel my hands clench.
I want to follow her, hold her, listen to her, and make her feel safe.
I feel lousy for walking the other way.

'Hey, Aaron, sorry mate, I was on the phone,' I say, shaking his hand.
I practically run down the stairs. I want this truck unloaded and gone.
'In a rush, mate?' Aaron remarks.
'Yeah, big day.'
'You sure it's got nothing to do with the hot chick upstairs? I saw her last time
I was here and damn, she has some legs on her.' He starts undoing the straps.
I laugh half-heartedly and pretend not to be annoyed by his comment.
'Yeah, no, I have a to-do list for today longer than my arm.'
'She single?' He asks.
'No.' I give him a look.
'You and her?' He asks.
'Yes.'

It takes about thirty minutes to unload the truck and sign the paperwork.
The moment Aaron left, I practically run back upstairs.
'Liz! Babe?' I call out.
Then I realise the house is completely quiet; no music, no humming, nothing.
Panic starts to set in.
I race to her bedroom, it's empty.

So is her bathroom.
I check the rest of the house, calling her name.
Her phone is still on the bench, so are the ingredients she was going to use.
'FUCK!' I yell out loud.
'What's got you all worked up?'
I turn to see Amber standing at the door.
'Where's my girl?' She asks.
'I don't fucking know, she was just here… I went to unload a truck and came back and now she is not here.' I start pacing the kitchen.

'She wanted to talk but…' I stop mid-sentence as dread fills me.
I race back to her bathroom.
'Dominic?' Amber calls and follows me. 'What, Dominic?'
I search through the vanity cabinets.
'Pills! They aren't here, where are they, Amber?'
I'm really starting to panic.
I grab the vanity top.
'Liz stopped taking them, she made me get rid of them,' Amber replies.
I look up at Amber's reflection in the mirror. She still has the vials though, I think to myself.
'Why?' I ask, turning to Amber.
'She didn't want them anymore. Liz and I spoke about it and she asked me, so I did.'
'I don't understand, what about her dreams?' I ask, looking at her.
'Simple: She has you, you are all she needs.'
That means she hasn't taken an overdose.
The beach! I need to get to the beach, I'm sure she is there.

'I have fucked up, big time,' I say as I barge past her back to the kitchen, and straight into Liz.
A huge flood of relief washes over me.
Before I can say anything, she grabs her phone and my hand.
I notice her face is red as she pulls me out the door, then lets go of my hand and runs.
Amber and I take off after her, wondering what's happening.
She runs while making a call.
We head next door and I can hear screaming.
Liz races in without a thought.
She turns to Amber.
'Amber, grab her and calm her down,' Liz says as she slides along the floor, then takes over CPR on a child no more than ten years old.

I realise what's going on.
I watch Liz, and she has complete control.
I have never seen her like this.
She is ordering the father around, and he is grabbing all sorts of stuff.
Straw, pens, tea towels, knife, duct tape, and vodka.
'Dominic,' Liz calls my name without even looking at me.
She has cut away the young boy's shirt.
'Dominic, can you please pull this pen apart, put it in the tray with the knife and pour the vodka over it.'
I nod and do what she asks me.

'Okay, he is breathing, pupils are reactive, but slow. I'm going to make a small incision,' She tells someone on the other end of the phone.
She pours vodka over the child's chest and the father's hands.
'Dominic, can you pour the vodka over my hands, please?' She asks.
I do as she asks, watching her work.
'Dominic, please go outside and flag down the ambulance. They will be coming under full lights and sirens.'
She looks up at me.
I don't need to be told twice.
I wait in the driveway for about ten minutes before I hear the sirens.
It's not long before I see them and wave them down.
I run back inside as they turn into the driveway.
'They are here,' I announce, reaching the kitchen.

Liz is still tending to the child.
That's when I notice she has blood on her hands, legs, and her clothes.
Amber is with the mother, who appears to have fainted, and the father is sitting on the floor, in shock and very pale.
'Dominic,' Liz says my name without even looking at me.
She is applying pressure around the pen's empty tube.

'Yes?'
'Can you help Matthew, please?' She motions towards the boy's father.
'Sure,' I reply.
I can hear Liz talking to the child.

I help the dad move, as the paramedics get to the kitchen and start tending to the boy with Liz.
I watch as she starts to go through everything.
She has had to cut the boy's chest and insert a straw.
Liz gets up and walks over to Amber to check on the mother.

She turns to the father who is trembling with shock in the reclining chair and
still looks really pale.
Liz says, 'Matthew, go grab some clothes and toiletries for yourself and Renae.
I'll stay with Shaye till you come back.' She has her hand on his shoulder.
He looks at her and nods.
'What do you need me to do?' I ask her.

'Best stay with Amber. Renae might wake up freaking out.' She smiles at me.
I'm mesmerised watching her like this. I see this is who she really is—completely
capable, in control, and in her element.
I go to Amber and watch Liz working confidently side-by-side with a male
paramedic.
She talks easily as her hands move effortlessly.

'I told you, Dom. She is ready to go back to work—look at her,' Amber is
watching her as well.
More paramedics arrive and take over the care of the child.
The first responders come over to me to take over the care of Renae, the boy's
mother.
I move out of the way.
'Traumatic Pneumothorax.'
'What?' I turn to Liz
I didn't even realise she is standing beside me, with everything going on.
'Broken ribs caused massive internal bleeding, which in turn caused the chest
cavity to fill with blood and the lung to collapse.' She is watching the paramedics
tend to the child.

She looks up when the dad comes back downstairs.
She goes over to him and explains what's happening.
He starts to cry and hugs her.
I start to go over to her when Amber stops me.
I look at my hands to see them shaking, and I look over at Liz and hers are
completely still.
She is calm and focused.
I'm not going to lie, I'm beyond rattled.

It's another thirty minutes before they put the child on the spinal board, and
another twenty before the boy and his parents actually leave for the hospital in
the ambulance.
The three of us head back inside the house.
Liz tells us to go so that she can clean up and lock up the house.
I go to protest, but Amber shakes her head and we leave.

I look back to see her standing there, looking at the blood and medical paraphernalia left behind. She bends down and starts cleaning up.

Amber and I go back to Liz's house to wait for her.

We walk into the kitchen and I start to tell her about what happened with Simon.

'When I came back from seeing Simon off, Liz was going to tell me something, but the truck driver interrupted us.' I sigh.

'I felt like crap for walking the other way, but I needed him to go.' I lean on my elbows against the bench, letting my hands fall and bowing my head down.

'I panicked when I came back upstairs and couldn't find her. I immediately thought the worst of her, Amber, I thought she was going to...'

I can't even bring myself to finish what I was going to say.

I look back up at Amber and she stares at me with a heated glare.

I know she isn't happy with me and I don't blame her.

'I fucked up, didn't I?' I ask her.

'No, you didn't, Dom, but maybe you could have given her more credit.' She gets up and puts on the kettle.

'What I am about to tell you cannot be repeated. Don't even hint to Liz I told you anything, but I need you to understand why she is the way she is.'

'Okay,' I agree.

'The guy that Liz was with, Michael—he's a monster. He's your worst nightmare,' She pauses.

'He's so bad, he could be featured in one of those crime shows. He's a total psychopath.'

I look at her, trying to wish the truth of what she was saying away.

I am really struggling to think of Liz, my sweet, beautiful Liz, with such a person.

I can't get my head around it.

Amber continues, 'Liz never had a boyfriend when she was at school.

She had a great group of friends and did a bit of travelling with them after leaving school, then she started University. But throughout, she never dated anyone.'

'She was pure, innocent, had never even been kissed, let alone slept with anyone. And then, at some point, she met Michael. He became her first boyfriend and she thought she was in love.'

I wince, not at the thought of Liz loving another man, but that this guy stole her innocence.

I want so desperately to erase that experience for her.

I wish like hell that her first love had been with someone who deserved her.
I wish it was with someone who treated her the way she is meant to be treated.

I'm battling to listen to Amber's words, each bit stabs a little further into my heart and makes me angrier.
'She dated Michael, but didn't sleep with him,' she continues.
'She wasn't exactly waiting for marriage, she was nervous, she didn't think she was enough for him.
He had a good job, nice homes, cars, and money. Liz was a student with uni debts, and working three jobs because she wouldn't let her parents pay for her education. She had no idea who Michael really was, nor what he was capable of doing. He completely manipulated her and ultimately controlled her without her even knowing it to begin with.' Amber pauses and I see her catch her breath. 'Liz hasn't told us everything that happened to her. I'm still putting some things together between what she has told me and what the doctors have picked up,' she says, and the colour drains from her face as she remembers what she's seen.

'Michael managed to isolate her from everyone. In a few short weeks, he managed to influence her so much that he got her to quit her jobs and go to work for him as a medic. Once she did that, he revelled in the control he had over her. She could never have seen what was about to come. His control over her had taken hold and he knew it, but she didn't. He wanted more of her and was going to take it no matter what she wanted. They had only been dating a few weeks when they went out one night. He got drunk and wanted to have sex, she said no. She wanted it to be special and didn't feel she was ready. Dropping the mask of pretence, he beat the hell out of her and then raped her. That was her first sexual experience. That's how she lost her virginity. That's how it began and from there it got worse, far worse. She was trapped.'

I sit there listening, every sentence violating my sanity.
My head is in my hands and I feel like throwing up.
'She suffered horrendous beatings, rape, forced abortions—and that's only the beginning,' Amber continues.
I look up at her through misty eyes and can see her struggling to hold back her tears too.
'When she was first found,'
'Wait, first found?' I look at Amber, confused.

Amber takes a moment before she continues.
'Michael Webster is one of the biggest drug- and human traffickers that Australia has ever had. The Federal Police starting tracking him after he made a small mistake...'

'Elizabeth,' I state, more than asking a question.
'Yes, we had suspected him of importing drugs, but it was something she said to an undercover fed unwittingly that lead us to delve deeper...'
'Wait, you had someone undercover and didn't get her out sooner?' I stare at her, stunned.
'We weren't entirely sure of her involvement, so we investigated her as well. We found out too late that she was innocent and caught in a trap she couldn't get out of. We lost track of her for a while and thought she was murdered.'
My whole body feels numb and bile is rising in my throat.

'She was found in one of Michael's homes that was raided. When the police went in, she was handcuffed inside a large animal travel crate and had a broken leg, and a dislocated hip and shoulder. She was hemorrhaging badly, Dom, she was pregnant, but lost the baby. DNA proved that Michael was the father.' Amber pauses and looks outside, sighing deeply.
'When she was in the Royal Perth Hospital we made a call to Michael as he was listed as the next of kin. Her hospital room had cameras installed, so when he came to see her we could watch what he did and what he said to her.'

Amber pauses to sip her coffee before continuing.
'She was there for a week before he came to see her. His visits were an education for her, not that of the loving partner that she was brainwashed into believing he was. He told her what to say, how to act and to not eat. We kept her in hospital longer than she needed to be.
The doctors wrote in her charts that she suffered systematic abuse and torture over a very long period of time.'

I have to sit down, my legs are just buckling underneath me.
It's breaking me, hearing all of this.
I repeat the word 'torture' in a broken voice, and ask Amber, 'How long? How long was she tort...' I can't even say it again.
I look up at Amber questioningly.
'How long?'
She looks at the floor.
'Amber, how long?' I repeat.
She looks down, shaking her head, not wanting to answer me.
'How fucking long Amber?' I insist.
She looks up at me, and says, 'The doctors said years.'
'Fucking years!' I yell.
I'm in utter shock.
I actually can't even speak.
My head is spinning, thinking of my Liz with that monster for years!

Amber hands me my coffee.

I can't hold it, my hands are shaking so bad that she puts it on the table next to me, and places a hand on my shoulder.

'She's strong, our Liz, after everything she went through, she agreed to go back and help us build a case against him.'

'You fucking sent her back to him!' I yell at her.

Now I'm livid.

Amber looks down and goes quiet for a while before finding her words.

'You have to understand, Dominic, we had nothing without her. We needed her so we could stop him. Apart from the drugs and trafficking, we believe he has killed more than Sam Little, America's worst serial killer, not to mention the number of executions he has ordered. She was made aware of the risks involved, but agreed to it anyway. She signed the waiver without any coercion from us. She wanted to help put him away, in exchange for her safety as well as her family's.

We leaked false interviews and recordings to him, in which the police threatened to take him away from her, telling her she would be put in jail, but she wouldn't budge. She made out that they were in love and he would save her, and that he never touched her, claiming she was clumsy and fell down. Her medical files were leaked and Michael bought it, hook, line and sinker.'

'She told me he hurt her,' I say, 'I could tell it was worse than what she was telling me, her nervousness gives that away, but I never expected this! Why? How could someone be so cruel?' I look at Amber.

'To Michael she was his, she belonged to him. She was his possession to use as he saw fit. I first met Liz in Brisbane when she came out of the coma. When she finally started talking, she admitted to me she wouldn't do anything without being told to do it. She had lived for so long being told what and when to do things, what to wear, what and when to eat, everything, including even going to the toilet, that she didn't function at all as a normal person.' Amber sighs and looks up at me.

'I remember the first time I asked her what she would like to have for dinner and what movie she would like to watch. She had a panic attack and just couldn't cope with it. She thought it was a trick, and that by answering it, she would be beaten.' Amber has a mouthful of her coffee and continues.

'Michael's associates weren't allowed to touch, kiss or hurt her. But she was used in ways to keep their focus on her so Michael could do what he needed to. Only Michael would inflict the rapes, beatings, and torture. Michael would tell her she was worthless, undesirable and completely disposable. There are only four trusted men who could touch her other than Michael, and even that was strictly limited to orders given by Michael.'
'Wait, what do you mean by 'they'?' I ask, looking at Amber.

My fists clench.
I am losing it.
Amber wipes her eyes and doesn't answer my question.
'You, Dominic, are the first male she has, subconsciously, given herself permission to allow close enough to touch her. All the staff at the hospital, the police, and legal team, are all female. Any time a man would come anywhere near her, she would completely freak out and her body would just shut down. That part of her conditioning has been so ingrained that most of the time she doesn't even realise what is happening. Her body recognizes that touch from a male means severe punishment for her. The shutdown is purely self-preservation.'
'Okay, but she is out now, and she is with me. Why did she react when Simon hugged her?' I ask.
I can feel myself calming down a little.

'Simple, you haven't given her permission to touch another man.'
'But she doesn't need my permission.'
'Easy for you to say, not easy for her. You need to understand that on some level, subconsciously, she still needs your permission, because she is with you. Watch her, Dominic, everything she does it is to please you. Liz doesn't even realise she is doing it.' Amber stops and sighs as she looks at her cup.
'She is my best friend and I love her. I stopped seeing her as my client and informant a long time ago. Dom, the fact that she has let you touch her, kiss her and be intimate. I don't...' Amber stops.
'Dominic.'

I look up and follow her gaze to see my girl walk into her backyard.
I don't even think, I just run to her, pick her up and hold her tight.
She giggles.
'Dom, put me down, I'm gross.'
'No, you're not,' I look at her, 'Well, maybe a little messy.'
I let her back down and kiss her.

I smile and she returns it, she is amazing.
'Are you okay? You looked a little freaked out,' she peers at me nervously.

'Um, yeah, I panicked when I couldn't find you earlier,' I reply as I take her hand.
'Sorry about that, I was hanging out the washing when Shaye's mum called out to me. I didn't think to grab my phone till theirs went flat.'
Amber's right, Liz is cautious.
'Babe, don't apologise, you were amazing!' I assure her as we head inside.

'Hey, Amber.'
'Hey, hon, I'm so proud of you. You rocked it!' Amber says, hugging her.
'Thank you, I'm going for a shower. I'll make us something when I get out.'
'How about you shower and we make you something to eat?' Amber suggests.
'Well, in that case, I'll have my favourite.' She smiles and heads in for a shower.

'What's her favourite?' I ask Amber.
'Would you believe, it's good old Vegemite on toast. She eats the stuff by the spoonful.' Amber says.
'Amber, can I ask you something? And I want you to be completely honest with me.' I sit at the bench across from Amber.
'Of course.'
'Is Liz concerned that I would hurt her in any way?'

'No,' Amber answers without hesitation, 'The thing that scares her is you turning away from her when she tells you what happened to her. To Liz, that would mean everything Michael said was the truth, and she may as well go back to him.'
My phone rings as I look at Amber.
'This conversation, by the way, is not finished,' I answer my phone.
Amber nods.

🔭 ELIZABETH 🔭

I hop out of the shower and dry off.
I sit on my bed, wrapped in the towel, going over the events of the morning.
I saved a little boy's life!
It felt so good to be useful.
I miss working, I miss my job and can't wait to go back.
I never wanted anything else in the world as much as I wanted to be a paramedic.
Not being called mum, girlfriend or even wife.

I look up when I hear knocking on my door.
'Hey hon, how are you feeling?' Amber asks as she walks in.
I stand up and hug her tight.

'A little rattled, but I feel great, it was nice to feel useful.'
'Hey, you feed me so not only is that useful, you're a lifesaver—for me and for Shaye!' Amber laughs and hugs me again.
'Thank you, Amber,' I say.
'Any time, I'll leave you to get dressed while I make you a cuppa.'

I get dressed and pick up my clothes.
I end up throwing them in the bin as Dominic walks in the bathroom.
He doesn't say anything, he just holds me tight.
He knows all I need is him, and nothing else.
He leads me to my bed, and we lay down together.
His hand runs up my arm, I look up to him as his hand brushes my cheek and he softly kisses me.
'Babe, you are an amazing person. I'm so proud of you.' He leans in and kisses me again.
'You are going to do amazing things when you go back to work.' He smiles.
'You're okay with me going to work?' I ask him.
'I want you to do what makes you happy.' His fingers stroke my cheek.

I smile, pull him down and kiss him passionately.
He has no idea how much what he just said means to me.
We head out to the kitchen.

Amber is on the deck chatting to Luke.
'What's Luke doing here?' I ask Dominic.
'He is working here with me now that I will be here full time, as the other jobs are now complete.'
'Oh, so what are your plans for today?' I ask.
'Well we are finally starting to build the side deck extension. The last of the material arrived this morning. Luke has brought the machine to dig the holes for the new posts, and your new fire pit for the deck. Not to mention, you need to sign off on the new drawings for your other changes.' He raises an eyebrow.

He hands me a pen and the new drawings and permits.
I sign them and hand him his pen back.
I look at him and smile, and he leans in and his lips brush mine.
'You make it very hard, Elizabeth,' he says as he kisses me.
'Yo, Dom, you're not getting paid to make out with the owner, I would like to start sometime today, yeah?' Luke yells with a huge grin on his face.

Dominic smiles as he continues to kiss me and grabs my arse.
'Gotta go to work,' he says.

'Well, I'm sure I'll enjoy the view,' I say toying with my lips suggestively.
'Not fair, Elizabeth!' He groans.
'I know,' I say as I wink and turn away.
Amber comes in as Dominic slaps my arse again and heads outside.

'So, what's my girl up to today?' Amber asks.
'I'm meal prepping for Fraser,' I smile, 'And for you,' I add.
'Well, it's all approved, we just ask that you make contact with us twice a day, every day, and wear this.' She hands me a bracelet.
'Med alert bracelet?' I look up at Amber. 'What does it do?'
'It's a tracker and if your file is accessed, it's flagged automatically. Now there is one more thing; there will be AFP agents there—only as back-up.
'Amber…'
'Hon, I know what you're thinking. We all want you to go, but we also want to make sure you are safe. Michael may be behind bars, but we're just not sure of his reach. It could be further than what we know of. We're just taking precautions so you can go and enjoy your holiday with Dominic.' Amber hugs me.

'Have you told Dominic anything more about me?'
'No, I only told him what he needed to know the day you collapsed. The rest is for you to tell him. When you are ready.'
I nod and look down.
'What's wrong, Elizabeth?'
'It's nothing, really.'
'Don't say that, I know you.'
'I have never been away from you. What if I annoy Dominic? What if he doesn't want me to stay with him this long?'
'Liz, stop. Dominic wants you. Do you trust me?'
'Yes.'
'Then trust me when I say, go have fun and enjoy your time together. This is exactly what you need.'

Amber hugs me.
'Now I have a list and you need to cook.'
'Okay, but I have to go shopping first.'
'How about you order online and I pick it up. I'll get my card.'
'No, you won't, I cook, you eat. That's the deal, remember.' I look at her.
'Fine, I'm on drinks, then.' She smiles and walks to her room.
I look over the lists I have been given and go through my pantry and fridge.
Good thing I love cooking, I smile and laugh to myself.

I make coffee and grab the laptop and my list.
I order and pay, then send Amber on her way.
I've ordered extra as I know Cassie will be sleeping over.
They eat enough food between the two of them to feed a small country.
I laugh to myself.
I look outside to see where the boys are.
It looks like they have just finished digging some of the holes for my deck.
Must be time for morning tea.
I make a jug of iced coffee and put it on a tray with cups and a plate of Luke's favourite: vanilla slice.
I also take down the last mini lemon meringue, Dominic's favourite.

'I thought they were all gone!' Dominic smiles as I hand it to him.
'I saved you one,' I rest my hands on his waist and smile.
'You are amazing.' He smiles as he leans in and kisses me.
'Where's Amber? There is food and she is nowhere to be seen.'
'Picking up the groceries I ordered.'
'Did you get my list?' Luke asks.
'Let's see if I got this correct. Lots and lots of vanilla slice and lamingtons?' I smile.
'Is that all you wrote?' Dominic laughs as he looks at Luke.
'No,' Luke quips, 'I also wrote please and thank you.' He grabs another vanilla slice.
'Simon's list is the same as Luke's,' I smile.
Dominic shakes his head and eats his lemon meringue.
I leave them to it and head back upstairs to get ready for Amber's return.

Before I know it, the week is gone.
Dominic and I are packing the final things into his camper at his home on Saturday night.
I am excited and nervous, all at the same time.
Two weeks away from Amber, and alone with Dominic.
I hope I don't disappoint him.
'Liz,' I look up at him. 'Babe, are you okay? You're looking a little pale there.'
'I, umm…'
'It's okay, just breathe and talk to me. What can I do to help you?'

I nod and take a few deep breaths.
'I have never been away from Amber this long.' I look down at my feet, feeling stupid.
'Babe, please look at me.'

I bring my eyes slowly up to him as his hands come up to my neck, and his lips to mine.

'If at any time you want to come home, I will bring you home. There are a few spots where you can get phone service and you can call her. Amber has made me aware of what you need, so it's okay. She has also made me promise that you will enjoy yourself and have fun! Besides, I need all ten of my fingers.' He smiles and brings his lips back to mine.

His kiss calms me and his hands make me feel safe as they move over my body. I pull him in tight against me and kiss him more forcefully.

'Now off to bed. We have a date with the beach tomorrow, and I have to carry a rather large cooler.' Dominic scoops me up and carries me upstairs.

'Correction, you have two rather large coolers,' I smile as I snuggle in.

'Let me guess. Luke and Simon?'

'Yes, along with Amanda and David.'

He laughs.

On Sunday morning, Luke and Simon drop in to help load the coolers into Dominic's Ute.

They do, however, unload a container each; something to eat on the drive.

Dominic shakes his head at them as he walks over to me.

'Hey, you.'

'There's my girl.'

We follow Luke and Simon to the beach, and it's another perfect day.

As per the previous beach day, cricket becomes a contact sport.

Both of my coolers are empty and Dominic takes me out on the jet-ski.

There are no waves today, unfortunately, so no surfing, but the water is beautiful and warm.

I sit with Chantelle and watch them play football.

I notice that every few minutes or so her toes curl and her body stills.

I also notice her breathing changing, and I start to mentally calculate times and start an internal check-list, because if I'm right, Chantelle is going into labour.

I look down at my watch.

An ambulance would be at least twenty to twenty- five minutes away, but that's just to the beach access. We still need to get off the beach and that in itself will be a challenge.

'How far apart are your contractions?' I ask Chantelle.

'Six minutes.'

'How long do they last for?'

'Maybe ten to fifteen seconds.'

'I'll get Shaun,'

'No, not yet.'
'What's wrong, Chantelle?' I ask as I take her hand.
'I'm scared, I don't know if I can do this again. What if...'
'Well, I'm going to stop you right there. You are a strong woman, Chantelle, and Shaun is absolutely in love with you. You will do great!'

I watch Chantelle as she has another contraction.
'Breathe through the contraction and tell me what you feel.'
Chantelle nods and breathes.
Five minutes apart and at least thirty-five seconds long.
Her pulse is fast.
'I feel a lot of pressure.'

I calm and manage Chantelle through her contractions for another fifteen minutes more.
During this time I monitor her breathing, her blood pressure and watch for her anxiety to flare.
Everything is moving along as it should.
I smile and run my hand along her arm, a small reassurance so that she knows I'm here for her.
She's managing well and has relaxed a lot more, so I tell her, 'I'm getting Shaun.'
She's ready.

I go to get up as I see Dominic walking towards us.
I walk down to him.
'Dominic, can you please get...'
'Elizabeth! My water broke!' Chantelle calls out behind me.
'Shaun and Simon!' Dominic says as he runs back down to the game.
I run back to Chantelle, she's beginning to cry out in pain.

'Contractions are so close.' She breathes and grimaces.
'Hey, Chantelle, look at me,' I touch her arm reassuringly. 'I'm right here, okay. You are doing fantastically.'
Chantelle nods and breathes through another contraction.
'Okay, I'm going to remove your underwear,' I look at her and she nods.
I move my hands up under her sarong and pull her underwear down.
'Okay, Chantelle, at your last ultrasound, where was bub's head?'
'The baby was turning,' She breathes through another contraction. Three minutes from the last contraction and forty-five seconds long.

'Babe!' Shaun calls from behind me.
'Shaun!' Chantelle moans.

She breathes through another contraction.

Shaun races to her side and holds her hand, kissing her forehead.

Simon kneels down beside me.

'Simon, she won't make it off the beach. The contractions are too close and too long.'

'Oh my god, Liz, what do we do?' Simon asks.

'Get David and Amanda to call an ambulance and meet them at the beach entrance. Where's Dominic?'

'Right here,' he says from behind me.

'I need zip ties, metho, water, and a sharp blade.'

'On it.' Dominic runs off to tell Amanda and David what to do and to get the stuff from his Ute.

'Metho?' Shaun looks at me.

'No alcohol,' I reply as I watch Chantelle.

'What can I do?' Luke asks.

'Clean towels, and get Shaun's car.'

Shaun hands Luke his keys and Luke races off.

We get Chantelle to lie down.

'I've got what you need. I also have some hand sanitiser,' Dominic says as he reaches us.

'Thank you.' I look back up at Chantelle.

'Okay, Chantelle, I'm going to check and see how dilated you are. I'm sorry, but I don't have gloves. Can I proceed?' I ask her.

Chantelle nods through another contraction.

Using hand sanitiser to clean my hands, I look back up at Chantelle, but her eyes are closed, so I look to Shaun and he nods.

Dominic moves away from behind me.

'How far is she dilated?' Simon asks.

'Maybe about eight centimetres. How are you doing, Chantelle?'

'I'm okay.' She breathes out heavily.

'Babe, you're doing great,' Shaun says, looking down at her and smiling. 'I love you.'

He moves down and kisses her.

Chantelle cries out with more contractions.

They are really close, almost verging on each other. After a few more minutes I need to check again.

'Chantelle, Shaun. I need to check dilation again, is that okay?'

Chantelle nods and Shaun holds her hand to his lips and smiles.

'Ten centimetres. Ok, you're fully dilated now, Chantelle. Dominic, please kneel behind her so she can rest her head on your legs. Shaun I need you beside her so she can hold your hand and when she pushes. Simon, can you let her push on you and hold her other hand. Okay, Chantelle, we are going to help you. Push against Simon and I with your feet. With the next contraction you need to push.'
Chantelle nods. I lift up her sarong.

She starts to have another contraction.
'Push, Chantelle, and breathe.'
Chantelle cries out and pushes.
'You're doing great, babe,' Shaun tells her.
'Push, Chantelle!' I look up at her, 'Excellent, you're crowning.'

A few pushes later and I see more of the baby.
'Okay, here come the shoulders, you're doing great, Chantelle!'
'Neck is clear, no cord.' Simon remarks.
'David is driving the paramedics down. Amanda is staying with the ambulance,' Luke says, getting off the phone.
'Okay, push Chantelle, slowly, you're doing great. Luke, towels.'
'Liz,' Simon whispers beside me, 'She is tearing.'

I nod. Chantelle continues to push through more contractions.
'Okay, Chantelle, one more push should do it. Are you ready?'
Chantelle nods.
'Okay, one big push!' I say, stroking her leg, 'You are doing great.'
Chantelle pushes hard and the world is blessed with a new, precious life.

'Shaun, remove her top,' I instruct.
Dominic and Luke look away.
I hold Chantelle and Shaun's baby face-down in my hand, with his body along my arm and his head angled down.
I rub his back gently and he starts to cough a little, dispelling the mucus.
'Meet your beautiful and perfect little man,' I say, laying the baby boy on her chest and covering her with a towel.
Shaun kisses the top of Chantelle's head as the baby starts to cry.
'How are you feeling, Chantelle?' I ask as I wet a towel to clean her and check the tear.
'Apart from the fact I just gave birth on the beach,' Chantelle looks up at Shaun and smiles, 'I'm great and I don't think life could get any better,' she gushes.
Shaun and Chantelle's eyes are glued to their new baby.
I look away as they share a tender kiss.

I manage to refrain from shedding a tear; they have the one thing I could never give Dominic.
After giving myself a mental slap, I pull myself back to the moment and bask in what has just transpired.

'How's bub?' Simon asks.
'Looking for food,' Chantelle says, exhausted.
'Like his dad, then,' Simon laughs.
Shaun gets up and finds his phone before turning back to Simon and I.
'I'll have that any day,' Shaun says, shaking Simon's hand then hugging me. My body stiffens, but I accept his gesture.
'Thank you both so much,' Shaun gushes excitedly.
'I didn't do anything, it was all Liz,' Simon nods in my direction.

I watch as Shaun returns to Chantelle and their baby.
He takes photos of Chantelle holding their baby in between kissing her hand and gently running his fingers lovingly over his newborn son.
I feel blessed to have had a hand in their happiness.
'Dominic, pour metho on the zip ties and hand them to me, please.'
Simon and I use the ties to clamp the umbilical cord once it stops pulsing.

'How are you feeling, Chantelle?' I ask.
'I'm good.'
'You're better than good, babe, you're incredible!' Shaun gushes.
'Pour the metho over the blade, please, Dominic.' Dominic does as I ask.
'David's here,' Luke says.
'Okay, we will let the paramedics take over.' I look up and see Dominic smiling.
'Luke, can you please get a shovel and dig a deep hole near the tree line?' I ask.
'A hole?' Dominic asks.
'It's for the placenta,' I reply as I clean my hands with water and hand sanitizer, then check Chantelle's tear.

'Hey, Simon,' One of the paramedics says, coming up to us.
'Brad, good to see you.' Simon gets up and shakes his hand.
'You don't do enough at the hospital, you have to work at the beach now?' He jokes.
'Yeah, no. I just assisted, Liz did all the work. Elizabeth, I would like you to meet Brad. Brad, this is Elizabeth.'
I look up and smile.
'Elizabeth Miller? I have heard all about you. David is chomping at the bit to get you in. Your record and reputation precedes you. Bummer I missed watching you work.'

I clean my hands with metho and hand sanitizer and look back at Dominic.
He has swapped spots with Shaun.
Dominic comes to my side, helping me up; he smiles at me proudly.
I hold Dominic's hand tightly as I shake Brad's hand.
'It's nice to meet you. Shall I give you the rundown?'
I proceed to give Brad the rundown on the contractions, dilation, tear and birth.
Brad hands Shaun the scissors to cut the cord.
I help Brad with the afterbirth while the other paramedic, Jack, checks over the baby boy.

'Elizabeth!' Chantelle calls out for me.
'Can you come in the ambulance to the hospital with me? Shaun is getting my bag from home.'
'Of course,' I smile as she hands me her baby and gets carried to David's car.
I sit in the back of the car with her and she begins to feed him.
'Have you thought of a name yet?' Brad asks.
'Jonathan,' Chantelle smiles.
I follow Chantelle in as she is wheeled into the emergency department.
Shaun arrives not long after with her bag, and I leave them to themselves.

I wait outside for Dominic to come and pick me up.
'Elizabeth,' Brad calls, 'Why aren't you inside?'
'I wanted to give them time alone,' I say, taking a step back. 'Besides, my boyfriend will be here soon to take me home.'
'Bummer, I have finished my shift and was kinda hoping we could have a drink,' he smiles.
'I'm flattered, but I can't.' I look down, starting to feel nervous.
'Is your boyfriend tall and tanned, with a tattoo?'
'Yes.'
'I think that's him walking up now,' he points behind me.
I turn to see him walking towards me.
He smiles as he sees me.
I feel a wave of relief wash over me, but resist the urge to run to him to get away from Brad.

'Hey, you.'
'There's my girl,' he says getting to us, pulling me in and kissing me.
He can feel my nervous trembles.
'Dominic, this is Brad, he is one of the paramedics from the beach. Brad, this is Dominic, my boyfriend.'
Dominic shakes Brad's hand.
'Sorry, Brad, but I'm stealing my girl. I think chocolate is on the menu.'

'Surf and Turf?' I ask.

'Already ordered.' He smiles.

'Well, I'll leave you to it. Bye Elizabeth, Dominic.' Brad nods and walks off.

I wave as Dominic takes my hand and we walk back to his car.

We drive back to Moore Park and Dominic hasn't said much.

'Have I done something wrong?' I ask him.

'No, of course not. Why do you think that?'

'Because you haven't said anything nearly the whole way here.'

'Did Brad ask you out?'

'Yes, he asked me out for a drink. I said no, I have a boyfriend.' I look at the floor of the car and start to tremble.

He is angry with me. 'I'm sorry, Dominic, I won't talk to him again.'

'Babe, you haven't done anything wrong. He did, though,' he says, pulling into the tavern's car park.

He finds a parking space, and switches his car off, turning to me.

'He knows we are together, I heard Simon tell him on the beach. It was a bit weird that he asked you out and didn't extend the invite to me when I picked you up. But I get it, you are gorgeous! Why wouldn't he want to ask you out? What you did today, the way you took control of the situation? Amazing!'

He kisses me tenderly.

'I'm so proud of you. How did you do that?' He looks at me, still smiling his beautiful smile.

'Can we stop at my house first? I want to pick something up that I need to show you.'

He kisses me again, with more urgency, and I moan softly. He groans as he pulls away.

'Now let's get the pizza and raid the vending machines for chocolate,' Dominic says against my lips.

'Yes, please,' I smile.

I send Amber a message asking for the USB we had spoken about.

She replies, I'll have it ready for you.

We stop at home and I grab my laptop and the USB from Amber.

She hugs me tight.

'I'll be right here if you need me.'

'Thank you,' I nod.

I nervously walk back downstairs.

Dominic is waiting in his Ute.

We head to his home.

We shower and eat dinner before I set my laptop up in his lounge and pull out
a file from the laptop bag pocket..

I'm about to show him a part of my past that hurts me the most. He knows I
can't have children.
What he doesn't know is that I have lost babies because of Michael and how I
lost them.
The scars are a constant reminder of what I endured, but what I'm about to show
him… Those scars will forever haunt me.

'Michael would film my every move to make sure I was doing as I was told.
His doctor trained me as a medic, so that when Michael would go on one of his
missions, I would be useful.
As part of my cover, the Federal Police set up a file that states what I am capable
of.
Due to the nature of how I came to be has been redacted.
This is a copy of what the QAS has, it states, Classified Field Medic, and as you
can see, certain things have been censored, except my skill set, that's why David
wants me there.'

I watch Dominic glance over the file before looking back at me.
'The only reason I'm studying paramedics now, is for the changes in procedures,'
I answer the question he was about to ask.
I take a deep breath, pausing before continuing.
This is tough.
I am anxious about how Dominic will feel, watching what I'm about to show
him.
I take another deep breath, plucking up more courage.

'I've been pregnant, Dominic. In fact, I've had babies of my own. I have had to
deliver my own stillborn babies, on my own, in a cage no bigger than a public
toilet cubicle. All the babies I birthed, except one, were stillborn. I gave birth to
one absolutely perfect little girl. I fed, held, and loved her.'
I can feel the tears surfacing.
I feel an old wound rip open, and the pain of it is just as raw as if it was happening
again.
I struggle to suck in the sobs that begin wracking my body.

Dominic wraps his arm around me, holding me.
Saying nothing, but letting me do what I need to do.
With the USB inserted into the laptop, I mute the sound and press play.
I can't bear for him to hear it, and I can't bear to hear it either.

Dominic watches as I give birth with no help, no pain relief.
He watches me hold her and feed her.
I can't watch any further.
I get up and go upstairs and leave him to watch the rest of the footage alone.

🔟 DOMINIC 🔟

Liz leaves, I understand why.
I sit and watch the footage of her giving birth by myself.
I watch as she holds her baby girl, and despite who and what the father is, I see the look in her eyes: She instantly loves her.
I watch as she kisses her head, and places her to her breast to feed her.

Then something happens off screen.
I watch Liz shield the baby with her own body.
I watch Liz getting beaten as she holds her baby.
I feel sick, and rage wells up within me as I watch.
Nothing can prepare me, or compare with what comes next.
Someone manages to get the baby off her, and holds her just out of Liz's reach.

I watch as her baby girl is shot.
I watch as Liz crumbles.
The men walk away, leaving her, destroyed.
Liz crawls over to her baby girl and desperately tries to save her, even though she knows she can't.
I watch her break.

The footage changes.
Liz has a gun pointed at her head as she performs surgery on a man.
She couldn't save him, and I watch her get beaten for it.
More footage of her performing surgery.
I scroll through and there are hours of her doing surgery.
I notice that she is having trouble standing in one, and every time she stops, she is hit.
She looks absolutely exhausted.
I turn the volume up and hear her cry out, she is her on her knees begging as a gun is pointed at her stomach.
My god, she is pregnant again.

'Please, no, Michael!'

Gun shots ring out and her body crumbles as she falls to the floor, blood pooling around her.
I stop the footage.
I can't watch anymore, and I close the laptop.
My whole body is convulsing and I feel physically ill.
I try to get into control.
I don't want Liz to feel any worse than she already does from showing me the video.

My beautiful Liz.
I get up and practically run upstairs.
I find her sitting on the end of our bed, curled up, rocking and crying.
I pull her in and hold her tight.

'That's not everything, Dominic. I can't…' She sobs, her whole body heaving with sorrow and loss. 'There is so much, I just wanted to be able to show you what really happened so you would understand some of it. So you would understand why I can't have children.'
'It's okay, babe, I know. But I'm still here, not letting you go.'
I hold her till she stops crying and her body stops trembling.
We're both exhausted from the sheer emotional drain of what we've seen.
Liz of letting go and taking the enormous step to show me, and me from watching it, trying in some way to process it.
We fall asleep holding each other.

CHAPTER 7

Holiday

I wake the next morning before her and she is still in my arms.
I just lie there and watch her sleep.
It's hard to believe, after everything, she is still here.
Her bravery and strength just astound me.
Even now, I can't comprehend it.
I also can't believe I am lucky enough to hold this amazing woman every day.

I watch as she starts to stir and I run my fingers along her arm, down to her fingers.
I bring her fingers to my lips as she starts to wake, she smiles as soon as her eyes meet mine.
She touches my face.
'Are you okay?' She asks me.
'As long as you are in my arms and I get to see your smile every day, I am a very happy man.'
'What would you like for breakfast?' Liz smiles up at me.
'Do you mean besides dessert?'
She giggles and pulls me down to her.
We eventually made our way downstairs for breakfast, can't argue with leftover pizza.

'Are you ready to go, babe?'
Liz looks at me and nods, 'Yep, let's go.'
Two weeks without any reminders about anything to do with Michael and the case will be good for her.
A chance for her to breathe, really breathe.
I take her hand as we walk out our front door together.
She looks absolutely beautiful today, you could almost say she is glowing.

She drifted off to sleep on the way to River Heads to get the barge over to Fraser Island.
We find a spot on the beach just south of the S.S Maheno shipwreck and set up camp.

I set up for the first of the surprises I have planned for her: A double sun lounger and a double hammock with a sunshade.
Her smile is radiant and she holds me against her.
'It's perfect, thank you Dominic.'
'Anything for my girl.'
We spend most of the day cuddled in the hammock.
Tomorrow is Champagne Pools and Orchid beach.
I wake up and find Liz standing outside, watching the sun come up.
I walk up behind her, wrapping my arms around her and burying my face in her neck, taking in her scent and warmth.
'Hey, you,' Liz says, hugging my arms to her.
'There's my girl,' I kiss her neck.
'I'm making breakfast, Vegemite on toast.'
'Best breakfast ever,' Liz chuckles.
'I'll make the coffee.'

ᛒ ELIZABETH ᛒ

We head for Champagne Pools and the water is beautiful and clear.
The waves crash over the rocks into the pools.
We set up the sunshade and spend the morning swimming and laughing.
Dominic holds my hand every chance he gets, when I'm not in his arms.
'Are you okay, Dominic?' I ask as we enjoy the water.
'I'm fine, why?' He holds me close.
'Did I show you too much?'
'No, I just want you to know that you will never be alone again. I'll be right beside you.' He kisses me softly. 'Are you hungry?' He asks.
'A little.'
'Come on, there is a pub at Orchid Beach.'

We pack up and head for Orchid Beach.
As we drive to the pub, Dominic points out a dingo and her pups, they are adorable.
We sit on our picnic rug on the open grass paddock across the pub, which also doubles as the RACQ Life Flight helicopter pad, overlooking the ocean.
I opt for chips and gravy for lunch and it is perfect.

'Shall we go see the shipwreck before we go back to our campsite?' Dominic asks, pulling me onto his lap and resting his head on my chest.
'Mmm, sounds good.' I close my eyes as I kiss the top of his head and take a deep breath.

We hold each other for what feels like forever.
No place I would rather be than in his arms.
I really do love him.

The shipwreck is amazing.
We even see a couple more dingos at the water's edge. Another perfect day coming to an end.
I make a platter as Dominic gets the drinks and we lie on the double sun lounger on the back of his Ute. Watching the waves roll in, the sky changes colour and the stars appear.

'Dominic,' I kiss his hand.
He has drifted off to sleep.
I pull a light blanket over us and snuggle into him, listening to his heartbeat and the sound of the ocean.
I run my hand up his arm and feel him tighten his hold on me.
I bring his hand to my lips and kiss each one of his fingers.
His fingers brush my cheek, lifting my face up and his lips find mine.
His hand moves to my neck as he deepens the kiss.
I whimper softly and dig my fingers into his sides.

'Elizabeth,' Dominic groans.
'Yes, Dominic.'
His hands move over my body as his lips move along my neck.
I see car lights turn towards us.
'Dominic, we have company coming our way.'
He groans as he moves to see a car pulling up near our camp set up.

A group of people get out and walk around before they are joined by two more cars.
I can't see them properly, but judging by the voices, it's a group of men on a camping trip.
Dominic gets off the back of his Ute and helps me down.
We clean up and head to our shower enclosure.
He turns on the hot water on demand and we quickly wash off.
I send Amber a good-night message, then Dominic and I head to bed.
He pulls me in, and we drift off to sleep holding each other.

I wake the next morning, it was a night with no bad dreams and in the arms of the man I love.
Life can't get any better.

I carefully get out of bed so that I don't wake Dominic, put the kettle on the gas stove and turn it on.
I get out the bacon and eggs and start making breakfast while I listen to the waves.
I hear the zipper behind me.

Dominic wraps his arms around me and rests his chin on my shoulder.
His hand brushes my hair aside and he gently kisses my neck.
My skin tingles at the sensation of his warm breath against my neck.
'Morning,' I whisper, 'How did you sleep?'
'I slept well, but I woke a little lonely.' He kisses my temple. 'Looks like we have neighbours.'
'I saw that when I got up.'
I turn my head and smile.

Dominic smiles as he kisses me.
The kettle starts to whistle, and Dominic turns it off before holding me tight again.
'So, what have you got planned for us today?' I ask as I finish cooking.
'We are packing a cooler and spending the day at Eli Creek.'
'Sounds perfect.' I turn in his arms and smile up at him.
Dominic pulls me in and holds me tight.
I can feel him trace the scar on my back before reaching for my butt.
'Shall I make the coffee?'
'Yes please.'
We clean up after breakfast, get ready and I pack the cooler.
I have managed to hide a few of Dominic's favourites so he doesn't eat them all at once.
I start putting stuff in Dominic's car.

'Excuse me,' A man's voice comes from behind me.
I slowly turn around as Dominic comes to my side.
'Hey mate, what can we do for you?'
'Can I borrow milk, please? We seem to have forgotten to pack any,' the man asks.
'We only have long-life milk, is that okay?' Dominic asks as I reach into the back seat of his car.
'That would be great, thank you so much.' He smiles at Dominic and then at me.
He looks familiar and it makes me nervous.
I hand the carton to Dominic, who passes it to the man.
He thanks us again and walks away.
Dominic turns to me and he can see my hands shaking.

As he takes them in his and kisses me, I feel my body calm.
Dominic opens my door and we head to Eli Creek.

Eli Creek is a fresh-water creek that flows out to the ocean, and from what I have read, it's a popular destination for anyone who comes to visit Fraser Island. Fraser Island itself is amazing, it is the world's biggest sand island, sitting off the Queensland coast in the Pacific Ocean, a short ferry ride from River Heads or Inskip Point.
I'm giddy with excitement as we drive to Eli Creek, but in the back of my mind I can't help but think about the man who was looking for milk.
He is familiar, I know it, but I can't place him, and it makes me feel unsettled.
Dominic takes my hand and squeezes gently.
'Why are we parking here?' I ask when he parks his Ute.
'Well, every man and his kids will want to be up there, close to the boardwalk. We will be crammed in like sardines. Here we can spread out a little, and we get to watch the idiots pass through at high tide.' Dominic smiles and winks.

We set up the batwing awning on the driver's side and around the rear of his Ute.
We lay out the sand mat and set up our table and chairs.
Dominic blows up two of those inflatable donuts with the portable air compressor.
'Come on. I'll take you up a few times before all the holiday-makers on Fraser end up here,' Dominic says as he hands me a donut and takes my free hand.
The tide is low at the moment and the water is cool.
We make our way along the boardwalk.

'At high tide we will be able to float all the way to our car,' Dominic smiles as we reach the end of the boardwalk.
'Okay , so because it's fresh water, it can be quite cool.' Dominic gets in and I pass him my donut.
He helps me in, he wasn't lying.
'Oh my goodness, that's cold!' I squeal excitedly.
We float down on the steady current.
'Wow, this is beautiful, Dominic.'
'You think this is beautiful, wait until I take you to lakes McKenzie, Wabby and Birrabeen. We can also do Basin Lake, you hike there from Central Station.'
'Can't wait,' I smile at him.

We float down the creek a few times before we head back to Dominic's Ute.
I start to feel nervous as I look around and see the ever-growing crowd of people, and reach for Dominic. We get back to his Ute and I put my sundress over my bikini.
I turn around and Dominic is standing right behind me, looking at me.
'What?'
'Bummer, I really liked what I was seeing,' he grins.

I blush and keep looking at him even though I want to look away, which I know he doesn't like.
He slides his hands over my hips and around to my arse, pulling me against him.
I run my hands up his arms and wrap mine around his neck as he leans in.
His tongue teases my lips before kissing me passionately and squeezing my butt cheeks.
'You are so beautiful, Elizabeth,' he whispers against my ear, making me shiver.
'Don't you ever forget that.'
I can feel myself blushing again.

'Dominic…' I'm cut off before I can say anymore.
'Hey, it's the milk man and his lady.' The man from this morning walks up to us.
I duck a little more behind Dominic. Where do I know him from? Maybe he went to uni with me before I met Michael?
I feel frustrated and anxious.
'Need more milk?' Dominic asks.
'No, I just thought I should repay you for this morning,' he laughs.
'I'm Will, by the way,' he says, offering Dominic his hand.
'I'm Dominic.' He shakes Will's hand.

'And this is Elizabeth.' Dominic says as he takes my hand and squeezes it gently.
'Hello,' I hesitantly shake Will's hand.
It feels familiar.
'It's nice to meet you.' I move back a little further, avoiding his eyes.
'Don't worry about the milk,' Dominic says, shielding me.
'Well, the beer is cold if you and the missus would like to join us later.' Will nods as he walks back to his group.
Shit, I think to myself, Will is Nadine's brother. We were all living in a house while we were studying at uni, before I met Michael.

'Breathe, babe.' Dominic turns back to me and holds me, kissing the top of my head. 'Are you okay?'
'I don't know, I just, I have a weird feeling. I'm…'

'Don't apologise, babe.'
I need to tell Dominic.

👀 DOMINIC 👀

I grab the shovel and dig out a small semi-submerged seat on the water's edge, as Liz puts on a rash vest and grabs the container of snacks and drinks.
We sit in our little water seats and watch as people play cricket and football in the water, as the tide comes in.
Liz gets nervous as more people arrive.
I watch her closely for any signs I need to get her away from here.
She won't say anything, but I know something is going on.
She has grown quiet and I've seen her rub her scars.
'Do you want to go?' I ask, taking her hand.
'No, I do want to stay. I have to get used to being around people.' She looks down, ashamed.
'Okay, babe. But if you need to leave, let me know, I don't care. We can go back to camp and be lazy in our hammock.'
Liz looks at me and smiles.

I kiss her hand. 'Now, what goodies have we got?'
'All your favourites,' she answers as her smile shines.
Amber's right, everything Liz does is to please me, to make sure I'm happy.
'What's your favourite?' I ask.
She looks nervous.
'Umm, I like them all.'
'I know your favourite. Wait here.' I get up and go to the toolbox on the side of my Ute and find the hidden box.
I get back and hand her the box and watch as she opens it.
Liz giggles as she finds the box is packed with Vegemite Snacks.

'I cleaned out most of the Woolworths and Cole's stock. So you should have enough for two weeks.'
Liz looks at me and smiles.
'Best gift ever, thank you.' She leans in and kisses me.

After a couple hours of incoming tide, we have to move our seat a little further up the bank and the idiots don't disappoint.
At least four four-wheel-drives pass us on the back of tow trucks, and one starts to float but is now firmly wedged on the south bank of Eli Creek and partially submerged.

It will need to be dug out at low tide.
I get my small Weber BBQ ready and Liz hands me her lamb and rosemary sausages and Greek lamb kebabs.
It's not long before we have company.

'Hey, Dominic, we have a cold beer with your name on it.' Will calls out as he walks over to us.
I can see Liz trying not to feel uncomfortable.
'Thanks, mate.' I take the beer and Will offers one to Liz.
'No thank you, I don't really drink alcohol much,' Liz says, trying her best to look at him and smile.
'No worries, more for Dominic then,' Will laughs.
'Your missus can drive you back, you should come join us.' Will looks at me before glancing at Liz.

I really don't like the way he is looking at her, I don't trust him.
'We are just about to eat…' Liz starts to say.
'Well, come after, Dominic,' Will cuts her off. 'She can clean up and join us after, and bring some of that food. It smells great.' Will waves and walks back to his group.
I glare after him.
I hate that he just spoke like that about her.

'Like fuck that's gonna happen, what an asshole!' I fume quietly, turning to Liz.
'I'll get the plates.' She turns away.
'Babe, wait.' I reach for her and pull her against me.
I kiss the scars on her shoulder through her rashie.
Liz is trying so hard not to show the effect he has had on her.
'He sounds like him,' her body trembles. 'His demeanour just then, it reminds me of…' She can't say his name.

'If you want to have a beer with him, I won't mind, I just can't be near him. I'm…'
'You don't have to apologise. I don't like the way he spoke to you. I'm not going to go where you're not comfortable going, and we are here together. This is our time to be just us.'
I turn her around and bring her face up so I can see her eyes.
I run my fingers along her cheeks and down to her neck, covering her scars, and I feel her body calm down.
She closes her eyes and her breathing slowly returns to normal.
I wait for her to open her beautiful, big green eyes again and smile.
A moment later her smile returns and she opens her eyes.

'Don't you ever stop smiling.' I kiss her softly and she brings her hands to my sides.
'I had better get back to the BBQ before I burn your sausages and kebabs.'
Liz giggles.
I love it when she smiles and giggles.
I smack her arse and kiss her before going back to the BBQ.

I watch Liz make a small salad as I finish cooking the meat.
After lunch, we manage to avoid Will and his friends.
We have another float down the creek before sitting back on our edge-of-the-water seats.
Liz lays her head on my lap, reading a book, as I sit back with one hand behind my head and my other hand playing with her hair.

'We should get going,' I say, breaking the silence. 'I'm hungry for dessert, how about you?'
I look down at her and wink.
'Sounds like a good idea to me,' Liz looks up at me and smiles.
We get up and pack everything away.
We head off and make our way back to camp.
I grab Liz's phone and hand it to her.
'Music,' I wink.
She laughs and selects an INXS playlist.
I pick her up and she wraps her legs around me as we head inside our camper trailer.
I sit her on the bed.
She removes her sundress as I zip up the door before turning back to her.
I remove my shirt and claim her lips forcefully.
I slide my hands up her thighs, gently squeezing as I go.
Her body feels wonderful in my hands, and she responds to my touch no matter how soft my hands move over her.
She groans softly as her hands move from my sides slowly up to my neck, before tangling in my hair.

I climb up onto the bed and remove her bikini bottoms and my shorts.
I take her breast in my mouth as I enter her and she whispers my name.
She wraps her legs around me, pulling me in tight, and drags her fingernails down my back.
I push up on my hands and roll my head back at the sensation.
'Fuck, Liz,' I groan.
'Yes…'

I move and bring Liz around to be on top, move my hands to her sides and squeeze.

I can feel light shudders running through her body.

I start to thumb her clitoris as my other hand moves up to her breast, pinching her nipple.

I love the way she moves along my cock.

She leans back, resting her hands on my thighs.

She throws her head back as she starts to orgasm.

I sit up and bring my mouth to her breast and hold her tight as I climax.

I press my lips to hers as I turn and lay her down under me.

We are both breathing heavily, but I'm not finished with her.

'A little black box is in the pocket beside you,' Liz whispers as I kiss her.

I start to move against her as she sighs.

'Mmm, Elizabeth, what are you suggesting?' I ask as I gently bite her earlobe.

'Just something for my hot-for-me builder to ponder over,' she moans and breathes heavily as I kiss her.

Liz fuels my desire by returning my kiss and digging her nails into my lower back, making me shudder.

I look up as cars approach. Fuck! It's Will and his mates, they get out of the cars and look intoxicated.

'What's wrong?' Liz asks, 'Have I…'

I cover her mouth gently.

'No, Will and his mates have just got back.'

We can hear them talking.

'I'm telling you, she looks like Chantelle Watson. Dead fucking ringer, even covered in those gnarly scars.'

I look down at Liz, there is pure fear in her eyes.

She tries to move, but I won't let her.

'Liz, ssh,' I look at her.

She nods as the tears fall, her whole body trembling.

'Man, she was fucking hot as fuck back when she raced motocross.'

'Didn't she win the State and Australian Champs?'

'Three years in a row. But she just stopped and then no one heard from her again.'

I can feel Liz really starting to panic. I move my hand from her mouth and claim her lips with mine, trying everything I can to calm her.

'Didn't your brother have a thing for her?'

'Yeah, James,'

Liz pushes me off her and sits up.
'James!' She starts to cry.
I pull her in and hold her.
I look out the top of the tent window.
Will and his mates are walking over towards our camp.
'Fuck!' I grab my clothes and hers.
'Get dressed and stay in bed. Do not make a sound and do not come out. Do you understand me?' I look at her as she gets dressed.

Liz nods, fuck, she is retreating now.
I get dressed, then I kiss her softly and with as much passion as I can.
'I'm still by your side, not letting you go. I'll be back as soon as I can get rid of them. Now where's my girl?' I ask as my fingers brush her cheeks, then cover the scars on her neck.
'Hey, you.' Liz smiles wanly.
'There's my girl.'
'Yo, Dominic!' Will calls out.
I smile at her and hand her the phone and headphones.
'Out in a sec!' I call back to him.
'Beer is getting hot.'
I roll my eyes.
Liz puts her headphones on, turns away and curls up.
I can see her body still trembling. I walk outside to Will and his mates.

Will introduces me to his mates Rick, Brad, John, aka Little John, Daniel, and Steve—all from Margaret River, Western Australia, of all places.
They have brought over a cooler full of beer.
'I won't have too many, Liz has a headache.'
Will rolls his eyes. I swear to god, I'm about ready to knock him the fuck out!
Will proceeds to tell me in great detail all about Chantelle Watson and his brother's infatuation with her, right up until his accident and death.
Will makes out that he and Chantelle were an item, but his mates laugh.
'She never said no to me,' he says, looking at me.
You wish, dipshit!

'Will, she was a fucking virgin, everybody knew that. That's why half of the motocross guys were chasing her,' Rick cuts him off.
'She was a nice person.' Steve adds.
'I went to her funeral, they had people outside, not everyone could fit in the church for the service.' Brad sighs.

'I'm telling you that Chantelle is not dead. Elizabeth is Chantelle. Died in a car accident my arse, she could drive just as well as she could ride a bike. Just look at her scars…'
'Will,' John cuts him off, 'You are being a dick, sit the fuck down and shut up!'

Will gets out his phone and starts scrolling.
I continue to talk to his mates and watch the time.
'I'll be back in a sec,' I say, getting up.
I check on Liz and she has fallen asleep.
Tear-stained and still absolutely beautiful.

I go back to Will and his mates.
I sit down on my cooler and Will hands me his phone, showing me clips on YouTube.
I watch them.
I can see it's Liz, but I don't give anything away.
'Well, sorry to disappoint you, Will, but that's not Elizabeth. She is not whoever you said. We have been together since high school. Liz was in a car accident with her family; she was the only survivor.' I say, giving them part of Elizabeth's backstory as Amber told it to me.
'I am sorry though, you seem to still have it real bad for… What's her name again?' His mates laugh.
'Chantelle,' Will glares at me.
He is unsteady on his feet.
He will be easy to put on his arse if he keeps going.
 'I'm going to prove it,' He slurs.

Please keep going.
I will really enjoy putting you down.
He starts walking unsteadily towards me.
'The only thing you're going to do, Will, is make a complete dick of yourself. Now sit down before you fall.' John stands up.
'Fuck you, Little John! I'm outta here.' Will stumbles away.
'Sorry about Will, Dominic,' Rick looks at me apologetically.
'Don't worry about it. Can I ask you all a favour, though?'
They nod.
'Elizabeth heard him talk about her scars and it made her uncomfortable and upset. She has suffered enough and is still suffering without him making it harder. Please keep him away from her.'
They nod and we say our goodnights.

I send Amber a message regarding Will and his friends.

I managed to get a picture of him so Amber can look into it.

I also ask if she can somehow make up pictures of Liz and I in a relationship that could pass for being from 13 years ago. I need Will to back the fuck off, I need Liz to heal and want to talk to me, not feel she has to because of him.

I raid the goodie container and find more mini lemon meringues.

I smile, I have a few and crawl into bed with my girl.

👀 ELIZABETH 👀

I wake a few times during the night and every time, as much as I tried not to, I woke Dominic.

'I'm so…'

'Babe, don't apologise.' He smiles and kisses me tenderly.

Dominic looks at his phone as he stretches and yawns.

'It's almost sunrise. Would you like to sit in the hammock with me and watch the sun come up?'

'I would like that,' I say as I look down at my hands.

'Come on, I'll meet you in the hammock. I'll bring a spoon with some Vegemite.' He smiles as his fingers tilt my chin up.

'I don't suppose we could have dessert first?' I look at him nervously.

He grins.

'Yes, dessert does sound better.' Dominic's hand moves up my thigh. 'On one condition.'

I look at him uncertainly.

'Is it because you want it, or are you making sure I'm happy?'

'Are you happy?' I ask him.

My hands tremble.

'Yes, I get to hold you and see you smile. That's what makes me happy.'

'Is that it, is that all?'

'Babe. Are you happy? Do you feel safe with me?' He asks.

'Yes, I do feel safe with you. You make me happy, but I don't want to disappoint you.'

'Elizabeth, the only way you could ever disappoint me is if you give up. Don't ever give up on your dreams, follow them, fight for them. All I ask is to be a part of your life.'

'I want to be with you, Dominic,' I look at my hands. 'For as long as you will have me.'

'Elizabeth, please look at me.' He takes my hand. 'You are my someone. I'm not planning on walking away from you, ever.'

I look up at him and smile, I really do make him happy.
I actually make someone happy, without being hurt.
'Do you want dessert?' Dominic asks.
I remove my shirt and pull him to me.
'You really are beautiful.' Dominic's lips move against my neck.
His tongue moves along the scars on my body and I feel his hands move up my thighs and remove my underwear. I groan as his tongue teases my nipples.
'Dominic,' I breathe, 'I want you.'

Our bodies move as one.
I bring my elbows to my side, and push up and roll my head back.
Dominic wraps his arm around me and I push to get him to roll onto his back.
I move along his cock as his hands grip my hips, squeezing as he groans.
I drag my nails lightly down his chest, before leaning back with my hands against his thighs.
'Elizabeth,' Dominic grunts my name, 'My god, Elizabeth, don't stop. Fuck me, you are...'
I move and claim his lips with mine, kissing him passionately.
He sits up as I continue moving along his cock.
I throw my head back as he buries his face in my cleavage.
I can feel my body start to tremble. Dominic holds me tighter.
I tangle my hands in his hair, he moves to bring himself back on top and puts his hand over my mouth. His body shudders and he groans deeply as he orgasms with me.

Dominic removes his hand, kisses me softly and I hold him to me as we enjoy the moment.
He is breathing heavily as I move my hands up and down along his back.
I can feel his body tense and he groans.
'Elizabeth.'
'Dominic.'
He lies beside me and I rest my head on his chest, listening to his heartbeat.

His breathing changes, he has drifted off to sleep.
I get up and let him sleep.
I get dressed, fill the kettle and turn on the gas stove.
The sun is just above the horizon and the day is going to be overcast.
The kettle starts to whistle and I turn it off.
I make myself a cup of tea and sit on the sun lounger.

I am happy, Dominic makes me happy.
I make Dominic happy, life is perfect.

I lie there enjoying the quiet when I feel something wet on my elbow.
I look down and see the face of a dingo, sniffing my elbow.
'Morning,' I say to the dingo.
The dingo steps back, sits and looks at me, tilting its head.
'I don't have any food for you,' I say, sitting up.
It whines.
'I'm sorry, but Dominic doesn't like to share.'

I swing my legs over the side of the sun lounger.
'And even if he did, I'm not allowed to.'
It whines again.
'Please don't, I feel bad.'
The dingo makes a barking noise.
I might go back inside the tent now.

I slowly stand up as the dingo watches.
It whines and dips its head.
It is absolutely gorgeous. I slowly move towards the tent.
'Liz,' Dominic's voice startles the dingo.
'She's right, I don't like to share.'
The dingo whines again as I move closer to Dominic.
It tilts its head to the side before running off down to the beach.
I watch it run to the water's edge before being joined by three other dingoes.
Dominic wraps his arms around me and kisses my shoulder.

I turn in his arms and rest my head on his chest.
'Should I be concerned about the dingoes stealing my girl?' Dominic chuckles.
'Only if you don't keep the Vegemite and chocolate in stock,' I snicker.
'I need to talk to you about something. Let's go for a walk down to the beach.'
'Okay,' I let go of him, averting my gaze as I take a step back.
'It's about Will,' Dominic takes my hand and we walk down to the water's edge.
He stops and looks at me and smiles.
'Chantelle Watson, Western Australia and Australian Motocross Champion, three years in a row.'
I look at him.
'Will showed me footage. I knew it was you straight away.'

I look at the ground.
What do I say?

What do I do?
My hand moves to my wrist.
'Babe, I don't want you to rush to tell me anything,' he says as he takes my hand and kisses the scar on my wrist.
'But he is adamant that you are Chantelle Watson. His mates believe the story about your death; one of them even went to the funeral.' Dominic pulls me in and kisses my hair.
'I told them the backstory Amber gave me, but I also added that we are high school sweethearts.'
'Really?' I ask.
'I really do wish I had found you a lot sooner. So how does it feel to be my girlfriend of, let's say, thirteen years?'
I laugh and say, 'I think I can handle thirteen years.'

'Okay, so we went to Shalom Catholic College. I left in year ten to do my building apprenticeship and you graduated in nineteen-ninety-eight.'
'Anything else I should know?'
'Well, judging by what Will showed me and what I see now, you are as hot-as-fuck now as you were back in high school.' Dominic kisses me and grabs my butt.
'Shall we head back up for breakfast?'
'As long as you're cooking,' I smile.
'Right, Vegemite on toast it is, then,' he says, taking my hand.

We just get back to camp when it starts to rain lightly.
Dominic moves his car so we can open the awnings and put up the second gazebo.
The weather looks pretty set in, so it's a lazy day of snuggles and reading.
Maybe even seconds on dessert, I smile to myself.
Dominic hands me my phone and I send Amber a check-in message.
I make coffee as Dominic makes breakfast and we spend the day revelling in each other's company, with no-one else around.
A late afternoon storm rolls in and we watch the lightning over the ocean.
It goes on for a couple of hours, so does dessert.
I watch him sleep.

I love him, but it's also on my mind that I want to keep him safe.
I start to formulate a plan that will accomplish that.
I will send Agent Smith a message tomorrow and start getting things ready.
I need to know that the man I love will never get into the hands of Michael, even if that means Michael takes me; even if it costs me my life.

I have trouble sleeping.
I wake up feeling hot and bothered despite the cool breeze.
I get up without waking Dominic, go outside and sit in the hammock with a sheet.
There are still flashes of lightning and I can just make out thunder in the distance.
The ocean sounds peaceful, and I can see dingoes running along the beach chasing a kangaroo.

'Babe,'
I turn as Dominic reaches my side and kneels down.
'I couldn't sleep,' I say as he kisses my hand.
'Mind if I join you?'
'I would like that,' I smile.
Dominic gets up and walks around to the other side.
He lies down, wraps his arm around me and pulls me against him.
His free hand moves slowly along my arm and I feel myself drifting off to sleep.
'I love you, Dominic,' I mumble softly.
We fall asleep in the hammock.

I wake as the sun hits us and the day is beautiful; not a cloud in the sky.
We decide to have breakfast at Eroung before heading to Lake McKenzie.
I can't get over just how beautiful Fraser Island really is.
Dominic parks his Ute and sets up the beach cart with large wheels for pulling on the sand.
We load it with our stuff and head down to the lake.
Dominic is right; it's stunning. The water is clear, with amazing shades of blue contrasted by the white sand.

We find a spot and set up the sun shade, lay out the beach blanket and our towels.
Dominic helps me put on sunscreen and I return the favour.
He takes my hand and we walk down to the water.
It's cool at the outset, but it feels good against my skin.
Dominic sinks down into the shallow water and I follow.
I feel his chest against my back and he wraps his arms around me, resting his chin on my shoulder. He kisses my neck.

I watch the people around us.
Women look at Dominic, but he doesn't return their glances.
I'm not jealous if he looks, it's human nature, but it does make me feel like I make him happy.
That may sound silly, but to me it means a lot.

Michael would always point out the attractive women in the room, and then list all my faults.

Dominic never does that to me.

'Elizabeth,'

Dominic moves around in front of me.

'Yes?' I look at him.

'What are you thinking?' He pulls me in closer.

'When Michael did take me out, he would point out all the beautiful women and tell me all my faults. He loved the attention he would get from other women, and I had to watch.'

A tear falls and Dominic wipes it away as he brings his lips to mine.

'Babe, I see them, but I only want you. You are my everything, my special someone.' He smiles as he puts his hands on my arse.

I wrap my legs around him as he holds me.

'I could never understand why I was never good enough, what I did that made him…'

'It was never you, Elizabeth. He needs you, he is weak without you. He needed you to make himself feel important. He is the weak one, not you. You never needed him, you will never need him. We have each other and that's all we will ever need.'

He rests his forehead on mine and we close our eyes.

'I'm still here, not letting you go, Elizabeth.'

I open my eyes and see him smiling. His smile is infectious.

'There's my girl.'

Dominic pulls me in and holds me tight.

'Thank you, Dominic.'

'Anything for my girl.'

After a while, I start to feel cold and we head back to our spot.

I wrap myself in a towel as Dominic lies down.

I lie down on my stomach and start reading my book.

Dominic rolls on his side to face me, he rests his hand on my back, and drifts off to sleep.

Such a simple touch from him sends warmth through me and I feel myself relax and enjoy my surroundings.

I let him sleep.

I have woken him a lot the last few nights, he must be tired.

The little kids in the family next to us yell out, 'Dingo!', and wake Dominic.
'Are you okay?' I ask him.
'Yeah, no, I'm good.' He sits up and stretches.
'Are you hungry?'
'Starving,' he smiles. 'What are we having?'
'I have made some mini pizzas and quiches to heat up in your little Weber.'
'Yum, let's go.'

We pack up and head back up to his Ute, put away the beach stuff and load the cooler and BBQ into the trolley.
Then we head to the fenced picnic area.
Dominic heats up the BBQ and the food as I go to the bathroom.
I get back and take over the cooking while Dominic goes to the bathroom.
'Smells good!' Will's voice comes from behind me.
Oh crap! I start to panic.
'You just missed Dominic, he will be back in a minute.'
'I didn't come to talk to him, I came to talk to you, Chantelle.'
'My name is Elizabeth.'
'Damn, he has you trained well,' Will says, moving towards me.
'I'm sorry, I don't understand what you mean.'
Dominic, where are you? I look around for him.
'He took you, made you fake your death and change your name. Did he have James killed?' Will moves closer.
'Please leave me alone.' I start to cry. 'Go away, please.'
My whole body trembles and I struggle to breathe, my vision starting to blur.
I hear Dominic call for me. He reaches me and pulls me in.

'I've got you, babe, I'm here. Breathe, babe.' He kisses the top of my head.
I start to breathe normally and wrap my arms around him.
'Dominic.'
'I'm here.'
I look up at him and smile.
Dominic turns to face Will, shielding me from view.
'Now would be a good time to fuck off, Will.' His voice is thick with anger.
I turn away from them.
I do my best to pretend everything is normal, turn the BBQ off and start getting lunch ready. My hands tremble uncontrollably.
I don't hear Will say anything, but I do see him leave out of the corner of my eye.
Dominic holds me as I finish setting everything up and we sit down to eat.

'What do you want to do, do you want to leave, babe?' Dominic asks me.
I look up at him, he is watching me intently.

'I don't want what's happened to ruin our holiday. I want to stay, is that okay, do you think?'
'As long as that is what you want, I'm happy to be wherever you are.' He smiles.
We finish eating and clean up.
We stop at Central Station before heading back to camp.
Thankfully Will wasn't at his camp.

'Dominic?'
'Yeah, babe?'
I can't bring myself to look at him.
'Do you, um, do you know how to hurt…to hurt someone?'
'Yes. I did Muay Thai for a while and some MMA. I can look after myself and I can look after you, Liz.'
He reaches for me and adds, 'But I'd never hurt you.'
'I know you wouldn't.'
'Why do you ask?'
'I can't… Amber has shown me how to do some basic self-defense. But it was more about removing some restraints and lessening the injuries I could receive. They also showed me a few things before I went back Michael, I couldn't really use self-defense against him otherwise he would have known something was up so I took the beatings. But I, would you…'
'Show you?' He asks before I finish.
I nod, still not looking at him.
'I'm not sure how well it would go, having to hold you so I can demonstrate some moves,' he says, trying to lighten the mood and help me relax.
'You make it very hard for me to let go of you.' He lifts my face so I can look at him. 'But, I will endeavour to try and teach you.'
'Thank you, Dominic.'

He smiles and kisses me softly, before holding me tight.
It looks like we are in for another storm tonight; we can hear the rumbling in the distance.
Dominic hands me my phone and I send Amber the check-in message.
I don't tell her about Will.
I don't want her to worry or feel she has to end our holiday.

'Mmm, dinner smells amazing,' Dominic says as he brings his hands to my hips, resting his chin on my shoulder.
'Sichuan pork with jasmine rice,' I smile and lean back into him.
'What's in the foil?'
'Dessert: Triple choc brownies.'
'So, you're not on the menu?' Dominic smiles as he softly kisses my shoulder.

I smile and shrug as Dominic wraps his arms tighter around me.
We hear cars pull up near us. Will and his friends have just arrived back at their camp.

'Elizabeth, did Will ever try anything with you?'
I stiffen at the memory, and my body starts to tremble.
'He did, once. He snuck into my room one night while we were away at a comp. I was getting dressed for bed when he came up behind me. He made a comment about the birthmark on my back.'
'Which birthmark?'
'Michael had it removed. He said it was ugly. The only marks allowed on my body were ones that were left by him. I had to have laser hair removal. He had my hair dyed black and gave me breast implants. They had to remove them when I was in hospital. One of them had ruptured.'

I feel Dominic's hands move under my shirt and cup my breasts.
'Well, I'm glad they are gone. Your breasts fit perfectly in my hands.' He kisses my neck.
My body enjoys the sensation of his hands.
I serve up dinner and ask him more about New Zealand as we eat.
After dinner I go and open the gas freezer and pull out two individual servings of ice cream to go with the triple choc brownies I warmed up.
'Yum, what ice cream is this?' Dominic asks as he basically inhales his dessert.
'Kahlua and vanilla.'
'Well, we are definitely buying this again.'
'You can't buy it!' I chuckle.
'Is this yours?' He asks, looking at me incredulously.
I nod and smile.
'Well, I'll make sure we always have a bottle of Kahlua in the cupboard, then.'
I smile at him as he finishes his dessert.
After we clean up and shower, we lie in the hammock, listen to the distant rumble and watch the light show over the ocean.
I get woken by Dominic getting up. He picks me up and carries me to bed.
I drift off to sleep in his arms.

The next few days are spent exploring the island and its hidden beauty.
Thankfully, Will has kept his distance.
We have lunch at the Happy Valley pub and buy fuel and take-aways from Cathedrals.
I am really starting to feel like I can breathe.
Dominic is helping me to heal.

I know he said that seeing me smile makes him happy, but I still need to be sure of it.

I still worry that I will do something one day that will disappoint him.

🔖 DOMINIC 🔖

The last few days with Liz have been amazing.

Amber sent me some photos she had made up, but thankfully Will has kept his distance.

Amber also mentioned that Liz hasn't said anything about Will in her messages.

I think she is worried Amber will make her come home early.

I still see him watching her when we are at camp.

I watch Liz and she is oblivious to it.

I notice that she is breathing easier and is relaxing.

Her smile isn't forced, it's easy and natural.

I can tell when she interacts with other people from when we had lunch at the Happy Valley pub. Elizabeth's smile is all she will ever need to give me.

'Hey, you,' Liz smiles as she sees me coming out of our camper trailer.

I love her smile, it makes her eyes shine brighter.

'There's my girl.' I slide my hands over her hips and around to her bum.

'What would you like to do today?'

'Would it be okay if we stay here today? I just...'

'You have met quite a few new people and need time out.' I finish her sentence.

Liz nods against my bare chest.

'Okay, lazy day it is, then. I hope you're not planning on seducing me? Because that's my plan.'

She snuggles into me and giggles coyly.

Fuck, I love it when she giggles.

I've really fallen for her.

I put up the gazebo and the fly walls.

We set up the cooler inside the gazebo, along with the double sun lounger.

Liz made up a platter with all my favourites, along with her Vegemite snacks.

I'm starting to see more of what Amber referred to; how Liz moves, her demeanour around men and beautiful women, her mannerisms, how she always makes sure I have everything before she does anything for herself.

Liz makes sure everyone is happy with everything she does, and doesn't even know she is doing it.

That is going to change.

I will make sure she starts putting herself first.

I get her to lay with her back against my chest, slowly moving my hands along her shoulders, down her arms to her hands, and hold them.

I kiss the top of her head, breathing in her smell.
I move my hands back up her arms to her shoulders and gently massage them.
'Mmm, that feels so good,' Liz says, 'Remind me to return the favour.'
'This is me returning favours.' I can tell she doesn't understand.
'All my favourites you made for our holiday; I got very spoilt. Now I'm going to spoil you.'
'You don't have to,'
'I want to. I want you to be happy, because I am.'
'I am happy with you, Dominic.' Liz says, sitting up and turning to me.
'You brought me here and showed me so many beautiful places. I don't know how to thank you for what you have done.'
'You don't have to thank me, babe. I do what I do because I want to show you things, take you places.' I bring my hand to her neck as I sit up.
'I know this is all new to you, but what we have is real. You are absolutely amazing. You survived, please remember that.' I kiss her softly.
'Now I have some photos to show you, courtesy of Amber.' I reach over for my phone.

'Okay, this is us at high school.' I start flicking through the photos.
'Is that Luke and Simon?' She asks.
'Yep, and behind them is David and Amanda.'
'You look quite dashing in uniform!' Liz laughs.
'Year twelve formal,' I look at Liz. 'Babe, what's wrong?'
'That dress, my mum helped me pick it out.'
She runs her fingers over the screen of the phone. I go to put my phone away.
'Please don't. Can I please see them?'
'Are you sure?'
Liz nods and I continue showing her the pictures.
Amber has done heaps: Liz's year twelve graduation, Christmas, birthdays, random photos of Liz and I together.
Even photos of Elizabeth's back story. I can see Agent Smith as her father.
I don't know who is playing her mum.

'Thank you, Dominic.' She snuggles in and I hold her close. 'I really miss my family.'
'I know, babe,' I kiss her hair.
'But you have a new family now. You have Luke and Simon, David and Amanda, Shaun and Chantelle with their little baby boy. Not to forget Amber and Cassie. You also have me and my family.'

'So, the accident part of the story is true, then.' Will's voice comes from behind us.
I turn around but Liz doesn't. She starts trembling.
'Yes, I told you that. I also asked you not to keep going, but you did. Elizabeth lost everything.' I say, standing up and walking over to the fly door.
'I'm all she remembers.' I walk out as Will backs away.
'Come near her again and I promise, you will not be walking away.'
'But…'
'Don't push it, Will.'
'Chantelle and Elizabeth, they are the same person.' He says, looking towards Liz.
'I won't tell you again, mate; you're out of line and wrong.' I move to stand in his line of sight and move closer to him.
I show him the photos of Liz and I together.
I notice I'm taller, and bigger.
I know how to fight, but I also know never to underestimate the other person.

'Will!' His friends call out behind him.
'I want to talk to her,' he says, looking at me. 'I have to talk to her.'
'You need to back up. You have already upset Liz enough.'
Unbelievably, he tries to move around me.
I plant my hand firmly on his chest, and shake my head.
His friends reach us.
'Will, what are you doing?' Little John asks him.
Stepping forward even further, he says, 'I'm trying to prove…'
That's as far as he got before I knocked him on his arse, out cold.
I glare at him on the ground, and throw a look of disgust at his mates, who rush to pick him up, before turning and walking back to Liz.
She hasn't moved from where I left her.
'Are you okay?' Liz asks me, her eyes on the ground.
'I'm fine. Are you okay?'
'I… yes.' She takes my left hand and sees the redness on my knuckles. 'Is your hand okay?'
Liz checks my hand.
The paramedic in her is coming out.
'Yes, but I'm not concerned about it.'
'There is no break or dislocation. I'll get some ice for it.' She still hasn't looked at me.

I let her go and get ice from the cooler, keeping an eye on Will's friends carrying him back to their camp.
I let Liz tend to my hand to distract her.

'Have I scared you?'
'No, I just...' Liz stops. 'I'm scared that he will say something that will get back to Michael, and he will find out about you. I don't know what to do.'
'What do you mean?' I ask, sitting next to her and tilting her face up so I can see her green eyes.
'If Michael finds out he could really hurt you.'

'Well, I'm not leaving you. The only way for Michael to hurt me is for him to hurt you. And I promise you that he will never get to you while my heart still beats. We are in this together, you and me.' I trail my fingers over her cheek, tucking her loose curls behind her ears.
'I won't allow you to face this on your own. I am going to stand by your side and help you rise above everything that happened to you. Besides, I can't be anywhere you're not.' My lips brush gently over hers as she rests her hands on my hips.
We lie down on the double sun lounger and I hold her close.
She finally stopped trembling and has drifted off to sleep.
I run my hand through her hair as I get my phone and look at the pictures Amber has done.

I imagine thirteen years of her in my arms. It would not be long enough.
Suddenly Liz's body jolts, knocking the phone from my hand, as if she's trying to get away.
I wrap my arms around her and hold her tight.
'Dominic,' Liz says, breathing heavily, her voice laden with fear.
'I'm here, I've got you, you're safe.' I kiss the top of her head.
'Did I hurt your hand?'
'No, but I think you should kiss me just to be sure my hand's not hurting.'
'Just a kiss?' Liz sits up and looks at me.
I sit up and bring my hands to her neck.
'No, I'm thinking more along the lines of thirteen kisses, to start with,' I smile.
'Thirteen?' Liz looks at me, confused.
I nod.
'One for every year. We have a lot of catching up to do,' I answer as my thumb moves over her lips.
Liz smiles as I bring my lips to hers.
'I think this will be a daily quota.' I smile and bring her lips back to mine.

Liz softly whimpers.
I turn and lay her down on the sun lounger under me.
I look down at her and smile as my thumb brushes her cheek.

She moves her hands up my chest and wraps her arms around my neck, pulling me down to her.

I put my head on her chest and slide my hands under her shirt, resting them on her sides.

'Dominic,'

'Yeah, babe?'

'Thank you for being so understanding and patient with me.'

I sit up and look at her.

'You don't…' I shake my head, but Liz cuts me off.

'Yes, I do.' She holds my face in her palms.

'Well, in that case, you are very welcome,' I smile.

I lay my head back down on her chest and enjoy the sound of her heart beating and the touch of her hands.

'Are you hungry?' Liz asks after a while.

'What have you got me cooking?'

'I've got some meat patties for burgers.'

'Your patties?'

'Yes.'

'Yum, I'll get the BBQ heated up.' I get up, offer her my hand and help her up.

I look over to Will's camp, they seem to be having a good time.

Music is up and I can hear them laughing and carrying on.

As long as they stay over there and Will doesn't try to talk to Liz, I won't need to show them how hard I can actually hit.

I walk over to the camp kitchen, giving Liz a quick love-tap on the bum as I pass her.

She looks at me with a raised eyebrow and a smile on her face.

I turn the BBQ on and watch as Liz gets the rest of the food out for lunch.

I sit down and pull her onto my lap.

'Dominic!' Liz giggles.

My hands move up her back and I bring my lips to hers.

She sighs softly as her hands move to my neck.

'Excuse me, ranger doing permit checks.'

'Yep, just a minute.'

We get up and I get the permits for him to check over.

Liz starts cooking the patties and the onion.

'Sorry to disturb your lunch. Can I also check your license, please?'

'Yep, it's in the car.'

I walk to my car, grab my wallet and pull out my license.

'Where did you get the patties from? They smell great!' The ranger remarks as he looks over at Liz.
'My girlfriend, Liz, made them,' I reply.
The ranger looks over everything.
'Excellent, all good. Thank you. Enjoy your lunch.'
He smiles and leaves and moves along to Will's camp.

My phone beeps with a message from Amber.

Ranger is AFP checking on Liz. Will is going to be raided in about 40 minutes, he has a record for drugs and so does one of his friends, the others are clean. Also, he posted Elizabeth's picture on Facebook. It's been taken down and his profile suspended. Make sure you aren't there when they raid him, or at the very least distract her.

That fucker took her picture! Oh, now I really want to knock the fucker out hard, not a soft one like I did earlier. A hard nose-breaking, needs-plastic-surgery knock the fuck out!

Thanks, Amber. I reply and go back to Liz.

We have lunch and clean up.
I'm trying to think of a way of distracting her, like maybe a walk to the shipwreck.
'Hey babe,' I call out to her, 'I want to go for a walk to the shipwreck, are you keen for a walk?'
'I would love to,' Liz walks over to me.
I take her hand and we walk hand in hand along the water's edge.
It takes about fifteen minutes to reach the shipwreck.
We sit together in the soft sand watching the waves roll in and wash over sections of rusted metal.
Tourist buses stop and visitors file out, taking photos.

'Dingo, dingo!' A tourist calls out.
I follow their points and sure enough, about twenty meters away from Liz and I is a dingo lounging on the sand, watching everything and hoping for some free food. It's not long before one becomes three, but they stay their distance.
Every now and then they lift their heads, sniffing the air around them.
'They are beautiful,' Liz says as she leans against me.
I pull her into my lap and hold her against me.
She is feeling the drop in temperature.
'Are you ready to go back?' I ask, kissing her hair.
'Not yet, can we stay a little longer?'

'Just let me know when you are ready to go.'
Liz pulls herself into me a little more, causing me to grin like a Cheshire cat.

🐾 ELIZABETH 🐾

Dominic holds me while we sit, watching the waves roll in and out. It's almost hypnotic and I could happily sit like this forever.
Just me and the man I love with every fibre of my being.
I watch people come and go; parents stopping their children from trying to climb on the shipwreck.
I close my eyes and take in a deep breath, inhaling the fresh ocean air, listening to Dominic's heartbeat and the sounds around us.
Before long I feel Dominic gently shake me, rousing me from sleep.
I didn't even mean to fall asleep.

'I'm sorry, did I sleep long?'
'No, but it's going to be dark soon, so we should head back.'
Dominic stands before helping me up.
I take one last look at the S.S Maheno, it's hard to believe that it's been in that spot since 1935.
'Do you know what Maheno means?' Dominic asks as we are walking back to camp.
'No,' I shake my head.
'It's Maori for island.' He answers, smiling down at me.
'Well, considering where she wrecked, the name is fitting.'
'It's also the name of a town on New Zealand's South Island, about three hours south of Christchurch.'
'Looks like we should go there for a holiday next,' I smile suggestively.
Dominic nods his head with a mischievous grin on his face.

We have a light dinner and head to bed early.
I don't bother wearing anything to bed, I love the feeling of his body touching mine without the barrier clothes provide.
'Liz, are you okay?'
'Yeah. Why?'
'You have been quiet.'
'I'm okay, Dominic, maybe just a little tired.'

I smile as he lies on his side beside me.
I close my eyes and enjoy the feeling of his hand moving slowly over my body.
I open my eyes and turn my head to face him.

His eyes meet mine and I can feel myself blush.
Ugh my body! His fingers brush my cheek and follow the scar on my neck.
I want to know what he is thinking when his eyes follow my scars.
Why does he trace them with his fingers?
Do they disgust him in some way?

'What are you thinking right now, Dominic?'
He sighs and looks back up at me.
'I saw the way you were watching the children. I saw the pain in your eyes, despite the smile on your face. I hate that look in your eyes.'
'You want to know which ones caused it?'
He doesn't answer, but he doesn't have to.
'Come with me.' I take his hand and get off the bed.
He puts his shorts back on and I get him to sit on the step to the bed.
It takes a lot of courage to stand in front of him, naked, about to bare my most painful scars.

'This one,' I take his hands, 'And this one. He shot me twice with a low calibre gun when I told him I was pregnant.'
'Twice?' He looks at me.
'He used the ultra sound machine and pressed down on my stomach to know where to aim and made sure he got both.' I say, holding back my tears. 'His doctor made sure I was able survive.' I can see the anger in Dominic's face.

'This one,' I move his hand to one below my belly button.
'I was seven months pregnant when he decided he didn't want my baby boy. He shot me again with a low calibre gun and they gave me an injection to bring on labour. I had to give birth to him on my own with no drugs and a bullet wound. He came to this world forever asleep.' My body trembles. "Michael sat back and watched while his doctor made sure that I survived. 'This one,' I move his hand over my lower abdomen.
'His doctor removed the babies when they died after a 12 hour operation I was forced to perform, and the subsequent beating that followed due to my failure. They pumped me full of adrenaline but no pain relief.
I was tied to the bed and felt everything until I passed out due to the pain and trauma.' Tears fall.

Dominic's eyes swell with tears.
'These ones here, here, and here. He stabbed me. I gave birth to a beautiful, live baby girl before he...'
'The baby girl from the footage.' He cuts in before I can say anymore.
I nod as the tears sting my eyes.

'Yes,' I murmur softly.

Dominic stands and brings his lips to mine.

'I'm sorry, babe, what he did to you and your babies is just inhuman. I promise you, he will never, ever touch you again. You will never know pain like that again. I am yours and you are mine, and I will do whatever I can to make sure you are happy and feel safe. I will give you whatever you want.'

'Dominic, all I need is you. All I want is to be happy and have someone to share every day with.'

Dominic smiles and kisses me softly.

He looks over my body and smiles at me.

'What?' I ask him nervously.

'You are wearing my favourite.'

'But I'm not wearing anything,' I say before he finishes.

'Exactly,' he says, picking me up and taking me back to bed.

We get up the next morning have breakfast and head north for the day.

I realise on our return to camp the Will and his friends are no longer there.

Finally alone, I smile.

'Now that's another of my favourite things you wear,' Dominic says, pulling me against him.

'What's that?'

'Your smile. I love the way your eyes shine when you smile. That's how I tell when you are really smiling, and when you're just being polite.'

'What else? What else do you like about me?' I ask, not looking at him.

'Honestly, it will be quicker to tell you what I don't like.' Dominic brings my face up to meet his. 'There is nothing about you that I don't like. Everything about you, Elizabeth, I love everything about you.'

He smiles and kisses me softly.

I can feel myself blush.

'Are you hungry?' I ask him.

'Yes, what are we cooking?'

'I have T-bone, and brownies.'

'Ice cream?'

'Yes.'

'Your ice cream?'

'Yes.'

He smiles and holds me close. I listen to his heart beating.

'Liz, I need to tell you something.'

'Okay,' I step back.

Dominic takes my hand and leads me to the sun lounger.

He sits and pulls me onto his lap.

'I have been keeping Amber up to date about Will, and I sent her a picture of him, along with one of his friends.'

I sit up and look at him. I'm not angry, just shocked.

I don't say anything, I just let him continue.

'The ranger that checked our permit, he was AFP checking on you. I didn't know that until I got a message from Amber.' Dominic gets his phone from his pocket and opens Amber's messages.

He hands me his phone and I read them.

'Will has a record for drugs, so it was easy for Amber to do what she needed to.'

I look at Dominic.

'So I suggested going for a walk to the shipwreck.'

'You planned this?' I ask him.

'No. I didn't know anything until I got the message. I didn't want to lie or hide this from you.' Dominic takes the phone from my hands and puts it on the seat.

'I'm sorry, Elizabeth.'

I look at Dominic as my hand moves along my wrist.

'Are you mad at me for not telling you?'

I shake my head.

'What is it?' He looks at my hands.

'What's wrong, babe?' Dominic takes my hand in his, his other hand covering the scar on my neck.

'You have to leave me. I'm not safe for you to be near. I need to disappear.'

'No,' He cuts me off, 'I'm not leaving you.'

'But Will posted my photo. If Michael finds out and finds you…' I shake my head and my whole body trembles with fear. I feel cold.

I look away.

'Babe, look at me, please.' Dominic turns my face, making me look at him.

'I told you, I'm standing by you, I'm not going anywhere. Wherever you go, I go.' Dominic brings my lips to his and kisses me, wrapping his arms tightly around me.

'Dominic, I would never forgive myself if Michael hurts you.'

'Babe, I want you. I know your past is hard for you to leave behind, but I'm still here, not letting you go.'

I let Dominic pull me into his embrace.

I feel nervous and unsettled, worried.

'I should get dinner ready, you will be hungry.'

'Dinner can wait. Right now I have you right where I want you, in my arms.'

I relax, he has that effect on me.

No place I would rather be than right where I am.

'Thank you, Dominic.'
'Anything for my girl.' I feel Dominic kiss the top of my head.

We lie there together for ages, not saying a word.
I listen to his heart beating and notice his breathing has changed while his arms
were now heavy.
He is asleep.
I manage to get up and cover him with a light sheet.
I set about getting dinner ready for when he wakes.
I peel the potatoes while the BBQ heats up, and bring the water to boil while
humming along quietly to Powder Finger and Eskimo Joe.
I cook the meat low and slow, while the potatoes boil.
I place a small steaming tray over the potatoes and add some green beans.
I wrap the brownies in baking paper, then in foil, and place them on the BBQ
plate after I turned it off.
I make some pepper gravy and mash the potatoes.

👀 DOMINIC 👀

I wake to find Liz has gotten up. I hear her behind me, and I can smell dinner.
I quietly move so I can watch her.
Her phone lights up, but she ignores it.
Then my phone vibrates with a message from Amber.

What's going on? Elizabeth hasn't sent the check-in message and she isn't
answering my calls and messages. I can't find her because her tracker isn't
working.

Liz is fine. I'll get her to send in the message and find out why the tracker isn't
working. I reply.
I also told her about Will.

WHAT!!!!!! WHY!!!!!! Amber responds.

Because she is opening up and talking. I didn't want to hide it from her and then
she finds out from somewhere else.

She is talking!? What about?

Her babies. I'm going to go to Liz now. Night Amber.

OK, Dom, thank you. Hug our girl for me. Xoxoxo

I put my phone down and get up.
I turn around and come face to face with Liz.
'I was coming to see if you were awake and get you for dinner, but I saw you texting so I waited.' Liz looks down, 'I wasn't reading over your shoulder.'
I pick up my phone and open the messages.
'You can read them. I don't have anything to hide.'
'That's not what…' Liz stops and takes a step back.
That's when I realise what I said, and how it must have sounded to her.

'Shit, sorry, babe, that came out wrong. Amber was worried because she hasn't got your check-in message, and you haven't answered her texts or her calls.' I pull her into me.
'I know you have things that you're not ready to talk about. I don't think of it as you hiding things from me. I just want you to know you can trust me, I don't want you to feel I'm hiding things from you.' I turn her face up so I can see her eyes.
'I trust you Dominic, it's my past I don't trust.'
I kiss her softly as she rests her hands on my sides.
'Now, wasn't I supposed to cook dinner?'
'You were sleeping, I know you have been tired. I have woken you a lot the last few nights. I wanted you to sleep so I made dinner for when you wake up.' I kiss her softly before she finishes.

There it is again, Elizabeth making sure I'm pleased with her, with what she does.
I take her hand and we walk to the table.
I get her to sit as I serve up dinner.
I go to the drinks cooler, and she has refilled it with beer and Canadian Club and Dry.
I look for her drinks and can't find any, so I grab a beer for myself and Canadian Club for her.
'I couldn't find any of your drinks,' I say as I open the can and place it in front of her, 'I will get some more for you tomorrow.'
I sit down across from her.
'It's okay, you don't need to.'
'I know, but I want to.' I smile at her.
'Thank you.' She smiles.

We sit and eat.
Liz doesn't say much, she is still processing what I told her about Will.

We clean up after dinner and I pass her phone to her.
Liz nods and sends Amber a message.
She passes me her bracelet.
The clasp has broken, and she had put it in the slide-out cupboard with the aluminium foil and utensils.
I send Amber a message and a picture of the bracelet's broken clasp.
'I'll fix it in the morning for you,' I say to Liz as I hand it back to her.
'Thank you.'

I hold her and she snuggles in.
We shower while the brownies finish heating up, Liz has heated up two for me and doubled my serving of ice cream.
We sit in the hammock, under the gazebo with the flyscreen walls.
I snuggle into her and kiss the scars on her shoulder as I breathe in her scent.
I feel her hands move over my arms.
I pull her in tighter and we fall asleep.

'Dominic, Dominic, wake up!'
I wake with a jolt and cause her to fall out of the hammock.
'Shit, babe, are you okay?' I ask getting to her, 'I'm sorry.'
'It's okay, I'm fine,' Liz replies, her voice is shaky and she is hiding her face. 'Are you okay? You were dreaming about something.'
 I help her up. 'I don't remember. Are you sure you're okay?'
'You called out my name and were holding me tight,' Liz says as she nods.
I bring her face up so I can see her eyes.
I notice her lip is bleeding.
I take my shirt off and press it gently against her lip.

'I did this? I'm…'
'Don't be, it was an accident.'
'Babe, you were hiding it.'
'Only because I didn't want you to feel bad,' she smiles, and her eyes shine.
She isn't scared of me.
Elizabeth pulls me down and kisses me softly, and I smile.
I pick her up and Liz snuggles in.
I carry her to bed and fall back to sleep with her in my arms.

We spend the last few days on Fraser visiting all her favourite places.
I watch her carefully.
I want to make sure I didn't scare her the other night.
She still gives me all of her, and spoils me with my favourites.
We get up really early on our last day and pack up camp.

I want to spend the last morning here with her at Eli Creek.

We get to Eli Creek and set up the awning and the two gazebos.

I grab the big portable Weber and turn it on to heat up.

Liz starts making pancakes, bacon, and eggs while I get the table and chairs ready.

I use the water heater to make coffee and a cup of tea for her.

A steady stream of people start arriving.

We spend the morning floating, and I devour pretty much all the treats Liz had left over for me.

For lunch I heat up the sausage rolls Liz had made and defrosted.

I feel like a kid in a candy store when I see her wrap up the last of the brownies and place them on the BBQ to warm up.

'Ice cream?' I ask.

Liz smiles her amazing smile and nods.

'I got a message from Shaun, we are invited over to their place for Jonathan's naming day ceremony tomorrow afternoon. Do you feel up to it?' I ask, resting my chin on her shoulder.

'I would love to. Do you?'

'Only if you want to,' I kiss the scars on her shoulder, 'Would you like to have dinner with me at the tavern tonight?'

'Are you asking me out on a date?' Liz giggles.

I slide my hands up her thighs.

'Will I get dessert?' She asks, leaning back into me.

'You know I can't say no to dessert.'

'What are you having for dessert?' A small voice asks from beside us.

We look down and see a little boy, no older than five.

'Triple choc brownies,' I answer him.

'Can I have some?'

'If it's okay with your parents, I'll give you some to share,' Liz answers, 'I still have some frozen.'

'MUM! DAD!' The boy turns and runs to his parents.

I watch as he points and his siblings look towards us.

I wave and his parents wave back.

'They said yes!' The little boy runs back to us.

Liz gets the container out and wraps five brownies in baking paper and foil.

'I thought there weren't any left.'

'I was saving them for you and the drive home. There is also another small container of goodies you haven't found yet,' Liz smiles.

His parents come over to us and Liz explains how to heat them up.
The kids hug Liz as they say thank you, and head back to their spot.
I look back at Liz, I can see how hard that was for her, and she is trying hard not to let it show.
I pull her into me and I can feel the tears on my chest.
I know how much she wants to be a mum; we will find a way for her to have that.

We leave Eli Creek just after twelve.
On the way home, Liz books a table at the pub for dinner.
She drifts off to sleep, so I park the Ute in front of the shed.
I sit and look at her for a moment.
Would she say yes if I ask her to move in with me?
She starts to stir and I touch her gently.
'Babe, we are home.'
'Hey, you,' Liz smiles.
'There's my girl.'

I help take the washing to the laundry and we unpack the trailer.
Liz hangs out the washing and puts another load on, and I give the Ute and trailer a wash.
She comes back to help and we clean up.
'I prefer the first time we washed the car,' Liz giggles and goes to hang out the next load of washing while I finish cleaning the camper and gear.

👀 ELIZABETH 👀

It feels good to be back, even though I could have stayed longer.
I hang out a load of washing and go back upstairs for a shower.
I have just finished showering when Dominic comes into his en-suite.
'Bummer,' he smiles as he undresses and turns on the shower.
I take a deep breath and drop my towel.
I hop back in the shower with him.
'Dessert doesn't always have to be after dinner.'
'Now how can I argue with that,' he smiles as he pulls me into him.

We drive to the pub for dinner and I can't help but notice the smile on Dominic's face.
'What are you smiling for?'
'I just had the best two weeks' holiday ever.' He looks at me as he parks his car.
'So did I. I didn't really want to come home.'

'I was thinking about tomorrow. We jump on the bike and go for a ride before going to Shaun and Chantelle's,' he says, reaching into the back seat.
Dominic hands me a bag. I look at him as I open it.
'You bought me a helmet?'
'Yep. I know you have one, but this one matches my bike and my helmet.'
'Thank you!'

We get out of his car.
Dominic comes around and takes my hand and we walk into the pub.
'Yay, they're back!' Simon calls out.
I look over as Simon rushes up and hugs me and I hold Dominic's hand tight.
'Thank god you're back!'
'Let me guess, you ran out of goodies?' Dominic laughs.
'Ah yes, but I'm also happy to see our girl, and you.' Simon shakes Dominic's hand.
'Luke and Cassie are about five minutes away, Amber's at the bar. David and Amanda are at the table.' Simon points to the table.
'Did you plan this?' I ask Dominic.
'No, but I was in on the plan,' Dominic smiles, and wraps his arm around me as we walk over to the table. We spend the evening showing photos of our holiday and laughing.

🦉 DOMINIC 🦉

I watch Liz. Her smile is infectious.
'Oi, are you playing pool or are you just going to stalk your girlfriend?' David jokes.
'Haha, very funny.'
'Can you just tell her already and put a ring on it? We are all waiting.' David says, handing me the pool cue.
'How long did it take you to ask Amanda?' I laugh.
'Too long,' he replies, looking at Amanda, 'Hurry up and have your go, it's your shout.'

I have my go and pass the cue back to David as I head to the bar.
I look around and see Louise with Stephanie and Daniel.
I fucking hate Daniel, and Louise knows that.
I pay for the drinks and start walking back when Amber walks towards me.
'Amber,'
'That's me,' she smiles.
'Daniel is here.'

That's all I have to say.
She nods and heads to the bar.
I place the drinks on the table and go to Liz.

'Would you mind driving home tonight?'
'Drive your car?' She looks at me, shocked. 'Are you sure?'
'Of course.' I pull her into me and lean in. 'From what I've been told, you can drive just as well as you race bikes,' I whisper in her ear.
Liz blushes and smiles.
'Okay.'
I kiss her, not caring who sees.
'Dominic, pool, dude, you can do that later.' Luke grabs me and takes me back to the pool table. 'Man, you have it bad.'
'I've told him already.' David passes me the pool cue.

👀 ELIZABETH 👀

I get up to go to the bar to order the next round of drinks.
'Mmm, unguarded.' I feel a hand touch me.
Oh, crap, where's Amber and Dominic?
'How many times have I told you, she's not interested,' Amber says, walking up and standing beside me.
'Come on, it will be fun, I'll make sure of it.'
'Did you not hear me? Walk away before I taser you where it hurts most men.'
I give Amber the money.
I need to get out of here before I panic and lose it.
I run to Dominic's car and pace behind it.
He touched me and it felt so wrong. Breathe, Elizabeth, just breathe, in and out, in and out.
Just calm down and go back inside to Dominic. Oh god, he touched me.
I find the nearest tree and throw up.

'Babe,' Dominic comes running towards me.
'Don't come any closer.' I lean against the tree.
'I'll get you some water.'
'Dom!' Simon calls out.
'Water!' Dominic calls back to him.
'On it.'
'What happened, babe?'
'I was at the bar about to order drinks when…' I lean forward, the thought makes me want to vomit again.

'And he, he…' I stumble and Dominic catches me.

'He what?'

'Touched me, I could feel his hand move down my back. He smells like, like…' My whole body is shaking. 'He scares me…'

'Babe, look at me please,' Dominic holds my face so I can see him, 'I've got you, you're safe, he can't hurt you.'

He kisses my forehead. 'Please trust me.'

'I trust you.' I close my eyes and lean against Dominic.

'Dom, water,' Simon says, getting to us.

'Babe, here try and drink some water.'

'I'll tell the others you have gone home.' Simon puts his hand on Dominic's shoulder.

'Thanks, mate.'

CHAPTER 8

It's All in the Name

I don't remember getting back to Dominic's, or getting to bed, but I wake in his arms.

I manage to get up without waking him and brush my teeth.

I stand under the rain head shower, letting the hot water wash over me.

I feel so embarrassed by my moment last night.

I guess with what happened with Will, and then last night, I just couldn't deal with it.

Thankfully I didn't pass out.

'Babe…'

I turn and see him smiling.

'Hey, you.'

'There's my girl.' He wraps his arms around me. 'How are you feeling?'

'Stupid.'

'Don't.' He kisses my shoulder.

'I'm sorry I didn't drive home. I tried so hard.'

'Babe,' Dominic turns me around, 'You didn't make it to the car before you passed out. I carried you to bed.'

'Oh,' I look away.

'Please don't.' He brings my face back up and kisses me with urgency. 'No one knows. I didn't even tell Amber.

I sent her a message saying we went home, that you were tired and not feeling well.

And Simon promised not to say anything.'

'Simon?' I look away, ashamed. 'I'm trying so hard…'

'Don't. Don't push yourself, you will get there in your own time.' He holds me. 'Are you still feeling up to going this afternoon?'

I nod against his chest.

We finish showering and get dressed.

I'm really looking forward to getting on the back of a bike, even if I'm only the pillion passenger.

Damn, he looks good in leather.

Dominic walks up to me and hands me my helmet, and I hook it over my arm.
'Ready?' He asks.
I nod and smile.
He takes my hand as I grab the backpack, and we head down to the shed.
Dominic pulls the cover off his bike as I watch.
'Ducati 1198S. Top speed, just shy of three hundred kilometres per hour, and around 131NM of torque.' I say, running my fingers over his bike.
'She was my baby till you came along,' Dominic says as he grabs me.
'You had her customised." I smile as I continue to examine his bike.
The carbon fibre fairing at the front.
Wheels anodised with red trim, and the colour; matt black with red gloss frame.
Not forgetting the highly chromed exhaust.
The bike is incredibly sexy.
He starts her and it sounds amazing.
We head off for breakfast at a cafe somewhere, I don't care where, I just enjoy the ride.
We stop again at a cafe in Bundaberg, then grab some fuel and before I know it, we are at Woodgate.

Chocolate Paddle Pops, on a beach with Dominic.
'My brothers loved the Bubble O Bill ice creams.'
'Is that the one with a bubble gum nose?'
'That's it, but my favourite is…'
'Let me guess,' Dominic cuts me off, 'Good old chocolate Paddle Pop.'
'That and the Weis bars.'
'I still prefer your ice cream,' he smiles as he lays his head on my lap. 'How did you get into motocross?'
'My step-dad taught me how to ride. I hated going slow, so he signed me up, much to my mother's dismay. I raced for about twelve to thirteen years. I loved it. My brothers signed up as soon as they were allowed to, and I used my sponsorships to help them with gear, money and so on.'
'Do you miss it?'
'Riding yes, the racing side—not really.'
'But you were great at it. I mean, Australian Champ three years in a row. Why did you stop?'
'Injury. I dislocated my knee and with rehab and uni, I just didn't go back. I was happy.'
Until I met Michael, I think to myself.

'Babe,' Dominic looks at me.
'That happened just before I met Michael. I had a Honda CBR nine hundred.
I loved that bike. I saved for ages to buy it. I even painted it red and black to
match my dirt bike. He made me take it to my family's workshop and leave it
there. Ladies don't ride bikes, he would tell me.'
'Mine's right there, you can ride it whenever you want.'
'Thank you, Dominic. But I don't…'
Dominic hands me the key.

'Go, take it for a spin.'
'It's been over seven years since I last rode a bike.'
Dominic stands up and pulls me up to him.
We walk up to his bike.
'Get on,' he says, looking at me.
I get on, he hands me my helmet and I put it on.
I put my hands on the handle bars.
He turns on the bike, I put it into gear and slowly accelerate.
I do a lap and head back to him.
He looks up from his phone and stands as I pull up.
I drop the stand before turning the bike off and removing my helmet.
'Well?' He asks, smiling.
I look at my hands and they are shaking.
He takes them in his and brings my fingers to his lips.
I smile as I watch him kiss my fingers.

'You look good on a bike,' he winks.
'Shall we head to Shaun and Chantelle's now?'
I nod hesitantly, I really want to go, but it's more people I don't know.
'If you need to leave at any time, just tell me and we can go.' He holds me.
'Thank you, Dominic.'

We pull up to Shaun and Chantelle's home and there are heaps of cars.
It reminds me of the day Dominic took me to the beach for the first time.
Breathe, I tell myself. You will be fine, Dominic is here, you're not alone. Just
breathe.

'Babe,' I get startled by a touch.
'Sorry, babe, are you okay?'
I take his hand and look up at him.
He smiles at me and it's infectious.
'I will be,' I smile back.
He kisses me softly and we head through the side gate to the back yard.

Shaun sees us first and hugs me.
I return it, but don't let go of Dominic's hand.

'So glad you came! Chantelle will be stoked that you're here now.' He shakes
Dominic's hand. 'Drinks?'
'Yeah, that would be great,' Dominic smiles.
'Right, well the white cooler is alcohol and the blue is soft drinks and water, or
I can offer tea and coffee.'
'Soft drinks will be fine, thanks, mate.'
Shaun nods and grabs a couple of cans and then goes and gets Chantelle.

Before I realise it, I'm swamped by three pregnant women asking all sorts of
questions.
'I'm sorry, but I'm not a midwife. I'm a paramedic on leave for study.'
'Elizabeth,' Chantelle comes up with her baby boy and hugs me before letting
me hold him.
I see Dominic watching me, he smiles and I find myself blushing.
'I want you to meet my parents,' she smiles excitedly.

'Okay,' I nervously follow her, while holding Jonathan, who is wide-eyed and
absolutely perfect.
'Elizabeth, these are my parents, Karl and Abby,' Chantelle smiles.
'Hello, it's nice to meet you.'
Her parents hug me.
'We have heard so much about you. It's nice to actually put a face to the name,'
Karl says, hugging Chantelle around the shoulders.

'When we got the call from Shaun, and he told us what happened and what you
did… We just don't know how to thank you.' Abby smiles as she runs her finger
along Jonathan's little arm.
'Just love this beautiful little man, and that's thank you enough for me.' I watch
him yawn and suck his hand. 'I think this little guy is hungry.'
'Would you like to feed him?' Chantelle asks. 'I express milk so Shaun can feed
him.'
'I couldn't!'
'Yes, you can. Shaun won't mind. Besides, expressing helps with the mastitis.'
Chantelle takes me inside.

I sit in the lounge while she gets his bottle ready.
I remember holding my little girl for the first time.
She was perfect in every way.
I held her and fed her.

I gave her a name and a lifetime of love in the fifteen minutes I had with her.
I still to this day miss her and love her.
I can feel the tears in my eyes as Chantelle comes over with his bottle.
I sit there watching him feed, his tiny fingers wrapped around my little finger.

DOMINIC

I watch Elizabeth from a distance feeding bub.
I can see how much she wants this, even though she is trying to hide the hurt that is brought on by this tender moment.
'When are you and Elizabeth going to have kids?' Shaun asks.
'She can't.'
'Sorry, Dominic,' Shaun puts his hand on my shoulder, 'I can get Chantelle to…'
'No, don't. As much as it hurts her, Liz will be loving the moment. Can I ask you a favour, though?'
'I won't say a thing to anyone, and I will let Chantelle know so she won't make any comments.' Shaun says before I can finish.
I nod and walk inside to my girl.
Liz has finished feeding him and Chantelle takes him to get ready for a sleep.

'How are you doing?' I ask as I pull her into me.
'He is perfect,' she says, snuggling in and avoiding the question.
'Babe, tell me what you are feeling. I want to help you.'
'Ebony Jade,' Liz's voice trembles.
'Ebony Jade?'
'That is the name I gave my little girl before she died. She was perfect and I got to hold her for fifteen minutes. Fifteen minutes and a lifetime of love. And now I'll never get to have that again. I can't give you that.' Liz cries. 'I know you want kids and I can't, I can't give you children.'
I look up and see Chantelle with a look of shock on her face.
I motion for her not to say anything and she nods, leaving us alone.

'You don't have to give me anything other than yourself.' I make her look at me.
'You have given me you and that's all you will ever need to give me.' My thumbs wipe her tears.
I hold her tight and kiss her like it is our last.
We spend the rest of the afternoon enjoying the party.
'Attention, everyone!' Shaun calls.
We stop and turn around.

'Chantelle and I would like to thank all of you for coming today. It means so much to the both of us. There are two reasons for today. We are celebrating the birth and naming of our son, Jonathan Michael West, and,' Shaun reaches into his pocket and gets down on one knee.
Chantelle says yes before he even asks.
'Well, that was easier than expected,' Shaun says, putting the ring on her finger and kissing her.
'Okay, before the party continues, can I please have Dominic, Elizabeth, Amanda and David join us.'
I take Liz's hand and walk up. She stands nervously beside me. I can feel her shaking.

'Do you Dominic, Elizabeth, David, and Amanda accept the honour of being the godparents of our son, Jonathan Michael West?'
Elizabeth squeezes my hand.
I look at her and I can see what the names and this gesture mean to her.
This kid is going to be absolutely spoilt.
I smile.
The four of us sign the register and Shaun introduces Liz to his parents and family.
I notice she has gone really quiet.
I watch as she heads inside.
I think I need to take her home.

'Dom,' Simon comes up to me. 'Is she okay? She is not her usual self.'
'I'm taking her home now.'
'Is she pregnant? You are more protective of her than normal.'
'Nah, mate, she's not pregnant,' I sigh.
'Oh, judging by what I've seen today, that's a waste. I'm sorry.'
'Don't…'

'Dominic,' Chantelle comes up before I can say anymore.
'I'm sorry about earlier. I didn't know about your baby girl, are you both okay?'
'What?' Simon looks at me.
'Elizabeth lost a child before we got together. Please, for the love of god, do not say anything to anyone, especially Liz,' I ask them.
They nod as she comes up to us.
'I'm going to take my girl home now, 'cause I want attention. Your baby stole my girl and I'm feeling left out.' I grab Liz and pull her into me.
'You want food,' Simon laughs.
'That too,' I laugh, 'Ready?'
Liz nods and we say our goodbyes.

I watch Liz get some of her frozen meals out of the freezer. She hasn't said a thing, she's not even humming.

I watch as she puts them in the microwave to heat up.

She has completely zoned out.

'Babe,' I get up and walk into the kitchen. 'Liz,' I touch her on the shoulder and she doesn't move. She has completely frozen.

'Babe, it's me, Dominic.'

'Sorry I was…' I don't let her finish.

My lips claim hers, she sighs as I lift her onto the bench and run my hands through her hair.

I feel her hold me, her hands move under my shirt and rest on my sides.

I love her touch.

I groan at the sound of the doorbell.

👀 ELIZABETH 👀

I giggle as Dominic pulls away.

'Don't you move, I'm not done with you,' he winks as he goes to answer the door.

'Hey Louise, what's up?'

'Can I talk to you for a minute? In private.' Louise stares daggers at me.

Dominic looks at me and smiles as he closes the door.

I turn back and look out the sliding back door, over the ocean.

I can hear them talking, so I walk outside and close the door behind me.

She is trying to talk Dominic into leaving me.

Will he leave me? I would let him go, at least he would be safe.

I lean against the railing, resting my head on my hands, and close my eyes, taking a deep breath.

I open them and go for a walk down to the beach.

I sit on the sand and watch the waves wash up onto the shore.

I love him so much that I would walk away without questioning him.

I know he has told me he is happy, and that I make him happy.

If he leaves me I would move away.

I would be happy for him, but I don't think I could stay in the house with the memories of our time together.

I would leave Amber behind as well, because she is happy with Cassie, more than she would be following me around.

'Elizabeth!' Dominic calls.

I stand up, time to face the music.

I turn around, only to have him grab a hold of me as his lips devour mine.

His hands hold me to him, and I feel his fingers dig into my sides before knotting in my hair. I rest my hands on his sides.

'Elizabeth,'
'Yes, Dominic?'
He sighs.
'I'll go now,' I say, stepping back.
'What?' He looks at me, not letting me go.
'I heard some of what was said, that's why I came down to the beach. I can leave now, I'll pack my bags.'
'No!' Dominic says, abruptly cutting me off.
I look at him.
'You are not going anywhere other than back inside with me.' He brings his hand to my face.

'I told Louise I'm not leaving you, and she needs to cut her crap, it's ridiculous.'
I think he doesn't know she is bi-polar or it's possible she has told him something else.
If my suspicion is correct I'm not going to tell him, it's not my secret to share.
'Please, Elizabeth, I'm not letting you go.'
His eyes search mine, he still wants to be with me.
I smile.
'Now we have a date with a microwave meal, our lounge and the second Lord of the Rings movie.' He smiles.
'Now how can I say no to that?' I giggle.
We walk back to his house hand in hand.
I still don't make it through all of the movie.

I wake to the sound of the alarm.
I go to get up, only to have him pull me back into his embrace.
'I don't want to get up,' he groans.
'Well, you have to. You have work and I have a builder to perve on,' I giggle.
'Do describe this builder.'
'Umm, well. He's about your height, brown eyes, dark brown hair, left handed, has this amazingly intricate tattoo from his left hand up to and around his shoulder, onto his neck, and will do anything for pats and food.'
He laughs.
'Oh, I forgot, he looks really good in leather, and on a bike.' I pretend to fan myself.
'Too bad he's a Warriors fan, but in his case I think I'll make an exception.' I giggle as he pins me under him.
His look is almost predatory.

I lick my lips and bite my bottom lip.
Then I smile as I move my leg along his.
'Breakfast in bed?' I query.
'Mmm, best breakfast ever.'
I have to agree.

'About time you turned up,' Luke grins.
'I've had to make my own coffee, and there's no vanilla slice in sight.'
'Freezer, bottom shelf, under the frozen vegetables, in a labelled container.'
'I'll put the kettle back on!' He yells from the top of the steps.
'I don't think I've ever seen him move that quick before,' Dominic laughs.
Dominic and I walk inside to find Luke eating frozen vanilla slice.
'It's like the best ice cream ever.' He says with a mouth full.
Dominic goes to get one and Luke pulls the container out of reach.
'Luke I can make more.'
'Fine.' Luke rolls his eyes.
I giggle at his childish behaviour.

Dominic gets a slice and takes a bite.
'It is good but I prefer the ice cream you made for the brownies,' Dominic says
as he eats the frozen slice.
'What ice cream? What brownies?' Luke asks with a mouth full, looking at
Dominic and I.
'Liz made some for the Fraser trip.'
'Please?' He asks.
'I guess I'm going grocery shopping then,' I smile.
'I'll call Simon and see what time he finishes. He can pick it up,' Luke says as
he calls Simon.
Dominic laughs and shakes his head.
'I better make a list then,' I smile at Dominic.

I walk over to the pantry and open the doors.
'LUKE!' I shout.
'What's wrong?' Dominic asks.
'Yes?' Luke answers as he smiles at me.
'Care to explain?' I ask, pointing to the very full pantry.
I walk over to the fridge and freezer and I open the doors.
They are full as well.
'Simon, Amber and I thought we should repay,'
'I don't cook for repayment, Luke.'
'We know, but we wanted to. We also went through your cookbooks and made
lists.' He grins.

'So the phone call to Simon…' Dominic asks.
'To see where he was. He's bought more containers and,' Luke pauses.
'And what, Luke?' Dominic asks.
'A chest freezer for your shed.' He smiles as he eats another vanilla slice.
'Chest freezer!?' I look at Dominic.
'Well, I guess I should get started then. Would you like coffee?'
'I'll make the coffee,' Dominic smiles at me.
'I'll eat!' Luke calls as he sits at the outdoor table.

Dominic shakes his head and makes coffee.
I read over the lists and then ponder over my music choices.
I end up going with The Rat Pack, Buddy Holly, Ritchie Valens and Elvis.
I set about getting all the prep done for the frozen dinners and savoury snacks.
I open one of the cupboards.
'LUKE!'
'Do you like it?' He calls back. 'There is a note inside it!'
I pull out the ice cream maker and put it on the bench.
I read the card.

PLEASE AND THANK YOU
LOVE
LUKE, SIMON & AMBER

I smile and open the lid, pull out the note and read their requests.
Looks like I'm making ice cream, I smile to myself.
I sit down and read through the manual.
I have never used an ice cream maker before.
Simon arrives with the chest freezer and containers of various sizes.

I spend the day cooking and absolutely loving it.
We end up with Simon, Luke, Amber, and Cassie joining Dominic and I for dinner.
I enjoy myself, but I am glad when Luke and Simon go home, I am tired.
Amber comes into the kitchen.

'Cassie and I are going now, I'll drop in tomorrow before I go to work.'
'You and Cassie are really good together. I'm glad you found someone that makes you happy.'
Amber hugs me.
'I have always been happy with you, don't you forget that.' Amber smiles at me.
'I am so proud of you.'
'Proud of me?'

'You are allowing yourself to heal, to love and be loved, to feel and really laugh and smile. I didn't know you before Michael. But from what I have heard and read about you not to mention what I see right now. You are an incredibly strong woman. Your strength gives me strength.'
I look at Amber shocked.
'Dominic agrees with me.' She winks.
'What am I agreeing to?'
'How awesome our girl is.' Amber smiles as she hugs me again. 'See you both tomorrow.' Amber walks out the door blowing kisses.

I lean into Dominic.
'How are you feeling?' Dominic asks as he hugs me.
'Apart from tired and wanting a shower, I feel good.'
'How about I finish cleaning up while you have a shower.' Dominic smiles.
'It's okay, all I need to do is finish packing the dishwasher.'
'Go and have a shower I'll finish packing the dishwasher.' He kisses me softly.
'Thank you.' I smile and head in for a shower.
The shower feels so good it was hard to get out. I dry off and don't even bother getting dressed.
I just climb into bed.
I fall asleep before Dominic gets out of the shower.

I wake to the sound of Dominic on the phone.
It's 3:30 in the morning.
'When?' He has his back to me sitting on the end of the bed.
'Yep, alright I'm on my way.' He hangs up.
'Dominic, what's wrong?'
'Louise is in the hospital and is asking for me.' He doesn't turn around.
'I'll make you a coffee to go while you get dressed.' I get up and pull my robe on.
I just finish making him a coffee in a travel mug and heating up a sausage roll when he comes out.
'I'll text you later, okay?'
'No, don't text me. Louise doesn't like me and texting me while you are with her will only upset her. Take my car, it's auto, that way you can eat your sausage roll.' He smiles at me.
'Thanks, babe.' He pulls me and kisses me before grabbing his coffee and food.
I watch him walk out the door. I can't get back to sleep so I end up cooking.

I don't realise the time until I see Luke at the top of the stairs.
'Don't tell me Dominic is still asleep.' He says walking into the kitchen.
'No, he is at the hospital with Louise, he left just before four this morning.'
'What happened?'

'I don't know. I told him not to text me while he is with her because she doesn't like me.'
'I'll call him now. How are you?'
'I'm fine, I just couldn't get back to sleep.' I look at him.
'Are you sure?'
I nod and smile.

Luke goes outside to ring Dominic as Simon comes to the top of the stairs.
They both look at me before going downstairs. Louise is winning, I sigh.
I know it's not a competition but it's hard when you suffer so much and finally open up only to have everyone walk away.
A short time later they come back upstairs.
'Is everything okay?' I ask not looking at them.
'Yep, we just spoke to Dominic. He should be here any minute.' Luke replies as he opens the fridge.

'Hey Liz, I hope you don't mind but I have been speaking to Brad and David at QAS about you. I have seen your file.' Simon sits at the bench across from me.
'I took it to my boss, and he has been speaking to David and your previous superiors. Would you consider coming to work in the ER?'
I look at Simon, completely shocked.
'I'm not qualified,'
'You're more qualified than half the staff at the hospital. Classified field medic. I mean, well can you explain just a little.'
Oh crap! I think to myself.
'I can't say too much but, I would go on certain assignments, I was the field doctor. I saw a lot of bad things happen. I had to perform surgery under extremely dangerous, difficult, and stressful circumstances. Sometimes under duress.'
'Military?' Luke asks.
I nod.
'Can you please think about the offer?' Simon asks me. 'Pretty please.'
I smile.
'Okay I will think about it. I'm going to go and lie down for a while. I have labelled containers for you.'

'Oh before I forget,' Luke says with a mouthful.
I look at Luke and he has a huge grin on his face.
'Simon just dropped off the fridge to go with the chest freezer.'
I giggle and open the fridge grabbing out a couple more containers and putting them on the bench.
'I have already put heaps in the chest freezer all labelled. Amber is getting a shed key cut for each of you.' I turn and put the kettle on.

'Okay kettle is on. There are more labelled containers in the fridge. You can put them in the shed fridge,' I turn back around and look at them already eating the food from the containers I just put on the bench. 'Try not to eat it all at once.' I smile as I walk to my room.

I lay on Dominic's side of the bed, snuggle into his pillow and drift off to sleep.
I get woken by Dominic snuggling in behind me and holding me tight.
I turn in his arms and he rests his head on my chest.
I run my fingers through his hair and he takes a deep breath.
'Do you want something to eat?'
'Yeah but right now all I want is you.' He sighs.
'What's wrong, Dominic?'
'While I was at the hospital with Louise my ex turned up. I had to sit in the same room with her and I hated every second of it. All I wanted was to be at home with you. I didn't want to be there. Does that make me a bad person?'
'No, it doesn't. If she wasn't there it wouldn't have felt like that.' I kiss the top of his head. 'Is Louise okay?'
'Yeah, she was in a car accident. She hit a large Kangaroo and her car rolled. She will be out in a couple of hours.'
'Can I ask you something?' I ask nervously.

Dominic sits up on his elbow and looks at me.
'Simon has offered me a job in the emergency department,'
'Congrats, babe, that is awesome.' He smiles and kisses me.
'Are you okay with that?' I ask looking at my hands.
'Why wouldn't I be?' His hand covers mine.
'Because I would be working with men and I could come into contact with Brad.' I look at him nervously.
'Babe, I don't care who you work with as long as you feel safe and you are happy.'
'What if I panic?' I look away.
He gets up and removes a band from his wrist, I sit up and watch him.
'My parents gave me this when I last saw them.' He takes my left wrist and puts it on. '
Now whenever you're feeling like you are going to panic or feel nervous I want you to run your fingers over this. I want you to know that even if I'm not by your side I am still with you, not letting you go.'
'Dominic, I can't,'
'Yes you can. Besides my parents would kick my arse if I didn't.' He chuckles.

I look at him and smile.
I can feel myself blushing.
I look at the band and run my fingers over it.

It has his family's name on it.
'Taumata.' I say to myself.
He brings his hand to my face and I look up and see him.
'Thank you, Dominic.'
'Anything for my girl.' He says as he brings his lips to mine.

I go out to the kitchen to get Dominic something to eat while he has a shower and gets ready for work.
I find Simon and Luke sitting at the bench with huge grins on their faces and an empty container in front of them.
'You ate it all?' I ask them.
'No, Amber helped.' They say together.
'Hey, hon,' Amber comes up and hugs me.
'Lunch for work?' I ask.
'I packed it all on my own.' She grins.
'Oh, my baby is growing up.' I giggle.

Amber smiles when she sees the band on my wrist.
'Right well. No rest for the wicked. I'll see you later. Hands off my containers.'
She looks directly at Luke and Simon.
'That hurts, Amber.' Luke grins.
'It's like you don't trust us.' Simon adds.
'When it comes to food, no.' Amber blows kisses as she walks out the door.

I get out bacon and eggs.
'Luke, Simon, are you still hungry?'
They grin.
'I'll heat up the BBQ.' Luke gets up and goes outside.
'I'll make coffee.' Simon says getting up.
'What should I do then?' I ask.
'Be in my arms.' Dominic says coming into the kitchen and holding me.
'What will be Liz's position at the hospital?' Dominic asks Simon.
'Dem Nurse.' Simon looks at me. 'We are waiting to hear back from our head of department but fingers crossed it's a yes.' Simon smiles as he holds both hands up and crosses his fingers.
'Shifts?' Dominic asks.
'Day shifts and on call if required.' Simon looks at me with pleading eyes. 'So, is that a yes?'
I nod and snuggle into Dominic.
'YAY!'

Luke and Simon make a late breakfast while Dominic and I snuggle together on the lounge.
'Food's cooked and coffee is hot.' Simon calls from the kitchen.
'Shall we?' I smile up at Dominic. 'What?' I ask him.
Dominic pulls me in tight and kisses me.
'I suppose I better have something to eat and get some work done.' He smiles.
'I'm going to check my emails then I'll be out. I'm waiting for my results.'
He kisses me as he helps me up.
'I'll see you outside then. Don't be too long.' He smiles.
'Come find me if I am.'

He chuckles as he walks outside.
I open my laptop and check my emails.
I find what I'm looking for.
Taking a deep breath, I open the email.
I get a sense of pride reading my results; HIGH DISTINCTION.
One step closer to what I have always wanted.

I go out onto the deck when I get a message from Amber.
'Hey hon, I wanted to call but on a job at the moment. I got a phone call and need to chat to you tomorrow about your case.'
I stare at my phone and my hand starts to shake.
'Liz, what's wrong?'
I look up when I hear Dominic's voice.
I'm shaking.
I look back down at the phone, not knowing what to do or say.
Before I realise it, Dominic is beside me.
He puts one arm around me, takes my phone, and reads the message from Amber.
'Maybe I should get Luke and Simon to leave,'
'No!' I didn't let him finish. 'Sorry I didn't mean to snap at you.' I say looking at the deck and feeling ashamed.
I take a deep breath.
'The last couple of months with you have been amazing.' I look up at him.

He is watching me as I keep mum.
'Luke and Simon have been good to be around. I don't want them to have to leave because of this.'
'If that is what you want then. I am happy to do whatever you want.' He says, holding me tightly and kissing the top of my head.
We sit at the table together.

'So did your uni results come through?' Dominic asks, taking my hand.
'Yes.'
'Well how did you do?' Simon asks.
'I got High Distinction for all my subjects.'
'I told you that you are more qualified than most of the staff at the hospital.' He smiles as he and Luke serve up breakfast.
'I was on shift when Shaye was brought in, and I was there when you delivered Chantelle's baby.'
I blush and look away.
I feel Dominic kiss my hand and I look up to see him smiling at me.

'I can see why David wants you there. Royal Flying Doctors, RACQ Lifeflight and QAS all want you. How much longer have you got left to study?' Simon sits down and looks over at me.
'It's a six-year course. But with my previous experience and my module completion I think I have about eighteen months left.'
'When did you start?' He asks.
'February this year.'
Simon drops his fork and looks at me.

'Can you email me your course and results?' Simon asks as he picks up his fork again.
'Sure.'
We enjoy a late breakfast.
I clean up, Dominic sees Simon off and Luke heads down to start work.
I set about getting some more cooking done.
I have just put tins in the oven and set up my laptop when Dominic comes in.

'Can I get something for you?'
'Nope I'm just getting a drink. What are you up to?'
'Cakes and brownies are in the oven, vanilla slice trays and cheesecakes are in the fridge, ice cream is in the freezer. Now I'm going to do some study.'
'Did you…'
'Yes, I made your favourite ice cream.' I smile.
'You're the best.' He kneels beside me, smiling.
'What?' I ask him.
'How did I get you?'
'Shouldn't I be asking that about you?' I blush looking away.

'Babe,' He lifts my face.
'No.' He kisses me softly.
'How about I call an early finish and you and I go to the beach.'

'I need a couple of hours. By then everything should be cooked and ready and cleaned up.'
'It's a date.' He smiles.

He heads back downstairs and I look over my next modules and study block.
I need to do nine weeks of on-the-job training and my final weeks on Campus in Rockhampton.
I'll try and see if I can get it all done at the start of next year and ask Dominic if he wants to join me for some of it.
A couple of hours later everything was cooked, iced, cut up, and in containers.
I clean up then grab a small cooler and start getting some food ready.
I had just finished cleaning and packing the cooler when Dominic comes in to take a shower.

I wait out on the deck with the cooler and blanket.
I close my eyes enjoying the cool breeze when familiar arms envelope me and his scent fills my nose.
'Hey, how are you going?' I ask
'I'm much better now that I have you right where I want you.' He kisses me softly. 'I'm great, just tired.'
'How about we get the spare bed mattress and lay it on the deck. I have the cooler with food and drinks and we can fall asleep under the stars.'
'Let's do it. Is Amber coming home?'
'No, tonight she is staying with Cassie. She stopped in earlier for food and a change of clothes. So, we are all by ourselves.' I smile.

'Did she mention anything about your case?'
'No, I did ask but she wants to tell me tomorrow. She is still waiting on a couple of things.'
I laid the blanket out and Dominic got the mattress.
I grab our pillows and doona.
I have The Rat Pack playing softly and we snuggle in together.
'I was looking over my next lot of modules and study block. I have to do a nine week on job placement and my final two weeks on campus. If I can do it all in the space of three to four months at the start of next year would you like to come to Rockhampton with me?, I'll pay for everything,'
'Liz, babe, you don't have to pay for everything. If it goes to plan, I could look for work.' He sits up and looks at me.
'So, is that a yes?' I ask sitting up.
'I'll go wherever you go.' He lays me down and rests his head on my chest.
I run my fingers through his hair. He tightens his hold on me.
'Thank you, Dominic.'

We lay there together enjoying the sounds of the ocean and the company of each other.

It's not long before he drifts off to sleep and I lay there holding him.

It's not long before I also drift off to sleep.

'Elizabeth, babe, you need to get up.'

'Why?' I groan, pulling the doona over me.

'It's starting to rain.'

I sit up and realise we are outside on the deck.

We lean the mattress under the eaves on the deck, and by the time we pack up we are both soaked and I'm freezing.

Dominic looks at me and smiles.

'What?' I smile back.

'You're wet, in a white shirt and no bra.' He grabs me hard and picks me up.

I wrap my legs around him and smile.

He kisses me hard as he walks us into our en-suite.

He puts me down in the shower and he pushes me against the wall as he turns on the shower.

I feel his fingers dig into my hip as his other hand slides under my shirt.

'Do you trust me?' Dominic asks.

'Always.'

'You need to tell me to stop if it's too much for you. Tap me if I'm too rough.'

I nod as I move hands up his arms.

'Liz...'

'I promise I will tell you. But I want to try. I want to have all of you. I can feel you holding back every time.'

Dominic smiles and his hand moves to my waist as he undoes my shorts and pushes them down, my underwear follow my shorts.

I go to undo my buttons, but Dominic shakes his head and pushes my hands to my sides.

I watch him remove his clothes, my eyes move over his naked body and I shiver with anticipation.

He grabs my shirt pulling me hard against him.

I go to move my hands along his arms, but he shakes his head and I drop them to my sides.

He kisses me hard and although he is showing dominance, I can feel his passion.

I whimper and bring my hands to his sides.

'No, you don't get to touch me yet.' He kisses me hard and I drop my arms back to my sides.

He pulls away and looks over me like a predator about to pounce on its prey.

I blush and look away.
'Look at me, Elizabeth.'
I do as he asks.

He brings his hand to my throat but doesn't squeeze, he gently pushes me against the wall.
"Tell me if you need me to stop." He says softly against my ear
I nod letting him know that I will tell him if I need him to stop.
Michael's movement were never gentle when it came to sex, it was all about him and his pleasure.
But Dominic is different; he is all about dominance but it's my pleasure he is chasing.
His pleasure is all to do with mine and my body's reaction to him.
He steps back a little under the shower and rolls his head back, I watch as the water cascades over his body.
I can feel the anticipation building in me and I'm breathing heavily.
He looks back at me and smiles as his hands move to the collar of my shirt.
His hands move slowly to the first button and undo it.
Then a devilish grin crosses his face, and he gently removes my shirt back.
He pulls the shirt down to my wrists and is about to tie them behind me.
"Please don't tie my hands." I ask looking away from him.
His hands move slowly as he drops the shirt to the floor.
"Look at me, babe," He says as he brings my face back up so I can look at him.
He smiles and kisses me softly.
"I won't do anything that you don't want to do. I want you to enjoy this, not fear it or me." He makes me stand there as he showers.

He gets my body wash and begins to wash me.
His hands move over my body and his fingers tease my nipples.
I so badly want to touch him but I'm not allowed to yet.
I lick and bite my bottom lip as I look over him, knowing full well what that does to him.
He grabs my arse with both hands pulling me under the shower and the water washes over me.
His hands move over me.
'Close your eyes and rest your hands against the wall.'
I close my eyes as he begins to finger me.
Everything feels heightened because I can't use my hands and now I can't see.
I moan his name.

Dominic pushes me hard up against the wall, he presses himself against me.
I can feel his lips brush against my cheek.

Dominic's lips follow my scar down to my breast, his tongue teasing my nipple before he bites.
I gasp and my whole body shivers as he moves down.
His hands grab my hips and his fingers dig in.
His tongue teases my inner thigh, and he pulls my hips to him as he begins to give me oral.
I crave to touch him, to see him.. My whole body erupts with pleasurable fire.
The intense feeling is unlike anything I have experienced with him.
Dominic goes harder, gently bites and I shiver at the sensation.
I can feel the heat of desire coursing through my body and so can he.
This spurs on Dominic and he goes harder.
His thumb massages my rim as his other hand moves up, grabbing my breast and pinching hard.
I can't hold back and I orgasm.
He moves back up, claiming my lips and pressing hard against me.
My body is craving more.

'Open your eyes.'
I smile as I open my eyes.
'Say my name.'
'Dominic.'
He slides his fingers into me hard.
'Say it again.'
'Dominic.' I cry out.
Dominic brings my fingers to his lips.
'Get on your knees.'
I slide down to my knees.
'Are you okay, babe?'
I smile and nod taking his cock in my mouth.
He has one hand on the wall as his other hand tangles in my hair.
Dominic's hips match my rhythm and he pushes my head on his cock aggressively.
I suck harder.
I want to give him as much pleasure as I can, I want all of him.
I take him deep causing him to tighten his grip.
I look up at him and his head has rolled back as he groans.

'Liz,' He looks down at me. 'Harder.'
I take him deep again and let him push my head hard, causing me to gag a little.
I dig my nails into his legs as I go harder.
'Fuck me,' He cries.
I now have both of his hands tangled in my hair.
'Don't stop,' He tells me.

I go harder, taking him deep.
My hand moves along his shaft as my other hand teases and plays with his balls.
I look up as he rolls his head back, moaning.
He is close and I'm going to take it all.
I go harder and faster, he tries to pull back but I won't let him.
Both of his hands pull my hair tightly.
He spreads his legs a little more and leans back pushing my head down hard.
He starts to orgasm and tries to pull out but I take his cum and swallow it.
He leans against the wall recovering, as I use mouthwash to rinse my mouth out.

He turns the shower off and grabs me, forcing me out of the bathroom and onto our bed.
Holding my arms to my sides, he begins to kiss and nip at my body.
I arch my back and whimper at the sensation.
His grip tightens on my wrists as he reaches my breasts.
'Dominic,' I cry. 'Don't stop.'
He releases my wrists and cups my breasts burying his face in my cleavage and biting.
I don't stop him.
I dig my fingernails into his shoulders before dragging them into his hair.
He moves down my body; he gently bites along my most sensitive scars; my body shudders at the sensation.
His hands grab my legs pulling me to the edge of the bed before he pushes my legs open.
 His tongue teases my clitoris before taking it hard in his mouth and sucking.
My hands tangle in his hair as my body reacts to the feeling.

Dominic sucks hard as he shakes his head.
I orgasm and he keeps going.
I feel myself getting hot, my whole-body aches with wanted desire.
He goes harder the more I cum and call his name.
He bites a little too hard and I tap his head with my finger and he stops biting and kisses my clitoris before he starts sucking and tonguing it again.
'OH MY GOD, DOMINIC!' I call out as I orgasm again.

He moves up, claiming my lips with a hard kiss.
There is nothing passionate about this kiss, it is pure dominance.
He is giving me all of him.
Dominic moves me up the bed.
I feel him enter me.
He pushes hard and deep before getting to his knees and lifting my feet up to his shoulders.

I watch as he rolls his head back and starts to go harder.
His hands grab my hips and I touch his hands.
He leans forward, sliding his hands up to my breast.
My legs are still against his chest; the more he leans towards me the more intense it feels for me.
He moves back upright and lifts my hand up, bringing my fingers to his mouth and sucking them.
He then moves my hand down to my clitoris and gets me to rub myself.
I watch the pleasure he takes from watching me masturbate as he fucks me.

He spreads my legs, giving my hand better access to my clitoris and using his spit to lubricate my fingers.
His fingers dig in as I start to whimper and he rolls his head back.
Dominic's fingers dig in harder, I tap his hand gently and he softens his grip.
His hands slides up to my breasts, pinching my nipples.

He puts a pillow in between my head and the wall, grabbing my hair with one hand, he pushes the side of my head into the pillow and starts to go harder.
It feels amazing, although he is letting go and being harder and rougher with me, I don't feel unsafe or scared.
I feel him bite and kiss my right shoulder, sending waves of heat through my body.
His hand moves to my hip and wraps around me, I run my hand along his.
I start to whine and he knows I'm close.
He starts to get rougher, but I don't tap his hand, I let him go.
I want to know how far I can go.
He softens a little, he could hear it in me.

He pulls me against his chest as I orgasm; my whole body craves him.
Dominic moves back, pulling me with him.
He grabs my hands and pushes me down.
I can feel him deep inside me.
'Yes, Dominic.' I cry out in ecstasy. 'Yes, don't stop.'
He lets go of my hands and grabs my waist.
I let him go harder.
I don't need to tap or tell him, he knows when I have reached my limit.
'Fuck, Liz.' He moans.

He lays down and brings his knees up, I lean against his legs as I move along his cock.
I feel his hands move up my back.
He grabs my waist with one hand as he tangles his other hand in my hair.

I go harder on him.
He growls and arches his back.
He moves and pins me on the bed, kissing me hard.

Dominic gets to his knees with one of my legs under him and my other leg against his chest, he enters me again.
Grabbing my hand, he sucks my fingers.
I know exactly what he wants.
I move my hand back down to my clitoris and begin to masturbate again as he watches.

He starts getting rough.
He pushes deep and digs his fingers into my leg and waist.
He leans back and groans, he is holding back and trying not to cum.
He moves me up the bed and reaches for the little black box.
He looks at me and I pull him down to me.
'I want you, Dominic.' I say as I bring my lips to his and kiss him as hard as I can.
He returns it.
'Tell me if you need me to…'
'I trust you.'
Dominic grabs my leg and pushes hard and deep.
I reach for him, pulling him down to me.
'I'm not going to stop you.' I say against his ear.
I gently bite his earlobe and moan.
He pushes up on to his hands and I wrap my legs around him.
Every movement he makes goes deep, hard, and fast.
I bring my hands to his side and dig my nails in.
I feel his body shudder.
He groans and pulls out.
Dominic pulls me up and kisses me before turning me around and making me bend over.

He enters me again and fingers my rim, I shudder at the sensation.
I want this, I want it with him. His other hand grabs my arse as he goes harder.
I whimper loudly.
'Liz, babe.' He slows.
'No, don't stop. I want more.'
I throw my head back as he continues.
His hands follow the scar on my back from the top to the bottom before grabbing my arse hard. He groans and starts to go harder.
'Elizabeth,'

He stops but I keep moving, I hear the foil being torn.
He moans as he slowly pulls out.
I feel his hand move over my arse and the cold sensation of the lubricant.
He slides in slowly before grabbing my arse hard.
'Elizabeth.'
'I want it, don't stop.'

I let him go as hard as he wants.
My body responds to his every movement and touch.
He only stops to apply more lubricant.
He is not gentle but still makes sure I'm ok, he knows instantly if I can't take it and slows.
Once I'm ok, he pushes the boundary a little further and I'm loving every second of it.
'Dominic,' I cry.

I start to orgasm, my whole body shakes.
He doesn't stop or slow, he goes harder.
I push back into him, letting him know not to stop.
It's not long before I can feel him getting close.
He leans forward pushing deep.
His grip tightens and he growls loudly, he grabs my hand and brings it up to my clitoris.
Dominic keeps his hand over mine as I masturbate.
We orgasm together and it is the most intense one I have ever had with him.
Dominic pulls me up and holds me, he brings his lips to my shoulder.
We are both breathing heavily.

'You, Elizabeth, you are amazing. Your body is fucking perfect.'
I lean back into him and close my eyes, taking a deep breath.
I turn my head as I open my eyes and look up at him. He is smiling.
'Are you…' He kisses me before I finish asking him.
'Are you okay?' He asks me. 'Please be honest.'
I nod, I move as he gets up, goes to the bathroom and comes back a moment later.
He lays on the bed next to me.
He lies on his side, facing me and resting his hand on my side.

'I trust you, Dominic. You knew when I couldn't take much more. You didn't pressure or push me. I loved every second of it.' I smile and run my fingers along his cheek.
'Did I hurt you?'

I look away.

'Babe, I want to know so I don't do it again.'

'It hurt a little but at the same time it was extremely intimate and intense. I want it again.' I look at him nervously. 'I want you to be satisfied.'

'I am with you every time. I love the way you feel in my hands. You fit perfectly against me. But I don't want to do anything that you are not comfortable doing.' Dominic pulls me in, and I snuggle into him. I feel his hand follow the scar along my back. I fall asleep as he plays with my hair.

CHAPTER 9

I'm Broken

I wake alone and cold, it's three in the morning.

I pull on my robe on and get up.

I walk out of our room and see Dominic sitting outside at the table.

'Dominic?' I walk up to him.

He turns and smiles as he reaches for me, pulling me onto his lap.

'Are you okay?'

'Yeah, Louise rang and woke me, she wanted to talk. She fell asleep while we were talking then I couldn't get back to sleep.' He sighs. 'I asked her to get help. I'm worried about her.'

'You are a good friend, Dominic. Would you like me to get you something to eat or drink?'

'No, let's go back to bed.' He kisses my fingers. 'I just need you wearing…'

'Let me guess,' I look at him. 'Nothing.' I smile.

'It's my favourite look on you after your smile.' He smiles as he tucks my hair behind my ear.

We get up and head back to our bed.

I remove my robe and climb into bed.

I pull him into me and he rests his head on my chest.

I feel him drift off to sleep as I run my fingers through his hair.

I lay there holding him as I think of more ways I can keep him safe.

Agent Smith and I have come up with a few, but I need to have a plan B and C.

'Blood' I think to myself, Michael loves it when I bleed.

I need to draw blood and send it to Agent Smith so they can plant it for Michael to find.

I will also need to write letters to Michael in code that only he would understand. That should keep him at bay for a while.

Dominic stirs and mumbles in his sleep and I hold him tighter.

I kiss the top of his head and I feel his arms tighten around me.

I love Dominic so much that I would sacrifice my own life to ensure Michael never touches him.

I don't know how long I laid there holding him before I finally fell asleep, but I have plans formulated and waiting to get put into action.
I wake up to find him getting dressed for work.

'Hey, you.'
'There's my girl.' He smiles as he walks up to me and sits on the bed.
'What are your plans for today?' I ask him.
'I'm about to leave and go pick up some stuff. Would you like to come? We could have breakfast somewhere.'
'Give me 20 minutes and I'll be ready to go.' I smile and get up.
I have a shower and get dressed.
I find Dominic out on the deck.
He is on the phone and he sounds annoyed, so I make some coffee to go while I wait for him to finish.
I'm almost done when he comes up behind me, wrapping his arm around me, and burying his face in my neck, taking a deep breath.
'Is everything okay?' I ask him.
He turns me around, holds me tight, and kisses me.
Thank god he is holding me because my knees weren't, my knees suck.
He pulls back and I stumble slightly.

'Dominic,'
His lips silence mine. I sigh softly as his hands tangle in my hair.
'Dominic, what's wrong?'
'I just need you.' His hands cup my face and he smiles. 'That was Stephanie on the phone, I thought it was Louise, it was her name as the caller.'
Dominic lays me down on the lounge before covering me with his body.
'Is everything okay?' I ask trailing my fingers through his hair as he lays his head on my chest.
'No. Louise is having some problems and now that I'm not dropping everything to run and help her I'm the bad guy.'
He holds me tighter and continues. 'Louise and I have been friends since grade five. We have always had each other's back through good and bad. '
He presses his lips on my chest.

'Louise is jealous, Dominic. You have someone and she doesn't, it's completely natural.'
'I understand that but why throw it at me like she has been doing. Getting Stephanie involved is just childish.'
'People do strange things when they feel like they have lost a huge part of themselves. Just give her time, the friendship you both have is strong. Everything will work out in the end.'

Dominic sits up on his side to look at me.
He gives a solemn nod before resting his forehead on mine and closing his eyes.
'Thank you for listening.'
'Anytime.' I plant a soft kiss on the tip of his nose.

We have breakfast in town before heading to Bunnings, then we go shopping for groceries.
Luke is just arriving by the time we get back home.
I leave him and Dominic to unload while I get coffee and vanilla slice ready, along with Dominic's favourite.
Amber arrives not long after and joins us for coffee.
She keeps looking at me.
I know she needs to talk to me.
Dominic and I clean up after while she is on the phone.
Amber walks in as she hangs up.
'Hun, I really need to talk to you. We have had a development in your case.' Amber says as she gives me an uneasy look.
'What kind of development?' I ask.
'Michael.' That's all she needs to say
Dominic glares at her and I feel weak and physically sick.
I run my fingers over Dominic's band.

'I'm sorry, Dominic, I can't discuss this in front of you.' Amber says.
I close my eyes and hold onto the bench, trying to breath.
'Do you want to go for a walk, hun?'
My eyes are still closed, and I breathe deeply.
'Okay,' I whisper.
'Liz,' Dominic moves to my side and wraps his arm around me.
I turn and snuggle into his embrace, taking a deep breath.
'Babe.' His hand lifts my face and I open my eyes.
'I'll be okay.' I hope that sounds convincing because I don't believe it myself.
'I'll be right here if you need me.' He kisses me softly.

I turn to Amber.
'Let's go.' I nod.
Dominic glares at Amber and walks out.
I have told him too much too soon.
Amber's phone rings.
'I'll meet you on the beach in five minutes.
I just have to take this.'
I nod and head down to the beach, my head is full of what ifs and fear.
Amber joins me a short time later.

'Sorry,' She says, sitting next to me.
'All good, what's going on?' I ask, taking a deep breath.
'The bail hearing has been brought forward.' Amber says.
'So, what does that mean for me?' I ask as I stare over the ocean.
'At this point, I need you to come with me tomorrow. There will be a video link and you need to be there in case you need to speak. Now this is just a formality because he will be doing his via video link from prison.'

Pure dread and fear set in and Amber picks up on it.
'He can't hurt you, Liz.' Amber says as she wraps her arm around me.
'We have been feeding him false information about you under the assumed name of Gena Newman. He won't be able to see you. Besides, the pictures we leaked to him show you still have your implants and long black hair.'

'I hated the black hair and implants' I say, looking at my feet as my fingers brush over the band on my wrist.
'I know, hun.'
'What will happen if he makes bail? I know he will come for me personally.' I look at her.
'I don't know. But bail would come with restrictions,'
'Oh, come on, Amber, restrictions? He is Michael Webster. Do you honestly think restrictions will stop him? I'd rather die than go back to him, Amber.'
'Not going to happen, Liz, you are protected'

'I have made preparations to ensure Dominic will be safe.' I say, standing up and running my hand over Dominic's band.
'What do you mean?' Amber asks.
'I'll see you tomorrow. What time?'
'9 am at the courthouse. I'll take…'
'No, I'll meet you there.' I say as I walk away.
'Wait, Liz, what preparations?' She calls out. 'Lizzy!'
I don't answer. I just keep walking and thankfully she doesn't follow me.

AMBER

'Amber, where is Liz?' Dominic asks me.
I let out a big sigh.
'Amber?'
'She wanted to be alone, so she went for a walk' I say as I walk up onto the deck.
'She's alone? You left her?' Dominic goes to leave towards the beach.
'Dom, leave her.'

'What's going on?' Luke asks, walking up to us.
'Her fucking ex.' Dominic replies.
'I wouldn't worry mate, she won't leave you.' Luke says.
'Not worried about that, he used to…' Dominic didn't finish.
'He beat her?' Luke asks.
'That's only the beginning of it.' I reply.
'Luke, can Dominic and I have a moment please?' I ask.
'Sure.' He pats Dominic on the shoulder.
Luke looks at me.
'Look after our girl.' Luke smiles and walks off.

I turn back to Dominic.
'Liz said something that concerned me, and I need you to promise me something.'
'What did she say?'
'She won't go back to him. She would rather die than be taken by him. She has made preparations to ensure that you are safe.' I look away from him.
'What precautions do you think she has taken?' Dominic asks me.
'I don't know and I gather you don't either, so I need you to help me.'
'What do you need?'
'If you notice anything, anything at all no matter how small, I need you to tell me. It's really important.'
'Okay, anything else?
'I need you to promise me something. When the time comes, and I think it will be sooner rather than later, when she tells you everything, promise me you won't run. She's going to need a friend, boyfriend or more. Just for goodness sake, don't leave her at that moment, okay?' I look at him.
'I have no intention of leaving her.'
'Good because if you do,' I say, walking closer to him with my arms folded.
'I have a particular set of skills that would make Liam Neeson from Taken look really cute and cuddly.' I say, looking directly in his eyes.

He nods and walks back to Luke.
I head back inside and wait for Liz.
I open the case files and read them even though I know it word for word.
I need to find something to make sure I can keep her safe.
The 'Precautions' she mentioned really has me rattled.
I don't notice the time until my phone rings, shit, Liz, where are you?
'Agent Carter speaking,'
'AMBER! My office now!' Call ends.
'Shit!' I say.

⚭ ELIZABETH ⚭

I just walk and walk, not even thinking about where I was going.
It isn't until I reach the surf club that I realise how far I have walked but I don't really care.
I end up sitting on the beach and watch the waves roll in.
Life is so much simpler when you're out on the water; there's nothing but the sun and surf.
How am I going to face the man who beat, raped, stabbed, shot, and tortured me for years?
He passed me as entertainment to his associates.
Thankfully, they weren't allowed to touch me.
I lost five babies and the ability to have children altogether.
I hate him, he is a monster and I want my revenge.

I finally have happiness, a home I feel safe in, good friends and someone I love, and now that he's raising his evil head, it's all at risk.
I make myself promise to have my revenge on Michael.
I will show him I am someone who can have love and happiness.
After everything he did to me, after everything I lost, I now have something to live for; I look at my left wrist and sigh.

It was Christmas day in 2009 and a moment of weakness.
I was sitting on the steps of my deck, looking out to the ocean and clutching a knife.
I watched the blood drip down the steps as I ran the knife up my arm.
I don't remember feeling the pain.
It wasn't until Amber found me, and slapped my face as she yelled at me,
'You fucking bitch! How dare you let him win!'
I realise she is right.
Why should I fall and let Michael stand tall?
I will have my revenge one way or another, in this life or the next.
I will never let him hurt the people I love.
I have Amber to thank for showing me the light in the darkness, and now I have Dominic.

I look down at his band and smile.
I just want to shed everything that has held me back.
I know I have only been with Dominic a short time, but he is all I want and I'm in love with him.
I'm not ready to admit it to anyone, especially him.
I don't think he is ready to hear it and I don't want to change anything.

I stand and walk down to the water, letting it wash over my feet.

What Dominic and I have right now is perfect.

I'm determined not to let Michael win.

I stand there for what feels like ages as I think of the time I have spent with Amber and Dominic.

How they have helped me more than I could tell them.

I need to get back home, back to Dominic.

I can't wipe the smile off my face as I start walking home. I'm going to meet the man I love.

'Heading home?' A familiar oily tone says from behind me.

I roll my eyes

'Yes,' I reply 'Dominic is waiting for me.' I run my hand over Dominic's band

'Can I join you on the walk?' Daniel asks.

I really don't want him to but I have a feeling he won't take no for an answer.

'I can't stop you from walking on the beach.' I say not even looking at him.

I wrap my arms around myself and keep walking, wishing Dominic was with me.

'Well, I'll take what I can get,'

I can feel his eyes on me, and I try not to let him get to me.

'For now, anyway. But I would really like to get to know you more.' He continues.

He's arrogant and slimy. I don't like the feeling he gives me.

I make sure there is a good distance between us.

He talks and I mostly ignore him. I'm relieved when I get to my beach entrance.

'Goodbye,' I say politely.

'Can we…'

'No.' I look directly at him. I'm really starting to feel uneasy.

My hand covers Dominic's band as I try to stay calm.

'Sounds like a challenge.' He tilts his head to the side and grins devilishly.

'Mmm you're really not playing fair here, Elizabeth,' His eyes change, and I slowly fill up with dread.

I quickly turn and leave the beach.

Suddenly, someone grabs me from behind, spins me around, and slams me into a tree.

'I love it when you play hard to get, but I know you want it.'

He kisses me and I manage to knee him in the groin.

He stumbles back but doesn't let go of my arm.

'You bitch!' He hits me so hard that I spin and hit the tree, splitting my lip and eyebrow in the process.

I can taste the blood in my mouth.

I call for Dominic and the blood stings my eye.
Feeling dazed, I try to run but Daniel grabs my wrist and I cry out in pain.
'Dominic!' I scream as I try to hit Daniel.
'NO!' I cry out as I manage to push him away.

'Fucking bitch.' Daniel pulls me back.
'NO! Let go of me!' I yell.
'DOMINIC!' I scream as loud as I can.
I manage to punch him in the face, but he doesn't let go of me.
He throws me hard to the ground.
I feel my head hit a rock and start to feel dizzy, but I know I need to move.
I roll over to my stomach and stumble as I try to get up.

'Dominic!' I scream again as he kicks me, causing me to roll on to my back.
I scream for help as he pins me to the ground, and I try to fight him.
I attempt to remember what Amber and Dominic taught me.
But Daniel is strong and I find it hard to fight him off.
I manage to get him off me and get to my feet.
'Dominic!' I scream again.
 Daniel tackles me from behind and I manage to turn and twist his arm before pushing him away.
He grabs my shoulder and punches me hard in the stomach, causing me to bend over.
He then grabs the back of my head and rams his knee into my face but misses my nose.
I fall backwards to the ground, hitting my head hard.
I'm gasping for breath and I feel very light-headed but I need to keep fighting.

I roll to my stomach and try to crawl away.
My vision is blurred.
I can't even tell if I'm crawling to or away from my house.
He kicks my side again causing me to fall before he pins me to the ground.
This time he manages to hold me down.
I try to scream but he is on my chest and I can't breathe properly.
He is holding my wrists above my head.
The pain is unbearable.
'Beg for it, Elizabeth.'
'Please don't do this' I manage to say as tears fill my eyes.
I can feel his free hand move over my breast and he squeezes hard.
I try to get my hands free not minding the pain.
'Daniel, please stop.' I beg him.

'Mmm, say my name again.' His voice is laced with venom purpose.
I shake my head. He slaps my face.
'Say my fucking name!' He yells at me.
I can feel the blood from his nose dripping onto my cheek.
'Daniel.' I cry.
I don't turn to look at him.

Still holding my wrists, he slides down on me and grabs me hard by the jaw.
His smile is intensely evil.
He wraps his hands around my throat and squeezes, then repeatedly slams my head onto the ground.
I try to dig my fingers into his eyes, but I feel like I'm going to pass out.
'I'm going to have so much fun with you, your lips, your…'
'Get off her, you fucking asshole!' Dominic yells as he yanks Daniel off me, and lands a punch that sends him flying.
I roll onto my stomach and try to crawl away.
I can't get up, I feel so tired and sore.

'Dominic…' I weakly call out as he rolls me onto my back.
'Shh, babe, it's okay. It's me, Dominic. I've got you.'
'Dominic,' I whisper with a mouth full of blood.
I turn my head and spit out the blood, I feel so light-headed.
Luke reaches us as he calls the police.
Dominic removes his shirt and begins to carefully wipe the blood from my face.
I can feel myself fading.
'Dominic…' I try to reach for him but I can't lift my hand.

'Stay with me, Liz. Come on, babe, don't close your eyes.' Dominic says, his voice breaking.
'Daniel, he, he…' I can't finish, my mouth hurts too much.
'Sshh it's okay, don't worry about that mongrel. Hey look at me, don't close your eyes. Come on, babe, please keep your eyes open.' Dominic's voice sounds shaky

'So tired.'
'Can you sit up?' He asks. I hear his voice break again.
Dominic holds me up and I see Daniel, out cold, and that's when the gravity of the situation hits me, and I start to cry.
I try to get away, but Dominic holds me close, my eyelid feels heavy and it's hard to keep them open.
'Hey, I've got you, I've got you. Please, babe, keep your eyes open and look at me. Where's my girl?' Dominic says as he tries to sooth me.

'Police and ambulance are on their way.' Luke says.
'Can you call Amber please?' Dominic asks as he passes Luke his phone.
'Tired. I'm so tired, Dominic.' I whisper.
'Liz, I'm going to carry you to the house okay? Just keep your eyes open.'
I manage to look up at him. I can't open one eye, it feels swollen.
I look over at Daniel and he is starting to move, I panic.
'Liz, look at me, not him, just breathe. I'm right here' Dominic says as he kisses my head softly.
I look up at Dominic, his eyes are red as he softly wipes my tears and smiles.
I rest my head against his chest as he carries me home.
I listen to his beating heart.
 Luke half drags Daniel back to the house and zip-tie him to the railing.

'Babe, I'm so sorry for letting this happen to you. I was out the front, on my phone, packing stuff away. I was about to come look for you.' He says as we get inside.
He sits down with me on his lap at the kitchen table, holding me close to him.
'I'm sorry, I didn't mean to make you worry.' I whisper. 'Please don't be mad at me.'
Luke enters and Dominic motions for him not to come any closer.
'Is she alright?' Luke asks.
I can feel Dominic tense up and kiss the top of my head.
'I'll make her a cuppa,' Luke says.
'White and one.' Dominic replies.
I start to shake, I can't breathe.
Dominic tries to calm me down.
'Babe,' He says, pulling me in.
'I'm here with you. Just breathe with me in and out, in and out.' He says as he plays with my hair.

'I've got you, I won't go anywhere.' His fingers trace my scars.
I hear the cup being put on the table and a phone ringing.
'Luke, can you talk to Amber please?' Dominic hands Luke the phone.
I know Amber is going to be pissed.
'Dominic?' I whisper.
'Yeah, babe.'
'I said no, I was walking,' I paused.
'I know, babe.'
'I said no, I was coming home to you. He…'
'Liz, babe, look at me please.'
Dominic gently lifts my head.
'I said no,' I say softly

'Liz,'
'I don't want him, I want you and I told him that.'
'I know and he will pay for it.' He says pulling me in.
'I tried to get away but, but he, he…'
'Babe, I'm here now. I've got you.'
'Amber is on her way, I hope the cops get here before she does.
She scares the crap out of me.' Luke says as he re-enters.

I start replaying the events of the attack.
My mind starts playing the what-ifs game.
What if Dominic wasn't here?
What if I couldn't fight him off?
What if he did rape me?
Would he have continued to hurt me?
What if he hurt Amber?
What if he hurt Dominic?
What was he really capable of…?
Darkness.

'Elizabeth,'
I can feel someone touching me on the shoulder and my head hurts.
'Elizabeth,' A voice says softly.
One eye starts to open while the other one feels sore and swollen.
'Elizabeth.' A man's voice says, it's calm and smooth.
'My name's not Elizabeth, it's Chan…,'' I stop mid-sentence.
I realise where I am, and that the voice belongs to Dominic.
The look on his face makes my heart drop.
'Are you okay?' He looks so worried.
'Um, I think so, I'm a little confused.' I answer, scared to look at him.

He doesn't say anything.
He just gets up and leaves my bedroom.
I stare at the door, surprised at his odd behaviour.
He walked out just like that.
He just left me alone without even looking back.
He doesn't want me anymore.
I look at my now empty wrist, his band is not there.
He took it back.

I replay the conversation with Amber and the altercation with Daniel.
I struggle to get up on the side of the bed only to see Amber walk in.
'Hon, how are you feeling?'

'Fine, where's Dominic?' I ask.
'He is outside. The police is waiting in the kitchen with the paramedics.
I asked them to wait till I give them okay to come in. I'll send them in.'
'No.' I start to cry again.

Amber holds me.
'He's left me, Amber.'
'Who? Dominic? Why on earth do you think that?' She is incredulous.
'He just got up and left, he didn't say a word, didn't look back.'
Amber doesn't say anything, she just sits with me.
'Why am I so unwanted, broken and…?' I pause and take a deep breath.
'And what?' Amber asks.
'Still here, why am I still here? Everything I want just walks out my door without
looking back. Why did you save me that day?' I ask.
'Because you are worth something to me. You are my best friend and I love you.'
'Stop lying to me, Amber,' I cry. 'You saved me because I'm more useful to you
and the case alive. You only need me to put him away.'
'Hey, that's not true, Elizabeth.' She looks at me angrily.

I push her away and stand up.
'Please, just leave me alone. I don't want to be here. I just don't care anymore.' I
walk into the bathroom without looking back and close the door.
I turn on the shower and sit under the water, not even bothering to get out of
my clothes.
I watch the water turn red with my blood.
I should be used to this by now; beaten, bleeding, and alone just like Michael
said I would end up.
I guess I can't fight fate.
I should never have left him. This brief moment of loving someone was never
going to last.
I was a fool to think I could ever have that or amount to anything.
I can hear people talking but not what they are saying, which is fine.
I look at my wrist and run my fingers over my scar, willing it to open again so I
can stop hurting.
I start to cry again.
I am alone, with no one to hold me, no one to love me.

Why did Amber save me that day?
She has all the reports, the evidence, and statements.
But it can't be compared to a living victim.
She needs me on the stand, broken, to show the world that Michael Webster is
not the man everyone thinks he is.

I hear my bathroom door open, but don't bother to look behind me.
'Don't worry, Amber, I'm not dead… yet.' I say.
No response.
The door closes and I hear footsteps come closer.
'I'll make sure it's clean, and I'll even leave a note for you. That should help you, right?' I go on.
'Soon you will be rid of a victim that felt so alone when everyone left, Michael finally broke her completely. At least you won't have to pretend anymore; you will finally be rid of Chantelle Watson.
You can move on and be happy, you deserve to be happy.
Dominic will be safe, Michael will never know about him.
Dominic can move on and find someone who can give him what I can't, children.
I'm only holding you both back.'

'Well, I'm not going anywhere,' Dominic says.
I freeze. I feel him sit behind me, his arms wrap tightly around me.
'I'm not going anywhere, and neither are you.' He says.
'Now the ambos and police are here for you, and to take you to the hospital.'
'I don't want to go.' I say.
'Well, you are. You have cuts all over your face and the back of your head.'
I sigh, I know he is right. I rest my head on my knees.
'Okay,' is all I manage.

He turns the tap off and wraps a towel around me.
I don't say anything and I'm too scared to move.
I'm not scared of him.
I'm not even sure I can look him in the eyes after everything I just said.
'Now, I'm going to get you up, okay?'
'Okay.' I whisper.
My whole body is shaking.
I don't even look at him.
I'm too ashamed and I just know he is disappointed in me.
He removes my wet clothes and then wraps me back up in the towel.
Dominic starts to dry my hair and I flinch in pain.

'I'm sorry, babe.' He says, pulling me into him.
'Dominic…' I whisper
'Yeah, babe.' He says as he tries to gently dry my hair. I can feel the cuts start to bleed again.
'Is he, is he still here?' I tentatively ask.

'Yes, the police handcuffed him and put him in the back of their car. They are going to leave as soon as the other police car arrives. The ambos didn't check him, they came straight up here to check on you.'
'Please don't make me go out there, I can't. Please don't,' I say, still not looking at him.
'Okay.' He replies.
'Thank you.
Are you angry with me?' I ask.
He stops and I start to shake again.
'I'm sorry I disappointed you. Please don't be mad at me. If you keep me I will do better.' I can feel the tears coming.
'Babe, I'm not angry or disappointed in you. I'm proud of you.' He replies
He gently lifts my head, he is smiling at me.

'I don't understand. I said bad things, I gave up, you told me not to and I did. I disobeyed you. I'm so sorry,'
'You fought back and didn't stop. I saw him tackle you to the ground. He is bigger and stronger than you but you didn't give up. You broke his nose, babe.'
He begins to laugh.
It was not what I expected to hear and hearing him laugh makes me smile.
I lift my left hand to see it bruised, swollen, and deformed.

'Shit.' Dominic gently holds my left elbow.
'There are at least two breaks and some dislocated fingers.' I noted.
'How do you know?' He asks.
'Not the first time my hand has looked like that. There's no hammer this time so that's a bonus'
'Hammer?' He looks at me.
'Um, I dropped a five hundred dollar bottle of wine when I was serving him dinner one night, so I got punished for it. I got a broken wrist and fingers, and no food for three days.'
Dominic didn't take that well.

'Dominic, I'm sorry about what I said when you came in, I...' I look down at my feet as I tremble.
'Liz, look at me please and hear what I have to say.' His hands move to my neck, covering my scars.
I take a deep breath, and do as he requests.
He kisses me softly.
'Liz, I care for you a great deal and I'm going to stand by you. I want you.'
Dominic kisses me gently again.
'You want to keep me?' I look at him in surprise.

'Please don't say it like that, but yes…' he smiles.
'I don't want anyone else, I just want you. I want to be yours and I want you to be mine.'
'What do you want?'
'You.'

Dominic smiles and kisses me softly. He grabs another towel and removes his wet clothes.
'Come on, let's get you dressed, okay?' He says.
He helps me get dressed and packs a bag.
I know I will be there for a couple of days.
There is a knock at our bedroom door.

'Come in.' Dominic answers.
My door opens and I hear a man's voice.
'Hi, I'm senior constable Matthew Layfield. I'm here to see your wife. The paramedics want to take a quick look at her. Is that okay?'
I come out of our walk-in closet and nod.
'My wife will be out in five.' Dominic says.

The policeman nods and closes the door.
I sit on my bed as I stare back at the floor.
'Why did you call me your wife?' I ask him.
'If they have it in your file as Mr. and Mrs., it's less likely to stand out to anyone looking for you.' Dominic says as he sets my bag on our bed.
I watch as he kneels in front of me.
He takes my right wrist and puts back his band on it.
'It came off during the struggle. Luke found it.' Dominic sits beside me and wraps his arm around my waist.
'Besides, I have realised something. I prefer Elizabeth over Chantelle. Liz is so much easier to say when I have you in bed.' He whispers in my ear.

'Can I come in?' Amber is standing at the door.
Her eyes are red, I hurt her. I get up and hug her tightly.
'I am so so so sorry, Amber, You didn't deserve any of what I said. Please forgive me.'
'Chocolate cake and you're forgiven, and I'm not sharing it with Dominic.'
'There is chocolate cake in the fridge and your favourites in the freezer.' I smile at her.
'Oh, come on, first, Simon, and now, Amber? I'm not going to have anything left, What about me?' Dominic pouts.
'Well, there is more than one cake in the fridge.' I reply.

Dominic picks my bag and we head to the kitchen.

'So, what's my cake?' He asks.

'Well, technically it's not cake because I didn't get around to cutting up the extra vanilla slice I made. There are also your favourites and cartons of beer in the shed fridge.' I tell him.

The paramedics examine me and insist I come with them due to my head injury and loss of consciousness.

Dominic nods in agreement.

The police, Amber, and Dominic will meet us at the ambulance's entrance.

'I'll meet you at the hospital, okay? I need to stop at Cassie's first then work. I need to make changes for tomorrow.' Amber hugs me.

'Tomorrow?' Dominic asks.

'I'm supposed to go to Michael's hearing in case I'm required to speak.' I answer, holding his hand. 'It's via video link, he's not in Queensland.' I finish.

Amber looks at Dominic.

He looks at me.

He is clearly not happy, but he understands.

Simon meets us at the entrance to the hospital.

Amber must have got a hold of him.

He looks at me.

'What the fuck, Dom?' Simon looks at him.

'Daniel. He… he hit her and tried to rape her.' Dominic's voice cracks.

'What?! No, what an asshole!! I just saw him, well I thought it was him being brought in.'

I panic and try to leave.

I don't want to be in there with him.

'Hey, no you don't. He can't hurt you.' Dominic says, grabbing me.

'No, please don't. He, no, no, I…' I can't breathe. My whole body is shaking.

'He is under police custody in a separate area.' Simon tries to calm me but it's not working

I know he can't hurt me, but I'm so scared to see him again.

My anxiety is hitting me hard.

The adrenalin has worn off and there is nothing left to hold me up.

All I want to do is roll up into a little ball and shut the world out.

'Elizabeth, look at me now!' Dominic shakes me and his voice is strangely demanding.

My body instantly stops. I stare at him blankly.

'Yes, master. Sorry, master.' I whisper.

Dominic sighs and pulls me into him.

I offer no resistance.

'Sorry, babe, I didn't mean to sound angry. Please forgive me?' He asks.
I don't move or shake. I just stand there and nod in submission.
Simon looks at Dominic.
They take me to get CT and x-ray straight away.

🦉 DOMINIC 🦉

I watch Liz as the nurses help her onto the bed for x-rays.
I feel the tears and I don't care. I feel like I let her down.
I keep seeing her on the ground bleeding and hurt as that monster hit her.
I can still hear her screams.
Her screams for me, and I wasn't there.
Like I promised her.

'What the fuck was that about, Dominic?' Simon asks, turning to me.
'I've never in my life seen anything like that. It was like she was in some kind of trance.'
'Simon…' I sigh. 'It was her ex, he…'
'Fucker…beat her?' Simon says before I finish.
'Really bad, and for a very long time.'
'Is that how she lost the baby?' He asks me.
I nod.
I can't hold it back and I start to cry.
I sit down and put my head in my hands.

'But she is so….Fucking scumbag! Now it all makes sense. I wondered why she reacted so weirdly when I hugged her this morning. No wonder you and Amber are so protective of her. Amber called me and told me to expect her and that no male staff was to go near her except me. I was so confused by that, now I get it.'
Simon sits next to me and puts his hand on my shoulder.
'Please don't say anything to her, she feels really bad about it. And make sure no one mentions Daniel near her.' I tell him.
'Dominic, I have been in this job for a while and I can tell systematic abuse from normal abuse. But her reaction was on a whole other level. Do me a favour?' He asks, standing to check on Liz.
'What?' I ask as the tears keep falling.
'Look after our girl.' He says, putting his hand on my shoulder.

'Mr. Miller?'
'Yes.' I look up.

'I'm looking for your wife, Elizabeth Miller. We met at your home earlier this morning. I need to get her statement.'
'She is being x-rayed at the moment but she will be done soon. Can you wait, please?' Simon answers before I do.
'Of course, I'll wait in the staff room.' The officer nods and leaves us.

'See, even he thinks you should put a ring on her, and he only met you both this morning. I'll try to change shifts and see if I can stay tonight and keep an eye on her.'
'Thanks, mate, I would appreciate that.' I nod.
I can't believe what's happened, I should have ignored Amber and went after her.
I could have protected her.
Daniel would never have touched her.
I don't know what I would do if I lose her.

My phone rings.
It's Mum.
I was on the phone with her when Daniel attacked Elizabeth.
When I was helping Elizabeth, I asked Luke to tell her that I'd call back.
I had forgotten to, until now.
'Hey, Mum,' I answer the phone. 'We are at the hospital now.' I start to cry again.
'I don't know anything yet. Can I call you back when I know something?' I take a deep breath.
'Thanks, Mum. I love you too.'
I put my hands behind my head and gaze at the ceiling, trying to get a handle on my emotions.
'Dom,' Simon calls out.
I turn as they wheel Elizabeth back out and I race to her side.

👀 ELIZABETH 👀

All my scans and x-rays come back clear except for my left hand and wrist.
I have a dislocated thumb and two fingers.
 My middle finger, hand, and wrist are broken.
I also have a concussion and a perforated eardrum.
They pump me full of pain killers, but I still feel everything when they try resetting my fingers.
I do my best not to show the pain but I end up screaming anyway.
It is excruciating!
Dominic does his best to help but Simon has to escort him out.

He couldn't handle it and it isn't helping me.
I pass out from the pain.

They move me to a private room after they do another x-ray.
My fingers are back in, so once the swelling goes down, I'll need to have a bit of surgery because the injuries are severe.
'Are you okay?' I ask Dominic.
'Of course, why?'
'You have been really quiet and distant. I'm sorry if I have done something to upset you. I… I… I can do better. I will be better,'
He stops me with a soft kiss.
'I don't want you to change.' He looks at me.
'You don't? I don't understand.' I return his look nervously.
He gets up and looks out the window with his hands behind his head.
'Liz, you haven't done anything wrong,' He clears his throat as he turns back to me.
'I should be apologising to you.' He walks back to me.

I can't read his expression, but I can tell he is tired.
'Dominic, what's wrong?' I reach out and grab his hand. 'Talk to me.'
'I wasn't there.'
'Weren't where, Dominic?' I am lost.
'I wasn't there to stop him,' He answers.
I grab his shirt, look him in the eyes, pull him down onto me, and kiss his lips.
I flinch at the pain but I don't care.
I just need him.
He pulls back and looks at me as his thumb brushes softly against my lips.

'Babe, your lips…'
'Are all yours.' I smile at him.
He smiles back as I lean into his hand and kiss his thumb.
'Excuse me, sir,'
'Yes,' Dominic turns to face the door.
'Visiting hours are over. I'm sorry but I have to ask you to leave.' The nurse explains.
'Okay but can I have just five more minutes, please?' He flashes his best smile at her.
The nurse looks at her watch.
'Elizabeth's next set of ops are in about twenty minutes, you have until then.
'Thank you very much, nurse' Dominic smiles.
The nurse smiles as she leaves.

'Knock, knock.' Simon walks up to my bed.

'Hey, Simon.' I say.

'Hey, I made some calls. I have already done a few doubles this week so I can't stay. But I am going to stay at one of the nurses' place down the road. I'm like a two-minute run away. I told them they have to call me if you need me, okay?'

'Thanks, mate, I appreciate that.' Dominic shakes his hand.

'Thank you, Simon.' I smile at him.

'See you tomorrow, yeah?' Simon nods as he waves and leaves the room.

We are finally alone.

Dominic lays on the bed with me and I rest my head on his chest.

He plays with my hair as I fall asleep to the sound of his heartbeat.

I am woken up by a gentle touch of fingers running down my cheek, over my lips, and down my neck.

I slowly try to open my eyes, but the light and the painkillers are making it difficult.

'Mmm Dominic.' I whisper.

My eyes focus on the face before me, and it's not Dominic.

My eyes widen in horror.

'Hello, Chantelle.'

No no no no no God no!

'It took me a while but here I am.' His voice is calm and drips with venom. 'Miss me?'

I don't answer.

'Do not make me repeat myself. You know I hate to repeat myself.'

His hand grabs my jaw and squeezes as he leans in.

'You're in shock.'

He slaps my face, causing my lips to bleed again which only excites him more.

He looks at my lips as he licks his.

'Mmm… I have missed those lips.'

'How did you find me?' I whisper.

'You, of all people, should know what I'm capable of.' He says as he rubs my lips.

He climbs on top of me, with his eyes still glued to my lips.

I see the knife in his hand.

'I have returned to take back what belongs to me.'

He grabs my hand and squeezes it.

I scream in pain but he covers my mouth.

I feel the knife run down my body as he starts to cut away the hospital gown.

'But we are going to have some fun first.'

He kisses me and forces my lips open but I can't kiss him back.

He grabs my broken wrist and squeezes till I comply.

I start to cry.
I feel physically sick and the tears sting my eyes.
He pulls away and my blood is smeared on his face.

'Stop crying, I didn't say you could cry.'
He hits me hard in the face.
I can't stop crying.
I don't want to go with him.
He starts to punch my chest but I manage to turn and get him off me.
It's hard to breathe.
I need to get away.
Michael slams me onto the ground and drops the knife.
I manage to get to it and drive it into his back.
He roars in pain as he pulls out the knife, stumbling against the wall.
He comes at me.
I grab the IV stand and hit him with it.
He drops the knife and I fall to the ground, struggling to breathe.
I pick up the knife as he grabs me again.

'That was not very nice, you will be punished for that.' Michael says as he throws
me at the wall.
He stumbles towards me and I ram the knife into his leg.
He hits me hard and pulls the knife out of his leg.
I try to stand but he kicks me up against the wall, my hands slip in the blood.
I feel him punch me in the back.
He lifts me up by the throat, and starts punching me again.
He stumbles back and the knife drops.
I know I have to kill him; it's the only way to save Dominic.
I reach down and grab the knife.
I run at him and drive the knife into his body.
He punches me and I crawl back towards the wall.
I manage to pull myself up and hit the critical button.
Alarms sound and he looks at me with fury.

'You fucking slut! You are going to fucking pay for that, you dumb fucking
bitch!'
He runs at me, grabs me by the throat, slams me into the wall, and yells at me
so much that his saliva hits my face.
I ram my thumb nail into his eye.
He manages to pull back and hits me so hard in the face that I briefly black out.
I feel cold metal on my temple.
I can taste the blood in my mouth.

'Screw you, Michael, you are nothing!' I yell and spit blood in his face.
'What the fuck did you say to me?' He wipes his face, looking confused.
'You heard me, you fucking coward!' I yell.
His grip tightens.

'What? Too soft to pull the trigger?' I challenge him.
'Fuck you, bitch.' Michael stumbles back and drops to the ground.
Blood gushes from the wound on his leg and abdomen.
I feel myself slide down to the floor.
Michael crawls over to me and his hand grabs my throat as he brings the gun back to my head.
The last thing I see as I hear the bang is Dominic's face smiling at me.
I love you, Dominic.
'Dominic is safe.'
Freedom.

CHAPTER 10
Please Don't Give Up

👀 DOMINIC 👀

My phone wakes me up.
'Hello,'
'Dominic. It's Amber, you need to get to the hospital. Where are you?'
'I'm at home why? What's going on?' I yawn and stretch.
I look at the time, it's 3:30am in the morning
'Amber, what's happened?'
'Just get to the hospital.' Amber hangs up.
'Fuck!' I yell.

I get dressed, feed the dogs, and drive the fastest I have ever driven to Bundaberg.
I find the closest parking space to the hospital and race to her room.
It is empty and ransacked.
I don't even see the police tape.
All I can do is stare at the blood on the pillow and hold the end of the bed.
'No, no. no. no, Please god, no!'

I notice blood on the wall, window, and floor.
I move around the side of the bed.
There is so much of it everywhere.
That's when it hits me.
My hands are shaking as I pull the sheet back; it's also stained blood red.
My heart drops.
She is gone.
He found her and killed her.
My girl is gone.
I feel weak and sick.
I don't want to be without her.
I'm going to kill that fucker.
My legs are buckling under me but I'm fighting it.

I need to find Liz.

I feel the anger and pure hatred I have for her ex along with the overpowering grief of losing her.

'Dominic.' A voice breaks through my thoughts.

I look up to see Amber at the door.

'What happened, Amber?'

The look in her eyes fills me with dread. I can't… She was right here.

'Where is she, Amber?

I want to see her now.

I need to see her.'

'Amber, is Dom here yet?' Simon calls.

Amber turns and nods as Simon enters the room, his eyes are red.

'She's gone, Simon,' I stumble.

'No, mate, she's not, she put up a hell of a fight though. Come on, the doctor is ready to see you.' He says as he grabs me.

'What? She fought back and beat Michael?' I steady myself.

'It wasn't Michael, it was Daniel.' Amber spoke.

Her eyes are red, she has been crying.

'She is alive but it's not good. The doctor needs to talk to you.' He grabs my arm.

'What fucking happened? How did he get to her? I told her she would be safe. I asked her to trust me. She fucking trusted me Simon.' I yell as I push him away.

'She fucking trusted me!' I cry.

Simon tries to reach for me again but I push him away hard causing him to stumble slightly.

'Excuse me, Mr. Miller, the doctor is waiting. Your wife has just come out of surgery'

'Thank you,' Amber nods.

'Come on, I'll take you.' Simon says as he reaches for me again.

'I'm sorry, Simon. I…'

'Dominic, don't, mate, it's alright. I understand. It's okay.' He puts his arm around my shoulder.

I nod and we follow Simon.

It is a solemn walk.

When we get to the doctor, his eyes don't give anything away.

Amber and I are taken to a small room where Simon is told to stop.

There are two men in suits already in the room.

The doctor motions for Amber and I to sit, and he hands her a clipboard as he leaves the room and closes the door.

'Can someone please for the love of god tell me what the fuck is going on?' I am furious at this point.
I'm angry, scared, and I'm not sure how much more I can take.

'Mr. Taumata,' A suit behind me speaks. 'We have been briefed by Agent Carter about your relationship with Miss Miller. We need to speak with you about something.'
He pauses briefly then continues as he comes to stand in front of me.
'My name is Agent Reilly. You have met Agent Amber Carter, the other gentleman behind you is Agent Smith.'
I turn to look at him. It's weird but he reminds me of that Agent Smith from The Matrix movies. I turn back to Agent Reilly.
'How is she and what happened?' I ask.
'I will get the doctor to let you know.' Agent Reilly says as he stands and opens the door.
'Doctor, if you would like to step in.'
The doctor walks in. He has a file in his hands and his face doesn't give anything away.
'This is Dominic, he is Elizabeth's…husband.'

'Mr. Miller, your wife is lucky to be here. She died three times on my table, but we managed to get her heart started. She is a fighter.' The doctor clears his throat.
'Her body is very weak and with all the previous trauma it has endured, we are not sure how well she is going to recover. Her injuries are very substantial: she has bleeding on the brain, bruised ribs, punctured lungs, and multiple stab wounds.'
I sit there in a complete daze. I can't believe what he is saying.

'She is in an induced coma at the moment. I regret to say but I don't know if or when she'll come out of it and if she will wake up without permanent damage. The injuries to her brain are extensive and coupled with her past injuries, we just can't tell what is going to happen. We're hoping for the best, but the risk of losing her is still high. Rest assured that we will do everything we can for her but now, it's all up to Elizabeth.' The doctor looks apologetically at me.
Agent Reilly clears his throat, 'We will leave you and Agent Carter, you both have a lot to discuss. Agent Carter is aware of our position and together with Doctor Jack Montgomery they will brief you. I am sorry I had to meet you under these circumstances.' Agent Reilly says as he stands and opens the door to leave.
I nod in agreement but I'm so dazed by everything that has transpired. I watch them leave.

'Can I see her please?'
The doctor nods. I stand up and look at Amber. She takes a deep breath and stands up too.

'I can't go in that room, Dominic.' She looks at the clipboard.
'And I can't sign that.' She hands me the clipboard.
I look at the clipboard, D.N.R - Do Not Resuscitate and organ donor register.
I look at Amber then back to the doctor.
'That,' The doctor starts to say, 'Is for when you bring her out of the coma.' I finish for him.
He nods solemnly.
'Take me to her now.' My hands have never shaken as much as they are at this moment.

We follow the doctor to the ICU ward. I can't bring myself to speak.
I don't know what I would do if I can't hear her laugh, see her smile or even just hold her again.
My whole body aches with pain, anger, and fear.
The doctor stops when we get to her door and turns just as Simon reaches us.
'I'll wait out here with Simon. I'm not ready, sorry, Dominic.' Amber says quietly.
I hug her and turn back to the doctor.
'Now Mr. Miller,' the doctor sighs, 'there are a few things I need you to be aware of before you go in.'
'Okay,' I nod.
'She has extensive swelling, bruising and cuts to her face. She is in a neck brace due to injuries caused by the attempted strangulation.' The doctor stops and takes a deep breath. 'During the attack, her already broken wrist was squashed and her thumb was dislocated. The machines are doing everything for her right now, from breathing for her, to feeding her. When we put her under she had a bad reaction, it appears she was drugged and hallucinating. She thought Daniel was her ex-boyfriend Michael who we have now all been made aware of.' He says uneasily.

'Mr. Miller, the next forty-eight hours will be critical. We'll do all we can for her, but the risk of her becoming brain dead whilst in the coma is still there. But I promise you that we will do everything we can, but as I mentioned, the real magic is going to have to come from Elizabeth.'

I steady myself as much as I can. I'm reeling.
This just can't be happening.
Simon comes up beside me and puts his hand on my shoulder.
I can see the tears in his eyes.

I'm in total disbelief and don't know what to do.
I feel helpless and, to be honest, fragile.
I'm terrified Liz won't pull through this and I'll lose her.

'Whatever you or Elizabeth need, just ask us. We are all here for you both.' Simon interrupts my thoughts.
I nod, I can feel the tears stinging my eyes. Simon goes back to Amber and hugs her.
'Mr. Miller, I personally believe that some people can hear what's happening around them and can respond better. I can see how much you care for your fiancée,'
'Fiancée?' I interrupt him
'Sorry, your wife.'
I nod and take a deep breath.
'Okay as I was saying. It's clearly evident that you love her so please talk to her, touch her. It's the small things that just might get her through this, if she is still with us…' he says trailing off.
If she is still with us. Those six small words absolutely crush and rip my heart out. I can't lose her, I won't lose her. I can't be where she's not.

'This isn't going to be easy, Dominic, if I can be so informal? It's going to be tough, she will need all the strength you have to pull through this.'
All I can do is nod as he opens the door and leads me into the room she lays broken and beaten.
He closes the door.
My feet become glued to the floor and I can't move.
I can't even begin to comprehend what's in front of me.
My Liz, my beautiful Liz, lying in a hospital bed.
Her face covered in cuts, swollen and bruised.
The length of her arms are covered by bandages.
The swelling and damage to her face is so bad, I can hardly tell it's my girl.
There are tubes coming from her mouth.
She has on a neck brace.
Her eyes are taped shut.
Machines to her left beep, her breathing looks almost robotic.
I have to grab the end of her bed to hold myself up.
The doctor grabs my arm and helps me to a chair which he positions next to the bed.

'I'll give you a moment alone. I'll come back soon and answer any further questions you will most likely have then.'
'Excuse me, Doctor, sorry I missed your name.'

'It's Jack, Jack Montgomery,' He replies
'Dominic,' I say, shaking his hand. 'Where are her belongings?'
'They should be in the cupboard next to her bed.'
'Thank you.'
He nods and leaves the room. I sit beside her bed and hold her uninjured hand to my lips.

I feel the tears roll down my face and I don't even care.
My girl is laying in this fucking bed, hurting! I would give anything for it to be me instead of her.
'Hey, Dom.' Simon enters her room.
'Can I get you anything? I'm going to the cafe down the road.'
'Um sure, just coffee thanks, mate.' I can't even think about eating, I still feel like throwing up.

'No problems, I'll be back in about twenty minutes.'
'Simon.'
'Yeah?'
'Can you please call Luke? I'm going to be late, real late.'
'Already done and favours called in.'
'Thanks, mate.'

I get her bag out of the cupboard and look for her phone.
Shit! It needs a passcode.
I sit for a minute and look at her, thinking of everything she told me and the things Amber said.
Her book. I flip through and stop at the bookmark; it is a photo of us on the beach.
Amber took a photo of our first kiss, sneaky girl Amber. I turn it over.
There is a message from Amber.

Hey Hon,
You're welcome
Xo

I grab my phone and scroll through the pictures, till I find what I'm looking for.
Photos from the day I took her to the beach.
I look through them meanwhile I only have one photo of her.
She is sitting with her legs crossed on the sand, watching a butterfly on her finger.

I sit there for I don't know how long just looking at the photo.

I remember Luke and Simon telling me that if I don't go to her, someone else will.

I look at the date, January 16. It's worth a shot and so I type in 1601.

Shit, it actually works.

I open her photos, there are none, no contacts, no messages.

Just music and food.

I start playing music from her phone to cover the machine's constant beeping.

I take her hand again, bringing it to my lips.

'Please don't give up, because I'm not going to give up on you.' I kiss her hand as the tears roll down my face. 'Please come back to me, I don't want to be where you're not.'

'Dominic.'

I look up to see Amber at the door, she is staring at the floor.

'Hey, Amber, how are you holding up?' I ask as I wipe my face.

'I won't lie, I'm struggling more than I expected I would.'

'I get it, you love her, she's your best friend. Come in and sit with us'

She walks in slowly, still not looking up.

I get the other chair for her and we sit in silence.

The doctor walks in not long after to check on us, and a nurse follows to take Liz's ops.

I hand the clipboard to Dr. Montgomery.

'I can't sign that,' I say to him.

'That's fine, Mr. Miller, I understand. But it's routine procedure.' He nods and smiles.

'Now, there is a small visitor room down the hall with vending machines, tea and coffee facilities. If you bring food there is also a fridge there, just label your containers, and a microwave. Next to that is a restroom with a shower. Now concerning visitation, there are strict rules and limits to the number of people in the room at a time.'

'Knock, knock, I come bearing gifts, oh sorry, Doc.' Simon walks over and hands me a coffee. He's also brought me something to eat.

'Thanks, mate,' I sigh.

'Simon, is it?' Doctor Montgomery asks.

'Ah, yes it is, I'm a DEM nurse here and their best friend.'

'Jack Montgomery,' He offers his hand to shake.

'Right, well, I'll leave you all to it. If you have any questions regarding your wife's care, Simon can answer most questions and anything he can't cover, I will be here keeping a watch on Elizabeth anyway. Plus there are the ICU nurses who will be more than happy to help too.'

'Thanks, Doc.' I say.

I watch him leave with the nurse when I turn to Amber.

'She's not going anywhere, Liz is a fighter and she's coming back to us. She is coming back, Dominic, isn't she? I cannot be without my best friend.' Amber says.

I put my arm around her.

'I'm not giving up on her, either. She is coming back to us. We have our whole life together to plan.'

I look at Simon. He has a huge smile on his face and is giving me the thumbs up.

'Simon, is Liz sedated as well as being in a coma?' I ask as I look at Liz.

'Without looking at her chart I'd say definitely. She is probably on some sort of Ketamine type drug. It paralyses the body to allow them do what's needed. I think she will be like this for the next forty-eight hours. They will slowly reduce the drug till they think she is ready to do it on her own. They may do more blood transfusions though, she lost way too much.'

Amber and I sit next to Liz while Simon sits on the other side looking over her chart.

I manage to eat and drink the coffee, but I taste nothing.

I just feel numb.

I don't know how I'm going to cope, I don't even think I am coping.

So many emotions are bristling to the surface and I can't unravel them.

I take Liz's hand, bringing it to my lips.

It's the only thing I can do that makes sense.

I close my eyes, thinking about what else I can do to help.

I look at Simon.

'I have to go, can you stay?' I ask him

'Of course, my shift isn't till this afternoon and the couch looks good so I'll hang out with Amber.'

'Where are you going, Dominic?' Amber asks me.

'Liz hired me to do a job. I need to do it for her. I want as much done as I can for when I bring her home.'

Amber nods.

'Can I ask you a favour?' I look at Simon and Amber.

'Sure.' They reply.

'Please make sure her music doesn't stop playing.'
Amber stands.
'I really need that passport.' I say quietly as I hug Amber.

I get to my car and call Luke.
His brother is helping him.
He tells me not to leave the hospital but I need to do this for her.
I want to surprise her when she gets home, it needs to be perfect.
I'm going to extend the deck to allow for her new spa and build her a daybed.

The following few days and week are hard.
I spend every moment either with Liz, holding her hand, kissing her, talking to her or at her house, working to get her wish list done in time for her homecoming.
It is hard being there without her.
I spend the entire weekend with her and help the nurses when they need it.
I would ring my parents from the hospital to let them know how she is doing.
I convince them not to fly over from New Zealand, and promise I will bring Liz to see them when she is up to it.
They have heard so much about her from me, they know how I feel.
For now, it is all about focusing on Liz and helping her to heal.

I would sit there in the hospital room and show her pictures, even though she can't see them.
I'd tell her about my day, and change her music.
Everyone came to see her.
Simon would sit and have lunch with her, even some of the nurses would also sit with her.
Every now and then her hand would flinch.
I take that as a sign that she is coming back to me.

The following Saturday, I tell Luke to have a day off but he declines.
He and his brother were going to start on the kitchen.
Today is the day they are going to remove the life support and see if Liz can breathe on her own.
My stomach is in knots, I'm so nervous and hoping like hell she will be able to.
Each day, the swelling on her face has gone down, and the bruises have begun fading.
Her vitals are slowly improving, and she is responding to stimuli.
I get to the hospital early, I can't sleep.
I need to see my girl, I need to be with her.

'Morning, Dominic.'

'Morning, Jane, how are you?'

'I'm good thank you, you are just in time. I'm about to do Elizabeth's ops. Our girl is looking well.' Jane smiles.

'Hey, Dominic, you're back.'

I roll my eyes, and turn around as the young nurse walks seductively towards us.

'Of course, I'm back, Erin.' I really don't like her.

'So, my shift finishes in about thirty minutes, would you like to join me for coffee?' Erin is ramping up the seduction today.

'No, thank you, I'm here for my wife.'.

Jeez woman, take a hint! How many times do I have to decline your advances?

I turn away from her, shaking my head, and walk to Liz's room.

'Oh, come on, Dominic, what she doesn't know won't hurt her.' She smiles.

I turn and look at her.

She really is a revolting person.

Who does that when their partner is laying in a coma?

I'm disgusted by her comment.

'Do you like your job? If you do, don't speak to me again.' I virtually spit at her.

I turn and follow Jane to Liz's room.

Jane looks totally embarrassed.

It's become more comfortable referring to Elizabeth as my wife.

What started as a mistake by the police and hospital staff was encouraged by Amber and her superiors.

It feels good calling Liz my wife, I have to admit.

I find myself wanting it to be true, and I think I've even found the perfect ring.

But are we ready for that? Is Liz ready for that?

I sit there with her, just holding her hand while Jane and I talk about what's going to happen today.

Jane leaves after about fifteen minutes.

I feel her fingers move and I smile.

'There's my girl.' I say as I brush strands of her hair behind her ears.

I lay my head next to hers.

'Please come home to me, I need you. Nothing feels right without you.'

I feel her fingers move; it feels like she is trying to squeeze my hand.

I softly touch her head with my free hand, run my fingers through her hair, and rub her hand with my thumb.

'I miss you, your laugh, your touch, your smell. I need you back.'

I drift off to sleep.

Amber wakes me up.

'Hey, Dom, how's our girl?'

'She is beautiful and amazing and coming home.' I say as I stretch.

Simon joins us about twenty minutes later—he' swapped shifts to support us at this critical moment. Doctor Montgomery joins us not long after as well, followed by half a dozen other medical staff.

'Good morning, everyone.'

'Morning, Doc.' I shake his hand.

'So, as you all are aware, we have been reducing Elizabeth's sedation so she can wake up on her own.'

We nod.

'Today we are going to start removing all the tubes, and we hope she will be able to breathe on her own.'

'For anyone that hasn't seen this process before, there will be quite a bit of noise with alarms going off—this is normal. We ask you to keep calm and let us do our job.'

'Can I hold her hand please?' I ask.

'On one condition, if I tell you to move don't question it, just do it.' He looks at me.

'Of course.'

He nods and turns back to the medical team.

I sit next to Liz, holding her hand.

'This is it, babe, it's going to be all up to you.'

Simon walks over, puts his hand on my shoulder and leans down.

'She is a fighter, Dominic, she will be home before you know it. Then can you please put a ring on her finger?' He winks before kissing Liz on the cheek.

He moves to the side for Amber to do same.

She touches my shoulder and goes to stand with Simon.

The doctor is going through the last of the checklist.

'Please come back to me, babe.' I kiss her hand.

The doctor nods at me.

'Let's do this.' I say

They start working on her, alarms sound as the tubes are removed, and after about five minutes she's free of the machine that has been helping her breathe. Now it's all up to her.

'Come on, babe, breath, please.' I will her to breathe.

Alarms sound.

'MOVE!' The doctor yells.

I jump out of the way and stand next to Amber as they immediately start CPR and pump in adrenalin.

'CLEAR'
Her body jolts as the Defibrillator shocks her.
'No rhythm.'
They commence CPR again and administer more adrenalin.

'CLEAR'
They shock her with the defibrillator again, and continue with CPR and administer more adrenalin.
I can't do anything.
I'm out of my mind, scared, and willing her to breathe.
God, I hope she comes back to me.
I scream in my mind 'fight babe, fight!!!'

'CLEAR'
Her tiny body is shocked again.
'We have rhythm.'
Amber and I look at each other, then at the doctor.
I look back at Liz and see her chest moving on its own.
I race back to her side and hold her hand.
The doctor and his team talk amongst themselves.
I feel tears sting my eyes, and with the wave of relief come tears of happiness.
We just jumped one hurdle.

'Dominic?' The doc's voice breaks through my thoughts.
I look up to see him standing at the end of the bed.
'The good news is, she is breathing on her own which is great, but we won't know how the attack has affected her brain until she wakes up'
He looks over at Amber and Simon then back to me to ensure we understand him.
'I will leave you to it and be back later, okay?' He says as he puts back her chart.

I get up and go to him. He offers me a handshake, but I hug him instead.
'Thank you.' I say.
I turn to Simon and Amber and hug them.
Simon leaves to do his shift but promises to come back tomorrow.
Amber sits with me and I realise that I never actually asked Amber what happened.
'How did this happen, Amber?' I ask, looking at Liz.

'Daniel had help, he got a hold of Rohypnol. We still haven't found out who snuck it in yet, but we think we know who helped him inside the hospital. He managed to get out of his room and we think the people that helped him told him where Liz was. On the hospital security footage, we discovered that he was hiding across the hall, watching and waiting.' She pauses. 'He waited for you to leave with the nurse, timed her ops then…'
'I was there while he was waiting? I was right fucking there! Right fucking there all over again!' I was so angry. 'It's like I failed her all over again, it's all my fault.'
'No, Dom, you didn't fail, he got past all of us.' She stands up and hands me a file.
'He blocked the door with a chair and injected her IV with the Rohypnol, it didn't go to plan for him'
I flip through the file and read the nurse statement.

'We believe he intended to rape her then cut her wrists to make it look like a suicide. But when he woke her up, she hallucinated.'
'Which is why she called him Michael?' I ask.
She nods.
'She didn't call for help until she turned the knife on him and stabbed him three times. Judging by his injuries she fought hard'
In the statement, the last thing Liz is reported to have said before her heart stopped is 'Dominic is safe now'. She really fought with everything she had thinking it was Michael who was attacking her.

'Amber, have you read this?'
'Yes, she thought she was saving you. She didn't even realise that she had been stabbed. She was high on the Rohypnol and, acting out of pure adrenalin, did everything she could to protect you at the expense of her own safety,' Amber stops and takes a deep breath.
'She doesn't care about herself, she's not thinking about herself. She is only thinking of how she can protect you. Elizabeth has seen what Michael has done to people who have even looked at her without permission. One man touched Elizabeth one time, and Michael forced her to watch as he cut off the man's arm. Then he made her watch as he beat the poor man to death with the arm he cut off.'
I sit there looking at Amber then back to Liz.

'She would die to protect you. Elizabeth won't even give it a thought if she knows it's the only way to protect you.' Amber collects the file from me. 'How do you feel about her now, knowing what you know, and how dangerous it is for you to be in her life?'
I look at Amber.

'I'm not going anywhere. Where is Daniel now?'
'Dead.'
'Good' is all I can say.

'Oh, before I forget I came bearing a gift for you and our girl.'
Amber hands me a yellow envelope, I open it and tip out the contents.
'Liz's passport?' I ask her.
'Yep, but it comes with conditions though. We need to know all your travel plans and they need to be approved. Other than that, enjoy.'
'Hell yes!' I stand up and hug her.
'Thank you so much, Amber.'
'I'll leave you to it. Call me if anything changes, okay?'
'Of course.'

I sit back down next to Liz, looking at her passport. I hold her hand and lay my head next to hers.
'Hey, babe, I got you something.' I kiss her cheek.
'Amber helped me get you a passport.'

'Hello, Dominic. Am I disturbing you?'
'Hey, Doc. No, not at all.' I shake my head as I sit back up.
'How are you doing? I'm sure watching the events of the morning would have come as quite a shock. It can be quite harrowing to watch for most people.'
'Yeah,' I nod.
'Hey, can I ask you a question?'
'Of course.' He nods as he moves to the opposite side of her bed.
'Once she is out of the coma, how long until she is able fly?'

'Um that is a big if. But if all does go well and she heals, maybe, and I mean maybe.' He looks at me like a father laying out terms for dating his daughter. 'I would say possibly 3-4 months at a push.'
'Ok, thanks, Doc.'
He goes about doing his checks while I sit looking at Liz and then at her passport.
I don't even know when he leaves.

Elizabeth Marie Miller born 26th of December 1980.
My Elizabeth, my girl.
I kiss her softly.
I hold her hand.
'We should do Fiji first then New Zealand, what do you think, babe?'

I swear I can feel her hand squeeze mine.
I fall asleep holding my girl's hand.

'Dominic,' I wake to hear a soft whisper and fingers touching my face.
'Dominic,' There it is again. 'Hey, Dominic, wake up. Please wake up'
'Mmm,' I murmur.
'Hey, you.'
Opening my eyes, I sit up shaking the sleep away.
It takes me a second to realise where I am.
I look around to see who is in the room.
'Dominic,'
I turn back around to see where the voice is coming from.
Her eyes are open, she is smiling.
'Babe, Liz, you're awake; you're actually awake!'

I run to the door and call out that she's awake then run back to her side.
I gently brush her hair behind her ear and kiss her forehead.
'My god, babe, I have missed you so much.'
'How are you?' She asks me, her voice is hoarse.
It's hurting her to talk, I can tell.
'I'm fine, even better now that you're awake. Try not to talk too much.' I kiss her
hand.

She is blushing, you can still see it even with the bruising, and it makes me smile.
Her doctor comes in followed by Jane.
'Hello, Elizabeth, I'm Dr. Jack Montgomery. How are you feeling?'
'I'm good thank you, just sore, and a little cold.' Elizabeth struggles to talk clearly
'I'll get you another blanket,' Jane smiles.
'Thank you.' Liz smiles and looks back at me.
My god, I have missed her so much.

The doctor says, 'Okay, I'm going to do a bunch of…'
'Cognitive and reflex tests.' Liz finishes.
'Correct,' he says and laughs remembering she's a paramedic.
'Okay, Elizabeth, I'm going to give you something for your throat first. It's going
to be sore for a few days due to the damage and the tubes we had to insert. Try
not to talk too much.'

I watch Jane hand her something to drink and some water as well as some ice
for her to suck on.
I message Amber, Simon, and Luke while they continue with the tests.
Amber's reply is colourful.

Luke wants to know when 'his girl' is coming home, he misses her vanilla slice.
Simon must be on shift or asleep because I am yet to receive a reply from him.
I look up when Doc Montgomery starts asking Liz what she remembers.
She looks at her broken hand, trying to remember.
She starts rubbing the scars on her neck and collarbone, then the scar on her left wrist.
She looks up.
'Dominic was eating cake after we got back from surfing.'
She looks at me and starts to panic; she senses something is wrong from the look on my face.
She is missing an entire month of memories.
'What? What is it? What's wrong? I...I'
'Liz, Shh no it's not important, just boring stuff.' I say, trying to keep her calm.
'I'm sorry, I'll try to remember.'
'Babe, don't worry, it will come back to you when it's ready,' I softly touch her cheek, wiping a tear away.

'He is right, Elizabeth'
'But...'
'But, nothing, you can't rush this Elizabeth. Trying hard to remember could do you more harm.'
'Okay,' she looks at her doctor.
'Good, please stay calm and rest. I'll come back later this afternoon to check on you.'
'Thanks, Doc' I say, getting up to shake his hand.

I close the door after they leave and return to her side.
'Why did you lie?' She asks, not even looking at me.
'Liz...'
'Please tell me,' She begs.
'Babe, it's really not that import...'
'Yes it is! I saw the look on your face. I could tell it was really important.' Liz looks at me.

I smile, and it's my turn to blush a little as I remember what happened after I ate the chocolate cake.
I let out a kind of stifled kind of laugh and scratch the back of my head.
Her eyes never leave my face.
'Okay, but I just want to say something before I go into any details.
It means a lot more than it may sound, but it was just as important to you as it was to me.'

I sit back with my hands behind my head and take in a deep breath.
She is sitting up, watching me intently with her big beautiful green eyes.

'Okay,' I lean forward and hold her hand.
'Right, so you remember me in your kitchen eating the chocolate cake. Well you cornered me, and we had nothing but my towel, your towel, and a plate between us,'
I narrate what happened.
I want to tell her about the shower, Fraser, and the birth of Chantelle's baby but I decide against it.
I need her to remember that on her own.
She watches and listens as I tell her just how important she is to me.
How I wish I could trade places with her because seeing her like this kills me.
Liz holds my hand and as much as it hurts her, she smiles.
I so badly want to taste her lips but first they need to heal; she needs to heal.

'What are you thinking, Liz?'
I see a tear fall.
'Babe. Hey, look at me.'
She looks at her fingers.
I take her hand in mine as I wipe her tears away.
'Please, babe, what's happening? Do you want me to get the nurse?'
'No, it's just...'
Something is wrong.
'It sounds stupid...'
'So? I want you to tell me. What's upsetting you?'
Her fingers start to trace the scars on her neck and collar bone, her breathing changes.
I take her hand and bring it to my lips, then trace the scars with my fingers.
I can feel her calm down as she closes her eyes.

'I heard things while I was in the coma, and I feel stupid.'
'What did you hear?' I ask as I kiss her fingers.
Liz closes her eyes and takes a deep breath.
'One of the nurses wants to get you into bed, I heard her on numerous occasions. Even down to the explicit details. She feels that I'm not able to satisfy...'
'Liz...'
'See, I told you it was stupid. Now I sound like a jealous girlfriend,'
'Liz...'
'Is it true?' I can see the hurt in her eyes.
'Yes, one of the nurses tried and I turned her down. I didn't for one second think about anyone else but you.' I kiss her fingers again.

'So what else did you hear?' I raise my eyebrow and smile.

'Umm, at first it was more mumbles, but it got clearer. I heard you talking about my renovations. .I think I heard Simon and Luke and a few other voices I don't know. Nurses and my doctor, I felt pain, but I couldn't move. Amber and something about a...'

Liz stops mid-sentence and looks at me.

'Babe, what?' I ask her.

'Are you leaving?'

'Leaving?' I'm not sure what she means.

'Leaving me? Did I do something to disappoint you?'

'I...'

'I heard Amber and you talking about a passport.' She says, cutting me off.

I smile, relieved, 'Yes, Amber got me a passport, but it's for you" I reply.

'I don't understand, am I going to have to leave? Are you sending me away? Dominic, I...'

'No, I'm taking you on a holiday, just you and me.' I say, watching her eyes widen.

'Really? Why?'

'Once you are given the all clear to travel and Amber's boss approves. We are off to Fiji and then New Zealand. I want you to meet my family,' I kiss her hand.

'Really?'

'Yep, I do.' I smile at her.

'What if they don't like me?'

'I have told them about you. I had to convince them not to fly over. I had to promise to take you to meet them.' I brush the hair from her face.

'I think they love you more than me.' I laugh.

'They call me every day and it's all about you.'

I can see her blush even through the bruises. I love when she blushes.

'Hey, a heads up, the staff here believe that we are husband and wife.'

Liz looks at me, unsure.

'It started as a mistake. Amber's bosses put it on the medical records thinking it's better for you.'

'Are you okay with that?' Liz asks me nervously.

'Yes, I'm more than okay with it.' I smile.

Liz blushes again.

'Dominic, can you hold me please?'

'Are you sure? I don't want to hurt you.'

'I have missed you' She looks at me then at her fingers.

I lay next to her and she snuggles in, that's when I realise how much weight she has lost.

I kiss the top of her head, she doesn't even smell the same.

'Thank you, Dominic.' She says just loud enough for me to hear.
She starts to drift off to sleep.
'Please don't leave me here,' she mumbles.

👀 ELIZABETH 👀

I am woken by Dominic trying to move, we both must have fallen asleep.
'Sorry, Babe, the doctor is coming in and I think Amber is almost here.' He says getting off the bed.
'There's my girl!' Amber exclaims as she walks through the door.
'I have been waiting for about twenty minutes for them to wake up.' Simon says, following Amber through the door.
Amber gives me a huge hug.
Simon walks up to Dominic and they shake hands.
My doctor knocks on the door and walks in, followed by a young nurse.
I notice Dominic's body language change immediately.
He comes over and holds my hand, practically standing between me and the nurse.
Judging by the look she is giving him, I know it's the nurse that was hitting on him.
She isn't exactly hiding her feelings.
I nod at Amber and she winks back with 'WTF but I'll follow your lead'.

'How are you feeling, Elizabeth?' Dr. Montgomery asks.
'Tired, and wanting to go home.' I reply.
I look at the nurse and she is staring at Dominic.
I smile at Dominic.
I squeeze his hand as he sits next to me and kisses my hand.
My fingers brush his cheek and I wink at him.

'Well, about that…'
'Just a minute. Excuse me, nurse.'
Dominic's hand tightens around mine and he shifts in his seat.
'My name is…'
'I don't care what your name is. Just because I'm in a coma doesn't mean I'm dead or can't hear what is said in my room.'
Her eyes widen, Simon steps closer to Amber.

'I could hear what you said about me while I was in the coma,' I pause dramatically, making her squirm. 'While I was in a coma, in your care, you had the nerve to proposition my husband right at my door.'

The doctor, Simon, and Amber stand in stunned silence as they look from me to the nurse and back. Then they look at Dominic to see if what I'm saying is right.
The nurse starts to speak.
'Don't bother responding.' I look at Amber. 'Agent Carter.'
'Yes, Special Agent Miller.' Amber replies.
'Can you please escort the trash from my room?'

Amber smiles and pulls out her handcuffs.
'It would be my pleasure.' Amber says, spinning the handcuffs on her fingers.
'Carter?'
'Ma'am?'
'Be gentle, she is a nurse.'
'Just a little?'
'No.'
'You're a buzz kill, ma'am.'
'Carter, one more thing…'
'Yes?'
'All your weapons are to remain holstered.'
'Ma'am,' Amber nods.
Amber and the nurse leave the room and I turn back to the doctor.
'Right, so when can I get out of here?' I ask.

I hide my hands so no one can see them shaking, but I feel Dominic's hand tighten around mine and his thumb move gently over the scars on my hand.
I close my eyes and take a deep breath.
Dominic's warmth spread through me as I start getting flashbacks of Michael attacking me in my hospital room.

In my flashback, I see Michael hitting me in the chest and yelling at me.
I stab him and yell back at him.
I fight back against Michael to protect Dominic.

The doctor, still somewhat stunned, looks at Simon then Dominic.
'Right, well, umm, well. We are moving you to a general ward on Monday after your surgery,'
'I meant hospital, Doctor, I need to go home.'
'Well, the surgery is for a wedge resection' He tells me.
The doctor continues talking but I'm not really listening to him, I'm getting more flashbacks of the attack in the hospital.
Michael kisses me and tears my clothes; he hits me again, again.
'So, if the surgery goes well and you heal, you can be discharged possibly Friday. Elizabeth?'

I look up,
'Sorry, what?' I ask.
'Are you okay?' He asks.
'Yeah, no, just in a little pain that's all.' I answer, looking at Dominic.
He is still beside me, holding my hand and watching me.
I need to tell him what I did, what happened, and I need to know if I killed him.
Is Dominic safe?
I need to know if I have kept him safe.
'Elizabeth?'
'Yes,' I reply.
'You could be home Friday.'
'What! A whole week?' I sigh, closing my eyes.

The flashback returns as I remember him waking me up.
I remember him touching me, kissing me, asking who has touched me.
Telling me he has come to collect what belongs to him.
That no one takes his property, no one takes his Chantelle.

'Elizabeth?'
'Yes.' I look up at my doctor.
'Are you sure you are okay?
'Yes, I just want to go home.'
'Okay, well, if you don't have any other questions, I'll see you tomorrow.'

Amber walks back in, looking at Dominic as my doctor leaves.
'Well, Simon and I are going so we'll see you later.' Amber practically pushes Simon out the door.
Amber nods at Dominic and he returns it as she closes the door, and then he turns to me.
'Are you going to tell me what was happening just then?' Dominic asks.
'I'm remembering the attack at the hospital. I remember you holding me, and I fell asleep. I remember fingers touching me, I thought it was you.' I run my fingers along the scar on my neck as the tears fall.

'Hey,' Dominic climbs onto my bed and holds me, kissing the top of my head.
My whole body trembles.
'Babe, breathe. I'm here now with you.'
His fingers trace my scars.
'Liz,' His lips touch mine and my body calms.
'Do you want to talk about it?' Dominic asks against my lips.
'Yes.' I whisper.

I take a deep breath.
I need to tell him.
He moves beside me and carefully pulls me into him.
I snuggle in and take another deep breath as he plays with my hair.
'I felt fingers on my face, it was so strange that I felt weird. He was there when I opened my eyes. I was so scared I couldn't move or scream. He was kissing me, and forcing me to kiss him. I didn't want to but he grabbed my wrist and squeezed it. I cried out in pain and he bit down on my lip causing it to bleed again. I felt physically sick. I didn't want him, I didn't want to go with him' I say looking up at Dominic.
'What do you mean go with him?' Dominic asks me.
'He wanted me to go with him. Right then I knew I had to do something. I knew he would find out about you. I had to stop him. I had to fight to protect you. I wouldn't tell him anything, so he started hitting me, but I managed to get him off me and I hit him. When I fell to the floor, I saw his knife. I knew I had to, I had to stop him. I knew if I didn't, he would come back and I couldn't live with myself if he... He would have done horrible things to you before he...'

'Liz, it wasn't Michael.' Dominic sits up and looks at me.
'What do you mean? I was there, I saw him, I felt him.'
'Remember how you said you felt weird?' Dominic's hands move along my neck down to my hands bringing them to his lips.
'Yes.' I whisper, closing my eyes as he kisses my fingers gently before laying back down beside me.
'Well, it was Daniel attacking you. He injected Rophynol into your IV so that you would hallucinate. Someone sneaked it to him and helped him find you.'

I just sit there looking at him. I am so shocked I don't know what to say.

'So, I didn't protect you?' I whisper to myself.
That means he is still out there, and he could still find me and that means Dominic is not safe. I need to tell him.
'Liz, are you okay? I didn't hear what you said.'
'Where is he? Where is Daniel now?'
Dominic sits up and puts his hands behind his head.
He looks at me before holding my hands again.

'He's, um, he died'
Dominic doesn't look at me, he just looks at my hand and holds it.
'Because of me?'
'No!' Dominic doesn't even hesitate.
'He died because he attacked you and nothing else.' He looks at me.

'I'm okay, they are beautiful. I'm just feeling a little emotional, that's all and I just want to go home.'
'I'll get some water for you now.' Nurse Judy says.
She comes back a few minutes later with water and a vase, accompanied by my doctor.

'Morning, Elizabeth and Dominic, how are we all this morning?' He asks.
'I'm ready to go home.' I reply.
He smiles.
'Yes, well, about that. You are booked in for surgery tomorrow morning at 8am. Once that is done, you will be moved to another ward to recover.'
'So when can I go home?'
'As previously stated, by the end of the week.'
'Fine.' I moan.
'I'll see you tomorrow morning to prep you for surgery.' He says as he reads my chart.
'How long will she be in surgery for?' Dominic asks.
'It's hard to say, we won't know until we get into theatre. Liz's wrist is healing well, it's just more removing the pins. The lung wedge resection will take some time. Do you have any other questions?'
'No, I think that covered everything.' I answer him.
'Okay, well, I'll leave you to it then, and I'll see you in the morning.'
'Thank you.' I say.
'Oh and one more thing, Mrs. Miller, NO WALKING! Total bed rest.' He looks at me and then Dominic, like a parent walking in on the boyfriend making out with his daughter.
Dominic closes the door and then sits on my bed.

'Right, spill it out, why did you lie?' He asks me.
'I, well, umm,' I'm beginning to feel nervous.
I start to rub the scar on my neck and collarbone, my hands are shaking.
He grabs my hand and traces the scars on my neck and smiles as my body calms down.
'It's stupid really.' I don't look at him.
'Babe, tell me.'
'No one has ever bought me flowers, and I don't, I don't have anything to give you in return.'

His hand lifts my chin so he can see my face.
I hesitantly meet his eyes.
He holds my face and rub my cheeks with his thumbs.
He smiles as he brings his lips to mine.

'You have already given me everything I want.'
My lips part as my head tilts back, giving him all the access he needs.
Oh, my god, I have missed this.
Although his kiss is gentle, I can feel just how much he has missed this as well.
He sits back and I look at him angrily.

'What?' He asks.
'You stopped, I didn't...'
I didn't finish, he smiles and kisses me again.
'Good thing I really, really love kissing you.' He says.
His lips brush against mine before he kisses me.
I sigh as I pull him against me and hold him there, he doesn't even stop me.
It may look like just a kiss to some but for us it is an intimate moment filled with passion, desire, and a sense of belonging.
I belong to him and he belongs to me.
'Are you satisfied now?'
'Maybe, not sure, you may have to repeat it.'
'Is that so, Mrs. Miller?'
'Yes, Mr. Miller'
We laugh as he kisses me again. His lips feel good against mine.
'Is that better?'
'Yes.' I smile
I hold him to me. Apart from cooking he is my happy place.

We spend the rest of the day talking about my kitchen renovations and the arrival of my fireplaces. Dominic shows me photos, I snuggle in and we both sleep.
It is getting late and he is getting ready to go when his phone rings.
'It's my mum, give me a minute and then I'm all yours again.' He smiles.
'Don't worry, answer her, it's not like I can leave.' I tell him.
He kisses the top of my head as he answers his phone.

'Kia ora mama.' He says as he stands.
'No, I'm at the hospital with her now' He continues
'Do you have me on speaker?' He rolls his eyes. 'Kia ora papa'
'Ae papa' He looks over at me. 'Kaore.'
'Mum, what is dad doing?' He asks, walking over to the window.
While he chats with his parents, I put on my headphones and try to google some of the words he is saying.

'Ok, ok, kei te pai papa.'
I really need to learn if I'm to be a guest in their home.

Kia ora - Hello
Haere ra - Goodbye.
Mama - Mum
Papa - Dad
Ae - Yes
Kaore - No
I google thank you (Tena koe) just in case. Dominic walks up to me.

'They want to speak to you.' He says, handing me his phone and mouths the words.
'I'm sorry, I.O.U.'
'Okay,' I take his phone nervously.
'Kia ora,' I say hoping that it sounds correct.
They cheer so loudly that I have to pull the phone from my ear.
I look at Dominic and he has a huge smile on his face.
He ends up putting the phone on speaker and we chat with his parents for almost an hour.

'Alright, we have to go now,' He says.
'Haere ra.' I say hoping that I say it correctly.
I get more cheers from his parents.
He hangs up and kisses me.
'You're amazing,' He praises me with his lips still against mine.
'My parents definitely love you, and will make it very difficult for us to have alone time when we go.' He says as he continues to kiss me.

I can't help but smile as I put my hand on his chest.
'You have to go,' I say.
'Ten more minutes.' he smiles.
I pull him to me, and his lips touch mine.
My whole body shivers under his touch.
I do love him.
I love how he makes me feel safe and cared for.
He groans deeply as the nurse knocks on my door.
'Now I really have to go.'
'I'm sure that you'll be okay till Tuesday' I smile.
'Tuesday?' He questions.
'I have surgery tomorrow, so I'll be pretty out of it, no point in coming in. Besides, you have to work.' I remind him.
'Ha, I'll be here tomorrow.' He smiles at me.

Dominic runs his hand down my cheek and his fingers trace the scar on my neck.

His kisses me before walking towards the door.

Just before he leaves the room, he looks back and winks at me.

I lay back and close my eyes.

I'm so glad that I took the chance to let him in, now I just need the courage to tell him everything about my past.

A past that I'll never be able to escape because the scars I see every day are a reminder.

I fall asleep and dream of him and I on a beach without a care in the world.

I wake to the sound of rain.

I love rain.

It gives a good excuse to stay inside cooking, with music and a good book.

I look at my flowers and smile as I re-read Dominic's note.

I must have dozed off because I get a fright when the nurse touches my arm.

'Sorry, we are just getting you ready for surgery.' She says

'No worries, Can I ask you something?'

'Yes?' Jane asks.

'This note, is there a way I could take it with me to surgery please?' I ask her.

'I'll see what I can do for you.' Jane smiles as she puts her hand on my shoulder.

A few minutes later, my doctor, surgeon, and anaesthesiologist are in the room.

They explain the drugs that will be administered, what they will be doing, and the risks involved.

I have already had my pre-med, it was administered earlier.

This time the ventilator will be easier to insert as there is no swelling in my throat.

So apart from a wedge resection on my lung, which doesn't seem to want to heal, and my wrist, I'm just great.

'Right, well, let's get this done, shall we? I would love to go home.'

They nod and the orderly pushes my bed to the theatre room.

🔍 DOMINIC 🔍

I'm running through the hospital hall looking at my watch.

'Shit 7:59am.'

I reach her room to find Jane packing up Liz's things to move them to her new room.

'Crap!'

'You just missed them Dominic, take the elevators L2 and follow the signs.'

'Thank you, Jane.'

Following Jane's instructions, I run to catch up.
I turn the last corner and see Liz's doctor opening the restricted access door.
'Wait!' I call out as I run to them.
'Dominic, what are you doing here?' Liz asks as I get to her.
'This,' I say as I lean in and kiss her.

Her hand touches the side of my face and it sets my whole body alight.
I don't care who is watching us.
I stand up and hold her hand.
Liz smiles and her beautiful big green eyes shine, it lights up my world.
'I told you not to worry about coming in but I'm glad you did.' She smiles at me.
'I was in the area and thought I would drop in.'
'Let me guess, Bunnings for supplies then a sausage on bread with onion and BBQ sauce.'
'How did you know?' I look at her.
She points to a spot on my shirt.
'Right,' I nod.

She smiles. I lean back down and kiss her.
'Right, well, I'll see you this afternoon.' I say.
I look at the surgeon and Liz's doctor.
'Look after my girl.' I say.
'Of course, Dominic, your wife is in excellent hands. We will let you know as soon as she is out of theater.' He says.
I shake their hands before turning back to Liz and holding her hand.
I feel something in her hand and look down, it's paper.
'So, I'll see you this afternoon before or after your next Bunnings' run.'
'You're mocking me?' I raise an eyebrow.
'Me? Never,' she laughs, holding her hand over her heart.

I kiss her again before watching them take her away.
I realise that the paper in her hand is the note I left her.
She still has it with her.
I have a huge grin on my face as I remove my phone from my hand pocket.
There's a message from my mum wanting to know if I saw her Liz this morning.
I reply back,

Good Morning, Mother.
Yes, I just left MY Liz.
I am well thank you for asking.
Love from your SON
Dominic.

I get back to my car, yep, Liz is my girl.

The drive back to Moore Park Beach feels longer than usual.

I hate that she is there all alone.

I wanted to stay.

Simon said he would keep me updated.

I'm sure Mum will ring a few times to check on her Liz.

I smile because I know exactly what Liz would say if I did stay.

Anyway, I have the cabinetmaker, plumber, and electrician coming tomorrow so I really need to get stuff done.

The doors and windows are still a week or so away.

I pull into Liz's driveway and stop behind Luke's car.

There are other cars there that I have never seen.

I see Amber with some men in suits and uniforms, it's a good thing I packed up Liz's vials.

'Amber,' I call out and wave.

She looks up and waves back, gives some directions to the people with her then walks over to me.

'Hey, Dom, how's our girl doing this morning?' She asks.

'Good, but missing her friend.' I reply.

Amber's smile fades.

'What is it, Amber?'

'Dom!' Luke yells.

'Yeah,' I answer, not looking away from Amber.

'Did you get the gear? I'm out downstairs.' He says walking up to us.

'Yeah, in the back of the Ute, mate.' I answer, still looking at Amber.

'Sweet, when you're done catching up, do you think you might actually do some work?' He laughs.

'Be with you in a few. Do you want a cuppa?' I ask him.

'Do koalas shit in the bush?' He replies.

'Dom, Michael made bail.'

'For what he did to Liz? How long was he in?' Luke asks.

We all stand there—deathly quiet.

'After what she did to Daniel, Michael might be in for a shock if he turns up.' Luke says

I turn to find him standing behind me.

'Michael makes Daniel look like a teddy bear.' I say before looking at the ground.

'Sorry…' He starts to say.

'How the hell does a vile monster like him get bail after what he did to her? How many times did he almost fucking kill her?' I ask Amber as I walk away

'Friends in high places.' She replies, following me.

'Dominic, he made bail. How am I supposed to tell her? She is so happy, it will break her. You know how she reacts just hearing his name let alone his voice, or worse seeing him! Remember how she was last time? She went into a trance for days. She doesn't move, eat or sleep, just sits on the floor in the corner with a blank expression.' She says as she puts on the kettle.

She stands there looking out the window as I make coffee.

'Dominic, you know her life with him even on a good day, which there really wasn't, was the worst. Her bedroom was smaller than a toilet cubicle. She was shackled every night and slept on a mattress with a blanket. The only time she slept on a bed was when he was raping her. Even then she was still shackled to the bed' she says.

I can see the immense strain already wearing on her face.

'How the fuck am I supposed to tell her?'

'Well you are just going to have to come straight out with it.' I say.

'But…'

'No, Amber, Liz has been through enough I know, but hiding anything from her is going to be worse than telling her. You can't soften a blow like that and it's not your fault he's out.' I say, cutting her short.

'So, when are you going to tell her?' She inquires, turning back to me.

'What, me?' I ask.

'Yes, I think you're the closest person to her now, it might be easier on her if you tell her.'

'Do you remember when you first met her Dom?' She asks me.

'Of course, how can I forget.' I smile.

'Right, well, Liz and I have special codes and messages she gives or sends me. Kind of like an SOS.' She says. 'Do you know how many tradesmen she had come here?'

'No, how many?' I answer her.

'Before you, six and they all ended with me getting the code from her to come now!'

That surprises me.

'What happened, Amber?'

'A couple tried to ask her out, one guy lingered around longer than he needed to.'

'I had a hard time trying not to ask her out. The whole time I was with her, I just can't explain it.' I stretch and scratch the back of my neck. 'What did you do to get rid of them?'

'I would come racing home and act like the jealous girlfriend, they'd bail.'

Amber said after each incident, Liz would shake and retreat back into her shell. I imagined how hard that would have been for Liz.

I feel myself getting worked up and annoyed until I remember the day I first turned up and was lucky enough to meet her.

Her back was to me.

She was wearing an oversized white shirt with her shoulder exposed, showing that red bra strap.

Her shirt lifted as she moved just enough to expose her red panties.

When she turned around, her eyes and those lips were mesmerising.

Auburn hair falling just below her shoulders.

I had never been left speechless until I saw her that day.

'Careful, Dom,' Amber's voice breaks through my thoughts.

'Huh, what?' I ask.

'Careful?' I am still lost.

'You look like a lovestruck puppy' she laughs.

'Your eyes light up and you smile whenever you see her, it's like no-one else exists when she's around. It's really something to see.'

'Ha, she is mesmerizing' I say.

'You know she would never have come to the beach that day, right? You're welcome by the way. Now pick a ring and make sure you look after my girl.' She winks.

'Hahahaha, thank you, Amber.' I say, giving her an overdue thank you as I pour the coffee into mugs.

I head down to Luke with his coffee.

'You're welcome, lover boy.' She calls out.

I hand Luke his coffee.

'Thanks, took you long enough, lover boy.' He says as he sips a mouthful.

'You heard?' I look at him.

'Enough.' He points to the hole in the floor where the stairs are going and nods.

'You know, Amber is right.' He says.

'About?' I ask him.

'You and Liz. Mate, I have seen you with past girlfriends—none has had the same effect on you like Liz. Not even close. If you can't see that you're head over heels in love with her, you're blind because we sure as shit can! I've gotta tell you bro, if I have even half of what you and Liz have, I would be a very happy man. You're a lucky guy, Dom, and she's a lucky gal—you have the magic most dream of'

'Luke…'

'Mate, all I'm saying is, Liz is worth whatever is coming. You two have something special, so look after our girl and don't fuck it up.' Luke says as he takes another mouthful.

'Get back to work.' I stifle a laugh.
'You know I'm right.' He shrugs.

I know he is. Liz is all I think about.
I hate not being near her, holding her, talking to her, and waking up next to her.
Liz is my last thought when I go to sleep and my first thought when I wake.
She is all I want in my life.
I'll always be grateful to Amber for making sure she came to the beach that day.
Mum rings a few times wanting updates.
Simon calls too to update me on Liz.
Amber rings to tell me the same and that my travel plans are with her bosses.
The day seems to just drag on. It feels like I am looking at my watch every five minutes.
I hardly get any work done.
I look at my watch again at 12pm, surely it can't be much longer.
'Dom, mate, just go.'
I look at Luke.
'Go, I'll finish up here and prep for tomorrow,' Luke says.
'Thanks mate.' I pat him on the shoulder.
I don't need to be told twice.

I run to my car and race home to have a quick shower.
I arrive home to find that Greg and Thelma have collected their dogs.
They left a gift basket on the bench, gotta love them.
I also have a freezer full of home-cooked dinners. I have to admit that I miss the dogs.
On the plus side, no more bruises on my legs from hurricane Clyde's tail.
I have just found a car-park when Amber rings to tells me that Liz had been brought into recovery and everything went well.
I run to where Amber told me to go only to be denied entry.
'What do you mean I can't go in? I'm her husband' I question the nurse.
'I'm sorry, sir, but no males are allowed to go in the room. I'm sorry even her doctor was sent out.' The nurse turns and walks away.

Fuck it, I think.
I need to see my girl.
I make a quick stride past the nurses' desk to Liz's room.
I slip inside and see Liz out of it still with Amber sitting in the chair next to her.
'What's going on?' I ask as I walk over to her bedside.
'She is still a bit out of it.' Amber answers.
'Dominic.' Liz says my name.
'Sir, you can't be in here' a female nurse says.

'He stays.' Amber says sternly.
'Okay.' The nurse smiles and leaves.

'What's happening?' I ask Amber, I can clearly tell something is up but can't tell
if it's that nut case ex-boyfriend or Liz's health.
I take Liz's hand, she looks so pale.
'Is she okay?' I ask.
'Surgery went well, Dom. She panicked when she woke up and tried to punch a
male nurse taking her ops. I did stipulate that no male staff were to enter until
I gave the all clear, I guess the memo wasn't passed on. I locked down her room
to just women staff until she's conscious, for everyone's safety.' Amber smiles.

'I'm going to go now. I'll let the medical team know you're safe, at least I hope
you will be' she laughs.
'I'll be back later. This is a private room so I'll also let them know you can stay
here with Liz tonight. I've already packed you some nibbles and drinks in the
hope you can, can you stay?'
'Of course, thank you, Amber. I'll look after our girl.' I reply.
'See you later.' Amber leaves.
'Amber…' Liz whispers.
'No, babe, it's me, Dominic.' I sit on her bed and hold her hand.
'Hey, Amber, I…' Liz mumbles, still groggy.
'Liz, hey what's the matter?' I ask.
'I need, tell Dominic…'
'Tell me what?' I ask.
'I love him.'

I just stare at her.
She just said that right?
Will she remember what she said?
I really hope so because I feel so elated, like the luckiest man on earth.
Smiling from ear to ear, I look to grab her hand and notice the plastic.
I want to remove it but it's stuck to the bandage. I gently get up from the bed to
take a better look when my phone rings.
'Hey, Amber.'
'Good news, well, it's more like great news for the day, and you will love me. I
have just been told your travel plans have been approved.'
'Thanks, Amber, that is fantastic news, yes we love you heaps.' I say, walking
around to the other side of the bed and removing the plastic from her hand.
'I will finalise and sign off everything, give her a hug for me, love ya.'
'Will do thanks, Amber, talk later.' I hang up and put my phone back in my
pocket.

I open the plastic bag, tip out the contents and bin the plastic bag.

It's my note to her.

I smile as I sit on the end of her bed, realising she took my note into surgery.

It's amazing how a small gesture can mean so much to someone.

'Knock, knock.'

I look up as I put the note in my pocket.

'Hey, Simon.' I get up and shake his hand.

'Hey, I thought I would pop in to see if she is awake. I'm finished for the day, do you need anything?'

'No, I'm all good thanks anyway. I'll pop out and grab some dinner later once she's awake and settled.'

'I have made arrangements to stay with my friends just down the road and changed some of my shifts to nights. Since she's woken up, I'll pop in tomorrow.'

'Thanks, Simon.'

He waves and leaves.

'Dominic.' Liz whispers.

'Hey, babe,' I lean down and gently kiss the top of her head.

'Do you need anything?'

'Water please,' Liz replies, her voice is a little dry.

'I'll let them know you are awake and get you some water.' I say as I brush the hair from her face.

'Thank you.' She smiles as the colour returns to her face.

I return with the nurse and her doctor, the nurse brought a jug and a cup with her. Something is wrong. I can see it in her eyes.

'Elizabeth, how are you feeling?' Doctor Montgomery asks.

'Apart from some pain and discomfort I feel good,' Liz replies and has some water.

Lie, I think to myself.

'Good to hear, now your surgery went well though a little longer than we wanted but at the end of the day, you won't need to go back in.' He opens the file as the nurse takes Liz's ops.

He reads over some notes and sits on her bed.

'Now you will be moved to the general ward, BUT, Mrs. Miller, please no walking till at least tomorrow afternoon and that's only with a nurse to the bathroom. I don't want torn stitches.'

'Ok, thank you.' Liz nods and drinks more water.

'Right well, with all that out of the way let's get you moved and settled. The nurse has left a hospital menu for you to fill out for dinner tonight and breakfast tomorrow.'

After he leaves, I sit next to her and hold her hand.
'Liz, why did you lie? What's bothering you?' I ask her.
She removes her hand from my hold and starts to rub the scar on her neck and collarbone, her breathing also changes.
I take her hand and trace the scars while I kiss her fingertips.
She closes her eyes and takes an uncomfortable breath.

'This is going to sound really stupid I know but…' She looks at me nervously.
She remembers what she said, and wants to take it back.
I won't lie, my heart sinks.
'I took the note you left with me to surgery and now I can't find it.'
Relieved, I pull the note from my pocket and hand it to her as I kiss the top of her head.
'Thank you.' She whispers.

I lay down next to Liz and hold her till they come to move her.
We get to her new room and Liz settles in.
'Hey, would you mind if I duck off for half an hour or so and grab some dinner?'
'As long as you bring back something chocolate and real coffee.' She smiles.
'Now that I can manage.' I say as I lean in and kiss the top of her head.
'Thank you.' She smiles.

I have just finished eating when I hear someone call my name.
I look up to see Stephanie walking towards me.
'What! No hug for me?' Stephanie says.
'No.' I answer, 'Anyway, I have to go.'
Stephanie stands in my way, she puts her hands on my chest and looks at me.
'My offer…' she says, running her hands down.
'Is not wanted.' I grab her wrists.
'I'm with Liz,' I say pushing her hands away.
'Can't we be…'
'Stephanie! My answer is no, not now, not ever again. Get the hint and leave me alone.'
I brush past her and walk away without looking back.
I call Luke on the way back to let him know about my run in with Stephanie, give him updates on Liz, and that I'll be staying for the night.

I'm about to enter Liz's room when I hear Amber's voice from inside.
Judging by Liz's voice, she has just found out about Michael.
I compose myself for a bit before heading in.
'I need to go, I need to hide, I need to keep Dominic safe.' Liz's voice trembles.
'No, you are going to stay here, I will protect you. You won't have…'

'If you protect me, who protects Dominic? I have to leave Amber, I'm too weak to fight him and too weak to protect Dominic against Michael. The only way to protect him is if I leave.' Liz's voice breaks.

'Liz, look at me, you are stronger than you know, look at what you have done. Bought a house, and made it a home. Met Dominic and made a new start.' Amber comforts her.
'Oh, Amber, what am I going to do? I have finally found my first everything. I finally thought I had my chance at happiness, that I actually mean something to someone other than what I…'
Liz sniffles and I can hear Amber trying to soothe her. 'I have never actually told you, have I?' Liz pauses. 'I didn't realise it at the time but the hospital psychologist said that I didn't actually love him because Michael groomed me.' Liz pauses again.

'I thought he loved me and I loved him. I wanted my first time to be special, I wasn't saving myself for marriage or anything. I was nineteen almost twenty years old, never had a boyfriend, never even kissed a boy, and I told him that. He seemed to be happy with that. Before I realised what was happening, I was all alone with him, just what he wanted. He would come home drunk and smelling of perfume, he didn't even hide it. He even called me once while he was having sex.' Liz's voice trembles.
'He managed to isolate me from everyone. I was only allowed to leave the house with him or go to uni. When I was at uni, he had people watching me, I wasn't allowed to talk to anyone. He terminated all my jobs. Michael paid for my uni and I had to pay him back by working for him. I saw horrible things, Amber, horrible things. He made me do horrible things. Amber, the people I saw Michael tortured and killed…' Liz's voice shakes as she tries not to cry.

'It's okay, hon, you don't have to tell me anymore' Amber says.
'Not everything is in your files, Amber, and I can tell you. Maybe I can find the courage to tell Dominic everything. Besides, I took important documents and downloaded stuff off Michaels computer and didn't hand them over.'
'What, why?'
'Insurance, I guess, at the start I wasn't sure who I could trust so I have kept them hidden.'
'And now?' Amber asks.
'I think I'm ready to try.' Liz's voice shakes but she sounds determined.
'We went out for dinner for my birthday. He needed to put on a public appearance as the happy couple to dispel some rumours. He got so drunk that he passed out at home before he had the chance to shackle me in my room. When I saw my reflection in a mirror, I knew there and then I needed to leave.

'I packed up what clothes I had and went to the bathroom to pack my toiletries. That was where he cornered me; he had come to and wanted to give me my birthday present. I was so angry with myself that I just didn't run instead of wasting time packing my things. He tried to take off my clothes. I said no, so he beat me up then held a knife to my throat and raped me.' I can hear Liz breaking as she talks.

I so badly want to go comfort her but my feet feels like stone and remain rooted to the floor.
I'm torn from wanting to go in and wanting to stay where I am so she can unburden her pain to Amber. In the end, I feel she needs Amber more than me right now.
'It's okay, hon, take a breath.'

'He raped and beat me for three hours. That was the first time I was penetrated, and the first time he showed his true colours. I couldn't walk for a week, and couldn't talk for three days due to the swelling in my throat or see. That was also the start of the next seven and half years of my servitude. I was good for cooking, cleaning, fucking, entertainment, I was his punching bag. His beast-tamer, so he called me. He made me work with Dr. Spencer.'
'Dr. Spencer Mengele? He has been linked to Michael but it's been hard to actually place them together, he is a German doctor, correct?'
'Yes. Dr. Spencer Mengele is German and takes great pride in his ancestry. He is a descendant of Josef Mengele, The Angel of Death from the Auschwitz Concentration Camp. Dr. Spencer performed the abortions. Sometimes he didn't even bother with sedation; he enjoyed the pain he would inflict.'
'Liz, hon, why did not tell me some of this at the start?'
'I was ashamed. I still am.'
'Ashamed?' Amber asks her.
'He never asked me if I wanted to be his girlfriend. He just took me and all my firsts. I never fought back; I was terrified. I let him break me.' Liz starts to cry
'Elizabeth. I'm telling you that you should never be ashamed of yourself. Michael made you believe that, but it's not true. I know Dominic would say the same thing.'

I stand there completely shocked.
I feel physically sick.
How could anyone be so vile and repulsive?
How could anyone do that to her?
My girl alone, scared, and hurt at the hands of a, a fucking monster!
My fists are clenched at my sides.

I shake them out to release the pressure I can feel in them and go for a walk to cool off.

That fucker is going to pay for what he has done to her.

I make myself a promise, well, more of a vow.

I'm going to stand by Elizabeth, she will not face Michael alone.

I send Amber a message telling her I'm on my way back.

I wait for a minute, no reply.

I decide to head back to Liz's room.

I stop again when I hear Amber's voice.

'Do you love Dominic?' Amber asks her.

My heart stops, please say,

'Yes, I do love him, I'm just not ready to tell him yet,'

I stand in the hall, going a little 'Yes!' to myself and smile.

'I need to be sure of myself. I need to trust myself to be able to tell him everything. Dominic is really my first boyfriend, my first love. He is everything I ever wanted. He never pressures me into anything, he is caring, patient and understanding. When he asked me to be with him, I didn't even stop to think about it, I didn't need to. Just to be asked told me everything I needed to know at the time about him. I just need to be sure I'm good enough for him, I don't want him to be ashamed or embarrassed of me.'

'Why would he feel that?' Amber asks.

'Because of my scars, I'm ugly. And when men come near me or hug me, I panic and become awkward—that's embarrassing. I can't give him children. I'm broken.'

'Hun, I believe that Dominic really cares for you and he sees past all that.' Amber says.

'I was ready to end it.' Liz continues.

My heart just about stops beating. What?

'When?' Amber questions.

'After I said all those horrible things to you. I sat on the floor of the shower, I just felt so lost.' Liz starts to cry.

'You remember that?' Amber asks her. 'Oh hun, I could never stay angry with you. I love you like a sister.'

'I remember parts but a lot is still blurred and… and fleeting. Liz's voice starts to break.

I stand in the hall, listening. I feel like I need to help her realise, to see what I see when I look at her.

'What did Dominic say?' Amber asks her.

'He sat behind me and held me. He told me he wasn't going anywhere, and neither was I.' Liz sighs.

'I'm happy with you, Liz. I don't think of you as a witness, victim, or informant. I see you as my best friend and I love you. Besides, I can't cook, so I kinda can't do without you.' Amber and Liz laugh.

'Dominic has given me something I thought I would never have. He has given me so much to fight for, something to live for. But I'm scared that my past will hurt him or worse. If something happens to him I will never forgive myself. I'm also scared that I'm never going to be enough or be good enough for him. I really do love him, but what do I have to give him in return?'

'You give him you, nothing more, nothing less. I know you wanted to be a mum, but I know for sure you and Dominic are meant to be together. And he will love you regardless. You are an amazing person, Liz.'

'Thank you, Amber.'

'Anytime.' Amber replies.

I get a message from Amber saying two minutes.

'I have to go, hon, are you going to be okay?'

'Yeah, I think Dominic is due back soon.' Liz replies.

I hear Amber get up off the bed so I wait in the hall, leaning against the wall. Amber sees me as she comes out the door and holds her finger to her lips. I nod.

'Hey, Amber,' Liz calls her back.

'Yeah, hun.' She replies standing at the door.

'I know I will never see my family again, but are they okay? Are they safe?' Liz asks.

Amber looks at me then turns to Liz.

'Your mum and stepdad are on a cruise at the moment and they are doing well. Your brothers are still racing motocross.' Amber pauses. 'Jonathan is engaged and has a daughter named Chantelle. Travis is going to be a dad soon. Your brothers go to visit your grave and change the flowers regularly. They don't believe the car accident story, but they haven't told your parents. Your brothers still have your motor bikes and surfboards at the family work shed. We have a team that checks on them just to be sure. They all still live in Margaret River.' Amber says looking at the floor.

I am stunned, her family is alive and she can't see them? It's hard for me to wrap my brain around it, especially since my family are so close and I couldn't even comprehend how hard it would be to know they are there and not be able to see them.

'Can I have pictures of them?' Liz asks.
'I'm sorry, hun, I can't,' Amber replies.
'Ok, bye, Amber.'
I hear Liz cry. Amber sighs and motions me to follow her. We reach the elevator
when she turns to me.
'How much did you hear?' She questions me.
'I heard her talk about Michael and the rape. I went for a walk then came back
and heard you ask her if she loves me.'
Amber paces the hall in front of the elevator. 'How do you feel about what you
heard?'
'Honestly, angry, useless, frustrated, and amazed, but I really care for Liz. All I
want from her is just her and nothing else.' I say scratching the back of my head.

I sigh and lean against the wall.
Amber watches me, she knows I am falling in love with Elizabeth.
But I am not falling in love with her, I am in love with her.
But I'm worried that if I tell her, she will let the fear of Michael hurting me get
in the way of her putting him behind bars.
Amber smiles at me and presses the button for the elevator.
'Well, I know that you two are meant for each other, and when you realise it,
I want to help you pick out the ring. And another thing, I better be the first
person you call when she says yes!'
'Ring, marriage, a little early, don't you think?' I reply.
I know I want it now, but is Liz ready for that? I ask myself. She said she loves
me but marriage is a big step and I want my forever to be with Liz...

'Dominic.' Amber smiles at me.
'You love her, you have for a while now. Everyone can see it. But YOU need
to be ready for it from the looks of it. I know Liz is ready, she was from the
moment you kissed her.'
Amber walks into the elevator, blows me a kiss, and winks as the doors close.
I can't wipe the smile off my face as I walk back to my girl and replay Amber's
parting comment over in my head.

👀 ELIZABETH 👀

I look up as Dominic enters the room and try to hide the fact that I have been
crying.
His smile lights up my world.
'Hey, you.' I say as he walks over to me.

He doesn't say anything, he just walks up to me and in one movement, he cups my face with his hands and kisses me.
Everything in me tingles, I love how he has that effect on me. 'I missed you.' He says as he continues to kiss me.
I give him all the access he demands in his kiss.
I use my good hand to pull him to me.
He refuses my attempts at first, but he gives in.
I grimace a little, but I don't care, I just need him.
He rests his head on mine breathing heavy.

'Liz,' He whispers.
'Don't stop.' I look at him.
'But you're hurting, I'm hurting you.' He says sitting up.
'I don't care, it's worth it.' I say smiling.
He takes my hand and kisses me softly then lies down beside me and pulls me in gently.

'Do you want to talk about why you have been crying?' He asks as he kisses the top of my head.
I take a deep breath and feel my body tremble.
'Michael made bail, he is free.' I pause trying to calm myself.
My fingers start to trace the scars on my neck.
Dominic runs his fingers through my hair.

'Liz.'
'I don't trust him, and I'm scared. Scared he will find me and take me back, I can't go back…'
'Liz.' Dominic sits up.
He helps me sit up.
'I'm going to say something, and I need you to be honest with your answer, I'll respect your decision. Can you do that for me, Dominic?' I ask him.
He nods, his eyes don't leave mine and he holds my hand in his.
I take a deep breath.

'Michael is a vile, repulsive, and purely evil man; he is a monster. The scar on the right side of my neck…' Dominic traces the scar with his fingers. 'I picked up his phone to clean the coffee table. This one on my arm is from a compound fracture from my punishment when I tripped over and grabbed the arm of a man sitting in the room. This one on my shoulder, he shot me for not cooking his meal the way he wanted it. I have so many scars, each one was a lesson he said I needed to be taught. He took away my chance to bear children.' The tears start to fall. ' What I'm trying to say is…' My hands are trembling, tears are falling, and I look directly at him.
He moves closer using his thumbs to wipe away my tears.

'I know what I want, I want you. But I live in a constant state of fear, looking over my shoulder, scared he will find me. If he finds me, he can't hurt me anymore than he already has. He took everything from me. But…' I close my eyes and shake my head.
'If I'm with you and he, he, he will hurt you to punish me.' I summon the last of my courage.
'If you want out, I understand. I'll move away, pay you to finish the house and you will never see or hear from me again. You will be safe.'

'Liz, I'm not leaving you now or ever. I'm going to stand by you no matter what. I want you Liz, I want you.' He says as his hands brush my cheek.
'Dom…' That's all I get to say as his lips devour mine.
'I want you, I need you.' He says as he kisses me.
Dominic's kiss reminds me of the day that I made the layered chocolate mud cake and is as dominating just as much now as it was then.
I love every second of it.
I love him.

Suddenly, everything comes back.
My night with Dominic, from the chocolate cake to the little black box to our long shower.
I delivered Chantelle and Shaun's baby boy, Jonathan Michael West.
Our holiday on Fraser Island.
Will.
The attack on the beach.
Me screaming for Dominic.
The taste of blood in my mouth.
When I punched Daniel.
All the pain.
Getting angry with Amber.

Wanting to end it all.
The attack in my hospital room and me fighting back.

'I remember.' I say in between breaths.
'Dom, I remember.' I repeat.
'Remember what?' He asks, his lips still brushing against mine.
I look at him and touch his face and run my fingers through his hair.
'Everything' I say biting my bottom lip.
'Everything?' He asks.
'I cornered you while you were eating chocolate cake, I pulled your towel off you.
When I gave you the little black box you asked if I was sure. When you told me
to tell you if I needed you to stop. When you asked if I trusted you, you pinned
me against the shower wall and the spa. Delivering Chantelle and Shaun's baby
boy and the naming day. Fraser Island, Will and the quota of thirteen. The night
when you let go.' I ramble through all my memories excited that I can remember
the moments shared with Dominic. It feels like I'm being pulled in a hundred
different directions.

'Babe, slow down that's a lot to recall all at once. Just close your eyes and take a
moment. Remember what your doctor said.'
'I need to let Amber know about the hospital...'
'Babe, stop.' Dominic grabs my hands and brings them to his lips.
'I don't want to think of that right now, I just want you to focus on the good
things now.' He says as he kisses my fingers.
I nod my head and close my eyes, relaying the memories of delivering a baby
and our holiday to Dominic before opening my eyes again.

His smile gives me the feeling that I have everything.
'Everything?' He smirks with a raised eyebrow.
'Did I miss something? I'm sure I remembered everything.' I look at him.
'No,' He replies. 'You got it all.' He smiles and kisses me tenderly.
He lays next to me and I rest my head on his chest.
I can feel him run his fingers through my hair.
We lay there in complete silence, I could really get used to us like this.
Happy, with great friends, everything else just isn't important right now.
'Before I forget.' Dominic's voice breaks through my thoughts.
'When I was having dinner, I ran into Stephanie. She did not like me calling my
moment of weakness with her a mistake. And in making a hasty exit, I forgot
your chocolate and coffee, sorry,'
'I'm bummed that I missed it,' I say looking up at him.

There is a knock at the door and a nurse walks in.

'Sorry to interrupt, we need to do your ops and dressing change,' She looks a bit shocked seeing a male in the room and her eyes flick between Dominic and I.

'Sorry, sir, but I'm going to have to ask you to wait outside.' She finishes.

'Please don't make him leave, I want him to stay,' I say, feeling a little embarrassed.

'Okay, I'll be back with new dressings, would you like warm water for a wash down? She asks.

'Thank you, I would appreciate that.' I reply.

'Of course, I'll be back shortly,' She says and leaves.

'I can't wait to have a real shower and wash my hair properly.' I say sitting up.

'I can't wait to get you home,' He says.

'Oh, really why is that?' I smile.

'Well we had a deal,' He sits up and moves in front of me.

'I work, you make lunch,' He pauses, leans in, and his lips brush against my ear.

'And then I make you scream my name,' He whispers as he kisses my neck.

I tremble with desire.

'Yes, we do have a deal,' I say 'But.'

'But what?' He asks, moving so he could see my face.

I lean in.

'I could get used to you,' I pause as I pull him in and our lips touch.

'Used to me what?'

'Behind me.' I reply.

He groans and kisses me hard, his tongue demands access and I happily give him.

His hands caress my hair, and I hold him to me.

Suddenly he stops and pulls away looking very flustered.

'What? Did I do something wrong? I thought…' He cuts me off by putting his fingers on my lips.

'God, no, you did everything right.' He says, 'It's been a while since we were…'

'Oh.' I say. 'I'm sorry I didn't mean to,' I say, bringing my hand to my mouth.

'Shhh… it's okay, believe me,' He smiles. 'I had to stop or you know,'

'Are you alright?' I ask, trying not to enjoy this too much.

'Yep, just give me a minute,' He lets out a stifled laugh.

'Okay,' The nurse interrupts our moment. 'We have your dressings and warm water with soap and a towel, we will also change your bag and IV while we are here.'

The nurse says as she wheels in the trolly while another nurse enters with her.

'Thank you.' I say looking at Dominic.

'I'll just sit here.' He says, moving to the chair and pulling a pillow onto his lap.
He tries to adjust himself without making it too obvious.
He smiles at me as he shakes his head.

👀 DOMINIC 👀

I sit back in the chair and watch as the nurses remove the hospital gown.
She has lost more weight and her shoulder blades stick out.
Her spine all the way down to her hips protrudes, her skin is white and spotted with bruises.
There are bruises on her arms under the pressure bandages.
When I have held her arms, she has never once complained.
She becomes aware of me staring at her.
I smile and wink at her, she is still beautiful.
Her hair has gotten longer.
The nurses get her to lay back after they wash her back then start to change the dressing on her chest.

'Ouch.' She says wiping a tear away.
I move to her and hold her hand.
'I'm okay.' She says with her eyes closed.
'Okay, Elizabeth, we will get you to sit back up and we will put on new pressure bandages then do your hand.' The nurse says.
'Why does she have the bandages on?'
'To help with swelling and clotting.' The nurse replies.
'Are you okay, Elizabeth?'
'Yeah it just hurts a little.' She says.

They put new pressure bandages and gown and we help her lay down.
I can tell she is in more pain than she is letting on.
'Hey, I'm okay, it only hurts at the moment due to the changes.' She flinches.
'Not very appealing to look at right now, am I?'
'You are always appealing to me' I say cutting her off.
'Liar.' She smiles.
'Need I remind you of earlier?' I whisper in her ear.
She blushes and turns to face me, I kiss her forehead gently not caring who is in the room with us or what the nurses think.
I feel her grimace and flinch in pain.

'Hey,' I brush the hair from her face.
'You will be home by the end of the week' My fingers trace along her jaw.

'Mmm sounds good, sitting in the sun watching you work.' She giggles.
'What's so funny?'
'I have the best-looking pool boy.' She replies.
'Pool is not finished,' I smile at her.
'Fine, builder cum gardener, cum server, ouch!' Liz squeezes her eyes shut and a tear escapes.

I look over at the nurses and they are changing the dressing on a wound I hadn't seen before, running along her inner thigh from her pelvic area to her knee.
'Hey,' She touches my face. 'Dominic…'
I turn to look at her.
'What? How did that happen?' I go to look back, but her hand stops me.
'Dominic, it looks worse than what it is, and it's almost healed.'
'I didn't know.' I say looking at her.
'Sorry I thought you did, that's why they didn't want me walking too early. They think Daniel was trying to cut my femoral artery, lucky for me he was unable to do so. He may have tried my wrists if I hadn't…' She stops.
'Oh god, Liz. Hey look at me.' I lean in and kiss her softly.
'It was you or him, he attacked you remember that. He did this. Not you, don't you dare feel guilty.' I say to her.

'He is right, Elizabeth, everyone here thinks you were incredibly brave and we were all so relieved when you woke up. Well, all except one nurse who has been asked to leave.' The nurse says as she smiles at Liz.
'I think the DEM staff were the most relieved. I think they wanted another container of your cooking. Simon made us very jealous bringing in the food you had cooked for him.' The other nurse says resting her hand on Liz's shoulder
'I'm happy to spread the food around.' Liz smiles.
'As long as I get mine first.' I give her my best puppy dog look.
'I'm sure you will, you're lucky enough to be married to a great cook.' She says.
Liz blushes, I love it when she blushes.

'Okay, we have done your dressings and bag, we just need to change the IV bag, so I'll be back shortly with our RN. Is there anything else I can get for you?' She asks Liz.
'Um, if it's okay, can I please have another blanket?
'Of course and Mr. Miller can I get anything for you?
I look at Liz and smile.
'Nope I'm all good, just look after my girl.' I reply.
'Of course.' The nurse replies.

We are finally alone after they get her blanket and change her IV.
I lay down beside her holding her close.
'I can't wait to get you home and in the shower. I don't like the smell of hospital soap,' I say as I kiss the top of her head.
'I can't wait to sleep in our bed Mr. Miller,' Liz laughs 'And have real coffee.' She adds.
Liz yawns as she starts drifting off to sleep.
'Dominic,'
'Yeah babe.'
'Can you get my books from my bedside table, please?'
'Sure, now go to sleep.' I reply.
'Thank you.' Liz says kissing my hand.
'Anything for my girl.' I say gently running my fingers through her hair and kissing the top of her head.

I message Amber asking her to bring Liz's books from her bedside table tomorrow morning if she is able to.
I get a reply back almost instantly.
'Of course, I have an early start so I will see you there. P.S have you asked her yet??'
As I lay there holding Liz, I think about what Amber said at the elevator.
I was with Stephanie for two years before I was ready, I loved her.
That was until I found her in our bed with Daniel.

I left work early and went to her house to surprise her, I wanted her to move in with me.
I wanted everything with her, marriage, a home, and kids.
And that all came crashing down when I opened the door, they didn't even bother to stop.
I drove home, packed up all her stuff, and left it on her doorstep.
I even changed the locks on my place and blocked their numbers.
I didn't want to see or talk to them, it gutted me.

I know Elizabeth is different, what I feel for her I can't explain.
I know she can't give me children, and I want children.
It tears at me, and plays on my mind.
Can I be with her knowing that?
Will I be regretful or resentful?
Liz moves in my arms snuggling in more.
'Dominic' She mumbles my name in her sleep.
'I'm here' I say as I gently touch her face.
Yes, I can be with her.

And if we are meant to be and want kids together, we will find a way together. 'My Liz…I'm here to stay.' I kiss the top of her head and drift off to sleep holding my girl.

'Dominic.' I hear Liz say my name.
'Mmm.'
'Dominic,' Liz says gently, touching my face and tracing my jaw line and down my neck.
I slowly open my eyes and see her beautiful smile.
'What time is it?'
'After 6:30,' She replies.
'Crap' I say sitting up.
'What? What's wrong?' She asks me with a concerned look on her face.
'I unfortunately have to get going.' I get up and stretch.
I turn back around to see her pale with her hand on her chest.
'Babe, what's wrong?' I ask reaching for her.
'I'm okay, it's just,' She pauses and takes a few shallow breaths.
'Sometimes it hurts when I take a deep breath. I'll be fine, don't worry.' She says smiling.

For a brief moment I get lost in her eyes and find in them everything I want in my future, her. She's perfect and she's mine to love.
'So, what's the plan for today?' She asks.
I sit on her bed and hold her hand in mine.
'The cabinet maker, plumber, and electrician are coming. We are mapping out your kitchen today, and I believe that your white goods are due to be delivered today. Your stove on the other hand will take longer to come.'

'Thank you, Dominic.' Liz smiles at me.
'What for?'
 She looks down. She is nervous, her hand traces the scar on her neck.
'Whatever you are trying to say is okay.' I say.
I reach my hand up to her face and run my fingers along her cheek and down her neck tracing the scar and holding her fingers, as I lift her chin so her eyes meet mine.

'I just need you to know how much you mean to me. You mean so much more to me than just my boyfriend,' she says.
She takes a tentative breath before continuing.
'I have a lot of baggage and crap that I need to deal with and I understand that at times I may be frustrating…'.
I watch a tear fall.

'Elizabeth, you are the bravest and most amazing woman I have ever known.' I say as I lean in and my lips brush against hers.
She tilts her head back and parts her lips. 'You, Elizabeth, are mine, and I am so grateful that you are in my life.' I say.
My hands are in her hair as I kiss her…
My kiss is tender but primal.
My need for her is unlike anything I have ever felt.
It is ignited by her returning my kiss.
She moans as she grabs a handful of my hair pulling me in to her.
It takes all of my self-control to pull away from her, groaning as I do.
She clutches her chest.
'Babe.'
She puts her hand up.
'I'm okay, just catching my breath.' She says laying back in the bed.
'Sorry babe.' I touch her cheek.
I watch her grimace, I'm annoyed with myself.

'Don't ever apologise for that, that kiss was, was, it was wow.' She closes her eyes as she takes an uncomfortable breath.
'I'm sorry.' I say.
She looks at me with a raised eyebrow.
'You will be if that kiss was a once off cause then yeah I will be pissed.'
'I promise that was not a once off.' I say holding my hand over her heart.
'Good, don't make me get Amber on to you.' Liz giggles.

'She's right, I'm all sorts of crazy. I was wondering when you two were going to stop sucking face.' Amber pipes up.
We laugh as I wink as Liz.
'I really have to go now,' I say, kissing Liz.
'I'll be back later with chocolate and coffee.' I promise her.
'I got Amber to bring you your books.' I kiss her one more time.
'Thank you.' Liz smiles at me.
'Bye Amber.' I say as I leave.
'See ya lover boy.' She winks at me and walks over to Liz.

I walk to my car and get in, resting my head on the steering wheel.
'This week is going to take forever.' I groan.
My phone beeps with a message from Amber.
'Liz doesn't like big chunky rings, xo.' I smile as I read the message.
I put my phone down and laugh to myself as I start my car and head home to shower and get ready for work.

CHAPTER 11

Homecoming

🔲 ELIZABETH 🔲

The week is slow.

I am up walking albeit slow and sore but, hey, it is nice to be on my feet again.

I am able to use a toilet, so that is an added bonus, and shower.

Oh my god it feels so good to actually do that.

Dominic still doesn't think I smell right even though he brought my body wash and shampoo from home. As promised, he brings me chocolate and coffee every day, refreshes my flowers, and goes to Dymocks to buy me more books when I am done reading the ones I have.

Everyone comes to visit me including Gavin.

He even brings me flowers.

I find out he gets kind of shy when he likes someone and because of Dominic he keeps his distance.

It is only Louise that doesn't visit but that's okay, I know how she feels about Dominic.

I don't want her to fake it around me or make her feel uncomfortable.

My pain levels have gotten better since all my stitches are out, and a special cast for my wrist was fitted.

I am ready to go home, to sleep in my own bed and have Dominic with me, and not be practically dragged out by the nurses and making them promise to take extra good care of his girl.

He never corrects them when they call him Mr. Miller or refer to me as his wife.

In fact, I think he enjoys it judging by the smile he would get on his face.

They asked him how long we have been together and he replied, 'Not long enough'.

I have Amber meet me at the hospital to pick me up.

I told Dominic that I would call when I am ready to leave but I want to do a couple of things first and then surprise him.

'So where are we going?' Amber asks me.

'I, um, want you to take me shopping…'
'Yay I know exactly where to go, anything else?'
'I have a couple of errands to do, pick up some DVD's and CD's that have arrived, and then pick up my new car.'
'Do tell. When did you exactly buy this car?'
'I have had it pre-ordered and the sales guy came to the hospital so I could sign off on the paperwork, make some payments, and voila a new car.' I say excitedly.
'What did you buy?' Amber asks me.
'Only my dream car,'
'You didn't.'
'I did. Clubsport, manual, and I get to pick it up today.' I say trying to contain my excitement.
'Did you…?'
'Yep, she has been remapped, loud, lowered, black with red accents and heavily tinted windows.' I feel like a kid on Christmas morning.

I enjoy the drive home even if my wrist doesn't.
I am in love with my car.
But all I can think of is getting home, back to Dominic, and how I need to be with him.
I pull into my driveway and see Luke first, he turns back to the house.
I think he is calling Dominic.
I pull up behind Dominic's Ute.
When I see him walk down the path, it feels like my heart skips a beat.
I feel excited but nervous all at the same time.
He is looking over my car as he lifts tools into the back of his Ute.
I start to get out when he sees me, and before I can say anything he is in front of me.
His smile makes me weak at the knees.

Dominic wraps one arm around my waist, locking me to him, as he caresses my cheek down to my neck and kisses me.
His body pushes me against my car as he deepens our kiss.
'You're home.'
'Yep,' I reply as I wrap my arms around his neck and smile.
'Finally, I have missed you not being here,' He says in between kisses and his hands slide down and grabs my arse.
I pull him in and hold him to me.
'I have missed being here to watch you work.'
'Let's get you upstairs, would you like a cuppa?' He asks.
'Sounds good.'
His lips feel so good against mine.

'Get a room, will ya.' Luke interrupts our little moment.
'Hey Luke, how are you?' I ask him.
'I'm great, looks like you're doing well. Glad you're back, now he can stop pining and looking at his watch every ten minutes. Maybe he might even get some work done.' Luke laughs.
'He's lying, it was every fifteen minutes' Dominic says, getting my bag out of my car and taking my hand.
'See you tomorrow, Luke.' Dominic waves at him.

'Working weekends? I also didn't think tradies worked past three on a Friday afternoon.'
'I want as much as your renovation done before Louise's birthday party. And it's 10 past 3 on a Friday afternoon.' He says looking at his watch then smiling at me.
We head upstairs and Dominic puts the kettle on while I have a shower.
I come out of my room and my cuppa is on the bench, he is on the phone with his back to me.
I grab the mug and head out onto my beautiful new big deck and lean against the railing, closing my eyes and listening to the ocean as the cool sea breeze washes over me.
I don't hear him walk up behind me but he wraps his arms around me, cuddling and taking a deep breath.

'Mmm much better.' He says kissing my neck and sending shock waves through my body.
'How are you feeling?' He asks me.
'Tired and hungry.' I reply turning in his arms.
'My keys are on the bench, take my car when you go get the food.'
'The new car?' He looks at me kind of shocked.
'I trust you, just don't be long.' I smile.
'I'll duck home, shower and grab a change of clothes, then grab some dinner okay.' He says, tucking my hair behind my ear and running his fingers down my neck.

'You weren't staying here?'
'Not without you. It didn't feel right even being inside while you weren't here.'
'Well,' I pause and take a deep breath. 'It can be your home too, if you want that is,' I look at him, I start to feel nervous and start shaking, I look to the ground.

'Hey.' His hand touches my face then traces the scar on my neck. 'Look at me,' His hands bring my face to look up at him. 'I would love nothing more than to hold you every night,' He smiles and brings his lips to mine. 'We will talk about it later.' His kiss is soft but it still puts my body into a trance and I can feel the heat rise through me.

'Okay,' is all I can manage to say as he leaves.

I turn back around and smile, taking in a deep breath, the cool sea breeze feels good against my skin.

I light the bamboo citronella lanterns and light my new fire pit.

Making myself another cup of tea, I sit down on my daybed watching the flame and listening to the waves.

'Liz,' A voice says softly and a gentle hand touches my face.

I start to open my eyes.

'There's my girl.' Dominic says.

'Hey, sorry I fell asleep' I smile sleepily at him.

'Are you still hungry?' He asks, helping me to sit up.

'Yep, what are we having?' I yawn and stretch then cross my legs in front of me.

'Fish and chips from the pub.' He replies looking directly at me.

'Awesome' I say smiling back at him.

He laughs and says, 'I missed you,' then leans in and kisses me.

'Wait here and I'll get some cups.'

I nod as he stands up and turns away, he grabs a large bag and takes it inside.

I can't help but smile.

He returns with two coffee cups and some napkins, and notices the look on my face.

'I thought about what you said while I was gone,' He says, sitting next to me.

'Now we have only been together for a short time, but in that time…' He says lifting the food up onto the bed, '…in that short time I have come to care about you more than I would have thought, and being away from you is difficult. I want to be with you, and I would love to stay here with you. I would like to try it, but if it's too much for you, let me know and we will go back to the way it was. How do you feel about that?' He looks at me.

'I love it, I feel the same about you.' I reply smiling back at him.

He smiles as he looks at a bottle like he knows something I don't.

'Well, let's celebrate with a cheap bottle of champers and some take out.' He says as he opens the bottle, pours it into our cups and hands me one.

'Cheers.' we say together.

We sit and eat, we talk about his childhood, New Zealand, our up and coming holiday, and my renovation. We sit for what feels like hours, talking and laughing. It feels good to be with someone and not fear them. We clean up and Dominic gets more timber for the fire while I make some hot chocolate with a hint of Kahlua.
We sit together on the daybed and chat some more.
At some stage, we end up laying down and he wraps me tightly in his arms.
I wake feeling a little cold and find that the fire has died out. I am alone.

I sit up as Dominic comes out onto the deck.
'Where did you go?' I ask him.
'Bathroom, I had a quick shower. I was coming back to get you and take you to bed.' Dominic replies, helping me up.
'Thank you for tonight. It was amazing, I really enjoyed it.' I say.
His hand brushes my cheek.
'Good to know you're easy to please.' He jokes.
'Nothing big and flashy, except for that car.' He says with a smile.
'Yeah, she is pretty flashy.'

He kisses me softly.
He takes my hand and we head inside.
He helps me wrap my wrist and I wash my hair and brush my teeth.
When I come back into our room he is already asleep.
I drop my towel and climb into bed beside him and fall asleep looking at him.

I wake the next morning to find him already up.
I sit up as he comes in and the covers fall, exposing my breasts.
'You don't make it easy.' He groans looking at my breasts.
'Sorry.' I say, biting my bottom lip and looking up at him.
Before I can say anything else, he is on top of me, his kiss is hard and dominating.
I surrender to his kiss, and start to undo his shirt buttons.
He groans as he stops and rests his head on mine, before putting his hands on either side of my head to support his weight.
I slide my leg up to hold him to me and smile.

'As much as I want to take you right now, Luke has just arrived and believe me, it's not easy to walk away from you.' He kisses me again.
I look at him and pout, not moving my leg.
'I really have to…' He growls and kisses me again.
'Luke is waiting for me, one more then I really have to go.' He smiles as his lips meet mine.

He stands up and smiles, buttoning up his shirt, and running his fingers through his hair.

'I have a cuppa tea on the bench for you,' He smiles as he walks out our bedroom door.

I get up, get dressed and head out to the kitchen.

I grab my cup of tea off the bench and walk out onto the deck into the crisp morning air.

'Hey, Liz,' Dominic calls out from the bottom of the stairs.

'Yeah,'

'Can you please move your car, there is a truck coming shortly.'

'Yep give me a minute.' I grab my keys and head down.

'Can you put her in the garage? I need the shed space.' He asks

'Sure.'

He grabs my arse as I go to walk past him and kisses me.

'As much as I want you to take me right now,' I smirk as I use his own words against him. 'I have a car to move.' I wink and turn away.

No sooner had our cars been moved that the truck arrives with more timber, plasterboard for downstairs, and other supplies.

I am in the garage when one of the guys from the truck comes in.

'Nice car.' He says looking at it.

'Thank you.' I smile politely and look away.

'Boyfriend's?' He steps closer to the front of the car.

I give a little chuckle, 'No she's mine, I picked her up yesterday.'

'Manual?' He moves to the front side of the car.

'Yes' I reply looking for Dominic

I can't move around the back of the car as there is no room and he is blocking my exit.

He moves towards me, I look at the ground and I begin to panic.

'We should go for a drink some time.'

'No thank you, I'm with Dominic,' I reply.

'Come on, it's just a drink.'

'She said no, and she said she is with me.' Relief floods through me when I hear Dominic's voice.

'You get paid to unload a truck not to chat up my girlfriend, now fuck off.'

'Whatever, mate.'

Dominic comes up to me.

'Are you okay?' His hand traces the scar on my neck.

I can feel myself calm as he kisses the top of my head.

'I'm okay, Dominic, thank you.'

He kisses me.
'Go upstairs, I'll be there shortly.'
I look up at him and smile.
'There's my girl.'

He takes my hand, leads me out of the garage, and kisses me again.
I head upstairs to make breakfast and about thirty minutes later, Dominic comes inside and pulls me into him.
'Hey babe.'
'Hey you, would you like some breakfast or coffee?'
'Coffee for Luke and I please. But I have a favour to ask, two actually.'
'Okay, but you're making the coffee.'
'Can you do a hardware run, some stuff didn't come on the truck and I need it.'
'Sure what's favour two?' I ask.
'It's actually for Luke, he will ask you.' He says.
'Okay, I will have a talk with Luke.' I say walking towards him to grab my bag and keys.

Dominic grabs me by the waist and pulls me in again.
'Thanks,' He says as he kisses me.
'You're lucky I like you.' I say smiling at him.
'Just like?' He questions.
'Okay, like you a lot.' I giggle.
He smiles and kisses me again.
'Likes me a lot.' He grabs my arse with both hands and kisses me hard.
I trail my hands down his chest to his waist, I pull away.
'Looks like you like me a lot too.' I grab my bag and keys and smile at him.
'I'll tell Luke you're making coffee.' I wink.
My look tells him exactly what I'm thinking
'You're evil,' He says smacking my arse. 'Luke has the list.' He finishes.

I head downstairs to Luke.
I find him on the phone so I wait for him at my car.
'Hey Liz, how are you?'. He walks over to me.
'I'm really good and you?' I reply.
'Yeah I'm good but I need to ask you a huge favour,' He says folding his arms.
'Okay, what do you need?'
He takes a deep breath,
'Is it okay if my kids hang out here over the weekend with me, my ex has to work,'
'Sure, no problems' I say before he finishes
'Really?' He says looking a little stunned.

'Really, it's no problem at all, as long as you need.'
He walks up and hugs me, I tense up.
'Hands off she's mine' Dominic strides over and jokes.

Luke releases me as a car pulls in my driveway.
'Get ready, cyclone Sheila has arrived,' He takes the cup from Dominic.
'Who the fuck is this, Luke?' The woman yells as she gets out of the car and walks up to us.
'Shelia, stop!' Luke says, looking embarrassed.
'Don't tell me to stop, is this little floozy the reason you haven't been around?' She looks at me.
'Sheila, stop, that's enough.' Dominic says.
'Oh, shut up, Dominic' Shelia doesn't even look at him.
'My name is Eliza-'
'I don't care what your name is!' She cuts me off.
'You should.' I say to her.
'Liz…' Luke goes to stop me.
'It's okay, Luke, let the bimbo speak,' She huffs.

I take a deep breath.
'As I was saying, my name is Elizabeth, this is my home. I have employed Luke to work here. He was thanking me for allowing him to have his kids here.' My hands start to shake. 'Besides, I'm Dominic's bimbo.'
'Whatever,' She glares at Luke then walks back to her car.
I watch her get the kids out of the car, say goodbye to them, and then leaves. I walk over to them.
'Hello, I'm Liz.' I say kneeling down to their level.
'Are you Daddy's new bimbo?'
'Jack!' Luke says.
'Mummy says it won't last.'
'Lily!' Luke starts to get angry.
'Are you why he won't come over?'
'No, I'm not your daddy's new bimbo, I'm Dominic's. I'm your daddy's boss, he is building new parts of my home.' I say before Luke says anything.

'Oh, I'm Jack and this is my sister Lily.' Jack smiles.
'We are six,' Lily pipes in. 'We are big and at school.'
'Well, Jack and Lily, it's nice to meet you, I'm about to head into town, would you like me to get you anything?' I ask.
'Ice cream.' They say together.
'And a PlayStation.' Jack adds.
'No,' Luke says.

'Can we have a Wii then?' Lily begs her dad.
'No,' He replies.
'What about movies?' I ask them.
'Anything Jurassic Park, Marvel, DC, and Transformers.' Luke replies.
'Toys, and we like soccer,' Jack starts to say.
'Jack, that's enough.' Luke steps in and looks at me.
'Whatever you spend I will pay you back.' He finishes
'No you won't, I won't accept it.' I smile and walk back to the garage.

Dominic leans up against my new car.
'I'm not taking her, I'll take my old car, it's auto.'
He stands there smiling at me.
'What?' I ask him.
'Just checking out my bimbo, She's pretty hot.' He laughs.
Luke heads up the path with the kids, as I walk over to my old car. 'Yes, I suppose I am.' I say looking at him.
'I'll take the kids upstairs and raid the biscuit and cake tin. Frozen cake and biscuits is better than no cake and biscuits,' Luke waves from the bottom of the stairs.
'Leave some for me.' Dominic calls out.
'No promises!' Luke replies.

'Do you have the list?' Dominic asks, pinning me against the car.
'Yes,'
'Luke and the kids are raiding your freezer.'
'Yes they are.'
Dominic's head drops down and his lips brush against my ear.
'We are alone.' He whispers.
'Yes we are.' I stutter as his warmth assaults my senses.
Dominic places his hands on my waist, he can feel my body's reaction to his touch.
His hands slide under my loose top finding my breasts and his lips brush against my neck.
His lips leave a trail of kisses up my neck and along my jawline.

His kiss starts off soft as he pushes harder against me, his hand travels down and up under my skirt.
His kiss hardens as his hand travels up my inner thigh, I wrap my arms around his neck.
I gasp and moan as his fingers slide into me, moving his hand back and forth, rubbing my clitoris and fingering me.
His other hand slides my bikini top aside and gently squeezes my nipple.

His kiss becomes more demanding as his tongue presses against mine and he gently bites my bottom lip. I can feel myself getting close to coming and so can he.

My body begins to shudder and he pushes against me harder.
'Dominic.' I whisper.
I start to orgasm, he kisses me harder stifling any sound I make. I feel a small sting in my chest but it is worth it.
'Liz.' He says against my lips.
'Dom,' is all I manage before he kisses me again and both of his hands slide to my arse grabbing hard and lifting me, I wrap my legs around him.
He rests his head on my shoulder, I can feel his lips on my neck and I hold his head there. 'Well, umm, well.' I say catching my breath.
'Sorry.' He smiles.
'Don't apologise. If it wasn't for the three other people in the house my back seat would have been tested.'
He groans.
'You are very hard to let go of, Elizabeth.' He looks at me.

'Then don't.' I say softly.
He leans in and kisses me, his hands squeezing my arse, and he drives my body wild.
Our kiss is hard, rough and full of desire.
He wants my body under him as much as I do, I feel breathless.
He releases me as he opens my car door.
I feel him press against me as I turn to get in.
His hands slide under my skirt and run up the front of my thighs.
I feel his breath against my neck.
I relish the feeling and lean against him.

'Don't be long' He says as he kisses my neck and smacks my arse and then walks back to the house.
I get in the car smiling to myself.
I return a few hours later bearing gifts, food, and supplies.
Lily and Jack are very happy with my ice cream selection not to mention other 'gifts'.
Luke, not so much.
While I was gone, they had put my old stove back in the kitchen with the promise of chocolate cake for good behaviour.
I get Dominic and Luke to remove the spare bed and put it in the garage and not long after that, the trampoline, furniture and TV arrives.

Luke is still not too impressed with me.

While the boys set up the furniture, TV and Wii, Lily and I make lunch and put chocolate cake in the oven. After lunch, I teach the kids the fine art of getting their butts whooped at Mario Kart, Brain Freezes, and how to hide and not share the chocolate cakes and other goodies with Uncle Dominic and their dad.

We forget the time till there is a knock at the door.

'Enter!' Jack calls out.

Luke opens the door and walks in.

'Alright you two, time to go.' He says.

'I'm staying here with Aunty Lizzy.' Lily tells her dad as she shoots him with a nerf bullet.

'No, I'm taking you home, your mum will be waiting.' He replies as he leans up against the door frame.

'Please.' They say in unison.

'I suggest a deal. If it's okay with your dad, you can stay for dinner and desert. You can come back tomorrow but you have to behave and go home with your dad when he says so.' I look at Luke with my best puppy dog eyes.

'Fine' He rolls his eyes.

'YAY!' The kids and I high five each other.

'Dominic, deal with your bimbo she is corrupting my kids.' He calls out as he walks back towards the kitchen.

I hear Dominic laugh.

'Let's go cook dinner.' I say.

'What are we having?' Jack asks.

'I can make spaghetti bol…,'

'Yes!' They say before I finish.

🔳 DOMINIC 🔳

Liz comes out to the kitchen with the kids and I pull her in and kiss her softly.

'Uncle Dom.' The kids whine.

'What? She is my girl.' I smile.

'Go wash your hands while I get everything ready.' Liz tells the kids.

She watches them run to the bathroom before turning and walking into the kitchen.

I watch her move around the kitchen getting things ready.

I walk up behind her resting my hands on her hips and kissing her neck.

She turns in my arms and smiles her beautiful smile.

I run my fingers along her cheeks and bring my lips to hers.
Her hands rest on my sides as she sinks further into my embrace only feeding my desire for her.
I feel my shirt being tugged.
'Uncle Dom,' Jack whines again.
I turn and look at the kids. Jack and Lily smile, they start to push me out of the kitchen.
'Okay, I'm going. I'm going.' I say with my hands up.
I laugh and grab a couple of beers from the fridge and head out to Luke on the deck.
'Here you go, mate.' I say handing him a beer.
'Thanks, Dom.'

We sit watching Liz and the kids in the kitchen laughing, singing and dancing while cooking dinner.
I can't help but think about what Liz said when we first got together.
I could see how much it hurt her when she told me she was unable to have kids.
'She's good with them.' Luke says while looking at the ground.
'Yeah she is.' I reply.

'They have never taken to anyone I've been with.' He laughs.
'I think your ex may have something to do with that one.' I say, having another mouthful of beer and going back to watching my girl.
'Probably, I mean she tells the kids I left her for someone else. I just couldn't stand being made to feel like I was never good enough. It was the hardest thing I have ever done. Not being able to hug them, talk to them whenever I feel like it.' He stops. 'But you have a keeper with Liz, mate, I mean look at her.'
I shift in my seat and lean forward, resting my elbows on my knees.
'I mean she is smart, funny, loves cooking, cars, and you,' He slaps me on the shoulder. 'And fucking alright to look at.' He laughs.
I know he would never go there but I still get that 'fuck off that's my woman' feeling.
I look down at my beer and start to pick at the label.

'Hey, do you boys need a refill?' Liz calls out.
'Sounds great please, Liz.' Luke replies.
'All of the above and cold beer in the fridge, mate look after her.'
'I plan on it.' I say as I have the last of my beer.
'I reckon we should get this fire going.' I suggest.

I look up and see Liz walking towards us with our drinks.
I get up and go to her, grabbing her and pulling her in.

I kiss her while wishing we were the only ones here but also to show she is off limits.
'Thank you.' I say, taking the beer from her.
'You're welcome.' She winks at me.

I walk back to Luke, hand him his beer and get the fire going.
'So you and Liz look like you are both in a good place together?' Luke asks, breaking the silence. 'Do you want children? Does Liz?'
'Umm,' I reply.
'Come on, mate, kids are the best thing ever,' He stops and clears his throat.
'Don't let the chance pass you by, you're great with kids. My kids love you. It's Uncle Dom this and Uncle Dom that. The sooner the better I say.'

'No,'
'What do you mean no?' Luke looks at me shocked.
'No what?' Liz asks.
I freeze up hearing her voice and look up at her as she walks over to us. I didn't even hear her come out.
'Kids, when are you and Dominic going to have a team of them?'
I put my beer down, get up and go to her.
'Dom's always wanted them, and mine absolutely love him and you,'
'Luke.' I shake my head.

I pull her into me.
'It's a bit early for baby talk, isn't it?' I can hear the hurt in her voice.
'I think for now I'll just hang with yours.' Liz says.
'Liz…'
'Dinner's ready.' She says with a fake smile.
'Liz, babe.'
She shakes her head and walks back inside, I turn to Luke.
'What?' He asks.
'Stop with the baby talk.' I say kind of angry.
'Oh, had the talk and didn't go well? Don't worry…'
'Mate, stop! Liz, Liz can't have kids.' I say quietly so she doesn't hear me.
'There's IVF…'
'Luke, no, she can't, just fucking stop alright!' I snap at him.

He looks at me kind of shocked, I have never spoken to him like that.
'I'm sorry, mate, it's just, Liz was, um, her ex…' I pause and take a deep breath.
'She lost the ability to have children altogether. She wanted more than anything to have kids.' I sigh.
'Shit, that is fucked! I'm so sorry,' He says me.

'Yeah it is, so let's not go there again, okay? I'm good with it and I'm staying, she is amazing and she's mine, that's all I care about.' I reply.
'Put a ring on her already for god's sake. She loves you and you love her, even I can see that.'

'See what, Daddy?' Lily asks, coming to the door.
'I'm going to have trouble getting you two to leave.'
'Does that mean we can have a sleepover?' Jack asks
'In Aunty Lizzy's room?' Lily adds.
'I propose another deal.' Liz says getting down to their level.
'Okay!' They run over to her.
'After dinner you go with your dad. He will tell me if you have been good, and then you can come back another time for a sleepover, deal?'
'Deal,' They say, giving Liz a high five.
'Dom, your bimbo,' Luke looks at me and tilts his head in Liz's direction.
I shrug and smile.

'Uncle Dom,'
'Yes, Lily' I reply.
'I like Aunty Liz. You should keep her.'
'I like her too,' I say smiling at Liz.
'I'm going to marry her.' Jack says with a huge grin on his face looking up at her.
'Wow, I'm very flattered but I'm with your Uncle Dominic.'
'But you hid the chocolate cake and goodies from him and told us not to tell him.' Jack says as he looks up at her.
Luke and I look at her and she shrugs.

'Yes, thank you, Jack, but in all fairness, I hid it from your father as well, so we didn't have to share with them.'
'Fine, but if you get in trouble and you break up, I'll marry you.'
'Yeah not going to happen little buddy, Liz is my…'
'Bimbo.' Lily says.
We laugh and much to my dismay Liz ends up between the twins. I notice Liz has hardly touched her food. Her hand runs along the scar on her neck as she plays with her food.

'Jack, Lily. Eat up please, I need to get you home.' Luke remarks.
'Can we stay at your house, Daddy?' Jack asks
'Sure buddy, I'd love that.'
'Can I ask Mummy now?'
'Sure.' Luke hands Jack his phone.
Jack goes outside to call Sheila.

Liz hasn't shifted her gaze from her plate.
Luke taps my foot and I look at him; he nods in her direction, he can see it too.
I look back at Liz and watch tears start to fall.

'Aunty Liz.'
'Yes sweetie,' Liz says, still looking at her plate.
'Can we have more ice cream and cake?'
'Sure, go grab some bowls,'
'Jack, we can have more ice cream and cake.' Lily yells.
'Mum says we can stay with Dad.' Jack says from outside.
'I'll be back in a minute.' Liz says getting up.
'Liz,' She ignores me and goes to our bedroom.
'Go, I've got this' Luke says.
I walk in to find her pacing and she turns to me.
'I'm so sorry, Dom.' I don't let her finish.
I bring my lips down on hers and hold her.

She gives up trying to push me away and kisses me back.
'Don't apologise, Babe,' I say, running my thumb across her cheek.
I kiss her again still holding her against me.
'Do you want me to get Luke to make other…'
'No, I really enjoyed today, besides, I made a deal.' I feel her take a deep breath.
I stand there holding her and running my fingers through her hair.

'Are you okay?' She asks me.
'Of course why?'
'What Luke said outside, and I…'
'Liz, I don't care, all I want is you and your beautiful smile'.
I lift her face so I can see her eyes. I smile at her as I trace her scars.
I feel her relax, she starts to smile.
'There's my girl.' I kiss her softly.

'Aunty Lizzy!' Lily calls out.
'Ice cream is ready.' Jack calls out.
'Better get out there before they come in looking for you, Aunty Liz,' I say walking out behind her and grabbing her arse.

The rest of the night goes by quickly although Luke and I end up with dish duties, while Liz and the kids face off for one last race.
Judging by the faces, Liz won just.
Jack starts telling Luke his plans for winning tomorrow's big race as we walk downstairs to say goodbye.

'Uncle Dom.' Lily pulls my hand and motions for me to get down to her level.
'Yes, princess.'
'You can't let Aunty Liz practice,' She whispers in my ear.
'What do I get in return?'
'I'll tell you where she hid the other chocolate cake.'
'A second cake? Now this is interesting, does your dad know?'
'I'll tell him.' Lily looks at the ground.

'What's wrong, Lily?'
'I saw Aunty Liz cry and I don't want her to get into trouble for hiding the cake.'
'When was she crying?'
'After we finished making the cakes and hiding them. Jack asked if we could call her Aunty Liz.
 She tried to hide it but we saw it. Is she in trouble?'
'No, of course not, she hides them so that we can have it tomorrow.'
'Do you love her, Uncle Dom? You have to.'
'Yeah I guess I do, but it's our little secret. I want to surprise her. Can you help me with that?'
'Can Jack help?'
'Of course.' I wink at her.

Lily has the biggest smile on her face and hugs me.
Jack comes running up and hugs me too.
I look at Lily and nod.
She grabs Jack's hand and they run to hug Liz and then they get in the car quickly.
'What was that about?' Luke asks.
'I found out about cake number two, Lily didn't want Liz to get into trouble.' I reply watching Liz say goodbye to the kids and walking back to me.

'Right, well, I'll see you two tomorrow morning then, night.'
'Goodnight, Luke.' Liz waves.
I pull her in. 'I hardly saw you all day. If that happens tomorrow, I'm staging an intervention.'
'I'm guessing Lily told you about the second cake.'
'She did.' I say taking her hand.
'In exchange for?'
'Helping them beat you tomorrow, and she saw you upset after they asked if they could call you Aunty Liz. Do you want to talk about it?'
'Not tonight, today has been special.'

We walk back up the stairs and sit by the fire after I add more timber.
I watch her as she stares at the flames.
'Liz,' I say.
'Hmm.' She turns to me and smiles.
I lean in to her.
'I like you a lot.' I say to her as I bring my hand across to her waist.
My lips brush against hers.

'I like you a lot too.' She says as I pull her on to my lap and hold her against me listening to her heart beat.
I feel her lean back and loosen my hold on her and watch as she lifts her shirt over her head.
'Liz,'
Her lips press against mine as she runs her hands through my hair, she only stops to remove her bikini top before kissing me again.
Our kiss deepens as I run my hand up her back and remove her hair clip, letting her hair cascade down her back.
She starts to undo my shirt buttons.
I run my hands over her breasts and feel her nipples harden.
I tangle my hand in her hair as I pull her head back giving my mouth access to her neck.

She gasps as my mouth finds her breasts.
'I need you Dominic,' She whimpers. 'Please,'
I slide my hand under her skirt grabbing her arse as my other arm runs up her back and holds her to me.
I turn and lay her on the daybed.
She feels so good under me.

Liz manages the last few buttons of my shirt.
When I stand to remove my boots and shirt Liz begins to undo my belt and shorts.
She takes my cock in her mouth all the way and I grab fists full of her hair, my hips match her rhythm.
I sigh as Liz teases me with her tongue before taking me all the way and her hand touches and plays with my balls.
I roll my head back and moan loudly, lost in the pleasure she is giving me.
'Liz,' I growl, 'My god.'
My breathing quickens, I need her under me.
I pull her up and kiss her hard.
I unzip her skirt and let it fall to the ground, the last of her underwear joins it.
She feels so good naked against me. I lay her down and enter her.

She whimpers and wraps her legs around me, I hold her good wrist above her head pining it there while making sure I'm not hurting her.
She uses her forearm around my neck and pulls me to her.

'Dominic,' She murmurs my name seductively.
My god, I love the way my name sounds coming from her lips as I make love to her, I never want her to stop.
I trail bites down her neck to her breasts.
She arches her back and gasps as I tease her nipples with my teeth and tongue.
I trail bites back up and claim her lips hard, her hunger matches mine.
I release her wrist and grab the frame pushing deeper and harder.
'Dommmm, Dominic.' She cries again her voice thick with desire and it drives me wild.
Her tongue traces my neck up to my earlobe and using her teeth gently bites me, sending shockwaves through me.
Her fingers trail down my back she digs them in and buries her face in my neck.
I can feel her body start to shake, Liz starts to orgasm, I push deeper again as she arches her back.
I take her breast in my mouth and feel her body react.

'Dominic.' She calls my name.
'Liz.' I call her name as she pulls me back to her lips.
I run my hand down her side and grab her thigh as she climaxes.
Hearing her orgasm and calling out my name brings out my primal urge to fuck her harder and she isn't stopping me, I can't hold back anymore.
I push up to my knees and grab her hips rolling my head back and growl my whole body tenses.
'Elizabeth.'
I run my hands up and down her thighs as I rub her clit, her back arches again as I bring her to climax again.
'Elizabeth.' I call her name.
Liz pulls me back down to her.
'Dominic.' She says my name as our lips touch.
'Liz, I,' I say kissing her hard as I orgasm.

I swear every time with her gets better.
Liz returns my kiss with everything she has to give me.
I can feel it, this woman is mine and mine alone.
'I want you Liz.' I say, running my thumb along her lips.
'I want you all to myself.'
I look down at her.
She smiles and kisses my thumb, her eyes shine and never leave mine.

'I need you Elizabeth.' I say to her.
'You have all of me Dominic, for as long as you want me.'
I lay next to her resting on my elbow, trailing my fingers along her body watching her body's reaction to my touch.
The light from the fire highlights the scars on her body, but she is still absolutely fucking beautiful.

👀 ELIZABETH 👀

I see him looking at my scars, I start to feel self-conscious.
'Hey, Liz look at me.'
I bring my eyes up to meet his gaze.
'You are beautiful,' He says.
'Your scars are part of who you are and I will kiss every one of them.'
I feel his hand move along my body.
'I want you Liz,' His lips brush against mine 'I want you.'

I shiver under his touch as his hand moves along my leg and pulls my leg up on to him, and moves back to my arse.
'I want you, Dominic.' I whisper against his lips 'I need you.'
I tease his lips with my tongue and groan as I feel him harden.
'I'm yours.' I say as I kiss him.

Dominic's hand moves up to my face, his fingers brush my cheek as he kisses me.
His kiss becomes hard and dominating but in a way that shows he cares for me making sure I enjoy it just as much as he does.
I push myself against him enough for him to pull on top of him.
I slide on to him and begin to move against him.
My body is ignited by his hands moving over my breasts and down to my hips and grabbing hold as he breaths deeply, my name leaves his lips.
His eyes stated with heated desire never leave mine.
He grabs my arse and grabs it hard.
I start to feel the heat rise.
I try to hold back, he sits up and holds me against him as I move back and forth on him.
Dominic's hand tangles in my hair as his lips tease along my neck down to my breasts and back up to my lips.
'Cum with me Dominic.' I whisper in his ear.
'Fuck Liz,' He growls deeply and kisses me hard.

I moan into the kiss knowing how much he likes it as my movements become faster and my body starts to shake.
'Dominic' I call his name.
I feel his hands holding me tighter.
'I need you Dominic, Please Dominic take me.'

He takes over, it feels so good under him.
Every movement becomes deeper, harder, faster.
Dominic holds my hand above my head, his fingers intertwined with mine.
His head is buried against my neck, it's getting harder to hold back.
His hand holds mine tighter, I can feel I'm getting closer, his other hand slides under me as my back arches.
His lips claim mine, he wants as much as I can give him.
The sounds of pleasure leaving my lips is only feeding his desire.
'Dominic, oh my, Dominic,' I begin to orgasm.
'I, I, lo…' His lips are on mine.
He is getting close and I try holding back but I'm already there.
He lifts himself off me still holding my hand above my head and I watch him cum with me.
'Liz.' He calls out my name as he cums.

I pull him back down to me, we are still breathing heavily when our lips meet.
He is still on top of me looking at me.
'You are amazing, Elizabeth, you know that,'
'Really, I don't…'
'Yes, you are,' He cuts me off.
'You made me the happiest man alive when you came to the beach that day, when you kissed me, when you gave yourself to me, and said yes to being my girlfriend.'
I feel a tear escape my eye.

'You have given me more than I ever thought I was allowed to have. For so long I believed I was nothing, a nobody and completely disposable.'
'Liz I…'
'Dominic, if what we have ends please know that I will be forever grateful to you and this time we've spent together.' I say brushing his face with the fingers of my broken wrist.
'Elizabeth, you are not nothing, you are my everything, my someone. I will do everything in my power to make sure you never feel like that again.' He says. 'I promise you Liz, I will do whatever I can to make you feel protected.'
His kiss is tender, it almost feels loving.

'Come on, let's get you to bed.' He says helping me get up.
I pick up my clothes to start getting dressed.
'Yeah no you don't' He says, grabbing me.
I let out a little scream and giggle as he scoops me up and carries me inside.
'Dominic, our clothes.' I giggle.
'They will be fine, I'm going to sponge bath you.' He says.
'Yes sir,' I giggle coyly.

He carefully wraps up my wrist and helps me shower, he washes my hair gently.
Using my body wash his hands move over my body sensually, it feels so good.
He uses his fingers to tease my body and lingers over my breasts.
His hands move along my thighs and starts to rub against my clit and begins
to finger me.
'Dominic,'
I lean back against him and he turns my face towards his, my arm wraps around
his neck as our lips meet.
'Dominic,' I whisper against his lips.
The kiss is hard and erotic.
It excites my body and I want more.
Dominic holds me tight against me as he brings me to orgasm.
'Well, umm wow, remind me to return the favour.' I say breathing heavily as he
still holds me against him.
I turn in his arms.
'I'm so lucky to have you.' I smile at him.
'No, I'm the lucky one,' He says as his lips brush against mine.

He kisses me softly but he still manages to make me weak at the knees.
I turn the water off as he wraps himself in a towel and gets mine.
He wraps me in my towel and gently unwraps my wrist then begins to dry my
hair then brush it carefully.
I close my eyes enjoying the moment and a small tear escapes.

'What's wrong?' He asks me.
'It's nothing.'
'Liz, babe please tell me.' He pleads.
'I want to be there for you.' He holds me tight.
He's right, I do need to talk, and I need to tell him.
I suck in a breath, turn to face him and nod as I take his hand and lead him to
our bed.

'It's sweet actually. Having you wash, dry and brush my hair made me feel special. It's just… no one has done that other than my mum when I was little. It just brings to the forefront that I…,' I look down at the floor and my hands pull at the seam of my clothes.
'You miss your family,'
I nod and smile at him before turning my gaze back to the floor.

'It was the hardest thing I have ever had to do. We were so close and I feel like I hurt them, failed them. And I will never get to see them again. Chantelle Watson the name I was given when I was born, died on Thursday the 26th of July 2007.' I reach over to my bedside table opening the drawer and pulling out a red jewellery box.
I hand Dominic the box.

'A car accident, it was so bad the only way they could identify me—Chantelle was through DNA. The victim of a drunk driver hit and run, never caught.'

'So, you were in an accident?' He asks as he opens the jewellery box.
'No, it was all Michael, I wasn't trying to escape after he hurt me.' I pause.
'From what I was told when they found me, I was shackled to a bed and almost dead. I was like that for about three to five days. My jaw, nose, eye socket, both arms and legs and most of my ribs were broken. My hips were dislocated and my pelvis was shattered. I had lost so much blood that…' I looked at him and his face was in utter shock.
'Sorry, too much information, I…' I look back at the floor, my hands begin to tremble.
'No Liz, I just. Babe you're here now, with me. What shocks me is you managed to survive, you are a fighter. Don't ever think that you are not. I'm so sorry you had to experience that, alone and scared. I want to know everything, the good, the bad, and the really bad. I want to know everything about you. I'm here for you and I want you to tell me whatever you want, whenever you want okay?'
'Yes, thank you.' I smile at him.

He pulls me in.
'That box is all I have left of who I was.'
He starts to look through the contents, my student ID, a locket with a photo of my dad and a bit of his ashes, and a ring my mum and stepdad gave me when I turned eighteen. The newspaper clippings of the car accident and my funeral that almost five hundred people turned out to, my funeral notice and memoriam, and lastly a picture of my grave.
'Amber managed to get those few things for me but stopped at getting me photos of my family.'

I take a deep breath and watch him go through all that's left of who I was.
He stops and pulls out my eighteenth birthday notice from the local newspaper.
'Your date of birth,'
'My real date of birth is one day after yours. The 26th of May 1980.'
I look at him and smile.

'Sometimes I feel ashamed of myself for what happened like I let it happen to me even though I know that it is not the case. It's like for someone so smart I was really stupid. I...'
'I can tell you for certain that you are definitely not stupid and should never feel like that. I'm not ashamed of you, your scars or your past. You are still here and I'm lucky enough to share every day and night with you.' Dominic says before I can finish.

He reaches over and picks up my book opening the cover.
He lifts the note he wrote for me and puts it in the red jewellery box.
'I'm thankful for Chantelle, she gave me you.' He kisses the top of my head.
'Come on, let's get you to bed, you have a big day tomorrow. Mario Kart Supercar finals so I'm told, and I have to find that chocolate cake.' He smiles and winks at me.
I discard my towel and climb into bed.
Dominic slides in beside me and reaches for me.
He feels so warm and good to hold.
He pulls me in, and I fall asleep in his arms.

CHAPTER 12

The Lovebirds

👀 MICHAEL 👀

'Is everybody in position?'
'Yes, Michael, the house is surrounded,' A voice says over the phone.
'Good, where are they?' I ask getting out of the car and walking up the driveway.
'Second floor master bedroom, they are home alone and just gone to bed.'
'Excellent, let's pay them a little visit shall we.' I say giving the signal.

Once inside we make our way to the master bedroom.
I don't bother to put on gloves because the law won't touch me.
I sit on the bed and cover her mouth forcing her to wake up, her eyes open and greet me with a look of pure fear.
It's my favourite look in a woman's eyes.
'Well, well ,well, how is my girl?' I whisper as I pull the covers down to reveal her naked body and run my hand over her breasts.
'I missed you,' I say looking at her as I remove my knife from its holster.
I run the knife down her body and rest it against her pussy, her body is shaking, and it turns me on.
'You are going to get dressed now and then…' I press the knife against her and the tears start to fall.
'You, the new boyfriend and I are going to have some,' I remove the knife from its resting place and smell it. 'Fun.' I smile.

I remove my hand from her mouth and punch her mouth, busting her lip.
I watch the blood run down.
I grab her by her hair and pull her up.
She hasn't made a sound yet.
I watch the blood drip down onto her breast and then lift my gaze up to meet her eyes.
I lean in and lick her lips and taste her blood and tears.

'I brought you a gift and you are going to love it.' I say grabbing her face and squeezing hard.

'Get him up.' I don't bother to whisper anymore.

I turn back to her, her lip has stopped bleeding.

'Get dressed now.'

She nods as I push her into her closet and watch her start getting dressed.

I turn back to the boyfriend, he is trying to put up a fight.

I walk over to him and smell my knife again as I look at him.

'Please by all means put up a fight, I'll only enjoy it more when I take it out on her.'

He stops instantly and looks across the room at her, as she walks out of the robe dressed in a shirt and jeans.

'My girl here and I might start the fun early. I have some toys in the car, you remember my toys don't you?' I ask her as I walk over to her.

She doesn't say anything or even move.

I backhand her, sending her to the floor.

'Answer me when I ask you a fucking question!' I yell as I kick her.

'Yes. Yes, I remember your toys.' She says as her voice trembles.

I feel myself getting excited and hard, it's been a while and controlling myself is getting difficult.

I grab the back of her head and pull her up and turn around.

'Get dressed, I hate looking at naked men' I say looking at the boyfriend.

I drag her by her hair to the car and get her to straddle me and I rest my head on her chest.

Her heart is racing and her body is trembling.

She can feel me harden against her.

'Kiss me.' I command her.

She brings her lips to mine.

I can taste the blood and her tears and I bite her lip hard causing her to gasp in pain.

The boyfriend joins us.

'Li-'

'NO!' I cut him off and punch him in the nose.

'You do not speak unless spoken to.'

I pull the gun from the pocket in the car door and turn the safety off.

I point the gun at him and look him in the eyes then bring it back to her, I run it down her breasts.

'Have you ever fucked a woman with a gun?' I ask without looking at him.

'I have, haven't I?'

'Yes.' She says.

'Remove your shirt.'

I watch as she removes her shirt and her body trembles.

'Impress me or he gets a bullet where it becomes useless for reproduction.'

The drive to the warehouse takes about forty minutes, the whole time she is trying to impress me by sucking my engorged cock as my gun is pressed against him.

'Sam.'

'Yes, Michael.'

'Tie him up but don't gag him, I want him to watch and get Drew to dress her up in her gift.' I say walking into a room.

'Are they here?' I ask.

'Yes, they are waiting for you.'

'Excellent, tell Brian to come in.' I say.

'I'll get him now,' Sam says as he finishes tying up the boyfriend.

I look around the room and the fridge is stocked with her blood and other supplies.

The medical equipment is next to the hospital bed. I look at the boyfriend, he is watching me.

Next to his chair is a table covered with a sheet that has all my toys on it.

In front of him is a bed that has a range of shackles and cuffs on it.

I pull the sheet off the table and his eyes widen as he sees my toys for the first time.

'Don't worry, they aren't all for you.' I say grinning at him as I sit on the bed.

'She is good, isn't she? I bet she makes you scream just as much as you make her scream.' I look over to the door as she is brought in wearing my gift, her uniform.

'I always liked a woman in uniform so,' I say as I look at the boyfriend.

'Anthony, I would like you to meet Lilith Baxter, one of the undercover rodents that stole my property and I want her back. She stole my Chantelle and hid her from me.'

'I know who she is,' He says.

'She told you?'

'Lilith left the force and is studying medicine, forensic medicine. I'm still with the police.' He replies, his eyes never leave mine.

'Did the bitch tell you what she did to me? Did she tell you that she stole Chantelle from me?' My anger is reaching a pivotal point where I either control it or go full blood lust. She nods at him.

'Lilith was undercover in a special task force in conjunction with the federal police. But told me nothing about what she did in that task force or where they hid Chantelle. She was undercover police not Federal she doesn't know anything. Please she is good, please let us go, we won't say anything.'

'Of course, she doesn't know, but she knows the next in line, the person she had to report to and that's the information I want.' I look over to her. 'I got her name from the one under her and so on and so forth.' I stand and stretch. 'Now whether you walk out of here is up to her.' I say as they bring in a sledgehammer and some timber. 'You have read Misery right?' I ask him.

He shakes his head.

'No.' I smile. 'Well this is a treat.' I grin as I place the timber between his ankles and rest the sledge hammer against the table.

'Right, well, there are a few ways this can go,' I say walking over to her and grabbing her by the hair, forcing her to her knees as she faces him. 'Lilith Baxter.'

'Yes Michael.' Her voice trembles.

'Option one, you tell me, and you can both leave here… alive. Not my favourite option but, I'm pressed for time.'

I turn to the table and run my hands over a selection of knives before selecting one.

'Option two, I torture him till you tell me.' I say standing next to him.

'Option three, my favourite.' I say walking over to her, grabbing her hair and pulling her head back.

I run the tip of my knife over her throat while looking down at her. 'I have my way with you, using my toys, while he watches. Then my friends with questionable desires have their way with him and you. This will be followed by torture and death.' I say looking between them both.

'So, Lilith what's your decision?'

She takes a deep breath and her body trembles. She begins to cry.

'Agent David Ryan' She says.

I look over to Brian.

'Check it!'

'I'll have an answer in fifteen minutes for you.' Brian leaves the room.

'Fifteen minutes, I could have some fun I guess.' I grab her and throw her on to the bed and get on top of her.

'You see, Anthony' I don't bother to look at him.

'Women are only good for three things, cooking, cleaning, and fucking. And when they don't do as they are told, I punish them.'
I start slapping Lilith, only stopping when her lip and nose bleeds.

'Our Lilith here was one of the rats that found Chantelle after her punishment. I was having a very bad day only to come home and find that she didn't cook my dinner how I told her to.' I say getting off the bed. 'Chantelle spent four days cuffed to that very bed. I beat her for three days, she looked perfect—a masterpiece. I broke her nose, jaw, eye socket, and both collarbones. I fucked her so hard her hips dislocated.' I take a breath. This is getting me somewhat excited and very hard.
I look at Anthony and he looks pale. I laugh at the sight of him.

'From what I remember I broke her arms, legs and pelvis. I believe that she was also bleeding internally. I hit her hard with this.' I hold up my gun.
'I cracked her skull. I remember the sound of her bones breaking and her screams. She knows how much hearing her screams and begging for me helps soothe the beast in me. Chantelle needs me, she is lost without me. The best part is, I film it all so I can watch it over and over again—such pleasure. Do you want to see my favourite?' I ask him as I grin with evil intent.
He shakes his head.
'No? Oh come on Anthony. It's perfect jacking off material.' I say 'Sam, bring in the laptop.'
Sam nods and leaves to get it. A couple of minutes later he comes back with a laptop on a trolly.

I drag Lilith over to watch my masterpiece.
'I've taken the liberty of shortening it since we don't have time to watch it all. You'll be watching all the best bits! Lucky you!' I laugh.
Oh, I'm enjoying myself. I laugh as Anthony throws up and Lilith cowers. I make sure they watch the video of me as I break Chantelle's bones.
'Michael,' Brian says walking in.
'Yes, Brian,' I put my hand up to signal just a minute, my eyes don't leave the laptop.
'Anthony you need to watch this, this is where I break her pelvis with a baseball bat.' I say to Anthony and Lilith.
Hearing Chantelle scream as she chokes on her own blood is fucking beautiful, pure poetry.

Anthony throws up again, fucking pussy, I laugh at him.
'Intel is good.' Brian says.

'Right, party is over let's pack up and get these two love birds home.' I look at Brian.
'Brian.'
'Yes, Michael,'
'Can you please take them home and tuck them in?'
'Of course.' Brian replies with a grin.

The boys pack up everything back onto the truck as I'm driven back to the airport.
I read over Chantelle's hospital records and it reads like a Shakespearian masterpiece.
I get to the part where they removed her implants due to being ruptured but they didn't replace them, that pisses me off.
They were big and beautiful with her long auburn hair and green eyes.
I fucking want her back, she is mine, I own her.
But, I think to myself, I will have to thank them for fixing her for me to break all over again.

My phone rings.
'Brian.'
'Done.' He says directly.
'Excellent, see you at home.' I hang up.
'Sam, I would like to meet the surgical team that worked on Chantelle.' I request as I close the files.
'Of course.' Sam replies as he drives.

☷ ELIZABETH ☷

I get woken by Dominic leaving a trail of kisses down my back.
'Morning' I say rolling over.
'Morning' He replies, pulling me into him.
'What time is it?' I ask.
'A bit after five-thirty, do you want to go for a walk on the beach?' He asks as his finger brushes the hair from my face and tucks it behind my ear.
'Sounds great.' I smile
'You get dressed and I'll make coffee,' He says.
'The clothes.'
'Already picked them up.' He answers before I finished.
'Thank you.'

He gets up from our bed and helps me up.
'Now that's a view that gets better every day.' He says kissing me.
He leaves me to get dressed.
I'm standing in my walk-in closet looking down at my locked cabinet. It has everything in it footage, photos, my medical files, interviews.
I will show him when I work up the courage.
I brush my teeth and walk out onto the deck, he is standing with his back to me.
I walk up behind him and slide my arms around him.
'Hey you,' I say to him.
'There's my girl.' He says turning in my arms and holding me tight.
'How are you this morning?' I ask him.
'Great and you, how are you feeling?'
'I feel,' I breathe in. I love his scent. 'I feel fantastic.' I reply.
I feel him hold me tighter and kiss the top of my head.
'Let's go for our walk.' I say.

He hands me my travel mug and takes my hand. We walk hand in hand to the beach. We walk where Daniel attacked me. I don't realise I have stopped till Dominic touches my face.
'Liz…'
'Sorry, I just…' I pause. 'I…'
'Hey look at me.' He says as his hand brings my eyes to meet his.
'Do you want to go home?'
'This was my safe place, and now it's tarnished. I don't know if it will ever feel safe again.'
'Liz. If you want to, you could…'
'I'll be okay, Dominic, I have you. Thank you.' I smile at him.

He has become my whole world.
'For what?'
'Making my scars easier to bear, accepting me and helping me heal. I feel like I'm slowly becoming who I was before everything.' I blush as his hand brushes my cheek.
'I'm not going anywhere, I'm here for you.' He says, leaning in and kissing me softly.
'Come on, the beach awaits us.'

We sit on the beach and Dominic sits behind me, holding me against him.
I tell him about my family.
My mum Janice, a primary school teacher, and my three grandmothers taught me my love of cooking.
My dad, Philip, who passed away when I was two.

How my grandfathers taught me to shoot and cricket.

My stepdad, Mark, a mechanic who taught me cars, motorbikes, football, and how to surf.

And lastly my twin brothers, Jonathan and Travis.

I may have been the older sibling but they still looked after me like I was their little sister.

I tell him that I never had a boyfriend at school, high school or when I travelled with friends, not even when I started studying and working, and how I never kissed anyone.

I tell him my regrets and how meeting him changed who I thought I would become by making it better.

'Of all the things that have happened and the events that have led me here,' I turn to face him.

'I will always be thankful for everything you have done and given me.' I say reaching up and touching his face.

He smiles as he leans in and kisses me.

It's not a hard kiss or one that shows dominance, but it still causes my body to react to him.

It's just after 7am when we get back home, and Amber is having breakfast on the deck.

'How's my favourite lovebirds?' She asks.

'We are great.' Dominic replies. 'How about…'

'I'm great.' She smirks, cutting Dominic off.

'Would you like a cuppa?' I ask her.

'I would love a nice big hot coffee.' Her grin is huge and she looks very smug.

'I'll go make them.' Dominic says as he kisses my cheek and hastily retreats.

'What?' I ask her.

'Oh, you know.' Amber winks.

'You have lost me, where are you going with this?'

'I just love seeing you and Dominic together. You two are like the perfect couple.'

'Okay, I'll go help Dominic.'

'You do that. Don't rush.' She still has a huge grin on her face.

I walk inside, Dominic has just finished making coffee.

'What's with Amber?' He asks.

'I don't know, it's like she knows something we don't.' I answer.

He shrugs.

'I'm game if you are.' He looks at me.

We walk back out and I hand Amber her coffee as Dominic sits down.

'Okay, we will bite what's going on?' I ask as I remain standing.
'Oh my dear Liz, you really are a saucy little minx, and you my dearest Dominic,'
She pauses.
'You two look really good on the daybed together.'
I look at Dominic and then to Amber, my cheeks burn red with embarrassment.
Well, fuck me, she is never going to let us live this down.
Amber is like a dog with a bone, a big scary police dog.
'So is this a regular thing for me to find when I come home late?' She asks.
'Well, the daybed is sturdy.' I shrug as I have a mouthful of coffee.
Amber sits there, stunned, looking at me, as Dominic chokes and spills his
coffee then drops the cup as he tries to put it on the table.
'I'm going for a shower.' I say and I quickly retreat.
I wrap my wrist and get in the shower.
I feel a sense of pride that I made Amber blush and completely lost for words.
I have never really made suggestive comments like that, she must be rubbing
off on me.

'Sturdy,' Dominic says behind me with a stifled laugh.
'The daybed is sturdy.' He repeats my sentence.
'Well it's true.' I say turning around to face him.
Dominic is leaning up against the door frame, his arms are folded and he is
holding his shirt covered in coffee.
'What?' I ask him, as I turn the water off and wrap myself in a towel.
'Sturdy' He says again with a stifled laugh.
'Well it's true, it's not like we were exactly easy on it.'
'No, I guess we weren't,' He says, walking towards me.

His eyes haven't left mine.
'We could compare it to your lounge, although it's been a while,' I smile.
'You may have to.'
I start to remove my towel.
'Remind me,' I say biting my bottom lip and dropping my towel.
Turns out I need another shower, apparently, I missed a spot.
Good thing my shower wall is also sturdy.

Luke and the kids arrive not long after our 'shower', and I'm whisked away to
the playroom, leaving Dominic and Luke to fend for themselves as they hunt
for chocolate cake.
'It's behind the beer, Uncle Dom,' Lily calls out.
'Thank you, princess.' Dominic sings out from the kitchen.
'And the vegetables.' Jack adds.
'Thanks, bud.' Luke replies.

After a Mario Cart series win, I leave them to play and head into the kitchen.
The cake container is sitting on the bench and most of the cake is gone.
I smile, best I make another cake and some biscuits and cupcakes as well.
I turn on the oven and head downstairs to put on a load of washing.
Dominic is on the phone out on the grass and Luke is cutting timber.
I notice Dominic is still eating cake while he is on the phone and judging by his body language, it's his mum.
I check on the kids before I start cooking, they are asleep on the sofa bed cum indoor trampoline cum pillow fight arena and nerf gun battle cover.
I smile again as I head into the kitchen and start cooking.
I check on the kids again, they are still asleep when I head down to hang out the washing.
I hum to myself while thinking about groceries and takeout for lunch.

I feel familiar arms wrap around me.
'Hungry?' I ask him.
'Yep, I'm thinking take out.'
I giggle.
'What?' He asks, kissing my neck.
'That's exactly what I was thinking.' I say turning around in his arms.
'Really?'
'Yep, I was thinking either a bakery run or take away from the pub maybe Steak Sandwiches.' I reply, wrapping my arms around his neck.
'Bakery run.'
'Okay, I'll head into town. Do you have a list for me?' I smile.
'You're the best but I'll come with you.' Dominic says as he kisses me.
 How can a simple kiss make my body tingle with warmth from my head to my toes.
The twins have woken up and promise they won't let their dad sneak any of the treats I have just gotten out of the oven.
We have a deal.
Luke looks at Dominic, shakes his head and walks back downstairs.

Dominic and I head into town to the shops.
I have a list with strict instructions to buy more ice cream, cones, topping and this time I had better not forget the sprinkles.
I'm walking through the aisles grabbing a few extras for dinner tonight and lunch tomorrow.
'Elizabeth?' A voice says from behind me.
I turn to see Sheila walking up the aisle towards me.
'Hi, Elizabeth.'
'Hello Sheila, how are you?' I ask her.

'I'm good thank you. I'm sorry about my embarrassing outburst yesterday.'
'Look, don't worry about it. I'm happy to make out like it never happened. Besides, I'm sure you had your reasons and I won't judge you.'
'I appreciate that. But I still shouldn't have acted that way. I am very sorry.'
Sheila smiles.
I see Dominic walking up the aisle towards us.
'All forgiven.'
'Hello, ladies.' Dominic says as he walks past Sheila and stands next to me.
'Bye Elizabeth, Dominic.' She says brushing past us.
He puts his arm around me.
'What was that about?' Dominic asks.
'She was apologising for her outburst yesterday.' I reply.
'Take what that woman says with a grain of salt. You are paying Luke, so you are her meal ticket. You are also friends with Luke, and you are with me.'
'She doesn't like you?'
'She doesn't like rejection unless she is the one dishing it out.'
'Oh!'

We just pull into our driveway when my phone starts beeping.
'Who's that?' Dominic asks.
I look at him nervously and my hands start to shake.
Dominic stops his car and puts his hand over mine.
'Babe, it's okay, what's up?' He smiles and traces my scars.
I feel my body relax as he brings his lips to mine.
'Ahh, I get it, you think I'm upset about you getting a message? Liz my friends are your friends.'
I look at him and he smiles. He has just unknowingly given me permission.
Even though I have spoken to Luke and Simon by myself, I always worried about what Dominic would think.
I know it sounds stupid but it feels like a whole weight has been lifted off me.

I smile and touch his face.
He kisses me and manages to pull me onto his lap.
He holds me tight and deepens our kiss.
Oh, he makes me swoon.
He always knows just how to take me to another level of joy and pleasure.
Dominic's hands slide under my shirt and gently squeeze my sides.
I remember his question and answer, 'Umm it's Simon, he wants to come over this afternoon with a few people to finalise the party. I tell him to come around five-ish. I'll order pizza and pick it up from the pub.'
'I'll go,' He says his fingers move along my cheek as his other arm still holds me to him.

'Take my new car when you go.'
'You have driven your car once Liz'
'My hand hurts if I do, and I don't want her just sitting there not being driven. Besides broken wrist plus gear changes equals not nice feeling. But I'm looking forward to getting her on to a skid pad and having some fun. I'm going to book her in to have some work done to the engine. I reckon I can get a few more horses under the hood.'

Dominic smiles and shakes his head
'What?'
'Next you'll be wanting a dirt bike?' He kisses me softly.
'Now that sounds like fun, I had a Yamaha and a Honda but I've always wanted a Ducati road bike. Looks like I'm going shopping.'
'You can ride mine, I have two dirt bikes, just need to get them fixed. The Ducati looks better with you riding it anyway.'
'I would love to. Give me a few weeks for this cast to be taken off, then we will see how it handles holding on to the handle bars of a bike..' I say holding up my hand.
'How about you and I go for a ride next week to Agnus for a short getaway?'
'I would love that.' I smile at him.
'Right well we will go and get you some more gear.'
'I already got some, I just need boots. I had to get them ordered, they should be here by the end of the week.'
Dominic groans and kisses me. I can feel him smile.

Dominic and Luke head off around 5:45pm for the pub run and alcohol restock. Simon arrives with Sally and Sarah not long after, and Amber arrives with Cassie.
Jack and Lily has just let it slip that Luke bribed them to let him have some biscuits and cupcakes, but they stopped when it came to the cake.
They also give a full insight into their eventual victory over me in Mario Kart.

'We talked to mummy today and she is picking us up at six-thirty.' Jack says.
'Ok well maybe you and Lily should have showers and you can take the cupcakes with you.'
'Mummy won't let us.' Lily says looking at the ground
'Oh, I'm sure that it will be fine.'
'Nope, Jack said you cook better than she does, and then she started yelling at daddy over the phone. Daddy tried to be really nice and told her that your cooking isn't that good' Lily says looking at the deck.
'Is Daddy in trouble for lying?' Jack asks.
'I'll make a deal with you.'

'Okay!' They say in unison
'We won't mention this again and you can come over with your dad anytime you like. Deal?'
'Deal!'
'Okay, head in for showers, Lily you can use my bathroom and Jack you use the main.'

The kids run inside and I turn back to the table where they all start laughing.
'Oh man, I can just imagine what Sheila was like. I would have loved to have been here for that conversation.' Simon laughs.
'She is like a rodeo bull with lipstick, poor Luke.' Cassie says.
'Poor Luke, what?' Luke asks as he gets to the top of the steps.
'Hey, Luke, the kids are in the shower.'
'Thanks, Liz.'
'You finish up with them, I'll help Dominic.'
Luke nods and I head down to the garage. Dominic has just got the last of the stuff out of my car.
'Hey you, I came to help. Luke is with the kids.' I said.
'Good so I have you to myself for five minutes.'
'Just five minutes?' I ask him.
'I'll take what I can get.' Dominic grins as he pulls me to him.

He kisses me like he hasn't seen me for days.
I untuck his shirt and slide my hands under his shirt as his kiss intensifies, we don't even hear a car pull up.
We are lost in each other.
'Really!' A voice says.
We turn to see Sheila.
'Rub it in, why don't you!' She snaps.
'Sorry, Sheila, I…'
'Don't bother. Where are my kids?' She cuts me off.
'Upstairs, I asked them to have showers so you didn't have to worry about it.'
'Wow, mother of the year material, aren't you!'
'That is enough Sheila!' Dominic yells at her and steps between Sheila and I.
'Whatever, Dominic.' She says sarcastically and walks off.

Dominic sends Luke a warning message and turns back to me.
'Hey, come here. Are you all right?' He hugs me.
I nod and let him hold me.
'I booked my bike to get serviced. I will take it in tomorrow.' He says as he runs his finger through my hair.

'I booked our Agnus weekend from next Friday night to Sunday night.' I sigh and hold him tighter.

'You look upset babe...' Dominic says as he lifts my face.

'I'm tired and I hate feeling like a bad person when I haven't done anything wrong.'

'Shelia?'

I nod.

'Don't worry about her. She can say what she wants but we all know the truth about her.'

Dominic kisses me softly.

'Let's get this food up there before they come looking for it.' He smiles.

Dominic and I take the pizza upstairs and Sheila is in the kitchen going through the kids bags.

'I'll put some pizza in a container for the kids.'

'I can cook!' She snaps

'I'm sorry, I didn't mean, I...' I turn and walk outside sitting at the table.

Simon and Amber look at me, I'm trying not to show how much this is affecting me.

'Bye, Aunty Lizzy,' The kids say running up to me and hugging me as Luke and Sheila walk out of the house.

'Bye, now you be good, deal?'

'Deal,' They high-five me.

'Hey, Mummy,'

'Yes, Jack.'

'Uncle Dom is going to marry Aunty Lizzy, but if he doesn't, I want to marry her.' He says grinning.

'Yes, and they will have twins like us.' Lily adds.

'I highly doubt that.' Sheila says looking at me.

'Why, Mummy?' Jack asks her.

'Well Aunty Lizzy here is barren. She made sure that she can't have kids and Uncle Dominic wants kids. He would never really love someone like her. He will tire of her, they won't get married and he will leave her for someone who he can have kids with. And you, Jack, you are too good to marry someone like her.'

We are all in shock as she grabs the kids' hands, smiles at me and leaves.

'I'll get some plates.' I say getting up before anyone could say anything.

'Liz...' Luke stops me

'Don't,' I cut him off and walk inside.

I don't even look at him.

I stand at my bench with my arms wrapped around myself.

I feel sick and my chest hurts.
I don't understand why she would say such horrible things.
I have never done anything to her.

'Liz,' Amber says coming inside and touching my shoulder.
'Why?'
'Why what, hun?'
'I have more right than anyone to be mean, horrible and rude, instead…'
'Instead what?'
I put my hands on the bench and I feel my tears fall.
'Instead I have to look at myself every day, knowing the one thing I wanted most in my life was taken from me. I have to look at the man I love more than anything in the world knowing I can never bear his children to give him the one thing he wants. I already don't feel good enough for him let alone a stranger telling everyone I'm not,' I start to cry.
'Liz,'
'I love him, Amber'
'Liz…'
'What am I going to do?'
She doesn't answer me.
I wipe my face and pick up the plates and turn around.
No, no, no he is standing there.
I hand Amber the plates.
'I should probably go, yeah I should um…' I say looking at the floor.

I walk to our room, my whole body is shaking as I pick up my bag and keys.
I hear the door close and I take a deep breath and turn around.
He removes his hat, sunnies, boots and socks.
Not once does his eyes leave mine.
He begins untucking his shirt as he walks towards me.
I watch his hands start to unbutton his shirt. He comes to stand in front of me.
His fingers begin to unbutton my shirt.
His hands move to my neck before sliding under my shirt, pushing it from my shoulders and letting it fall to the ground. My shorts join my shirt.
'Dominic, I…'
'Shh.' He says quietly.

He removes my bra and pants.
My body reacts to him, my breathing gets quicker.
I lick my lips and take a deep breath as his hands move up my body.
I start to undo his belt but my hands are shaking, he finishes it and removes his shorts and pants.

He brings his hand to rest on my neck as he runs his thumb along my jaw.
I feel his other hand rest on the small of my backm holding me to him.
His eyes look at my lips as I bite my bottom lip.
Dominic pulls me in tighter, his kiss starts off soft and becomes hungrier.
He lays me down on our bed, looks at me and smiles.

'I don't care about what she said. I know you can't have children and I'm still here not letting you go.'
He kisses me again. 'I'm not letting you go, Elizabeth.' Dominic says as he rests his head over my heart and holds me.
I run my fingers through his hair and close my eyes.
This intimate moment wasn't about sex, it is about Dominic and I together.
My safe place in his arms.

'Liz, Dominic,' Amber knocks on our door.
'Just give us a minute we will be out shortly.' Dominic lifts his head and replies.
'Ok, we will wait for you.'
He looks back down at me and smiles, I melt every time he smiles at me.
'I'm not done with you.' He winks.
Dominic helps me up off the bed and pulls me into him.
I am in love with this man.
We get dressed and head back out onto the deck, everyone is still here.
Amber quickly comes over to me followed by Luke.

'I'll make her pay for it.' Amber says.
'And how do you think you will do that?' Luke asks.
'Oh, my dear Luke, that's the beauty of having this badge, gun, handcuffs and a get out of jail free card.' Amber replies, winking at him.
'You're a…'
'Yep, a bona fide special cop who moved here with her bestie.' Amber says hugging me.
'Now who is hogging 'my' girl?' Dominic says as he grabs my arse and kisses me.
He winks as he hands me a drink.
'Shall we eat? I'm…'
'Hungry? Shocker.' I say cutting her off.
'See, she is my bestie.' Amber smiles.

We spend the next couple of hours planning the final touches of Louise's birthday party.
I have the menu set so tomorrow, I'll book extra tables and chairs along with a cooler trailer to hold all the extra food and drinks.

Sixty people, I won't lie, I'm more than a little nervous, especially with the loss of my wrist for a while.

It also means there will be people here in my home that I don't know.

After the thing with Sheila, I'm a bit nervous.

Everyone has left except for Amber and Cassie.

They look really happy together, Cassie is absolutely adorable.

Amber has this look on her face and I know something is going on.

'Okay what?' I ask Amber.

'How did you know?'

'You are my best friend, so what's up?' I smile at her.

'I need, sorry, we need to ask you a favour.'

'Yes.' I answer her, I know what she is going to ask before she even asks.

Amber and Cassie look at me.

'Yes, Cassie can move in.' I smile at them.

'It won't be for a couple of months till my lease is up.' Cassie says.

'That's fine, it's plenty of time. I'll get Dominic and Luke to make some more changes downstairs and it's all yours.'

'I have a better idea.' Dominic says walking back onto the deck.

'And what is your idea?' I ask him as he comes up alongside of me.

'You could move in with me, if you want, and Amber and Cassie can rent this house.' He looks at me.

'You mean, I, you want, I…' I start to panic.

He wants me to live with him!

He just asked if I want to move in with him.

I look at the ground and start to rock and shake.

'Liz, look at me,' He moves in front of me.

'You don't have to say yes or no right now. All I want is you and me together wherever you are. But I mean it, please just,'

'Yes,' I whisper.

'Yes?'

'Yes, I'll move in with you.' I answer him.

Dominic pulls me in and holds me tight.

'Thank you,' He says.

'What for?' I ask him.

'For taking a chance on me and saying yes.' He replies.

'Really I should be…'

'No,' He cuts me off and smiles.

He kisses me softly.

I don't realise that Amber and Cassie has left till Dominic and I move to the daybed.

We lay down and look at the stars and listen to the ocean.

He holds me against him running his fingers through my hair.

He asked me if I wanted to move in with him, not tell me, just asked.

I can't explain what that means to me but I'm so happy right now.

We just lay together in silence holding each other.

'Dominic?'

'Yeah, babe,'

'About what I said in the kitchen. I'm sorry, I know that you are not ready to…'

'Don't apologise, you were being honest. I suspected that you felt that way and honestly, I feel good about it.'

'Even though I can't give you children?'

He sighs, releases me and sits up.

'Liz, just because you can't physically give me children doesn't mean we can't have kids. If we want kids together, we will find a way.' He turns to me and smiles.

His hands cover mine and I look up at him and smile.

'I'll be a surrogate.' Amber says behind us.

'So would I.' Cassie adds.

I turn to face them.

I didn't hear them come back.

'Really?'

'Amber told me about your ex. He sounds like an asshole abusing you for not being able to have kids. You deserve to be happy, and if you and my brother from another mother asks, my answer is hell yes!' Cassie says smiling.

'You know I love you. I would do it even if you weren't with Dominic.'

'Wow, I was totally not expecting that. I don't know what to say, thank you doesn't seem to even be enough.' I get up and hug them both.

'See after everything you have endured, being a good person and a loving person. It draws people to you and they will support you no matter what.' Dominic says as he kisses my cheek and hugs Amber and Cassie.

'Goodnight, ladies, my girl and I are going to bed.' Dominic says as he takes my hand.

'Oh, before I forget,' I say, turning to Amber and Cassie.

'There is a box under the daybed with blankets now.' I wink at Amber.

'Yes, the daybed is sturdy,' Dominic says and winks before scooping me up and putting me over his shoulder, taking me inside.

I wake up before Liz the next morning and sit up on my elbow watching her sleep as my eyes follow her curves.
Her old scars mixed with new ones.
I think over everything that has happened in the time I have been with her.
I look at Liz and I know without a doubt I want it all with her now.
I want to tell her I love her.
I would marry her today if I could.
But I want to wait, I want it to be perfect for her.
I want to wait till this case is over so she can enjoy it.
I need to talk to Amber.
I don't want anything to stop her from nailing that fucker to the wall.
He is never going to get her.
'Hey you, what are you thinking?' Liz touches my face.
'You look like you are deep in thought, intense even...'
'No...' I answer her before she finishes asking me. 'Do you want to go for a walk on the beach?' I ask her.
'We could wrap my wrist and take the boards down.' She suggests.
I look at her and smile, she is definitely my girl.

'I'll go check the conditions. I'll be back asap.' I lean in and kiss her.
I jog down to the beach. It's beautiful but also as flat as a lake.
Oh well, walk it is.
I turn to walk back and stop where Daniel attacked her.

I remember her screams for help, calling my name, fighting back and trying to get away.
I remember seeing her trying to get back to me.
Her statement to the police.
She told them how she got slammed into the tree.
Seeing her bleeding and hurt but still trying to get away from him and get to me.
I drop to my knees.
I came so close to losing her it's hard to bear.
I feel physically sick remembering him on top of her.
His hands on her, hitting her, and yelling at her.

'Dominic? Dominic? What's wrong, are you okay?'
I look up to see her running towards me.
I get up and go to her, picking her up and holding her tight.
'What happened?

I came out onto the deck and saw you drop.'
I kiss her like it's going to be our last.
'Sorry to worry you.' I look up at her.
'Dominic please what happened? Did you hurt yourself?' Liz asks me.
I sigh and rest my head on her chest listening to her heart beating.
I feel her kiss the top of my head and her hands trying to soothe me.
I put her down and look in her eyes, my Liz, beautiful and incredible Liz.

'No, I'm not hurt, but the pain of thinking I almost lost you buckled me. I almost lost you because I wasn't there for you—I feel like I failed you' I looked at her.
'Hey look at me, You did not fail me.' She takes my hand and puts it over her heart and smiles, her eyes shine.
'You know how I feel about you, do you want me to give you some time to yourself?'
'No!' I say. 'I don't want to be where you're not.'
'Do you still want to go to the beach? Or do you want to go back to the house?' Liz asks me.
'Let's go sit on the beach, I just want to hold you.' I say, playing with her hair.
'Sounds good.' Liz says, taking my hand.
We walk down to the beach and I sit behind her holding her tight.
I replay our first kiss. I was sitting behind her like I am now.
I softly kiss her shoulder and run my hands along her arms and intertwine my fingers with hers.
It's having the same effect on her now as it did that day.

'Did you bring your guitar?' She asks me.
'You remembered.'
'Of course,' She giggles.
She turns and looks at me.
'I was so scared, I almost cancelled that Friday morning before the beach day with your friends. It was the reason Amber left me a note asking me to cook all that food. We arrived and you were surrounded by beautiful girls and then there was me. Plain, boring, damaged, and nothing to offer you. I wanted just one night with you, one night to know what sex felt like.' She looks at me.
'All my shrinks told me the same thing. I wasn't in love with him, and looking back now, I can see it. I was groomed from day one. We went out for my birthday. It was one of the last times I saw my family. He got so drunk and when I got him home, I decided to leave. My mistake was that I didn't tell anyone. I packed my bag and went to the bathroom to get my toiletries. That's where he found me.'

She starts to shake her voice breaks, my fingers trace her scars trying to sooth her. 'He wanted sex, he demanded it, he said that he owned me, I was his to do with whatever he wanted. I politely declined and he started to beat me with whatever he could get his hands on—I've never experienced such fear before in my life. I managed to get around him when he stumbled but he caught me and threw me across the hallway into a glass cabinet. He used the broken glass to cut my shoulder here.' She says pulling her shirt down to show the three jagged scars on her shoulder blade.
'He then held a knife to my throat while he raped me. When he was done, he told me it was my fault and like an idiot I believed him.'

I wipe her tears away and kiss her softly.
'I would do it all again if it was my only path to you.'
I pull her in and hold her tight. I know she has given me a watered down version of the real event.
God, it's got to be hard for her to open up about it when all she wants to do is probably forget it.
I don't press her. If she needs to drip feed it to me, then I'm totally fine with that—whatever she needs to do.
I don't want her to be ashamed.
I will love her unconditionally.
'Thank you for telling me, Elizabeth.'

We sit for ages not saying anything.
I just hold her till she stops shaking.
She has had so much taken from her, and I want to give her my everything to make up for it.
'What's your plans for today?' I ask her.
'Shopping for the party and Louise's gift. I remember her saying that her sister is overseas so I was thinking of getting her a travel voucher so she can go visit her.'

'Can I ask you a question? Don't answer if you don't want to.' I ask her.
'Okay.' She replies.
'The money?' I ask her.
'When I was helping them, a group of agents managed to skim money and assets on the down low. At the time I thought it was for evidence. It turned out that it was for me. They did it in a way that couldn't be traced and gave it to me when I went into hiding. The problem is they don't know all of Michael's businesses and I wasn't privy to everything. What they managed to seize was only a small portion of his wealth'
'How much?'

'Um 6.8million. Some was cash and the rest were liquidated assets classed as proceeds of crime and seized by the government. Amber calls it legal laundering.'

'Um wow.' I'm a little shocked.
She looks at me with a questioning look.
'So, I'm dating a super sexy millionaire.' I look at her and give her a wink.
'The dating and millionaire parts are correct.' She blushes.
'Oh no the super sexy is definitely correct. I still think about your red underwear and oversized white shirt. Best greeting ever.' I smile at her.
'You did see? I was kind of hoping that you didn't.'
'Yep, you were opening the kitchen window and I almost dropped my book. I was almost completely speechless.' He laughed.
She blushes again.
'Your shoulder was exposed and that red bra strap. Your hair is longer now. I was so happy when you sat beside me, you smelled amazing. I had to work hard to maintain my dignity that day—it was so difficult. By the end of the appointment all I wanted to do was kiss you.' I say with a smile.
'I wanted you to as well! I was too nervous to tell you, and then your phone rang and I lost any courage I did have to tell you what I wanted you to do to me.' She giggles as she blushes.
'What?' I ask her.
'Amber would not shut up after you left, she picked up on whatever was going on and I had no idea, of course, I thought it was just my wishful thinking. I have never made so much cake in my life. She wanted to take me shopping as she thought my wardrobe was lacking some essential outfits required to keep you interested.'
'I don't know, that shirt and red underwear definitely have my approval.'
'I'll be sure to remember that.' Liz blushes again.

'Come on, I have to work unlike some other people I know.' I say standing up.
'So, when do I get to see your pool boy skills?' She asks looking up.
'What makes you think I'll be your pool boy?' I ask, helping her up.
'I did buy a red bikini,' Liz looks at me.
'My place this afternoon,'
She laughs as I pull her in and kiss her.
'I may have to purchase a strong daybed,' I say smiling at her.
'I'll bring the little black box,' Liz winks at me.
Ahh she's killing me, I think, as I pick her up.
She wraps her legs around me and returns my kiss.

Liz ends up ordering all the party food for delivery the week before the party.
After I get back from dropping my bike off, I have to endure watching her move around the kitchen and house. It is pleasurable torture.
Every time I see her, I smile.
I finish up and find her in the shed packing food into the freezer.
'Hey, would you like a hand?' I ask as I pick up some containers.
'Yes please.' She smiles.
'You've been a little distant today, is everything okay?' she asks me.
'I've just been thinking about what you said. I know you're giving me the PG version of what happened to you.' I say.

She is nervous, I see her fingers trace the scars on her neck and collarbone which she always does when she's nervous.
Her fingers then trace the scar on her wrist when she wants to say something but doesn't know how. When she goes into protection mode, her body language stiffens and her breathing becomes rapid.
'Liz, I'm not ashamed of you, your past, or your scars. I'm only interested in you, your heart, your soul, you inside, but I am totally loving the you on the outside too!' I smile.
I tuck loose locks of hair behind her ears and trace her scars. Her body starts to calm as she smiles too. I hold her tight.
'Thank you,' she whispers
'So, I have some good news, well kind of.' I say kissing the top of her head.
'Mmm.'
'Well with the delay in some materials, I called it a day. So now I get to show off my pool boy skills if you're up for it.'
'My bag is already in your car.' She giggles.
'Thank god, because I have endured just the thought of you in a red bikini all day and it has not gone well.'

'I thought I heard a lot of swearing. What happened?' Liz looks up at me concerned.
'Made a couple of mistakes, Luke thought it was fantastic and wanted to know what had me so, flustered.' I reply.
'And my suspicions have been confirmed.' Luke says walking into the shed.
'What did you do or say to him? Because I have never enjoyed watching him struggle to focus as much as I have today. Every time he saw you he would gush like a school boy over the hot teacher. Liz, did he tell you he walked straight into a wall?'
'Are you done, Luke?' I chuckle.
'A solid wall, Elizabeth, while he was watching you, it was great.' Luke was laughing.

'How many times did you drop your hammer, Dom?'
'Fuck off, Luke.' I say.
'Aw man best day ever, even better than the day after he met you,' he says continuing to laugh his head off.

'Okay, okay, okay…cold beers in the fridge upstairs.' I cut him off.
'Right well, before I completely embarrass my boy anymore, I'll go and get the beer. Oh, but before I forget, the stove guy rang. They found it in Sydney. It won't be here for at least another week or so.'
'Thanks, Luke. And we need to have a chat, I'm interested in knowing more about our boy Dominic here.' Liz says.
I look at her.
'No, no you don't.' I say to her.
The smile on her face gives it away that she is totally enjoying herself. She looks from me to Luke as he says, 'It can be arranged, information in exchange for food.'
'Asshole! You're supposed to be on my side.' I give him a stifled laugh.
'If roles were reversed?' He looks at me.
'True.' I shrug.
Luke laughs as he walks out.
'I hate you!' I call after him.
'No you don't.' He replies.

'So, do I get to hear about what happened the day after we met?' She asks me.
I look at her.
'I could always ask Luke. I'm sure he would be,'
I silence her with a kiss, I can feel her smiling. I hate Luke.
'Come on we have a date with my pool, and my bruised ego needs tending.' I smile at her.
'Two minutes,' she winks at me.

'Can you please grab the bag off the back seat of my car?'
'Sure.' I open the back door of her car.
'I'm not sure how long you will be in it though.'
'In what?'
'The bikini.'
'Well there isn't much material anyway, so…'
'Shit!' I say as I slip and hit my head on the door frame.
She laughs and says, 'you okay?' before laughing again.
'Yep just great.' I say lying on my back on her back seat.
'Poor baby, do you want me to kiss it better?'
'Yes.'

Liz climbs in as I sit up. She removes my hat and runs her fingers through my
hair as I pull her on to me.
Liz gently kisses the top of my head.
'Is that better?'
'No, you missed it. Just a little lower.'
'Now?'
'No, lower.'
'Now?'
'Lower.'
Her hand touches my cheek.
'Now?'
'Little to the left.'
Her lips touch mine.
'Now?'
'Perfect.'
I hold her to me, she matches my hunger, my desire.

'Come on, pool boy.' Liz smiles at me as she gets out of the car.
'So, what's in the bag?' I ask as I get out of the car.
'It's, um, kind of a gift for you.' She smiles and looks at the floor.
She is nervous.
'Kind of a gift?' I raise my eyebrow.
'Well I um, and then you…' Liz says blushing and running her fingers over her
scars.
She is really nervous.
'Ok, well I shall open it when we get home.'
'I um, kinda need it first.' She says with a quickening of her breath.
I put the bag on the car and smile as I walk up to her.
I hold her hand while my other hand traces her scars.
I bring my lips to hers and kiss her softly till she begins to relax.
'How do you always know what to do? Thank you,' she smiles
'Anything for my girl, so what do you want to do for dinner?' I ask her.
'I made your favourites,'
'Now we really have to go.' I say grabbing her hand, closing the car door and
getting the bag off the car.
She is laughing as I lead her out of the shed and up towards the stairs.

'Oh, guess what?' She asks.
'What?'
'I made some purchases a while ago and they are now ready for delivery. And
now that I will be living at your house,'
'Our house.' I correct her.

She stops for a second and looks at me, and I smile.
'Can I have them delivered to our home?'
'Of course, Can I ask what they are?'
'Juke box, pinball machine, arcade game and a pool table.'
'Can you get any sexier?'
'Well, hopefully the barely there clothing article in that bag you are carrying helps.'
'Shit!' I trip on the last step and end up on my back on the deck.

'Elizabeth, you broke him.' Luke laughs as he walks over with a beer for me.
'Funny, Luke,' I say sitting up and taking the beer.
'What have you done to him?'
'Nothing, I just told him that I bought a jukebox and a pool table.' Liz replies, picking up the bag.
'You forgot to mention the arcade game and pinball machine.' I say leaning up against the back of a chair having a mouthful of beer.
Luke is loving this. 'Asshole', I laugh to myself.
'All you need now is a dart board.' Luke says looking at me.
'There is one in the shed.' Liz replies.
'Sweet now teach her to surf and ride dirt bikes.'
Liz has a huge grin on her face as she walks between Luke and I.
'What?' Luke asks.
'I raced motocross as a kid till around nineteen, and I grew up surfing.' Liz turns back around and heads inside.
'You raced motocross?'
Liz nods as she walks in the door.

Luke stares after her for a while and has a few mouthfuls of beer before turning back and looking down at me.
'What the fuck, dude?' He grins.
I shrug.
'Do not fuck this up!' He points at me.
'I won't...'
'I'm serious because I will kick your arse if you do.' Luke cuts me off before I can say anymore.
'Aren't you supposed to be on my side?' I laugh.
'Vanilla slice, mate, I'm on the side of vanilla slice and whatever else comes out of that kitchen.'
'Well you'll be happy to know I asked Liz to move in with me. I asked her last night.'
'Fuck yeah! That's what I'm talking about, good!' He points to the 'ring' finger of his left hand and leaves.

I look down at the deck and smile to myself.
I have already organised the ring. It will be here in a few days.
I just need to have a chat with Amber and then wait for the perfect moment.
I'm lost in thought.
'Are you planning on staying down there?'
I look up
'No, I don't plan on…' I don't finish my sentence. I'm gob-smacked.
She walks out in a long coat and red high heels.
'I'll be in the car. Can you grab the containers off the bench for me please?'
I nod as she walks down the stairs.
I manage to carry the food and get to the Ute without falling or dropping it all.
I get in our Ute and smile at her.
Liz smiles back as her fingers trace her scars.
I hold her hand and kiss her fingers.

'Let's go home.'
'I would like that.' Liz replies.
She moves in her seat and I catch a glimpse of what looks like red lace.
My mind wanders, imagining my hand resting on that red lace, my fingers exploring in between her legs.
I only just manage to drive home and walk inside with the containers without making a fool of myself.
I'm completely taken by her.
'So can I please unwrap my present now?' I ask.
'I guess I should let you, considering that you have been flustered all day.' Liz looks up and smiles at me.
'You really are beautiful, you have no idea just how much.' I say as my fingers brush her cheek.
I watch her blush, her beautiful green eyes hold my future.

'You are my everything, my whole world and I will do whatever I can to give you everything you desire.'
'Liz, everything I desire is standing right in front of me.' I pull her in and kiss her.
'But, you're wearing too much.' I say, pushing her against the bench.
My hand traces the scar on her neck down to her collarbone.
I trace the scar softly with my fingers down to the first button and her breathing quickens while her hands hold the bench behind her.
I undo the button, and my fingers brush against her soft skin and lace.
I move the coat from her shoulder, mmm strapless I think to myself, as I kiss along her collarbone and shoulder.

My fingers then slide down to the second button.
'Knock, knock, Dominic, your front door is open,' Thelma my neighbour sings.
'Shit.' I say against Liz's shoulder and look up towards the front door.
'Hi, Thelma, I'll be with you in a minute.'
I place my hands either side of Liz and rest my head against her neck.
'Go, I'm not going anywhere. I'm home.'
I groan.
'Stay right where you are, don't move, don't,' I kiss her and pull away to look at her.

'Hi Thelma.' I say walking to the front door.
'Hello Dominic, sorry to bother you. Greg needs a hand, are you busy?' Thelma asks.
'No, I was just unwrapping some…' I pause, 'someone,' I think to myself.
'What does Greg need?'
'He is having trouble with the caravan, he has been trying to do it himself but we are leaving tomorrow and are you able to give him a hand for a bit?'
'Sure, I'll be over in a minute.'
'Thank you, Dominic.' Thelma smiles and leaves.

I close the door and walk back to Liz. She hasn't moved from where I left her.
'Can we continue later?'
Liz smiles and nods.
'I'll be right here.'
I kiss her like it's my last, smile and head to the front door.
'Dominic.'
'Yeah, babe?' I reply, turning around.
'Don't be long,' Liz says as she drops her coat to the floor, and turns to go up the stairs.
Fuck me! She looks um… oh fuck.
'Fuck!' I sigh.

She removes her hair clip and her auburn hair cascades down.
'Oh come on, Liz…Fuck!' I groan.
I watch her walk upstairs. I slowly walk backwards straight into my front door.
'Oh come the fuck on!'

All I can see is her tiny frame in delicate red lace.
Her strapless bra with red ribbon and silver heart dropping from her cleavage.
And the red lace panties low cut at the front and wraps around hugging her hips.

The back has a red ribbon criss-cross and the delicate lace sits perfectly on her arse.

It's not a G-string, it hides just enough to show exactly what she wants.

It doesn't help my predicament when she is holding the little black box.

And those red heels are just DAMN!

Just a bit turned into two hours. Greg and Thelma offer me a beer when we finish.

'Sorry as much as I would like to, I need to go.'

'So, when do we get to meet her?' Greg asks.

'The one who has you so smitten,' Thelma adds.

'You two are as bad as my parents.' I laugh.

'Yes, we probably are. We have caught a few glimpses of her, she is very beautiful Dominic.' Greg says with a smile.

'We will be back in a week Dom. We would love to meet her.' Thelma says. Greg takes her hand.

'Come on dearest, let's go finish packing so he can get back to unwrapping her.' Thelma chuckles.

I look at Greg.

'Hey, I may be old but I ain't dead.' They both laugh and wave as they walk away, hand in hand.

Nearly fifty years of marriage and they are still falling in love with each other every day. I love that.

I run home to my girl.

I walk back up the steps and look in. Liz is in the kitchen.

I stand there watching her move around the kitchen.

Her coat is on the back of the lounge, she still has the heels on but has a short red silk robe on.

I open the door as she looks up and smiles at me.

'You're home early.'

'What do you mean early?' I ask her.

'Well last time was long enough for me to make and ice a layered mud cake.'

'What are you making now?' I ask her.

'Your lunches, mini quiches, savory foods. I was just cleaning up, are you hungry?'

'Define hungry,' I say walking towards her.

Liz starts to untie her robe.

'I might have something to your liking.' She winks.

I look at my hands. They are covered in dirt and grease and I'm covered in sweat.

'I should shower,' I say looking up at her.

'Correction we should,' She smiles at me.
The doorbell rings.
'Hold that thought,' I say, as the doorbell rings again.

'Dominic? It's Louise.' Louise calls out.
'I'm coming, just a sec.' I call back, as I wash my hands.
'I'll go change. Your pool's heated right?'
'Yes, it is.' I smile.
Liz slides her high heels off and makes her way towards the stairs as I go to the door.

What the fuck does Louise want now?
I'm reaching the end of my patience with this shit.
I open the door and Louise walks in. Something is bothering her.
'Dominic, we need to talk about Elizabeth.' She says walking over to the kitchen and sitting on the bar stool.
'Oh yeah? Why?' I ask standing on the opposite side of the kitchen leaning against the stove.
'I've been speaking to a few people, she is a liar, she is not who she says she is.'
I roll my eyes.
'Who have you been speaking with?' I ask her.
'I asked around and did some research. I couldn't find anyone matching Elizabeth's description on social media. Sheila told me that Luke said Elizabeth tried to make a move on him and was trying to get with Daniel. Stephanie told me she found out Elizabeth paid someone to attack her and Daniel was trying to help her, you pointed the finger at the wrong person. I also know…'
'Just stop, Louise!'

I sigh as I run my hands over my face.
'Louise we have been best friends for a long time, that is the only reason I haven't told you to fuck off and get out.' I say looking at her. 'I'm over this bullshit, I really am and I have been extremely forgiving, it's getting old and you need to stop.'
She winces and looks taken aback by my comment.
'Dominic, she is lying to you. I'm your friend. I won't sit back and watch you get hurt. I had to tell you and as a friend I need to be there for you.'
I walk over to the buffet and pick up a folder and return to the kitchen. I drop it in front of her and open it.

'So, this is what Daniel did to her.' I say pointing to the pictures.
'These are when he attacked her the first time.' I say as I pull out photos and show her.

'These ones are her hospital room, when he attacked her the second time.' I say showing her the pictures of her battered and bloody.
All the colour drains out of Louise's face.
She looks from the pictures to me and I can tell she can't even comprehend it, she's shocked by them.
'Liz died on the table three times and had twelve blood transfusions. Over a week in a coma. This is what she looked like.' I show her the last few photos on my phone.
'Louise, I'm telling you, you don't know Elizabeth and you have treated her unfairly. You ignored her from the first day you met her. Stephanie was disgusting to her. Sheila was absolutely fucking horrendous to her. Elizabeth has been nothing but kind, warm, and welcoming to you all and everyone else I have introduced her to.' I was starting to get mad.
'But, Dominic I...'
'Enough Louise! I was there. I saw Daniel attack so did Luke.. I pulled him off her, Luke called the police. Simon treated them at the hospital.' I say with a raised voice.

'Dominic,'
'Did you come to the hospital?' I asked her.
'No.'
'Right, of all the people I introduced her to, you were the only one who didn't. You didn't see what we did.' I close the file and put it back and turn back to face her. 'I almost lost her. I almost fucking lost her!'
'I...'
'Don't bother, Louise. You need to ask yourself what you want, friendship or nothing, the ball is in your court now. It won't be a hard decision for me if you continue to push.'
'But, Dominic...'
'Fuck off and get out!' I turn and walk away from her.

I walk upstairs to my girl and find her sitting at the top of the stairs.
I can tell she is trying not to cry.
'Are you okay?' She asks me.
'I'm more concerned about you.' I say sitting on the step in front of her.

'She is right though. I am hiding things from you.'
'I know but you are not ready to tell me everything, I understand that. It doesn't mean you are lying'
'But I have files, tapes, photos, videos. I could show you at any time.'
'Are you ready?' I ask her.
My fingers trace her scars.

'No.' She whispers and sighs.
'Then that is good enough for me.'
I move up and hug her.
I hate that people have singled her out to say hurtful things.
She has been so kind to everyone and welcoming.
Allowing Luke to bring his kids over and spoiling them.
Giving away my treats to Simon.
She has even opened her home to host Louise's surprise birthday party.

'I hate coming in between you and your friends.' She says looking at her hands.
'Look, I don't know Louise's reasons for what she just did. But I have a feeling
that it has something to do with Stephanie and Sheila.'
I pull her onto my lap and rest my head on her chest, listening to her heartbeat.
We sit there for ages.
I don't want to let her go.
Every now and then, I feel a tear drop.

'Are you hungry? I'll make you something to eat.' She gets up.
She is retreating again, I can feel it.
'Liz,... I say grabbing her hand.
'Yes?' She doesn't even look at me.
'Don't shut me out okay?' I pull her back to me.
My fingers trace her scars and I kiss her cheek.
Her breathing changes and I can feel her smile as her arms wrap around me.

'Now I'm going to make you dinner, you like Vegemite toast right?' I say.
She smiles and giggles.
'There's my girl.' I say lifting her chin.
Her eyes are red, but she is still absolutely beautiful, I kiss her softly.
I notice that she never got changed.

'Please don't stop being friends with Louise because of me. She wanted you
before I came into your life. It would be hard for her to see us together.'
It surprises me that Liz is still concerned about my friendship with Louise even
after the vile way Louise has treated her.
'Liz,' I sigh. 'I don't want to have someone that toxic in my life. I appreciate what
you said. But the way she is pushing right now, that will end our friendship.'
'Even a friendship as long as the one you have had with Louise?'
'Yes. But right now I don't want to think about Louise and her,' I wave my hand
in a circle. 'Whatever it is that she is doing. I will deal with it later.' I rest my
forehead on hers. 'Right now all I want is you.'
I run my fingers down the side of her face and trace the scar on her neck.

I hold her tight and kiss her like she is my reason for living.

'Come on, I got you a new jar of Vegemite and a spoon with your name on it.' I say as I pick her up.

She giggles as I pick her up.

'Wow a whole jar, just for me?'

'It's a big jar,' I reply.

'Well I feel very special. Thank you.' She rests her head on my shoulder as I carry her downstairs and sit her on the bench.

'Sorry our night didn't go as you planned.' I say as I tuck a strand of hair behind her ear.

'It's okay. I haven't technically moved in yet so we can always have a redo. It does give me another reason to go shopping. But...' She wraps her legs around me and I place my hands on her thighs.

'The night is young and if your Vegemite on toast is amazing, then I might just let you have dessert.' Liz winks at me.

'Are you doubting my mad toasting skills?' I ask her.

'Gosh no, you make amazing toast but...'

She releases me and slides off the bench and walks towards the lounge.

'But what?' I ask her.

She turns back to face me.

'You don't work well flustered.' Liz drags her bottom lip into her mouth with her teeth.

She knows exactly what that does to me.

Liz unties her robe, turns, and lets it fall as she bends to get something out of her coat.

I hold the top of the bench.

Fuck that arse looks good in red.

Liz turns back around, holding the little black box.

'So, I propose a deal.' Liz looks at me blushing.

I can see her hands tremble, she is trying so hard not to be nervous.

I forget sometimes how new all this is to her.

'A deal, I'm listening.' I say walking towards her.

Her breathing is becoming quicker, but every now and then it catches—her chest still hurts her sometimes.

'We sample dessert to see if it's to your liking,'

'Well they say you eat with your eyes, and so far I'm very, very impressed.'

Liz looks up at me and smiles. Her smile is amazing and her eyes shine.

I take the box from her and put it down. I hold her hand and run my fingers over left her fingers. I want so badly to have her wear my ring.

I want to spend the rest of my life falling in love with her every day.
I want to shout to the world how much I love her.
'Tell me how you feel.' I ask her.
'Feel about what?'
'About me, I want to hear it, I want to see your face as you say it.'
'I love you, Dominic.'

CHAPTER 13
A Change In Plans

👀 MICHAEL 👀

Dalkeith, Western Australia.

'What do you mean you can't find him, Brian?!' I yell.
'Sorry Michael, he is overseas somewhere and, with no known family, I can't trace him. I do have a contact trying to locate him, though.'
'FUCK, FUCK, FUCK!' I yell slamming my fists against my desk.
'I want her back, she belongs to me, I fucking own her. I spent years training her she was fucking perfect and those fucking rats stole her from me.' I yell.
I'm so fucking angry I can feel the saliva leave my lips and I can hear my heart beating.
I need her back; she calms me, her cries soothe the savage beast in me as I fuck her.
Chantelle needs me; she loves me, she will do whatever I ask of her.

'Fucking find her, Brian!' I snarl.
'Michael...' Sam says, walking into my office.
'What?' I snap.
'The merchandise has arrived at the warehouse.' He replies.
'Excellent, when's the next shipment due?' I say as I try to calm myself.
'Fifteenth of September.' He replies, handing me the inventory.
'All survived, good it will be a tidy profit. I'll change the docking time and dock of the next shipment. Keep our friends with badges guessing.'
'I'll wait for your orders then.' Sam nods.
'Right, Sam, let's make some visits.'

I turn back to Brian.
'Brian, you find her, no one steals my property and gets away with it. When you find her, call me and watch her. I want to pick her up.'
'On it, I follow up some leads in Sydney, Melbourne and Tasmania.' Brian says before leaving my office.

I walk into the bathroom off my office to compose myself.

It's been more than two years without her, and it's getting harder to control myself.

I need her back, I fucking need her.

All these other bitches are nothing, but my Chantelle is perfect.

Remembering the sound of her blood dripping through the thin mattress on to the floor below makes my cock stiffen.

Her gargled criess as she chokes on her own blood.

The way her eyes roll into the back of her head as she passes in and out of consciousness.

Her screams as her hips dislocate.

Aaahh, I feel myself wanting to cum and I need the release.

Mmmm Chantelle.

I finish off, shower, and put on a fresh suit.

I walk back to my office.

Sam stands up and opens the door for me.

'How are the preparations going at my new property in Margaret River?'

'Ahead of schedule. Chantelle's room will be completed next week, and all the supplies will be there the following week.' Sam replies.

'Excellent, we will head there after we visit a couple of clients. I want to see it myself and find something to fuck.'

'I know just the place. Shall we head there now?' He asks.

We start walking downstairs.

'Yes.' The visits can wait a little longer.

'I need some attention,' He sneers.

The maid meets us at the bottom.

'Pardon, sir, this was just delivered to the gate.'

I look at her as I take the large envelope from her, she disgusts me.

'Make sure you have my bag packed. I'll be gone tonight for a minimum of three days.' I don't even look at her.

'Sir.' She nods and walks towards the kitchen.

The maid has no grace or aura of sweet perfection.

Chantelle on the other hand is pure, her movements are full of grace.

She fits perfectly against me and no one dares to question our love.

'May I ask what is in the envelope?' Sam asks as he opens the door for me.

'I had Donald blow up the file photos they took when they found Chantelle and stole her.'

Sam drives me for thirty minutes to a seedy brothel that is also owned by one of my clients.
'Matthew,' I say walking through the door.
'Michael,' He says as he walks up and shakes my hand.
'Visit, business or pleasure?'
'Both.' I nod and smile.
Sam hands Matthew a file.

'I'll get the girls for you.'
He reaches over the counter and pushes a button.
A minute later, five bitches walk out and stand in front of me.
I walk along the line up and stop in front of one with auburn hair.
Her body trembles slightly, bringing a smile to my face.

'When was her last client?' I ask.
'Fresh, you'll be her first,' He says pointing at the bitch.
'Michael, don't break the merch. You break it, you buy it.'
I grin because I do like to road test.
'Don't worry, Matthew, she's not my type.'
Chantelle is my type, and this bitch is no Chantelle.
Chantelle is soft and delicate, Chantelle is the red rose in my garden of thorns.
Her smell, her voice, her screams for me.
Chantelle will do anything for me without question.
Just the mere thought of her gets me hard.
I follow the bitch to her room.

I remove my suit jacket and lay it over a chair as I watch her.
I unbutton my cuffs and shirt and smile as I see a tear fall.
This is going to be fucking fun.
'Don't just stand there, I'm not the one putting on a show.'
I watch as she moves towards me and gets on her knees, her body trembles.
'Impress me.'

👀 DOMINIC 👀

I wake up, startled, to an empty bed.
I look at my phone and it's two in the morning, where is she?
I see the light on downstairs, I chuck on some track pants and go down.
I'm almost at the bottom of the stairs when I hear the hum of the dishwasher.
I see her sitting on the bench with a book.

She can't sleep, the jar of Vegemite is sitting on the bench and she has the spoon in her mouth.

I lean against the wall and smile as I watch her.
She looks at the stove, she is cooking something that smells good.
The last few months with her have been amazing.
She has been trying so hard to get better and heal.
I know she hasn't been sleeping well, it's the little things that can trouble her the most sometimes.
Last night, it was a news report about a missing police officer and his partner who had both left the force and moved to Melbourne from Western Australia.
The report went on to say that this is the fifth and sixth former police offers to go missing.
It really hit home when they mention the link to Australia's biggest organized crime syndicate.
I felt her body tremble so I pulled her in tighter and caress the scars on her neck.
She didn't have to say a thing, I knew exactly what she was thinking… Michael is coming for her.
He can come but he ain't going to get any fucking where near her.

Liz slides off the bench and bends down to look at the oven.
As she stands, I notice her hand as she pulls the spoon from her mouth, it's bandaged.
I smile as I watch her move around the kitchen quietly.
I get to watch her every day, my girl home with me.

She pulls the trays from the oven and sets them on the bench before turning off the oven.
Biscuits, they smell amazing.
I walk up behind her and wrap my arms around her.
'Hey you, what are you doing?' She says as she runs her hands along my arms.
'What are you doing is the real question?' I bury my face in her neck and take a deep breath.
'Sorry, did I wake you?' She asks, turning in my arms.
'I tried to be quiet.'
She pulls me in and kisses me softly.

'Why can't you sleep?' I ask as I run my fingers along her cheek before resting my hand on her neck covering her scar.
'I was like this whenever I moved after I left the hospital. Now that I'm going to live here with you, I just need to get used to my surroundings, smells, sounds.

This is what I do, I'm sorry if it annoys you.'
I smile at her and shake my head, she could never annoy me.

'And this?' I ask, lifting her right hand.
'Hot handle.' She replies.
'May I have a look?'
'I treated it, it will be okay.'
'Elizabeth?' I look at her.
She nods, and I lift her on to the bench and carefully and slowly unwrap her hand, she flinches.
'Geez, babe,'
'It's fine, Dominic. It looks worse than it is. It will be healed by Louise's birthday and I can still cook.'
'Liz…'
'I only just did it so don't worry. I could use your help though.'
'What do you need?' Holding her hand gently and kissing her fingers.
'I did the first lot of tempered chocolate but I may need you to pour the next layer.'
'Is that how you did this?'
'Yes.' She replies as I wrap her hand again.

I hold her against me.
It feels so good to have her here with me.
I kiss her head softly.
I stand there, holding her for a while before I realise she has fallen asleep.
'I love you, Elizabeth.' I say as I kiss the top of her head.
I gently carry her upstairs to bed, and fall asleep, holding her close to me.
I wake to find her already up and a note on her pillow.

You wouldn't wake up.
I'm on the beach
xo Liz.
P.S Coffee is on the bench.

I chuck on a shirt and some board shorts and head to the kitchen.
My travel mug and towel are on the bench with another note.

Dressed in red
xo

I pick up my mug and towel and look out towards the beach.
The sun is up with no clouds in the sky.

It's going to be a beautiful day, the perfect start to spring.
I look to find her, but I can't.
Smiling, I turn towards the stairs just as I hear the door downstairs.
I race down and see her walking towards the beach, dressed in a red sarong and holding a towel.
I run after her.
'Liz,'
She turns around and smiles.
She looks tired, she hasn't slept well, I can tell.
Still absolutely beautiful though.
'Hey you.' Liz smiles as I kiss her.
'There's my girl,' I look at her and smile. 'You didn't sleep well did you?'
'No, I woke again around 3:30. But on the plus side you have heaps of goodies and enough to share with Amber, Simon, and Luke.' She says taking my hand.

We walk down to the beach.
'How was it last time?'
'Not good, hence the sleeping pills. Not sleeping, bad dreams, stress, anxiety, it was not fun.'
'Do you want them?'
'No.' She lays her towel down and sits.
'Babe if you need them I would rather you have them if it helps you.'
'No,' She shakes her head. 'I never liked taking them to begin with.'
She covers her mouth and yawns.

'I'll take the day off and we can lay on the lounge. Maybe you could make the second Lord Of The Rings movie.'
'We will have plenty of time for that after Louie's birthday.
I'm thinking another weekend in Agnus, 1770 or even Bargara.'
'Just you and me sounds like the best weekend ever.' I smile
'How long were you up the first time before I came downstairs?' I lay my towel next to her and sit.
'About three hours, I don't even remember going back to bed.'
'I lifted you onto the bench. You were showing me your hand, I gave you a hug and you fell asleep. I carried you to bed.'
'Well that explains a lot.' She giggles.
'How so?'
'All the biscuits were there when I went back downstairs.'
'What can I do to help you?'
'Just be you.' She smiles at me and winks.

She unties her sarong and lies down. Holy crap, I look her up and down.

'Can I have dessert instead of breakfast?' I ask.

She looks at me and smiles. I rest my hand on her waist as I kiss her and slowly slide my hand under her.

'So, what's your plans for today?' I ask her.

'Simon is dropping off packing boxes for me around 10ish and Luke has more stuff for the party. And I'm doing more cooking. Poor old stove is just hanging in there.'

'I'll bring the trailer for furniture today.' I kiss her softly.

'Thank you.'

'You're welcome.' I say against her lips.

Liz feels so good in my hands and I'll never get enough of kissing her.

'I'll help you pack after work.'

'There isn't much, just some clothes, books, cookbooks, and my study textbooks. So, it won't take us long.'

She pulls me back down to her.

She fits perfectly against me and I get to hold her every day.

Liz is mine and I'm hers.

I love her and I will continue loving her till the day I die.

'Good morning, Dominic,'

I turn behind us to see Greg and Thelma walking up the beach with the dogs. Bonnie and Clyde both bypassed me and went straight to Liz as she finished tying up her sarong.

'Good morning, Greg, Thelma'

I look down at Liz and the dogs are practically laying on her as she pats them.

'Got some competition for the next week by the looks of it.' Greg says as I shake his hand.

'Looks like it.' I reply, hugging Thelma.

They both have huge smiles on their faces as they look at me.

'Greg, Thelma I would love you to meet Elizabeth.' I say helping her up.

'Hello, it's nice to meet you.' Liz goes to shake their hands but they pull her in for hugs.

Liz stands next me, she is nervous.

'You are beautiful, we can see why he is so in love with you.' Thelma smiles

'I don't know about that.' Liz says looking at the ground as she moves a little more behind me.

Greg and Thelma look at me. I nod and wink at them.

'Well, Bonnie and Clyde love you that's for sure, they never bypass Dominic.' Greg says, looking at the dogs who were now sitting at her feet.

'Well, they are great and they both have Dominic wrapped around their paws.' Liz smiles at me.

'Hey, are you saying that I'm soft?' I look at her.
'Maybe just a little.' Liz smiles back at me.
Her eyes shine in the sun and it's hard to look away.
For a brief moment it feels like we are the only two people here.
We look back at Greg and Thelma and they are both smiling at us.

'We will drop them over later before we leave.' Greg says.
'No worries, the key is in the same spot.' I shake Greg's hand and hug Thelma again, and then put my arm around Liz.
'You know where we live when you have our invite.' Greg smiles as he holds Thelma's hand and they start walking home.
'What invite?' I ask.
'The wedding.' Greg says winking at us.
'Whose wedding?' Liz asks looking up at me.
'Yours and Dominic's,' Thelma replies.

I can feel Liz start to tremble.
'Um, wow, they really want to see you married to just anyone.' She pulls away and picks up her towel.
'Liz…'
'I should get ready. I need, I mean, work.' She turns to leave.
I stop her from walking away.
'Liz, I.'
'It's okay, Dominic, you're not ready and I need to be able to give you everything first. I'm not even expecting you to say it back or even want to, let alone marry me. You're happy with what we have and that's good enough for me.' Liz says not even looking at me.
I don't let go of her.
'Liz.'
'Don't, please don't. Please don't say it if you don't mean it, just to make me happy.' She still won't even look at me or come back to me.
I pull her into me and hold her till she stops trembling.
I want to tell her, but I want the moment to be perfect after everything she has been through.
I need it to be perfect for her.
It's getting harder to keep my secret every time I look at her.
We walk back to the house, holding hands.
Liz hasn't said a word and she is pale.
This is not good.
If she retreats back even just a little, it will be harder to get her back and for her to heal.

'Liz, babe. Please look at me?' I ask her as we get to the kitchen.
Liz stops and looks at me and I can't read her expression.
Her body language is different and she is starting to build walls again.
I can't let her retreat, I can't be where she's not.

'I was with Stephanie for two years before I was ready. I thought I wanted everything with her, house, marriage, kids but I was wrong.' I look at her.
Her face softens.
'I'm sorry, Dominic, what she did to you was horrible and unforgivable.'

I move closer to Liz and run my hand down her cheek, she closes her eyes and turns her face into my hand before opening her eyes again.
Her eyes completely captivate me and hold me to her.
'You came along and completely bowled me over. I fell for you quicker than anyone I have ever been with. When I asked you if you wanted to move in with me, it was because I realised I don't want to share you and I just need you with me. I just want to hold you every chance I get.'
I watch her face, her hand touches the scar on her neck then moves down to her wrist.
'You are beautiful, amazing, and stronger than you give yourself credit for. Every day that I'm with you is better than the last. I'm not prepared to let you go, Elizabeth.' I say as my fingers trace her scars. 'I don't see your scars. I see you, my beautiful, smart and incredibly sexy woman.'

I pull her into me as her hand touches my face.
I lift her up onto the bench and bring her lips to mine.
I kiss her with everything I have to give.
She surrenders to me as I hold her tighter against me.
Her hands slide under my shirt as her legs wrap around me holding me exactly where I want to be, with her.

'Dominic.' She calls my name and I feel her hands slid up to my chest.
I lift my shirt over my head, and I feel her lips on my chest as it leaves a trail of kisses up to my neck.
Her lips find mine and her tongue tease mine.
My hands slide down to her waist and squeeze gently, then slide down to her thighs, squeezing a soft sigh from her lips.
I bring my hands back up to her neck and run my thumbs along her jawline.
I take a moment to look at her and she gives me her amazing smile.
'There's my girl, don't you ever stop smiling'.
She pulls me back to her.
I untie her sarong and run my hands over her body.

I feel the goosebumps on her skin as I slide my hands under her bikini bottoms and give her arse a hard squeeze.

Her lips are on mine, her arms are around my neck, and her legs are wrapped around me.

Liz brings her lips to my ear.

'I want you, Dominic.' She whispers.

I look at her as I run my fingers along her cheek.

Liz slides off the bench and takes my hand.

I follow her upstairs to our bedroom.

I stand behind her and wrap my arms around her holding her tight.

My lips brush against her neck as my hands move over her body.

I untie her bikini top and let it fall to the floor.

Running my hands over her breasts as she leans back into me.

I trace along her body with my fingers down over her hips and back up.

Liz's body reacts to my touch and it feels amazing.

I start kissing along her collarbone to her shoulder.

My hands move over her breasts, teasing her nipples, as her breathing quickens.

She turns around in my arms and I stare into her eyes.

I feel her fingers move down and her hands undo the tie on my boardshorts, her bikini bottoms follow my shorts to the floor.

I bring my hands to her face and my lips to hers remembering my promise to her about the kiss.

I slowly run my tongue along her lips as she parts them and I gently bite her bottom lip.

I feel Liz's arms wrap around my waist pulling herself closer to me.

I tangle my fingers in her hair pulling her head back more.

I am hungry for her and I want to let myself lose control but I know she is still tender and I need to take care.

She feels so right in my arms and against me.

I start to kiss her harder, more dominating, more primal.

I need her, I crave her, I love her.

She returns my kiss, she is giving me all of her, and I fucking love her.

👀 ELIZABETH 👀

He lays me down carefully on our bed and continues the kiss that is driving my body wild.

His kiss may be hard, dominating and primal but it's also tender, so whatever he is doing it's causing my body to surrender to him.

His hands start to move along my body leaving a trail of heat behind them.
I can feel his lips on my neck. He is breathing heavy trying to control himself.
He slowly begins using his tongue to tease me along my neck.
I whimper, I can feel myself wanting to lose myself in this man.
'Dominic.' I whisper his name. 'I want you, all of you.'
I feel him enter me as he slowly buries his face into my neck, moaning.

His hand slowly moves down the back my leg to my knee, squeezing, then slowly back up and grabs my arse as his lips find mine.
Every one of his movements makes me want to feel him against me more than the last time.
Every movement, every touch drives me wild, my body reacts to the touch.
Dominic's fingers trace slowly back up and grabs my breast.
His lips trace along my neck as he hisses deeply.
My breathing hitches as I tilt my head back.
I arch my back as his mouth finds my breast and his hands slides around to my back holding me as he pushes harder and deeper.
'Dominic.'
'Liz.' He buries his face against my neck.
His hands move up, holding my arms above my head, as he leaves kisses along my neck back down to my breast.
His tongue teases my nipple before he takes my breast in his mouth again.
Dominic's body feels good moving with mine.
I can feel his body shake as he tries to hold back.
His eyes meet mine, it's hard to explain how much I love this man.

I run my fingers down his back causing him to shudder violently.
'My god Elizabeth you are beautiful.' Dominic says as his lips hungrily claim mine.
His hands slide under me as he moves and rolls to bring me on top of him.
His arms hold me to him as he sits up.
I roll my head back as I move on him.
He brings his mouth to my neck and makes his way down to my breasts.
His hands grab my hips and he squeezes hard and pulls with my movements.
I can feel the heat rise in my body as it responds to his.
Dominic can tell I'm close.
'Dominic,.
My hands in his hair, his lips brush against my breasts.
My body shudders as I growl, his hands squeeze my hips.
I lean back resting my hands on his thighs as I move along his cock.

Dominic's hand moves slowly up my back before tangling in my hair and pulling me back to him.
His arm runs up my back holding me as I begin to climax calling his name.
He pulls me down onto the bed under him.
'Mmm Dominic,'
His breathing becomes heavier and faster, his lips find mine and his tongue demands mine.
His hand moves through my hair more, pulling my head back as his other hand holds my breast and his fingers pinch my nipple.
He growls deeply as his hips roll and his thrusts become harder and deeper.
My arms wrap around his neck and my legs hold him to me.
He brings me to climax again.
'Cum with me, Dominic, cum with me.' I say breathing heavily.
'Tell me again, Elizabeth,'
'I love you, Dominic,'
Dominic's body shudders as he begins to orgasm with me.
His lips crash down on mine and he pushes deep into me.
He buries his face into my neck, breathing deeply, as his kisses make their way back to my lips.

'You are amazing, Elizabeth,' He kisses me softly.
'Absolutely fucking amazing, and all mine.'
'So are you.' I smile and blush.
He lays down beside me holding me, I feel his fingers move along my back.
I sink into his embrace and start to fall asleep when his phone rings.
'Do you want to get that?' I ask him.
'No, I'm busy with you.' He says rolling back on to me.
I giggle as he kisses me. His phone rings again.
'Dominic,' I say as he kisses me.
'No,' He says as he begins kissing my neck.
It rings again.
'Shit, fine, I'll answer it.' He sighs into my neck.
He rolls over and picks up his phone.

'Luke what's up,'
Dominic turns to look at me.
'Are you sure?'
He lays down and puts his hand on his head.
The doorbell rings.
'Don't worry I think it's just rang the doorbell, thanks mate.' He hangs up. 'Shit!'
'What's wrong?' I ask him.

'Ex girlfriendish of three weeks. I was with her twelve or more months ago, stage five clinger. Hated my friends especially Cassie and doesn't like taking no for an answer.'
Doorbell rings again.
'And she is ringing your doorbell now?'
'Yep.'
'Put this on.' I hand Dominic a towel.
'Follow me down in a minute.' I say smiling at him.
'Okay.' He looks at me.

👀 DOMINIC 👀

I smile as I watch her put on her bikini bottoms on and walk off pulling on her red robe.
I wrap the towel around myself as I reach the bottom of the stairs and Liz winks at me as she opens the door.
'Hello, can I help you?' Liz asks.
'I'm looking for Dominic. I know he is home, his Ute is here. I want to see him now.'
'And you are?' Liz asks leaning on the door frame.
'I'm his…'
'Lana,' I say walking up to the door.
'Mmm, hello, Dominic,' Her eyes look me up and down.
The look on her face makes me want to cringe, the thought of her touching me makes me want to scrub every inch of my body with a steel brush.
'What are you doing here?' I ask her directly.
'To see you.' She smiles at me.
'I'll have a coffee,' Lana looks at Elizabeth. 'White with two sugars.'
She tries to come inside.

Like fuck you're stepping inside this house!
Man she has not fucking changed, still likes to think the world is her doormat.
'We are kind of in the middle of something.' Liz says.
'Who is this, Dominic?' Lana asks angrily and crosses her arms.
I'm going to fucking tell you exactly, and you will never be it, I think to myself.
'I'm Liz, his…'
'Fiancée.' I cut in putting my arm around Liz and kissing the side of her head as I pull her closer to me. I can feel Liz tremble. I start to close the door.
'What!' Lana looks at me then at Liz with disgust.
'Goodbye Lana.'

'Wait, I really need to talk to you.' Lana puts her hand on the door, trying to push it open so she can walk inside.
'What, Lana? I'm really not interested in anything you have to say.' I sigh.
'I really need to talk to you. It's important, Can I come in?' She asks.
'No, you can't, you can tell me here.' I replied.
'In private,'
'No,' I cut her off. 'You can tell me right here in front of Elizabeth.'
'But…'
'But nothing, Lana, just get to the point please. I have a pressing engagement.' I say losing my patience.

'Right, well, um, I had a baby and you're the father.'
'What the fuck!' I think to myself.
I stand there in complete shock.
You are only just telling me this now!
Liz pulls away from me.
I try to stop her but she pushes my hand away.
'I doubt it, we used protection.'
'No, we missed it once.'
'I'll give you both some privacy,' Liz says and walks away.
'Liz, no.' I say.
She doesn't even look at me; she just keeps walking.
I turn back to Lana, she stands there with her arms crossed and a smirk on her face as she looks me over.
Like fuck I'm going back to you.
'Can I please come in, Dominic? We need to talk about this.'
'No, Lana. You are not welcome here.'
She hands me a picture of a baby boy.
'Ethan Taumata, your son.'
'He is not my son.' I look at the picture of the smiling baby boy. 'Congratulations, Lana, he looks happy and healthy.'
'He needs his dad. He needs you. I need you, we had fun together.' She moves closer to me.
I feel her hand touch me and I pull away from her and shake my head.
'I can make you very happy and very satisfied.' Lana smiles seductively.
I could vomit right about now if I didn't find it so funny.
'Not going to happen.' I laugh. 'Get me the proof, then we will talk.' I say handing the picture back and closing the door.

She tries to object but I ignore her and run upstairs to my girl, the only person I want in my arms.
'Liz,' I hear the shower but the door is closed.

I go to open the door but she has locked it.
I rest my head on the door and knock.
'Liz, can you please open the door? Liz.'
She doesn't answer and I stand at the door and wait for her.
Liz opens the door, she looks fragile and pale, it breaks me to see her like this.
'Sorry I just needed a moment, are you okay?' She asks, unable to look at me .
'Don't apologise, I'm concerned about you. I don't believe her.'
'Dominic, it's okay. You weren't with me, if it's true we will work through it unless you…' Liz's voice trembles as she looks at the floor.
'Unless I want to?' I ask her.
'You want to break up with me,' Liz trembles again as her hand covers her wrist.
'Liz,'
'I'll understand,'
'Liz,'
'I won't interfere,'
'Liz,'
'I can pack now,'
'No, I don't want to break up with you. Even if it is true I do not want to be with her. Ever!'
'You don't, even if it's true?' She looks at me.
'I want you and only you. The only packing you are doing is to move in here.' I say touching her face.
I love it when she blushes, I pull her in and hold her.
'Thank you.' I say.
'What for?'
'For standing by me and for being you, my beautiful, amazing and sexy…'
'Bimbo.' Liz finishes.
I smile and chuckle.
'You better have a shower and get ready for work if I'm to finish packing today.'
'Yes ma'am, give me fifteen minutes.' I say kissing her.

I have just come downstairs when my phone rings.
'Hey Luke,'
I look for Liz, the front door is open.
'No, her phone's on the bench,' I pick it up 'It's flat. What's up?'
I see her walk through the door, and she smiles when she sees me.
'Okay, we will be there in about ten, thanks, mate.' I hang up and drop my phone on the bench.
I walk over to meet her.
'What's wrong, Dominic?'
'The police are at your house, they need to talk to you about what happened.'
'Okay.' She looks at the floor as her hand touches her neck.

'Hey, I will be there with you okay.' I hold her, replacing her hand with mine and tracing the scar with my fingers.

'Have you put everything in the car already?' I ask her.

She nods against my chest, Liz has gone completely quiet.

'Fucking Daniel,' I think to myself.

We drive to her house and she doesn't say a word, we pull into her driveway and she goes completely pale.

I look over and they are waiting at their car.

I turn back to Liz and her expression has changed to pure fear. Fuck! Michael has found her.

'Dominic, don't say anything, don't do anything, and do not touch me. Call Amber, they are not police.' She doesn't even look at me.

'Liz,'

'No, Dominic. Try to remember everything, Amber will need the information.' She gets out of the car and walks towards them. I try to make a note of everything as I walk up to the house. I have my phone out, ready to call Amber. Wait! What?! They're fucking handcuffing her! I watch them place her in the back of their car and start to drive off.

'LUKE!'

'Yeah,' He jogs towards me.

'Get your fucking keys now!' I yell at him. I can't use my car, it has the trailer still connected to it. He grabs his keys and runs with me to his car.

'Follow them.' I say as I call Amber on speaker.

'But not too close.'

Come on, Amber, answer your phone. I wait for a minute or so before I ring her again.

'Come on! Where are you?' I scream in my head.

'Fuck!' I yell.

'Dom?' Luke asks.

I keep watching the car in front of me.

'What's going on Dom?' Luke asks me.

'They aren't police,'

'The ex?'

'I think so.'

We keep the distance between us and them. I call Amber again.

'Hey Dom…'

'Two men dressed in black and blue posing as detectives handcuffed Liz and took her!' I cut her off, putting my phone on speaker.

'WHAT?!' she screeches down the phone.

'Black Ford number plate 253 QPD. Luke and I are following it now.'
'Where are you?'
'Murdoch's Road heading towards the servo.'
'Okay, dispatching units now. Did Liz say anything to you? What did she say precisely?'
'Um, not to say anything, not to do anything, and do not touch her. Call Amber, they are not police.' My voice breaks, I can't lose her. 'She said to try and remember everything, Amber will need the information.'
'Ok describe them.' She says urgently.
'Um my height, one has thinnish brown hair, the other is blond.'
'Sounds like Daniel's accomplices judging by the descriptions we have from hospital staff.' Amber mumbles as she relays the information to someone. 'Besides Michael wouldn't trust just anyone with Elizabeth. The two men who took her do not match who Michael would send.'
'What!' I look at Luke.
'It's not Michael, Liz will know that by now.'
'How, how would she know?' I ask her.
'Ok, Dom, where are you now? I need to relay the information,' Amber ignores my question.
'Moore Park Road coming through the 'S' Bends and past Booyan Road.'
'Dominic, did you see any guns or any weapons?'
'I don't know. Luke?'
'Um, sorry I didn't see, they just showed me a badge and I rang Dom.' Luke answers.
'I need you to think, Dominic, it's important, Elizabeth is depending on you.'
I try to think.
'Yes, the guy who handcuffed her had one on his hip. I didn't see if the other guy had one.' I'm really starting to panic.
I swear to god if they fucking hurt her!
'Okay, Luke, hang back, don't get too close. Dominic stay on the phone and tell me everything.'
I hear Amber relay the information.

'All cars approach with no light or sirens. Extreme caution, occupants considered armed and extremely dangerous. Female passenger is a hostage and is considered a high valued target. Black Ford with number plate 253 QPD. Number plates are fake. Female hostage is to be handed over to Dominic Taumata and Luke Preston.'
'Amber, Liz has just laid down.' I say watching the car in front.
'Good! She's remembering what I taught her about handcuffs. I've shown her how to escape them by dislocating her thumb and fingers. Sounds extreme, but in a life and death situation, it's effective.'

Oh god!
I am torn between cheering her on to break free and feeling like I'm going to
throw up knowing she'll be injuring herself to do it.

Luke and I watch.
I see Liz sit up and look behind her, she has been gagged.
Liz turns back around and there appears to be a struggle, the car swerves on the
road.
Luke and I watch as the car leaves the road and then comes back on.
Those fuckers are going to pay!
'Dom, chill, mate.' Luke says.
Suddenly the car swerves back off the road and hits a tree on the driver's side.
'Shit! Amber, they hit a tree.'
Luke skids to a stop.
'Dominic!' I hear Amber call my name, but I chuck the phone at Luke and run
to the car.
I can't open the doors, they are jammed but I can see her laying still in the back.
The handcuffs are around the handbrake and it's been pulled up and the
passengers belt has been undone.
Both men are out, alive or dead, I don't know and don't care right now.
I just need my girl to be okay.
She's not moving and panic courses through my body.

'I need something to break the glass!' I yell to Luke who is coming towards me
while relaying everything to Amber on the phone.
He races back to his car and grabs a crowbar from the back, and sprints towards,
me shoving it in my hands like a relay baton.
I break the glass and climb in.
Luke grabs the crowbar to try and prize the door open.
We can hear the police coming.
'Liz, Elizabeth. Babe! Can you hear me? I'm here babe, Liz...' I unwrap the
seatbelt from around her and remove the gag.
'Dominic...' I can just hear her.
Relief rushes through me.
'Come on let's get you out of here.' I say as I help her up.
'Ow!' Liz winces in pain.
'Oh god, so sorry babe'
'My shoulder, it's....I'm going to pass out.'
'Dom!' Luke calls out.
'She's breathing but hurt bad,' I yell to him.
'Fucking door is jammed!' He mumbles in frustration.
'Liz babe, come on, say something.' I kiss her forehead and hold her to me.

I can feel her breathing softly.
'Dominic.' Liz says my name softly.

Luke finally gets the back door open and helps me get her out. I carry her back to his car.
'Elizabeth, talk to me.' I say trying to keep her awake. 'Liz, keep your eyes open and on me.'
Luke helps me get her in the car.
'Stop!' An officer yells and runs up to us.
'Who are you?' He asks as he draws his gun.
'Dominic Taumata.' I reply.
'Luke Preston.' Luke says as he closes my door and gets in the driver's seat.
He nods and goes back to the car that's still holding the fuckers who tried to take her as he is joined by additional police.
Judging by the look of the car they will definitely need to be cut out.

'Liz?'
She has passed out.
'Let's go Luke! Let's get her to the hospital.'
'Got it.' He nods.
Luke is about to leave when the officer returns.
'Follow that unit they will escort you to the hospital.'
Luke nods and guns it after the police car.
I sit in the back with her and call Amber on our way to the hospital.
We follow a police escort all the way to the hospital.
Amber is at the ambulance bay with Simon and a couple of other nurses.
I get out and lay her on the bed.

'What happened?' Simon asked.
'Daniel's mates. Trying to finish what they started.' Amber replies flatly.
'Fuck! Poor girl.' Simon sighs as they cover her with a blanket and wheel her in.
'Agent Carter…'
Amber turns around.
'Excellent!' she says, 'the uniformed officers are here.'
Addressing them, Amber says, 'You remain here with her, and DO NOT leave her unguarded. You two at the back, you watch the perps when they are brought in. They are to remain cuffed to their beds at all times. Under NO circumstances, and that includes pissing, are they to be uncuffed or removed from their rooms. Understood?'
'Ma'am.' They nod and move to their positions.

Simon and Luke look between Amber and I.

'Um, what's going on here? Care to explain?' Luke asks.

'You're an actual agent? I thought you were a plain clothes cop.' Simon adds.

'Yes, I'm a Fed. Liz is…um, a state secret.' Amber replies.

'Liz is one of the good guys.' I add.

'You know?' Simon asks, looking at me incredulously.

'Not all of it, but Liz is slowly telling me bits and pieces as she feels comfortable to.'

Simon looks at Luke questioning if he knew as well.

'It's news to me too, Simon. I know that Liz has this ex-boyfriend Michael, who is apparently a real sick shit. That's all I know,' Luke says to him.

'He's the worst of the worst.' Amber sighs and moves to Liz's bed, resting her hand on Liz's arm. 'Makes Friday the thirteenth look really tame, and I would die to protect my best friend and stop him from taking her.' Amber finishes flatly.

The look in Amber's eyes right now is plain and simple.

They fucked with the wrong person and she's the one who will make them pay for it.

'Well I hope whoever this Michael is, I hope that the fucker burns in hell.' Luke remarks then looks up at me. 'Mate, that will be the only time I don't tell you to fucking chill.' He looks back at Liz.

I can see just how much he cares for her as a friend.

'This conversation does not leave this room, understood?'

Simon and Luke nod.

'Dominic,' Liz says softly.

I rush to her side. She tries to smile at me.

'How are you feeling?' I ask her.

'Give me a new cast and a fuck load of painkillers. Put my shoulder and fingers back in and I'll be good to go home.' Liz grimaces.

'Your shoulder is out?' Simon asks.

'Yep, and I really need it back in. Simon can you hold my elbow and shoulder then slowly maneuver and push it back in?'

'Um no, but I'll get someone who can. I'll be back shortly.' He says rushing out.

'Shit,' Liz's pushes back on the pillow. 'Luke, I left the food in Dominic's car, when you…'

'Don't worry, Liz, I'll sort it.'

'Thank you, Luke.'

'Dominic,' Amber touches my shoulder. 'You and Luke can go. I'll stay and drive her home.' Amber says sitting down.
'No, I want to…'
'Hey…' Liz reaches for me with her broken hand.
'Go, I'll be there in no time. The containers are all labelled; Amber, Luke, Simon, Dominic, and Party. There is also a box labelled Jack and Lily.' Liz grimaces in pain.

'Okay, Elizabeth, let's have a look at this shoulder, shall we?' Dr. Marcus MacDougall says as he walks in with Simon.
He stops and looks around at everyone.
'Okay so we have the over-protective best friend, over-protective husband, and…'
'Over-protective best friends, Luke and Simon.' Amber joins the doctor in lightening up the mood.
'Right, well, Simon, will you be okay to assist?'
'I'm fine with that, are you okay with that, Liz?' Simon asks, looking at her.
Liz nods.
'Dominic?' Liz says, touching my face with her left hand.
'Yeah babe.'
'Go, I'll be fine.'
'Tell me again, please?' I ask leaning in.
Elizabeth smiles even though she is in pain.
'I love you, Dominic.'

I kiss her, not caring who is in the room with us. I look up and see that Luke, Simon, and Amber have huge smiles plastered on their faces. I look at her doctor who is still standing at the door of Elizabeth's room.
'Look after my girl, Doc.'
'Of course, Mr. Miller, your wife is in good hands.' He replies.
'Dominic.'
I turn back to Liz.
'I don't want to leave you.'
'I know you don't, but I will be fine. Amber and Simon are here with me. I'll be home as soon as I can.' Liz closes her eyes and takes a few shallow breaths.
I touch her cheek softly as she opens her eyes and I kiss her softly.
I stand and look at Amber and Simon; they both nod in silent agreement, they won't leave her side.
I kiss her one more time before I leave with Luke.

Luke and I get into his Ute.
'You love her, don't you?' Luke asks as we put our belts on.

'Yeah mate, I really do.'
'Have you got a ring yet?' He grins as he leans over and puts the key in the ignition.
'Yeah, mate,' I say looking at him. 'I got her a ring.'
'Sweet! I have the perfect best man speech, Simon can MC it. Amber can be the Maid of Honour with Jack and Lily as page boy and flower girl.' Luke slaps my shoulder.
Laughing I say, 'Wow, how's you?! You already have it all worked out! Exactly how long have you been planning that?' I ask him.
'When you first kissed her, we all saw it. None of us have ever seen you like that with anyone.' Luke laughs as he starts his car.

On the way back to Liz's house I tell him about Lana and Louise's visit.
Luke is so pissed off, he is ready to cancel the party.
'No, Liz wouldn't let me, we spoke about it, so she won't let you cancel it either. She wants to do this for her.'
'Why would she want to after what Louise said to her?' Luke asks.
'Because Liz feels sorry for her. She feels for Louise since she still carries a flame for me.'
'I'm so done with them bitches,' Luke says.
'Shelia is being a bitch because the kids are Aunty Liz this and Aunty Liz that. Jack let it slip that I liked Liz's cooking better than hers. And Liz does cook better, it's also that they love her and Sheila hates that. You rejected her too, she told me about it. She will never forgive me for leaving her, never forgive you for rejecting her, and won't forgive Liz for being in our lives and her kids' lives. And Stephanie, well she is just a nasty piece of work, Louise should know better.'

'How did Sheila find out about Liz not being able to have kids?'
'Me,' Luke sighs and shakes his head.
'Sorry, mate.' He looks absolutely gutted.
'It was a heat of the moment argument with Sheila over the phone. I felt like absolute crap afterwards. I just didn't think she would be so, so fucking callous.' Luke says turning into the driveway.

We walk upstairs into the house and I kind of feel lost without her here.
I go and sit on our bed and rest my elbows on my knees as I cover my face with my hands.
How did she know?
Why did she go with them?
A million questions run through my mind.
I see her jumper on the bed and pick it up.
'Coffee is hot' Luke says as he knocks on the door.

'Thanks, mate.' I get up from the bed, still holding her jumper.
I bring her jumper to my face and take a deep breath.
I want her home, safe.
It's unnerving her not being here where I can keep a look out for her.

I put her jumper back on the bed and walked to the kitchen.
Luke has already sorted the containers and put the party stuff in the cooler room.
I open mine and it's packed with mini quiches, mini pies, mini sausage rolls, lamingtons, vanilla slice and mini lemon meringues.
I smile as I put the container back in the fridge.
Simon and Luke's are in the shed fridge and Amber's is in her fridge.
I look in Jack and Lily's box—peanut butter and choc chip biscuits.

'Hey, are you alright?' Luke asks me.
'Um, yeah.' I say looking at my phone, it's 9:30 am.
I look back at Luke, he can see the concern etched on my face.
I turn back to the fridge and get the last of the chocolate cake out.
My phone rings, it's Amber.

'Hey Amber,'
I look at Luke as Amber tells me what's going on.
'Ok, thanks Amber I'll see you soon.'
I nod at Luke.
'Yep, no worries.'
I give him the thumbs up.
'Thanks. Bye Amber.
'What's happening?' Luke asks.
'They have put her shoulder back in. She dislocated three fingers getting out of those cuffs, god she's courageous! Amber said they've fixed them, and done some x-rays and scans which thankfully have all come back clear. Liz is getting her new cast now and they should be back here within the hour.'
'Awesome, it's weird not having her here.' Luke says.

'You better not be eating my goodies!' Simon says as he walks through the door.
'It's a tempting thought.' Luke asks.
'Piss off!' Simon says, laughing as he punches Luke's shoulder.
'Coffee?' I ask Simon.
'Yes, please.' He replies.
'When did your shift finish?' I ask him.

'I was walking out when I ran into Amber. She didn't have to say a thing. I just turned around and followed her. Her look said everything.' Simon pulls up a stool and sits next to Luke. 'I helped put her shoulder in then the head nurse told me to go because I had already overstayed my shift and pulled too many back to backs. Jane and Judy came down to see her as I was leaving.'

'Thanks mate.' I shake his hand.

'We have gotta look after our girl.' He nods

'Did Dominic tell you about Louise's visit?' Luke asks Simon.

'No, he has not.' Simon looks at me.

Luke proceeds to tell Simon what happened while I made Simon's coffee and cut up the cake.

By the end of it, Simon is just as pissed as Luke.

'Cancel it, and just have a house party for Liz.' Simon says.

'No, Liz won't let us cancel it. Liz still wants to have it.' I say looking at him.

'That's mad. I'm not okay with that, it's wrong of Louise, but I don't want to upset Liz and what she wants.' Simon sits down and drinks his coffee.

'So, have you told her?' Simon looks at me.

'No, he hasn't.' Luke answers for me.

'Hurry up already!' Simon smiles.

'He's got one!'

'Hell yes!' Simon says.

'I'm waiting for the right moment,' I say looking at him.

'Right moment? Have you seen what she has gone through? Yep even Amanda mentioned it. And don't forget Amber. I mean, I know it's her job and all but they are best friends. She is extremely protective of her, Amber wouldn't let it go on if she doubted you.' Simon adds.

I laugh.

'Amber wanted to help me pick the ring.' I look at them.

'Liz met Greg and Thelma and they are waiting for the wedding invite and…' I look up…

'What the fuck is she doing here?'

I look at Sheila as she walks towards us.

Simon and Luke turn around.

'You're not welcome here!' Simon says before anyone else speaks.

Simon turns his back to her.

'Leave!' Luke adds.

'Is Elizabeth here?' She asks.

'No.' I reply.

'What do you want, Sheila? Haven't you done enough?' Luke says as he looks at her.

'I need to talk to her.'
'You! You are not going anywhere fucking near her!' Luke snaps at her and turns his back to her.
'I need to apologise,'
'Again?' I ask looking at her.
'I know what I did was wrong,'
'Wrong!' Luke yells as he turns back around to look at her. 'What you did was horrendous! It disgusts me to even think that I even loved you and had children with you. You cannot come back from this, Sheila. What you said is unforgivable. And you did it in front of the kids and other people knowing full well the damage it would cause and how much it would hurt her.'

I have never seen Luke like this; he is beyond pissed.
Simon completely ignores her as he walks out.
'Luke, I'm sorry I really am. I was angry and hurt,'
'Hurt! What the fuck would you be hurt for? You have been pregnant and you have two healthy kids and you're fucking hurt! You have no fucking idea...' Luke points his finger at her.
'I apologised to the kids about all the horrible things I said about Elizabeth. It hit me when the kids started crying asking why I was being so mean.' Sheila says with tears in her eyes.
'What else did you say?' Luke asks her.
'Liz will be home soon and I really don't want you here or anywhere near her.'
'Please, Dominic.' Sheila pleads.
'Do you promise to apologize and leave straight away?' I ask her.
I don't want her here but I know Liz.
She will hear her out for the sake of Luke and the kids.
'Yes.' She nods meekly
'You can see her another day.' I nod my head hoping that I have made the right decision.
Luke looks at me.
He is fuming and not happy with me.
Even when I told him about Sheila, he never looked at me like he is now.
If looks could kill I would be dead.
'Fine!' He gets up and walks out onto the deck with Simon leaving me with Sheila in the kitchen.

Sheila walks over to me.
'Dominic,' She says, touching my arm
Her fingers move along my arm and I cringe at her touch.
'Don't, don't you ever touch me again.' I say
'Leave. Now.' I say as I walk outside to meet Luke and Simon.

'Are you okay?' I ask Luke.
'No, I'm fucking not!' He replies.
'Are we okay?' I ask looking at him.
He turns to face me and sighs.
'Yeah mate we are. Just do me a favour.' He says looking at me.
'Anything.'
'Now is the right time don't wait. I have seen the scars on her arms and legs, I'm not stupid. Simon told me about her reaction at the hospital. I have seen you at your lowest with Stephanie. That's nothing compared to what I saw in you with Liz the day Daniel attacked her and every day she was in hospital. As sappy as this sounds, the love that you two have for one another and the bond you share is something I can't even begin to put into words. Mate, just tell her, marry her.'
Luke looks at me, I can see the unshed tears in his eyes.

'Luke can I talk to you please?' Sheila asks, walking up to us.
'Fine,' Luke's face changes to one of anger and disgust.
He walks down the back steps and towards the beach.
'Luke's right you know.' Simon says looking at me.
'Don't make Elizabeth wait any longer.'
I nod, they are both right.
'Shelia's going to try and sweet talk him, isn't she?' I ask Simon.
'Do you know he pays her rent plus child maintenance?' He replies as we watch them.
'Yep, I pay him extra when he works for me. Do you reckon he will pull it?'
'Judging by him pulling away from her now, yep. About fucking time.'
'Are you going to talk to Louise about what she said?' I ask.
'Nope, she will know that I know and…'
'Uncle Dominic!' Jack and Lily call out behind me. 'Hey, Uncle Simon.'
Jack and Lily run up to us.

'Hey, what are you doing here? Aren't you supposed to be in school?' I ask as they hug us.
'Mummy gave us the day off and asked us to wait in the car. But we wanted to see Aunty Lizzy,' Jack says as I pick him up.
'Where is she?' Lily asks as Simon puts her down.
'She will be back soon so you can go and play while we wait for her.'
'Is there any cake?' Lily asks.
'Um, no sorry, Uncle Simon ate it.'
Lily and Jack look angrily at Simon and I laugh.
'So did your dad and Uncle Dominic.' Simon laughs.
Jack and Lily look at me and cross their arms, clearly not impressed.
'But she did make you some treats. How about we wait and surprise her, deal?'

'That's what Aunty Lizzy says.' Lily looks at me with her arms still crossed and a stern look on her face.

'So, do we have a deal?' I ask them.

'Yes!' They say in unison.

We high-five then they run inside and a few minutes later, Luke comes back upstairs.

'Are they inside?' He asks.

'Yep, in their games room.' I reply.

He nods and walks inside.

'Games room?' Simon asks with a raised eyebrow.

'Yeah, Liz set it up for them.'

'Why am I only just finding out about said games room?' Simon pretends to be hurt.

'Wait for me, Luke!' Simon calls as he runs after him.

I smile and shake my head as I walk over to the table.

I sigh as I sit down and wait for Liz to get back.

I hate that she is in hospital again but at least she is coming back to me today.

'Goodbye, Dominic.' Sheila approaches the table.

'Just leave.' I turn my back on her.

I sit there going through photos on my phone, photos of Liz and I on the beach, at home, her asleep.

Even in pictures her smile is infectious.

After a while I hear a car pull into the driveway and Amber's voice.

I get up and start to head downstairs when Jack and Lily intercept me.

'Hey we had a deal!' I laugh.

Luke and Simon follow me downstairs.

I find Liz swamped by Jack and Lily.

'Hey, you two, she is my...'

'Bimbo we know, Uncle Dom.' Lily rolls her eyes.

'Hey, what are you doing here?' Liz asks, returning their hugs with one arm in a sling.

'Move over, I want to hug Aunty Liz.' Simon tickles the kids. 'Thank you for the goodies.' He hugs her.

Liz was a little taken back by the hug but returned it, that's my girl.

'My turn.' Luke hugs her as well, Liz smiles and returns his hug too.

That's my girl. I smile.

'Is everything okay? Why are the kids here?' Liz looks confused.

I hold her and feel her sink into me.

I look down at her and see her smiling at me.

I lean down to kiss her.
'Uncle Dom.' Jack whines.
I groan.
'Yes,' I look at the twins
'Oh, right, the treats. Sheila was here she wanted to talk you.' I say to Liz.
Amber is pissed, I can tell she is ready to blow a fuse.
'Okay,' Liz says, picking up the plastic bag off the ground which I take from her.
'I told her it can wait for another day. I told her to leave.'
We head upstairs to our room.
Amber, Luke, and Simon take the kids to the games' room to give Liz a few minutes before she gets swamped again.

'Do you want me to do the packing while you rest?' I ask her.
'No, I just want you to hold me.'
'That I can do.'
'Thank you.' She says.
'Come on let's get you a cuppa..' I take her hand and walk out to the kitchen.
The first thing I see is Shelia waiting by the door.
Her checks are stained red from crying.
'What the fuck are you doing here?' I ask her while shielding Liz behind me.
'I have to apologise, Dominic.' Sheila replies meekly.
Liz moves to my side and faces Sheila.
Shelia looks between Liz and I.
'I'm really sorry, Elizabeth.'
Liz doesn't reply she just nods and walks back into our room.
I watch Liz walk away before turning back to Shelia hoping she would see the pure hatred in my eyes.
'Right, you have said your apologies. Now would be good time for you to fuck off!' I snap at her.
I don't wait for a response, I just slide the door shut and turn my back on her.
I don't say a thing when I walk up to Liz, she doesn't need it.
All she needs is for me to hold her.
We stand there together reveling in our unspoken love for one another.

'Aunty Lizzy!' The twins call for her.
'Brace yourself, you are about to have a ton of questions thrown at you. We think Sheila may have said something to them or they overheard conversations.'
'I might need you to hold my hand then.' She gives me that amazing smile of hers.
I kiss her softly.
'Found her, Uncle Dom is…'
'Are they making babies?' Lily cuts in.

Liz and I laugh.

'Hey, Jack, what's up?' Liz asks him.

He grabs her shirt and pulls her into the kitchen.

'Are you angry with us?'

'Why don't you want kids?'

'What is barren?'

'Is that what you did so you don't have kids?'

'Why did you take Uncle Dominic from our mummy?'

'Is it your fault our daddy left mummy?'

'Why did you let Daniel hurt you if you loved him?'

What the fuck!

I stand there completely stunned by their questions.

I look at Liz and she has remained completely calm; her face doesn't show anger or hurt.

'Jack and Lily, that is enough.'

'It's okay, Luke.' Liz cuts in.

Amber is not impressed by the questions either.

Simon shakes his head and walks away in disgust.

'Okay, I see I have some answers to give you.'

'Liz…' Luke looks at her.

'No Luke, it's okay, it's not their fault.' Liz answers before Luke could finish.

'No, I am not angry with you.' Liz smiles at them. 'I wanted nothing more than to be able to have children, but, I was in a really bad car accident and almost died. That accident is the reason why I'm barren, which is another way of saying 'unable to have children' like your mum put it.' Liz takes a breath and continues. I can see her hands starting to shake and she is getting pale.

'No, I didn't take your dad away from your mum. They broke up a long time before I met your dad. I'm sorry but I didn't know that your mum liked Uncle Dominic, but they were never together. I didn't love Daniel or even like him. He hurt me because he's a very bad man.' Liz says.

I hear her voice break.

'I'll be back in a minute,' Liz walks back into our room.

The twins look towards the door then back at me.

'So, you didn't stay the night with our mum and tell her you love her?' Jack asks me.

'No buddy, I didn't.' I reply.

'Is Mummy in trouble for lying?' Lily asks.

'Yes, she is. When anyone lies they get into trouble.' Luke answers.

'Is Aunty Liz okay?' Jack asks as he looks between Luke and I.

Both Jack and Lily look like they are about to cry.

'I'll go check, while your dad gets you your treats.'
'Do you still love her, Uncle Dom?' Lily whispers.
I kneel down and smile at Jack and Lily.
'Yeah I do.'
They smile and hug me.
I give Luke a nod.
I leave them to it and head into the room to check on Liz.

'She really doesn't like me, does she?' Liz asks as she paces at the end of our bed.
'No, but that's her loss. Sheila plays mind games, she did it to Luke for years before he walked away.'
'That must have been so hard for him.' Liz leans into me.
I sit down and pull her onto my lap.

'Yes it was, only because he didn't want to leave the kids. She got really nasty, but somehow managed to sweet talk him into getting what she wanted. She would use the kids to make him feel guilty. So, if you are feeling sorry for her in any way, don't. She turned up at my place one night and tried to come on to me. I turned her down and told Luke everything the next day.'
'How did he take it, was he angry with you?'
'He was when I first told him, but it was more of a shock, I think.'
Liz looks at me and I can see her fingers trace the scar on her wrist.
'What's bothering you?' I ask her.
'After everything that has happened to me, what I have now is beyond what I could have hoped for. Why me? What drew you to me? You could have anyone that isn't…' Liz struggles to find the right words.
'Isn't what?' I ask her.
'Isn't so damaged and so broken.' I watch as her hand covers her wrist and a tear drops.
'You are not damaged or broken and you are beautiful. I don't want anyone else, I want you.' I lift her face so I can see her eyes.
I kiss her as I run my fingers along her wrist and up to her neck.
'They are kissing again!' Lily yells from our bedroom door.
Liz and I smile at each other.
'How about I make you the cup of tea I promised you earlier?' I ask her.
'Yes please.'
We head back into the kitchen.

'Hey hun, I made you a cup of tea and I have to go back to work now. I need to report back, at some stage I will need to get a statement from you as well as Dominic and Luke.' Amber says.
'Okay, email the forms through and I'll type them up for you.'

'Love you, you're a gem.' Amber hugs Liz. 'No eating my goodies. I know how to get away with… stuff.' Amber looks at Luke and I as she walks out the door.

'Okay, who wants some yummy treats that I hid from a certain dad and Uncle?' Liz asks the kids.
'Yes please!' Simon yells from the kids' games room.
Jack and Lily laugh.
'Not if he doesn't come out here!' Luke yells back.
Simon makes it to the kitchen in record time.

'What did you hide?' I ask Liz as I hand her a cup of tea.
She winks at me as she takes a sip. Liz opens the fridge and pulls out some containers from the fruit and vegetable drawers.
'Who likes apple turnovers, brownies, and chocolate fudge?' Liz asks.
'We do!' Simon answers excitedly.
Liz opens the lid and slides them over to Luke and Simon.
'Share,' She winks at them. 'Oh, before I forget, Simon, here are some of your other goodies.'
Simon opens his container and slaps Luke's hand away, making the twins laugh.

After a while, the twins and Liz go to the games room and I see Simon off.
When I get back upstairs, I can hear Luke working downstairs.
I go to the kids' games room to check on them and Liz.
'Hey, where's Aunty Liz?'
'Don't know.' They reply not looking up.
I find her asleep on our bed.
I move the boxes and cover her up.

👀 ELIZABETH 👀

I wake to find the house in darkness and Dominic asleep beside me.
I carefully get up and go to the bathroom.
I need a shower and a cup of tea.
I brush my teeth and struggle to undress for ten minutes.
'Babe, how are you?' Dominic asks from behind me.
'I'm okay, just trying to get undressed to have a shower and not succeeding.' I say turning to face him.
'Why didn't you wake me, babe?' He asks me.
'Because you were asleep, and I know that I have been waking you a lot during the night.' I smile at him.
He walks up, kisses me softly and helps me undress and wrap my wrist.

Then he gently helps me wash my hair and my body.
The bruising is starting to show on my shoulder, ribs, and hand.

'How did you know they weren't police?'
'I have been around these kind of people long enough to know, and besides Amber would have told me. I then realised it wasn't Michael, he would come personally to collect his 'property'.' I reply as he dries me up and helps me get dressed.
'Do you want something to eat? You have been asleep for twelve hours.'
'No, just a cup of tea and then back to bed with you.'
'Okay.' He smiles then kisses me softly.
We head out to the kitchen and I watch him make me a cup of tea.

'Dominic.'
'Yeah, babe,' He turns around and places the cup in front of me.
'Thank you for what you did yesterday.'
'Anything for you.' He smiles.
'Can we go home please? I don't want to stay here anymore.'
'If that's what you want,'
'Yes, please, it doesn't feel like home anymore.' I look up at him.
He smiles.
'I would love to take you home.' He smiles as he walks over to me.
'You finish that while I go and get dressed and leave a note for Amber.' He says kissing the top of my head.
The drive home is quiet, I feel sore and tired.
I just want to be in our bed, in our home.
Dominic helps me out of his car.
I want to hold his hand but he won't let me, he knows how much pain I am in.
Instead he picks me up and I snuggle in as carries me to the front door.
My safe place in his arms.

'I'll go and check on Bonnie and Clyde, then I'll be up okay.'
'Okay.' I nod and walk upstairs.
I sit on the end of our bed looking out the glass doors and wait for him as I run my fingers over his band.
I'm starting to believe that we really do have a future together, but, before he commits to me I need to tell him everything.
It's time.

⊙⊙ DOMINIC ⊙⊙

She looks up and smiles as I walk into our room.
I will never tire of her smile.
I notice her fingers running over my band.
'You're supposed to be in bed.'
'I'm waiting for you.'
'Well I'm here now,' I smile as I lean in and kiss her.
'Do you want to talk about Lana and the baby?' She asks me.
'Nope, not really. I don't believe her. I just want to hold you and listen to you talk about whatever you want to want to talk about.' I slide into bed pulling her in to my embrace.
'Will they arrest me for killing Daniel?' Her questions throws me for a loop.
'I don't think so.' I hope that I'm correct. 'I don't think that Amber and her bosses will allow it to go that far. We can talk to Amber, if anyone knows for certain it's her.'
'Tell me more about New Zealand.' Liz asks, snuggling more.
'Well for starters they have the best NRL and Cricket team,'
'I beg to differ, the Raiders and Australia are the best teams.' Liz smiles at me.
'Raiders? Well it could be worse you could support the…'
'Broncos, no thank you.' She laughs.

I pull the covers down and Liz snuggles in as I lean back against the bed head.
I lay there for a while running my fingers through her hair.
'Liz,'
She's asleep, I hold her closer and kiss the top of her head.
'I love you, Elizabeth.' I whisper to her.

I wake up as the rising sun breaks through the curtains.
I'm still holding her.
I carefully move and lay her down.
I sit there and watch her for a while.
I can't believe she is here with me, that she said yes to me.
I go to get up for a shower when I feel her touch.
'Hey,' she smiles.
'Hey, babe. Are you hungry?'
'A little hungry. You go shower I'll make you breakfast, you like Vegemite on toast, don't you?' She smiles and sits up.
I smile at her, my girl, all mine to love.
'How about we shower and then I make you breakfast?'
'Now how could I say no to that?'
I pick her up and carry her into the bathroom.

I help her shower and dress.
I notice more of the bruises and the pain she is trying to hide.
I also notice that she hasn't gained much weight since leaving the hospital.

'Liz, are you sure you are okay?' I ask her.
'Of course, why?' She looks at me, her fingers trace the scar on her neck.
I get her to sit on the bed with me.
'Okay, I'm not saying this to upset you in anyway, I'm just concerned,'
'What's wrong with me?' Her body trembles slightly.
'Babe, nothing is wrong with you. When you were in the hospital you lost a lot of weight. You don't appear to have regained much of what you lost and I want to be sure that you are okay.' I say taking her hand carefully.
'Stress and pain. Not sleeping much isn't helping much.'
'What can I do to help you?' I ask as I brush the hair from her face.
'Just be you and keep the Vegemite in stock.'
'That I can do for you.' I kiss her softly.

I carry her downstairs just because I want to.
Sitting her on the bench, I hand her a spoon and smile as I open the jar of Vegemite and give it to her.
'Tea or coffee?' I ask her.
'Um, tea please.'
'My mum rang last night.'
'How is she?'
'She is great. I told her you were asleep and then she's like 'Oh well I'll call back tomorrow to talk to my girl.' Then she hung up, she didn't even talk or ask about me.' I say walking over to her.
'You know you can always give her my number.' She smiles as she wraps her legs around me.
'No, she will never leave you alone, this way she will have to talk to me.' I laugh.
'Was she like this with Stephanie?'
'Nope, if anything Mum avoided her. I look back at it now and my whole family pretty much avoided us nearly the whole time we were together.'
'Why didn't you go back to New Zealand with your family?' Liz asks.
'I wanted to go back and have Stephanie meet the rest of my family but she didn't want to. By the time we split I had bought the land, built the shed, and started building my home that is now ours.'
Liz blushes. I watch her lick the spoon and put it in the sink.
'I'm really nervous about meeting them.'
I stop her hand before she touches her neck.
'Don't be, they love you more than they love me.' I say as I tuck a lock of hair behind her ear.

'They are all waiting to meet you.'
Liz blushes, I love it when she blushes.
I kiss her fingers softly then my lips find hers.
My god, I love this woman so much.
'So, what's on today?' I ask her.
'White Chocolate mud cake and a crap load of painkillers. Along with…' Liz trails off staring at the door.
I follow her gaze.
Lana is standing at the glass door, watching us.

I look back at Liz.
'Don't move, I'll be right back.' I pull her in and kiss her.
Liz pulls me in closer and kisses me back; she knows exactly what I am doing.
I am showing Lana that I'm not going back to her even though she claims to have my child.
I walk over and open the door, and she hands me a yellow envelope.
'What's this?' I ask her
'Can I come in and talk?'
'No,'
'Dominic?'
'Yeah, babe.' I turn to Liz.
'Let her come in. I would love to hear what she has to say.' Liz winks.
'Okay.' I walk back to Liz and she wraps her legs around me.
I pull her in close.

'You have five minutes, Lana. What's in the envelope?'
'Your son's birth certificate.'
I can feel Liz's body tense up.
'It will take a lot more than a birth certificate to prove that Dominic is the father.' Liz says politely.
I can feel her shaking, trying to hold it together.
Lana opens the envelope.
'The date of birth proves it, we were still together when you go back nine months. And you're listed as the father.' Lana slides the document over to me and I slide it back to her.
'You see, Lana, I know for a fact that I wasn't the only one you were screwing, and I know who it was.'
Her eyes widen in shock.
'I have a doctor in town, be here at nine o'clock.' Liz says writing down the address.
I pass it to Lana, she looks at me.

'Get me DNA proof then we will talk, until then, don't come around here. Now please leave.'
We watch her walk out the door.
'How did you know she was with someone else?'
'A friend told me about one of her flings. It's one of the reasons I broke it off with her.'
'Who was it?'
'One of the guys who used to work for me. Enough about her. I need you to…'
That's as far as I get before she pulls me to her, her lips on mine.
There is no place I would rather be and that's right where she is.

'I have a phone call to make, and a favour to call in,' Liz smiles then writes down the address for me.
I watch her slide off the bench and look for her phone.
I smile as I pick her phone off the bench and hold it up.
'Looking for this?' I ask her
Liz looks up and smiles, walking back to take it from me but I pull away from her.
'Trade?' She asks
'Yep,' I smile.
I pull her in and kiss her, I smile as she moans and tightens her hold around my waist.
I pout as she pulls away, I love it when she giggles.
I watch her walk over to the lounge as she makes a phone call.
'Hello, this is Elizabeth Miller for Adam Miles please.'

After about ten minutes she comes back to the kitchen.
'Can you be at that address at 11:30 please?
'Yep, that I can do.'
'Adam will do the test and send it away and it's all paid for.'
'Liz…'
'Dominic, don't stress. If you feel the need to repay me I can think of a couple of ways.' Liz looks at me seductively.
I pull her in carefully against me and kiss her like I did that morning in the hospital.
'Now about this cake, how about I order one and you rest?'
'No, I want to cook,'
'Liz,' I look at her
'But…'
'I think it would be best, you're in pain, Luke and Simon will agree.' I smile, kissing her again.

My phone rings.

'Hey Simon, what's up?'

I look at Liz and smile.

'No, she hasn't why?'

I kiss Liz's fingers softly.

'Sounds like a perfect idea, I'll let her know. Thanks mate.'

I hang up and claim her lips again.

'What?' Liz asks me.

'Simon and Luke had a chat and agreed with me, they have decided to order a cake.'

'Oh, so I'm not cooking today?' She looks a little disappointed.

'Nope you have a free day to rest and enjoy here. Or you could watch a certain hot for you builder.'

'So, it looks like I'm packing then.' Liz smiles.

I pull her back in and lift her up onto the bench as I kiss her softly.

She has taken the sling off but still has some pain.

The bruises look bad, but she is adamant that they look worse than they feel, anyway I have been extra careful with her.

'I wonder if Amber can wrangle a free day and take me shopping?'

'What do you need?'

'Well, once I'm out of this cast and fully healed, I need a new outfit for our redo. You like red, don't you?' She winks at me.

'On you yes, I like it even more taking it off you.' I say running my fingers along her cheek and down her neck.

'Well, I better ring Amber then.'

I smile and kiss her again.

👀 ELIZABETH 👀

I slide off the bench and grab my phone, Amber doesn't answer so I send her a message asking for her help today.

'You are required to take me shopping today. Special outfits required wink wink.'

I get a replay ten minutes later.

'Hell yes, all sorted, see you soon xoxox'

'Well it's all sorted, I'm shopping for an outfit.'

'I'm looking forward to the unwrapping.' Dominic winks at me.

'Maybe I should also look for a sturdy daybed and a storage box.' I look up at him and I can feel myself blush.
'And a spa.' I add.
Dominic clears his throat and looks a little flustered.

We head to the house after Dominic feeds Bonnie and Clyde, Luke arrives shortly after us.
'Morning Dom, Liz.'
'Hey, Luke, let me pay for the cake. I did say I was going to make it.'
'Yeah, not happening, Liz, you have done enough.' Luke smiles, giving me a hug.
It still feels strange, but I return it, then turn to Dominic and he wraps his arms around me as he leans against his car.
'Where is my girl?' Amber yells as she practically runs down the stairs to us.
'Okay, so I have the whole day planned. Cafe for food and caffeine stop, shopping, brunch, shopping, more food, shopping then to the pub. I have a list of shops we have to visit and your painkillers on standby,' She looks at us. 'What?' She asks.
'How long have you been planning this?' I ask her.
'Two years and since the day you met each other, the beach, and after what I walked in on the following day.' She smiles at me.

'Coffee, Dom?' Luke winks and heads up to the house.
'Yep thanks Luke.'
'I'll be in the car.' Amber says and I hand her the keys.
I turn and look up at Dominic and he smiles.
'What? Is there something I'm missing?' I ask him.
'Nope'
'Ah yes I think I am…'
Dominic pulls me against him, his hand holds the small of my back as his other hand holds my cheek.
I lean my head into his hand.
I love the warmth of his touch.
'I'm going to miss you.' He says smiling at me.
'I'm only going shopping, I'll be back in a few hours.'
'You're going shopping with Amber.' He looks at me and smirks.
'True,' I smile and bite my bottom lip.
'Maybe you should remind me,' I start to say.

He knows exactly what I want, him.
I can feel all his lust, passion, desire and hunger.
He gives me weak knees every time he kisses me this way.
His kiss lets me know I am his and he is mine.

'Remember now?' He smiles at me.
'Kind of, you may have to remind me again this afternoon.' I say.

His lips find mine as he turns and pins me against his car.
I love his dominating kisses.
I sigh and feel him smile.
'Tell me,' He says as his lips brush against mine.
'I love you, Dominic.' I say breathlessly.
He smiles and kisses me again.

'I'll see you when I get back.' I say as he pulls away.
'Looking forward to it.' He winks at me.
I turn towards the garage as he smacks my arse.
I'm smiling as I get into my car.
Amber looks at me.
'Finally.' She laughs and starts my car and I put my window down.
'What?' I ask her.
'You know I love you right?' She says to me.
'And I love you. What's going on, Amber?'
'Well you and Dominic are moving in together and that means I'm not going to
see you as much.' Amber says as she starts to drive out of the garage.

Dominic is still standing there waiting for us to leave, he walks up to my car
and bends down.
'Look after our girl, Amber.' He says.
'Like my life depends on it.' She smiles.
'Try not to be too long, I would,'
'Now my dearest Dominic, here's the thing. I have been waiting for this this day
for two years. Two years of waiting to take my girl on a serious shopping day.
Now I have eight shops, three cafes, and one pub to visit. I'll send you pics.' She
winks and blows him a kiss.
'Okay then.' He smiles as he leans in and kisses me.
'Miss you.' I smile at him.

I look in the side mirror as we drive away, watching him turn around and walk
back towards the house with his hands in his pockets, I sigh.
Amber stops the car and puts it in reverse.
'What did you forget?' I ask her.
She re-enters the driveway.
'Go,'
I look at Amber trying to understand.
But before I can ask her, my door opens and she unclicks my belt.

Dominic pulls me out of the car.

He groans as his hand tangles in my hair and he kisses me hard.

'I'll see you for dinner.' I say turning around to be back in the car.

'It better not be that late.' He says grabbing my arse.

'The longer she takes getting in the car, the longer it takes for me to get her back to you.' Amber laughs.

I smile as Amber drives out of the driveway, everything feels perfect even with this whole Lana thing.

But I'm still scared I will lose him if the baby is his and after I tell him everything.

He knows that Michael is an evil man and if he is the father, he will need to protect his child.

I would not stop him when he leaves me and I will make sure that he never sees me again.

I have plans to make sure he is safe whether he is with me or not.

I run my fingers over his band and whisper his name.

Amber can tell I have something on my mind and she manages to get me to sing and laugh with her all the way into Bundaberg.

By the time we get to the first cafe my ribs are killing me.

Amber hands me my painkillers and we head into the cafe.

'Good morning, ladies, what can I get for you this morning?' The waitress asks.

'Can I please have pancakes with ice cream and strawberries. A side plate of bacon, a toasted ham cheese and tomato sandwich with cracked pepper, a large chocolate thick shake and a mugachino with two sugars to start with.' Amber says.

'No worries and for you?' She asks.

'I'll have pancakes and strawberries and a mugachino with two sugars as well thank you.' I say as I turn to Amber. 'Go and get us a table.' I say.

I get the table number and head over to Amber.

'So what goss have you got for me?' She asks as I sit down.

'Um, well I do have something to tell you or talk to you about', I ask nervously.

'Of course, is something wrong?'

'Um yes, well no, I mean not really, I think.' I sigh.

'Liz, you're shaking, what's wrong?' She asks, looking really concerned.

'Well this is a lot harder than I thought it would be.' I look at the table.

'Just breathe and tell me, I won't judge you, you know that. I will support you no matter what.' She reaches over and touches my hand.

'Okay,' I take a deep breath. 'I, I'm ready to tell him everything. But I want to do it before I move in with him, because I'm scared. So I'll do it now, that way I don't…' I take a few deep breaths.

'Don't what?' She asks me.
'Don't have to move out if he leaves me.'

'Nope, not going to happen. He will not leave you.' Amber says confidently.
'How can you be so sure?' I ask her.
'Because of what I see.'
'What do you see?' I ask her.
'From the moment you met each other, you were drawn to each other. When you look at each other it's like there is no one else around. You love him and he loves you.' Amber smiles.
'No he doesn't, he cares for me very much but he doesn't love me. He is happy with what we have and I'm fine with that. Besides…'
'Okay, here is your coffee's and thick shake. Your food will be served shortly.' The waiter smiles.
'Thank you.' I say politely
The waiter leaves
'Besides what?' Amber asks me.
'Dominic might be a father and if he is, I'm not good for him and I…'
'What the hell do you mean a father? And what do you mean you're not good for him?' She asks me
'His ex-girlfriend turned up claiming her son is his'
'What does that have to do with you and Dominic? If it is his child, I know you will love it like it's you own.'
'Well if it his?'
'It's not.' Amber cuts in, so completely sure of her answer.'
'If that baby is Dominic's, the best way I can protect him is to…'
'No, hell no you are not leaving.' Amber cuts me off.

'Okay, I have pancakes with ice cream with a side plate of bacon and a toasted sandwich.'
'Me please,' Amber smiles.
'So that means you have pancakes with strawberries.'
'Thank you.' I nod
'You're welcome, please enjoy.' The waiter smiles and leaves.

'You are not leaving.' Amber says as she points her fork at me 'Besides, I won't let you and neither will he.' Amber smiles at me.
'So, what do you propose?' I ask her.
'Let me think about it and get back to you. I think better when I have eaten anyway.'
I laugh. 'So very true.' I say.

We finish our breakfast and coffee and head to our first shop.

'Liz, can I ask why you are still having Louise's birthday party at your home after the shit she has pulled.'

'I have already answered that question enough times. I'm tired of the fighting, and the hating. I'm willing to give her one more chance to accept Dominic and I as a couple or move on.'

'You're too nice, Liz.' Amber rolls her eyes. 'Shelia better not be coming '

'She's not.'

'Good, one cray person is enough.' Amber remarks as she directs me to a seat.

I sit while Amber goes about picking our outfits for Louise's birthday party and before I know it, she has ten outfits for me to try on.

I come out of the dressing room to find Amber not in the seat with our stuff.

I start to panic and look around the shop.

'Sorry, I had a work call.' She says walking up to me.

'Oh, is everything okay? I ask her.

'It is now.' She smiles at me.

That's not the truth, I think to myself, but I know now is not the time or place to discuss it.

I end up picking a few outfits but my three favourites are: a knee length navy blue cotton wrap dress that tied off to one side with shoulder length sleeves and more cleavage on display than I would usually wear.

A mid-thigh length black light weight wrap dress, with a frill detail down to a V cut also showing cleavage.

The third one is definitely my favourite of the three though.

A beautiful white off the shoulder not quite knee length cheesecloth dress perfect for days at the beach.

Amber is in her element and I am fully enjoying our time together.

'Come on, Liz, now we have shoes and accessories to get and then…'

'Let me guess, food,' I giggle.

'You know me so well.' She laughs.

We put the bags in my car and head off to the next shop on her list.

Once again Amber makes me sit as she goes through the shoe shop with the sales assistant.

I choose a pair of black high heels with thick black heels and black ties around my ankle and up my calf, they also have delicate criss-cross straps over my feet to my toes.

Amber manages to talk me into a pair of black thigh high boots in faux suede that zip up along the back with a cute bow tie at the top to finish it off.

I do, however, find a pair of boots on my own that Amber doesn't mind.

Tan leather with a zip and thick heel that finish just above my ankles and will go perfectly with my cheesecloth dress.

I also buy the other shoes that Amber picked out for me.

Apparently a girl can never have too many shoes.

We put our bags in my car and head back inside to continue our shopping adventure but first it is time for a coffee break.

'So I have been thinking about what you said at breakfast.' Amber says as our order is brought to the table.

'I haven't changed my mind. I have to leave if he is the father or else, Michael will use the child,' I look at Amber.

'Liz, I am telling you. You are not leaving, and Dominic is not the father.' Amber says as she has a bite of her chocolate muffin.

'But what if he is?' I ask her.

'You're still not leaving.'

'But Michael is looking for me. What aren't you telling me…?'

'No we are not having this conversation yet. I don't have all the information, besides, I want to sit down with you and Dominic. Agent Smith has made me aware of the documents you signed regarding Dominic and what you want if something were to happen. But until I have everything in front of me, it would be pure speculation on my part. Now we are best friends having a girl day and we still have a couple of shops before we stop for a late lunch. So drink your coffee and eat your muffin.' Amber smiles at me.

'Fine, but as long as we still have this conversation.'

'Shit what time is it?' Amber looks at her watch. 'Crap I need to ring Cassie, give me twenty minutes and I'll be back with you.'

'Go.' I smile, shooing her away.

I watch her walk outside.

I wait for a few minutes to make sure I'm in the clear.

I also have a phone call to make.

'Hello, Agent Smith, it's Elizabeth. I need your help with something.'

After about forty minutes, I have made new arrangements and plans.

I finish my coffee as Amber finishes talking with Cassie and returns to our table.

'Sorry it went a little longer than twenty minutes.' Amber says as she sits back down.

'Don't worry about it. I was just looking at my up-and-coming study roster and plan. I also looked at some more property and checked my emails. I had a really productive half hour.' I smile at her.

'Ha ha. Right, well, let's go smart arse. No rest for the wicked.' She grins at me.

We head off to her next shop which happens to be swimwear.

I end up buying fifteen bikinis.

I liked them all and couldn't decide.

'Lizzy look, jewellery, quick come on.' She looks at me excitedly and pulls me to the window.

I find a beautiful silver heart pendant wrapped in an infinity link of black tungsten.

But I absolutely fall in love with a four layered necklace composed of black tungsten and silver with New Zealand pearls.

The first layer is a simple silver chain with a pearl.

The next layer is in black tungsten with an infinity drop around a pearl.

The third layer is a silver chain with a flat silver circle and a heart-shaped pearl center.

The last and longest layer drops down to my cleavage.

It's tungsten with a metal bar with pearls.

I buy both necklace sets; they both come with earrings and a ring.

We head back to the car, Amber's arm hooked in mine.

'Where are we off to now?' I ask as we drive out of the car park.

'Across to the sports club, I'm absolutely starving and it's my shout.' Amber smiles.

I sit back in my seat and close my eyes, listening to the song playing on the radio.

'How are you feeling?' Amber asks me

'A little sore and tired but I'm okay. What's your plan for after lunch?' I ask her.

'I saved the best for last. Lingerie, lots and lots of lingerie. Maybe even some toys.' She winks as she turns into the restaurant car-park.

'NO!' I cry out. 'No toys please, Amber.' I start to panic and have trouble breathing.

'I'm sorry, hon, I didn't even think.' Amber looks at me.

'I um,'

'Liz, breathe.'

'I can't. I, I need to get out.' I try to open the door but my vision is blurry.

'Shit, hang on I'm parking now, just breath, hon. Liz, breathe.'

'I'll call Dominic for you.'

'NO! No need to do so, I need to do this on my own.' I say as I stumble out of my car and clutch my chest.

I'm trying to focus but it's not working.

I run my fingers over Dominic's band as I start to cry even though it hurts to breathe.

'Liz.'

🔭 DOMINIC 🔭

My phone rings, it's Liz.
'Hey babe,' I answer
'Sorry, Dom, it's Amber.'
'What's up? You…'
'You need to talk to Liz.' Amber says cutting me off.
Something is very wrong.
I can hear it in Amber's voice.
'Where are you?'
'Um at the sports club next to Bunnings in the car-park.' She replies.
'I'm at Bunnings. Hang on I'm coming.'
'Liz, breathe, hon, come on breathe.' I can hear Amber talking to her and I can just make out Liz struggling.
I drop the stuff on the trade counter and run, yelling to Dylan the sales guy, 'I'll be back later to get those.'
'No worries, Dominic, I'll put them aside for you.' He calls back.
'Thanks mate.' I sing out.
'Amber, talk to me I'm coming!'
Amber doesn't reply but I can hear shuffling.
'Amber! Talk to me! Amber!'
'I can't calm her, Dom. She is pale and shaking. If she passes out, I'll have to call an ambulance and they will delay her return to work again.'

'Amber, I'm coming.'
'Liz, hun, just breathe,' I can hear Amber say.
'Don't close your eyes, just breathe, hun, he is almost here.'
'NO! No, no, he will take me.' I hear Liz say as she panics and struggles to breathe.
'Hun, it's Dominic. Dominic is coming, not Michael. It's Dominic,' Amber tells her.
I can see Liz's car.
'Amber, I can see her car.' I tell her.
Amber stands up and waves before ducking back down.
'Liz, hun, look at me don't close your eyes. Dominic is almost here, just breathe, please hun.' Amber tells her.
I can hear Liz struggling.
'Liz, babe,' I call out to her hoping she will hear me.
'Dominic's almost here,'
'Amber,' I say as I reach Liz's car.
Amber moves out of the way.
I grab Liz and pull her up into me.

Her whole body is trembling, there is no resistance in her, she doesn't even make a sound.
Liz is just leaning against me with her hands at her sides, I stand there and support her weight.
'Shh babe, I'm here now.' I say as I trace the scars on her neck.
I hold her tight, kissing the top of her head.
My fingers run along her neck, up and down along the scar.

'Come on, babe,' I say as I kiss the top of her head.
'I'm so sorry, Dom. I didn't mean to upset her, I didn't even think,'
'Amber, it's okay. I know you would never mean to hurt her.'
Liz's body is still trembling but she has started to calm down.
'Come on babe, come back to me. I need you, I can't be where you're not.'
I run my fingers through her hair as I kiss the top of her head.
My fingers move across her cheek and down to her neck and along the scar.
After a while I can start to feel her body relax, she is calming down and her breathing is returning to normal.
I just stand there and hold her.
I rest my lips on the top of her head and take a deep breath.
I love her smell.
I close my eyes and just rock with her.
'It's okay, babe, I'm here.'
I feel her arms wrap around me.

👀 ELIZABETH 👀

I slowly start to relax, listening to his heart beating.
I take a deep breath, he is so warm and intoxicating.
I take another deep breath.
Dominic continues to hold me, running his fingers along my neck.
'Dominic.' I whisper.
'I'm here.' His fingers touch my cheek.
I hold him tighter and take a deep breath.
I can feel his lips on the top of my head.
I look up at him and smile.
'Hey, you.'
'There's my girl.' He says as he smiles.
I feel him kiss the top of my head as I take a deep breath.
I close my eyes as his fingers move across my cheek and down my neck.
I look up again at him and smile.
'Don't you ever stop smiling.' He says.

He brings his lips to mine.
His kiss starts off soft, I feel his hand tangle in my hair as he pulls me in.
I feel my whole body relax into him, his kiss is the same as the morning when he woke up next to me in the hospital.
I am his and he is mine.
My knees feel weak, Dominic's arm around my waist holds me even tighter.
Amber's right, I can't leave him unless he tells me to go.
I need to tell him everything.
He rests his forehead on mine, my eyes are closed.
'Dominic?'
'Yeah babe.'
'Thank you.'
'Anytime.' He says as he kisses my forehead.

I don't know how long we stand there but I don't care, I just need him.
'Amber,' I whisper.
'She's here.' He replies.
'Is she okay?'
'Yeah I'm fine, I'm just worried about my bestie.' Amber replies.
'I'm sorry I panicked over something so stupid.' I say holding Dominic tighter.
'You don't need to apologise, hun.'
My body has finally stopped shaking.
'Dominic?' I look up at him.
'Yeah babe.'
'I love you.' I smile.
He smiles and brings his lips to mine.
'Will you join us for lunch, Dominic?' Amber asks.
'As long as I'm not intruding on much needed best friend time, I would love to.' Dominic says, still holding me tight.
'Of course not, come on I'm starving and it's my shout.' Amber replies.
I turn to Amber and smile, I know what she is doing.
'Thank you.' I mouth to her.
Amber winks and smiles.

Dominic makes a call to Luke before we head into the sports club.
We order lunch and find a table.
Dominic heads to the bar to get drinks.
'Okay, Lemon lime and bitters for Amber, Bundaberg Ginger Beer for you and me.'
'Thank you, Dom.' Amber smiles.
'So, where to next?' Dominic asks as his hand slides onto my thigh.
His touch is warm, gentle and calming.

'Home.' Amber replies.
'No we are not.' I say.
'But,'
'No, as you so excitedly put it and I quote, 'Lingerie, lots and lots of lingerie.' I blush.
Dominic drops his phone.
'Right, well, I'll um head back to Bunnings then back to the house to finish up.' He is a little flustered.
'Hun, are you sure?' Amber asks.
'Yep, I promised you.' I smile.
I feel Dominic's hand on my knee, I smile at him as he gently squeezes.

'Maybe we could stop at Yamaha first, there is this new dirt bike I'm looking at.' I say as I bring up the picture to show Dominic.
I look at Amber.
'What?' I ask her.
'New house, new boyfriend, new car, bike. What's next?
'A couple of surfboards, then I will be fine. Why?' I ask her.
'Sounds like a midlife crisis.' Amber smiles at me.
'I'll take you. I have to drop mine off while we are on holiday so they can have a look at the clutches.'
'What's wrong with them?' I ask him.
'Not sure.'
'What gears?'
'The YZ250 2nd gear and the YZ450F, the clutch won't engage at all.' He replies.
'Sounds like the flywheel and or clutch rods.' I say smiling. 'Could even be a build-up of gunk. I could have a look later, it may just need a good clean. I have the tools to do it.'
I feel Dominic's hand on my leg and it makes me blush.
I look at the table and take a deep breath.
Then I look up at him and smile.

'You two are the cutest.' Amber says
'Ok we have a large pizza with everything?' The waiter asks.
'That's me please.' Amber smiles.
'Steak with pepper gravy?' He asks
'Yep that's me.' Dominic says moving his phone and wallet.
'And that leaves you with a BLT.'
'Thank you.' I say as I try to open my bottle of pain meds.
'I'll do that for you.' The waiter says, taking the bottle from my hands.
'Um, thank you,' I say quietly.

He goes to hand them back.
'Thanks, mate, I'll take them.' Dominic says as he holds out his hand.
The waiter hands them over, smiles and leaves.
'Liz?' Amber says tapping my foot.
'Babe?' Dominic grabs my knee.
'I'm okay really. I'm just still getting used to being around men I don't know touching me.' I say
'The car salesman?' Dominic asks.
'I had help with that.'
'Who?' Amber asks.
'Agent Smith,'
'As in my boss Agent Smith?'
I nod.
'Well he does have a soft spot for his Elizabeth.' Amber says.
'How so?' Dominic asks, looking annoyed.
'The daughter he never had.' Amber replies.
'We bonded over cars and reruns of Bathurst from the last…' I pause and look down.
'Last what?' Dominic
'The last seven years that I missed.' I whisper.
Dominic reaches over to me and lifts my face to meet his. He runs his fingers along my cheek and down my neck.

'Don't worry, Dominic, Liz is all yours.' Amber winks at him.
'He can't play a guitar or build a deck.' I say smiling at him.
'There's my girl.' He smiles as his hand moves to my leg squeezes.
We finish lunch and head back to my car.
As much as I want to go home with Dominic, I also want to spend time with Amber.
Not to mention buy lingerie, lots and lots of lingerie.
And that's exactly what I do, three different shops and almost $2000 later.

Amber and I stop at the Moore Park Beach Tavern on the way home.
Much to my dismay, Sheila, Stephanie, and Louise are there as well.
'Aunty Lizzy,' Jack and Lily come running.
'Hey you two. How are you?'
'We are good.' Lily says.
'Is Uncle Dom here?' Jack asks.
'No but you can call him if you want?' Amber says.
'Yes please.' They say in unison.
'Okay, here's my phone, it's already calling him.' I say handing the phone to Jack.

'Hey, Uncle Dom, we are at the pub drinking with Aunty Lizzy,' Jack says, handing the phone to Lily.
'Can you please come? Aunty Lizzy is sad without you.' Lily says
'Okay, I will tell her. Bye, Uncle Dom.' Lily hands me the phone.
'He is on his way.' She smiles at me.

I call him back so he doesn't worry.
'Hey.' I say.
'What's wrong?' He asks.
'Nothing's wrong. I'm not sad, but I do miss you.'
'I'll go home and shower. Then I can meet you and Amber at the pub for dinner.'
'If you want, Amber can pick you up. She is dropping some stuff off at Cassie's so she can pick you up on the way back. You can then drive my car home.'
'Done. I'll be ready in about 45 minutes.'
'Okay I'll see you soon. Uncle Dom is coming, he will be here soon.' I say hanging up.
'Yay!' They say in unison.
'Liz, maybe you should come with me,'
'No, Amber, I need to do this. I can't always rely on you or Dominic to be next to me. I know it's hard for me but I still need to do this. Besides, you are only a phone call away if I really need you.'

Amber leaves and I get dragged out the back to play soccer with Jack and Lily.
We end up with another six kids joining us, thank god for pain killers.
Sheila, Louise, and Stephanie just look at us, I still don't trust Sheila.
I raid my purse for change so the kids can raid the vending machines and we continue to play. I
 end up playing with no shoes as my thongs broke.
'Daddy!' Jack and Lily run to Luke.
'Uncle Simon, Uncle Ben.'
Simon and Luke pick up the kids, give Ben their drinks order and walk straight past Sheila, Louise, and Stephanie without even acknowledging them.

'Hey Liz, my brother Ben is joining us. I'll introduce him when he comes back with the drinks, is that okay?'
Luke and Simon hug me.
I still shake a little when they hug me but I'm getting better.
'Of course. Is Ben the brother that helped while I was in the hospital?' I smile.
I look up and see Ben chatting with Louise and I get an uneasy feeling.
'Yep.' Luke nods. 'Come on Aunty Lizzy, Uncle Simon and I need your help beating these gremlins.' Luke says as he tickles Jack and Lily.
'Not to mention the other half dozen kids that has appeared.' Simon adds.

'Let's kick some butts.' I say laughing.
'Look out Aunty Lizzy!' Lily yells pointing behind me.
I turn and Dominic comes up behind me, picking me up and carrying me to the picnic table.
'Hey, you.'
'There's my girl.'
He kisses me as he sits me on the picnic table, his hands on either side of my face.
My arms wrap around him.

'I hate you being away for that long.' He says looking at me.
'Uncle Dom?' Jack calls out.
'Yeah little buddy.'
Jack grabs Dominic's hand and pulls him down to whisper something in his ear.
Dominic looks at me and smiles as Jack points at me.
He turns back to Jack and nods and says something.
They both look at me and smile before doing a fist bump and Jack runs back to the soccer game.

'What are you two scheming?' I ask Dominic.
'Boy stuff,' He replies.
'Boy stuff, right.' I say wrapping my legs around him, pulling him in.
His hands brush along my cheeks as his lips touch mine.
'Tell me again.'
'I love you.'

He kisses me softly.
'Okay, lovebirds here are your drinks.' Amber says as she places the drinks tray on the table.
'Hey Amber, do you have my keys? I need to get some shoes out of the, car my thongs broke.'
Amber hands me the keys as I get off the table.
'Don't be long,' Dominic grabs my arse when I start to walk away.
I turn to face him as I walk backwards.
'If I'm not back in two minutes come find me.' I wink and bite my bottom lip.
'Do not tempt me, Elizabeth.'
'But…'
'Aunty Lizzy are you leaving?' Lily asks me before I can finish replying to Dominic.
'No just getting some shoes out of my car because my thongs broke. Go back and play. I'll be back shortly.' I say as Lily hugs me.
'Okay.' Lily runs off and joins the other kids.

👓 DOMINIC 👓

'Who is Miss Sex on Legs walking away?' Ben asks, walking up with drinks.
'That's Elizabeth,' Simon replies.
'Please tell me she is single.' He takes a mouthful of beer and watches Elizabeth.
'No!' We all say at once.
'Who is the lucky bastard?'
'Me.' I reply as Amber, Luke, and Simon point at me.
'Ha, yeah right. Like you would have a chance with her.'
'And you would, brother?' Luke asks.
'Hell yeah, and I'm going to introduce myself.' He smiles at Luke.
'I wouldn't,' Simon starts to say.
'Ask Jack and Lily and they will tell you with great pleasure.' Luke laughs.
'No, I'll ask her.' Ben says.

My phone beeps. It's a message from Liz.
'Walking back lonely. Did you get a better offer? Xo'
I smile as I look up and see her, there's my girl.
Jack runs up and pulls on her shirt and she drops to his level.
What is he up to?
Lily runs over and points to us.
The three of them look over at us, I bet they are dobbing on Simon, Luke, and I for eating the last of the goodies.
Judging by Lily's reaction, Liz has promised to make more.
I can see Louise, Sheila, and Stephanie watching Liz like predators stalking their prey.
'Mine,' Ben says, walking towards Liz.
I go to stand up but Jack and Lily grab Ben.
Liz walks straight past him not even looking at him as he tries to get her attention.
My girl and she only has eyes for me.

👓 ELIZABETH 👓

'So, Luke,' I say, walking up to the group.
'What are those two up to?' He asks me.
'Apparently you, Uncle Simon, and Uncle Dominic ate all the treats. Now I have been engaged to make more under strict provisions that I don't tell you where I hide them.' I smile at Luke, Simon and Dominic.
'What did they eat?' Simon asks.
'The last of the fudge and brownies.

I also have to make more chocolate cake and…' I freeze as someone walks up and grabs me from behind.
Dominic stands and pulls me behind him, my whole body is trembling.

'What the fuck, Ben! I told you she is with me.' Dominic snaps.
His voice sounds almost malicious, not like him at all.
'Dom, mate. Chill, just chill alright.' Luke says pushing Ben back.
Simon moves back and shields Jack and Lily.
Dominic's body language is hard, protective, and very territorial.
He hasn't moved his arm and no one is stepping between them.
There is obvious distrust between Ben and Dominic but this doesn't need to go any further.
'Dominic.' I gently touch his arm, his body language instantly changes and he turns to face me.
His expression softens as his eyes meet mine.
'Can we go home please?' I ask, my body still shaking.
'Sure.' He holds me close.
'I can drop Amber home later.' Luke says.
'Thanks, mate.' Dominic shakes his hand.
Amber comes up and hugs me.
'We will bring him up to speed or I can break all ten of his fingers, your choice.' She smiles.
'Just bring him up to speed. He did help while I was in hospital.' I look at Amber.
'Are you sure you are okay?' Amber asks me.
I nod as Dominic wraps his arm around me, shielding me from Ben as we walk to my car.
He opens my car door for me before getting into the driver's seat.

'Are you okay?' I ask him.
'I'm fine.' He sighs as he places both hands on the steering wheel and pushes back into the seat.
'Are you angry with me?' I am feeling ashamed.
'Babe,' He takes my hand. 'Of course I'm not angry with you. I'm just annoyed at Ben.' He looks at me.
'You sounded very different.' I say as I run my fingers along his.
'I'm sorry if I freaked you out.'
'It wasn't you that freaked me out. Your body language was territorial and hard. I thought you were about to hit him.'
'I was close. If he made another pass at you or utter a pathetic and stupid comment about you, I would have. It wasn't until you put your hand on me and said my name that I snapped out of it.' He smiles at me.

'Come on let's go home.' I say.
'Anything for my girl.' He says as he leans over and kisses me softly.

As we drive home, I can tell something is bothering him.
We pull into the driveway and park next to his car.
'Right, tell me what's bothering you.' I look at him.
'It's not you.' He sighs.
'What is it? Can I do anything to help?' I ask, putting my hand on his arm.
'You can't do anything. It's this baby thing with Lana. Then at the pub it was the way Sheila, Stephanie, and Louise were looking at you. I just don't trust them.' He looks out the windshield.
'What? Even Louise?'
'No, not even her anymore.' He shakes his head.
'Ok, well I won't go to the birthday party tomorrow night. I'll stay home'
'No. I want you with me. I'm not going for her anyway.'
'Good thing, I didn't get her the travel voucher then, huh?'
'What did you end up getting her?'
'Day spa vouchers.'
'Let's go put my mad toasting skills to use.' Dominic smiles at me.
'After,' I wink at him.
'After?'
'You show me your pool boy skills. I have a new bikini.' I say biting my lip.
'Yes, definitely after the pool. But I have a surprise for you.'
'A bigger jar of Vegemite?' I ask.
'Even better.'
'Two big jars?'
'Come on.' He laughs.

We open the boot of my car as I look for my new bikinis, my phone rings.
I don't know the number, so I ignore it.
'Hey, no peeking.' I smile.
'I found your bikini.' He smiles as he holds up a small piece of black material.
'There is more than one.' I wink at him.
'So, your day was productive then.' He grins
'Very, was yours?'
'Yes but this evening will be much better.' He says as his fingers brush along my cheeks.
'Now I am intrigued. Do tell.' I say as I feel myself blush.
'I'll show you.' He says, pulling me in and kissing me. 'Come on, pool awaits.' He smiles

I hand him some bags as I grab a few.
The rest can wait till tomorrow.
I go into the bathroom and change into one of my new bikinis.
I choose one of emerald green, the bottom is a low cut Brazilian at the front and it doesn't cover much of my arse which I know for a fact that Dominic will like.
The top is held together at the cleavage by a silver loop, adjustable triangles with skinny neck and back ties.
I cover up with an emerald green sarong and take a deep breath.
I know I shouldn't be nervous with Dominic but I still feel like I need to please him.
I try hard to be more confident in myself but the anxiety is still present.
I take another deep breath and open the bathroom door.

Oh dear lord, he is not wearing a shirt and his board shorts sit perfectly, showing off the V thingy that makes a girl go mmm....
My knees feel weak and I hold onto the door frame.
I still hate my knees and the way my mind goes blank whenever I am around him.
I run my fingers over his band.
'Hey you.' I manage to say two words and not sound like a complete loser.
'There's my girl.' He grins walking up to me.
He kisses me softly.
'Okay I have three surprises for you.'
'Can I guess?' I ask.
'Okay.'
'Um, a cheap bottle of champers, fish and chips, and a really big jar of Vegemite.'
'Not even close, but I'll keep those in mind. Come on.'
'Lead the way.' I smile as he takes my hand.

His touch still manages to send shockwaves through my body.
We head down to the bottom floor.
I can see Bonnie and Clyde out the side door of the laundry, feasting on huge bones on the grass.
'Okay, now you need to close your eyes, I'm going to carry you.'
I nod and smile as he lifts me up.
I close my eyes and rest my head against him, wrapping my arms around him.
I snuggle into him as he carries me outside.
'Keep your eyes closed while I put you down on your feet.'
'Okay,' I giggle excitedly.

He gently puts me down and moves away.
I can feel the warmth of the late afternoon sun.

'Dominic?'
'Just a second, don't move, and keep your eyes closed.'
I stand there nervously waiting.
'Liz?'
'Yes.'
'Are you ready?'
'Yes.' I say nervously.
I feel his hands touch my neck and his lips against mine, he pulls me in holding me tight.
'Okay open your eyes,' He says moving behind me.
I open my eyes to see a big beautiful day bed with a sunshade.
It's a beautiful dark solid timber, perfect for a lazy day with my man.
Beside the day bed is a big wrought iron fire pit.
'Dominic.' I turn to him.
'Do you…'
'I love it, thank you!' I say before he finishes.

I wrap my arms around his neck pulling his lips to mine, his arms wrap around me as I deepen the kiss.
His hands travel up to my neck sending shock waves through my body.
'May I?' He says as his fingers trace my jawline.
'Yes,' I nod nervously as he brings his lips back to mine.
I moan softly as his fingers untie my sarong and I feel it fall away.
He removes the clip from my hair and he tangles his hands in my hair.
He deepens the kiss and his hands move down my body, holding me tighter.
I feel his hands squeeze my hips as they move to my arse, he stops and pulls away looking over my body.
'What?' I ask him. 'Do you not like it?' I say nervously.
He grins and takes another step back.
'Well damn!' He smiles and gets me to spin around.
'F.Y.E.O.' I say smiling.
'What?'
'For your eyes only.' I say nervously.
He smiles.
'I take it that you like it?'
'Very much,' He says as he lifts me up.
I giggle as I wrap my legs around his waist.
He walks into the pool and sits on the corner spa seat.
'Well I have to say, so far your pool boy skills are impressive.'

He smiles as his hands move from my hips to my arse and squeezes hard.
'So are the rest as good as this one?' He asks as he squeezes my arse again.

'Well one has a lot less material than this one. A couple has more and the rest are around the same. I also bought a surf rashie.'
'So how many did you buy?' He looks at me smiling.
'Well I tried on a few and I couldn't decide, and Amber was no help at all. So I decided to buy all of them.'
'Which is?'
'Fifteen.' I say biting my lip.
'Fifteen of these!' He grins.
I nod.
'What are you trying to do to me?' He groans.
'Well as Amber says, keeping you interested.' I say nervously and blush as I look at Dominic.
'Well I can tell you for certain. I'm not interested in anyone else. But I have to say, I absolutely love seeing you in little to no clothing at all.'
I blush even more and look away.

'Liz babe, look at me.' He asks.
I look at him.
'I see past your scars. You are the most beautiful person I have ever met.' He kisses me softly. 'So are you going to tell me what's in the rest of the bags?
'Some shoes, a few dresses, jewellery, and lots and lots of lingerie.' I blush again. Ugh my body sucks!
He groans and buries his face in my neck.
'Please tell me this cast comes off soon.' Dominic groans.
'I have an x-ray on Monday afternoon and then I'll know. But I'm pretty sure it will be taken off on Monday.'
He groans.
'I'll wear some tomorrow for you, and you can unwrap, if you're a good boy.' I say smiling at him.
He kisses me hard, his hands grab my hips pulling me against him then slides down to my arse and squeezes hard.
I fold my arms around his neck and run my fingers through his hair.

'Oi!'
We look up to see Simon, Luke, Amber, and Ben on the veranda.
'What are you doing here?' Dominic asks.
'We come bearing food, drinks, and dumb arse here needs to talk to you.' Luke replies.
I start to shake and it's not because I'm cold.
Dominic looks at me and touches my face.
'Hey, Liz, look at me. He won't touch you again'
I nod.

'Um ok, but it's also F.Y.E.O.' I say looking at him and blushing.
He kisses me softly.
'I'll get you your towel, wait here.'
I nod and move to let him get up.
'We will meet you inside,' Simon calls out.
Dominic gets out of the pool to get our towels.
I nervously look up and see Ben looking at me before he goes inside.
I get an uneasy feeling.

Dominic makes sure they have gone inside before helping me out of the pool
and wrapping me in a towel
'I'll give you surprise number three later when they leave.'
I smile at him, he touches my neck and trace my scars.
I close my eyes and take in a deep breath.
His hands move up to my cheeks and his thumb moves along my lips.
I open my eyes.
'We better get up there.' I sigh.
'What's wrong, babe?'
'I just wanted to be alone with you after what happened today. I'm sorry I made
you leave the pub early and now,' I blush and look away.
'I'll make sure they don't stay long.' He pulls me in and holds me.
'Thank you, Dominic.'
'Anything for my girl.'

We head upstairs.
Dominic heads over to the lounge as I go upstairs to get dressed.
I choose my new pair of black fitted jeans, loose light purple jumper similar to
my oversized white shirt that Dominic loves.
I put my hair up in a clip but leave a lock out, Dominic always plays with it
when I snuggle with him on the lounge.
I head downstairs and see Dominic in the kitchen.
He looks up and smiles, I smile back and walk to him.
'I made you a cuppa.'
'Thank you,' I smile and wrap my arms around him resting my head on his chest.
Dominic's arms fold around me and I can feel him kiss the top of my head

'Elizabeth?'
I feel my body tense and I release Dominic.
I move behind him and hold on to his arm.
'Yes,' I reply looking at Ben.
'I just want to apologise to you, I really didn't mean to upset you.'
'Thank you.' I reply.

Ben moves close but Dominic stops him and shakes his head.
Ben sighs and walks back to join the others.
I take a deep breath as I release Dominic's arm and pick up my cup of tea.
I close my eyes and take a sip, enjoying it.
I open my eyes to see Dominic smiling at me.

'What?' I ask him.
'My girl, my beautiful, smart, amazing, and incredibly sexy woman.' He says as he leans in and kisses me softly.
I can feel myself blush.
'I must say I like this new jumper, it reminds me of...'
'My white shirt. Which is the exact reason why I bought it.' I smile at him.
He smiles and kisses me again.

'Hey lovebirds. While the food is still hot, yeah?' Amber calls out.
Dominic takes my cup and then my hand and we walk over to join the group.
I sit between Amber and Dominic while Luke hands Dominic a beer.
We all chat and laugh while eating pizza.
I still won't look directly at Ben, but I can feel his eyes on me and it makes me really uncomfortable.
Dominic senses it and rests his hand on my leg, squeezing my knee every now and then.
Amber's phone rings.
'Shit, it's work I have to take this. Excuse me.'
Amber heads out onto the veranda.
I watch her, something is wrong, her body language is different.
She looks straight at me.
I have seen this look before.
It's right before I have to run again.
I'm not ready, this is not part of the plan.
I start to panic and Dominic picks up on it.

'Liz, what's wrong?' Dominic asks.
Amber comes back inside.
'Liz, I need to talk to you.' Amber looks at me then Dominic.
I nod and walk outside with her.
'Agent Smith is on his way, he will be here tomorrow. He has some things for you to sign as per your request. And...'
She looks up at me.
It seems Agent Smith has changed the plan.
'I have to run again, don't I?'
'No,' She replies.

'Has Agent Smith changed the plan?'
'No.' Amber shakes her head
'But,'
'Liz, I need you to listen very carefully. I have just been informed about some information that has come to light.'
'Okay.' I whisper. My whole body starts to tremble.
'What else is in Margaret River other than your family?'
'I um,' I can't focus. My family lives in Margaret River. Oh god no.
'Liz, your family is safe but I need you to focus.'
I shake my head trying to think.
'Think Elizabeth! This is important. Why would Michael go there?'
'I um,'
'Elizabeth!' Amber snaps at me and grabs my arm.
Than it dawns on me like a sinister fog creeping slowly over my body, severing what resolve I have built.

'His farm. He bought a farm there.' I look at Amber as fear runs through me. 'Oh no, Amber he, he will be building my room. He IS coming for me.' I stop and shake my head. 'I need to go now, it's too soon. I'm not ready.'
'What room?'
'After you released me back to him, I heard him talking to Sam and Brian about the farm and building me a special room. An underground bunker for me.' I grab the railing and close my eyes trying to focus on my breathing. 'He would have bought the farm under a different name.'
'A bunker? Why Margaret River? Elizabeth,' Amber pushes me for information.
'Elizabeth,' Amber snaps at me again.
I flinch at the sound of her voice
'Elizabeth, I need you to focus. What bunker? Why Margaret River?' Amber grabs my arm hard, causing me to wince in pain.
'My family, I'm going to be just out of reach and it will be my tomb. I'll be right there and they will never know.' I look at Amber as the tears start. 'It's his way of gaining control over me before he breaks me all over again.' I cry.

'Elizabeth—focus. Where in Margaret River?' Amber snaps at me again.
'It will have everything in it. His toys, my bed, the chair. He is going to torture and rape me there, he told me he was. He will also have blood, drugs, and other medical supplies to keep me alive. He is going to kill me only to bring me back, heal me, and then break me all over again. When he gets me in there I will never be found.' I close my eyes trying to get my body to stop shaking.

I need to change the plan, I have to do this on my own.
I need to run alone, I need to let Michael take me.

This is the only plan that will work.

But first, I will make Michael think I'm coming to him.

This will give me time to formulate a plan.

'I won't go back, Amber. You promised me, Agent Smith promised me. I was promised this will work and that Dominic and I will be safe. I'll make sure that he never finds out about Dominic and he won't take me alive. I won't let the system fail me again.' I look at Amber.

'Liz,' Amber says, putting her arm around me.

I pull away from her.

'Don't,'

'Liz,'

'Just don't, Amber. I need you to stop being my best friend for just a moment and get what I asked you for. I need the Amber that will do her job first and not worry about my well-being. I need you to be part of the system I know I can trust.'

'Liz,'

I put my hand up to stop her.

'I need to be alone for a while.' I say as I walk back inside.

Amber follows me.

'Liz, wait!' Amber calls out.

I ignore her.

'Liz,' Dominic calls out.

I ignore him as well.

I head upstairs to the bathroom, close the door, and sit at the window overlooking the ocean.

I sit there and focus on my breathing, running my fingers over Dominic's band and trying to think of all the good things I have now so I won't black out.

👀 DOMINIC 👀

I watch Liz ignore me and I look at Amber.

'Amber, what the hell just happened? What's going on?' I ask her.

Amber pulls me aside.

'Michael has been spotted in Margaret River.'

'Liz's family?'

'They are fine. Michael is not interested in them; they are just visual bait for Liz.'

Amber looks at her hands and back up to me.

I'm starting to worry, are they taking her away from me? Does Liz really have to go? Why can't she stay? Can I go with her? I can't be where she is not.

'So?' I look at Amber.
'I need to check on something first and update the team ASAP. Agent Smith is coming to talk to Liz tomorrow before the party. We have something planned but Elizabeth has got him to organise other things. Whatever that is involves Luke, Simon, and Cassie as well. There have also been other developments I haven't told her about yet.'
'Amber, why were you yelling at her?'
'I'm sorry, Dominic, I knew it was the only way to get her to focus and not run. The developments could change the plan.'
'What plan?' I ask. 'Run? Amber what are you talking about?'
'The run and disappear plan.'
My heart drops

'Do I go with her?' I look at Amber.
'No..' Amber shakes her head.
'She can't'
'She isn't going anywhere. Liz is staying right here with you.' Amber says putting her hand on my shoulder.
'Dominic,'
'Yeah.'
'Liz told me today that she is getting ready to tell you everything. But with the possibility of you becoming a father, well, it scares the crap out of her. I convinced her to stay even if you are the father, Liz is worried that if Michael does find her and finds out about you.' Amber closes her eyes and takes a deep breath.

She opens her eyes and looks at me.
'He will use you and if the child is yours, use the child to get to her. She will cave to save you and the child, Liz won't even give it a second thought. I know Liz, she is preparing to go it alone. If I'm right she has a plan B that only she knows.'
'No, if she leaves I leave with her. I won't let her be alone ever again. I promised her Amber, I promised her.'

'Apparently Liz has had documents drawn naming you as her next of kin if something happens to her.'
'No, I don't want it.' I look at Amber
'Liz has also got you down as her assigned. You will be privy to all aspects of the case if you decide to stay.' Amber looks over at the lounge.
'I still haven't figured out what precautions she has taken. She said it again 'I'll make sure he won't take me alive.'
'She's a paramedic, Amber, it has to be a drug of some sort.' I sigh.

I know what they are. I found them all through her house along with the bats and knives.

'Good thinking but what?'

'Whatever she can get her hands on.' I reply. 'I can't, Amber, I can't lose her. I love her, I fucking love her.' I lean down on the bench.

'I know, Dominic. Everyone knows; everyone except Elizabeth.' She looks at me.

I nod and walk upstairs.

Elizabeth is my whole world, my everything.

She is everything I'll ever want or need.

The bathroom door is closed, I can't hear running water.

I take a deep breath and open the door.

I see her sitting, looking out the window with her fingers running over my band.

She turns to face me and smiles, with her eyes shining.

👀 ELIZABETH 👀

I look up and smile as he walks up to me.

I can't help but smile, he is my whole world, my everything.

He is everything I'll ever want or need.

He sits next to me and wraps his arms around me, he just holds me, not saying a word.

I move and sit on his lap, facing him.

I run my fingers through his hair and along his cheeks resting my hands on his neck.

I bring my lips to his.

'I love you, Dominic.' I whisper against his lips.

I tease his parted lips with my tongue and I feel his arms tighten around me.

I kiss him with all the passion, hunger, desire, and love that I have for him.

His tongue dances with mine as he holds me tighter.

'Liz,'

'Dominic…' I say against his lips.

'I…' Dominic groans. 'I'm not letting you go,' He says, wiping away my tears.

'Ever.' He says against my lips.

I smile as I lean back in and kiss him as he pulls me in tighter.

It starts off soft but gets harder.

He is holding me against him as his hand tangles in my hair.

I love this man and I will die protecting him.

I don't care what Amber or her bosses says.

I was a prisoner of Michael for more than seven years.
I know exactly what that monster is capable of.
I know exactly what he will do to me when he gets me back.
But if he finds out about Dominic, he will be enraged even more.
He will make Dominic watch as he tortures and breaks me all over again.
Michael won't touch Dominic straight away but will use him against me.
Dominic is my weakness and Michael will use that to his full advantage.
I tighten my hold on Dominic as I deepen our kiss.

'Liz,'
'Yes,' I reply breathing heavily.
'What was that? It better not be goodbye because I'll follow you.'
'I won't,' My lips silence him. 'It's my promise to you.'
'Promise?' He looks at me, I can see the pain in his eyes.
'To love and protect you or die trying.'
'Liz…'
'No more for today, I will tell you everything on Sunday.' I say as I run my hands through his hair.

Dominic nods as he rests his head on my chest and holds me tight.
I kiss the top of his head and run my fingers through his hair.
I memorise every detail of his face, his body, touch and smell.
It will be those things that will get me through what I'm now planning to do.
I'm going to end this one way or another.
We head back downstairs.
Dominic turns the kettle on as I get the chocolate cake and vanilla slice out of the fridge.
He comes up behind me and wraps me in his arms, kissing my bare shoulder.
'I really really like this jumper.' He whispers in my ear.
I smile
'That's why I bought it.'
'Shame about the jeans though, they ruin the view.'
'I'll remember that.' I giggle.

'Hell yeah, that better be yours, Liz.' Luke says coming to the kitchen.
I smile and nod.
'Sweet save some for me, don't let him eat it all.' Simon calls from the lounge.
'Snooze you lose!' Dominic and Luke call out.
Simon practically jumps into the kitchen.
He punches Luke in the shoulder and steals his plate.
'Hey, that's mine.' Luke says
'Snooze you lose.' Simon laughs as he eats.

'Here Luke,' I slide another plate over to him.
'Amber, Ben would you like some?' I ask them.
'Um when have I ever rejected your food?' Amber takes a plate.
'Sure,' Ben replies.
'Man I could eat this all the time.' Luke says helping himself to more vanilla slice.
'I'll trade double vanilla slice containers for information.' I say leaning over the bench.

'I'm listening.' He looks at me.
'You can finish your story from the other day when Dominic was…'
'Done.' He says before I can finish.
'Along with additional information.'
'Done.' He smiles at me.
'What's done?' Dominic asks.
'It's need to know.' I wink at him.

Dominic looks straight at Luke.
'No,' He points at Luke.
'Sorry mate the food is worth the risk.' Luke laughs.
'Can I make deals? I have heaps on Dominic as well.' Simon adds
'Fuck off, Simon.' Dominic looks at him.
'Ooh, tell me and then I can tell you about Liz.' Amber says
'He already knows.' I say.
'Really? Does he know that you stood in the kitchen looking out the window after he left the first time you met? You were glowing. You were on a whole other planet. I was talking and you were completely spaced out with your fingers on your lips and smiling.' Amber smiles.

I look at Dominic then to the floor, blushing.
'You could have sworn he kissed her.' Amber looks at Luke.
'I almost did, twice. But we were interrupted.' Dominic says as he touches my neck, bringing my eyes up to see his.
'She stood in the kitchen for like half an hour trying to remember how to make chocolate cake.' Amber giggles.
Dominic smiles at me, I bite my bottom lip.

'Dominic spilt coffee on himself when he saw Liz at the shops the next day and then tripped over the drawbar of the trailer trying to hide.'
'Okay, Luke, you can fuck off now.' Dominic laughs.
'But there's more,' Luke looks at Dominic.
'Really?' I look at Dominic.

'No.' Dominic shakes his head.
'He kept checking his phone and when it was Liz, he was like a kid at Christmas. And they would talk for ages.'
'Liz was the same, she would blush every time I would mention his name. She even burnt a pavlova due to her daydreaming.'

'Dominic at the pub on Friday. Panicking that you would ring and cancel.' Simon laughs. 'He was so nervous about Saturday he would jump every time his phone beeped and he completely ignored all the candy in the room.' He adds.
'I'm so glad I was able to entertain you both.' Dominic laughs, shaking his head.
'Don't worry, Amber was no better. I couldn't get her to shut up. I have never made so much chocolate cake and…'
'Well, you did succeed on a couple of occasions.' Amber looks at me.
'Right, I got you with chocolate and cream on the Sunday night after the beach. Followed by Liz and the sturdy daybed a while ago.' Dominic laughs and smiles at me.
Simon, Luke, and Ben look at us and Amber.
'Well,' Luke says looking at Amber.
'Do tell.' Simon adds.
'Well, I got home on the Sunday night after the beach and our dear Dominic hadn't left yet.' Amber winks.
'We had dinner and Liz said that she made cheesecake.
Judging by what I walked in on, I said I was surprised she found the time to which Dominic replied.' Amber looks at him.
'Well we did go through a fair share of chocolate and cream.' Dominic says, pulling me in and kissing the top of my head.

Luke, Ben, and Simon look at us.
'Oh but wait it gets better.' Amber says and they look at Amber.
'I got home late one night and found them 'busy' on the daybed. When I confronted them the next day Liz so beautifully said,' She looks at me.
'Well the daybed is sturdy.' I say.
They all laugh and Dominic holds me tighter.
'See, meant to be together,' Simon says.
Ben looks at the floor, Luke, Simon, and Amber look at Dominic and smile.
'Am I missing something?' I ask.
'He loves you.' Ben says.
'Um, yeah no Ben, I don't think so. Does anyone want coffee.'
'No we should get going, big day tomorrow. What time will you and Dominic be coming over?' Amber asks me.
'Um probably around lunch time I think.' I reply.

'Hey Liz, can I?' Luke asks.
'Of course I'll grab a container.'

'Hey, they are mine.' Dominic laments.
'I'll make you some more.' I smile.
'You better.' He says as he grabs me.
'Can I take some?' Ben asks
'Sure. Simon, Amber?
'Yes please.' Simon replies.
Dominic groans.
'I'm good, there is stuff at home.' Amber replies.
I look at Dominic and smile.
'Hey, Liz, where are your car keys?' Amber asks.
'On the buffet next to Ben.' I answer.

'Is that your beast?' Ben asks.
'Yep,' I answer Ben, not looking at him.
'Sweet, nice work on the wheels, Dom.'
'I didn't do a thing. That car is all Liz's doing.' Dominic replies as I hug him.
'So you can cook and appreciate nice cars. Call me if you ever end up single.'
Ben smiles.
'Yeah not happening.' Dominic replies, picking up on my nervous tremble.
'Get in line behind me.' Simon says.
'Way back in line.' Luke adds, slapping Ben on the shoulder.

Dominic looks at me and smiles, holding me tighter.
He kisses me softly and his hands slide down grabbing my arse and lifting me
up.
I smile as I return his kiss wrapping my legs around him and Dominic smiles,
deepening our kiss.
I know what he is doing and I love it.
He sits me on the kitchen bench as the others start to grab their stuff.
His hands slide under my shirt.
'Mmm… no bra.' Dominic says quietly with a raised eyebrow.
'I thought you might approve of easier access.' I wink.
His fingers play with the loose locks of hair on the side of my face.
I feel Dominic move his hands down and pull me in closer, he is looking past
me and his body language has changed.

'Elizabeth, Dominic.' Ben says.
'Yes, Ben,' Dominic replies.
I slide off the bench and stand behind Dominic, holding his hand.

'Luke, Simon and Amber explained a little about your ex and what happened with Daniel. I wouldn't have done what I did if I had known. I also didn't believe Dominic when he said you were together. I am really sorry.' Ben says sincerely.
'Thank you, Ben. We appreciate it.' Dominic replies.
'Thank you.' I say holding Dominic's hand tighter.
I still get a funny feeling about Ben.
I also get a small sense of mistrust from Dominic towards Ben.
'I guess I'll see you tomorrow then.' He smiles.
'Yep, see you tomorrow.' Dominic nods.

Dominic pulls me in front of him and kisses my bare shoulder as Ben walks away.
'Dominic,' I turn in his arms. 'Please don't leave me alone with him. I still don't feel right.' I whisper as I look up at him.
He smiles as he brings his hands up to my neck and kisses me softly.
'Wouldn't dream of it—I feel the same way.' He winks.

I wrap my arms around him, in his arms is my safe place.
'I should get the last of the bags out of the car.'
'I'll help you.' He says taking my hand.
We follow the others out and see them off before turning to my car. We start getting the bags.
'Hey no peeking I said.' I smile as I grab the bag off him.
'But,'
'No it's a surprise.' I say as I wink at him.
'How many surprises?'
'How long are we in Fiji?' I ask him.
'Seven nights.' He replies with a smile.
'Well more than seven.' I wink at him.
'New Zealand fourteen nights.'
'More than twenty-one.'
He groans and grabs some more bags and we head inside.

'Maybe I can wear one tonight.'
'Well after that green bikini, I won't complain. He smiles at me as I blush.
The best promise I ever made myself was to let myself move on from my past.
I know that I will never escape it but I can't let it rule my future.
Do I have a future with Dominic?
I watch him move around the bedroom as I sit on our bed.
He makes me feel like we do, he makes me feel loved even though he hasn't said it.
I admit I'm not expecting him to.

And I know it won't be for a long time even if he does.
I'm okay with that.
I'm living in whatever moment we are having right now.
Because what I am planning could put an end to everything.
It could bring an end to my life.

👀 DOMINIC 👀

Elizabeth is watching me move about our bedroom.
I know she has something planned and I'm scared it will be at the expense of her life.
Losing her is not something I'm prepared to do, I will not let her leave without fighting for her.
I love her and she loves me, hiding my secret is getting harder every day.
I want to tell her but the time is not right.
I lay awake at night sometimes and watch her sleep.
I know she is having nightmares but they haven't woken her up or affected her like they have in the past.
She is more relaxed and letting me in.
As hard as it is for her to talk about her past she is talking and healing.
I smile at her.
'Hey, you,' Liz says walking up to me.
'There's my girl,' I say as I wrap my arm around her waist and my other hand on her neck covering the scar.
I run my thumb along her jaw as my lips meet hers and her arms wrap around me, pulling herself against me.

👀 MICHAEL 👀

MARGARET RIVER, WESTERN AUSTRALIA.

'Sam.'
'Yes Michael.'
'I'm heading over to the barn to check on Chantelle's room. Tell Spencer to meet me there.' I say grabbing the medical files for Chantelle.
'Have you heard from Brian?' I ask him.
'Yes he was following up leads. He is on his way back now,' Sam looks at his watch. 'He is due within the hour.'

'Excellent, meet me in the barn when he arrives. I would like to see what he has for me immediately.'
'Of course, Michael.' Sam says leaving my office.

I look over Chantelle's files again, I have big plans for her.
New toys, new room, even her own hospital room and doctor.
I'm looking forward to getting reacquainted with my beast-tamer.
I get up and head over to the barn, Spencer is waiting for me.
Spencer is a German doctor with questionable desires and family links to Hitler and the doctors who helped with the genocide.
He is perfect for my organisation, he likes to experiment and I can supply the bodies.
'Michael.' Spencer smiles.
'Spencer, I have two new work rooms and a playroom for you.' I say.
'Excellent, I have been looking forward to my new playroom.'
I hand him Chantelle's medical files.
'Have you found her?'
'No, but Brian has a lead and he will be joining us shortly.' I reply.
I open the door to 'The Barn' and walk in.
I head over to a stable gate and open it.
In the stable floor is a metal door.

'To open the door you require a five digit pin code followed by the hash key, it's '02605#' I say as I put in the code and open the door.
I walk down the stairs followed by Spencer.
'Well done, Michael, you have some amazing toys for me.'
Spencer's face is like a kid in a candy store.

'What do we have here; x-ray, ECG, dialysis machine, defib, sterilizing autoclave. You even have drugs and blood.' Spencer says with a smile.
'I have a lab for you as well to play in, you can make drugs for me and what's required to treat Chantelle and my men.'
Spencer smiles.

'What else do you think you will need?'
'Well going by her file here, a CT and MRI wouldn't go astray.
I mean you are intending in keeping your plaything alive.'
'Done,' I nod and walk through the red doors to her new room.
It's coming along nicely.
The toilet and shower have been installed along with her bed.
Even some of the cameras, TV, and DVD player have been installed.
The hose and drains are in along with the washing machine and dryer.

My toy cabinet will be installed against the wall next to the stairs.
The black polished concrete floor will look good with her blood splattered and dripping on it.

'Michael.'
'Hello, Brian.' I turn to greet him.
'I have some good news and some bad news,' He says walking up to me.
'Brian,' I say annoyed.
'I hate bad news.' I look at him.
'I followed leads in Sydney and Melbourne which turned out to be nothing. But, a contact got me these.' Brian hands me an A4 envelope.
Pictures slide out, my Chantelle.
I start going through them.
'Who is this man and what is he doing?'
'That is Agent David Ryan, her personal bodyguard. He looks to be building a deck. Keep looking.' He says.
I look at him, then back to the pictures.
As I continue to look over the pictures, I start getting angry.
He is touching my property without my permission.
He is kissing her, and she is returning the kiss, he has fucking brainwashed her.
She's my fucking Chantelle, not his, mine!
The last picture sends me into pure rage.
He is in bed with my Chantelle!

'Where the fuck are they?' I yell as I feel my mouth dry up.
'Hobart.' Brian replies.
'Get a team ready and provisions. I'm making a house call.' I yell.
Brian and Sam nod then leave hastily.
I scream in murderous rage.

Chantelle is my fucking property to fuck, no one else's.
I will fucking draw and quarter anyone who touches her without my permission.
But first, they will watch as I fuck her, hit her, cut her, and watch her bleed.
They will hear her cries and screams.
I will make Chantelle watch me as I torture them.
I will cut their balls off with a rusty blade.
Take to their fingers with tin snips.
I will cut out their tongue and let them choke on their own blood.
Chantelle's punishment will go on for days.
I will fucking break her and break her again and again.
I will fuck her till she forgets him and forgets her own name.

No one will ever take her from me again, I will make damn fucking sure of it.
I am Michael Webster and I own her!

I will adopt a child and dangle it in front of her like bait, to keep her from leaving and keep her inline.
I could show her pictures of her family.
I'm Michael fucking Webster, I'm unfuckingtouchable and I'll burn them alive if they try.
I compose myself by watching footage of me fucking Chantelle.
I listen to her scream and beg.

I get hard watching her bleed as I run the knife from her neck to her collarbone over her breast and down to her belly button.
I watch as I lick the blood on her breast.
I undo my zipper, I need to cum.
I continue to watch.
I start using the leather flogger on her, her back starts to go red as it welts and starts to bleed.
Her arse is begging to be fucked.
I continue to watch as I jerk off.
I ram a lubricated butt plug up her arse causing her to scream in pain and bleed.
I start to cum as slap her arse in the footage.
I clean myself up and turn the footage off.
I grab the envelope with the pictures and head back to the house.

'Sam,' I say walking into the kitchen.
'Michael,' He replies.
'Spencer wants a CT and MRI machines. The bunker will need to be extended so get plans drawn up. Talk to Spencer and see what else he will need.' I say dropping the envelope with the pictures in front of him.
'They are expensive and hard to come by,'
'Do I look like I care? I have money and contacts.' I say cutting him off. 'I'm not in the mood to be told no.' Truth be told I'm never in the mood to be told no.
'I'll get on it.' He says as he opens it up and starts looking at the pictures. 'Is this Ryan with her?' He asks.
'Yes, and he is fucking her!'

'Michael?' Brian says walking into the kitchen
'Yes Brian?' I reply.
'Arrangements have been made, we leave tomorrow morning for Perth. There are a few things that require your attention first and then we fly out for Hobart.'
'Excellent.'

'Would you like the maid to make you something to eat?' Brian asks.

'Yes please, I'll eat that in my office.' I start to leave.

'Brian?' I say, turning back.

'Yes Michael?'

'We will need more Type O blood would you…'

'Of course, I'll go see Spencer after I get the maid.' He nods as he leaves the room.

'I'll go see him as well, I'm Type O too.' Sam stands.

'That's right, thank you, Sam.' I reply.

I walk up to my office smiling.

Just think, in forty-eight hours I'll have my property back with me, my Chantelle.

In forty-eight hours also, Agent David Ryan will be dead.

CHAPTER 14
Happy Fucking Birthday

👀 Elizabeth 👀

I wake up before Dominic.
I slept well after my late night phone call, things are finally starting to happen.
It was the first night in a long time with no bad dreams.
I quietly go to get up but he grabs me and pulls me to him.
He wraps his arms around me and brings his lips to my shoulder.
'Hey, you.'
'There's my girl.'

He holds me tight as he kisses the scars on my shoulder.
'Morning,' I giggle.
'Morning beautiful.' He says.
He rolls me over and climbs on top of me and I wrap my legs around him.
Dominic rests his head on my chest and I run my fingers through his hair.
We lay there for ages just enjoying each other's touch.
'We have to get up,' I say, kissing the top of his head.
'I don't want to,' He replies, holding me tighter.
'Dominic,'
'No.'
I giggle.
'Dominic,'
'No.' He groans.
He starts to kiss my chest, moving up to my neck, following my jawline, and finds my lips.
His phone rings.

'Dominic,' I say as he continues to kiss me.
'No.' He growls
I can feel his hands move along my body.
'Dominic,'

'Liz,' He says against my lips.
My phone rings and I reach over and grab it, it's Amber.

'Hey, Amber,' I answer.
Dominic trails kisses down my neck.
'No, I was up.' I say.
Dominic takes my breast in his mouth and I try not to moan.
'What? When?'
Dominic stops and looks up at me.

'Okay, we will be there in about an hour.'
I put my phone back on the bedside table and look at Dominic.
'Don't stop,' I look at him.
'What was that about?' He asks.
'Something special.' I wink at him.
'Do tell.' He asks.
'No.'
'Please?' He looks at me.
'Mmm no.'
I giggle as he moves back up.
'Pretty please.' He pouts.
'Mmm maybe.' I giggle. 'Mmm then again maybe not.' I smile.
'I just realised that I didn't give you your last surprise.'
'Well it can wait, I have something else in mind.' I say biting my bottom lip.
'Why, Mrs. Miller, are you trying to seduce me?'
My legs wrap around him and pull him down.
'Is it working, Mr. Miller?'
He grins.

We finally make our way to Amber's house.
'You're late!' Amber says I get out of the car.
'Sorry,' I say as I look at Dominic and smile.
'It's in the shed. What is it?' She asks.
'It's a belated birthday surprise for Dominic.' I reply.
'Right, well, I shall leave you both to it.' Amber winks and leaves.

Dominic and I walk into the shed.
There is a large box lying flat on the table and up against the back wall with 'fragile' taped all over it.
'Liz, what is it?' He looks at me.
I can't help but smile.

'Well I wasn't really able to get you the perfect birthday gift while I was in hospital. But I found something that I knew you would love more than anything,'
'Elizabeth.'
'I wanted to get you something that would hold meaning.'
'I missed your birthday.'
'My birthday is not till December.' I look at him.
'No, I mean your real birthday.' He looks at me.
I shake my head and smile.
'Open it.' I say handing him a stanley knife.

He takes the knife and smiles at me then starts to cut the strapping away followed by the tape.
Dominic lifts the lid of the carton and picks up an A4 envelope addressed to him.
Dominic looks at me as he opens the envelope and slides out the papers.
I watch him read the letter, and then he looks at me with a shocked look on his face.
I panic a little and run my fingers along my neck.
He starts to unwrap the contents and my hands start to shake.
Dominic stands there just looking at it and reading the certificate of Authenticity.
He just stands there looking at it, I slowly move towards him.
'Dominic,' I say softly.
'Um, Liz. Is this really what I think it is?' He asks, still not looking at me.

'Yes, it's the Auckland Warriors inaugural jersey from their first game in 1995 against the Broncos at Mt Smart Stadium. It's signed by the players and coach.'
'It's amazing, How did you get it?'
'Auction for a children's hospital in Auckland. I got the winning bid.'
'I, um, wow. Thank you.' He looks at me.
I blush and look at the floor. Dominic's hand lifts my chin up.
'You are amazing, you know that right?' He says as his hand moves along my cheek.
His other hand snakes around my lower back and pulls me in.
He leans in and kisses me softly.

'Now can we see it?' Amber calls from the doorway.
Dominic groans.
'If you must.' He replies.
Amber walks in followed by Luke and Simon.
Amber quickly glances at it before stealing me away.
'Cuppa?' She asks.
'Sure.'

We head upstairs into the kitchen, I know she needs to talk to me about something.
We make coffee and head out onto the deck.
'What, Amber?'
'I did what you asked me.' She replies, looking nervous.
'Is it exactly how I wanted it?'
'Yes, all the deliveries are due next week and while you are away, it will be done as per your request.'
'All clean?' I ask her.
'When traced it will lead back to him.'
'What else do you want to ask, Amber?'
Amber takes a deep breath.

'These precautions you spoke of. What are they?'
'Amber, I'm a paramedic. I spent a lot of time in hospitals. A bit here a bit there and before you know it I have my own stash. I may have also taken some heavy stuff from the paramedics when they were treating Shaye. I have also been around a lot of police and bad people.'
'So what do I do if you take it?'
'Nothing.'
'Elizabeth, I'm serious.'
'So am I, Amber, if I take it I'm dead,'

'Elizabeth, you can't. You have no idea the damage it would cause.'
'I have no idea! Seven years, Amber, seven fucking years! He has the farm now, don't you see, this changes everything.'
'Elizabeth, what about Dominic?'
'Dominic will be safe. He can move on, you both can.'
'I won't let you, Dominic won't let you.'
'Amber, just stop! You have read the files. I was the one who lived through it. He is coming for me, not you for me.' I close my eyes and take a breath. 'What I suffered before is nothing compared to what's coming. He is preparing for my return. That changes everything. I need to change things.' I turn to walk away.

'Liz,'
'I'm going for a walk, ALONE.' I say heading to the steps towards the beach.
'Liz,'
'What Amber?' I turn to her.
'I'm sorry but I love you,'
'Amber, seven and a half years. I lost seven and a half fucking years! Do you honestly think I will go back to that?'
'At least give us a chance,'

'If he gets me in the bunker there is no chance. What don't you understand about that? They let him out, when he takes me there you will not find me.' I turn away from her.

'Liz please!' Amber pleads with me.

'What's going on?' Dominic asks.
I turn around and see Dominic, Luke, and Simon on the deck.
'Babe, what's going on?'
'Ask, Amber!' I snap and start to walk away.
'Elizabeth.' Dominic calls out.
I turn back to him.

'Babe talk to me. Please.' He walks towards me.
'I can't.' I shake my head and step back from him.
'Hun, you can't do this.' Amber pleads.
I turn and walk away, I need to be alone.
'Elizabeth!' Dominic calls out.
'Don't! Please don't.' I call back and keep walking.

👀 DOMINIC 👀

I look at Amber, she looks completely defeated.
'What the hell was that about?'
Simon and Luke walk over to us.
'Is Liz okay?' Luke asks.
'No,' Amber replies. 'Something has happened, things have changed.'
'Where is Michael?' I ask her.
'Last report this morning has him heading to Perth by private jet. But he has logged flight plans and we can't get confirmation yet on what they are.'
'Why?' Luke asks.
'Friends in high places.' Amber looks at the ground.
'What do we need to do to protect our girl?' Simon asks.
Amber turns to Simon.
'Simon?' Amber says.
'Yeah.' He replies.
'What drugs did Liz get while she was in hospital?'
'Amber?' I look at her.
'I just found out Liz's precautions.'

'What precautions?'
We turn around to see Agent Smith at the top of the stairs.

'Sir, you're early.' Amber says.
'Where is Elizabeth?' He asks.
'What precautions has she got?' He looks at Amber.
'Drugs, I was just asking Simon what she could have gotten,'
'Where is she? Is everyone here?'
'Elizabeth has gone for a walk and Cassie is about five minutes away.' Amber replies.
'Good.' He walks up to the table placing his briefcase on the table. 'Go and get her back here now.'

'Amber put the kettle on, has my girl made any treats?'
'Your girl?' I ask.
He turns back to look at me.
'Do you have a problem with that?' He asks with a pointed stare.
'No, I guess not.' I say turning away and heading down to the beach to find Liz.

I find her standing on the water's edge, I stand there and watch her.
I need her to fight and not give up.
I remove my shoes and socks as she starts to walk into the water.
'Liz!' I call out as I run to her.
She turns around as I reach for her.
My lips crash down on hers, I kiss her hard.
Liz tries to push me away but I won't let her.
I just hold her tighter till she stops pushing against me.
Her arms wrap around my neck, her kiss is as hungry as mine.
I can taste her tears.
'Liz,' I whisper against her lips.
'Dominic,' Liz replies.
'Please don't give up, I need you. I can't be where you're not.'
'Dominic.' She looks up at me.

I grab her shoulders.
'I mean it, Elizabeth. I will find you, I will get you back. I won't lose you.' I say looking into her eyes.
'Dominic, I don't…'
'No Liz! You will fight. Michael cannot win, you cannot let him win, do you hear me?' I say angrily at her.
'I'
'Liz! You fight! You fight and I will find you, do you understand me? You will not give up!' I shake her.
'Yes, Dominic, I understand,' Liz stares at me blankly.

'Say it!' I snap at her.
'I won't give up, I will fight. You will find me.' Liz replies

I feel bad for snapping at her but I need to get her to focus.
I run my fingers along her cheek as my other arm snakes around her waist.
I feel her body language change, she looks me in the eyes.
'Tell me how you feel about me.' I ask as my finger traces the scar on her neck.
'I love you, Dominic. I love you more than life itself.'
I bring my lips to hers.
I need to tell her that I love her.
That I love her more than life itself and nothing will ever change how I feel about her.
I need to tell her so she won't give up.
'We need to head back. Agent Smith has arrived.' I say.
'He can wait a little longer.' Liz says as she pulls me back.
She whimpers as she deepens the kiss.
My hands slide down and grab her arse, lifting her, and she wraps her legs around me.
I walk out of the water, looking her in the eyes as I put her down.

'Shall we? Agent Smith is waiting.' I say smiling at her.
'Okay.' Liz replies.
I take her hand and we walk back, picking up my shoes on the way.
They are all waiting up on the deck for us.
'Liz,' Amber says.
Liz looks at her and nods.
Cassie, Luke, and Simon are sitting at the table with Agent Smith.

👀 ELIZABETH 👀

'Elizabeth, my girl. How are you?' Agent Smith gets up and offers me his hand.
'I am good thank you, and you?' I shake his hand but stay close enough to Dominic so that I can still hold his hand.
'I am well, thank you. Are you sure you want to still do this?' He asks me.
'Do what, Elizabeth?' Dominic asks me. 'What's going on?' There is anguish in his eyes.
'I'm not leaving you,'
'Against my better judgement.' Agent Smith interjects.

'What?' Amber asks.

'I have new information that I shared with Elizabeth late last night. I told her to leave straight away. Elizabeth refused. I still had to come here today and have this little meeting.'

'What information?' Dominic asks.

'Please let us all sit and have some coffee and treats. Elizabeth, would you mind?'

I nod and head inside. Dominic follows me inside.

'Liz, what's going on? I'm completely freaking out,'

I grab him and kiss him.

He wraps his arms around me tightly, no place I would rather be than in his arms.

'Liz please tell me. I'm not losing you,'

'You won't, I promised you. I won't leave unless you tell me to. You told me to fight and you will find me.' I say as I get the coffees ready.

'But,'

'Michael is on the move, he has his contacts looking for me.'

'He won't,'

'He is Michael Webster. This is one of the reasons for today's meeting, he is getting too close.' I turn back to him. 'Michael has gotten too close and things have had to change.'

I can see the fear in Dominic's eyes.

You could almost think he loves me.

'I need to be sure that I can keep you safe.'

'To hell with being safe! I made you a promise. I won't let you do this by yourself.'

'Dominic, please, you don't know Michael—he's a monster. I want to ensure the ones I love are protected and safe.'

I reach for him. 'I love you.'

My fingers brush along his cheeks and pull him down to me.

He kisses me softly before resting his head on mine and closing his eyes.

We walk out with the trays.

'Okay, shall we begin?' Agent Smith asks.

'Do you have the documents?' I ask him.

'Yes, I do Elizabeth. But…'

'May I have them now?'

He hands me a large folder with Yellow A4 envelopes and a pen.

'Shall we start now?' He asks.

I nod and begin to sign the documents.

Agent Smith watches me then looks at everyone in the room, 'Okay as you are all aware, Elizabeth has a past. What's happened to her is completely NOT her fault. It is all the doings of someone we class as a psychopath. Michael is extremely clever, cunning, and powerful.' He says.
Everyone in the room is intently focused on Agent Smith, taking it all in.

'Michael is also extremely wealthy and, as a result, has a lot of influence and people in the right places. Keeping Elizabeth safe even while Michael was in prison has been a big task. Even in the AFP and the police force, Michael has people on his payroll.' he says. 'However, we too have agents who have infiltrated Michael's organisation. These agents are the reason why we were able to put him away and how we initially found Elizabeth.
'What was he on your radar for in the beginning, Agent Smith?' asks Simon.
'At first we didn't even know what he looked like. Due to his love of using Russian muscle for some of his dirty work he was nicknamed 'Babayka' it's Russian for Bogeyman.'
'So did you know about Elizabeth? Where was she when you found her?' Simon quizzes Agent Smith again.
I look up and see Agent Smith look over at me, I nod and look back down.

'It was a tip off, the first time we found her,' I continue to sign the documents and not look up.
'First time? What do you mean? You rescued her twice? Dominic what the fuck?' Luke explodes.
'Luke, just listen.' Dominic puts a hand on his shoulder.
I finish signing the documents and look up to see Dominic looking at me.
With one hand still on Luke's shoulder to calm him, he reaches for me with the other, pulling me into his chest to hug me.
'The first time we found her, she was chained in a small cage under some stairs.' He answers.
'The second time we found her, she was unrecognisable. She was beaten so badly we all thought she was dead until we saw fingers move. She was pointing towards a cupboard. That's where we found the camera, he recorded everything.
'We were also able to get some money for Elizabeth so she could hide and we could protect her. We liquidated his assets and the team managed to extract funds via a few other methods. It was quite an operation in itself,' Agent Smith pauses for more coffee. 'Now our Elizabeth here being the extremely smart girl she is, did some pretty cool things too unknown to us. Her actions resulted in a significant pay off. We just need the last piece of the puzzle before we can put him away for good.

'None of this was easy. We deal with the dark side of the human race every day, but Michael is definitely one of the worst I've come across in my career. I think you really need to understand this. He's not just a bad egg or bully, he's pure evil. He is the Charles Manson of the crime world but the difference is, he likes to get his hands dirty, Charles didn't. He is completely fixated on Elizabeth. He calls her his 'Beast-Tamer'.

'He groomed her, and manipulated her for one purpose: to imprison her and do truly unspeakable things to her until he feels the raging beast inside himself calm down. Michael would torture Elizabeth for hours, sometimes days. Nothing including other people he tortured and killed would ever tame his beast, the man is a complete nut case, he's sick and twisted. The only thing that will stop him from continuing to do it and from pursuing Elizabeth is death.'

I can feel my hands shaking.
I close my eyes and try to focus.
I take a deep breath, filling myself with the warm familiar scent of Dominic.
He takes both of my hands.
'Hey, breathe with me Liz. We've got you, babe, it's okay, we're here.' He says as he runs his fingers over my neck.
I open my eyes.
He kneels in front of me, holding my hands till they stop shaking, our eyes never part.
'Don't you ever stop smiling.' Dominic says as he kisses me softly.
'Excuse me, Dominic. You are making me feel like an overprotective father with a loaded gun.' Agent Smith chuckles.
Dominic smiles as he helps me stand up.
Agent Smith walks over to us.
'How are you doing, Elizabeth? Are you okay?' He asks.
'Yes,' I say.
'I bought some sedatives with me if you need some, but looks like your man here is doing a brilliant job of calming and relaxing you.' He smiles at Dominic and pats his shoulder.
'I know my girl and know what she needs.' He says smiling at me.
'You do, and clearly you trust him Elizabeth,' He says.
I nod and smile at Dominic.

'You know, Dominic, I was with Liz every day for seventeen months before she even spoke to me. And that was only to correct me on who won the 85 Bathurst 1000.' He smiles at me.
'The James Hardie 1000. John Goss and Armin Habine, XJS Jag in six hours and forty-one minutes. Not Peter Brock.' I smile.
Agent Smith laughs.

'Right and today is the first time she has let me give her a hug'
I look down at my hands feeling ashamed.
'Don't you dare feel bad Elizabeth. You have come a long way and I'm very proud of you. When this finally goes to court, you will be stronger than Michael that's for sure.' Agent Smith says.
I smile and nod, I feel Dominic's hand gently squeeze my waist and I turn to smile at him.

'So, what's the plan from here, I assume there is one since I heard Liz say Michael is out of prison and is coming for her again?' Simon asks.
'Are we the only people that know all this?' Luke asks.
'Please tell me how we can protect our girl and kick this fucker's arse.' Cassie says as she stands up and walks over to me. 'I meant what I said that night. Dom is like a brother to me and I love the hell out of you, Liz. I'm here to support you both.' Cassie hugs me.

The plan is for you all to keep an eye out but not engage.' Agent Smith remarks.
'No not good enough.' Luke cuts in.
'Please let me finish. 'Agent Smith puts his hand up to stop Luke. 'Michael and his men are not to be taken lightly. When the time comes, we will need your help to move Elizabeth. With Michael closing in, it appears the leaks are closer then I first thought. So when she moves, it will only be Elizabeth and the person with her that will know the destination.'
'I move with her.' Dominic says more as a command than a request.
I shake my head. 'No you will meet me at the final destination.'
'NO.' Dominic stands up. 'We go together.'
'Dominic,' Agent Smith interjects. 'Please trust us. You are far too invested in Elizabeth that you could end up being the reason Michael gets her back.'
Dominic's body stills and the blood drains from his face. He flops back into his chair hanging his head.
'I won't let him take her.' He says not looking up. 'I can fight him.'
'That's just it, Dominic, he is not someone you can fight against and come out on top. He is not built to lose.' I place my hand on his shoulder before dropping to my knees.
'Right, now would you like to do the honours, Elizabeth?'
I stand up and hand Luke, Simon, Cassie, and Amber an envelope each.
I watch as they open them.
I feel Dominic take my hand and run his fingers over mine.

'Liz, this is a deed for my house. A deed in my name fully paid off.' Luke looks at me shocked.
'So is mine.' Simon adds.

'And mine,' Cassie says.
'Liz what have you done?' Amber asks.
'It's a small token of my appreciation to you all. You and Cassie have offered to give me something I thought I would never get the chance to have. Friendship and a family of my own.' I smile at Amber.
'It's a transfer of deed for this house; it's clean, debt free and all yours.' I add.
'Liz,' Amber starts to say something.
'Friends in the right places.' Agent Smith winks.

'Liz, I appreciate what you are doing but I'm not helping you so that I get something out of it. I don't, I mean I can't accept, this is huge.' Luke starts.
'You can and you will. Keep looking.' I smile at him.
He pulls out the rest of the papers and looks through them and stops. He looks at me completely stunned.
'Liz, this is too much.'
'No nothing is too much when it comes to children.'
'But…'
'It's an education trust fund for Jack and Lily. Sheila can't touch it and she can't claim anything against your property.'

Luke stands up and comes over to me.
'I love you,' He smiles and hugs me.
'Like a sister,' He slaps Dominic on the shoulder.
'I can love you like a sister and finally not be an only child,' Simon says as he hugs me as well.
'Thank you,' Cassie hugs me as well.
'Liz,' Amber comes up to me. 'I can't.'
'Yes you can, Amber,' I say, hugging her.
'But this is your…'
'Was my dream home, I have something better now. I don't care about the property or the money anymore.'
'But you never cared about the money.' Amber says.
'True,' I smile.

'So what's in that envelope?' Luke asks, nodding to the one I'm still holding.
'This one is for Shaun and Chantelle. They don't need to know but I want them to enjoy what they have and by doing this I know that I can help them do that.'
'And this one?' Amber points to the one on the table beside me.
'That will be up to Dominic to tell you.' I reply as I take Dominic's hand.
'Agent Smith, Amber. I will leave you both to it.' I say as I pick up the folder.

Dominic and I walk inside to our room.

I put the folder and envelope on the locked cabinet as Dominic closes the door.

'As promised, I will tell you everything tomorrow.' I say as I sit on the bed.

Dominic sits down on our bed.

He pulls me on to his lap and kisses the top of my head while running his fingers through my hair.

'Liz?'

'Yes.'

'Please don't leave,' Dominic says.

'I won't leave you but…'

'You have to fight, because I will fight for you. I love you, Elizabeth.'

I stand up and look at him as he stands.

I'm shocked he's telling me he loves me, I have been waiting for this moment. Is this real?

'Don't,' I say to him as I take a step back, putting my hand up to keep him at arm's length. 'Don't you dare.' My body trembles with nervous excitement.

 'Please don't say it if you…'

Dominic smiles as he reaches for me.

It's right at that moment I realise I now have everything I could ever want or need.

'I do mean it. I love you, Elizabeth.' He pulls me into his arms as his lips find mine and his hand tangles in my hair.

His hands move up my body to cup my face.

'I have wanted to tell you so many times and each time, something happened and we lost the special moment. I can't wait any longer so I'm telling you now before any other crazy stuff happens and before anyone bursts in on us.' he laughs.

'I love you, Elizabeth,' he move his hands down to my waist.

'I still can't believe you said it, and you mean it.' I say, as I feel myself blush.

'Why?'

'I don't know, it's just…' I look at the floor.

'What?' He asks as he lifts my chin.

I take a breath.

'For so long I was made to believe that I was nothing, a nobody, and utterly disposable. I guess I still find it hard sometimes to believe that someone actually wants to be with me. That someone can actually really love me.'

'Well I want to be with you, and I want you to stay with me and be with me. I love you, Elizabeth. I love you, including Chantelle, the person you used to be.' He looks at me.

I don't know what to say but I can feel the tears start to fall.
I never thought I would get to hear someone say that to me.
My life feels right despite what's happening.
I stare into the eyes of the man I love and see the love and desire he has for me.
Does this mean I could have a chance at having a family?
Now I know I have to fight.
I can't leave him.
I will do everything in my power to get back to him.

He wipes away my tears.
He leans in and kisses me, I part my lips as his tongue teases my lips.
I slowly slide my hands under his shirt, I feel his body tense under my touch.
Our kiss starts off soft, his hand tangles in my hair as his arm wraps around me.
Our kiss deepens and becomes more urgent, hungrier, harder.
He is kissing me with everything he has to give and I'm returning it.
I manage to get our shirts off, he stops and smiles at me.

'New?'
I nod.
My new bra is made with black lace over soft pink silk.
His fingers trace along the straps down to my breast and down my sides to my hips.
'Do you like it?' I ask him.
'Very much.'
'Then you will like the rest of it just as much.' I say biting my bottom lip and smiling.

His hands slide under my skirt to my arse.
He groans as he squeezes and lifts me up.
I wrap my legs around him, my arms around his neck, my hand in his hair holding his lips to mine.
He gently bites my bottom lip as he pulls my head back and his lips and tongue move along my jawline to my ear then down to my neck.
I gasp as his hand squeezes harder.
'Dominic.' I moan.

As soon as my feet touch the ground he turns me around, his chest against my back as he cups my breasts.
I slowly unzip my skirt and let it fall to the ground to reveal a very mini black lace over pink silk G-string.
I feel his lips move along my shoulder blade following my scars.

Dominic's lips and tongue trace the scar along my back, his hands grip my sides and squeezes.

The sensation makes my whole body shudder with anticipation.

He slides his fingers under the straps as he continues down with his kisses.

He slowly traces his fingers along my hips to the front of my thighs, I gasp as his hands slide up my thighs.

I touch his fingers.

His hand travels back up from my hip along the scar on my stomach up to my breasts, then to my neck where he turns my face to meet his.

'Dominic.' I whisper against his lips.

'Elizabeth.'

Dominic's tongue teases my lips as I turn around, pressing my body against his.

I wrap my arms around his neck as his arms wrap around me.

I part my lips and he gently bites my bottom lip.

'I love you, Elizabeth, with everything I have to give you.' Dominic says as his fingers brush my cheeks.

I look into his eyes.

I really do have my everything with him.

He loves me even though I'm broken.

I smile as a small tear falls.

'All I want is you, Dominic. A life with you, I don't care about anything else. I love you.' I say as his thumbs wipe away my tears and his lips claim mine.

This kiss feels different, it is still full of passion, desire and hunger, but now there is love.

He starts to kiss me harder.

Dominic's hands move around to my back and undo my bra.

He slowly moves his fingers to my shoulders, pushing the thin black straps down my arms as I move them down.

He takes my left hand gently, kissing each finger as he looks into my eyes.

'I can't wait till you have this cast taken off.' He smiles.

He removes his shorts and pulls me against his naked body, kissing me hard.

Dominic pulls away, his eyes travelling up and down my body.

I move my hand to my neck as I stand there nervously.

He covers my hand and his thumb traces along my jaw, I close my eyes and take a deep breath, savoring the moment.

I open my eyes to see him smiling.

'You are absolutely beautiful, Elizabeth.'

I smile and look at the floor.

'Babe, don't look away.' Dominic says lifting my face to meet his.

'But my…'
'I don't see them. I see you, Elizabeth.'

He pulls the covers down on our bed and eyes my body.
He sits on the bed and pulls me to him, his hands move over my hips and waist.
'I really like them a lot, but I really like them off you.' He says with a smile and raised eyebrow.
His fingers move up my legs to the thin straps of my G-string, he softly kisses my hips.
I run my fingers through his hair as I gasp, Dominic kisses along the top of the lace.
His hands move around and grab my arse, I sob, enjoying his touch and kisses.

Dominic stands up and kisses me as he lifts me up, I wrap my legs around him.
He turns and lays me down on our bed, I love the feeling of him on top of me.
He holds my arms above my head as he kisses me harder.
I can feel his erection against me, I want him so much, I want to feel him in me as we make love.
I want him as much as he wants me. Dominic begins to kiss along my jawline to my ear.
'I love you, Elizabeth.' He whispers as he gently bites my earlobe.
I sigh at the feeling, moving my legs alongside his.
Dominic continues to bite and kiss me from my neck to my breasts, making me whimper and yearn for more.

He moves down gently, teasing me with his lips and tongue.
Dominic fingers slide under the thin straps of my G-string, as he kisses along the top of the lace.
He slowly removes my G-string, his hands slide up my thighs squeezing as he moves up.
He enters me and I wrap my legs around him, our bodies move as one.
Dominic pushes deep as his lips devour mine, he growls my name against my lips.

'Elizabeth,' He moans. 'Elizabeth, I love you.'
He kisses me hard, his hands hold my arms above my head.
Dominic moves one of his hands down to my leg and grabs my arse.
His lips follow the scar along my neck sending my body into overdrive.
He trails his lips along my collarbone and down to my breasts.
My body shudders as he teases my nipples.
His kiss is dominating but I'm loving every moment of it.

I arch my back as I feel the warmth spread through me.
Dominic knows I'm close to coming and he knows I'm trying to hold back.

'Dominic,'
I feel his body shudder as he buries his face in my neck.
'I love you, Dominic.' I say against his ear.
He starts to push harder, and deeper and faster.
'Liz,' His voice is husky and deep.
'Yes,'
'I can't,' He grunts.
'Then don't.' I say as his lips find mine. 'Cum with me Dominic.'
I say against his lips as I look into his eyes.
His hand grabs my arse and squeezes hard, I can feel him starting to cum as I orgasm.
He orgasms as he buries his face in my neck, breathing deep and hard.

👀 DOMINIC 👀

I lay there with her under me, her legs wrapped around me.
I don't want to move, I feel her arms wrap around me.
Making love to her gets better every time, every touch, kiss, and smile just keeps getting better.
I love Elizabeth and I want the world to know it.
Her fingers move through my hair and up and down my back.
Her touch sending shockwaves through my body.
Elizabeth is beautiful, amazing and stronger then she gives herself credit for and she is all mine.
All mine to love, honour and protect till death do we part, even though I don't think death will ever part us.

I look down at her, my fingers brush the hair from her face.
My thumb moves over her lips as she smiles up at me.
'Where has your mind run off to?' She asks me.
'Everywhere with you.' I smile.
I love it when she blushes, her eyes shine brighter and I can't look away from her.
Laying down beside her, I pull her against me and hold her tight.
'Dominic,'
'Mmm.' I say running my fingers through her hair
'It was perfect.' She says before I could finish.
I smile as she snuggles in and I kiss the top of her head.

There's a knock at the door.
'Elizabeth? Dominic?' Amber calls out.
'Yeah?' I reply.
'Agent Smith would like to see you. He has a couple of things to finalise before he leaves.'
'Okay, we will be out in a few minutes.' I reply.
'Do we have to?' Liz asks as she climbs on top of me and pouts.
I smile as I sit up and hold her.

'Unfortunately, yes.'
'Fine, but I'm not happy about it.' She says wrapping her arms around my neck.
'Well,' I didn't finish.
Her lips are on mine, hungry and full of passion, desire and love.
I hold her tight.
'To be continued.' Liz says breathing heavily.
'Promise?'
'Yes,' Liz says as she teases my lips with her tongue.
'We better get out there before they come in.'
Liz sighs.

We get up and I get dressed, I turn and watch her get dressed, she catches me watching her and blushes.
I walk up to her and take her hand, running my fingers down her cheek to her neck then to her collarbone.
Liz closes her eyes and smiles, taking in a deep breath.
I lean in and kiss her, I can feel Liz smile.
'What?' I ask her.
'You like me lots.' She giggles.

My hands slide down under her skirt and grab her arse, lifting her up, Liz wraps her legs around me.
'Hell yeah, I like you lots.' I smile.
Liz kisses me.
'Are you dressed yet?' Amber calls out.
'Yes.' I call out, still holding Liz.
Amber walks in and smiles.
'I was starting to wonder when you two would be finished,'
My eyes haven't left Liz's. Her eyes shine as she blushes.
'You told her!'
'Yep.' I answer, still looking at Liz.
I let her down as Amber runs up and hugs her.

'Yay! It's about time.' Amber says excitedly.
'How long have you known?' Liz asks her.
'I figured it out before he even realised it.' Amber says hugging me.
Amber takes a step back, smiling at us.
'What?' I ask her.
'Come on lovebirds. Agent Smith has something for you.'
I look at Liz and smile as I take her hand and pull her into me.
I kiss her softly.
We follow Amber out on the deck and I take her hand again as Simon comes up and hugs her.

I look at Cassie and Luke, their eyes are red.
Cassie comes up and hugs me then Liz, Luke follows her.
'Dominic,' Agent Smith calls me over.
'I have something for Elizabeth but I want you to give it to her.' He smiles handing me an envelope.
'How much do they know?'
'Elizabeth asked me to give them the PG version, but I'm sure you are well aware that even that is very graphic.'
I nod.

'Now it is my understanding that Elizabeth has decided to tell you everything.'
'Yeah, she wants to tell me tomorrow.' I reply.
'Well I won't lie. When I spoke to her last night, I did try to talk her out of doing all this but she was very insistent. Elizabeth has never spoken to me the way she did last night.'
'How do you mean?'
'She argued and raised her voice with me. Elizabeth said if I didn't allow her to tell you, she would pull her statement and walk away from the case.' He smiles.
'Really?' I am shocked.

'I was actually impressed. But now that I'm here and see what she has, I know I was wrong. The way she is with you and how protective you are of her. I just need you to realise just how much she is going to need you.'
'I understand. I want to be there and I will be there for everything.'
'Good, because she won't be able to do this alone. When this goes to court she will be dragged through the dirt and made to relive all of it in front of strangers. She will have to face him and the hold he had over her was unlike anyone had ever seen. We had to break her just to get her to agree to help us.'

'What do you mean break her?' I ask him.
'We needed her to help us.'

'So you were one of the people who sent her back?' He could tell I was struggling with that.
'Unfortunately, yes. I'm sorry, Dominic, and I can never thank her enough. I owe her everything.'

'She almost died and then when you finally got her out she...'
'Dominic, believe me I know what you are feeling.'
'All due respect but no you don't. I love her,'
'And I can see that and from what I have seen and read she loves you just as much.' He says.

'This is for you, it's the results of a certain DNA test rushed through.'
'How did you know?' I ask.
'Elizabeth called me and asked for a favour. But I'm sure you will agree that she is owed a lot more.' He says as he shakes my hand.
'Thank you.'
'Excuse me, sir,' Amber says.
'Yes, let's finalize this.' Agent Smith says as he walks back to the table.

🔲 ELIZABETH 🔲

'What's that?' I ask Dominic.
'The DNA results you had rushed through.' He replies as he looks at the white envelope.
'I'll leave you to open it.' I turn to leave.
'No,' He grabs my hand. 'I want you next to me.'
'Okay.' I smile.

I watch him open the envelope and read the letter.
He smiles and I start to panic as he looks at me.
'No,' He says.
'No?'
'No, I'm not the father.' He says as he picks me up and spins me around.
He puts me down and kisses me hard.
'So, what's in the second envelope?' I ask him.
'I don't know, it's for both of us.' He hands it to me.
I sit down and open the envelope, it's from a fertility clinic.
I start reading the letter and my hands begin to shake.

'Liz,'
The tears start to fall, I look at Dominic as he takes the letter and reads it.

'Did I read it right?' I ask him.
He looks at me.
'Dominic,'
He kisses me.
'Yeah babe, you read it right. They have your eggs.' He says kissing me again.
'That means I can give you a child,'
'No, it means we can have a child together,' He says smiling at me as he brings his lips to mine.
'Liz, Dominic.' Amber comes over to us.
Dominic hands her the letter as he pulls me into him, kissing the top of my head.
'What's going on?' Simon asks as he joins us, followed by Luke and Cassie. Amber hands Simon the letter.

'They froze your eggs when they did the emergency hysterectomy?' He reads the letter.
'That's awesome, so when do I start?' Cassie asks.
'Start?' Luke asks
'Surrogate pregnancy, Amber and I have agreed to carry,'
'Hell yes! I finally get to be an Uncle.' Luke says, grinning from ear to ear.
'Let me deal with Michael first.' I say
'Let us deal with him. I told you I'm standing right beside you through everything. I'm not going to let you go through it alone.' Dominic says as he traces my cheek with his fingers.

'Elizabeth is right. Besides, let them enjoy the art of making babies without actually making babies.' Agent Smith says smiling.
'Well, we do have a sturdy daybed.' Dominic whispers in my ear.
'And a holiday to enjoy.' I look up at him and smile.

'Ben is going to be completely mad,' Amber laughs.
'Why?' I ask her.
'That is one thing I love about you, hun. You are completely oblivious to how men react around you,' Amber smiles.
I look at Dominic and back to Amber totally confused.

'The only reason Simon, Gavin, and I didn't try anything with you when we met you that day up the beach was because of Dominic.' Luke knocks his shoulder against Dominic's.
'But we weren't,'
'Yeah, you were.' Luke says before I could finish.

'Everybody could see it, he was completely taken by you and you, you only had eyes for him.' Simon adds.
'You still only have eyes for him.' Amber says
'What does Ben have to do with it?' I ask.
'He has it bad for you. He is hoping that you and Dominic split so he can be with you.' Luke sighs.
I can feel a shift in Dominic's body language. But I don't want to be with Ben, I don't even want to be near him.
'Dominic,' I whisper. 'Please don't let him, I can't…'
'He won't.' Dominic says before I can finish.

My hands shake and I try to hide it.
Dominic holds me closer and I feel him kiss the top of my head.
'Okay, let's finalise this meeting so I can head back to Sydney tonight.'
'Liz, babe, look at me.' Dominic says as his hands bring my face up to meet his.
'Liz, I love you and nothing, and I mean nothing, is going to change that.' He says as he caresses my cheeks down to my neck.
'I love you too.' I smile.
Dominic kisses the top of my head softly. I smile at the feeling of us.
'Hey you.'
'There's my girl.'
We join the others at the table.
'Right, Elizabeth, I just need you to sign these where indicated so all the deeds are sealed. That just leaves this one.' Agent Smith says looking at Dominic.
Dominic takes the documents from him and I hand him a pen.

'Liz, I can't.'
'Yes you can and you will.'
'Then I want it in both our names.'
'Do this for me now and I will do whatever you want when we return from our holiday.'
'Promise?'
'I promise.'
I watch as Dominic signs the documents.
'Oh before I forget, this one as well please.' Agent Smith says as he puts the last one in front of Dominic.
Dominic signs it and then Agent Smith hands it to me to sign as well. Dominic looks at me.

'What?' He asks me.
'Nothing,' I smile.
'You now have access to my entire file, case, everything.'

'Everything?' Dominic looks at me.

'You are able to sit in on classified meetings and if something happens to me, you are the only person who can act on my behalf.'

'Nothing is going to happen to you.' Dominic takes my hand and smiles.

I don't say anything, I just smile.

I smile at the man I love more than anything in the world knowing he loves me.

'Okay, all done. Now Elizabeth can I please borrow you for a few minutes? Then I'll be out of your hair.' Agent Smith motions for me to follow him inside.

'Are you sure about everything you have done here today?' He asks me when we get to the kitchen.

'Yes I am. They have helped in more ways than I can even imagine. I don't think I could ever repay them for what they have done for me and given me.'

'Are you sure that I can't persuade you to change your mind about your other plan?' He asks me.

'No you can't. It will work and then you will have what you need and I will be able to ensure Dominic's safety.'

'That's all well and good in theory, Elizabeth, but this could cost you your life.'

'I'm sorry but that is a chance I need to take. I need to ensure that Dominic is safe. My will leaves everything to him so that would also include my eggs, as well, correct?'

'Yes,' Agent Smith sighs. 'Elizabeth. Are you going to tell him?'

I turn and look at Dominic.

He is smiling and laughing with the others on the deck.

He looks up and sees me watching him.

He knows something is up.

'If I do, he won't let me go.'

'All right, Elizabeth.' Agent Smith sighs.

'These are the final documents you need to sign. They have all been post-dated and you have to sign as Chantelle Watson.'

I touch my face and take a deep breath before taking the pen from Agent Smith.

'My family is definitely protected? No one can take the money and assets from them?' I ask as I sign the documents.

'Yes that is correct, they are fully protected and this is the letter from the Governor General.'

I take the letter and read it.

'Your brothers are extremely suspicious, they don't believe that you are dead.'

'Has Will said something to them?'

'Yes.' Agent Smith hands me another document to sign. 'They are looking for you.'

'Who is looking for Elizabeth?' Dominic asks.
'My brothers.' I reply not looking up as I sign the last document.
'Done, Chantelle Watson is by all sense of the term officially dead.' I say handing the documents back to Agent Smith.
'What? Elizabeth what have you done?' Dominic asks.
'Chantelle had life insurance and assets. Now my family will have them and get the payout.'
'So, what did you have me sign apart from the deed, the next of kin and the case file documents?'
'I'll tell you tomorrow. I promise.'

'Liz,' Dominic looks at Agent Smith.
'Dominic look at me please.' I say touching his cheek.
Dominic looks at me, his expression is hard.
'Please trust me.' I plead with him.
He sighs as his expression softens.
'I trust you babe.' Dominic brings his hands to my face and runs his thumb over my lips.

I close my eyes and feel his lips on mine, I give a soft moan causing him to smile.
I open my eyes as he pulls away and I see him smiling.
'And that is my cue to leave.' Agent Smith says.
'Thank you Agent Smith.' I smile and hug him, granted I did feel a little uneasy but with Dominic by my side anything is possible.

Once he has gone, we begin to set up for the party. I start getting the food prep underway and the bain maries warmed up. Simon and Luke help Dominic move the cooler trailer to the back near the steps.
Luke and Simon gush when Sally and Sarah turn up to help. Even Gavin comes to lend a hand. When we finish, I serve up some food and beer. While everyone is chatting, I sneak away to look at the last envelope Agent Smith had left for me. I close our bedroom door and sit on the floor of the walk-in robe. I open the envelope containing photos of my family.

My brother Jonathan, playing with his daughter at his wedding.
My brother Travis and his heavily pregnant partner.
My brothers at my grave site changing the flowers and finally, my mum and dad.
I can't hold the tears back anymore and I begin to cry.
I would have loved to have introduced Dominic to them.
Let them meet the man who helped me heal and made me whole again.
The man who saw past my scars and loves me regardless.

I know my family would have loved him as easily and as much as I do.
I will be forever in Dominic's debt.

'Liz, babe?' Dominic sits behind me. 'What's wrong?'
'Sorry I just…'
'Hey look at me,' Dominic stops me.
 'Don't apologise. Whatever is upsetting you, I'm here for you ok.'
I nod.
'I love you, Elizabeth.' Dominic says wiping the tears from my face.
'I love you, Dominic,'
He pulls me into him and holds me tight.
He lets me cry, lets me grieve.

🔲 DOMINIC 🔲

We sit for ages on the floor of our closet.
I let Liz cry without saying anything.
I hold her close while running my fingers through her hair trying to soothe her.
I guess with everything that has happened, she has never really had anyone to comfort her enough to let it all out.
I kiss the top of her head then rest my cheek on the top of her head as I hold her tighter.
I run my fingers through her hair and play with the loose curls.
Liz eventually stops crying and falls asleep against me.

I close my eyes and take a deep breath letting her smell take over my senses.
I know she has something planned, something big, and I'm scared that it will cost her life.
'Liz, Dominic?' Amber walks in to check on us.
I look up and smile, Amber's expression is different.
I guess Liz isn't the only one who has been crying.
'What happened?'
'She signed the last of Chantelle Watson's documents. I think it's just the realisation that everything she had is finally gone.' I sigh.
'Poor thing.'
'Liz told me she felt like she failed them. I think in some way she regrets everything,'

'No, she doesn't.' Amber cuts me off.
 'I know that for a fact. Liz told me the only regret she has is you not meeting her family. She would do it all over again just to have you, even if it was only for one night.'
'I love her. I love her so much it hurts being away from her. I can't lose her ,Amber,'
'You won't. Can I get you anything?'
'No, I just need to be alone with my girl.'
Amber smiles.
'Of course, we will be out on the deck, just send me a text.'
'Actually, can you grab the pillows and doona off our bed please.'
Amber smiles and nods.

I manage to move and get comfortable, I lay down with Liz and hold her tight.
Elizabeth is everything I'll ever need or want in life and with the possibility of having biological children with her, it really is the best feeling.
Elizabeth is and always will be the love of my life.
I will spend the rest of my life showing her how much I love her and what she means to me.
I drift off to sleep holding my girl.

◷ ELIZABETH ◷

I wake in Dominic's arms on the floor of our closet.
I run my fingers across his forehead pushing his hair from his face.
He really is beautiful.
He stirs as I try to get up and his arms tighten around me.
 'No,' He groans.
I turn back to see him smiling.
'Hey you,'
'There's my girl,'
I smile and snuggle back into his arms taking a deep breath.

'Are you okay?' He asks me.
'Can I show you something?' I wipe my face and stretch
'Of course.'
We sit up and I find the envelope with the photos and hand it to Dominic.
He removes the photos and looks through them, I watch him.
He stops at the photo of my grave site where my brothers are changing the flowers.
Dominic looks back at me.

'Oh babe, I'm so sorry.' He says pulling me in.
I lay against his chest and close my eyes, listening to his heartbeat.
Dominic is and always will be the love of my life.
I will spend the rest of my life showing him how much I love him and how much he means to me.
The chance of having biological children with him is the best feeling.
I feel Dominic touch my cheek, his fingers lift my chin so our lips meet.
I feel his hand slide under my shirt and rest on the small of my back.
We both moan as we lose ourselves in each other.

'Knock knock.' Amber says walking in.
'Hey, Amber,' Dominic says.
'Hey, Amber,' I smile up at her as I lay against Dominic,
'How are my lovebirds?'
Dominic hands her the envelope that Agent Smith left me.
Amber opens it and looks at the photos.

'Oh, hun, I'm so sorry.'
'It's okay, Amber, really, I'll be fine. Today has been an emotional day and seeing those pictures topped it off.'
'I'll put the kettle on. Would you like something to eat?'
'What time is it?' I ask.
'Five thirty,' Amber replies.
'Crap! I'm sorry I was supposed to…'
'Liz, don't, it's ok. Everything is all sorted.' Amber smiles.
'Come on babe, let's get you some Vegemite and a spoon.' Dominic says kissing the top of my head.
'And chocolate?'
'Anything for my girl.' He smiles and kisses my forehead.
'I'll see you in the kitchen in about forty minutes,' Amber winks and leaves the room.
I look at Dominic and blush, he pulls me down and rests his head on my chest.
I run my fingers through his hair.
I can feel his hand slide under my shirt and grip my side.

'What's wrong, Dominic?'
'I know you're planning something big and I'm scared that I will lose you.' He says as he holds me tighter.
'Dominic I promise that I will do everything in my power to get back to you when he takes me.'
'Liz,'

'Michael has been in prison and I have been hiding for two years. He has a high sense of self-importance and likes to think he is untouchable, he can do what he wants when he wants and will not take no for an answer. It took them over a year to arrest him and then another month before they could get a judge to agree he is dangerous. He is angry and he is coming for me. I know exactly what he is capable of doing. When Michael finds me and takes me, I know exactly what is in store for me.'
Dominic sits up on his elbow and looks at me.
I reach up and touch his face as I look into his eyes.

'I love you, Dominic. I love you so much it hurts to be away from you. I am fearful of you leaving me, but the thing that really scares me the most, Dom, is Michael hurting you to get to me.'
Dominic smiles.
'I'm not going to leave you, Elizabeth.' He leans in and kisses me softly.
'Dominic,'
Dominic looks at me.
'I will die before I let him touch you, Dominic. I promise to do everything,'
Dominic kisses me again, his hand squeezing my hip.
He moves on top of me and deepens our kiss.
'I won't let you go without a fight,' He says against my lips.
'You will not go where I can't follow.' He kisses me hard.
'I won't let you,'
'Liz.' He says my name against my lips.
'I.'
Dominic kisses me harder.
'Liz.'
'But,'
'No.' He says not letting me finish.

His kiss is hard, my arms hold him tighter.
I'll tell him tomorrow why I can't let him go up against Michael.
Dominic groans deeply as he rolls and brings me on top of him.
He sits up, holding onto me and resting his head against my chest.
I hold him tight, resting my cheek on the top of his head as my fingers run through his hair.
We sit holding each other, knowing we are exactly where we want to be.

'I'm so sorry, Dominic. I never wanted to put you in danger.' I say taking a deep breath.
'I don't care about that. To be completely honest with you, I fell for you the day we met.' Dominic lifts his head to look at me.

'I felt a huge pull towards you that I couldn't even explain till now. I wanted you and it wasn't just sexual desire. I wanted all of you.'
Dominic's fingers brush my cheek as he tucks my hair behind my ear.
I can feel myself blush and a tear fall.

'Dominic, I wish more than anything that I could introduce you to my family and keep you safe. What I feel for you is beyond words. I was happy just thinking that I would have one night with you, but you stayed. You stayed even though you knew I was hiding and keeping things from you.' I look down at my hands, they are shaking.
'Liz,?' He looks at me with pain in his eyes.
I take a deep breath and look at him.
'You could walk out of this room right now and never look back. You will never have to work another day in your life. You could leave me with nothing but the memory of us.'
'Liz,'
'I could live the rest of my life in complete happiness with those memories knowing you are safe.'
'Liz, you didn't?' He shakes his head. 'I don't want any of your money.'
I smile as I run my fingers across the stubble on his cheeks.

'But it's your money,'
'I never cared about the money, Dominic. It got me here, it got me to you. I don't need it anymore.'
'I don't want it without you.'
Reaching over, I grab the documents I signed and hand them to him.
'I was going to give these to you tomorrow.'
I watch him read, his eyes narrow, and he looks up at me.
'Um, Liz, would you care to explain? This is a lot of money.' He says shaking his head.
'I liquidated some high valued assets. I was made a generous offer and I accepted it. You will now have joint control over everything I have. Whatever you owned before you met me is still one hundred percent yours, your assets are safe.'
'Liz, babe this is huge.'
I can't read his expression.

'Dominic, tell me how you feel. Are you okay? Happy or angry with me?'
'Liz,' Dominic puts the documents aside and takes my hands. 'Like I said before, none of this means anything if you're not beside me. Wherever you go I go, I will not allow you to ever feel alone, hurt and scared again.'
'You had best read the rest of the documents then.' I smile
I go to move but his arm prevents me.

I watch him read, and then he looks at me with a shocked expression on his face.
'Liz, when? Why?
'The transactions are not complete yet. When we go to New Zealand I will need to go to the bank, agent and the solicitor. If you're happy with it, I sign off and then transfer it to your name,'
'Our name.'
'If you would like to do that then we can,' I smile as he nods and returns my smile. 'And with all that done, we get the keys to all the properties purchased.'
'How many properties?'
'Six homes, a couple of units and one farm leased to a small company that makes cheeses.'
'How did you know I had thought about going back?'
'Well you do have all your family over there. Louise told me, one of the few times she actually spoke to me.'
'Would you…?'
'Yes, yes. I would move there if that's what you want.' I answer him before he finishes.

Dominic puts the documents down and takes my face in his hands.
He smiles as he looks into my eyes and pulls me down to meet his lips.
I feel his tongue tease my lips, I whimper as my hunger feeds his.
My body shudders as his hands slide down under my skirt and grabs my arse.

'Mmm Mrs. Miller.'
I giggle coyly.
'Mr. Miller.'
'Anytime you want to buy lots and lots of lingerie feel free.'
I giggle and blush.
'Unfortunately, we have to get ready for a party.' Dominic says against my lips, his voice deep and husky.
'So I get to show you my new dress, shoes, jewellery…'
I don't get to finish as his lips silence mine.
We return to the kitchen, Amber, Luke, Simon and Cassie are there waiting for us.
'Yay finally!' Amber runs up to me and hugs me tight.
Amber steps back and winks at us.
'About time you told her.' Luke remarks.
'Told her what?' Ben walks in.

I move to the other side of Dominic and look down at the ground.
'That he loves her.' Simon replies.

'So what time does this party supposedly start?' Ben says abruptly changing the subject.

His tone makes me uneasy and I find myself moving behind Dominic.

'Seven and Louise is due around seven thirty.' Cassie replies.

I look up and see Luke watching me.

He has picked up on my unease with Ben.

I feel ashamed because he did help and he is Luke's brother.

I feel Dominic hand reach back and touch me, he has also picked up on it.

'Right, well, we will head off and walk back down later,' Dominic says, still shielding me and trying to hide my unease.

'See you soon, yeah,' Amber says, hugging me.

I hold Dominic but I start to panic when I see Ben at the door watching me.

He is standing right where I need to walk.

'Hey, Ben, there is beer in the cooler next to the BBQ.' Luke says as he looks at us.

'Sweet,' Ben walks out. Something has made him angry.

Dominic nods at Luke, I feel so stupid.

'What's up his arse?' Cassie asks.

'Dominic.' Luke replies

'He has it bad for Liz.' Simon adds.

'Get in line then, Ben.' Cassie laughs.

Dominic and I say goodbye and head on to the deck towards the stairs.

'Liz?' Ben says.

'Yes, Ben.' I reply.

'Can I talk to you for a minute please? In private.' He asks.

I look at Dominic, my whole body is shaking.

'I don't think…' Dominic starts.

'Dominic?'

'Yeah babe,' He looks at me.

'He is Luke's brother I should try, shouldn't I?'

'I'll be right here.' Dominic smiles as his fingers move along my cheek and down my neck.

His lips meet mine and I feel my body start to relax a little.

I look at him and smile, Dominic winks at me.

I nervously walk over to Ben but try to keep some distance between us.

'Ben,' I say nervously.

'This was in my letterbox when I got home,' He hands me an envelope which I take as my hands start to shake again. 'I'm so sorry, Elizabeth.'

I don't notice Ben move closer as I open the envelope.
There is a written note on some A4 paper folded over some photos.

Dominic can't be trusted.
He is still fucking her.

My hands shake as I read the note and start to look at the photos.
The photos are of Dominic and Stephanie, some of them are quite intimate.
'If you need someone to talk to I'm here for you.' Ben says.

I don't realise how close he has gotten till he touches me.
His fingers brush my shoulder and he takes another step closer as he tries to pull me into him.
'NO!' I say
Dominic is at my side, putting himself between us, before Ben could say or do anything.
Ben glares at Dominic.
'You're a fucking coward, Dominic!' Ben says as Luke and Simon reach us.
'What's going on?' Luke asks.
'Ask Dominic! Having one woman at a time isn't good enough for him he has to fuck around. Nice photos, Dominic!'
'What photos?' Dominic asks, turning to me.
I hand them to him.
'What the fuck, Ben?' Dominic demands.
Luke takes the note and photos from Dominic and looks at them with Simon as I light the fire pit.
'Is that…?' Simon asks.
'Stephanie.' Dominic replies, still glaring at Ben.
'They were in the letterbox when I got home.'
'Bullshit!' Dominic yells.

I take the photos and note from Luke and Simon, throw them into the fire and walk back to Dominic.
'Liz I…'
'I know.' I smile at him, answering him before he even finishes what he doesn't need to.
How?' Ben asks.
'Well, Dominic's hair style is different in the photos and the scar on his right bicep, it is at least two to three years old now, but in the photos it's still bandaged.'
'But what about the note?' Ben asks.
'Simple, it's Stephanie trying to cause trouble, not the first time she has tried.' I reply as I take Dominic's hand and look up at him.

'Hey, you.' I smile.
'There's my girl,' Dominic smiles back at me.

'Fucking bitch, what is her problem?' Ben asks.
'I rejected her.'
'And she doesn't like being told no or put in her place.' I add. 'Can we please go home now?' I look up at Dominic.

'Anything for my girl.' Dominic smiles at me as he takes my hand and pulls me against him.
Dominic and I walk hand in hand back to our car, he opens my door but prevents me from getting in.
I look up to see him smiling.
'You are amazing.' He says
I smile.
'Thank you for trusting me.'
'Anything for my man.' I wink pulling him in.

My lips meet his, I can feel his hands on my hips, sliding under my skirt and grabbing my arse.
I moan.
I love the feeling of his hands on my body, his kisses, his body on mine, and the way he makes me feel.
'You need to take me home.' I wink at him.
'Yes, ma'am.' He smiles at me.

As we drive home, I run my fingers along his leg watching his body's reaction to my touch.
Dominic smiles and shifts in his seat as we pull into our driveway.
He parks beside his Ute. I get out and turn to him with a smile.
I open the back door of our car and get in, I start to remove my shirt as he opens the door.
He watches and grins, I reach over grabbing his shirt and pulling him onto me, he hungrily claims my lips as he reaches back to close the door.

My hands travel under his shirt up to his shoulders, lifting his shirt over his head.
I undo his board shorts and slide my hand, I feel him harden as he growls.
His hand moves up my thigh slowly, my body shivers as his fingers tease my senses and my body tenses.
Dominic's kiss becomes harder and more demanding as his fingers run along the thin straps of my G-String.

He pulls my G-string down and removes it. His hand moves back up my leg, squeezing as he goes.
I remove his board shorts.
'Liz,' Dominic moans as I take him in my hand again.

He pulls me up as he sits, I whimper as he enters me. Dominic's arms run up my back as his hands grip my shoulders.
'Mmmm Dominic,' I sigh, causing him to tighten his hold on me.
I feel his hands move slowly down my back causing me to shudder as his lips find mine.
I love the feeling of his hands as they move along my body and grab my arse.
His fingers trace up my spine to my bra, he unclasps my bra and grabs my breasts.
Dominic teases my nipples with his fingers before he finishes removing my bra.
I shudder as his mouth finds my breast and gently bites and sucks.

Dominic hand moves around and grabs my arse hard pulling me harder on to him as his other hand moves up my back and grabs my hair.
He pulls my head back, exposing my neck, before his lips find mine.
I can feel the heat rising through my body.
I try to hold back but Dominic can feel it.
My body tenses.
I begin to climax, Dominic holds me tight and kisses me harder as he climaxes as well.
His hands hold me to him as he breathes heavily against my neck.
'Liz,' He sighs.
'Mmm.'

'You feel so good against me. I can't get enough of you.'
'Good, I want you.' I say kissing him and wrapping my arms around his neck.
I feel his hands move up my back slowly, making goosebumps spread across my body.
I lean back and smile at him.
'I just realised something.' I say smiling.
'What's that?'
'We just christened our new car.' I giggle coyly.

'What's next?' Dominic smiles.
I watch him as his eyes move over my body.
I close my eyes enjoying his touch as his hands move over my hips to my arse.
'We have a few properties in New Zealand.' I open my eyes and blush.
Dominic's hands move to my hips and squeezes.

I lean in and wrap my arms around him, resting my forehead on his.

We eventually get dressed and head upstairs to get ready for the party.
I lay my dress, necklace, and shoes out on our bed and head into the en suite for a shower.
Dominic comes in as I am wrapping my wrist.
'Hey, you.'
'There's my girl.'
He delicately takes my wrist and wraps it for me.
I look up at him to see him smiling at me.
'What?' I ask him.
'Nothing, just admiring my woman.' He winks.
I smile as he leans in and kisses me.

'How are you feeling about everything?' I ask him.
'As long as you are next to me, everything is perfect.'
I can feel myself blush.
'Liz, can I ask you something about what you have done today?'
'Of course.' I reply feeling concerned.
'You have given up your dream home. You are moving in with me. And to top it all off, you said that if I ask you to move to New Zealand with me, you would. You said yes without hesitation. But what do you want?' He asks me.
'Simple, a home and someone to share it with.'

'And now that you have the chance of biological children.' He smiles at me.
'That chance means everything to me. I now have the opportunity to give you biological children. I don't care where we live as long as we are together. I mean, that is if you still want me after I tell…'
'Liz, I love you. There is no if, I'm not going to let you face what is coming on your own. We are going to face it together and beat him together.' He says cutting me off before I even finish.
I drop my gaze away from him, feeling nervous and ashamed.
'Liz, look at me.'
His fingers brush my cheeks and lift my face.

'I know that the locked cabinet in your closet has everything in it. I found your bats and the hidden vials which I never told Amber about. I know that what happened to you will not be easy for you to talk about. I won't lie, it won't be easy to hear it. But it will never change what I feel for you.'
'Dominic,'
'I see your scars, I see all of them and I still think you are the most amazing, smart, beautiful and incredibly sexy woman I have ever met or seen.'

He wipes away the tears that have begun to fall and he kisses me gently.
'Dominic,' I moan softly.
'I love you, Elizabeth.' Dominic says against my lips.
I melt into him.

Dominic helps me shower even though he doesn't have to.
Every time he touches me, kisses me and makes love to me, it just keeps getting better.
I feel Dominic behind me as he starts wrapping me in a towel.
I remember our first night together.
I just wanted to know what sex felt like when both people want it.
I felt so self-conscious when he stood in front of me without his shirt.
He is beautiful and I was so scared he would find me ugly and unsatisfying.

'Earth to Liz?' Dominic's voice breaks through my thoughts.
'Sorry what did you say?' I look at him.
'Where did you just go?' He says smiling at me.
I blush.
'Our first night together. You were, I mean, you still are beautiful. I'm so not and I was so nervous that you would find me ugly and unsatisfying. I had never had consensual sex so, technically, you are my first.' I reply looking at him.
His smile lights up my world.

'I just wanted to know what sex felt like when both people wanted it. I wanted just one night with you. That night would have been enough for me to live the rest of my life,'
'Liz, the moment I touched you that day I knew I could never let you go if I held you. Now that I have you, I'm not letting you go.'
Dominic pulls me in against him and holds me tight. I take in a deep breath letting his scent take over my senses. However long we have left together, I plan on enjoying every second of it.
'Come on, we better finish getting ready or we will never leave this room,' I wink at him.
'Yes ma'am.' He smiles.

I walk back to the bedroom to get dressed and my phone starts ringing, it's Agent Smith.
'Hello,'
I look over at Dominic. He is putting his jeans on.
'Yes, he is here.'
Dominic walks over to me.
'Agent Smith would like to talk to you.' I say handing Dominic my phone.

Dominic looks at my phone then back to me as he takes it.
'Hello.'
Dominic smiles at me.

'Yep, sure, give me a moment.'
Dominic grabs his socks, shoes and shirt.
He kisses me and smiles before heading downstairs.
I won't lie, this makes me nervous.
I head into the bathroom and brush my teeth before putting on mascara and
lip gloss.
I have just finished getting dressed when Dominic comes to the top of the stairs.
He stops and looks at me.
'What? You don't like it?'
'Wow! Babe you look amazing.' He smiles.
I blush and look at the floor.
'Liz,'
Dominic walks up to me and puts his hands on my waist.
'Babe, look at me.'
I look up at him, his eyes shine as he looks over me.
'You are absolutely stunning.' Dominic smiles.
'Thank you.' I say as he brings his lips to mine.

I feel his hands move from my waist to my arse and squeeze.
He groans as he deepens our kiss and my hands slide under his shirt.
'Come on, let's go to this party so I can show you off.
Then I can bring you home and unwrap you.' He says as he squeezes my arse
again. 'I love you, Elizabeth.' Dominic says against my lips.
'I love you, Dominic.'
I can feel him smile as he kisses me.

Dominic picks me up and carries me downstairs. I lay my head on his chest and
snuggle in.
'I could get used to this.'
'Anything for my girl.' He says kissing the top of my head.
I giggle as he sits me on the bench.
'How about I drive instead of walking?' He asks.
'Sounds good, we can get home quicker or just hang out in the backseat.'
'Why, Mrs. Miller? What are you suggesting?' Dominic leans in.
'Just something for my hot-for-me builder come pool boy to ponder over. Unless
he gets a better offer.' I smile and wink.
He runs his hands up my legs, I close my eyes and enjoy his touch.

I feel his lips on mine as his hands move up my thighs and squeeze causing me to part my lips and groan.

Dominic's tongue teases my lips as my body responds to him.
'Liz,' Dominic says against my lips.
'Yes, Dominic.'
'I love you, please don't leave me.'
'I won't leave you, I love you, Dominic,'
He kisses me hard. I wrap my arms around him and hold him tight.
Dominic's kiss becomes harder and more demanding, as his hands tangle in my hair.
I manage to pull back and look at him.

'What?' He asks, breathing heavily.
'What was that?' I ask him. 'You have never kissed me like that.' I look at him starting to panic.
'Honestly,' He takes a deep breath and looks at my hands then runs his fingers over his band on my wrist. 'I'm scared.' He says looking back up at me and holding my hands.
'Why?' I ask him.
'I'm scared that you are going to walk away and I won't be able to follow you.' He looks into my eyes.
'Agent Smith told you what I plan on doing, didn't he?'
Agent Smith doesn't know everything.
'Yes.' Dominic says with pain in his eyes.
'I will tell you everything tomorrow, I promise you, Dominic. I love you with everything I have.' I say as I bring my hands to his face.
'Let's enjoy tonight and...'
His lips find mine before I finish.
'I love you, Elizabeth.' He says in between kisses and breathes.
'Dominic.' I growl
 as his hands squeeze my sides.

He pulls away and looks at my hands before sighing and walking away.
I slide off the bench trembling.
Why did he walk away?
I hold onto the bench, breathe I tell myself.
He loves me, he is just scared.

'Liz, babe!' Dominic rushes to me. 'What's wrong?'
'You,'
Dominic pulls me into him.

'I, what, babe?'
'You just walked away, different, it felt different.'
'Sorry I didn't mean anything by it. I just went to get this.'
He hands me a small rectangle black velvet box.
I look at him as I take it from him.
'Dominic,' I look up at him.
He smiles.
'Open it.'
My hands tremble, his fingers touch the scars on my neck.
I open the box to reveal a beautiful silver bracelet with an inscription.

There's my girl.

'Turn it over.' He says softly.

Forever & Always.
Love, Dominic.

I can feel the tears coming.
'Dominic, it's beautiful.' I look up at him.
He takes my right hand and removes his band, putting my new bracelet on my wrist.
'I don't have…'
'I have you and that's all you will ever need to give me.' He says as his fingers trace the scar on my neck and his lips meet mine.

Dominic's kiss is soft and loving.
My hands travel up his chest and wrap around his neck, he grabs my waist.
'I love you so much, Dominic.' I smile at him.
He smiles as his fingers run over my left hand.
I pick up his band and tie it back on his left wrist.
Dominic takes my hand and we walk out the door.

We get to Amber's house and park the car in the shed.
Louise is due at seven thirty.
Everyone cheers as we walk onto the deck, Amanda runs up and hugs me.
'I told you he likes you.' She smiles at me.
'I still can't believe it sometimes.' I blush.
'You should have seen him while you were in hospital. He was so protective and doting. I don't think he ever let go of your hand. Simon told us he stood at the door and watched Dominic talk to you for twenty minutes before the nurse came in to do your ops.' Amanda smiles.

'It's funny because I can recall certain things while I was in the coma.' I say looking at Dominic as he talks to Ben and some other people I haven't met yet.
'Yes we all heard about the nurse.' Amanda laughs.
'Are you hogging my girl, Amanda?' Dominic asks as he hands me a drink.
'We are still waiting for the proposal, Dominic.' Amanda winks and hugs Dominic. 'Don't make us wait too much longer.' Amanda smiles and walks off. Dominic puts his arm around my waist and pulls me in.

'I would like to introduce you to some of my friends that you haven't met yet. Are you up to it?'
'I would love to.' I say as I hug him.
Dominic kisses the top of my head.
'Hey, Dominic, hello, Elizabeth.' Gavin walks up to us.
'Hey, Gavin. Didn't get the chance to talk to you earlier today, we haven't seen you for a while. Where have you been hiding?' Dominic shakes his hand.
'Training, they sent me to Brisbane for the final assessment.'
'How did you do?' I ask him.
'Passed. I'm now with the QFES.'
'Congratulations.'
'Thank you, Elizabeth.' Gavin says, still not really looking at me.

'Everyone, Louise is almost here!' Ben calls out.
'Shall we?' Dominic says, taking my hand.
I follow him inside, Amber is in the Kitchen with Cassie, Sarah, and Sally.
'Hey hon, hope you don't mind that we started without you. We thought you deserved the night off.' Amber says hugging me.
'No, of course not. Hello Cassie, is Amber behaving well?'
'Amber is, you know, Amber.' Cassie smiles and shrugs as she hugs me.
'Don't I know it?' I look at Amber.
'Hi Sarah, hi Sally.'
They smile and wave while eating.

'Hey, Liz, how is the shoulder?' Simon asks as he hugs me.
I squeeze Dominic's hand.
'Tender but good.' I reply.
'Stop hogging the bestie.' Luke says as he hugs me as well.
I squeeze Dominic's hand again.
'Hey, what am I?' Dominic asks.
'Arm candy.' Cassie smiles.
'No, he's my pool boy.' I correct her.
'Well, I can't complain when I have the perfect view.' He winks at me.

Dominic wraps his arm around my waist and pulls me into him, kissing the top of my head.

'Okay everyone, hide, Louise is here.' Ben calls out.

Dominic takes my hand and we head to our room and close the door.

'What are you doing?' I ask him.

'Spending time with you.'

'What about Louise's?'

'I don't care.' He cuts me off.

He sits down on our bed and pulls me onto his lap.

We lay down together, holding each other close.

We hear everyone call out 'Surprise!' and Dominic holds me tighter.

'Knock knock! We are coming in.' Luke calls out.

'Fine.' Dominic replies, not letting me go.

Luke and Simon walk in followed by Ben.

My body trembles but Dominic's hand moves along my cheek and down my neck.

I close my eyes as he kisses my forehead.

'Come on, if we have to smile at Louise so do you.' Luke says.

Dominic and I sit up, he is still holding me close.

'What do you mean? What's going on?' Ben asks.

'Luke, Simon. Liz and I will leave that up to both of you.' Dominic says as we stand up and leave the room.

I still get an odd feeling around Ben and I just can't figure out what it means.

I stop at the glass sliding door and I can see everyone hugging Louise and wishing her happy birthday.

I can also see Stephanie.

Dominic senses my mood change and we move to sit at the dining table.

I run my fingers over the bracelet Dominic gave me, trying to calm my nerves.

He takes my hand and pulls me onto his lap.

Dominic's fingers brush along my cheek as we look into each other's eyes.

'When you two finish drooling over each other, the birthday girl is outside.' Stephanie says spitefully, leaning against the bench.

'Yeah, we heard.' Dominic replies, still smiling at me.

'Dominic, why did you bring her? Louise doesn't even like her.'

Luke and Simon walk in with Cassie and Ben.

'This is Elizabeth's home for one reason.' Luke is annoyed.

'Elizabeth catered the party and she is with Dominic.' Simon adds.

'And no one in here likes you.' Cassie remarks.

Stephanie walks up to Ben, putting her hand suggestively on his shoulder.

'Ben does,'
'No I don't.' He says cutting her off and pulling away.
'I would appreciate it if you left. Just because you are Louise's best friend doesn't mean you are welcome here.' Dominic looks at Stephanie. 'Leave now on your own accord or Amber will have you removed by force.'
Stephanie leaves the kitchen in a huff as Amber walks in.

'I'm guessing no one outside this room knows what Louise said?' Ben asks.
'What did she say?' Amber asks.
'Not tonight, Amber, it's her birthday.' I say looking at Amber.
'Fine, but one wrong move.'
'And you can take out the trash, weapons unholstered.' I smile at her.
Amber has a huge grin on her face.
'What exactly does that mean?' Ben asks.
'Cop.' Luke replies.
'A special cop with friends in very high places.' Dominic adds.
'Right, well let's get this food out shall we?' I try to get up.
'It can wait a little longer.' Dominic pulls me in tight.
His mood is different.
Is it because he has told me he loves me?
Or is it because I'm telling him everything tomorrow?

'Drinks!' Amber says, breaking through my thoughts.
Amber and Cassie hand out the drinks
'Okay let's make a toast.' Amber says as we all stand at the bench.
'To Dominic and Elizabeth, forever together.' Amber says.
'Dominic and Elizabeth.' They say as Dominic and I look at each other.
'Cheers.' We all say.
'What are we celebrating here?' Louise asks, walking into the kitchen with Stephanie.
'Dominic and Elizabeth.' Luke says not looking at her.
'Together and in love.' Simon says not looking at her either.
Dominic pulls me in closer and kisses the top of my head.

'Happy birthday, Louise.' I hand her an envelope.
Luke, Simon, and Ben look at me.
'Thank you.' Louise says as she opens the envelope.
'Wow, Elizabeth. This is very generous, thank you.' Louise comes over and hugs me.
'It's from all of us.' I say tightly holding Dominic's hand as I return her hug.
'Thank you.' Louise says as she starts to hug everyone.
I look over at Stephanie and if looks could kill, I would be dead.

Dominic notices and moves to put himself between Stephanie's glare and me.
I lean back into him as his arms wrap around me tighter.
Louise returns to the deck.
'What did you get her?' Simon asks.
'Day spa vouchers.'
'You shouldn't have Liz. This party was enough.' Luke says
'Well, speaking of party. I have food to finish cooking and serve.' I say.
'Liz,'
I feel Dominic's fingers move up my arm.
'Yes,' I say softly as I turn in his arms.
He leans in and whispers in my ear.
'I'll be watching and waiting.'
'Waiting for what?' I ask him.
'The perfect time to steal you away.' He says.
I close my eyes as I feel his lips brush my cheek, I turn my head so my lips meet his.
'Don't wait too long.' I say against his lips.
I feel his hands on my waist as I tease his lips with my tongue.

'Mmm what are you doing Mrs. Miller?'
'Making sure Mr. Miller doesn't forget me.'
'I could never.'
'I love you.' I say as we kiss and he squeezes my waist.
I wrap my arms around him as our kiss deepens.
'Yo, Dom,'
I smile as he reluctantly pulls away.
'G'day, David.' Dominic says, shaking David's hand.
'Still have problems releasing the opposition player I see.' David laughs.
'Hi, Liz.'
'Hi, David.'
David walks over and hugs me, I tighten my grip on Dominic's hand as I return David's hug.

'So, when's the wedding?' David asks.
'I should ask you the same thing about you and Amanda.' I say trying to change the subject as I look at the floor. I need to wash the floor..
'Nice try.' David laughs.
'Okay, everyone get out of the kitchen and let me cook.' I wink at Dominic. Dominic pouts.
'Wow you have it bad.' David laughs.
'Haha, I'll be out in a minute.'
'I'll go get drinks then, shall I?' David says.

Dominic nods and turns back to me.
Dominic's fingers brush my cheeks as he brings his lips to mine.
'Dominic, out!' Amber says grabbing him and pulling him away.
'But I have a…'
'No buts, out.' She says pushing him out the door.
'Alright, I'm going, I'm going.' He laughs putting his hands up.
'You can have her back in about an hour.' Amber says pointing outside.
'Fifteen minutes.'
'Forty-five!' Amber counters.
'Twenty'
'Forty-five minutes. Come get her any earlier and I'll taser your arse.'
'Fine! I'll be back in Forty-four minutes and fifty-nine seconds.' Dominic says.
Amber grins as Dominic gets pulled away by Luke and Simon.

'You brought your taser home?' I ask her.
'No, but he doesn't know that.' Amber winks.
I laugh.
'He is screwed if you guys have a daughter.' Cassie giggles.
'Especially with you two as aunties.' I add.
'We need drinks.' Amber says, clapping her hands and opening the fridge.

I begin moving around the kitchen, cooking and organising trays.
I enjoy ordering Amber around, and Cassie is a great help, keeping Amber in check.
Amber keeps our glasses topped up and makes sure we are entertained.
My phone beeps, it's a message from Dominic.

'Tell Amber thirty minutes and counting! Xo'

I smile and look up.
I see him outside, leaning against the deck railing and talking with David, Luke, Simon, Gavin, Ben, and a few other people I don't know yet.
Amber takes my phone and reads the message.
She goes to her bag and gets out her badge and handcuffs.
She walks over to the window, knocks on it, and holds up the badge and handcuffs for Dominic to see.
He rolls his eyes as the guys lose it.
Luke slaps Dominic's shoulder.
I reply his message.

'27 minutes and counting.'

I watch him read the message.
Dominic smiles as he looks up and winks at me.
Amber and Cassie start taking the trays of food out and ask Dominic to heat up the BBQ.
My phone beeps again.

'20 minutes.'

'I take it that you haven't received a better offer.' I reply.

'Nope, no better offer,' came the reply.

I smile.
'What are you so happy about?'
I look up to see Stephanie standing on the other side of the bench with her arms folded.
'Um, I have a lot to be happy about.' I reply, starting to feel uneasy.
I look around for Amber, Cassie or anyone.
'Really? You're happy to take Dominic and lie to him along with everyone else?'
'I'm sorry, I don't know what you're talking about.' I say.

I drop my hands below the bench and dial Dominic's number.
'I'm going to fucking destroy you.' She smiles.
'What did I ever do to you?' I ask as my hands start to shake.
'I can't understand why he would even give you the time of day.'
I look around for Dominic.
He doesn't answer his phone so I let it go through to voicemail.
'That routine won't work with me.'
I have no way of getting away from her and she knows it.
She moves around the bench and corners me.
My hand moves to my neck as I look to the ground and my breathing quickens.
Dominic where are you?
'Are you serious, right now? You are fucking pathetic!' Stephanie laughs and moves closer. 'You are a pathetic slut! A nobody and nothing to everyone.' She continues.
'No, I'm not.' I say fighting the tears.
'What did you say? Speak up you stupid little slag.' Stephanie raises her voice.
'Please stop.' I beg her.
'What are you doing, Stephanie?' Ben asks from the glass sliding door.
'Just catching up with my new little friend here.'

'Leave her alone.' Ben says walking towards us.
I move past her but she sticks her foot out tripping me over and I fall, landing hard on my left wrist.
'Liz!' Ben calls out.

Stephanie laughs as she steps over me and returns to the party.
'Liz?' Ben kneels down beside and starts to reach for me.
I cower away from him and he stops.
'Are you okay?'
I shake my head and curl up as I start to cry.
'I'll go get Dominic.' Ben gets up and leaves quickly.

👀 DOMINIC 👀

'Dom!' Bens calls out to me.
'Yeah.'
Ben comes up and whispers in my ear.
'Get Simon.' I say as I hand him the tongs and run inside.
'Liz, babe.'
She is not where Ben said she was.

I race into our room and find her in the corner, hiding and crying in the dark.
'Babe?'
'I called you.' She sobs. 'I called you,'
'I'm sorry, babe. Amber borrowed my phone, hers was flat.' I sit down beside her and pull her onto my lap.
I notice her cast is broken.

'I'll take you to the hospital. Your cast is broken, we will get your wrist checked and a new cast.'
'No, you have been drinking. I'll be fine.'
'Liz, I have only had one light beer. I'll be fine to drive.'
'I still don't want to go. I'll tape it up and finish cooking.'
'How about you sit here with me until I'm sure that you are okay? Amber and Cassie can cook. Luke and Ben can do the BBQ.'
'Okay.' Liz snuggles in.

She stops crying after a minute or so.
I sit and hold her, kissing the top of her head.
I need to find out what happened and why Ben was vague on the details.
I swear to god, if he has anything to do with this, I will…

'Dominic, Liz.' Simon calls as he knocks on the door and enters.
'Simon, can you please examine Liz's wrist please?'
'Oh no! What happened?' Simon asks, kneeling down beside us.
'Stephanie and Ben happened.'
'No, it was just Stephanie.' Liz says quietly.
'Was Ben helping you?' I ask her.
'Yes.'
'Simon, Liz has a first aid kit in our closet. Left hand side, you can't miss it.'
Simon turns the bedside table lamp on and heads there.

I lift her face so I can see her eyes.
'Where's my girl?' I say as I brush the tears and hair from her face. 'There's my girl.'
I kiss her lips softly and I feel her fingers gently touch my cheek.
Simon comes back into the room, he puts the first aid kit on the bedside table and sits on the bed.
'Dominic, bring her up to the bed for me.'
I nod and carry her over to the bed.
Liz snuggles in.
I know she loves it when I carry her.
I sit on the bed with her on my lap.
'Liz, can I touch your wrist?' Simon asks her.
Liz nods as she lifts her hand.
'Shit.'
'What?' I ask him.
'Okay, Liz. This is going to hurt. I think you have dislocated your thumb and possibly...'
'It is.' Liz says softly.
'Are you ready?
Liz nods and snuggles in more, I hold her tight. Simon looks at me.
'On three. One, two, three.'
Liz cries out and her body goes limp.

'Liz?'
'She has passed out, Dominic.'
'Simon...'
'She is okay, Dom. Her wrist and hand will be very tender due to the breaks and surgery.'
I nod and kiss the top of her head.
'I'm going to take the cast off and check her wrist and the rest of her hand.'
I watch as Simon delicately does so.

Her wrist and little finger are dislocated as well.
Simon carefully puts them back in.

'Okay, good news. Nothing is broken, if anything I don't think she needs the cast. I will put it back on and tape it up anyway. It will help with the dislocation and swelling. When is her next appointment?'
'Um, Monday afternoon.'
Liz starts to stir as Simon finishes tapping up her cast.

⚇ ELIZABETH ⚇

'Dominic,' I whisper.
'Yeah babe, I'm here.' He says kissing the top of my head.
'Ouch.'
'Sorry, Liz. All done, I have taped it up tight but let me know if it's too tight. Now your little finger was dislocated as well as your wrist.'
'Thank you, Simon.' I say.
'Do you have painkillers?'
'Yes, I have,'
Simon puts his hand up.

'I don't want to know what they are or how you got them.'
'Okay. I won't tell them that you fixed the dislocations.'
Simon smiles and touches my shoulder.
'Thanks, Simon.' Dominic says.
'You're welcome.' Simon nods.
'Alright, I will leave you two alone.' Simon puts his hand on Dominic's shoulder.
'You know where I will be if you need me.'
Simon gets up and leaves the room, closing the door as he goes.
I get up and go to the en-suite to grab two painkillers.
I take them and, using my hand, I sip some water from the tap.
Dominic is still sitting on our bed.
I walk back to him and he pulls me back down.
He shifts and tightens his arms around me.

We sit for what feels like ages.
I'm in my safe place and Dominic knows all I want right now is him.
I can feel the Fentanyl working.
The pain is gone and I feel slightly high.
Thank you hospital medicine cabinet.
'Has it been twenty minutes yet?' I ask him.

He lets out a stifled laugh.
'Yep.'
'Good.' I get up and lock our bedroom door.
'Liz?' Dominic says as he stands.
'Dominic.' I walk up to him.
Using my right hand, I push him back on to our bed and lay down with him.

'Liz,'
'Forty-five minutes. Amber promised and you have been watching and waiting
to steal me away,'
'Liz, Dominic?' Amber says as she knocks on the door.
'Yes.' Dominic replies.
'Is everything okay?' She asks.
'Yep, we will be out…'
'In twenty minutes.' I cut him off.
'Okay.' Amber says.
'Twenty minutes?' He says looking at me.
'I'll take what I can get.' I say as I start undoing the buttons on his shirt.

I feel his arms tighten around me as he touches my hair.
I wrap my arms around his neck running my fingers through his hair.
I flinch as I bump my sore thumb with my other hand.
'Liz,'
'Don't stop. I…' I moan.
'Love you, Elizabeth.'

Dominic buries his face in my neck. 'I promise you forever and always.' He says
softly against my neck.
Dominic sits up and looks at me.
'Liz, promise me you won't go where I can't follow.'
I smile up at him and nod.

👀 DOMINIC 👀

I hold her tight and bury my face in her neck, breathing heavily.
My god, I love this woman so much.
I don't care about waiting anymore, I have the ring.
Together we will face Michael and beat him.
I come out of the bathroom to find Liz sitting on our bed holding her red
jewellery box.
I see my note and a dried flower in her hand.

'Hey, you.' Liz says looking up at me.
'There's my girl.'
'What's wrong?' I ask her.
'Um, nothing is wrong. Stephanie asked me something tonight.'
'What did she ask you?'
'What I have to be so happy about.'
'What did you say?'
Liz looks at me and smiles before looking back at the note and flower.
'I said that I have a lot to be happy about.'
'What's the flower for?'
'Well this is your note and the flower. The flower is from the bunch that you gave me the day after I woke up.' Liz says as she delicately touches the flower with her finger.
'I reckon I need to build you a chest.' I say as I play with a lock of her hair.

'I would love a timber chest. I have been looking for one but haven't found one that I like.' Liz looks up and smiles at me, her eyes shining.
Elizabeth's smile will light up the rest of my life.
When the ring arrives, I don't think I will be able to hold off till we go on holiday.
In fact, I don't want to hold off.
I want to ask her as soon as I can.

'Shall we re-join the party?' I ask her.
'We better before Amber breaks down our bedroom door.'
I stand up and pull her into me, kissing her softly.
Liz picks up her red box and puts it on her cabinet along with some envelopes.
She takes my hand and turns it over, placing the key on a chain in my palm.
'My life, in your hands.'
I pull the chain over my head and tuck it into my shirt.
I follow my girl out of our room.

👀 ELIZABETH 👀

Everyone is out on the deck.
Dominic sits and I go about prepping more food.
After a while, my left hand starts to hurt again.
I hold off taking more pain relief.
'Liz?' Amber comes into the kitchen.
'Yes.' I say looking up.
Amber looks angry.

'What the hell happened?' Amber asks, looking at me as she hands Dominic his phone.
I watch Dominic check his phone.
'Amber, don't worry,'
'Liz, what happened?'
'Amber, I'm fine, don't worry about it.'
'Don't give me that, Liz. I want to know what the fuck happened!'
'Here listen to the voice message.' Dominic says handing Amber his phone.
Dominic gets up and turns to walk out onto the deck.

'No, Dominic.' I call out but he ignores me and keeps walking.
'That fucking bitch!' Amber puts the phone down and follows Dominic.
I follow them, Luke and Simon manage to stop Dominic with the help of Ben, David and Gavin.
They miss Amber.
Amber walks straight to Stephanie and drops her with one punch.
Everyone stops but not one person steps into the scuffle.
'If you ever step foot in this house or Dominic's. If you ever come within yelling distance of Dominic or Elizabeth, I will fucking destroy you! Do you understand me?'
Stephanie stands and nods, she looks around for help but no one moves to help her.
'Get the fuck out of here before I have you handcuffed and dragged out.'
Stephanie leaves, looking very embarrassed.
Amber turns around and smiles at me.

'Right. I could use a drink.' Amber says as she walks up to me and hugs me tight.
'No one messes with my girl.' She winks.
Amber, Cassie, Dominic, and I walk back into the kitchen.
We are joined by Luke, Simon and Ben.
'What was all that about, Amber?' Louise asks as she walks into the kitchen.

Amber puts Dominic's phone on speaker and plays the voice message for everyone to hear.
'I'm so sorry, Elizabeth,'
'Was what you said and did any better?' Luke asks, interrupting her.
'No, it wasn't and I'm deeply embarrassed and ashamed.'
'What did you do, Louise?' Amber asks her with her arms folded in front of her, her deadpan expression levelled right at Louise.
'I forgive you, Louise.' I say.
Louise looks at me with some kind of shocked.
'I don't.' Luke and Simon say at the same time.

'I forgive you, Louise, but it won't happen again. I don't need or want any more stress in my life.' I level my gaze at her. 'The only reason I have tolerated what you did as long as I have was because of Dominic and the long friendship that you had. The choice is yours now, continue the friendship or lose it for good.'
Louise nods and walks out.
'Babe.'
I turn to Dominic and smile.
He pulls me in and kisses the top of my head.
I close my eyes and take a deep breath.
His scent fills my nose.
I'm home in his arms.
I wink at Sally and Sarah as they walk into the kitchen.

'So, Sally and Sarah. There are tables booked for next Friday night. Would you like to join Luke and Simon for dinner?' I ask them.
They both laugh at the look on the faces of Luke and Simon, it's absolutely priceless.
'Sure, what time?' Sally asks.
'Seven-thirty, I'll text you the details.'
'Perfect sounds like a date.' Sarah smiles.
Sally walks over and takes Luke's hand and they walk out.
Simon grins and walks over to Sarah, they also walk out together.
He looks back and gives a thumbs up as Sarah laughs.
'You planned that, didn't you?' Dominic asks me.
'I have no idea what you mean.' I reply.
'You know that you're evil right.'
'Good thing I'm cute then.' I wink at him.
'I can't decide if I like you better in red, emerald green or nothing.'
I blush.
'Come on, let's go and enjoy the party.' Dominic says taking my hand.
I smile and nod as we return to the deck.

'Elizabeth,' Amanda comes up to me. 'Are you okay?' She asks me.
'I never liked Stephanie.' David joins us.
'I'm fine really. Simon checked me over,'
'He said that your thumb was dislocated.' David says looking from me to Dominic.
'If anything, Amber, let her off easy.' Amanda says smiling.
'Simon taped up her cast and reset her thumb, wrist and little finger.' Dominic says pulling me tight against him.

I sit on the daybed near the fire and watch as Dominic talks and laughs, all within touching distance of me.

I head in and take some painkillers; my left hand is starting to become unbearable.

I start getting more food and sweets ready.

I just finish making a cup of tea when I hear someone behind me.

I take a deep breath and turn around.

'Ben!'

'Do you need a hand?'

'You don't have to do anything, I'm almost done.' I smile politely.

He walks towards me.

I take a step back, putting my hand up and looking away from him.

I am feeling embarrassed.

He stops then moves to a bar stool and sits.

I can feel him watching me.

'What's the deal with you and Amber?' He asks.

'We are best friends.'

'Nah. It's more than that. She is extremely protective of you, not as much as Dominic though, he is on a whole other level.'

'Well, um, before I met Dominic, Amber helped me escape from a bad relationship. We bonded and became best friends.'

'With benefits?'

I look at him confused.

'What do you mean?' I ask him.

'You know,'

I shake my head.

'Did you and her ever get together?'

'No never. So, did you ever work for Dominic?'

'Yeah, when I'm not at the mines and he needs a hand. Last time was about twelve to thirteen months ago, I helped out on a house before I got called back.'

'So you met Lana?'

The look on his face confirms my suspicion.

Now I understand Dominic's slight mistrust of Ben.

He doesn't blame Ben, but it must be hard all the same.

'We hooked up once. I didn't know she was with Dominic. I told him as soon as I knew. He was angry but not surprised. I don't think Dominic and I were the only ones on the job. I left a few days later and haven't really been back much.'

'Did you know she had a baby? She tried to pin the baby on Dominic, could it be yours?'

'Nope. Not a chance. I made sure that it didn't happen. Are you sure I can't help you?'

'Can you unpack and repack a dishwasher?'
'That I can.' He smiles.

Ben does the dishwasher as I clean the tables and arrange the trays with more food and sweets.
'Done. What else?'
'You can start taking the trays out with me.'
I follow Ben out with a tray and clean more tables.
I look around and see Dominic talking to Louise.
This makes me smile.
I really hope they can move on for the sake of their friendship.
I head back inside and start getting everything ready for the birthday cake as Amber walks into the kitchen.
'How is your hand? You landed that punch pretty good.' I tell her.
'Nurse Cassie checked me over and gave me the all clear.' Amber winks.
'Well I'm glad that you got the all clear to re-join us.'

'Hey Liz?' Ben says walking in.
'Yes.'
'Why did you forgive Louise?'
'Well, Louise and Dominic have known each other for a long time. I know how she feels about him, it would be hard for her to see us together. Besides, life is better with less hatred.'
'You didn't like me when we first met, did you? And...'
'Ben,' Amber interjects. 'Elizabeth didn't know you, and to be honest, we told not to but you pushed the boundaries,'
'None of us would have been able to stop Dominic from knocking you out. It would have only taken one hit, trust me I have seen it.' Luke says as he joins us.
Luke hugs me, my body trembles but I return his hug.

'Now my dear sneaky, Elizabeth. What are Simon and I going to do with you?'
'I take thank you payments in the way of Vegemite. Really big jars of Vegemite and wedding invites.' I smile and take a step back .
Luke turns back to Ben.
'Now, my brother, if Dominic was here when I hugged her, Liz would have been holding his hand and not shaking.' Luke turns back to me and winks before turning back to Ben.
'Now if you or anyone else scares her, make her shake or hurt her, I will not defend you from Amber and I'm especially not defending you from Dominic.'
'Let's get this cake out to the birthday girl, shall we? Then we can enjoy the rest of the night.' I smile lightly at Luke.

I walk outside behind Luke, Amber, and Ben.

I remember the chocolate coated strawberries and mango.

I head downstairs and get them out of the cool room.

They have just finished singing happy birthday as I reach the top of the stairs with the containers.

I set about cleaning off a table and setting out the chocolates.

I look up and see Dominic still talking to Louise.

I smile and head back inside.

I unpack and repack the dishwasher.

I look at the time it's after eleven-thirty.

I'm starting to feel tired and my hand is really beginning to hurt again.

I take some more painkillers and go to find Dominic to ask if I can go home.

I watch as Dominic hugs Louise and as he pulls away, she kisses him

'Liz,' Ben pulls me into him.

'I should go.' I say not taking my eyes off Louise and Dominic.

I run down the back steps.

'Liz!' Ben calls out. 'Liz wait!'

I run.

I don't want to be here, I need to leave.

I need to get to the shed and get one of the hidden keys for our new car.

☁ DOMINIC ☁

'What the fuck, Louise?' I ask pushing her away.

'I thought…'

'You thought wrong!' I say cutting her off.

I hear Amber calling out for Elizabeth and I look up to see everyone staring at us.

Shit!

Amber walks up to us.

'Congratulations, Louise and Dominic. Elizabeth saw all of that.'

I look around for Liz.

I can't see her anywhere, FUCK!

Ben isn't anywhere to be seen either and I know how he feels about her.

'Shit, Shit, Shit.'

'Oh you think, Dominic,' Amber yells at me. 'Liz let you in, she trusted you!'

Amber turns to Louise.

'Elizabeth forgave you once and against better judgement. If you think for one second I won't drop you where you stand, you are sadly fucking mistaken.'

Amber glares at Louise.

Amber's eyes are full of anger and hate.

'Dominic,' Louise says as she takes my arm and tries to hug me thinking I will protect her from Amber.

'Don't! Don't you dare touch or talk to me again. Our friendship is over. I don't want to see you ever again.' I say as I pull away in disgust. 'You know how I feel and you still pushed to do what you did here. Here of all fucking places.' I shake my head.

🆂 ELIZABETH 🆂

'Elizabeth!' Amber calls out.

I ignore her and keep running.

I stop and remove my shoes, I hear someone coming.

'Elizabeth, wait!' Ben calls out.

I drop my phone and my shoes then run around the corner to my neighbour's yard, thankfully they are not home.

There is a gap in the fence, near the shed, where the car is.

I sneak back into my yard.

I need to find the hidden spare key.

I can hear Amber yelling.

I find the key and get in the car.

I start crying.

He loves me.

He told me he loves me.

My eggs are at a fertility clinic, he wants to have a family with me.

My chest hurts, it hurts more than I can understand.

I cry to myself.

I need to go for a drive, to clear my head.

I just can't be here.

This house has been tainted further.

I push the door button.

The shed door opens and I start the car.

🆂 DOMINIC 🆂

'Fix it, Dominic!' Amber glares at me.

'Where did she go?'

'Ben went after her.' Amber says not looking at me.

I start to leave as Louise reaches for me one last time.

I pull away and make my way towards the back steps.
'You're too good for her, Dominic.' Louise calls out.
I turn to say something only to see Amber drop her with one punch.
Amber turns to look at me.
'You are next if you don't...'
'He will,' Simon interjects.
'He better.' Luke adds.
'Ben is less likely to share,' David begins to say as Amanda elbows him.
I get my phone out of my pocket and ring Liz's phone number.
I hear her phone ring.
'Liz, babe.' I call out as I run towards the sound of her phone.
'Dom,'
Ben comes up and hands me her phone and shoes.

'Sorry, mate, I tried to stop her but I didn't see where she went. I only found these because you rang her phone.'
I hear her car start.
'Shit!' I start running towards the shed.
I'm almost to the shed when I see her car leave fast.
'Liz!' I call out.
I keep running after her.
Babe, please stop.
I continue the chase as her car gets to the end of the driveway and stops.
I see the driver's side door open and Liz get out.
'Liz,' I run to her.
'Dominic, I'm so sorry. Please don't be angry with me, I just couldn't stay. I...'
'Liz,' I drop to my knees.
I feel her touch my face.
How am I ever going to be able to face her knowing how much she was hurt by what she saw

🦉 ELIZABETH 🦉

I drive down the driveway.
I look in the rear-view mirror and I can just make out Dominic running after my car.
Taking a deep breath I stop the car at the end of the driveway and get out.
'Liz,' Dominic says as he runs up to me.
'Dominic, I'm so sorry. Please don't be angry with me, I just couldn't stay. I...'
'Liz,' Dominic drops to his knees.
He is breathing heavily and not because he was running.

I kneel down in front of him and touch the side of his face.
I can feel the tears on his cheeks.
Running my fingers through his hair, I gently kiss the top of his head.
'Dominic.' I bring his face up to mine. 'Dominic, please look at me.'
Dominic looks up at me and his eyes are red.
'Liz, I'm so sorry. I didn't mean to kiss her, it just happened.'

I gently wipe away the tears on his face.
'Dominic, I know you love me. But I need to know. Did you and Louise ever sleep together?'
I already know the answer but I need to hear it from him. Dominic takes a deep breath.
'Yes. It was the weekend before I met you for the first time. But from the day I met you, I didn't want anyone else. I realised the day up the beach just how much more Louise actually wanted. It was a lot more than I was willing to give her.' Dominic sighs.
'Thank you for telling me. Please take me home, I would like to go home now.'
I stand up and get in the passenger seat.

I don't look at him or say anything on the drive home.
I know what I saw and I do love and trust him unconditionally.
I had a feeling that something happened between them but it never bothered me until now.
I forgave her for what she said about me, I even tried to be friends with her.
I wanted to preserve the friendship that they had.
Now, I don't ever want to see her again and I don't want Dominic to see her either.
I forgave Dominic the moment it happened but it doesn't make it any easier seeing the person you love more than anything being kissed by someone even if he didn't invite it.
The moment was like a knife to my heart.
'Liz, please say something.' Dominic asks as he parks the car.
'What are you planning on doing?' I ask not looking him.
'I told her that the friendship is over.'
'Good,' I get out of the car.
I can feel the tears roll down my cheeks.
I know he is hurting too.
Dominic didn't consent to Louise's kiss and I don't blame him, but it still hurts all the same.

👀 DOMINIC 👀

Liz won't even look at me, I can see her tears.
In one brief moment I crushed her, I broke her, I'm the cause of her hurt and tears.
I have no excuse.
I want to walk up to her and take it all back, hold her, and erase it from her memory.
I don't ever want to cause her anymore pain and tears.

I follow Liz upstairs and I can see her body shaking.
I would do anything to hear her say she loves me.
I sit on our bed and watch her remove her necklace and high heels.
She has gone really quiet.
What am I going to do?
I can't lose her, I can't lose my girl.
Elizabeth's phone rings.
'Hello,'
'Ben? Why are you calling? How did you get my number?'
Elizabeth starts pacing in the walk-in closet.
'I'm sorry, Ben, I'm really not comfortable talking about this with you.'
'Thank you for your concern. Goodnight, Ben.'

Elizabeth ends the call, she didn't even wait for the return goodnight.
I bury my face in my hands.
I'm so ashamed of what happened.
Will Elizabeth ever forgive me?
She let me in, let me love her, and I failed her.

👀 ELIZABETH 👀

I kneel down in front of Dominic.
'Hey, you,'
'My girl?' He asks looking up from his hands.
I look at my bracelet that he gave me and back up to him.
I lean into him.
'Forever and Always.' I say as I bring my lips to his.
'Forever and Always.' Dominic intones against my lips.
'I'm your...,' Dominic kisses me hard. I murmur, 'I'm your girl. I love you, Dominic.'
Dominic looks at me, he is hurting.

I can see his tears.
'Liz, I…,'
'Need to unwrap me.' I smile.
'I want to feel you against me even if you just hold me.'
He pulls back and looks at me.
'You don't want me anymore?' I stand and move away from him.
I look at my bracelet, my hands start to shake.
Dominic stands and takes my hands in his.

'Liz, babe, I'm really sorry. I will do whatever I have to do to prove I am worthy
of you. I love you, Elizabeth.'
'All you have to do is be honest with me.'
My hands move up his arms to his chest.
I unbutton his shirt.
I run my fingers up his body pushing his shirt off his shoulders.
Dominic's body is responding to my touch, his breathing quickens as my fingers
glide over his body.
I start untying my dress.
'Liz,'
I look up and smile as my dress falls to the ground.

'Hey, you'
'There's my girl.' Dominic says as a tear falls.
I wipe away his tears and smile.
'I forgave you the moment it happened, Dominic. Right now, I don't want to
talk about it, we can talk later.'
'You are amazing,' Dominic says as he holds my waist.
'Liz, I want to show you something.'
'Okay.'
Dominic helps me get dressed before picking up his shirt.

'What?' He asks me as he puts his shirt back on.
I shrug.
'Your shirt ruins the view.'
Dominic smiles and reaches for my hand, I turn my hand over and he runs his
fingers over my palm.
I close my eyes and breathe deeply, enjoying his touch.
I feel his hands move up my arms to my neck.
Dominic's lips brush against mine.

'Elizabeth.'
'Dominic.'

His tongue teases my lips as I part them in anticipation.
Dominic gently squeezes my waist before giving my arse a hard squeeze.
I sigh as he wraps my arms around his neck.
I feel him smile as he kisses me.
Dominic runs his fingers over mine.
I follow him to the shed.

'This is the last surprise I wanted to show you before we were interrupted. Would you mind closing your eyes?'
I smile and do as he says.
I feel Dominic's hands hold my face and his lips press against mine.
'Hey, you.'
'There's my girl.'
'Forever and always.' I say as I bring my hands to his waist.
Dominic kisses me softly.
'Are you ready?' He asks.
'Yes.'
I hear him open the door and turn the lights on.
'Keep your eyes closed.' Dominic says as he picks me up.
I snuggle in, my safe place in his arms.
I listen to his heart beating as he carries me into the shed.

'Okay, I'm going to put you down now. But don't open your eyes.'
'Okay,' I smile and take a deep breath.
My feet touches the ground and Dominic takes the opportunity to steal another kiss.
'It's after midnight and I'm making sure I get in the minimum quota.'
I smile as I pull him in.
'Okay, now this took me a while to get but I think it's worth it. I hope you like it.' Dominic says still holding me tight.
'I'm sure I will.'
'Alright, open your eyes.' Dominic moves behind me.
His arms are still wrapped around me as I slowly open my eyes.

I stand there looking at a dirt bike, but it's not just any dirt bike, it looks exactly like my old one.
Black and red with my racing number in hot pink.
I look over the bike and then notice the badge.
'Watson Family Motorcycles'.
My brothers built this bike.
Dominic got my brothers to build me a bike.
'Dominic,'

'Do you like it?'
'Dominic, I love it. How,'
'I had help because your brothers built this bike. I figured that this is the next best thing since you can't be with them.'
I turn and look at him.
'Do they know?'
'No, they don't. The bike arrived on Thursday, they still can't believe that I had to have it exactly the same and shipped all the way here.'
'You actually spoke to them?'

He nods, pulls out his phone and plays a recorded message.
'Travis.' I cover my mouth.
I start to cry.
It's the first time in over five years that I have heard his voice.
Dominic pulls me in.
'Liz, I'm sorry I didn't mean to upset you.'
'No, don't be. Can I please listen to the message?'
He plays the message again and it's almost at the end of the message when I hear,
'Jonathan.'
I turn and look at my bike.
It's exactly the same colours, the same stickers.
I smile as I run my hand over the seat up to the handle bar.
My fingers trace over my family's name.
I can't believe it!

I close my eyes and remember the last time I rode with my brothers.
We were riding through the state forest when it started to rain.
My chain broke and I got thrown into a large mud puddle.
I didn't tell my brothers until after we fixed the chain that my knee was dislocated, the padding on my bike leathers somewhat help to hide it.
We couldn't get it to go back in.
We had to ride over an hour back to the car, pack up camp.
This was then followed by a two hour wet and muddy car trip to the nearest hospital.
It was one of the best weekend camping trips we ever had as siblings.

'Liz,'
I open my eyes and turn to Dominic.
'Elizabeth Marie Miller, will you marry me?' Dominic asks me.
He is down on one knee and I watch as he opens the red velvet box to reveal a beautiful silver ring.

A square cut diamond centre stone with smaller diamonds along the band.
I gently touch the ring and look at Dominic.
'Yes,' I say as a tear falls. 'Yes, Dominic, I will marry you.'
The smile on his face lights up my world.
I watch as he delicately puts the ring on my finger.
He stands and kisses my fingers.
'Hey, you.'
'There's my girl.'
Dominic pulls me in and kisses me softly.

I can't believe what has happened.
I found someone, I let him in, I let myself feel and love him.
He loves me.
Not only does he love me but he wants me to marry him.
I look down at the ring on my finger, his ring.
I look back up at Dominic and see his beautiful smile and glistening eyes.

Dominic's phone rings in his pocket and he ignores it.
'I love you, Elizabeth.'
'I love you, Dominic.'
We put the ring back in the box as it doesn't fit my finger properly due to my injuries.
I stand there looking at the ring and run my fingers over it.
I really do mean something real to someone.
My hands tremble slightly and I look at the scar on my wrist.
Dominic loves me; he doesn't make demands of me.
He asks me about the things I like and has never made me feel like I'm a possession.

'Liz?'
I look up at Dominic.
'Where did your mind just go?' He asks as he plays with a lock of my hair.
I look at my bike and then back to his ring that he has given me.
'You let me love you, you love me. You actually asked me to marry you.' I look at him.
I feel his hands on my hips move up to the small of my back, pulling me in tighter.
'I said yes, my eggs are at a fertility clinic in Brisbane. My life is perfect. Our life will be perfect now that I can give you biological...,'
'We can have a biological child, it's not you giving me that. You gave me you and that's all you ever need to give me.'
'There is just...,' I close my eyes.

'Liz,' His fingers is moving along my cheeks.
'There's one thing left in our way.' I open my eyes. 'My past,'
'And it can wait a little longer. Right now I want you to enjoy this moment.'

Dominic takes my hand and leads me out of the shed.
I turn back to look at my bike one more time as Dominic turns off the light and locks the shed.
Dominic ignores his phone again as we walk back to the house, hand-in-hand.
We get to the front door and Dominic turns to face me.
'My god, I love you so much, Elizabeth.'
Dominic gives me the smile that always weaken my knees.
He opens the door and turns back to me.
'I promise you that I will spend the rest of my life loving you. I will not ever fail you again.'
'You didn't fail me, Dominic. I won't lie, it hurt to watch but I saw the start. I just couldn't stay. I had to leave. Ben followed me so I ran.'
His thumb rubs my cheek.
His phone starts ringing again and he ignores it as he starts to kiss me.

'Really, Elizabeth. You forgave him?' Louise butts in from the doorway.
Dominic looks up as he moves me behind him.
'What are you doing here, Louise?' Dominic asks her.
'What does she have that I don't, Dominic?'
'I love her.'
I go to move but Dominic's arm prevents me.
'I forgave you for what you said, Louise.' I say holding Dominic's side.

Louise moves and I see her holding what looks like a knife from our kitchen, Dominic sees it as well.
He pushes me further behind him.
I look down at his other hand.
He is calling Luke on his phone.
'Louise, please leave, you are no longer welcome here. Our friendship is over.'
'Was our night together a mistake, Dominic?' Louise stares at him, her eyes full of anger.
'No.' I answer before Dominic could.
Dominic turns and looks at me, I nod as my hand moves up his arm.
I move to his side.
'What?' Louise looks between us.
'No, it wasn't a mistake. He loved you but it made him realise that the friendship you both had was not something he was willing to risk. You meant so much more to him.'

'Please leave, Louise.' Dominic asks her again.
'You still didn't answer my question, Dominic.' Louise walks towards us.
Dominic moves back, pushes me behind him and holds me there.
'I can't give you what you want.'
'You never even tried!' Louise yells as she lifts the knife and points it at me, 'She turned up and I became invisible' Louise glares at me, her knife still pointed at me.
Dominic's body language changes.

'You are not the one I want Louise. I want Elizabeth, I love her and I'm going to marry her.'
'Oh please tell me you are joking! She is a nobody, a nothing, and…'
'Enough, Louise!' Dominic yells at her.
I see headlights coming up the driveway. Louise moves towards us.
'Don't come any closer, Louise, I'm warning you.' Dominic says, putting his hand up as his other arm protects me. Luke's car pulls up and he gets out with Simon and Ben.
'Louise,' Luke calls out as he walks towards the steps with Simon.
'Go away, Luke. Dominic and I are talking.' Louise takes another step towards us. She doesn't look away from Dominic.
'Louise, let us take you home.' Simon calls.
'This should be my home not hers.' Louise brushes him off as she continues moving towards Dominic and I.

I place my hand on Dominic's arm, I want him to look at me.
I feel his arm push me closer to him.
His body language is hard and defensive.
He is angry and ready to fight off whatever Louise has planned but I can feel small nervous shivers run through him.
'Louise, this is not you. What are you doing?' Luke asks as he joins Simon at the top of the stairs.
Louise looks directly at me and points the knife at me again.
'I'm going to take my place.' She tilts her head to the side and her look is inherently evil.
I feel Dominic stiffen
'No,' He starts to say.
'Dominic, I love you and I know you love me. ' Louise cuts him off. 'You told me that and I know that it's more than friendship. You're just confused, let me show you, Dominic.' Louise says as she takes another step forward.
I need to defuse the situation.

'Louise,' I move close to Dominic.
'Please, come inside. I will make you a cup of tea. Then we can pack my bags.'
Louise smiles.
'Yes, a cup of tea would be good.' Louise says.
We watch her walk inside and I move towards Simon.
'Simon, I have Benzodiazepines inside that should calm her.
'I don't want to know how or where you got those.' He looks at me.
'A med kit is in the boot of the new car, call an ambulance.'
Simon nods as he takes the keys from Dominic and heads to the car.

'Liz?' Luke looks at me.
'I suspect Louise may be bipolar and I need to calm her down before she hurts herself.'
'Or you.' Luke adds.
I look down at my hands, they are shaking.
'I won't let you go in alone.' Dominic kisses my fingers.
'Wait here, I will call you in shortly. Trust me.'
He sighs as he grabs my wrist and pulls me out of Louise' view.

'I love you. Please,'
'Dominic,' I place my hands on his chest and move them up to his face.
'Please trust me and go along with whatever happens in there. I love you.' I whisper.
'Liz,'
'I said yes to you.'
'What are you doing?' Louise asks.
My hands drop to my sides as I turn to Louise.
'Sorry, I was saying goodbye to Luke and Dominic.' I reply.
'Can we talk before I leave?' I ask her.
'Fine.' She sighs before turning back towards the kitchen still holding the knife.

I take a deep breath and follow her inside and go to close the door.
I look at Dominic.
He lifts his left hand up and points to his ring finger then to me, I nod and smile closing the door.
'How do you have your tea, Louise?'
'White with two sugars.'
Louise is standing in the kitchen with me, still holding the knife.
'Okay, the kettle is on. I'll go and change, I'll be just a minute.' I take a deep breath, walk past her and head upstairs.

👓 DOMINIC 👓

'Luke I need to be in there.' I say pacing as Simon gets to the top of the stairs.
'No you don't, let Liz handle this.' Luke says as he looks through the sidelite.
'Ambos and the police are on their way. I told them to approach without lights and sirens. I will meet them when Liz gives me the signal. Should we call Amber?' Simon asks.
'Not yet, give Liz time to do whatever she has planned.' Luke answers.
I continue to pace.
I can't handle the fact that I'm not in there with my girl.
She is on her own again.
'Dominic, chill, mate.' Luke looks at me.
My anger must be visible.
'Mate, you knocked out Daniel with one punch, Louise won't get up.' Luke adds.
'Then Elizabeth will be on her own.'
I have never raised my voice or hand in anger at a woman before.
I look down at my hands, they are clenched in tight fists.

'I won't let Louise hurt her, Luke. I can't just stand here, useless.'
'Dom, take a breath and chill. Elizabeth needs you, remember that.' Simon says as he puts his hand on my shoulder. 'Liz is going to slip Benzodiazepines into her tea. Louise will drink it and calm down. Our girl will be safe.'
'Where is Ben?' I ask them.
'Downstairs near the back steps just in case, he has been on speaker the whole time.'
I nod and continue to pace.
I put my hand in my pocket and hold the box with her ring in it.
I am going to marry her and nothing is going to stop me.

👓 ELIZABETH 👓

I reach the en-suite and close the door.
I find my pouch and change in the walk-in closet.
I get dressed in Jeans, ugg boots, and a light hooded jumper.
I send Dominic a message to let him know what's going on and tell him that I love him.
He replies back with 'My girl'.
I take a deep breath and head back downstairs to the kitchen.
'Right, we will have a cup of tea and then you can help me pack and make sure I get everything so I don't come back.' I say with my back to her.
'Good, the sooner you are gone the better.'

I place the Benzodiazepines in her cup with a little more sugar then add the hot water, stirring so they dissolve.

I put a little more milk in than I normally would in the hope she will drink it quicker.

I worry she will hurt herself to try and get Dominic to comply with what she wants.

'Would you like something to eat?'

'No.'

I place the cup in front of her and watch her drink from the corner of my eye as I drink mine.

'Right, what did you want to talk about?' She asks before having more tea.

'I want to ask you a favour.' I reply.

'Really?' Louise looks at me then sips more of her tea.

The knife is on the bench in front of her.

'I want you to promise me that you will look after Dominic and…,'

'Of course I will, I love him.' She cuts me off before having more of her tea.

'Give him children,'

'Children,' She smirks. 'I'll give him as many as he wants unlike you. I still don't understand why he would want you. You're barren and useless.' Louise grins.

'Yes, you are correct.' I say looking at the floor.

I know she doesn't know but her words still cut through me and I'm trying not to cry.

'You murdered Daniel. He was supposed to scare you into leaving. I didn't care how.' Louise has more of her tea.

'WHAT?' Dominic asks, I didn't even hear them come in.

I look up and see Dominic, his face is full of anger and hate.

Luke and Simon are standing behind him, shocked at Louise's statement.

I shake my head.

'I needed her gone. I saw him watching her and I know his reputation. He didn't need much convincing when I asked him.' Louise smiles and finishes her tea. 'I need to keep you safe, Dominic. Elizabeth will only hurt you.'

'Louise.' Dominic's voice is hard and he is trying to remain calm.

His fists are clenched at his sides.

Luke and Simon move in front of Dominic.

'I told Daniel he could do what he wanted, I didn't care. I even snuck the drugs and the knife into the hospital,' Louise stands and picks up the knife, walking towards me.

I could see the effects the Benzodiazepines are starting to have on her.

'But you!' Louise yells, lifting the knife towards me. 'But you! You fucking bitch you just had to fight back!'
I can't believe what I'm hearing, I just have to get out.
I don't want to hear anymore.
I walk backwards towards the glass sliding door as the tears surface.
I look up at Simon and signal 'two' with my fingers, he nods.
I look at Dominic, the hurt, anger, and betrayal is evident on his face.
Luke and Simon are preventing him from getting any closer.
'How does it feel, Elizabeth? How does it feel to murder someone,' Louise says walking towards me with the knife in front of her. 'How does it feel to be barren and...,'

I turn and open the door.
I run and don't look back.
I run down the stairs and around the corner of the house.
Someone grabs me from behind and a hand covers my mouth.
I panic, scream, and try to fight free.
I'm pushed against the wall.
'Ssh Elizabeth,' A voice whispers.
I stop.

'Elizabeth,'
I nod still facing the wall, too scared to move.
'It's me, Ben. Are you okay?'
I nod still not moving.
'Come with me, I'll take you to Dominic.'
I drop to the ground, curl up, and start rocking.
I hear my name being called, someone touching me, they shake me but I don't even respond.

👀 DOMINIC 👀

'Elizabeth!' I call her name but her stare is vacant.
Everything I have done in the past has helped her but this time it's different.
'Come back to me, babe. I love you.'
Simon rushes to me.
I look up at him and shake my head.
I sit there holding her, kissing the top of her head, and talking to her as Simon checks her over.
'Dom, she is in shock. Get her inside, the ambos have arrived and so have the police. They are with Louise. Amber will be here any minute.'

I lift her up and take her upstairs, Elizabeth offers no resistance and doesn't even make a sound.

Her stare is still vacant, her body isn't even trembling.

I sit on the lounge with her.

'Please come back to me.'

I whisper in her ear as I hold her tight.

'Dom!' Amber calls out.

'In here,' I reply.

Amber rushes to our side as Luke, Simon, and Ben look on.

'I can't get her back,' I say looking at Amber.

'Amber I can't get her back. I don't know what to do.'

'I can.' Amber looks at me and puts her hand on my shoulder.

'I can but you won't like it, and she will possibly freak out big time.'

I sigh and nod.

'We found this recording when we found her the second time,' Amber sighs.

'He took to her with a metal baseball bat.'

Amber gets out her phone and looks at me.

'Okay, babe, I need you back.' I say kissing the top of her head.

I nod and hold Liz tighter, burying my face in her neck hoping that I'm enough when she comes back.

'I love you, Elizabeth and I'm going to love you forever and always.' I whisper.

'Please forgive me.' Amber sighs and presses play.

'Come back here, Chantelle.'

'Please Michael, I'm sorry. I didn't mean to, I'm so tired.'

'You stupid fucking bitch. I said cooked rare, not medium rare!'

Gunshots are heard and screams of pain.

This is followed by something metal being dragged on the ground.

'Stop moving, you fucking ungrateful slut! You know what this is, so stop your snivelling.'

'Yes, I do. Please, Michael, don't. I will do better.'

'Come back here. I fucking own you and I will fucking punish you whenever and however I like!'

'Please no.' she pleads.

'Pick a leg, Chantelle.'

'Michael, please, the baby. I beg you.'

'I don't fucking care about the baby.'

'But it's your baby.' She cries.

You can hear her screams of pain as metal collides with something hard.
Hearing her whimpers of pain, I know he has hit her in the stomach.
She is still trying to plead with him as he hits her again.
'Shame it didn't break the first time, let's see if hit number two will break your leg.'
More screams, it sounds like he is dragging her.
'Poor fucking excuse, Chantelle! I hate excuses.'
It sounds like he has started to hit her with his own fists.
Everything has gone quiet.
'Chantelle,' Michael says her name.
'Wake up, Chantelle. Come on wake the fuck up!'
'CHANTELLE!' Michael screams with murderous rage.

'NO!' Elizabeth screams as she sits up trying to get free of my hold.
'Elizabeth, sshh it's ok.'
I grab her face and make her look at me.
'Elizabeth, it's okay, I have got you. You are safe.'
She is pale and her whole body is shaking violently, her eyes betray the pure fear she felt under Michael's dominance.
I run my fingers along her neck, covering her scars and trying to soothe her.

'Elizabeth, come back to me. I love you, Elizabeth.'
'Dominic.' Elizabeth looks at me, she is slowly coming around.
'I'm here, never letting you go. You are my girl forever and always.'
Liz sinks into my embrace and I hold her tight as she cries.
I look up at Luke, Simon, and Ben; the expression on their faces are of total shock.

'That is her ex?' Ben asks.
'Yes,' Amber sighs
'That was her…' He doesn't finish, he is still shocked.
Amber nods.
I can see how much it affects her.

'Dominic,' Liz whispers my name.
'Yeah, babe.'
She sits up and looks at me.
She's pale, tearstained but still absolutely beautiful and all mine to love, honour, and cherish.
'Ask me again, I need to hear it. Please.' She whispers.
I smile and reach into my pocket and pull out the red velvet box and open it.
'Elizabeth Marie Miller, will you do me the honour and marry me?'

Her smile lights up her face and her eyes shine.
'Yes, Dominic.'
I bring my hands to her face.
'I love you, Elizabeth, with everything I am.'
She leans in and her lips brush mine.
'I'm yours, Dominic. I love you.' Elizabeth says against my lips.
I kiss her softly as my fingers trace along the scars on her neck.

'Cough, cough.' Amber says, moving towards us.
I feel Liz smile, I sit back and look at Liz.
She is smiling and absolutely beautiful and all mine.
'Yay! It's about time!' Amber cheers and claps her hands.
'I've gotta call Cassie and tell her.' Amber hugs Liz before running outside.
'When did this happen?' Simon asks.
'Just before Louise turned up.' I reply.
'Well it took you long enough.' Luke says smiling.
'So when can we expect the big day? Sooner the better, I hope.' he adds.
'We have no idea. One thing at a time, we have a holiday to enjoy.' I reply.
And a scumbag to beat I think to myself.

Liz snuggles in more as her body trembles.
I hold her tighter.
I can feel Ben's eyes on us.
'Right, as best man and Amber as Maid of Honour we have some parties to organise.' Luke grins. 'Excuse me.'
I turn my head to see a police officer at the front door.

'My name is Senior Constable Debra Leads. I need to get statements from you all.'
'Um okay. Liz…' My fingers lift her chin up so I could see her eyes.
Her eyes are red and her face still shows fear.
'Babe, are you up to it?' I ask her.
'Okay,' She whispers.
Liz goes to stand but I pull her in and kiss her softly.
'I love you, Elizabeth.'
Liz smiles.
We head over to the table and sit, Liz looks pale.
'Babe do you want a cup of tea?' I kneel down beside her.
'Yes please.' She smiles at me.

I kiss her, she is still shaking.
I stand up and look at Simon.

He knows what I'm thinking.

We are both worried she is still in shock and, with what she has just heard, will have a panic attack.

I go to the kitchen and start making her a cup of tea.

'Is Louise okay?' Liz asks.

'Louise is fine, the Benzodiazepines worked. The ambos are thankful she was calm by the time they got here. Enough about her, what about you?' Simon asks her.

'I need a cup of tea, a hot shower, and bed.' Liz replies not looking up.

I look at her hands, her fingers run over her bracelet. I smile as I walk over with her tea.

'Do you think we can start now?' The police officer says abruptly.

Liz nods as I place the cup in front of her and take the seat next to her.

'Okay.' The officer sits down across from Liz, sets a digital recorder on the table and takes out a notepad and pen.

I take Liz's hands and watch her close her eyes.

'Elizabeth can you please start with your full name and then begin your account of what happened? I need to get to the hospital.'

'Excuse me...'

'Mr. Miller if you don't mind.' The officer cuts me off.

I look at the officer, shocked by her abruptness and the way she spoke to Liz.

Liz starts telling her account of the events right up to when Ben stopped her.

'How did you come by the Benzodiazepines? You drugged Louise against her knowledge. What were your intentions?

'Um...'

'It was a script and none of your concern. Her intentions were to calm a person who was clearly not in control so no one would get hurt. She is an off-duty paramedic who has done her job.' Amber says walking back inside.

'Excuse me, I think I will decide that.'

'Yeah no, you won't. You got your statement, you can leave now.' Amber cuts the officer off as she stands next to Liz.

'If you interrupt me again,'

Amber gets out her badge.

'Ma'am. I believe you have everything. If you require anything else you can contact Agent Carter.'

The officer packs up and leaves, I look at Amber.

'Liz, are you okay?' Ben asks her.

'Babe,'

Liz stands up and walks towards the stairs.

'Dominic,' Amber moves to my side.

'She heard his voice. She is replaying it in her head, just give her time to process it.'

'Amber what if she shuts down like she has in the past?'

'I don't believe that will happen this time.'

I nod and stand as I watch my girl walk upstairs.

'It's going to be hard for her when she tells me everything. I'm worried I'm not enough for her.' I say turning to Amber.

'You are, Dominic. I honestly think you are the only reason she is still here. The bond you share is unbreakable.'

I look at Amber.

'The scar on her wrist. The one she tries to hide and rubs when she doesn't know what to say.' I sigh.

'It's the only scar Michael didn't physically give her.' Amber says.

'How many does she have? And why did he call her Chantelle?' Ben asks.

I feel my fists clench. What the fuck does it matter to him? He is not with her, it's not his concern! Why is he still here?!

'We stopped counting at 397.' Amber replies.

I look over at Luke, Simon, and Ben.

'Dominic, chill, mate. Elizabeth needs you now.' Luke says. 'Dominic.' He calls my name again.

I glare at Luke, my anger is visible and my fists are clenched and shaking.

'Dom, mate. You need to think about Elizabeth.' Luke says.

'Dominic,' Liz's voice comes from behind me.

I instantly turn and go to her.

'I need you.'

I pick her up and carry her upstairs.

They can show themselves out, right now I'm with my girl and I don't care about anyone else.

I set her down at the foot of our bed and hold her tight.

'Are you okay?' Liz asks me.

'I am now that I have you in my arms.'

'Can we go to bed now? I'm so tired.'

'Anything for my girl.'

Liz goes to the bathroom and I start to remove my shoes and socks.

Elizabeth's phone beeps with a message from Amber.

I use my phone to send Amber a message.

'Gone to bed chat later.'

I put my phone down as Liz emerges from the bathroom.

Her demeanour has changed.

After quickly brushing my teeth, I come back out and get undressed.
Liz is sitting on the side of the bed staring at the floor.
I pull the covers down and reach for her.
'Liz, babe,' I wrap my arms around her.
'Dominic,' She whispers.

I pull her down on the bed, holding her against me as I run my fingers through her hair.
She feels so good against me, I take a deep breath letting her warmth spread over me.
'Dominic?'
'Yeah, babe.'
Liz turns in my arms and I run my fingers along her cheek and tuck her hair behind her ear.
'Can we have a small wedding in New Zealand? With your family? I'd love a ceremony with your heritage included.'
'I would love nothing more than that. How about we have two weddings?'
'Two?' Liz looks at me.
'Yeah. One in New Zealand and one here.'
'Okay'
'What? What is it, babe?'
'We would have to wait because,'
'Liz,' My fingers touch her face softly. 'I will marry you hundred times over, I don't care. I just want the world to know that you are mine and I am yours. I don't care about anyone else, I don't want anyone else. Just you and our life together.'
Liz smiles and lights up my world.
'Dominic, I love you so much.'

CHAPTER 15

Pandora's Box

🔟 MICHAEL 🔟

Hobart, Tasmania.

'ARHHHH! Where the fuck are they, Brian?' I yell throwing a chair.
'We will find them.' Brian watches me.
'You fucking better, Brian!' I start pacing the room.
'They left in a hurry. There are still clothes and toiletries upstairs.' Sam says as he reaches the bottom of the stairs.

I head upstairs to the bedroom.
I start going through drawers and cupboards.
I run my fingers over Chantelle's clothes, she is still wearing my favourites.
I start going through cupboards, pulling out draws and emptying them on the bed.
Out of the corner of my eye I see an envelope taped to the bottom of a draw.
I remove it and open it.
It's a letter addressed to me.

Dearest Michael,
If you are reading this, it means you are getting close.
You are getting close to being back in my arms.
I miss you so much, please come and find me. Please save me from these people.
I can't bear being apart from you any longer.
I need you, I love you.
No one is as good as you. No one does me like you do.
Forever Yours,
Chantelle.

She is waiting for me to save her, they are keeping her from me.
I am going to make them fucking pay for taking her.
I'm going to fucking slaughter them all.

She belongs to me.
I fucking own her.
Chantelle is my property.
'Michael'
'In here.'
'I've got confirmation from my informant, she has been moved.' Brian says as he walks up to me.
'Where?'
'Private Jet, Hobart Airport. They have just taken off.'

Brian hands me the iPad showing me pictures and footage.
They are dragging her out of the car, she tries to fight them off and run.
Someone grabs her and slams her to the ground and it appears they drugged her.
They fucking laid a hand on her, they fucking drugged her, they fucking hurt her!
I'm starting to have trouble controlling myself.
I love watching her fight them off, it turns me on, she is fighting for me.
'I will have flight confirmation shortly.'
'How long, Brian?'
'Hard to say, it's a classified federal jet.'
'Does it look like I care about classified or not? I want that information now.'
Brian nods and leave as Sam enters.

'Sam, make sure my jet is ready to go and can you please find me some bags?'
Sam nods and leaves.
I continue to search the room and I find more letters from Chantelle.
She has left hints from conversations she has overheard.
She really does love me and the very thought of her back with me, screaming my name, makes me hard.
Sam returns with bags and I begin carefully packing Chantelle's clothes and toiletries, and find one more note.

Dear Michael,
In the fridge labeled red food dye.
Something I know only you could truly appreciate.
Xoxo Chantelle.

I take the bags downstairs.
'Sam, please see these bags delivered to the farm please.'
'Of course.' Sam takes the bags and I head into the kitchen and start looking through the fridge.

I find the container labeled red food dye.
I open it and it's full of vials.
Vials full of her blood.
My Chantelle, my beast-tamer.
I smile, she has left me her blood.
Chantelle knows how much I love watching her bleed and how much it soothes me.

'Michael, it appears they are heading for South Australia. The information is being updated.' Brian says as he paces the kitchen.
I continue searching the house while I wait.
'Michael, they are en route to a small airfield outside of Adelaide. It's called Lyndoch Airport.'
'I have never heard of it. What's there?' Sam asks joining us in the kitchen.
'The Barossa Valley I believe, there is a second flight plan. You're not going to like it.' Brian says as he looks at me.
'Why?' I ask him.
'Because we can't land at it or anywhere near it.'
'Where, Brian?' I ask, starting to lose my patience.
'RAAF Base Tindal, in the Northern Territory.'
'FUCK!' I yell slamming my fists onto the bench.
'I'll keep an eye out for any changes in dates and times,' Brian looks at his phone.
'We are needed back in Perth, you parole officer has requested a meeting.'
'Fine but I want to see Lyndoch first.'
'Michael, does Chantelle have a sister?' Sam asks.
'No. Why?'
Sam hands me an envelope with a letter in it.
I read the letter.
Chantelle has written a letter to a sister she does not have.
'Brian! Change of plans, we are going straight to Perth. Lodge flight plans to Melbourne, Adelaide, Brisbane and Perth. I want to keep those fuckers guessing.'
I read the last line of her letter,

P.S. Say hello to Kathy Bates for me and tell her I'm sorry I lost Misery.
XO Chantelle.

I look at the bookshelf and find the book Misery, flicking through it, I find another letter.
On the envelope Chantelle has written 'Sweet Dreams'.
I smile to myself, I'm her drug and she is addicted.
I have a feeling she will be back with me very soon.
I can smell her perfume on the letter and I feel myself getting hard.

My Chantelle, she is planning on running, running back to me.
I close the book and leave the house with it.

'Sam, how is the farm coming along?' I ask as we drive to the airport.
'Ahead of schedule, the CT and MRI arrive next week and the additional bunker area has been built and lined. Should all be completed in about eight weeks not twelve like I first thought.'
'Excellent.' I smile.

🔖 DOMINIC 🔖

I wake to find Liz already up.
I put on some track pants and make my way downstairs.
I find her on the lounge dressed in her red robe.
She is resting her head on her knees and is gently rocking while staring out the windows with a vacant stare.
She is still processing hearing his voice.
'Liz, babe.' I sit next to her and pull her into me.
I lay back on the lounge as she snuggles in, we just lay there holding each other.
I can feel her body slowly stop trembling as I run my fingers through her hair.
Something is different. She sits up leaning on her elbow.
Her fingers trace along my face, down my chin and onto my neck.
Liz's fingers move down my body, and she watches my reaction to her touch.
I touch her face.
I watch her close her eyes and take a deep breath.
I sit up and bring my lips to hers.
'Hey, you.'
'There's my girl,'

I pull her onto me and hold her tight.
Liz presses herself against me and kisses me hard as her fingers drag along my back.
The sensation drives me wild.
I need her, I love her.
'Liz,' I call.
'Yes, Dominic.'
I untie her robe and push it from her shoulders, as my hands move along her body I can feel the goosebumps on her skin.
'I want you, Elizabeth,'
'Then take me.' She moans.

I stand up still holding her and she wraps her legs around me as I carry her upstairs to our bed.
Laying her down, I look at her and smile.
I stand to remove my track pants.

👓 ELIZABETH 👓

I watch him remove his track pants before bringing his lips to my thighs.
I reach for him, he slowly moves up my body, teasing me.
My body shudders under his touch.
'Dominic.'
My body shudders as he takes my breast in his mouth.
I arch my back and he slides his arm under me, lifting me up and claiming my lips with his.
I run my finger nails along his back and up through his hair.
'Dominic.' I sob as he enters me.
'Liz,'
'I want you, Dominic, all of you.' I whimper.
He pushes deep and his thrusts are hard.
His hand slides down and he grabs my arse as he groans against my neck.
My lips find his, my kiss is hungry, I want him, I need him.
He feels what I feel and returns it as he moves to bring me on top.

Dominic's hands move over my body to my arse as I move along his cock.
I lean back, placing my hands on his thighs as his hands move up cupping my breasts.
I move along his cock harder, he pinches my nipples harder and my body responds to him.
'Dominic. I begin to orgasm.
He sits up pulling me in and holding me to him.
Dominic's lips move along my neck and down to my breasts.
I pull his hair back, giving me access to his mouth.
'Liz,' He sighs as I push him back down.
Moving along his cock, I rake my finger nails down his chest to his abs.
My hands move to his sides and I squeeze, digging my nails in.
He groans loudly as I roll my head back.
'Dominic.' I call his name.
I can feel myself getting lost in this man.
My need for him, my love for him, I can't describe it.
Dominic sits back up, pulling me in and devouring my lips with his.
'Liz,' Dominic calls me as he kisses me hard.

'Dominic.'
'Liz, I want you forever and always.'
I look at him and smile.
'You have all of me, Dominic, forever and always.'

👀 DOMINIC 👀

My hands are in her hair as I kiss her.
I cannot describe the love I have for her.
Liz's body moves on me seductively, I slide my hands down her back and grab her arse.
Her arms wrap around my neck as she rolls her head back.
She is close, I can feel it.

'Dominic.' Liz pushes hard against me, calling my name as she climaxes.
I hold her as her whole body shudders.
I roll, bringing myself back on top of her.
Her nails dig into my back, grabbing the bed head I push hard and deep.
Liz calls my name out, her calls drives me wild.
I want to be gentle with her but my body is responding to her.
The more she calls for me, the more she digs in her nails, and the more I feel the need to please her.
Liz calls my name again as her body shudders.

I slide my arm under her as she arches her back lifting her up to me, my lips brushing against hers as I go harder, faster, and deeper in her.
Holding herself up on one elbow, her other hand pulls me in hungrily claiming my lips with hers.

I don't know what is happening but it feels like Liz is needing me on a whole other level and I need to be what she wants, what she needs.
The more she calls my name the more I lose myself.
I can't hold back.
I give her what she craves, what her body craves.

👀 ELIZABETH 👀

I can't explain what's going on but my need for him is heightened beyond anything I comprehend..
My body craves him, Dominic is everything I need.
He is all I will ever want.
I won't be able to hold off much longer, the heat has ignited and my body craves for more.

'Dominic.' I moan against his lips.
He starts to go harder, rougher.
My nails dig in and I drag them roughly down his back. I can feel him shudder.
He gets up on his knees, pushing deeper, his hands hold my hips.
I feel his fingers dig hard into my sides but I don't stop him.
'I love you, Dominic.'

I dig my nails into his thighs and his response is instant.
He moves my leg under him and pulls my other leg up along his body and begins to rub my clitoris.
I know what he wants.
I bring my fingers to my mouth and suck them then replace his fingers with mine and he watches me masturbate as he thrusts harder.

He pushes my leg to the side and leans in, I grab the back of his head and pull him in, his lips claim mine and I kiss him hard.
He is breathing hard and buries his head against my neck, his body tenses. He can't hold back for much longer.
I dig in my fingernails the more and call for him.
He gets harder and rougher, his lips find mine.
Dominic buries his face against my neck as I climax, calling his name.

His hand grabs my arse as he gets even harder and rougher.
He orgasms as he throws his head back.
I bring my hands to his face as he looks down at me.
'Liz, are you okay?'
We are still breathing heavily as he wipes tears from my face.

'I'm sorry, babe, I hurt you, was I…'
'Just what I needed you to be. You didn't hurt me, don't apologise.'
'Are you sure you are okay?'
I nod and smile as I pull him back down to me.

'Liz, you were different. Are you sure you are okay?'
'Were you not satisfied?' I ask him.
'My god, babe, yes, I couldn't hold back. The more you dug your nails in and called my name, the more I let go. I loved every minute of it,'
'And I loved every minute of it.' I say as I run my fingers along his face and brush the hair from his face.
'Liz, that wasn't goodbye sex was it?'
I look up at him.
'I don't know. Everything is about to change,'
'Not how I feel about you. I'm not letting you go.' Dominic cuts me off.
'I love you, Elizabeth, and I am going to marry you.'

Dominic's lips claim mine.
His kiss feels dominating and territorial.
He won't let me go, I'll be forever and always his girl.
He holds me tight as I hold him too, not wanting to let him go.
'Liz, you're shaking.'
'Sorry I,'
'Babe, don't apologise.' Dominic brushes my cheek and smiles at me.

I wrap my arms around his neck and pull him back down to me.
I sigh as he softly kisses me and his hand squeezes my sides.
I love the feeling he gives me as his hands move along my bare skin.
Every kiss no matter how hard or dominating makes me feel alive and desired.
Dominic moves beside me and sits up against the headboard.
I look up at him and watch as his eyes follow his hand as it moves along my body.

Why me?
How did someone like me find him?
What does he see in me?
'Liz, stop.'
'Stop what?' I ask him.
I am questioning myself again. But I can't help it, I heard Michael's voice. I'm trying to figure out and understand why he chose me.
'You are strong, amazing, beautiful and I love everything about you.'
'I wish I can see what you see,'

Dominic grabs my hand, pulling me off the bed and leading me into the en-suite.
We stand in front of the mirror.

'I want you to look at your reflection. You can see everything I can see. You just need to trust yourself.'
I look at the bracelet Dominic gave me and I close my eyes as I run my fingers over it.
I open my eyes again and look at our reflection.
I see Dominic smiling.
I look at my reflection.
I smile.
Dominic's smile is infectious.
He wraps his arms around me making me feel safe and warm.

I see myself smiling. I see myself in the arms of someone I love. I see myself in the arms of someone who truly loves me.
Dominic is giving me the strength to heal, the need to want to breathe.
I want to be here, I want to be with Dominic.
I have given up so much in my life, so much has been taken from me.
For so long, all I could do was dream of having someone who actually loves me.
No more fear, beatings, rape, and no more feeling alone.

I know what I need to do.
I also need to tell him everything.
Dominic gently kisses my shoulder.
I close my eyes and enjoy the moment.
I turn in his arms and he holds me tight, I rest my ear over his heart and listen to it beating.
'You are not alone anymore, Elizabeth.'
I look at him.

'I'm here with you. I'm never going to leave you.' He holds me tight.
I smile and nod.
It's noon by the time we get to Amber's.
I close my eyes and I start to shake.
You can do this, I tell myself, Dominic won't leave me.
I run my fingers over the bracelet he gave me, forever and always.
Dominic opens my door and holds my hand.

'Elizabeth, we don't have to do this today.'
I look at him.
'Yes, I have to, I need to.' my voice trembles.
'I'm here by your side.'

He helps me out of the car and kisses me softly before holding me tight and kissing the top of my head. We start walking upstairs, my chest feels tight and I'm beginning to feel hot.

I want to turn and run.

I'm about to open my locked cabinet, my Pandora's Box.

Amber is inside with Cassie. Amber walks up and hugs me tight.

'I'll be right here if you need me.'

'Thank you, Amber, I just need a moment alone.'

'I'll be right here when you're ready.' Dominic says as he kisses me softly.

He takes the key and chain I gave him from his pocket and hands it to me.

'Liz,'

'Yes, Dominic.'

He reaches into his other pocket.

He opens his hand, it's our engagement ring on a delicate silver chain.

I look up at him.

'I am going to marry you, and nothing is going to change that. I love you, Elizabeth.' I smile as he kisses me softly and holds me tight.

Dominic releases me and puts the chain with our ring around my neck.

He kisses me again before I turn and walk into our room.

🔯 DOMINIC 🔯

I watch Liz walk away and I hate it.

'Dom.'

I turn to Amber.

'Michael is following Liz's decoy and it won't be long before he realises it. I have been on the phone for the last few days. I got a phone call this morning just before you arrived.' Amber takes a deep breath.

I just know I'm not going to like what she is about to tell me.

'Michael has killed the of the agents who helped get her out, including the boyfriend of one of them. He is close, Dom, really close.'

'He won't. I won't let him.' I interrupt her.

'He will, don't you see, Dom? Someone close is helping him. He has acquired some inside knowledge, we only just got away from him last time.' Amber walks over to me.

'I need you to find out Liz's real plan.' Amber whispers, looking me dead in the eyes.

'What do you mean real plan? I thought…'

'Dom, I know Elizabeth. She has something else planned, and if I'm correct...'
Amber looks at me, she looks scared.
'If I'm correct, Dom, she is planning on confronting him, alone.'
'I won't let it come to that.'

👀 ELIZABETH 👀

I can hear their voices in the kitchen, but I don't know what they are saying.
I walk into my closet and stand in front of my locked cabinet.
My palms start to feel sweaty and my hands are shaking.
Taking a deep breath, I kneel down and put the key into the keyhole.
I close my eyes and try to focus, my whole body is trembling.

A warm familiar scent fills my nose and arms envelope me.
I lean back into his embrace letting his warmth spread through me.
'I love you, Elizabeth.'
I turn to face him and his lips find mine.
His kiss is hard and hungry but full of love.
His arms envelope me as he pulls me on to his lap. We sit together in silence.
My safe place is right here in his arms.

👀 MICHAEL 👀

Perth, Western Australia.

'Michael,' Brian knocks on my door.
'Yes, Brian.' I look up from my desk in my private office off my bedroom.
'I believe I have found where Chantelle might be now.' He says, walking up to me.
'How?'
'I had one of our rats look into Agent Ryan a little deeper. It appears he spoke to two agents in particular.' Brian hands me one of the files he is holding. 'Agents Reilly and Smith. It appears they are either her direct handlers or the ones her handler reports to.'
'And?' I glare at him. My patience is thin at best.
'Some chatter was intercepted, your name and hers came up.'
'Where?' I lean back in my chair.
'Queensland. I have my contact checking it but it will take time. I should have some form of confirmation in around forty-eight hours.'
'Why so long? What's the hold up?' I ask him before he finishes.

'High level classification due to the nature of your business.'
'Fuck!' I get up and pace in front of the window overlooking the city.

'I want everything ready to go when confirmed,'
'There's more, Michael.'
'More?'
'I have managed to get some documentation regarding an attack,'
'What? What fucking attack?' I yell.

'It appears that someone attacked her. Two builders working on a nearby house saved her.'
'Who attacked her?'
'I haven't read all the details, but I have some documentation and photos. From what I saw, it's not good.'
I slam my fists onto my desk.

'I will fucking kill whoever touched and fucking attacked her!' I yell.
Brian nods and hands me the folder.
'I'll leave you to read the files,'
'Where is Sam?' I ask as I run my hand over the folder.
'He got back around 1am this morning.'
'I need to see him, please send him up as soon as he is awake.'
'Of course.'
'Thank you, Brian.'

I watch Brian walk out the door and I turn towards my en-suite.
The bitch has woken up.
I stand up from my desk and walk to the door of my en-suite.
'Are you going to join me in the shower?' She asks me.
'No.' I reply as I lean against the door frame.
'Are you just going to stand there and watch me?'
'No.' I cross my arms. This conversation is boring me.
'What do you want?'
'I want three things from you.' I look at her, she is not my Chantelle.
This bitch disgusts me.
'And they are?' The bitch asks.
The more she talks, the more annoyed I become and it's less likely she will live long enough to see the farm.

'Number one, you are going to suck me off while I read over some important documents.' I walk closer to her. 'Number two, I'm going to fuck you so hard you will scream and…'

'What's number three?' She cuts me off, fucking pissing me off even more.
I tilt my head to the side and look at her with evil intention.

'You are going to bleed for me.' I smile.
'Bleed?'
I watch her face go pale and her wet naked body tremble.
I can feel myself harden, seeing the fear in her eyes turns me on.
'Bleed.' I grin.
'But I…'
'You're not here to talk and this conversation is boring me. You had better start using your mouth for its true purpose and usefulness.'
'I want to leave now. Please let me go.'
She is still standing in the shower, naked and trembling, I'm really going to fucking enjoy this.

'Michael?' Sam calls out, he sounds tired.
'Sam, sorry if I woke you up.' I turn and walk back into my office.
'That's all right, I have an appointment to get ready for.'
'It looks like we are going to Queensland.'
'No worries. I'll check on the farm, make a few calls. We have transport contacts in Queensland with federal transport permits.' Sam says as he scratches the back of his head and stretches.
'Excellent. I have a guest that I will need to keep for Spencer. She is also Type O. I won't damage her too much.'
'Of course, I'll leave you to your guest.' Sam nods and smiles as he leaves.
I nod and walk back to my en-suite.

'I want to leave now.' She stands in front of me, wrapped in a towel.
'Umm, no. You will do as you are told. I know of hundred different ways to make you bleed you and only one that is pain free.' I grin as I watch her process what I said.
'I'm not a man known for his patience and you are boring me to death.' I walk to my desk and remove my track pants.

I sit down as she walks out, I pull out my customised black and red Desert Eagle.
I run my fingers over it.
I remember all the times I fucked Chantelle with this gun.
I shot her with it many times too.
I smile, remembering the time I cracked her skull with the handle as well.
I feel myself harden.

I look at the bitch as I hold the gun up and rest the barrel along the side of my head.
Her eyes widen with fear and that is one of my favourite looks on a female.
'Incentive for you to impress me.' I say to her.
I watch her tremble as she walks towards me.

'Lose the towel.'
She stops, and I watch her hands tremble as she complies.
She kneels down in front of me, I see the tears roll down her cheeks.
'Open your mouth.'
She looks at me with pure fear in her eyes.

'Open your fucking mouth. Do not make me ask you again.'
I place the muzzle of my Desert Eagle in her mouth and remove the safety.
I pull her hair hard, causing her to whimper.
I lean in close, I can smell her tears and almost taste her fear.
I am really going to fucking enjoy this.

'Impress me.'
She nods.
I remove the gun from her mouth and put it on my desk.
The bitch begins sucking my cock, I lean back and begin reading.

Elizabeth Merie Miller.
Female
Age: 26
D.O.B 26/12/1980
Date of Incident: Monday 17/05/2010 and Tuesday 18/05/2010
Longreach QLD

NOTE: Victim escaped Federal Police protection three months prior and was located, hiding in Longreach. Federal Police decided to watch instead of acquiring the target. Victim was in possession of sensitive case material.

Police and paramedics were called to the victim's home. It was one female victim attacked by a single unarmed male. Builders next door heard her screams for help and came to her assistance.
I continue reading as the bitch continues her duty.
I read about her injuries: black eye, cuts to her face and scalp, broken wrist and dislocated fingers.
I thought Brian said it wasn't good, I'm still going to kill the fucker who attacked her.

I continue reading.
'Second attack,' I look down.
'I said impress me not suck a lollipop.' I grab her head and push her down, causing her to choke and gag on my cock.
I roll my head back, moaning, and grin.
'Better,' I go back to reading.

Multiple stab wounds, cuts to her face, fractured skull, busted lip, long cut along her inner thigh.
I'm starting to get very angry, no one and, I mean no one, touches a hair on my Chantelle.
'Defensive wounds,' I say to myself as I push the bitch down hard against my cock.
She starts sucking harder.

'My Chantelle fought back.' I growl as the bitch sucks harder, taking me deep.
I read about her death and revival.
There are notes regarding her surgery and more than a week in a fucking coma.
This motherfucker is going to die slowly and very fucking painfully.
I go through crime scene photos.
Auburn hair, her face swollen and bruised.
Her hospital room ransacked and blood everywhere.
I read the nurse's statement.

'Victim calling for help, calling for Michael to save her.'
'Stop!' I push the bitch off me before knocking her out with my desert eagle.
I pull my track pants up and grab the file.
'Sam, Brian!' I call out to them as I walk out to the hallway.

'Yes, Michael,' Sam says as he reaches my side.
'We are going to Queensland. It's Chantelle.'
I hand Sam the file, point to the nurse's statement, and watch as he reads it.
'I think you are right.' Sam looks up at me.

'My guest is sleeping on the floor at my desk, please see it delivered to Spencer.'
'Of course, I'll add it to the manifest. I have a truck with supplies heading to the farm tonight.' Sam says.
'Good. Now, Brian, they changed her name to Elizabeth Miller. I want to know who her handler is and where she is now.'
'What about her attacker?' Sam asks.
'She killed him with his own knife.' I reply.

My Chantelle, calling for me and killing the man who attacked her.
She knows she is mine, she knows I own her!
Chantelle loves me.
I walk through my room to my closet.
I pick up my brown leather bag similar to the bag doctors used to use.
I turn around and look at my shoe rack.
Running my fingers along the outside of my timber moulding, I find the concealed leaver.
I open my hidden cabinet and begin packing my favourites along with Chantelle's.
Chantelle's favourite is a long handled leather flogger.
I have choked, and gagged her with the handle and the leather knotted tails are stained with her blood.
It makes her back bleed beautifully, I can feel myself harden again.
 The mere thought of her bleeding, naked and screaming brings me great pleasure.
'I'm coming, Chantelle.' I grin.

👀 ELIZABETH 👀

'I love you, Elizabeth.'
I look at Dominic and smile as my fingers move along his jawline.
'I love you, Dominic.'
Dominic pulls me in and holds me tight.
'I couldn't let you open it on your own. I made a promise to you that you wouldn't be alone.'
He kisses the top of my head.
'Thank you, Dominic.'
'I don't want to be where you're not.'

I take a deep breath, letting his scent and warmth wash over me.
I turn back to my cabinet and touch the key.
Dominic's hand covers mine.
'Together.' He says.
He holds me tight and kisses the top of my head as we turn the key.
I slide open the doors.

'Seven and a half years of my life in four archive boxes.' I say as I lean into Dominic.
His fingers run through my hair as he pulls me into his embrace.

'You are not alone anymore and I promise you that you will never be alone again.'
I pull out box one and two as Dominic grabs three and four.
We walk into the lounge with the boxes and set them on the floor.
Dominic pulls me in and kisses me softly.
I leave him to get ready as I go into the kitchen to make coffee.

'Liz,' Cassie says as she comes up to me.
'Hey, Cassie, where's Amber?'
'She is on the phone outside.' Cassie replies as she gets the milk from the fridge.
'Any news on Louise?' I ask her.
'From what I heard she has been assessed by mental health. She has family interstate, once she is cleared she will be released into their custody.'
'What are you two talking about?' Dominic asks, coming into the kitchen
'I was asking about Louise.'
'Don't worry about her, babe. What happens to her now is her doing.'
'But I still…'
'Don't. She is gone and Amber has slapped a huge restraining order on her.' Cassie cuts me off.

Dominic wraps his arms around me as Amber walks in, she looks angry.
'You have forty-eight hours.' Amber snaps at me.
'Amber,'
'Don't Liz! I just got off the phone. This plan of yours, it sucks! I hate it!' She moves into the kitchen and stands next to Cassie.
'I'm sorry, Amber.'
'Yeah, well, Elizabeth. Fuck you and your apologies.'
'Amber?' Dominic says shocked by Amber's outburst.
Cassie stands there with her mouth open trying to gather her thoughts about Amber's sudden outburst at me.
'What, Dominic?'
'It will work.' I say looking at her.
'If it doesn't?' Amber challenges me.
'It will.'
'What do you think, Dominic?' Amber asks him as she crosses her arms.
'Honestly, I don't know what is going on.'

'Elizabeth leaked parts of her file to Michael. He will eat it up hook, line, and sinker.'
Dominic releases me and steps back from me.
I look at him and the anguish is written all over his face.

'No, Agent Smith was stalling. He wasn't keen on the idea, in fact, he was against it.' He places his hands on the back of his head.
'I changed the plan.' I say as I reach for him.
Dominic steps back even further away from me and shakes his head.

'No.' He says, his fingers scrap through his hair and down his neck.
'No?' I look at him, my fingers run over my bracelet.
'I'm the one who suffered at his hands,'
'And I'm the one who fucking loves you!' He yells and points a finger at me.
He is hurting but I never thought he would speak to me like this.

'And I said yes to you.' I say, trying to hold it together as my body trembles.
'Exactly! You said yes, as in you and me together!'
'That's why I did this. I need to end this, it's the only way I can ensure you are safe, Dominic,'
'Fuck being safe!' He yells. 'How much does he know, Elizabeth?' Dominic asks me.
'Only what I let him,'
'How much?' He yells at me and slams his fists on the bench.
I freeze.

'State, attack, death, and coma. She didn't leave much out, may as well roll out the red fucking carpet with a flashing neon sign saying HERE I AM!' Amber answers, waving her hands dramatically before turning around and leaning against the bench with her head hanging low.
'FUCK!' Dominic yells and turns away from me.
'Dominic, please,' I just manage to whisper as my hands tremble.
I remove the chain from my neck with the ring and put it on the bench along with my bracelet.
Tears start to fall as I look at the floor.
'I trust you, Dominic, and I have faith in you. You could have at least returned it.' I turn and walk out the door.

🔭 DOMINIC 🔭

'What the fuck?' Cassie yells at Amber and I.
'I'm disgusted by you both. You may not like what Liz is doing but you could at least be supportive.'
'Cassie,'
'No, Dominic!' She snaps at me.

'Cass,' Amber stops immediately as Cassie turns her death stare on Amber, immediately shutting her up.

'Either of you had no right to speak to her like that. I would have thought you would show her more respect than what you did.' Cassie shakes her head.

'After everything she has been through she did not deserve that. The way you both just spoke to her,' Cassie shakes her head as she walks up to me and holds out her hand.

I look at her, unsure what she is giving me.

'I may not know everything but I'm not stupid. I know what she has given up and what she has lost and when I look at you, Dominic.' Cassie sighs. 'I thought that maybe, just maybe, she had found herself. But you, Dominic. You yelled at her, slammed your fists on the bench, and then, just to drive it home, you turned your back on her. You have really disappointed me.' Cassie shakes her head as she drops the contents of her hand in mine and walks off.

I look down at my hand and my heart sinks as my chest constricts.

I hold back tears that threaten to fall as I stare down at Liz's bracelet and our ring. The ring that means for better or worse.

'Dom,'

'No, Amber.' I shake my head. 'Cassie is right we should trust her decisions even if we don't agree with them..' I sigh. 'I almost lost her. I made her a promise, like fuck I'm going break it.' I walk outside to meet my girl.

I get to the top of the steps and I can hear her crying.

I did it again, I hurt her.

I'm the cause of her tears.

I look down at her bracelet and our ring, I need to be better.

I'm the one who needs to protect her, love her, and trust her.

Elizabeth is my girl and I love her more than I can explain and, to be honest, I think I loved her the moment I first saw her.

I need her in my arms. I take a deep breath and go to my girl.

🔟 ELIZABETH 🔟

'Mind if I join you?' Dominic says behind me.

I wipe the tears from my face.

'Okay,' I mutter.

Dominic sits next to me, takes my hand and turns it over, and then he places our ring and my bracelet in my hand.

He pulls me in and kisses the top of my head.

My safe place in his arms.

'I'm sorry I made you angry,'
'No, babe, I'm sorry, you're right. But I just can't bear the thought of losing you. I can't lose you Elizabeth.'
'You won't. I made you a promise. I will fight and you will find me.'
'I trust you, babe, I just don't like your plan. The very thought of him being near you, touching you makes me want to…'
'Dominic, I will deal with him, your hands will be clean.' I say as I look up to him.
'So what is your plan, Elizabeth?' Ambers asks.
I turn to her.

'I don't trust the system anymore, after everything he did to me, not to mention what's not in your files. The system failed, they let him out, they are on his side.'
I feel Dominic's hand on mine.
'What are you going to do, Elizabeth?' Amber asks me.
'What I was too weak to do before. I'm going to kill him.'
The look on Amber's face is complete shock, she has never heard me say anything like that before.
I feel Dominic stiffen beside me.
'How?' Amber challenges me.
'By exploiting Michael's one and only weakness.'
'He doesn't have one, Elizabeth.' Amber says.
'Yes he does,'
'Why didn't you tell us at the start?'

'Amber, I am his weakness.'
'You will not be bait, babe.'
I turn to Dominic.
'Dominic, please trust me,' My fingers brush his cheeks.
'I know he has big plans for me. He won't hurt me straight away. If the plans are followed and everything goes right he will take me. I will have a small tracker, smaller than a grain of rice, implanted in my foot. You will be able to track my movement and I will end it when he gets to where he needs to be. Once he is dead, I will call and that's when you will come to me.'
'Babe,'
'I have already set things in motion. He will be getting all sorts of information. I have made sure he won't leave Western Australia. We still have time.'
'How do you know?' Amber asks.
'I have been sending him letters as per my agreement with Agent Reilly and Agent Smith.'
'What!' Dominic looks at me.

'I have written letters to him to make him think that they are keeping me from him against my will. I drew vials of blood and they were left at all safe houses for him to find as a gift from me. Michael loved watching me bleed. Also, before I went into hiding, Agents Reilly, Smith, and I staged crime scenes and footage of me killing people as I was trying to escape. Now I have also told him not to come because his rivals are following me, waiting to take him out. He also thinks I have stolen some of the evidence the feds were hoping to use against him. I told him I'm coming to him. That way he plays into the game that we have set.'

Dominic traces the scars along my cheeks and neck.

'Michael thinks I'm planning my escape because of my blind love and loyalty to him. So far Michael has believed everything I have planted for him and that I will contact him to let him know where I will be for him to save me.' I say as I close my eyes and take a deep breath, letting Dominic's warmth spread through me.

I open my eyes and see him.

'Hey, you.'

'There's my girl.'

'Forever and always.' I say as he puts the chain around my neck and claims my lips.

He puts the bracelet back on my wrist and kisses me like it will be our last.

I stand up and take Dominic's hand in mine and we walk back inside.

I can't be sure that my plan will work but Michael will have my back and this will all be over.

Dominic will be safe. At last.

👀 MICHAEL 👀

Perth, Western Australia.

'Pay off the rats I want to leave tonight.' I tell Brian.

'Of course. Sam reported back, they got to them. The Chantelle decoy is dead but she did squeal first. Apparently Chantelle was with them but got moved, and they have been interrogating her pretty hard. The letters have been confirmed, they are from Chantelle and the blood has been confirmed as Chantelle's. She mentioned that Chantelle managed to escape a few times.'

'How?' I ask him.

'You taught her to use the only asset she has, her body and she used your favourite weapon.' Brian smiles as he hands me some pictures.

It's crime scene photos.

'She did this?' I turned to him.

'Yes, and they did this to her.' Brian says handing me more pictures and video footage.

'They ran her off the fucking road!'

'Yes, and the footage I showed you in Hobart was from the first time she tried to escape.'

'Those fuckers are going to fucking pay for this.' I say as I continue to watch the footage.

They are hitting her! I'm the only person who lays a hand on her!

'FUCK!' I yell.

Brian's phone beeps.

'It's Sam. Ryan is on the way to the farm, he refused to give any details so far.'

'Excellent, well a dead rat is a good rat. Everything is ready to go, when is Sam due back?' I ask turning my back to Brian and pouring two drinks.

'In about two hours. Thank you.' Brian says as he takes the glass.

'All reports have her in Brisbane. Have you heard anything else?' I ask sitting on the lounge opposite Brian.

Brian takes a mouthful appreciating the amber liquid.

'Chantelle spent six weeks at Kangaroo Point before being moved to the Gold Coast, Ipswich, Caloundra, Eudlo, Palmwoods, and then escaping to Longreach. I'm still waiting for confirmation on her whereabouts now.' Brian takes another mouthful and relaxes back into the leather lounge.

'What are your plans?' He asks me as someone knocks on my office door.

'Yes?' I call out.

The housekeeper enters and hands me an envelope.

'This just arrived by courier.'

'Get out,' I say to her.

I wait till she leaves before answering Brian.

'My plan is going to the farm. I have questions and Ryan has the answers. I want to know who else he has been talking to apart from Reilly and Smith. I'm a little rusty on my torture techniques, but I'm sure that after some practice, it won't take me long to get back into the swing of it.' I grin. 'I've also got a new selection of saws that might help lubricate his vocal cords.' I settle back more into my seat.

'Do you think he will talk?'

'I hope I get to play for a while before he gives in?'

'Filming?' Brian asks me.

'Of course.' I smile.

I look at the envelope addressed to Mr. and Mrs. Michael Webster from Kathy Bates.

'Michael?'
'It's a letter addressed to Mr. and Mrs. Michael Webster from a Kathy Bates.'
I start reading, it's a warning.

Don't pay the rats, we are being watched.

I look at Brian.
'It's from Chantelle, she is warning me not to come yet. It's not just the rats after her,' I hand it to Brian.
'What do you think she means?' Brian asks, reading the letter.
'The rats are in bed with my rivals. They want her so they can get to me. Chantelle stole money and evidence,' I say, taking the letter back and continuing to read it.
'Chantelle is warning me not to leave Western Australia, she is coming to me.'
I sit back and take another mouthful of whiskey, savouring the warm amber of the 25-year-old single malt, and smile.
My beast-tamer is coming home to me.
She knows who she belongs to and she has killed for me.

👀 ELIZABETH 👀

'Hey Liz, are you ok?' Cassie asks as she comes up to me and rests her hand on my shoulder, shooting Dominic a look.
'I will be,' I say as I start making coffee.
'Amber and Dominic will come around.'
'I will support you as best I can, but I still don't like this plan,' Dominic says as he opens the fridge, getting out the food containers.
'Right, well, I will leave you both to it and go check on my girl.' Cassie shoots Dominic another look.
He smiles and nods, Cassie leaves and heads to their room.

Dominic comes up behind me and wraps his arms around me.
'Are you ready?' I ask him.
'Are you?' He kisses my neck softly.
'Honestly, no. But I need to do this before we go any further. You need to know everything. If you accept it, I need you to understand how much it scares me, and you will see this reaction every day,'
'Liz, I made you a promise and I have no intention of turning away from you, ever. I will love you every moment for the rest of our lives.'
'This won't be easy and my scars run deep,'
'And I will kiss every one of them. I will protect and love you fiercely.'
I turn in his arms and look up into his eyes.

'What I am about to tell you is like opening Pandora's Box. Once I start,' I look at him, 'you have to tell me if you need me to stop. I need you to be completely honest with me. Promise me.'
'Liz…'
'Promise me, Dominic.'
'I promise.'
I nod as he holds me tight, I close my eyes and take a deep breath.
His warmth spreads through me, giving me strength.
I turn back around and finish making our coffee.
Dominic rests his chin on my shoulder and keeps holding me.
He can sense my unease. His fingers move slowly down my arms and intertwine with mine.
His lips brush along the scar on my neck.

I lean back into him and smile.
'Elizabeth,' He whispers my name.
'Yes, Dominic.'
He turns me around bringing his hands to my neck.
'I love you,' he says as he brings his lips down to mine.
My hands rests on his sides as his kiss sets my senses alight.
It reminds me of the Monday after my collapse, when he got back from helping Luke.
His arm wraps around my lower back, holding me to him.
Thank god he is holding me, I smile, because my knees weren't… as usual.
He rests his forehead on mine, his eyes closed.
My fingers brush the side of his face.
'Dominic,' I whisper
He opens his eyes and smiles.
'Hey, you.'
'There's my girl.'
He kisses me softly. We take the coffee and food into the lounge.
This is it, there is no turning back now.

'I first met Michael………'

The End of Book One.